THE KING

BY J. R. WARD

The Black Dagger Brotherhood Series

Dark Lover

Lover Eternal

Lover Awakened

Lover Revealed

Lover Unbound

Lover Enshrined

The Black Dagger Brotherhood:
An Insider's Guide

Lover Avenged

Lover Mine

Lover Unleashed

Lover Reborn

Lover at Last

The King

Novels of the Fallen Angels

Covet

Crave

Envy

Rapture

Possession

J.R. WARD

THE KING

A NOVEL OF THE BLACK DAGGER BROTHERHOOD

New American Library

New American Library
Published by the Penguin Group
Penguin Group (USA) LLC, 375 Hudson Street,
New York, New York 10014

USA | Canada | UK | Ireland | Australia | New Zealand | India | South Africa | China
penguin.com
A Penguin Random House Company

First published by New American Library,
a division of Penguin Group (USA) LLC

First Printing, April 2014

LIBRARY OF CONGRESS CATALOGING-IN-PUBLICATION DATA:
Ward, J. R., 1969–
The king: a novel of the Black Dagger Brotherhood/J. R. Ward.
p. cm.—(Black Dagger Brotherhood; 12)
ISBN 978-0-451-41705-3 (hardback)
1. Vampires—Fiction. I. Title.
PS3623.A73227K57 2014
813'.6—dc23 2013048316

Printed in the United States of America
10 9 8 7 6 5 4 3 2 1

Set in Garamond
Designed by Patrice Sheridan

IN LOVING MEMORY OF

JONAH, A.K.A. THE BOO,
A.K.A. THE VERY BEST OF WRITERDOG.
R.I.P. AND SEE YOU AGAIN AT THE
END OF MY ROAD XXX

AND

W. GILLETTE BIRD, JR.

ACKNOWLEDGMENTS

With immense gratitude to the readers of the Black Dagger Brotherhood!

Thank you so very much for all the support and guidance: Steven Axelrod, Kara Welsh, Claire Zion, and Leslie Gelbman. Thank you also to everyone at New American Library—these books are truly a team effort.

With love to Team Waud—you know who you are. This simply could not happen without you.

None of this would be possible without: my loving husband, who is my adviser and caretaker and visionary; my wonderful mother, who has given me so much love I couldn't possibly ever repay her; my family (both those of blood and those by adoption); and my dearest friends.

Oh, and to my new WriterAssistant, Naamah.

GLOSSARY OF TERMS AND PROPER NOUNS

ahstrux nohtrum (n.) Private guard with license to kill who is granted his or her position by the King.

ahvenge (v.) Act of mortal retribution, carried out typically by a male loved one.

Black Dagger Brotherhood (pr. n.) Highly trained vampire warriors who protect their species against the Lessening Society. As a result of selective breeding within the race, Brothers possess immense physical and mental strength, as well as rapid healing capabilities. They are not siblings for the most part, and are inducted into the Brotherhood upon nomination by the Brothers. Aggressive, self-reliant, and secretive by nature, they exist apart from civilians, having little contact with members of the other classes except when they need to feed. They are the subjects of legend and objects of reverence within the vampire world. They may be killed only by the most serious of wounds, e.g., a gunshot or stab to the heart, etc.

blood slave (n.) Male or female vampire who has been subjugated to serve the blood needs of another. The practice of keeping blood slaves has recently been outlawed.

the Chosen (pr. n.) Female vampires who have been bred to serve the Scribe Virgin. They are considered members of the aristocracy, though they are spiritually rather than temporally focused. They have little or no interaction with males, but can be mated to Brothers at the Scribe Virgin's direction to propagate their class. Some have the ability to prognosticate. In the past, they were used to meet the blood needs of unmated members of the Brotherhood, and that practice has been reinstated by the Brothers.

chrih (n.) Symbol of honorable death in the Old Language.

cohntehst (n.) Conflict between two males competing for the right to be a female's mate.

Dhunhd (pr. n.) Hell.

doggen (n.) Member of the servant class within the vampire world. *Doggen* have old, conservative traditions about service to their superiors, following a formal code of dress and behavior. They are able to go out during the day, but they age relatively quickly. Life expectancy is approximately five hundred years.

ehros (n.) A Chosen trained in the matter of sexual arts.

exhile dhoble (pr. n.) The evil or cursed twin, the one born second.

the Fade (pr. n.) Non-temporal realm where the dead reunite with their loved ones and pass eternity.

First Family (pr. n.) The King and queen of the vampires, and any children they may have.

ghardian (n.) Custodian of an individual. There are varying degrees of *ghardians*, with the most powerful being that of a *sehcluded* female.

glymera (n.) The social core of the aristocracy, roughly equivalent to Regency England's *ton*.

hellren (n.) Male vampire who has been mated to a female. Males may take more than one female as mate.

hyslop (n. or v.) Term referring to a lapse in judgment, typically resulting in the compromise of the mechanical operations of a vehicle or otherwise motorized conveyance of some kind. For example, leaving one's keys in one's car as it is parked outside the family home overnight. Whereupon said car is stolen.

leahdyre (n.) A person of power and influence.

leelan (n.) A term of endearment loosely translated as "dearest one."

Lessening Society (pr. n.) Order of slayers convened by the Omega for the purpose of eradicating the vampire species.

lesser (n.) De-souled human who targets vampires for extermination as a member of the Lessening Society. *Lessers* must be stabbed through the chest in order to be killed; otherwise they are ageless. They do not eat or drink and are impotent. Over time, their hair, skin, and irises lose pigmentation until they are blond, blushless, and pale eyed. They smell like baby powder. Inducted into the society by the Omega, they retain a ceramic jar thereafter into which their heart was placed after it was removed.

lewlhen (n.) Gift.

lheage (n.) A term of respect used by a sexual submissive to refer to her dominant.

Lhenihan (pr. n.) A mythic beast renowned for its sexual prowess. In modern slang, refers to a male of preternatural size and sexual stamina.

lys (n.) Torture tool used to remove the eyes.

mahmen (n.) Mother. Used both as an identifier and a term of affection.

mhis (n.) The masking of a given physical environment; the creation of a field of illusion.

nalla (n., f.) or ***nallum*** (n., m.) Beloved.

needing period (n.) Female vampire's time of fertility, generally lasting for two days and accompanied by intense sexual cravings. Occurs approximately five years after a female's transition and then once a decade thereafter. All males respond to some degree if they are around a female in her need. It can be a dangerous time, with conflicts and fights breaking out between competing males, particularly if the female is not mated.

newling (n.) A virgin.

the Omega (pr. n.) Malevolent, mystical figure who has targeted the vampires for extinction out of resentment directed toward the Scribe Virgin. Exists in a nontemporal realm and has extensive powers, though not the power of creation.

phearsom (adj.) Term referring to the potency of a male's sexual organs. Literal translation something close to "worthy of entering a female."

princeps (n.) Highest level of the vampire aristocracy, second only to members of the First Family or the Scribe Virgin's Chosen. Must be born to the title; it may not be conferred.

pyrocant (n.) Refers to a critical weakness in an individual. The weakness can be internal, such as an addiction, or external, such as a lover.

rahlman (n.) Savior.

rythe (n.) Ritual manner of assuaging honor granted by one who has offended another. If accepted, the offended chooses a weapon and strikes the offender, who presents him- or herself without defenses.

the Scribe Virgin (pr. n.) Mystical force who is counselor to the King as well as the keeper of vampire archives and the dispenser of privileges. Exists in a non-temporal realm and has extensive powers. Capable of a single act of creation, which she expended to bring the vampires into existence.

sehclusion (n.) Status conferred by the King upon a female of the aristocracy as a result of a petition by the female's family. Places the female under the sole direction of her *ghardian*, typically the eldest male in her household. Her *ghardian* then has the legal right to determine all manner of her life, restricting at will any and all interactions she has with the world.

shellan (n.) Female vampire who has been mated to a male. Females generally do not take more than one mate due to the highly territorial nature of bonded males.

symphath (n.) Subspecies within the vampire race characterized by the ability and desire to manipulate emotions in others (for the purposes of an energy exchange), among other traits. Historically, they have been discriminated against and, during certain eras, hunted by vampires. They are near extinction.

the Tomb (pr. n.) Sacred vault of the Black Dagger Brotherhood. Used as a ceremonial site as well as a storage facility for the jars of *lessers*. Ceremonies performed there include inductions, funerals, and disciplinary actions against Brothers. No one may enter except for members of the Brotherhood, the Scribe Virgin, or candidates for induction.

trahyner (n.) Word used between males of mutual respect and affection. Translated loosely as "beloved friend."

transition (n.) Critical moment in a vampire's life when he or she transforms into an adult. Thereafter, he or she must drink the blood of the opposite sex to survive and is unable to withstand sunlight. Occurs generally in the mid-twenties. Some vampires do not survive their transitions, males in particular. Prior to their transitions, vampires are physically weak, sexually unaware and unresponsive, and unable to dematerialize.

vampire (n.) Member of a species separate from that of Homo sapiens. Vampires must drink the blood of the opposite sex to survive. Human blood will keep them alive, though the strength does not last long. Following their transitions, which occur in their mid-twenties, they are unable to go out into sunlight and must feed from the vein regularly. Vampires cannot "convert" humans through a bite or transfer of blood, though they are in rare cases able to breed with the other species. Vampires can dematerialize at will, though they must be able to calm themselves and concentrate to do so and may not carry anything heavy with them. They are able to strip the memories of humans, provided such memories are short-term. Some vampires are able to read minds. Life expectancy is upward of a thousand years, or in some cases even longer.

wahlker (n.) An individual who has died and returned to the living from the Fade. They are accorded great respect and are revered for their travails.

whard (n.) Equivalent of a godfather or godmother to an individual.

THE KING

PROLOGUE

SEVENTEENTH CENTURY, OLD COUNTRY

"*Long live the King.*"

At the sound of the deep, grave voice, Wrath, son of Wrath, had an instinct to look around for his father . . . a spark of hope that the death had not occurred and the great ruler was as yet still with them.

But of course, his beloved sire remained gone unto the Fade.

How long would this sad searching last? he wondered. It was such useless folly, especially as the sacred vestments of the vampire King were upon himself, the bejeweled sashes and silken coat and ceremonial daggers adorning his own body. His mind cared naught for such proof of his recent coronation, however . . . or mayhap it was his heart that remained unswayed by all that now defined him.

Dearest Virgin Scribe, without his father, he was so alone, even as he was surrounded by people who served him.

"My lord?"

Composing his visage, he turned around. Standing in the doorway of the royal receiving chambers, his closest adviser was like a column of smoke, long and thin, draped in dark robes.

"My honor to greet you," the male murmured, bending low. "Are you ready to receive the female?"

No. "Indeed."

"Shall we initiate the procession."

"Yes."

As his adviser bowed again and backed out, Wrath paced across the oak-paneled room. Candles wafted in the drafts that somehow infiltrated the castle's stone walls, and the roaring fire in the chest-high hearth seemed to offer only light, not warmth.

In truth, he had no desire for a *shellan*—or rather, a mate, as it inevitably was going to be. Love was required for the former, and he had none to offer a soul.

From out of the corner of his eye, he caught a flash of brilliance, and to pass the time before this dreaded meeting occurred, he went over and regarded the sets of gems that had been displayed upon the carved desk. Diamonds, sapphires, emeralds, pearls . . . nature's beauty captured and anchored by hammered gold.

The most valuable were the rubies.

Reaching out to touch the bloodred stones, he thought, It was too early for all of this. His being King, this mating arrangement, the thousand different demands he now bore and yet understood too little of.

He needed more time to learn from his father—

The first of three pounding knocks reverberated through the room, and Wrath was grateful that no one was about to see him flinch.

The second was just as loud.

The third was going to require his response.

Closing his eyes, he found it hard to breathe through the pain in his chest. He wanted his father with him—this should be happening later, when he was older, and not guided by a courtier, but his own sire. Fate, however, had robbed the great male of years that were his due, and in turn, subscribed the son to a sort of drowning even though there was air about him to breathe.

I cannot do this, Wrath thought.

And yet, as the third rap upon the panels faded, he squared his shoulders and mimicked the way his father's voice had always sounded. "Enter."

At his command, the heavy door swung wide, and his eyes were greeted by the sight of a full complement of courtiers, their somber

gray robing identical to that of the adviser who stood at the front of them. But that was not what registered. Behind the group of aristocrats, there were others, tremendous of stature, narrow of eye . . . and those were the ones who began to chant in a concerted growl.

In honesty, he feared the Black Dagger Brotherhood.

According to tradition, the adviser stated loudly and clearly, "My lord, I have an offering to bring before you. May I proceed with its presentation?"

As if the noble daughter were an object. Then again, tradition and social norms provided that her purpose was for breeding, and at court, she would be treated as any prized broodmare was.

However was he going to do this? He knew naught of the sexual act, and yet if he approved of her, he would be engaged in the activity sometime after nightfall on the morrow.

"Yes," he heard himself say.

The courtiers filed in through the doorway in pairs, splitting and forming a circle around the perimeter of the room. And then the chanting grew louder.

The magnificent warriors of the Brotherhood entered in a march, their tremendous bodies clothed in black leather and strapped with weapons, the cadence of their voices and movement of their forms so synchronized, it was as if they were one.

Unlike the members of the *glymera*, they did not part, but stayed shoulder-to-shoulder, chest-to-chest in a box-like formation. He could see nothing of what was in their midst.

But he could smell the scent.

And the change within himself was instant and immutable. In a single heartbeat, the plodding nature of life was washed away by a prickling awareness . . . one that, as the Brothers came closer, matured into an aggression that he was unfamiliar with, but utterly disinclined to ignore.

Breathing in again, more of that fragrance entered his lungs, his blood, his soul—and it was not the oils she had been rubbed down with or the perfumes that had been applied to whatever clothed her form. It was the skin underneath all that, the delicate combination of feminine elements that he knew was unique to her and her alone.

The Brotherhood stopped in front of him, and for the first time, he was not in awe of their deadly auras. No. As his fangs elongated into his mouth, he found his upper lip lifting in a snarl.

He even took a step forward, prepared to rip the males asunder so he could get at what they were shielding from him.

The adviser cleared his throat as if seeking to remind the assembled of his import. "Our lord, this female is being offered by her bloodline for your consideration for birthing purposes. Should you desire to inspect—"

"Leave us," Wrath snapped. "At once."

The shocked silence that followed was easily ignored on his part.

The adviser dropped his voice. "My lord, if you shall permit me to finish the presentation—"

Wrath's body moved on its own, pivoting itself around until he could match stares with the male. "Get. Out."

Behind him, a chuckle rose from the Brotherhood, as if they rather enjoyed the dandy getting put in his place by their ruler. The adviser, however, was not amused. And Wrath did not care.

There was also no more conversation to be had: the courtier had much power, but he was not King.

The males in gray shuffled out of the room, bowing, and then he was left with the Brothers. At once, they stepped aside and . . .

Revealed within their heft was a slender form draped in black robing from head to foot. In comparison to the warriors, the intended was slight of stature, narrower of bone, shorter of height—and yet hers was the presence that rocked him.

"My lord," one of the Brothers said with respect, "this is Anha."

With that simple and more apt introduction, the fighters disappeared, shutting him in alone with the female.

Wrath's body took over again, prowling his chaotic senses around her, stalking her even as she did not move. Dearest Virgin Scribe, he had meant for none of this, not his reaction to her presence nor the need coiling in his loins nor the aggression that had sprung to the fore.

But most of all, he had never thought—

Mine.

'Twas as a lightning bolt out of the night sky, changing his landscape, carving a gashing vulnerability in his chest. And yet even with that, he thought, Yes, this was right. His father's former adviser indeed had his best interests at heart. This female was what he needed to carry him through the loneliness: Even without seeing her face, she made him feel the strength within his sex, her smaller, daintier form filling

him out in his skin, the urge to protect giving him a priority and a focus he had been sorely lacking.

"Anha," he breathed as he stopped in front of her. "Speak unto me."

There was a long silence. And then her voice, soft and sweet, but quavering, entered his ears. Closing his eyes, he swayed on his feet, the sound echoing throughout his blood and bones, lovelier than anything he had e'er heard.

Except then he frowned as he had no idea what she had spoken. "Whate'er did you say?"

For a moment, the words that came from beneath the cover of the veil made no sense. But then the definitions of the syllables were verified by his brain:

"Would you wish to see another?"

Wrath frowned in confusion. Why would he—

"You have removed naught from my form," he heard her answer as if he had voiced his inquiry.

At once, he realized she was trembling, her robing transmitting the movement—and indeed, there was a heavy undertow of fear in her scent.

His arousal had clouded any further awareness of her, but that required rectification.

Collecting the throne, he brought the vast, carved chair across the room, his need to provide comforts unto her giving him superior strength. "Sit."

She all but fell into the oxblood leather seat—and as her draped hands clawed onto the armrests, he imagined her knuckles going white as she held on for dearest life.

Wrath sank down onto his knees before her. Staring up, his only thought, aside from that of his intention to possess her, was that he would never see her frightened.

Ever.

Beneath the layers of weighty robing, Anha was suffocating in the heat. Or mayhap it was terror that choked her throat.

She did not wish for this destiny of hers. Had not sought it. Would give it to any of the young females who had, over the years, envied her:

From the moment of her birth, she had been promised to the son of the King as the first mate—and because of that supposed honor, she had been reared by others, cloistered away, hidden from all contact. Raised in solitary confinement, she knew not the nurture of a mother or protection of a father—she had been adrift in a sea of supplicating strangers, handled as a precious object, not a living thing.

And now, at the culminating event, at the moment she had been bred and avowed for . . . all those years of preparation appeared to be for naught.

The King was not happy: He had thrown all and sundry out of whatever room they were in. He had not removed a single drape from her, as was his due if he wished to accept her in some fashion. Instead, he was stalking around, his aggression charging the air.

She had likely angered him further with her temerity. One was not supposed to offer suggestions to the King—

"Sit."

Anha followed the command by letting her weak knees fall out from beneath her body. She expected to meet the cold, hard floor, but there was a cushioned chair of some great mass to catch her.

Creaking floorboards informed her he was circling her again, his footfalls heavy, his presence so great she could sense the size of him even though she could see nothing. Heart pounding, sweat breaking out down her neck and between her breasts, she waited for his next move—and feared it would be violent. By law, he could do anything he wanted with her. He could slaughter her or toss her to the Brotherhood for their use. He could undress her, take her virginity, and then reject her—leaving her ruined.

Or he could simply render her naked and approve of her form, saving her virtue for after the ceremony the following night. Or even mayhap . . . as she had imagined in her most futile dreams . . . he would regard her briefly and re-cover her with gifts of special cloth, signaling his intent to rank her among his *shellans*—so that her life at court would be easier.

She'd heard too much about courtiers to expect kindness from them. And she was well aware that though she was to be mated to the King, she was on her own. If she had a small measure of power, however, mayhap she could remove herself from this to a certain degree, leaving the machinations of court and kingship to females of greater ambition and avarice—

The pacing stopped abruptly and there was protest from the floor directly before her, as if he had shifted position in some manner.

Now was the moment, and her heart froze as if it did not want to attract attention from His Majesty's blade. . . .

In one quick moment, the hood was off her face, and great drafts of cool air were free for her lungs' taking.

Anha gasped at what was before her.

The King, the ruler, the supreme representative of the vampire race . . . was on his knees in front of the chair he had provided her. And that should have been shocking enough, but indeed, his apparent supplication was the least of what struck her.

He was utterly beautiful—and of all the things she had sought to prepare herself for, this first, magnificent sight of him had never been contemplated.

His eyes were the color of pale spring leaves, and they shone bright as moonlight upon a lake whilst he stared up at her. And his face was the handsomest she had e'er beheld, although that was perhaps not compliment enough, given that she had not been allowed to look upon anything male before. And his hair was black as crows' wings, falling down a broad back.

Except even that was not what penetrated her consciousness most.

It was the concern in his expression.

"Be not afraid," he said in a voice that was velvet and gravel. "None shall e'er harm you, for I am here."

Tears pricked in her eyes. And then her mouth opened itself, words jumping out. "My lord, you should not kneel."

"How ever else would I greet a female such as yourself?"

Anha tried to respond, but caught up in his gaze, her mind became entangled—he seemed not real, this powerful male who bowed his honor afore her. To be certain once and for all, her hand lifted and moved to close the distance between them. . . .

Whate'er was she doing? "Forgive me, my lord—"

He captured her palm and the impact of the flesh upon flesh made her gasp. Or was that both of them?

"Touch me," he commanded. "Anywhere."

As he released his hold, she placed her trembling hand upon his cheek. Warm. Smooth from a blade's recent passing.

The King closed his eyes and leaned in, his great body shuddering.

When he just stayed as that, she felt a surge of power—not in an arrogant fashion, nor with any ambition for self-gain. It was simply from unexpected footing gained on what had seemed like an indelibly slippery slope.

How was this possible?

"Anha . . ." he breathed, as if her name were an incantation of magic.

Naught else was spoken, but the whole of their language was unnecessary, all parts of speech and vocabulary rendered worthless to offer any mere nuance, much less definition, to what bond was shaping and tethering them one to another.

She finally dropped her eyes. "Would you not care to see more of me?"

The King released a low growling purr. "I would see all of you—and looking would not be the half of it."

The scent of a male's arousal rose thick in the air, and incredibly, her own body responded to the call. But then again, that sensual aggression of his was well and truly bound by his singular will: he was not going to take her the now. No, it appeared that he was going to save her virtue until he had paid her the honor and respect of properly mating her.

"The Scribe Virgin answered my prayers in a miraculous way," she whispered as she blinked through tears. All those years of worry and wait, the anvil poised for three decades to fall upon her head . . .

The King smiled. "If I had known a female as you could exist, I would have beseeched the mother of the race myself. But I had no fantasies—and that is well enough. I would have done naught but sit and wait for you to cross into my destiny, wasting years."

With that, he burst up to his feet and went over to a display of robing. The colors of the rainbow were all represented, and she had been taught since an early age to know what each hue meant in the hierarchy of court.

He chose the red for her. The most valued of all, the signal that she would be the favored amongst all his females.

The queen.

And that honor should have been enough. Except as she envisioned the many he would take, pain struck in her chest.

As he came back toward her, he must have sensed her sadness. "What ails you, *leelan*?"

Anha shook her head, and told herself that sharing him was not something she had any right to mourn. She—

The King shook his head. "No. There shall only be you."

Anha recoiled. "My lord, that is not tradition—"

"Am I not the ruler of all? Can I not decree life and death o'er my subjects?" When she nodded, a hard cast came upon his face—and made her pity any who would try to deny him. "So I shall determine what is and is not tradition. And there shall only be you for me."

Tears sprang anew to Anha's eyes. She wanted to believe him, and yet that seemed impossible—even as he wrapped her still-clad form with the blood-colored silk.

"You honor me," she said, staring into his face.

"Not enough." With a quick turn, he stalked across to a table that had been laid with gems.

The largesse of jewels had been the last thing on her mind as he had lifted her hood, but now her eyes widened at the display of wealth. Surely, she did not deserve such things. Not until she gave him an heir.

Which abruptly seemed not a chore, a'tall.

As he returned unto her, she inhaled sharply. Rubies, so many she couldn't count them—indeed, a whole tray . . . including the Saturnine ring which she had been told had always graced the hand of the queen.

"Accept these and know my truth," he said as he once again lowered himself at her feet.

Anha felt her head shake. "No, no, these are for the ceremony—"

"Which we shall have here and the now." He put out his palm. "Give me your hand."

Anha's every bone was shaking as she obeyed him, and she let out a gasp as the Saturnine stone went onto her middle finger on the right. As she looked into the gem, candlelight refracted amongst its facets, flaring with beauty sure as true love lit the heart from within.

"Anha, do you accept me as your King and mate, until the door unto the Fade is offered afore you?"

"Yes," she heard herself say with surprising strength.

"Then I, Wrath, son of Wrath, do take you as my *shellan*, to watch over and care for you and any begotten young we may have, sure as I would and will my kingdom, and its citizenry. You shall be mine fore'ermore—your enemies are mine own, your bloodline to mix with mine own, your dusks and your dawns to share only with me. This bond shall ne'er be torn asunder by forces within or without—and"—here he paused—"there shall be one and only one female for all mine days, and you shall be that only queen."

With that, he brought up his other hand and laced all their fingers together. "None shall part us. Ever."

Although Anha did not have knowledge of it currently, in future years, as destiny continued to roll forward, transforming this present moment into past history, she would return to this instant over and over again. Later, she would reflect that they had both been lost that night, and the sight of the other had given them the solid ground they had required.

Later, when sleeping close to her mate in their bedding and hearing him gently snore, she would know that what had seemed like a dream was in reality a living, breathing miracle.

Later, on the night that she and her beloved were slaughtered, when her eyes latched onto the crawl space where she had hidden their heir, their future, the only thing that was greater than the two of them . . . she would have as her last dying thought that it was all meant to be. Whether the tragedy or the luck, all of it had been predetermined, and it had started here, in this instant, as the King's fingers intertwined with her own and the two of them became locked one into the other, for eternity.

"Who shall attend you this night and this day afore the public ceremony?" he asked.

She hated to leave him. "I should return to my quarters."

He frowned deeply. But then he released her and took his sweet time adorning her with the rubies until they hung from her ears and her neck and both of her wrists.

The King touched the largest of the stones, the one that hung over her heart. As his lids lowered, she believed that he had gone somewhere carnal in his mind—mayhap he was imagining her without benefit of clothing, nothing but her skin to frame the heavy golden settings with their diamond accents and those incredible red gems.

The last of the suite was the crown itself, and he lifted the circlet from the velvet tray, placing it on her head and then sitting back to survey her.

"You outshine it all," he said.

Anha looked down at herself. Red, red, everywhere, the color of blood, the color of life itself. Indeed, she could not imagine the value in the gems, but that was not what touched her. The honor he was paying her in this moment was legendary—and as she considered that, she wished this could have been private between them fore'ermore.

That would not be, however. And the courtiers were not going to like this, she thought.

"I shall take you to your quarters."

"Oh, my lord, you should not bother yourself—"

"There is naught else to consume me this night, I assure you."

She could not stop her smile. "As you wish, my lord."

Except she was not sure she could stand with all the—

Anha didn't make it all the way onto her feet. The King swept in and gathered her in his arms, holding her up from the floor as if she weighed naught more than a field dove.

And with that, he marched across, kicked open the closed door and strode out into the corridor: They were all there, the hallway full of aristocrats and members of the Black Dagger Brotherhood—and instinctively she turned her head into Wrath's neck.

Whilst being raised for the King's purpose, she had always felt like an object, and yet, that had gone away when she was alone with the male. Now, exposed to the invasive gazes of the others, she was once again in that role, relegated to a possession rather than an equal.

"Wherever goest thou?" one of the aristocrats demanded as the King strode by without acknowledging them.

Wrath kept walking—but clearly this one courtier would not be denied that which was not his due.

The male placed himself in their path. "My lord, it is customary for—"

"I shall attend her in mine own quarters this night and all others."

Surprise flared in a thin, pinched face. "My lord, that is the queen's honor only, and even if you have had the female, it is not official until—"

"We are duly mated. I performed the ceremony myself. She is mine own and I am hers, and surely you do not wish to be in the path of a bonded male with his female—much less the King with his queen. Do you."

There was a clapping sound of teeth meeting teeth, as if someone's jaw had fallen open and then been closed with alacrity.

Looking past Wrath's shoulder, she saw smiles on the Brotherhood's faces, as if the fighters approved of the aggression. The others in the robes? 'Twas not approval on their visages. Impotence. Supplication. Subtle anger.

They knew who held the power, and it was not theirs.

"You should be accompanied, my lord," one of the Brothers said. "Not out of custom, but in deference to the times. Even in this stronghold, it is appropriate for the First Family to be guarded."

The King nodded after a moment. "Fine enough. Follow me, but"—his voice dropped to a growl—"you do not touch her in any way or I shall rip from you the appendage that offends her physical form."

True respect and some kind of affection warmed the Brother's voice: "As you wish, my lord. Brotherhood, fall in!"

All at once, daggers were ripped out of chest holsters, black blades glinting in the torches that lined the hall. As Anha's fingers dug into her King's precious vestments, the Brothers let out a whooping battle cry, those weapons going over their heads.

In a coordination that was bred from long hours in each other's company, every one of the great warriors went down on their knees in a circle and buried the points of their daggers in the flooring.

Bowing their heads, and with one voice, they said something she could not comprehend.

And yet the verbiage was for her: They were pledging allegiance to her as their queen.

It was what would have happened at nightfall on the morrow, in front of the *glymera*. But she far preferred it here, and as their eyes lifted, respect shone forth—directed at her.

"My gratitude unto you," she heard herself say. "And all my honor to our King."

In the blink of an eye, she and her mate were surrounded by tremendous warriors, the vow that had been given now accepted, the work commencing at once. Flanked on all sides, just as she had sensed she had been whilst presented, Wrath resumed his striding in full protection.

Past her mate's shoulder, through the mountain of Brothers, Anha watched the assembled gathering of courtiers recede in their wake as they proceeded down the corridor.

The adviser in front of it all, the one with his hands on his hips and his brows down low . . . was not pleased a'tall.

A shiver of fear went through her.

"Shh," Wrath whispered in her ear. "Worry not. I shall be gentle unto your form the now."

Anha flushed and tucked her head back into that thick neck. He meant to take her when they came upon whate'er destination he had predetermined, his sacred body entering her own, sealing the mating viscerally.

She was shocked to find that she wanted that, too. Right now. Fast and hard. . . .

And yet, when they were finally alone again, when they had settled upon a fantastical bed of down and silk . . . she was grateful that he was as patient and kind and gentle as he promised her he would be.

It was the first of many, many times that her *hellren* did not let her down.

ONE

MANHATTAN'S MEATPACKING DISTRICT, PRESENT

"Give me your mouth," Wrath demanded.

Beth tilted her head back and leaned into her mate's arms. "You want it? So take it."

The growl that came out of that massive chest was a reminder that her man was not, in fact, a man. He was the last purebred vampire left on the planet—and when it came to her and sex, he was fully capable of going wrecking-ball to get at her.

And not in the stupid-ass Miley Cyrus poser-sex way—and provided Beth was willing, of course. Although really, when a woman had the opportunity to get with six feet, nine inches of hard-ass dressed in black leather, who just happened to have pale green eyes that glowed like the moon, and black hair down to the aforementioned concrete posterior?

No was not just out of her vocabulary; it was a foreign concept.

The kiss that came at her was brutal and she wanted it that way, Wrath's tongue thrusting into her as he shoved her backward through the open doorway of their secret hideaway.

Slam!

Best sound in the world. Well, okay, second-best—number one being what her man made when he came inside of her.

At the mere thought of it, her core opened even further.

"Oh, fuck," he said into her mouth as one of his hands slipped in between her thighs. "I want this—*yeah* . . . are you wet for me, *leelan*."

Not a question. Because he knew the answer, didn't he.

"I can smell you," he groaned against her ear as he ran his fangs up her throat. "The most beautiful thing in the world—except for your taste."

That gravel in his voice, the straining in his hips, that hard length pressing into her—she orgasmed right then and there.

"Fuck me, we need to do this more," he gritted as she ground herself against his hand, working her hips. "Why the fuck haven't we come down here every night?"

The thought of the mess that waited for them back in Caldwell drained some of the heat out of her. But then he started massaging her with his fingers, working the seam of her jeans against her most sensitive place while his tongue probed her mouth the way he did when he was . . . um, yeah.

Gee whiz, what do you know, surprise, surprise—everything about his being King and the assassination attempt and the Band of Bastards just floated away.

He was right. Why the hell didn't they make time for this slice of heaven on a regular basis?

Giving herself up to the sex, her hands tangled in his waist-length hair, its softness at odds with the harshness of his face, the strength in his incredible body, that iron core of his will. She'd never been one of those silly chippies who dreamed about a Prince Charming or a fairy-tale wedding or any of that Disney musical bullcrap. But even for someone who had had no illusions and no intention of ever signing a marriage certificate, there was no way she would have pictured herself with Wrath, son of Wrath, King of a race that as far as she had known back then was nothing more than a Halloween myth.

Yet here she was, head over heels with a straight-up killer who had a trucker's vocabulary, a royal bloodline as long as his arm, and enough attitude to make Kanye West look like a self-esteem reject.

Okay, he wasn't *quite* that egocentric—although, yup, he probably would cut Taylor Swift off in a heartbeat, but that was because rap and hip-hop were his music of choice and not 'cuz he was being a hater.

Bottom line, her *hellren* was a his-way-or-no-way kind of guy, and

the throne he sat on meant that personality defect was embraced on bended knee as the law of the land.

Talk about a perfect storm. The good news? She was the sole exception, the only person who could talk sense into him when he really got his hackles up. It was like that with all of the Brothers and their mates: Members of the Black Dagger Brotherhood, the race's elite group of fighters and meatheads, were not known for being easygoing. Then again, you didn't want pussies on the front line of any war, especially when the bad guys were of the ilk of the Lessening Society.

And those goddamned Bastards.

"I'm not going to make it to the bed," Wrath moaned. "I gotta be in you now."

"So take me on the floor." She sucked on his lower lip. "You know how to do that, don't you?"

More growling, and a big shift in the planet's orientation as she was popped off the ground and laid out on all that polished wood. The loft that Wrath had once used as a bachelor pad was right out of central casting: It had a cathedral ceiling, an empty warehouse's decor, and the matte black paint job of an Uzi. It was nothing like the Brotherhood mansion where they lived, and that was the point.

As beautiful as that place was, all the gold leaf and crystal chandeliers and antique furniture could get a little stifling—

Riiiiiiiiiiiiiiiiiiiiiip.

With that happy noise, she lost another outfit in her wardrobe—and wasn't Wrath proud of himself: Flashing fangs long as daggers and white as the driven snow, he proceeded to turn her silk button-down into a Swiffer, shredding the thing off her naked breasts, buttons flying everywhere.

"Now, that's what I'm talkin' about." Wrath tore off his wraparounds and smiled, exposing his dental hardware. "Nothing in the way . . ."

Looming over her, he latched onto her nipple while his hands went to the waistband of her black jeans. All things considered, he was pretty polite as he unhooked the catch and unzipped, but she knew what was coming. . . .

With a violent jerk, he laid waste to what had been a two-week-old pair of Levi's.

She didn't care. Neither did he.

Oh, God, she needed this.

"You're right, it's been way too long," she hissed as he went after his own fly, popping the buttons free, unleashing an erection that still managed to take her breath away.

"I'm sorry," he bit out as he grabbed her behind the neck and mounted her.

As she opened her thighs wide for him, she knew exactly why he was apologizing. "Don't be—*Jesus!*"

The blazing possession was exactly what she wanted—and so was the rough ride he gave her, his heavy weight crushing her, her bare ass squeaking against the floor as he pounded into her, her legs straining to link around so he could go even deeper. It was total domination, his great body pistoning in an erotic pump that got ever faster and more intense.

But as good as it was, she knew how to take things to the next level. "Aren't you thirsty yet?" she drawled.

Total. Molecular. Stoppage.

Like he'd been hit with an ice ray. Or maybe a truck.

As he lifted his head, his eyes lit up so brightly, she knew if she looked on the floor next to her, she'd see her own shadow.

Digging into his shoulders with her nails, she arched up to him and cocked her head to the side. "How about something to drink?"

His lips curled off his fangs and he let out a cobra's hiss.

The bite was like being stabbed, but the pain faded into a sweet delirium that carried her to another dimension. Floating and grounded at the same time, she moaned and pushed her fingers into his hair, yanking him even closer as he sucked at her throat and thrust into her sex.

She orgasmed—and so did he.

Duh.

God, after a dry spell of how long? At least a month—which was unheard of for them—she realized how much they both had to have this. Too much static from all the demands around them. Too much stress polluting the hours. Too much toxic crap they didn't have time to process with each other.

Like, after he'd been shot in the neck, had they really talked about it? Sure, there had been the *OMG, you're alive, you made it* stuff . . . but she was still flinching every time a *doggen* opened a bottle of wine in the dining room or the Brothers played pool after hours.

Who knew that a cue ball smacking into a rack sounded exactly like a gun going off?

She hadn't. Not until Xcor had decided to put a bullet into Wrath's jugular.

Hardly the kind of education she'd been looking for—

For no good reason, tears flooded her eyes and broke free, tangling in her lashes and seeping down her cheeks even as another round of pleasure flooded her body.

And then the image of Wrath's gunshot wound billboarded her vision.

Red blood on the bulletproof vest he'd worn. Red blood on his muscle shirt. Red blood on his skin.

The dangerous times come home, the ugliness of reality no longer a hypothetical bogeyman in her mental closet, but a scream in her soul.

Red was the color of death to her.

Wrath froze for a second time and jerked his head up. *"Leelan?"*

Opening her eyes, she had a sudden panic that she couldn't see him right, that that face she looked for in every room no matter the hour was gone, that that visual confirmation of his life wasn't going to be there for the taking anymore.

Except all she had to do was blink. Blink, blink, blink . . . and he was back with her, clear as day.

And that made her cry more. Because her strong, beloved man was blind—and though that didn't make him handicapped in her opinion, it did cheat him out of some fundamentals, and that just wasn't fair.

"Oh, fuck, I hurt you—"

"No, no . . ." She took his face in her hands. "Don't stop."

"I should have gone over to the bed—"

The sure way to get him refocused was to arch under him, and she did, undulating and rolling her hips so that her core stroked him. And Hello, big boy, the friction registered, rendering him tongue-tied and torn.

"Don't stop," she reiterated, trying to draw him back down to her vein. "Ever . . ."

But Wrath held off, stroking a piece of hair away from her face. "Don't think like that."

"I'm not."

"You are."

There was no reason to define what "like that" meant: Treasonous plots. Wrath at that ornate desk, strangled by his position. The future unknown and not in a good way.

"I'm goin' nowhere, *leelan*. You don't worry about a goddamn thing. Understand me?"

Beth wanted to believe him. Needed to. But she feared it was a promise far harder to keep than speak.

"Beth?"

"Make love to me." It was the only truth she could put out there that wouldn't burst the bubble. "Please."

He kissed her once. Twice. And then started to move again. "Always, *leelan*. Always."

Best. Night. Ever.

As Wrath pushed himself off of his *shellan* an hour later, he couldn't breathe, he was bleeding at the throat, and his Man of Steel cock had finally gone wet-noodle.

Although knowing the damn thing's stamina? He had five, maybe ten minutes before Mr. Happy got to grinnin' again.

The big bed in the center of the loft's vast space had been upgraded since his Beth had mated him, and as he stretched out on his back, he had to admit that having sex on the thing was so much better than doing it on the floor. That said, as he recovered, its sheets were unnecessary as he could have fried an egg on his chest from the exertion. Blankets were an absolute hell-no. Pillows had been lost quickly because there was no headboard, but the advantage was leverage from any compass point.

Sometimes he liked to put a foot down and really dig in.

Beth let out a sigh that was longer and more satisfying than a Shakespearian sonnet—and talk about a hell-yeah? Wrath's chest inflated like a hot-air balloon.

"I do you okay?" he drawled.

"God. Yes."

More with the smiling. It was *The Mask* all over again, nothing but Jim Carrey, Pepsodent white over here. And she was right: The sex had been beyond fantastic. He'd fucked her across the floor until they were in range of the mattress. Then, like the gentlemale he was, he'd put her on the bed . . . and had her another three times. Four?

He could do this all night—

Sure as an eclipse could wipe out the moon, his cosmic relaxation disappeared and took all warmth with it.

There was no *all night* for him anymore. Not when it came to kickin' it with his female.

"Wrath?"

"I'm right here, *leelan*," he murmured.

As she rolled onto her side, he could feel her staring at him, and even though his vision had finally given up the ghost and conked out on him entirely, he could picture her long, thick black hair and her blue eyes and her beautiful face.

"You're not."

"I'm fine."

Shit, what time was it? Had it been longer than the hour it had felt like? Probably. When it came to the grind with Beth, he could lose motherfucking days.

"It's after one," she said softly.

"Fuck me."

"Would it help to talk? Wrath . . . can you tell me where you're at?"

Ah, hell, she was right. He had been checking out a lot lately, retreating to a place in his mind where the chaos couldn't get to him—not a bad thing, but it was a solo trip.

"Just not ready to go back to work."

"I don't blame you." She found his mouth and brushed her lips against his. "Can we stay a little longer?"

"Yeah." But not long enough . . .

A subtle alarm sounded on his wrist.

"Goddamn it." Putting his forearm across his face, he shook his head. "Time flies, huh."

And responsibilities waited for him. He had petitions to review. Proclamations to draft. And e-mails in his inbox, those fucking e-mails that the *glymera* pulled out of their asses on a nightly basis . . . although those had been drying up lately—probably a sign that that bunch of fruit loops were talking among themselves. Not good news.

Wrath cursed again. "I don't know how my father did this. Night after night. Year after year."

Only to be killed brutally too young.

At least when the elder Wrath had been on his throne, things had been stable: His citizenry had loved him and he had loved them. No treasonous plots cooking in back rooms. The enemy had been from without, not within.

"I'm so sorry," Beth said. "Are you sure there aren't some things you can put off?"

Wrath sat up, brushing his long hair back. As he stared off ahead, seeing nothing, he wanted to be out fighting.

Not an option. In fact, the only thing on his dance card was going back to Caldie and rechaining himself to that desk. His fate had been sealed many, many years ago, when his mother had gone into her needing, and his father had done what a *hellren* should . . . and against all odds, the heir had been conceived, and birthed, and then nurtured long enough so he could see both of them killed by *lessers* right in front of his still-functional, pretrans eyes.

Crystal clear, the memories were.

It hadn't been until after his change when the ocular defect had begun to manifest itself. But that weakness was, like the throne, part of his hereditary due. The Scribe Virgin had had a prescribed breeding plan, one that had amplified the most desirable traits in males and females and created a caste-like system of social hierarchy. Good plan, up to a point. As usual with shit like Mother Nature, the law of unintended consequences had decided to slap a bitch—and that was how this King with his "perfect" lineage had ended up blind.

Frustrated, he jacked out of bed—and naturally hit one of those pillows instead of the floor. As his foot flipped out from underneath him and his balance went carnival funhouse, he threw out hands to catch himself, but didn't know where he was in space—

Wrath slammed into the floor, the pain exploding on his left side, but that wasn't the worst part. He could hear Beth scrambling through the messed-up sheets to get to him.

"No!" he barked, shoving himself out of her range. "*I got it.*"

As his voice ricocheted around the open space of the loft, he wanted to put his head through a plate-glass window. "Sorry," he muttered, yanking his hair back.

"It's okay."

"I didn't mean to bite your head off."

"You've been under a lot of stress. It happens."

Christ, like they were talking about him going soft during sex?

God, when he'd started in with the King shit, he'd done that internal-resolution bullcrap and made a commitment to rock that crown, be a standup guy, step into his daddy's boots, blah, blah, blah. But the unfortunate reality was, this was a marathon that was going to last his entire breathing life—and he was flagging after only two years. Three. However long it had been.

What the hell year was it anyway?

Shit knew he'd always had a short fuse, but being locked in the midnight of his blindness with nothing except demands he didn't jones over was making him volcanic.

No, wait, that was a little more temperate than where he was at—and the underlying issue was his personality. Fighting was his first and best calling, not ruling from a chair.

The father had been a male of the pen; the son was of the sword.

"Wrath?"

"Sorry, what?"

"I asked if you wanted something to eat before we leave."

He pictured going back to the mansion, *doggen* everywhere, Brothers in and out, *shellans* all around . . . and felt like he couldn't breathe. He loved them all, but goddamn, there was no privacy there.

"Thanks, but I'll just catch something at my desk."

There was a long silence. "All right."

Wrath stayed on the floor as she got dressed, the soft shifting of her jeans going up those long, luscious legs like a funeral dirge.

"Is it okay to wear your muscle shirt?" she asked. "My blouse is done for."

"Yeah. Abso."

Her sadness smelled like autumn rain and felt just as cold in the air to him.

Man, to think there were people out there who wanted to be King, he thought as he got to his feet.

Fucking. Crazy.

If it weren't for his father's legacy, and all those vampires who had truly, deeply loved his sire, he would have blown it all off and not looked back. But pulling out? He couldn't do that. His father had been a King for the history books, a male who had not just commanded authority by virtue of the throne he sat on, but had inspired honest devotion.

Wrath lost the crown? He might as well piss all over his sire's grave.

When his *shellan*'s palm slid into his own, he jumped. "Here are your clothes," she said, putting them into his hands. "And I have your wraparounds."

With a quick shift, he pulled her against him, holding her to his naked body. She was a tall female, but even so she barely came up to his pecs, and as he closed his eyes, he curled himself around her.

"I want you to know something," he said into her hair.

As she went still, he tried to pull something worth hearing out of his ass. Some string of words that were even in the same zip code as what was doing in his chest.

"What," she whispered.

"You are everything to me."

It was so incredibly, totally not enough—and yet she sighed and melted into him like that was all she'd wanted to hear. And a bag of chips.

Sometimes you got lucky.

And as he continued to hold her, he knew he'd do well to remember that. As long as he had this female by his side?

He could get through anything.

TWO

CALDWELL, NEW YORK

"Long live the King."

As Abalone, son of Abalone, spoke the words, he tried to gauge the response of the three males who had knocked upon his door, marched into his home and were standing in his library, staring at him as if measuring him for a shroud.

Actually, no. He tracked only one expression—that of the disfigured warrior who stood far behind the others, lounging against the silk wallpaper, combat boots solidly on the Persian carpet.

The male's eyes were hidden beneath the overhang of a heavy brow, the irises dark enough so there was no telling what color they were, blue or brown or green. His body was enormous, and even at rest, it was a bald-faced threat, a grenade with a slippery pin. And his response to what had been said?

No change in his features, that harelip nothing but a slash, the frown the same. No emotion shown.

But that dagger hand flexed wide-open and then curled into a fist.

Clearly, the aristocrat Ichan and the lawyer Tyhm, who had brought this fighter over, had lied. This was not a "conversation about the future"—no, something like that would suggest that Abalone had a choice in the matter.

This was a warning shot across his bloodline's bow, an all-aboard call to which there was but one answer.

And yet, even still, the words had come out of his mouth as they had, and he could not change them.

"Are you certain of your reply?" Ichan asked with an arched brow.

Ichan was typical of his breeding and financial net worth, refined to the point of femininity in spite of his gender, dressed in a coordinated suit and tie with every hair in place. Beside him, Tyhm, the solicitor, was the same only even thinner, as if his considerable mental prowess sapped his caloric intake.

And both of them, as well as the warrior, were prepared to wait for the answer they'd been given to change.

Abalone's eyes went to an ancient scroll that had been framed and mounted on the wall by the double doors. He couldn't read the small Old Language characters from across the room, but there was no need to go in for a close-up. He knew each one by heart.

"I was unaware that there was a question posed of me," Abalone said.

Ichan smiled falsely and strolled around, fingering a sterling silver bowl of red apples, the collection of Cartier desk clocks on a side table, the bronze bust of Napoleon on the desk by the windowed alcove.

"We are, of course, interested in your position." The aristocrat stopped in front of a pen-and-ink drawing on a stand. "This is your daughter, I believe?"

Abalone's chest got tight.

"She is about to be presented, is she not?" Ichan looked over his shoulder. "Yes?"

Abalone wanted to shove the male away from the image.

Of all things that were considered "his," his precious young, the only offspring he and his *shellan* had had, was the moon in his night sky, the joy that marked the household's hours, his compass for the future. And he wanted so many things for her—not in *glymera* terms, though. No, he wished for her what her *mahmen* and he had found—at least for the years until his female had been called unto the Fade.

He wished for his daughter abiding love with a male of worth who would take care of her.

If she was not allowed to be presented to society? That might never happen.

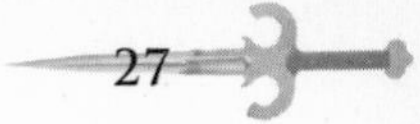

"I'm sorry," Ichan drawled. "Did you answer and I missed the reply?"

"She is due to be offered soon, yes."

"Yes." The aristocrat smiled again. "I know that you worry appropriately at her prospects. As a father myself, I am in your shoes—with daughters, you need to make sure they are mated well."

Abalone didn't release his breath until the male resumed his lazy loop around the room. "Does it not give you a degree of security to think that there are such clear demarcations within our society? Corrective breeding has resulted in a superior group of individuals, and we are required by custom and common sense to preserve our associations with like members of our race. Can you imagine your daughter married to a commoner?"

That last word lingered, carrying the pronunciation of an expletive and the threat of a cocked gun.

"No, you would not," Ichan answered for himself.

In truth, Abalone wasn't so certain. If the male loved her enough? But that was not the point of all this, was it.

Ichan paused to glance over the oil paintings that hung in front of the family's vast collection of shelved first editions. The artwork was, naturally, of ancestors, with the most prominent among them mounted over the marble fireplace's grand mantel.

A famous male in the history of the race, and of Abalone's bloodline. The Noble Redeemer, as he was known among the family.

Abalone's sire.

Ichan waved his hand around, including not just the room, but the house, all of its contents, and all the persons under its roof. "This is worthy of conservation, and the only way that happens is if the Old Ways are respected. The tenets that we, the *glymera*, seek to uphold are the very basis of what you hope to provide your daughter—without them, who knows where she could end up."

Abalone closed his eyes briefly.

And didn't that make the aristocrat assume a kinder, gentler voice. "That King you just spoke of so reverently—he's mated to a half-breed."

Abalone's lids flipped open. As with all members of the Council, he had been informed of the royal union, and that was the extent of it. "I thought he was mated unto Marissa, daughter of Wallen."

"In fact, not. The ceremony took place just a year before the raids, and the assumption was that the King had followed through on the promise to Havers's sister—but suspicions arose when Marissa was subsequently unioned with a Brother. Later, it came out to us through Tyhm"—he nodded to the lawyer—"that Wrath had taken another female—who is *not* of our race."

There was a pause, as if Abalone were being given the chance to gasp at the revelation. When he didn't become woozy from shock, Ichan leaned in and spoke slowly—as if to a mental deficient. "If they have offspring, the heir to the throne would be a quarter human."

"No one is of truly pure blood," Abalone murmured.

"More's the pity. Surely you will agree, however, that there is a tremendous difference between distant human relations . . . and a King who is substantially of that horrid race. But even if you are not offended—and surely that is not the case—the Old Laws provide the dictate. The King is to be a full-bred male—and Wrath, son of Wrath, cannot provide that for us in an heir."

"Assuming this is true—"

"It is."

"What do you expect of me?"

"I'm simply making you aware of the situation. I am nothing more than a concerned citizen."

Then why come with the violent backup? "Well, I appreciate your keeping me informed—"

"The Council is going to have to take action."

"In what form?"

"There will be a vote. Soon."

"To disavow any heirs?"

"To remove the King. His authority is such that he could change the laws at any time, eradicating the provision and further weakening the race. He must be taken down lawfully as soon as possible." The aristocrat glanced over at the drawing of Abalone's daughter. "I trust that at the Council's special session, your bloodline will be well represented by your seal and your colors."

Abalone glanced at the fighter leaning against his wall. The male seemed barely to breathe, but he was far from asleep.

How long until ruination came upon this house if he did not pledge his vote? And what form would it take?

He imagined his daughter mourning the loss of her only parent and being forsaken for the rest of her future. Himself tortured and then killed in some gruesome way.

Dearest Virgin Scribe, the narrowed eyes of that warrior were trained on him like he was a target.

"Long live the proper King," Ichan said, "is more like it."

On that note, the natty "concerned citizen" took his leave, filing out of the room with the attorney.

Abalone's heart thundered as he was left alone with the fighter . . . and after a moment of screaming silence, the male uncoiled himself and went to the silver bowl of apples.

In a low, heavily accented voice, he said, "These are for the taking, are they not."

Abalone opened his mouth, but all that emerged was a squeak.

"Is that a yes?" came a murmur.

"Indeed. Yes."

The fighter reached up to his chest harness and withdrew a dagger, the silver blade of which seemed long as a grown male's arm. With a quick toss, he flipped the weapon up in the air, the light flashing on the sharp edge—and with equal assurance, he caught the handle and stabbed one of the apples.

All without breaking eye contact with Abalone.

Removing his due from the bowl, his hard eyes drifted over to the drawing. "She's quite beautiful. For now."

Abalone put his body in the way of the depiction, prepared to sacrifice himself if it came to that: He didn't want the warrior even looking at the picture, much less commenting on it—or doing so much worse.

"Anon, then," the fighter said.

He left with the apple held upright, impaled to the core.

When Abalone heard the front door shut in the distance, he all but collapsed, falling onto the silk-covered sofa with limp limbs and a pounding heart. Even though his hands were shaking, he managed to take a cigarette out of a crystal box and ignite it with a heavy crystal lighter.

Inhaling, he stared at the picture of his daughter and knew true terror for the first time in his life.

"Dearest Virgin Scribe . . ."

There had been signs of unrest for a good year: rumors and rumbling indicating that the King was falling into disfavor among certain quadrants of the aristocracy; gossip that an assassination attempt had been made; insinuations that a cabal had formed and was prepared to move. And then there had been that Council meeting where Wrath had come forward with the Brotherhood and addressed the assembled with a bald-faced threat.

It had been the first time people had seen the King for . . . well, longer than Abalone could remember. In fact, he couldn't recall when anyone had had an audience with the ruler. There had been proclamations disseminated, of course—and edicts that had been progressive and, in Abalone's mind, long overdue.

Others didn't agree, however.

And were obviously prepared to force the hands of those who didn't concur with them.

Shifting his eyes to the portrait of his father, he tried to find some bravery in his deeper self, some kind of bedrock to plant his feet upon and stand up for what he knew was right: If Wrath had mated a half-breed, so what, if he loved her? A lot of the Old Laws that he was reforming were discriminatory, and if anything, the King's choice of *shellan* showed that he walked the talk of his modernizing.

And yet there was some old-school in the King, however: Two aristocrats had been killed recently. Montrag. Elan. Both violently and in their homes. And both had been associated with dissent.

Clearly, Wrath was not going to sit back idly whilst plots simmered against him. The bad news was that his enemies in court were stepping up the stakes as well, bringing their own muscle.

Abalone reached into the pocket of his smoking jacket and took out his iPhone. Pulling up a number from his contacts, he initiated a call and listened to the ringing with half an ear.

When a male voice answered, he had to clear his throat. "I need to know if you've been visited."

His cousin hesitated not a moment. "Yes. I have."

Abalone cursed. "I don't want any part of this."

"No one does. But this legal angle of theirs?" His cousin took a deep breath. "About the heir? People are responding."

"It's not right. Wrath has been doing good things, moving us in the ways of the modern world. He's abolished blood slavery and set up that home for abused females and their young. He's been fair and even handed with proclamations—"

"They've got him on this, Abalone. They're going to win this one—because there are more than enough left who are repulsed by the notion of a half-breed queen and a seriously diluted heir." His cousin's voice dropped lower. "Do not be on the wrong side of this, my blood.

They're prepared to do anything that's necessary to secure a unanimous vote when the time comes, and the law is what it is."

"He could change it. I'm surprised he hasn't."

"No doubt he's had a few more pressing matters to contend with than some dusty old books. And frankly, even if he reworded the provision? I don't know if there's enough support to carry him."

"He could retaliate against the aristocracy."

"What's he going to do—kill us all? Then what?"

When Abalone finally hung up, he stared into the eyes of his father. His heart told him the race was in good hands with Wrath, even if the King isolated himself in many ways. But his cousin made a lot of sense.

After a long while, he made another call that sickened his stomach. When it was answered, he didn't bother with any preamble. "You have my vote," he said roughly.

Before Ichan could laud his good sense, he ended the call. And promptly dragged over a wastepaper basket so he could vomit.

The only thing worse than having no legacy at all . . . was not living up to the one you'd been given.

As Xcor strode out of the aristocrat's house, he was annoyed to find that Ichan, the Council's representative, and Tyhm, the lawyer, were waiting for him in the moonlight.

"I think we were persuasive enough," Ichan announced.

So much pride in that haughty voice—as if the male had already placed his sagging arse upon the throne.

Xcor looked back at the Tudor mansion. Through the diamond-pane windows, the male they had confronted was on the phone, smoking a cigarette like his lungs required nicotine more than oxygen. Then he paused and stared up at something. A moment later, shoulders sloping in defeat, he put the cell back to his ear.

Ichan's phone went off and he smiled as he took it out of his pocket. "Hello? How lovely of you to call—" There was a pause. "Oh, I think that's so wise of you—hello? Hello?"

Ichan put the cellular device away with a shrug. "I shan't even be offended that he hung up on me."

And another one falls to the logic.

Xcor gripped his stolen apple and wrenched it from his blade.

With a sure hand, he began to peel the bloodred skin from its crisp, white flesh, whittling around and around until a curling strip formed beneath his weapon.

As opposed to his favored stance of assassination, this new legal approach to a forced abdication was going well. They had another half dozen members of the First Families to meet and brief, and then it was time to make this official at the Council level. After that? The killings would have to be done—no doubt one or all of the aristocrats they were dealing with would have delusions of the crownal variety.

Easily cured, however, and then he would have what he wanted.

". . . meal of our choice?"

As Ichan and Tyhm looked at him, he realized that he'd just been asked out to eat.

Xcor let the strip of skin fall to the snow at his feet. No doubt the dandy inside had groundspeople who would pick it up, although given how unsettled the dear boy was, mayhap he would venture out for a walk amongst his fucking topiaries and see it himself.

Threats were best made on multiple levels.

"The field awaits me the now," Xcor said as he carved out a section of flesh and bared his fangs, bringing his knife up to his mouth along with the piece.

The crack as he bit down had its desired effect.

"Yes, well, of course, indeed, for truth," Ichan said, his words like a ballerina spinning off her pointed shoes and careening into the orchestra pit.

How cute.

And then there was a pause, as if the adieu was to be repaid. When Xcor merely cocked a brow, the two dematerialized sure as if there were emergencies afoot at their respective manses.

So irrelevant these pawns were—he had used some up already and no doubt one or both of the pair that had just departed would find their graves in service to him.

Inside the great house, the Council member they had come to see was still hanging his head—but not for long. Someone entered the room, and whoever it was, the aristocrat didn't want them to know of his upset. He pulled himself together, smiling and holding out his arms. As a young female went unto him, Xcor figured her to be the daughter.

She was beautiful, it was true—the drawing had been accurate.

But she was not a patch on another.

Unbidden, memories flooded his mind, images of fair skin and hair, and eyes that were capable of stopping him in his tracks sure as a bullet, tangled his thoughts until he was the one tripping over his boots even as he remained standing.

No, however pretty and young that daughter was, she was but a far-off echo of loveliness compared to his unattainable Chosen.

"You must stop this," he said into the cold night breeze. "Stop this the now."

A fine command, indeed—and yet it was several minutes before he could calm himself enough to focus and dematerialize from the front lawn.

A blink later and Xcor was finally in his element: The alley before him was an urban armpit, the snow filthy from the tire grab left over after countless dump and delivery trucks had passed o'er this stretch behind half a dozen cheap restaurants. In spite of frigid December gusts, the stench of spoiled meat and denaturing green matter was enough to make the inside of the nose tingle.

Breathing in, he searched for the sickly sweetness of the enemy.

He had been born deformed and cast away unto the world by the female who had brought him forth from her womb. Reared in the Bloodletter's war camp, he had been honed as a blade in that sadist's fire pit of aggression and pain, any weakness pounded out of him until he was as deadly as a dagger.

This theater of combat was where he belonged.

And he was not alone for long.

Wrenching his head around, he braced his weight into his thighs. A group of human men came into view, clearing the corner, walking in a pack. When they saw him, they stopped and drew in on themselves.

Xcor rolled his eyes and resumed his promenade in the opposite direction—

"Whadafuckyadoin'," came the shout-out.

Turning back, he eyed the five of them. They were wearing some sort of coordinated theme of tough human: leather jackets, black skull caps, bandannas tied to the bottoms of their faces.

They had clearly intended to come upon someone or someones else.

Not the kind of foe he bothered with. For one thing, humans were so inferior physically, it was like biting into that apple. Secondly, they were liable to involve others of their species, either on purpose through that dreaded 911 thing or inadvertently, by causing a noise that alerted passersby.

"Whadafuckyadoin'!"

If he stayed silent, mayhap this would escalate into a coordinated song-and-dance number? How frightening.

"Go about your night," he said in a low voice.

"Go about your—whatreyasomekindaforiegnfuck?"

Or something to that effect. Their accents were difficult to decipher—moreover, he was disinterested in making much effort on that front—

From out of nowhere, a car careened around that corner, its tires losing traction as its driver pounded on the brakes.

Gunshots rang out, echoing through the night, scattering the assembled, including himself.

Wrong place, wrong time, Xcor thought as he caught a slug in the shoulder, the pain blazing through his head—and making it impossible for him to dematerialize.

He wanted nothing of this silly fight amongst the rats without tails. But it appeared as if he were going to have to engage.

He was *not* dying as the result of a human's bullet.

THREE

I-87, A.K.A. THE NORTHWAY

Oh, that new-car smell.

A combination of too-fresh carpeting, still-viscous hinge oil, and glue that was only surface dry.

Sola Morte loved a fresh start in the automotive department, which was why she always leased her Audi A4s. Every three years she got a new one—sometimes more often if there was a program that let her jump ship a month or two early.

So, yeah, this was familiar territory . . . except for the fact that she was getting a whiff of heaven from the trunk of whatever sedan she had been shut into.

Not the way she'd planned on ending her night, but sometimes free will was out on break when you needed it.

The question now was, how to survive the kidnapping and get back home.

Given her line of work as a burglar, she was used to improvising in dangerous situations. She wasn't exactly MacGyver-capable; it wasn't like she could build a nine-millimeter autoloader out of duct tape, a tube of toothpaste, twelve cents, and a Bic lighter. But she was smart enough to feel around, looking for a tire iron, a tool kit . . . a forgotten soda can. Anything she could use as a weapon.

When she'd been abducted from her house, she'd had nothing but the parka on her back and a desperate hope that whoever it was got her out before her grandmother made it down the stairs and was dragged into all this. The latter happened. The former? Bad news, because she didn't even have a cell phone.

And so far, her palm expeditions around the trunk had yielded a big fat nada.

She also had no clue where she was being taken. Going by the purr from the undercarriage and the lack of potholes? They must be on the highway—and had been for a while.

Man, her head hurt.

What the hell had they hit it with? A hammer?

Straining her spine upward, she patted under the small of her back, thinking she might be lying on the compartment that held the spare tire—and tools. She didn't feel any seams in the carpeting, though. Maybe you had to lift the whole thing up? Shit.

Reaching over her head, she rechecked the side walls, feeling the soft scratch of the carpeting and the undulation of the wheel wells . . . then the netting that might have held groceries in place . . . a folded sheet of paper that could have been a map, a receipt for some kind of purchase, a "Top Ten Ways to Torture a Captive" list. . . .

Drawing her knees into her chest, she turned herself around in the tight space, shoving with her hands and her feet, cramping her head into an angle it really didn't appreciate.

"Jeeeesus . . ." she groaned as she paused to catch her breath. "Cirque du Soleil is *so* out for a second career."

Resuming the stretching and twisting, she finally got her prize—the ability to check out the opposite—

"Well, hello . . ."

Digging her fingertips into a break in the carpeting, she followed the square cutout until she found latches on either end. Disengaging a compartment cover, she popped the panel free and found . . .

Toolbox? First aid?

A lottery win manifesting itself in a fully loaded Smith & Wesson?

As she navigated by touch alone, trying to decipher the shape and feel of what was inside, she was reminded of how much she appreciated her vision.

"Gotcha," she hissed, digging her nails into the box and fighting with the hold to get the thing free.

When it popped out, she realized there was a handle on the lid. Dumb-ass.

Its latch was simple to pop free, and inside . . .

The cylinder was about eight inches long and an inch and a half wide. On one end there was a cap with a rough patch on its top, and inside? Party time.

This flare was her only shot.

Tightening her hand on the thing, she refocused on trying to figure out where she was going to end up—other than a morgue, of course. The problem was, she had no idea how long they'd been en route—but if they were taking her to Benloise's house? Then they had to be closing in on their destination. West Point wasn't that far from Caldie.

And this was Benloise's doing.

Payback by the narcotics wholesaler for her little home invasion and redecorating gig. Which in turn had been her way of telling him to F-off over a payment issue.

That had involved Assail.

Closing her eyes—even though she couldn't see a damn thing—she imagined that man, everything from his glossy black hair to his deep-set eyes to that body that should have belonged to an athlete . . . as opposed to a drug dealer who was probably going to take over the entire eastern seaboard as his territory.

For a split second of insanity, she entertained a fantasy that he would come after her and help get her out of this mess. And yup, that was awkward on so many levels—one, she had never relied on anyone before, and two, the whole save-me-big-man bullcrap was enough to make her want to hurl on principle.

But her pride was taking a backseat on this one: She knew waaaay too much about Benloise. It was going to take a miracle to get her free, and Assail was the closest thing to one of those she'd met. Too bad he wasn't going to miss her anytime soon. They knew each other only because she'd been paid—partially—by Benloise to spy on him. Assail hadn't appreciated that and had turned the tables on her.

Which had led to . . . other things.

Shaking her head until the pain made things spin, she reminisced on all that had been so important before she'd gotten ambushed in her own kitchen: the cat and mouse between the pair of them, the seductive threat he threw off, the erotic charge she got just by being in his presence.

All of that had been so fucking important.

The current roll of the dice had wiped that slate clean, however. Now she was in survival mode—and if that didn't pan out, she just hoped her grandmother had something left to bury.

Because she wasn't fooling herself. Benloise wasn't going to cut her any slack just because she had been, for a time, almost like a daughter to him in some ways. She shouldn't have pushed him. Temper, temper, temper; her anger had been her undoing.

God, her grandmother.

Tears threatened, stinging her eyes, making her crack her lids and blink to keep them from falling.

Too much loss in her vovó's life. Too many hard things. And this was probably going to be the worst of it all.

Unless Sola got herself out.

As feelings too big and complicated to hold in threatened to short out her brain, she struggled to contain them . . . and the eventual solution for that was a surprise. She went with the impulse, however—in the same way she intended to use what she had found in the trunk wall.

Putting her only weapon down by her hip, she clasped her hands over her heart and bowed her head in prayer, chin to chest.

Opening her mouth, she waited for the rote passages of her Catholic childhood to resurface in her brain and tell her tongue what to do.

And they did. "Hail Mary, full of grace . . ."

The words formed a cadence, a beat like that of her heart, the rhythm uniting her with a whole host of Sundays in her distant past.

When she was finished, she waited for some relief or strength or . . . whatever you were supposed to get from this age-old ritual.

Nope. "Damn it."

Words—it was all just words.

Frustration made her kick her head back, slamming it into the compartment—in just the wrong place. "Fuck!"

Time to get real, she told herself as she tried to reach around and rub the sore spot.

Bottom line? No one was coming to save her. As usual, she had only herself to fall back on, and if that wasn't enough to get her out of this? Then she was going to die in a truly horrible way—and her grandmother was going to suffer. Again.

Talk about your prayers? Sola would have given anything just to go back and rewind the evening, hitting pause at that moment when she had come home and missed the strange sedan parked across the street. In her perfect, redo world, she would have gotten her gun out and put a silencer on it before setting a foot past the front door. She would have killed them both, and then gone upstairs and told her grandmother she was going to move the furniture around just as her vovó had asked the week before.

Under the cover of night, she would have then taken the pair of men out into the garage, backed the car up, and put them in her trunk. Or . . . more like one in the backseat and the other in the trunk.

Out to the boonies. Bye-bye.

After which, she would have packed up her grandmother and they would have left within the hour—even though it would have been the middle of the night.

Her grandmother wouldn't have asked questions. She understood where things were at. Hard life, practical mind.

Off into the sunrise, so to speak, never to be seen again.

See? Much better movie all around—and maybe that could become reality again, provided Sola took care of business when Benloise's bodyguards put on the brakes and finally let her out.

Grasping her flare, she started to prepare herself. What angle she was going to take. How to come at them.

Just mental masturbation, though, wasn't it—everything was going to depend on split-second timing that was ultimately unpredictable.

As her mind floated into the zone, her breathing slowed and her senses sharpened. Waiting was not a problem anymore; time ceased to have any measure. Thoughts were not an issue. Exhaustion didn't exist.

It was as she settled into that netherworld between now and later that something truly transformative happened.

She saw clear as day a photograph of her grandmother. It had been taken back in Brazil when she was nineteen. Her face was unlined and full in the best sense, youth gleaming out of her eyes, her hair down and flowing, not bound.

If she had known then what awaited her in adulthood, she would never have smiled.

Her son dead. Her daughter dead. Her husband dead. And her granddaughter, the only one who was left?

No, Sola thought. This had to end well. It was the only option.

Sola didn't say anything out loud this time—there were no rote phrases or clasped palms. And she wasn't sure she believed her own prayer any more than the other ones that had been taught to her. But for some reason, she found herself bending God's ear in earnest.

I promise, Lord, that if you get me out of this, I will leave the life. I will take vovó and get out of Caldwell. I will never, ever endanger myself or steal from another or commit an evil act. This is my solemn vow to You, on my vovó's beating heart.

"Amen," she whispered aloud.

THE IRON MASK, CALDWELL, NEW YORK

"Oh-God-oh-God-oh-God. . . ."

As Trez held the blond college student up off the floor, he had a good grip on the backs of her legs—but he was sorely tempted to drop her like a Hot Pocket. The sex was adequate—along the lines of the cold-pizza standard: Even if it's cold, it's still pizza.

But it ain't no Bella Napoli on 7th Ave in Manhattan.

And this about-to-see-God stuff? Total buzz kill, and not because he was religious in the human way or jel that she was having a great time while he was thinking of pizza. Her grating, squeaky YouPorn performance with the head throws that kept landing her extensions in his face was getting on his nerves.

Closing his eyes, he tried to concentrate on the feel of his cock going in and out of her. The woman had big fake tits that were as hard as basketballs, and a stomach that had some jiggle, and he couldn't decide what was worst: the fact that he wasn't attracted to her in the slightest; the reality that he was fucking this skank in the front bathroom of his own club—so his staff was going to catch him walk-of-shaming it; or the chance, however slim, that his brother might hear about this from somebody.

Shit, iAm. The male had a stare that could make a football player in full tackle gear feel like his bare ass was in a stiff breeze.

Not what Trez was looking for.

". . . God, oh, God, oh, God . . ."

FFS, if she could only spice it up with a couple JCs or something.

"OHGODOHGOD—"

Reaching between them, he decided to put himself out of his mis-

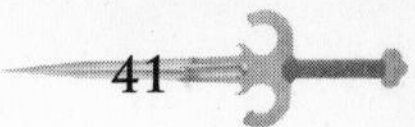

ery. Tickling her clit, he pitched her over that edge just in time for his erection to completely deflate and all but fall out of her.

Setting her back down on her feet, he immediately had to catch her, because her knees buckled.

"Oh . . . God . . . you're amazing . . . you're . . ."

Uh-huh, thanks, honey. The only thing he cared about was how long it would take to get her clothes back on. "You, too, baby."

Trez leaned to the side and picked up her—was it that bra thing she thought was a shirt? Or her thong? Or—

"Oh, I don't need my leggings yet . . . do I?"

These were for her legs? he thought as he held the black strip up. Hard to imagine it covering more than a hand or maybe one of those serving-bowl-size breasts.

Who had taken the pseudo-stockings off? Not him, he didn't think, but he couldn't remember, and not because he was drunk. This whole session, just like the last however many years of his love life, was not just utterly, but rather, purposely, forgettable.

Then why did he insist on pulling this shit again and again—

Right, no reason to channel iAm. His brother was more than capable of running through that rhetorical Every. Single. Fucking. Time. they were together.

"Daddy, I love you," the girl said as she gripped his biceps and hung off him like he was a stripper pole. "I love this."

"Me, too."

"You love me, right?"

"Always." He eyed the door and wished he'd scheduled a preemptive knock. "Lemme have your number, 'kay? 'Cause I gotta go back to work."

Cue the pouting—and didn't that make him want to bare his fangs and chew his way out of the bathroom wall.

"We could do it again," she drawled, getting up on her tiptoes to try to nuzzle against his neck.

Girlie, I could hardly get through it once, he thought. A repeat is not anatomically possible.

"Pleeeeeeeeeeeease, daddy . . ." More nuzzling. Then she eased back. "Please?"

Trez opened his mouth, frustration sharpening his temper and his tongue—

Except as he met her eyes, he saw an honest emotion in them and nearly recoiled. Talk about mirrors . . . he felt like he was looking at himself: sad. Hollow. Rootless.

She was half a woman.

He was half a male.

On that basis alone, they were Match.com time, two broken SOBs thrashing around the sex pool, trying to connect in ways that guaranteed their isolation would only continue.

"Please . . . ?" she begged, like she was getting ready for another loss in a string of them.

Staring down at her, he realized he'd common-denominatored her to her externals, but as with all strangers, there was a story behind how she'd ended up in a bathroom throwing around the L-word with a man who wasn't a man at all.

Hell, he wasn't even a normal vampire.

Trez brushed her cheek with his knuckles, and when she turned her head into his hand, he whispered, "Close your eyes—"

The knock was a one-and-doner, and considering how loud and to the point it was? Not like there needed to be a second.

"Boss? We got issues," came through the panels.

Big Rob's voice. So it was a security problem—and given that the guy hadn't gone to Xhex with it? She was either out for some reason . . . or, more likely, had sent for Trez herself.

The blonde's fake eyelashes lifted, but he didn't want that. "Gimme a minute, B.R."

"Roger that, boss."

"Close your eyes," he said again. As the blonde complied, he quieted himself, the muffled thunder of the club's bass beat drifting off, the smell of her too-heavy perfume abating, the pain in the center of his chest . . . well, that stayed right where it was, but the rest of everything went on the dimmer switch.

Reaching into her mind, he did what his brother had called him out on: As opposed to so many of these women, he took the time to erase the blonde's memories of them being together, from the inane conversation that she'd started up by the bar, to his taking her back here, to the religious experience she'd just had.

iAm was right. If Trez had been tidying up after himself like this all along? He wouldn't have gotten into the trouble he had with that other chick. And he and his brother wouldn't have ended up having to move into the Brotherhood's mansion. And that female Selena wouldn't have entranced him even more. . . .

Refocusing on the blonde, he decided not to just stop at the Wite-Out routine. Instead of leaving the twenty or so minutes as a blank zone, he gave her the fantasy she was after—that she'd met a guy who was googly-eyed over her and they'd had the sex of their lives five times in this bathroom before she'd decided she was too good for him.

Which in her new mind-set was going to be something she did frequently.

Finally, he inserted a thought that she should dress herself and check her makeup. And as a last-minute chaser, he tacked on that she was going to have the best year—no, decade—of her life.

Trez stepped out a moment later, fly up, shirt retucked, mask of all-good back in place. Big Rob was hovering in the shadows, discreet as any guy the size of a mountain could be.

Joining the guy, Trez crossed his arms over his chest and leaned against the cloth-covered wall. He didn't usually talk business out in the club proper, but the music was loud enough, the crowd self-absorbed in the way of the drunk and the desperate, and, last but not least, he felt compelled to keep an eye on the blonde. Make sure no one tried to get in there before she came out.

Plus he guessed he wanted some confirmation that he'd left her in a better state than he'd found her in.

At least one half of them could be improved.

"So what's up?" Trez scanned the dark, moody club, his monitoring both second nature and a matter of training: Shadows tended to be watchers, but after working with Rehv and now being the head of this den of iniquity, the shit was his primary interface.

Big Rob cracked his knuckles. "Alex broke up an argument about an hour ago between two non-regulars. Both men were kicked out, but the aggressor came back and is circling the sidewalk outside."

The blonde emerged from the bathroom, clothes where they needed to be, makeup retouched, hair pulled back instead of all over everywhere—but more to the point, her chin was level, her eyes calm and focused—and that secret smile on her lips took her essentially average looks into enticing territory.

As she walked into the crowd, Big Rob's eyes followed her and so did a lot of men's. But she didn't seem to care, her confidence all she needed as an escort.

Trez rubbed the center of his chest and wished he could whammy his own self and turn things on a dime like that. Then again, all the self-improvement in the world wasn't going to change the fact that the s'Hisbe wanted him back as a breeding stud for the rest of his natural life.

"Boss?"

"Sorry, what?"

"You want us to disappear the guy?"

Trez rubbed his face. "I'll go deal with him. What's he look like?"

"White boy, black clothes, Keith Richards hair."

"That narrows it down," Trez muttered.

"You'll see him out front. He's not in line."

Trez nodded and cut around the thick of the crowd, heading for the door. On his way, he looked over all the people, unconsciously searching for signs of conflict that could escalate from posturing bullshit to bowling-alley knockdown.

Even Goths could be frat boys if you pumped enough alchie into them.

Halfway to the exit, he caught a flash of something metallic off to the right, but as he stopped and reached out with senses other than his eyes, he couldn't find anything. Resuming his stride, he pushed his way out of his club, nodded to Ivan and the new guy, who were manning the entrance, and took a wander down the wait line, which was full of the usual suspects.

Although not the Kevin Spacey kind, of course. And more's the pity—he loved the guy in that movie.

No one out on the sidewalk fit B.R.'s description.

Guess whoever it was went for a wander.

As Trez pivoted to head back for the door, he got hit in the face with the beams of a trolling car, and the sting made him pull a vampire and shy away from the light. Blinking to clear his vision, he somehow made it to the front of the line and—

"What the fuck—he doesn't belong here! Why're you letting him in!"

As Trez realized he was the subject up for discussion, he stopped and looked over his shoulder. The mouthpiece with the attitude was about five-ten, one hundred and fifteen pounds—and not a girl.

Clearly, motherfucker suffered from terrier syndrome, his beady little eyes all fired up as he glared at Trez, his Stampy McStampy drill making him breathe heavy.

Probably played a lot of World of Warcraft or whatever it was—and that made him forget that if you were going to be a bigoted bigmouth, you'd better be able to back shit up.

Trez leaned down to the guy and gave him a moment to soak up the size difference—and what do you know, bitch's mouth closed and stayed that way.

"I own this place," Trez said in a low voice. "So the question is, why the fuck should I let *you* in." He glanced at Ivan. "He's not welcome here. Ever."

There was some conversating at that point, but he was done. As a Shadow, he was used to being stared at—regular vampires didn't know what to do with his kind, and frankly, he didn't really care for them, either. In fact, he'd been brought up to believe that the two shouldn't mix—at least until Rehvenge had stepped up to the plate and helped him and his brother in their exile. At first he'd been distrustful of the guy—until he'd recognized that Rehv was as they were: a foreigner in a closed club of folks he didn't respect.

Oh, and as for the human world? Everyone assumed he was black and attached their own racial associations, good and bad, to that—but there was the irony. He was neither "African" nor "American," so none of that shit applied to him in spite of the fact that his skin happened to be dark.

That was humans for you, though—self-absorbed to the point where they just had to see themselves in all situations. Meanwhile, there were whole other species walking among them, and they were none the wiser.

Although . . . that being said . . . if some misguided dumb-ass tried to pull the racial shit with him at his own front door? Then the idiot could fuck off.

Back inside the club, the strobe lights and the noise hit him like a brick wall and he had to force himself to break through the resistance. The flashes were just way too bright and the sound was worse, ricocheting around the inside of his skull until whatever was playing became an unintelligible mess.

What the hell was his staff thinking? Who'd made the call to crank it up so high—

Oh . . . shit.

Rubbing his eyes, he blinked a couple of times and . . . yup, there it was, in the right quadrant: a lineup of jagged lines that shimmered like sunlight through blown glass.

"Fuck me. . . ."

Courtesy of the sex sesh in the bathroom, the blonde had gotten herself a new hardwiring job—and he was about to enjoy eight to ten hours of barfing, diarrhea, and searing head pain.

As all migraine sufferers did, he glanced at his watch. He had about twenty minutes before the fun and games started, and he couldn't afford to waste them.

Walking faster, he pushed his way through the bodies, nodding to the working girls and his security team like everything was fine. Then he went into the staff-only back of the house, hit his office for his leather jacket and his keys, and exited stage left into the parking lot. His BMW was waiting for him, and as he got in, yanked the seat belt across his chest and hit the gas, he wished like hell he still lived at the Commodore—because then he could have had one of his bouncers do the driving.

Now that he'd taken up res at the Brotherhood mansion? Disinterested, third-party chauffeurs were a no-go.

Of course, he could call his brother. But iAm would offer his silent-treatment commentary the whole way home, and there was no need to subject himself to that loud noise: iAm was the only person he'd ever met who could make quiet harder on the ears than a jet plane taking flight.

As his phone went off, he thought, shit, he'd better call in and let everyone at work know he was down for the count.

Taking the cell out, he looked at the— "Great."

But it wasn't like he could send iAm to voice mail. Swiping his thumb across the screen, he put the thing up to his ear even though New York was a hands-free state.

His brother didn't even give him a chance to "hello" shit. "You're having a migraine."

"You're not supposed to be psychic."

"I'm not. I just pulled in as you tore out. I'm right behind you—and there's only one reason you drive off like that at one a.m."

Trez glanced in the rearview, and was quite proud of himself—if he cocked his head in a certain way, he could actually see the pair of headlights.

"Pull over."

"I'm—"

"Pull the fuck over. I'll come back for the car once I get you home."

Trez continued driving, heading for the Northway, thinking, nah, he could do this.

Good plan. At least until a car approached in the opposite lane—as it got closer, he was blinded completely and had no choice but to ease off on the gas. Blinking in the aftermath, he had every intention of nailing the accelerator and continuing on, except reality set in: He was running out of time, and not just in terms of the migraine.

The s'Hisbe were only going to up their warfare to get him back to the territories, and God only knew what their next move was going to be. So what this situation did not need was iAm watching his brother die right in front of him.

Trez had already done so much damage to the guy.

A Beamer fireball was *not* a good chaser to his track record.

Giving up, he pulled to the side, hit the brakes, and put his forehead down on his steering wheel. Even though he shut his eyes, the aura continued along its way, spreading out and moving gradually off to the upper edge. When it disappeared? Party time—and not in a fun way.

As he waited for iAm to stop next to him, he thought that it was ironic how doing the right thing sometimes felt like a total defeat.

FOUR

"Okay, what have we got here . . . ?"

The question was more, what *haven't* they got, Beth thought as she leaned over a freezer unit dedicated solely to ice cream.

Turned out pregnant women liked the sweet cold stuff. Okay, the pregnant Chosen, Layla, liked it—and Beth had delivered the same kind on schedule, every night for the last . . . how long had it been since the female's needing?

God, time flew.

And as she counted the days, she was well aware she wasn't thinking about Layla's progression. What she was really adding up was how many hours she'd logged in that room, sitting close by . . . hoping that for once an old wives' tale would come true.

She didn't just go up there to be a kind housemate or supportive friend.

Nope. Although why the hell she thought she and Wrath needed a baby in the middle of all this drama was a mystery. Mother Nature, however, had forced her around some kind of corner and there was no going back, no making sense of it, no reasoning with the urge.

Not that she'd necessarily talked to Wrath about it lately. As if he didn't already have enough on his plate. But come on, if she were able to kick-start her needing . . .

She just wanted to hold a piece of herself and of Wrath—and the more dangerous things became with the Band of Bastards, the more desperate that need became.

In some ways, it was the saddest commentary on where they were at.

At least something of him would survive if the Band of Bastards succeeded in killing—

The wave of pain at the thought was so great, she sagged against the freezer and it was a while before she could refocus on the mother lode of Breyers, Ben & Jerry's, Häagen-Dazs and Klondikes.

So much safer to stress over which flavor she'd have tonight. Layla was always vanilla—it was the only kind she could keep down. But Beth was wide open on that one, and thanks to Rhage's infamous appetite, there were, like, a gabillion choices.

As she searched for inspiration, the dilemma was a slice right out of her childhood, a modern-day echo of the days when she would palm up one of her hard-earned dollars, walk a half mile to Mac's Grocery, and take twenty minutes to get the same Hershey's Dixie cup of chocolate that she always did. Funny, she could still remember how the place had smelled like those cake cones Mac had handmade. And that cash register, the old-fashioned one that had had a hand crank.

When she'd check out, Mac would always give her a red plastic spoon, a napkin and a smile—along with her twenty-six cents in change.

He'd been extra nice to the orphans who'd lived down at Our Lady. Then again, there were a lot of people who had been kind to her and the other kids who had been either unwanted or unlucky.

"Mint chocolate chip," she said, reaching in and long-arming a stretch to the back.

As the cold air wafted up, she stopped to soak in the deep freeze. "Oh, yeah . . ."

Even though it was frickin' December, she found herself craving the chill, her skin goose-bumping, the pores on her face tightening, the inside of her nose humming from all the dryness.

Guess all that sex was still revving her up.

Closing her eyes, she went back to Wrath taking her down onto the floor and ripping her clothes off. So good. So what they needed.

Although she hated the way she felt now.

He was so damned far away, even though his body was just upstairs in that study.

Maybe that was another reason she wanted a child.

Refocus, refocus. "Vanilla, vanilla . . . where are you?"

When it turned out the vanilla was MIA, she had to settle for a trio'd half gallon that was polluted with strawberry and chocolate. No biggie. With proper surgical extraction, she'd be able to get the job done without getting any offending contamination in Layla's bowl.

Leaving the pantry and entering the kitchen proper, the sweet, earthy smell of sautéing onions and mushrooms mixed with basil and oregano was heaven in her nose. But the ambrosia wasn't for Last Meal and it wasn't a *doggen* at the sauce pot.

Nope. It was iAm—again. Which considering he appeared to cook when stressed suggested someone else's life was in the crapper.

The Shadow and his brother were the most recent additions to the Brotherhood house, and as the owner and head chef of the ultra-old-school Salvatore's Restaurant, iAm had more than proved his chops with linguine—although that was not to say Fritz approved of the guy getting out all those multi-gallon pots: As usual, the butler was hovering in the periphery, apoplectic that one of the household guests was doing any cooking.

"That smells delicious," she said as she put the containers on the deck-size granite island.

She didn't have a chance to get the bowls or spoons. Fritz sprang into action, pulling open cupboards and drawers—and she didn't have the heart to tell him not to wait on her.

"So what is it this time?" she asked the Shadow.

"Bolognese." iAm cracked open another spice bottle, and seemed to know the exact amount to put in without benefit of a measuring spoon.

Meeting his almond-shaped black eyes, Beth pulled her turtleneck higher to hide the bite marks on her neck. Not that he seemed to care either way. "Where's your brother?"

"Upstairs," came the tight reply.

Ah. Closed subject. "Well, I guess I'll see you at Last Meal?"

"I've got a meeting, but there's lamb for the rest of you, or so I've heard."

"Oh, I thought you were cooking for—"

"This is therapy," he said, banging the wooden spoon clean on the rim of the pot. "It's the only reason Fritz lets me use his stove."

She dropped her voice. "I thought you had special powers over him."

"Trust me, if I did, I'd use them." He turned down the flame. "S'cuse me. I've got to go check on Trez."

"Is he injured?"

"You might say." He gave her a brief bow and headed out of the room. "Later."

In his wake, the air seemed to change, the molecules in the kitchen calming down sure as if his dark mood had electrified them. Freaky, but she liked him and his brother: Another couple of trained killers in the house was not a bad thing at all.

"Mistress, I believe I have everything you need." The butler presented her with the accoutrements necessary for Breyer's imbibing on a silver tray. "For you and the Chosen."

"Oh, Fritz, how lovely—but, actually, I just need one bowl. I'm going to eat mine out of the carton as tacky as that sounds. But I could use a—thank you." She smiled as the butler handed over a scoop. "Do you read minds?"

The *doggen* blushed, his weathered, lined face breaking into a smile. "No, mistress. Occasionally I anticipate well, however."

Popping the top off the tri-flavor carton, she dug in, being careful to scoop the vanilla only. "Try all the time on that one."

As he flushed and ducked his already drooping eyes, she wanted to hug him. But the last time she'd done that, he'd nearly fainted from the impropriety. *Doggen* lived by a strict code of behavior, and although their fondest wish was to serve well, they simply couldn't handle it if they were praised.

And iAm had already stressed the poor guy out.

"Are you sure I may not apportion the servings for you?" the butler said anxiously.

"You know how I like to do it myself."

"May I carry the tray up for you, then?"

"No, I've got it." When he seemed ready to implode, she finished filling Layla's bowl and hedged, "Would you mind putting the ice cream away for me?"

"Yes, please, mistress. And the scoop. I shall take care of that."

As he made off like a bank robber with loot, she shook her head, picked up the tray and headed out into the dining room. Emerging on the far side into the foyer, she had to pause and take it all in. Even though she'd seen the three-story expanse every night for the last two years, the astounding space was still like entering into a different world: from its gold leafing to its brilliantly colored mosaic floor, from the muraled ceiling so high above to all the malachite-and-marble columns, it was pure magic.

And pure royalty.

In fact, the entire mansion was a work of art, each space in the house a new flavor of awe-inspiring luxury, a different tone set to perfection in every room.

She'd certainly never lived like this before Wrath had come into her life—or expected to. Dear Lord, she could remember after the two of them had first moved in here. Hand in hand, they'd gone through all the wings and floors, from the catacombed basement to the raftered attic. How many rooms were there? She'd lost count in the fifties.

Crazy, crazy.

And to think it hadn't been the only thing she had inherited from her father. Money . . . there had been so much money, too.

To the point where, even though she had shared half of it all with John Matthew after he'd come into their lives? Hadn't made a dent in spite of her half-brother taking millions and millions.

Totally nuts.

Crossing over the depiction of an apple tree in bloom, she hit the bloodred carpeted stairs and gunned for the second floor. An orphan all her life, it had been a shock to find out her father had known of her, had watched over her, had provided for her. But then from everything she'd heard, Darius had been like that. Never one to shirk duty.

God, she wished she'd known him.

Especially now.

As she reached the top of the stairs, she found the doors to the study open, and her man was where he hated to be—curled over acres of paperwork done in Braille, his huge shoulders blocking out most of the carved throne he sat in, his talented fingers tracing line by line, his brow furrowed trench-deep behind those wraparounds—

Both her man and George, his beloved service dog, looked over as if they'd caught her scent.

"Leelan," Wrath said on an exhale.

With a scramble, the golden retriever jumped up from his curled

position on the floor, flagged tail wagging, jowls scrunching into a grin that made him sneeze.

She was the only one he smiled for—although even as much as he loved her, he did not leave Wrath's side.

Putting the silver tray of ice cream down on a hall table, she strode in and waved to Saxton, who was in his usual spot on one of the pale blue French sofas. "How are the hardest-working menfolk on the planet?"

The attorney in the Old Laws stood up from his own pile of papers and gave her a bow, his fine bespoke suit accommodating the movement with ease. "You are looking well."

Yeah, well, nothin' like a little lovin'.

"Thanks." She went around the massive desk and took her husband's face in her hands. "Hey."

"I'm so glad you're here," he breathed—like it had been years since they'd seen each other.

Leaning down to kiss his mouth, she knew that he had closed his eyes even though she couldn't see behind the dark lenses.

And then she had to be about the dog.

"How are you, George?" Just like her hubs, she gave that puppy-soft face a smooch. "You taking care of our King?"

The chuff and the *thud-thud-thud* of his tail hitting the edge of the throne was a big, fat yes if she'd ever heard it.

"So what are you guys working on?" she asked as Wrath pulled her into his lap and stroked her back.

It was so odd. Before she'd met him, she'd hated the touchy-feely, cutesy cuddle stuff couples pulled. But what do you know, times changed.

"Just petitions." Read: Bullshit I'd rather light on fire than deal with.

"And we have another two dozen left." Saxton stretched his right arm as if it had kinked. "And then we have dispute resolutions and birth and death announcements."

Wrath let his head fall back. "I keep thinking there's a better way of dealing with this. I hate turning you into a secretary, Saxton."

The male shrugged over his legal pad. "I don't mind it a'tall. Anything to get the job done."

"On that note, what's our next one?"

Saxton took a piece of paper out of a thick folder. "Right. So this gentlemale wants to take on another *shellan*—"

Beth rolled her eyes. "What, like, *Sister Wives*, the vampire edition?"

"It is lawful." Saxton shook his head. "Although frankly, as a gay male, I don't know why anybody would want one, much less multiple—oh, I mean but for your good self, my queen. You would be worth making an exception for."

"Watch it, solicitor," Wrath growled.

"Kidding," the solicitor shot back.

Beth smiled at how comfortable they'd become with each other. "Wait, so is the two-wives thing common?"

Saxton lifted one shoulder in an elegant shrug. "It used to be more prevalent when the population was larger. Now, we have fewer of everything: matings, births, deaths."

Wrath put his lips by her ear. "Can you stay and have my break with me?"

A roll of his hips suggested his brain had taken a U-ie into horizontal territory. Or vertical—God knew he was strong enough to hold her off the floor for however long he wanted.

As her body began to warm . . . she thought of the ice cream she'd left in the hall. "Can you give me an hour? I have to—"

A loud crash out on the second-floor landing brought everyone's heads around.

"What the fuck is that?" Wrath gritted.

Downtown in that alley, Xcor crouched and covered his bullet wound as popping sounds rang out all around him and screeching tires announced the arrival of more gang members.

Cover. He needed cover—*now*. These humans did not care about him, but their gunfire was thick as a downpour and as unpredictable and undiscriminating as a stampede of bulls.

Leaping backward, he threw his body against the building, and the pain in his shoulder was a stunner. No time to dwell on it. Looking to the left . . . the right . . .

The only thing he saw was a door about fifteen feet away, and he dropped to the ground and rolled to it, outing his own gun in the process. Discharging two shots into the steel locking mechanism, he kicked hard and dove into the darkness beyond.

The air inside was fetid . . . and sweet.

Sickly sweet. Like the rot of death.

Rancid . . . like a *lesser*.

As he shut himself in, shots continued to be fired, and it wasn't going to be long before sirens would ring out. The question was, how many dead, how many wounded, and would any of that bunch of rats without tails find their way in here?

Alas, those silly questions would have to be answered after he figured out why this place smelled of his enemy.

Taking out his penlight, he flashed it around from his position on the dirty floor. The commercial kitchen had clearly been abandoned, spiderwebs hanging from the industrial fan over the stove and the empty racks above the counters . . . dust having settled on all surfaces . . . the detritus of a move hastily executed littering the way to the door.

Getting to his feet, Xcor panned his illumination in fat circles. Empty, tipped-over buckets that had once held commercial portions of sauces and yogurts cluttered a prep station, and topless tubs still full of mustard and ketchup revealed contents that had turned into solids, long since past rot and into a state of mummification. Farther in, a lineup of trays by a rusty industrial dishwasher had an errant spoon or fork in them, and opaque, half-broken glassware sat as if waiting for a ghostly washer to send them through the machine.

Crunching through the remnants of white china plates, he followed the scent that had commanded his attention.

The Lessening Society was made up of humans recruited into a war against vampires, weaklings transformed out of their pitiful state by the Omega—the side effect of which was a permanent stench somewhere between a two-day-old dead deer and spoiled milk.

One could always find the enemy by one's nose. . . .

The kitchen's meat locker was in the far corner, its prison-worthy door cracked open, its interior another pitch-black slice of God only knew what.

As he reached forward for the latch, his skin glowed white in the flashlight beam, and the creak of him widening the gap was loud enough to make his ears hum. A mad-dash scattering of tiny paws suggested actual rats were fleeing his arrival, and he felt them go over the tops of his combat boots.

The stink was enough to make his eyes water.

The beam entered first.

And there it was.

Hanging in the center of the walk-in unit, suspended on a hook through the back of the neck, a human male was doing an excellent bovine imitation.

At least, Xcor assumed it was a male, going by the pants and the leather jacket. Facial identification was impossible: The rats were eating him from the crown down, using the chain that was keeping everything up off the floor as a motorway to get to their fragrant meal.

So this was tragically not his enemy, but an actual dead body.

Such a disappointment. He had been hoping for something that pertained to himself. Instead, only more humans—

The crashing sound of somebody stumbling into the darkness had him clicking off his flashlight, his senses going on high alert.

Even with the stench from his friend with the meat-hook bow tie, the copper scent of fresh blood preceded whoever it was. As did the grunting of the wounded.

Awww. Someone had a boo-boo.

The flailing continued as sirens announced the Caldwell police's arrival—but the sounds were muffled, suggesting that the new arrival to the kitchen had had the presence of mind to shut them in together.

"Fuck!"

His visitor sent some of those empty plastic containers flying as he ran into the counter. Then there was more cursing. A groan as if he were laying himself down, likely on that stretch of stainless steel. Then shallow panting.

Losing patience with the entire drama, Xcor stepped free of the refrigerator. Unlike the injured gang member, he had some idea of the layout, and he managed to zero in on the guy, thanks to his hearing and a memory of where the center island was.

Things would have been much easier with sight, however. Apart from the obvious benefits of orientation, he did not enjoy the weightless feeling that came with blindness, nor the fact that he had to rely on his ears and sense of smell to navigate. There was also the reality that anything could be in front of his feet, ready to trip him up.

But he made it over toward the stricken human.

"You are not alone," Xcor drawled into the darkness.

"What! Oh, God! Who—"

"Do I sound like one of your own?" He was careful to roll the R a little longer than he usually would, just in case his Old Language accent was not perfectly clear.

More breathing. Heavy, very heavy. Accompanied by the acrid smell of true terror.

"You humans . . ." Xcor took a couple more steps forward, no longer bothering to muffle the fall of his boots. "The problem with you is that you have no true enemies. You fight amongst yourselves over the blocks of city streets or the lines of countries, because there is nothing external to unite you. My kind, conversely? We have an enemy that necessitates a certain cohesion."

Not enough to forestall his crown-ish ambitions, however.

At this point, the human started talking gibberish. Or mayhap that was a prayer of some sort?

Such weakness. It was deplorable—and exploitable as a moral imperative.

Xcor flicked on his flashlight.

In its beam, the gang member jerked around, his bloodstained body wiping clean a section of the countertop.

Plasma . . . as good as Windex, evidently.

Wide eyes strained the confines of their sockets, and hard breathing whistled out of an open mouth, the former tough guy taken down multiple pegs as pain and fear sliced his bravado into nothing but a memory.

"You should know that there are others who walk amongst you," Xcor said in a low voice. "Like, but not the same. And we are always watching."

The man cringed away, not that there was far to go. The counter was a workspace for cutlery and sieves, not a mattress for a grown-ass man.

Any more of that and he was going to end up on the floor.

"Who . . . who are you?"

"Mayhap a visual rather than a description shall suffice."

Baring his fangs, Xcor tipped up the flashlight and put his face within the illumination.

The loud scream was high-pitched, and did not last. Thanks to the overwhelming adrenal response, the man passed out cold, the stink of urine that wafted up suggesting he'd lost control of his functions.

Rather amusing, really.

Xcor moved quickly, navigating with ease over to the door, thanks to the flashlight. Assuming position against the wall, he clicked off the beam and let that scream draw its proper attention.

The Caldwell Police Department responded with admirable efficiency, a number of the officers throwing open the door, their own flashlights piercing through the dense darkness.

The instant they saw the gang member, they rushed forward, and that was Xcor's cue for a departure.

As he slipped out the door, he heard the word *vampire* rise up through a chaos of conversation—and thus it was with a smile that he dematerialized out of the way of the crowd.

Back in the Old Country, he and his Band of Bastards had kept the speculations and myths going by showing themselves from time to time, always to individuals, and ever in ways that fit the misconceptions that humans had of the species.

Defilers of virgins. Sources of evil that slept in coffins. Monsters of the night.

Such pish—although the latter did indeed pertain to himself.

And in truth, it felt good to do something similar here in Caldwell, rather as a dog marks its territory. Enjoyable, too, to give the irrelevance on that kitchen island something to haunt his memory during all his upcoming days in prison.

One needed to take one's amusement where one found it.

FIVE

When John Matthew had hit the mansion's magnificent staircase, the last thing on his mind had been the past.

As he'd ascended, he'd been focused on, in order of importance: getting his *shellan* naked before Last Meal; getting her naked in their bedroom; annnnnd getting his *shellan* naked and underneath him in their bedroom before Last Meal.

Whether or not he was fully clothed? Not a big concern except for the below-the-waist stuff. And if push came to shove, he could totally punt on the bedroom part—provided wherever they ended up offered even a semblance of privacy.

So, yup, on his way to the second floor, he was very much plugged into the present and the presence of Xhex—who, if everything had gone to plan, had left the Iron Mask about fifteen minutes ago and was now covering the "naked" and "bedroom" part of his preoccupation.

Fate offered a diversion, however.

As he arrived on the upper landing, the double doors to Wrath's study were open, and through them he saw a familiar tableau: the King seated behind his ornate desk; the queen in his lap; George, the golden retriever, at their feet; Saxton, Blay's former flame and Wrath's current solicitor, sitting off to the side on a sofa. As usual, the acre-size desktop was littered with paperwork, and Wrath's mood was in the shitter.

In fact, that grim expression was part and parcel of the room, just like the antique French furniture that struggled to support the Brothers during meetings and the pale blue walls that seemed better suited to the boudoir of some chick named Lisette or Louisa.

But what did he know from *Extreme Home Makeover*.

Pausing to offer the four of them a wave, he intended to carry on to his room, find his mate, take her in a variety of positions—and then go down freshly showered to the final meal of the day.

Instead . . . just before he turned away . . . he met the eyes of his half sister, Beth.

The instant the connection was made, some combination of neurons fired in his brain, and the electrical load was too much for his motherboard: Without warning, he went into a free fall, his weight listing backward as the seizure took over his muscles, rendering them at first spastic and then utterly rigid.

He blacked out before he hit the ground . . .

. . . and when he regained consciousness, the first thing that registered was the ow-ow-ow of his head and his ass.

Blinking slowly, he discovered that at least he could see, the ceiling above coming into clear focus first before a lineup of concerned faces registered. Xhex was right by his side, his dagger hand in between her palms, her brows down as if she'd wanted to come into the midnight of his pass-out and drag him back to her.

As half-*symphath*, maybe she could do that. Maybe that was the reason he'd returned so quickly? Or had he lost consciousness for hours?

Doc Jane was next to her, and on his other side were Qhuinn and Blay. Wrath was down at his feet with Beth—

The moment his sister's presence registered, the electrical activity started up again, and as a second go-around with the nightie-nights threatened, all he could think was, Damn it, this hadn't happened for so long.

He'd assumed this shit was over with.

Seizures had never been a problem for him until he'd met Beth for the first time—and after that there had been other episodes, always out of the blue, never with any kind of pattern he could discern. The only good news? They hadn't ever happened during fighting and had not endangered his life—

Unbidden, his body drew upward, his torso lifting itself off the carpet sure as if there were a rope tied to his rib cage and somebody far above was hauling him up.

"John?" Xhex said. "John, lie back."

Something welled inside his chest, some kind of cresting emotion that was both out of his reach and utterly visceral. Reaching for Beth, he willed her to take his hand—and as she crouched down and did, his mouth started moving, his lips and tongue finding unfamiliar patterns over and over again . . . even as no sound broke through his muteness.

"What is he trying to say?" Beth demanded. "Xhex? Blay?"

Xhex's expression became impassible. "Nothing. It's nothing."

John frowned and thought, Bullshit. And yet he didn't know what it was any more than Beth did—and he certainly couldn't seem to stop the communicating.

"John, whatever it is, it's all right." His sister squeezed his hand. "You're okay."

Looming above his *shellan*, Wrath's face shifted into an implacable mask—as if he'd picked up on some vibe and didn't like it.

Suddenly, John could feel his mouth moving in a different pattern, other things getting expressed now; although damned if he had a clue what they were. Meanwhile, Beth was frowning . . . so was Wrath. . . .

And that was it.

As his brain began to short out again, his vision closed in on Beth until all he saw was her face.

For no good reason, he felt like he hadn't seen her in a year or two. And the significance of her features, the big blue eyes, the dark lashes, the long dark hair . . . resonated in his chest.

Not romantically, no.

This was something else entirely—and yet just as powerful.

Too bad he couldn't hang on to consciousness any longer to figure it out.

"We are ready."

As Assail finished his second line of cocaine, he straightened from his granite countertop and regarded his cousins: Across the kitchen of his glass house on the Hudson River, the two of them were dressed in matte black from head to foot. Even their guns and knives didn't catch the light.

Perfect for what he had planned.

Assail screwed the top of his vial shut and tucked the stash into his black leather jacket. "Let us go, then."

Leading them out the back door by the garage, he was reminded of why he'd brought them over from the Old World to Caldwell: Ever prepared and never questioning.

In that regard, they were exactly like the autoloaders they carried upon their able bodies night and noon.

"We're going south," he ordered. "Follow my signal."

The twins nodded at him, their perfectly identical faces composed and grim, their powerful bodies prepared to uncurl and dispatch whatever was needed for any situation. In truth, they were the only ones he trusted—and even that pledge, grounded in their communal blood, wasn't an absolute.

As Assail pulled a black mask over his face, they did the same—and then it was time to dematerialize. Closing his eyes to concentrate, he regretted the coke. He hadn't really needed the buzz—considering where they were going, he was amped up more than enough. Lately, however, doing the powder was akin to pulling his coat on or holstering a forty under his arm.

Rote.

Focus . . . focus . . . focus . . .

Intent and will coalesced a heartbeat later and his physical form fragmented into a loose association of molecules. Zeroing in on his destination, he clouded toward it, sensing his cousins traveling through the night skies with him.

In the back of his mind, he recognized that this excursion was out of character. As a businessman, life for him was calculated on the basis of ROI: everything he did was predicated on a return for the investment made. Which was why he was involved in the drug trade. Hard to have better margins than selling black-market chemical products to humans.

So, no, he was not a rescuer; he was the anti–Good Samaritan. And when it came to vengeance? Any he wielded was on his own behalf, never another's.

Exceptions were going to be made in this case, though.

His destination was an estate in West Point, New York, a venerable old stone house that was set back on acres of lawn. Assail had been on the property once before—when he'd been following a certain burglar . . . and watched her not only break in through a very viable security system, but traipse throughout the mansion without taking a goddamn thing.

She had, however, pivoted one of the Degas sculptures about an inch out of position.

And the consequences for her had been dire.

Things were, however, going to be reversed.

Violently.

Assuming form at the lowest corner of the vast front lawn, he masked himself in the line of trees that bordered the estate's far edges. As the cousins materialized next to him, he recalled that first trip here, picturing Sola in the snow, her white parka blending in as she cross-country skied up toward her target.

Simply extraordinary. That was the only way he could describe every single thing about the woman—

A proprietary growl rose up deep in his throat—one more thing that wasn't like him a'tall. He rarely cared about anything other than money . . . certainly not about females, and never, ever about human women.

But Sola had been different since the moment he had caught her scent as she'd trespassed on his own property—and the idea that Benloise had taken her? From her home? Where her grandmother slept?

Unacceptable.

Benloise was not going to live through this choice he had made.

Assail began to stride forward, measuring the landscape with his sharp eyes. Thanks to a bright, winter moon, it might as well have been daylight as opposed to two in the morning—everything from the eaves of the house to the contours of the terraces to the outbuilding in the back clearly visible before him.

Nothing moved. Not around the exterior nor past any of the darkened windows of the house itself.

Closing in, he proceeded around to the back, reacquainting himself with the layout of terraces and floors. So old money, he thought. So established. As un–drug wholesaler as one could get.

Mayhap Benloise was less than proud of the way he made his paper.

"We penetrate here," Assail said softly, nodding to the plate-glass windows of a sitting porch.

Ghosting in through them, he re-formed in the interior, standing motionless as he listened for footsteps, a scream, a scramble, a closing door.

A glowing red light high up in a corner informed him that the security system was on and running—and the motion detectors hadn't yet been triggered by their sudden appearance. The instant he moved? All hell was going to break loose.

Which was the plan.

Assail first knocked out the security cameras. Then he triggered the alarm by reaching into his pocket and pulling free a Cuban cigar—in response, that light immediately started blinking. And whilst it discoed along, he took his time lighting his smoke, fully expecting any number of thick-necked strong-arms to come racing in.

When that did not occur, he exhaled over his shoulder and strode forward, going throughout the first floor with the cousins tight on his heels. As he went along, he ashed on the Oriental rugs and the Italian marble tiles.

A little calling card in the unlikely event they didn't meet up with anyone: Considering the retaliation the man thought appropriate for a statue's reorientation, cigar debris was going to send the bastard right over the edge.

When he found nothing in the public rooms of the house, he headed for the servant wing and discovered an empty kitchen that was modern and utterly uninspiring. God, how boring—the gray-and-chrome color scheme was like the pallor of the elderly, and the sparse furnishings suggested decor was not a priority in spaces Benloise did not frequent himself. But more to the point, and as with the reception rooms, there was no scent from Sola's presence nor that of gunpowder or fresh blood. There were also no dishes in any of the three deep-bellied sinks, and when he opened the refrigerator just because he could, he found six green Perrier bottles on the top shelf and nothing else—

A set of headlights washed across the windows, flaring in his face, casting sharp shadows among table legs and chair backs and stands of cooking utensils.

Assail puffed out a mushroom cloud of smoke and smiled. "Let us go out and welcome them home."

Except the vehicle passed by the house and zeroed in on the out-

building—suggesting that whoever it was had not come in response to the alarm being set off.

"Sola . . ." he whispered as he dematerialized onto the snow-covered lawn.

Emotions riding high, he nonetheless made sure to disable the monitoring cameras on the rear exterior—and then he ripped off his mask so he could breathe better.

The non-descript sedan stopped grille-first into the garage, and two white human men got out of the front, clamping the doors shut and going around to the—

"Greetings, my friends," Assail announced as he leveled his forty at them.

Ah, look. They were such good little listeners, each going statue as they jerked in the direction of his voice.

Walking over, Assail trained his muzzle on the man on the right, knowing that the twins would judge correctly his focus and concentrate on the other one. When he'd closed the distance, he leaned in and peered through the windows of the backseat, bracing himself to see Sola in some form of compromise. . . .

Nothing. There was no one back there, nobody bound and gagged, knocked out, or cowering in submission against the beating that would surely come.

"Open the trunk," Assail ordered. "Only one of you—you. You do it."

As Assail followed the man around, he kept his gun right at the back of the fucker's head, his finger twitching at the trigger, ready to squeeze.

Pop!

The trunk latch released and the panel lifted soundlessly, inner lights coming on. . . .

To illuminate two duffel bags. That was it. Nothing but two black nylon duffel bags.

Assail puffed his cigar. "Goddamn it—where is she?"

"Where is who?" the man asked. "Who are you—"

On a surge of pure hatred, his anger leaped ahead of his mind, taking over, taking control.

Pop! number two was the sound of a bullet leaving Assail's gun and blasting right through the guy's frontal lobe. And the impact sent a spackle of blood all over those nylon carry-ons, and the car, and the driveway.

"Jesus Christ!" the other guy barked. "What the—"

Rage, undiluted by any semblance of rational thinking, made Assail roar some horrible, ugly sound—as his trigger jumped the gun again. So to speak.

Pop! number three dropped the driver, the bullet entering right between his eyebrows, the body falling backward in a narcoleptic free fall.

As loose arms and legs flopped on the snow, Ehric's dry voice drifted over. "You realize we could have questioned them."

Assail bit into his cigar, taking a long puff just so he didn't do something to his own bloodline that he'd regret. "Take the bags and hide them where can we find them on the property—"

Down at the base of the drive, a car turned off the main road and came forward at a tear. "Finally," Assail bitched. "One would expect a faster response."

Brakes were hit at the house—at least until whoever was behind the wheel saw Assail and the sedan and the cousins. Then tires grabbed at the snow pack as the gas was hit once again.

"Take the duffels," he hissed to the twins. *"Go."*

Spotlit by the headlights, Assail lowered his gun down to his thigh so that it became lost in the folds of his three-quarter leather coat—and he ordered his arm to stay there. Much as it infuriated him further, Ehric was right. He'd just murdered two mouthpieces.

Further evidence that he was out of his mind in all this. And he could not make that uncharacteristic mistake again.

As the sedan slid to a halt, three men got out, and indeed, they had come prepared. Multiple muzzles pointed in his direction, and they were steady: These boys had done this before, and in fact, he recognized two of them.

The bodyguard in front actually lowered his autoloader. "Assail?"

"Where is she?" he demanded.

"What?"

In truth, he was getting so bored with these frowns of confusion.

Assail's trigger finger started twitching again. "Your boss has something I want back."

The enforcer's sharp eyes shifted to the first sedan with its open trunk—and given the immediate brow pop, it appeared he noticed the soles of his predecessors' shoes upon the asphalt.

"Neither of them could give me an answer," Assail drawled. "Perhaps you should like to give it a try?"

Instantly, that gun was back up into position. "What the fuck are you—"

From out of thin air, the twins made an appearance and flanked the trio—and they had far more firepower, what with all four of their palms locked on a quartet of Smith & Wessons.

Assail kept his gun where it was, out of the action temporarily. "I would suggest you drop your weapons. If you do not, they will kill you."

There was a heartbeat of a pause—which proved too long for Assail's liking.

In the blink of an eye, his arm shot up and *pop!* He shot the closest guard, putting a bullet through his ear at a trajectory that left the remaining two men still standing.

As yet another dead weight fell to the ground, he thought, See? There was still plenty of living and breathing left to work with.

Assail lowered his arm and released another plume of smoke that drifted into the headlights, tinting the illumination blue. Addressing the pair who remained vertical, he said levelly, "I shall ask you again. Where is she."

Rather a lot of talk sprang up, but none of it included the words *woman*, *held*, or *captive*.

"You're boring me," he said, lifting his muzzle once more. "I'd suggest one of the two of you start getting to the point now."

SIX

"Is he alive?"

Beth heard the words come out of her mouth, but was only half aware of having spoken them. It was just too terrifying when a guy as strong as John Matthew went over like that—and worse? He'd surfaced for a minute and a half, tried to communicate something to her, and passed out cold again.

"Good," Doc Jane said as she pressed a stethoscope to his heart. "Okay, I need my blood pressure—"

Blay pressed the floppy cuff into the doctor's hands and the woman worked fast, wrapping it around John's bulging biceps and puffing up its inner tube. There was a long hiss that was too loud, and Beth leaned back against her *hellren* as they waited for the results.

It seemed to take forever. Meanwhile, Xhex was cradling John's head in her lap—and God, that was a hard spot: Someone you love down and out, no clue what was going to happen next.

"A little on the low side," Jane muttered as she ripped the Velcro free of itself. "But nothing catastrophic—"

John's eyes began to open, the lids flipping up and down.

"John?" Xhex said roughly. "Are you coming back to me?"

Apparently he was. He turned to his mate's voice and lifted a shaking hand, clasping her palm and staring into her eyes. Some kind of energy exchange seemed to take place, and a moment later, John sat up. Stood up. Was only a little on the wobbly side as the pair embraced and stood soul to soul for a long while.

When her brother finally turned to her, Beth broke free of Wrath and hugged the younger male fiercely. "I'm so sorry."

John pulled back and signed, *What for?*

"I don't know. I just don't want— I don't know."

As she threw her hands up, he shook his head. *You didn't do anything wrong. Beth—seriously. I'm okay and it's cool.*

Meeting his blue eyes, she searched them as if the answer to what had happened and what he'd been saying could be read there. "What were you trying to tell me?" she whispered aloud.

The instant she heard what she'd said, she cursed. Now was hardly the time. "Sorry, I didn't mean to ask that—"

Was I saying something? he signed.

"Let's give him some space," Wrath said. "Xhex, you wanna take your man to your room."

"Amen to that." The broad-shouldered female stepped in, hooking a hold around John's waist and marching him off down the hall of statues.

Doc Jane put her equipment back in her little black bag. "It's time to find out what's causing those."

Wrath cursed softly. "Does he have medical clearance to fight?"

She got to her feet, her smart eyes narrowing. "He's going to hate me, but no. I want to do an MRI on him first. Unfortunately, for that, we're going to have to make some arrangements."

"How can I help?" Beth asked.

"I'll go talk to Manny now. Havers doesn't have that kind of equipment and neither do we." Doc Jane dragged a hand through her short blond hair. "I have no clue how we're going to get him into St. Francis, but that's where we need to go."

"What do you think could be wrong?" Beth interjected.

"No offense, but you don't want to know. Right now, let me start pulling strings and—"

"I'm going to go with him." Beth stared so hard at V's *shellan*, it was a wonder she didn't burn a hole in the woman's head. "If he has to get that test done, I'm going with."

"Fine, but we'll keep the team to an absolute minimum. This is going to be hard enough to pull off without taking an army with us."

Vishous's mate turned away and jogged down the stairs, and as she went, she gradually lost her form, her body's weight and presence dissipating until she was a ghostly apparition floating down the carpet.

Spook or solid, it didn't matter, Beth thought. She'd rather be treated by that woman than anyone else on the planet.

Oh, God . . . John.

Beth turned to Blay and Qhuinn. "Do either of you know what he was trying to communicate?"

Both of them glanced over at Wrath. And then promptly shook their heads.

"Liars," she muttered. "Why won't you tell me—"

Wrath started to massage her shoulders, like he wanted to calm the little woman down—and didn't that suggest that even if the particulars were unknown because of his blindness, he had read the emotions. He was like that. He knew something.

"Just let it go, *leelan*."

"Do *not* play boys' club with me," she said, pulling away and glaring at the cock-and-balls brigade. "That's my brother—and he was trying to talk to me. I deserve to be in on this."

Blay and Qhuinn got busy looking at the carpet. The mirror over the side table next to the study's open doors. Their fingernails.

Clearly, they were hoping a wormhole would open up under their shitkickers.

Well, too bad, boys—life wasn't an epi of *Doctor Who*. And you know what? The idea that pair—as well as every other male in the house—would always defer to Wrath made her even more pissed off. But short of stamping her feet and looking like a total ass, she had no choice but to shelve the fight for later when she and her mate had some privacy.

"Leelan—"

"My ice cream is melting," she muttered as she went over and picked up the tray. "It would make my night if any of you three would get real with me. But I shouldn't hold my breath for that, should I."

As she marched off, the sense of foreboding that followed her was nothing new—ever since Wrath had been shot, she'd felt like another shoe was going to drop at any moment, and gee, seeing her brother on the carpet did *so* much to improve that paranoia.

Not.

Coming up to the door that had been Blay's before he'd moved in with Qhuinn, she pulled herself together.

It didn't work, but she knocked anyway. "Layla?"

"Come in," was the muffled reply.

Balancing the tray awkwardly on her hip, it was hard to get a good hold on the knob—

Payne, V's sister, opened things up with a smile. And man, she was an impressive presence, especially in all that black leather: She was the only female on rotation to fight in the field with the Brothers—and she must have just come home from a shift.

"Good evening, my queen."

"Oh, thanks." Beth hitched her load up and entered the lavender bedroom. "I'm bringing provisions."

Payne shook her head. "I rather think it's going to be necessary. I can't imagine there's anything left in her stomach—in fact, I believe she's evacuated all the food she ate last week, too."

As retching sounds drifted out of the bathroom, they both winced.

Beth eyed the bowl of Breyers. "Maybe I should come back later—"

"Don't you dare," the Chosen called out. "I feel great!"

"Doesn't sound that way—"

"I'm hungry! Don't you dare leave."

Payne shrugged. "She has an amazing attitude. I come in here to get inspired—although not to go into my needing, which is why I need to leave now."

While V's sister shuddered again, like a female's cycle and the whole baby thing was nothing she was interested in, Beth put the tray on top of an antique bureau. "Well, actually . . . that's what I'm hoping for."

Payne's poleaxed expression made her curse. "What I mean is . . . um . . ."

Yeah, how to dig her way out of this one.

"You and Wrath are going to have a young?"

"No, no, no—hold on." As she put her palms up, she tried to develop a bailout plan. "Ah . . ."

Payne's embrace was fast as a gust and as strong as a male's, crushing the breath out of Beth's lungs. "This is *wonderful* news—"

Beth pushed her way out of those iron bars. "Actually, we're not there yet. I'm just . . . look, don't tell Wrath I'm in here, okay?"

"So you want to surprise him! How romantic!"

"Yeah, he'll be surprised, all right." As Payne gave her a strange look, Beth shook her head. "Look, to be honest, I don't know that my needing will necessarily be good news."

"An heir to the throne could really help him, though. If you're thinking politically."

"I'm not and I never will." Beth put her hand on her stomach and tried to imagine something other than three squares and a couple of desserts in it. "I just . . . really want a baby, and I'm not sure he's on board. If it happens, though . . . well, maybe it'll be a good thing."

Actually, he'd told her once he didn't see children in their future. But that had been a while ago and . . .

Payne gave her shoulder a quick squeeze. "I'm happy for you—and I hope this works. But as I said, I better go, because if that old superstition is true, I don't want to find myself in trouble." She turned to the bathroom's partially closed door. "Layla! I have to head out!"

"Thanks for coming by! Beth? You're staying, yes?"

"Yup. I'm here for the duration."

As Payne took off, Beth had too much energy to sit down, the idea that she was keeping something from Wrath not sitting well. Bottom line, they needed to talk this out; it was just a question of finding a good "when" for that.

And the whole needing/kid thing wasn't the only thing hanging over her. That confron with Wrath and the boys still stung. Men. She loved the Brotherhood—each one of them would lay down his life for her and had always put their flesh and blood where it counted with Wrath. But sometimes the all-for-one, one-for-all stuff drove her nuts—

More heaving. To the point where Beth winced and put her face in her hands.

Get ready for this, she told herself. It's all well and good to have delusions of dollies and plush toys, cooing and cuddles, but there was a ground level to parenting—and pregnancy—that she'd better be prepared to handle.

Although at this rate, her needing didn't seem to be in a big hurry to show up. She'd been in here every night for how long? And yeah, she was feeling hormonal—or it could be that life was just really hard right now.

Yeah, 'cuz that's exactly when you start trying for a kid.

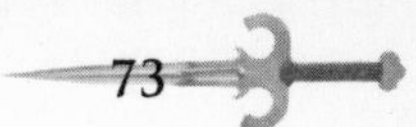

She must be insane.

Hitting the bed and stretching out her legs, she reached for her pint of Ben & Jerry's and attacked it with her spoon. Stabbing into the carton, she dug out the chocolate chunks and ground them between her molars, not particularly tasting anything.

She'd never been an emotional eater before, but lately? She was chomping down when she wasn't hungry, and it was beginning to show.

On that note, she lifted up her shirt and popped the button and the zipper on her jeans.

Sagging against the pillows, she wondered how it was possible to go from the heights of passion and connection to this morose depression so fast: At the moment, she was convinced she was never going to go into her needing, much less conceive . . . and that she was married to a guy who was a serious lunkhead.

Resuming her digging, she managed to excavate the mother lode of chunk veins and told herself to get a grip. Or . . . at the very least wait for all the chocolate to kick in and elevate her mood.

Better living through Ben & Jerry's.

Should be the company's tagline.

Eventually, there was the flush of a toilet followed by a course of running water. When the Chosen came out, Layla's face was as white as the loose robing she wore—and her smile was as resplendent as the sun.

"Sorry about that!" the female said cheerfully. "How are you?"

"More important, how are—"

"I'm fantastic!" she said as she went over to the ice cream. "Oh, this is beautiful. Just what I need to ease things down there."

"I had to weed out the straw—"

Layla threw a hand up. Brought her other one to her mouth. Shook her head.

On a choked breath, she muttered, "I can't even hear that word."

Beth waved things away. "Not to worry, not to worry. We don't even have the Flavor That Shall Not Be Named in the house."

"I'm sure that's a lie, but I will go with it, thank you rather much."

As the Chosen got in bed with her bowl, she glanced over. "You are so kind to me."

Beth smiled. "After everything you've been through, it doesn't feel like nearly enough."

Almost losing the baby—then the miscarriage stopping like magic.

No one really knew what had been wrong or how it had resolved itself, but—

"Beth? Is anything troubling you?"

"No, why?"

"You don't look right."

Beth exhaled and wondered if she could get away with lying. Probably not.

"I'm sorry." She scraped the inside of the carton, digging out the last of the mint ice cream. "I'm all . . . up in my head right now."

"Would you like to talk about it?"

"I'm just overwhelmed by everything." She put the carton aside and let her head fall back. "I feel like there's this weight hanging over me."

"With Wrath where he is, I don't know how you get through the nights—"

There was a knock at the door, and when Layla answered, it was not a surprise that Blay and Qhuinn came in. The two fighters looked awkward, though—and not because of the Chosen.

Beth cursed herself. "Can I just get my apology to you two over with now?"

As Blay went across and sat next to Layla, Qhuinn planted his shitkickers and shook his head. "You got nothing to sorry us about."

"So I was the only one who thought I jumped down your throats? Come on." And now that she'd cooled off and was properly chocolatized, she needed to apologize to her husband—as well as get him to talk. "I didn't mean to come across like a bitch."

"Rough times." Qhuinn shrugged. "And I'm not interested in saints."

"Really? You're in love with one," Layla chimed in.

As Qhuinn glanced over at Blay, his mismatched eyes narrowed. "Damn straight I am," he said softly.

As the redhead turned red—natch—that connection between the two males became positively tangible.

Love was such a beautiful thing.

Beth rubbed the center of her chest, and had to redirect things before she started tearing up. "I only wanted to know what John was saying."

Qhuinn's face closed down. "Talk to your hubs."

"I will." And there was a part of her that wanted to finish up here

with the Chosen and go directly to Wrath's study. But then she thought of all those petitions he and Saxton were working on. It seemed too selfish to barge in there and interrupt the pair.

Besides, she was two inches away from crying—and not even as in telephone-commercial tears. More like what happened to her at the end of *Marley & Me*.

Closing her eyes, she sifted through the last two years and remembered how it had been between her and Wrath back in the beginning. Knock-your-socks-off passionate. Heart and soul connected. Nothing but the two of them even when they were in a crowd.

All that was still there, she told herself. Life, however, had a way of clouding things. Now, if she wanted to be with her man, she had to get in line and that was okay—she understood jobs and stress. The problem was, so often lately, when they were finally alone together, Wrath would get that look on his face.

The one that meant he was only with her in body. Not in mind. Maybe not in soul.

That trip to Manhattan had reminded her of the way things had been. But it was only a vacation, a break from the real nature of their lives.

Placing her hands on her rounded stomach, she wished she were loosening her clothes for the same reason Layla was.

Maybe that was another piece to this whole kid thing for her. Maybe she was looking to get back that visceral connection she'd had with him—

"Beth?"

Snapping to attention, she looked over at Layla. "I'm sorry, what?"

"What would you like to watch?" Layla asked.

Oh, wow, Blay and Qhuinn had left. "Um . . . I say whoever threw up last gets to pick."

"It's not that much of a hardship."

"You are a real trooper, you know that?"

"Not really, no. But may I say that I wish for you the same opportunity to . . . how do you say, tuck it up?"

"Suck. It's 'suck it up.' "

"Right." The Chosen picked up the remote and got the Time Warner cable guide up on the screen across the way. "I'm determined to get this vernacular thing correct. Let's see . . . *Millionaire Matchmaker*?"

"I love Patti."

"Myself as well. You know, this ice cream really hit the stop."

"Spot. Do you want more? I can go down and—"

"No, let's see if this stays put." The Chosen lay her hand on her own belly. "You know, I truly do wish this for you and the King."

Beth stared down at her body, willing it to get with the program. "Can I be honest?"

"Please."

"What if I'm infertile." As the words blurted out, her chest burned with a fear so deep, she was sure it was going to leave a scar.

Layla reached out a hand. "Don't utter those words. Of course you aren't."

"I'm a half-breed, right? I never had normal periods when I was . . . you know, before I went through the change. I would go years without having one, and then what I did get just wasn't right." No reason to go into specifics with the Chosen, but what had presented itself as a period would be so light—not at all what other girls described. "And after my transition, all of that stopped."

"Well, I'm not overly familiar with the way cycles work down here, but it's my understanding that five years after the change you can expect your first needing. How long has it been?"

"Two and a half." Annnnnd now she felt really nuts. Why should she be worried about something that shouldn't even be on the horizon for three more years? "Before you say it, I know, I know . . . it would be totally early if I managed to kick-start it now. A miracle. But the rules for half-breeds are that there aren't any, and I'm hoping . . ." She rubbed her eyes. "Sorry, I'll stop. The more I say all this out loud, the more I realize how insane I am."

"On the contrary, I understand completely where you are. Don't apologize for wanting a young or for doing whatever it is you can to have one. It's perfectly normal—"

Beth didn't mean to hug the Chosen. It was just . . . one minute she was back against the pillows; the next she was holding on to Layla.

"Thank you," Beth choked out.

"Dearest Virgin in the Fade." Layla held on in return. "Whate'er for?"

"I need to know someone else gets it. Sometimes I feel alone."

Layla inhaled a great breath. "I know how that is."

Beth backed up. "But Blay and Qhuinn are totally with you in this."

The Chosen just shook her head, a strange expression tightening her features. "It's not about them."

Beth waited for the other female to fill in the blank. When she didn't, Beth didn't pry. But maybe . . . just maybe things were not quite as uncomplicated as they appeared on the outside. It was well-known that the female had been in love with Qhuinn at some point—but it had seemed as if she'd come to terms with the fact that he was destined for another.

Clearly, she was better at hiding her feelings in public than people assumed.

"Do you know why I wanted this so badly?" Layla said as they both resettled into their respective pillows.

"Tell me. Please."

"I needed something of my own. So does Qhuinn." She glanced over. "And that's why I envy you. You're doing it for a communion with your mate. That is . . . extraordinary."

God, what could she say in response? "Qhuinn loves you in a special way"? That was like soothing someone's compound fracture with an aspirin.

As the Chosen's pale green eyes shifted back to the television screen, she appeared far older than her youth.

It was a good reminder, Beth thought to herself. Nobody had it perfect—and as much as Beth was struggling, at least she wasn't carrying the baby of the man she loved . . . while he was happily with someone else.

"I can't imagine how hard this is for you," she heard herself say. "To love someone you can't be with."

Wide eyes shot back to her own—and there was an echo of something she couldn't decipher in them.

"Qhuinn's a good male," Beth said. "I can understand why you care about him."

Awkward moment. And then the Chosen cleared her throat. "Yes. Indeed. So . . . Patti appears displeased with this gentleman."

Great, Beth thought. So far she'd made her brother pass out, gotten on her husband's case . . . and now she was clearly upsetting Layla.

"I won't tell anyone," she said, hoping to make things better.

"Thank you," the Chosen replied after a moment. "I would be ever grateful for that."

Forcing herself into a refocus, Beth found that, yup, Patti Stanger was chewing some greasy-haired lothario a new one.

They'd probably violated her "Nothing in here, here, or here" rule. Either that or he'd jackassed out big-time on the date.

Beth tried to get into the blow up, but the vibe was off in the room, sure as if there were someone else in with them, a specter or a ghost, and not in the Doc Jane sense.

No, a weight had settled in the very air itself.

As the episode concluded, Beth checked her watch even though the TV flashed the time. "I think I'll go see how Wrath is. Maybe it's break time."

"Oh, yes, and I'm tired. Mayhap I'll sleep."

Beth got off the bed and collected the empty bowl and carton, returning them to Fritz's tray. Over at the door, she glanced back.

Layla was sitting against those pillows, eyes staring at the television as if she were mesmerized. But Beth didn't buy it. The female was a chatterer when it came to viewing, prone to lively discussion about everything from what people were wearing to how they expressed themselves to whatever drama she found shocking.

In this moment, however, she was pulling a Wrath—here but not here, present and disappeared at the same time.

"Sleep well," Beth said.

There was no response. And there would be no sleep for the female.

Beth slipped out into the hall of statues . . . and stalled.

In fact, she wasn't going to go see Wrath. She didn't trust herself at the moment. She was too up and down and back and forth emotionally—and she wasn't entirely sure she could not bring up the baby thing with him the second they were alone.

No, before she saw him, she needed some equilibrium.

It was in her best interests.

And everybody else's.

SEVEN

Assail killed his fourth human a moment after he dropped number three.

And the Scribe Virgin help him, he was itching to off the last of the trio who had arrived with such alacrity. He wanted to discharge a bullet into the man's gut and watch him writhe and suffer on the driveway. He wanted to stand over the dying and breathe in the scent of the fresh blood and the pain. Then he wanted to kick the corpse when it was over. Maybe light it on fire.

But Ehric was right. Whom would he question then?

"Retain him," he ordered, nodding to the remaining human male.

Ehric's brother was more than happy to oblige, stepping in and craning an arm around that thick neck. With a vicious crank, he bent the man backward.

Assail closed the distance to his prey, taking a puff from his Cuban and exhaling it into the bodyguard's face. "I should like to gain entrance into that garage." He pointed to the outbuilding, thinking mayhap they had her in there. "You are going to make that happen. Either because you supply the key or because my associate uses your head as a battering ram."

"I don't fucking know! What the fuck! Fuck!" Or something to that effect. The words were strangled.

Such crude language. Then again, given the Cro-Magnon cast of that brow ridge, one could assume one was dealing with very little in terms of higher reasoning.

It was easy to ignore all the babbling. "Now, will we be using a key or garage opener . . . or some portion of your anatomy?"

"I don't fucking know!"

Well, I have the answer to that, Assail thought.

Turning his cigar around, he regarded its glowing orange tip for a moment. Then he moved closer and put that hot spot a thin inch away from the man's cheek.

Assail smiled. " 'Tis a good thing my associate is holding you so tight. One jerk the wrong way and . . ."

He pressed the embers into the man's skin. Immediately, a scream pealed into the night, flushing an animal from the undergrowth, ringing in Assail's ears until they stung.

Assail retracted his cigar. "Shall we attempt a reply again? Do you wish to use a key? Or something else?"

The muffled answer was as unintelligible as the scent of burned meat upon the air was clear. "More oxygen," Assail murmured to his cousin. "So he may communicate, please."

When Ehric's brother relented, the man's answer exploded out of his mouth. "Opener. Visor. Passenger side."

"Help this man retrieve it for me, would you."

Ehric's brother was as gentle as a hammer to a nail head, dragging his captive around with no regard as to where the contours of the car were—in fact, it appeared as though he were using the man's body to test the structural integrity of the hood and engine block.

But the opener was procured and offered by a shaking hand—and Assail knew better than to put the thing to use. Booby traps were something he was very familiar with, and far better for someone other than him to do the triggering.

"Oblige for me, will you?"

Ehric's twin shoved the man toward the garage, keeping his gun within inches of the side of his head. There was rather a lot of tripping and falling, but missteps aside, the bodyguard did manage to get within range.

The man's hands were trembling so badly it took him several tries to depress the correct button, but soon enough two of the four doors

were rising up. And what do you know, that sedan's headlights were flashing right into them.

Nothing. Just a Bentley Flying Spur on one side and a Rolls-Royce Ghost on the other.

Cursing, Assail strode toward the building. Undoubtedly, some kind of silent alarm was going off, but he was not overly worried about it. The first round of cavalry had already arrived. There was going to be a lull before a second squad came.

The construction had two stories, and given its thermal-pane windows and historically inaccurate proportions, one could only assume it had been built in the current century. And stepping into the bay on the left, he was not surprised that everything was spotless, the concrete floor painted pale gray, the walls smooth as Sheetrock and white as paper. There were no lawn care apparatuses therein, no mowers, or weeders, or rakes. Undoubtedly there was a service for that kind of thing, and one wouldn't want that sort of dirty, smelly equipment around one's automotive babies.

As he moved quickly out of the direct lighting, the treads of his boots called his footfalls out sharply, the sounds echoing around. There didn't appear to be a lower level. And upstairs, there was nothing but a small office that was used to store off-season tires, tonneau covers, and other automobile accoutrements.

Heading back to ground level, Assail walked out of the place at a fast clip. Approaching the bodyguard, he could feel his fangs descend, his own hands shake, his mind hum in a way that made him think of cars roaring down the Autobahn. "Where is she?"

"Where . . . is . . . who . . . ?"

"Give me your knife, Ehric." As his cousin unsheathed a seven-inch blade, Assail holstered his gun. "Thank you."

Accepting the loaner, Assail put the point right to the man's throat, getting in so close he could smell the fear-sweat blooming out of those pores and feel the heat of the breath that pumped from that open mouth.

Clearly, he was asking the wrong question. "Where else does Benloise order captives to be taken?" Before the man could speak, he cut in, "I would urge you to be of care in your reply. If you are untruthful? I will know it. Lies have a stench all their own."

The man's eyes bounced around as if he were making an assessment of his survival chances. "I don't know I don't know I don't—"

Assail dug the knife in until it broke the skin surface and red blood welled onto the blade. "That's not the right answer, my friend. Now tell me, where else does he take people?"

"I don't know! I swear! I swear!"

This went on for quite some time, and tragically, there was no scent of obstruction.

"Goddamn it," Assail muttered.

With a quick slash, he silenced the nonsense—and the fifth useless human dropped to the ground.

Pivoting around, he glared in the direction of the house. Against its backdrop of roofing angles and chimneys, past the skeletal trees on its far side . . . a gentle glow had appeared in the eastern sky.

A harbinger of doom.

"We must needs go," Ehric said in a low voice. "Upon the nightfall, we will resume finding your female."

Assail didn't bother correcting his cousin's choice of words. He was too distracted by the fact that the shaking that had started in his hands had moved upward, a weed spreading throughout his flesh until even his thigh muscles were twitching.

It took him a moment to label the cause, and when he did, the largest part of him rejected the definition.

But the fact of the matter was . . . for the first time in his adult life, he was afraid.

"Where the hell is this place? Fucking Canada?"

Behind the wheel of the Crown Vic, Two Tone was ready to eat a bullet as the bitching continued. This five-hour drive through the middle of the night had been bad enough, but the waste of skin beside him in the passenger seat?

If he wanted to do the world a favor, he'd point the gun in *that* direction, not his own.

There would be such satisfaction in putting out the fucker's pilot light, but in the organization, the role of supervisor only got you so far—and the right to coffin a chatty bastard was just over that line.

"I mean, where the fuck are we?"

Two Tone bit down on his molars. "We're almost there."

Like the SOB was a five-year-old on the way to Grandma's house? Jesus Christ.

As he drove deeper into the absolute frickin' boonies, the sedan's headlights captured the immediate distance ahead, pulling the rows of pine trees and the two lanes that curved in and around the base of a mountain out of the night. Dawn was coming, however, a faint peachy light appearing over to the east.

Great fucking news. Sooner, not later, they were going to finally be off the road, and then they could deal with the merchandise, and get some goddamn rest.

Squinting, he leaned forward over the wheel. He had a feeling they were coming up to the turnoff. . . .

Two hundred yards later, an unmarked dirt road appeared to the right.

No reason to hit the directional signal—or slow down. He nailed the brakes and wrenched the wheel, their cargo thumping in the trunk.

If she'd fallen asleep, she was awake now.

The ascent was steep and the going got much slower: December meant a crap load of snow had already fallen on the ground this far north.

He'd only been to this property once before—and it had been for the same purpose. The boss man was not someone you wanted to piss off, and if you did, it got you snatched and brought up here where no one would ever find you.

He had no clue what that woman had done to offend, but that was not his problem. His job was to get her, disappear her—and hold her until further instructions.

Still, he had to wonder. The last asshole he'd delivered to the hidden place had embezzled five hundred thousand dollars and twelve kilos of cocaine. What the fuck had she pulled? And shit, he hoped he wasn't up here for as long as that other job had lasted.

He'd also gotten a rotator-cuff injury courtesy of that assignment.

The boss didn't like to do the torturing himself. He preferred to watch.

Hard to claim New York State worker's comp for the shit he'd done to the guy.

But, whatever, Two Tone didn't mind that part of the job. He wasn't like some guys, who were into it, and not at all like the big man, who didn't like getting his hands dirty at all. Nah, he was in the middle, happy enough to take care of shit provided he was paid well for it.

"How much farther are we—"

"Another quarter mile."

"It's fucking cold up here."

Gonna be colder when you're dead, motherfucker.

The boss had hired this asshole about six months ago, and Two Tone had been saddled with him a couple of times. He kept hoping that the dumb shit would be fired the good ol'-fashioned way, but so far, no luck.

Bastard would make an excellent floater in the Hudson River.

Or in a hole. Matter of fact, wasn't his name Phil?

Talk about inspiration.

After a final bend in the road, the underwhelming goal was reached: The single-story "hunting cabin" blended perfectly into the landscape, the low-slung building all but disappearing in the midst of the snow-covered underbrush and fluffy evergreens. In fact, the exterior had been deliberately constructed to look run-down. Inside, though, it was a fortress with a lot of fucking dark secrets.

And what was in the trunk was going to be added to that tally.

He'd never heard of a female being brought here before. Wonder if she was hot? Impossible to get a read on that when they'd been carrying her deadweight out of that house.

Maybe he could have some fun as he passed the time.

"What the fuck is this place? It looks like a fucking outhouse. Does it have heat?"

Two Tone closed his lids and ran through a number of fantasies that involved bloodshed. Then he cranked open his door and stood up, stretching the kinks out. Man, he had to take a piss.

Walking over to the door, he muttered, "Get the thing out of the trunk, wouldja."

No keys to worry about. Access was fingerprinted.

As he went along, he had to use a flashlight to zero in on the pseudo-decrepit entrance. He was about halfway to goal when he turned back, some instinct talking to him.

"Be careful opening that up," he called out.

"Yeah. Whatever." Phil went around to the trunk. "What the fuck can she do to me?"

Two Tone shook his head and muttered, "Your funeral. With any fucking luck—"

The second that latch was released, all hell broke loose: Their captive exploded out of there like her ass was spring-loaded—and she'd found a weapon. The red glow of a flare pierced through the darkness, illuminating the cluster-fuck she dealt out as she buried that brilliant tip right in the face of Two Tone's idiot backup—

Phil's howl of pain flushed an owl the size of a ten-year-old kid out of the tree right next to Two Tone and he was forced to hit the deck or lose his own head.

But then he had to be back up on his feet.

That woman took off at a dead run—proving, like that flare shit didn't, that unlike Phil she was no dummy.

"Son of a bitch!" Two Tone tore after her, following the ripping and tearing sounds as she went seriously off-road. Switching his flashlight to his left hand, he fumbled to get his gun out.

Not how this should be going down. Not in the slightest.

The bitch was fast as hell, and as he lumbered after her, he knew she was going to outrun him—and the last phone call he wanted to make to the boss was, "Oh, hey, I lost your project."

He could end up being the next person taken into the "cabin."

Discharging his weapon was the only shot he had. Ha-ha.

Skidding himself to a halt, he latched onto a birch tree, upped his muzzle, and started pumping off rounds, the shots echoing through the early dawn.

There was a higher-pitched curse—and then the sounds of running ceased. In their place? A concentrated rustling, like she was writhing on the ground.

"Fuckin' A," he panted as he jogged forward.

If it was a terminal wound, he was screwed nearly as badly as if she'd gotten away.

The flashlight skipped around the landscape as he closed the distance, highlighting trunks and branches, underbrush, the snowed-up ground.

And then there she was. Facedown in the needles, gripping one knee to her chest. Except he wasn't falling for it. God only knew what else she had up her sleeve.

"Get up or I'll shoot you again." He put a fresh clip into the butt of his gun. "Get the fuck up."

Moaning. Rolling.

He pulled the trigger and put a bullet into the ground right by her head. "Stand up or the next is through your skull."

The woman pushed herself off the ground. Debris hung from her black clothes and parka, and her dark hair was fuzzed up. He didn't bother rating her on his fuck scale. First and foremost was getting her into the secured location.

"Hands up," he ordered, training his weapon at the center of her chest. "Walk."

Her limp was bad, and he could smell the blood as he fell in behind her. No more sprinting for her.

It took them four times as long to get back to the car, and when they did, he found Phil still on the ground and not moving. Breath was going in and out of his open mouth, however, the subtle wheezing sounds suggesting that the pain was all-consuming.

As they passed, Two Tone checked out that face. Oh . . . shit . . . third-degree burns all over, and one of those eyes was not coming back. Except the bastard was probably going to live.

Right?

Fucking great. But he'd deal with that later.

When the pair of them came up to the door, he knew he needed to retain control of this situation.

With a quick move, he grabbed the back of her neck and slammed her headfirst into those hard-ass panels.

This time, as she slumped to the ground, he knew she wasn't coming up for air for a while. But he still gave her a chance to twitch it out before he put his gun away, pressed his thumb into the fingerprint reader, and opened the way in.

Flicking the lights on, he took hold of her armpits and dragged her inside. After locking them in together, he pulled her across the concrete to the stairwell . . . and then carried her down into the basement below.

There were three cells filling out the lower level, just like the ones on TV with iron bars, concrete floors, and stainless-steel pallets for beds. The toilets were functional not for the comfort of the prisoner(s), but for the boss's sensitive nose. No windows.

Two Tone didn't take a deep breath until he had her in the first of them and had locked the door.

Before he went aboveground to confirm capture with home base, put the camo tarp over the Crown Vic and deal with Phil, he went to the cell next door and urinated for what felt like an hour and a half. Zipping up, he stepped out and looked at the stained wall across from him.

The pair of shackles that hung from the two sets of steel chains were going to get used soon.

Complications with Phil aside, he almost felt sorry for the bitch.

EIGHT

Later that morning, an uppercut came flying at Wrath from the left, and in spite of the whistle it made traveling through the air, he couldn't respond in time: The knuckles nailed him square on the jaw and the crack rang his idiot bell, his head ripping around, blood flying out of his mouth.

It felt fucking *great.*

After another nightmare throne-al session with Saxton—seven to ten more hours of his life he was never getting back—he'd gone up to his and Beth's private quarters. Sex had been the only thing on his mind, the only release that was going to save the planet from his rotten mood.

His mate had been not just asleep, but passed out cold.

He'd lasted about an hour staring at the ceiling before hitting up Payne and telling her to meet him here in the training center's gym.

Like Rhage had always said, sex or fighting to take the burn down. Sex was out, so there ya go.

Harnessing the energy from the impact, he went with the momentum and redirected it into a kick that creamed his opponent in the side, throwing her off balance and sending her reeling. No to-the-mat for V's sister, though. Her landing was light and quick as a cat's, and he knew she had plans for him.

Triangulating the rushes of air, the scent of the female fighter, and the sound of her bare feet coming at him with a louder cadence, he knew she was approaching front-on in a crouch. Bracing himself, he sank into his thighs and loved the feel of his muscles tightening up and securing his two-hundred-seventy-pound body in the upright position. Tucking his elbows in, he waited for her to get in range and then punched outward. With her reflexes and the advantage of sight, she dodged the affront and dipped down to come up and cable him around his waist.

Payne didn't hit like a girl, whether it was with her fists or her feet or her entire body. She was more like an SUV, and as much as his ball sac would have preferred otherwise, she got him but good.

With a curse, he ass-over-elbowed and back-flatted like a little bitch. Not gonna stay that way, however.

And that turned out to be a problem.

As he fell into thin air, he was reminded of the way he'd yard-saled off the bed at the loft—and his inner ignition switch got tripped: True aggression came out—in the blink of an eye, this was not about training or keeping up his skills or getting some exercise. The war instinct was unleashed between him and his sparring partner.

With a growl that reverberated throughout the gym, he caught Payne's upper arms in a punishing grip and turned her tables, ripping her off him and slamming her facedown into the mats.

She was a solid female, well muscled and deadly—but she was no match for his strength and size—especially as he straddled her and snaked his arm around her neck. With her throat in the crook of his elbow, he locked his free hand on his thick wrist and leaned back into the choke hold.

Lessers. Enemies. Tragic deaths that changed the course of his life—and others'.

Distance from his mate. Sexual frustration. Suspicion Beth was keeping something from him.

Chronic frustration that downshifted quickly into an anxiety load that never left him.

Fear. Unacknowledged, well buried, and poisonous.

Self-hatred.

Against the dark backdrop of his blindness, everything went white, rage taking over when it had no place to go. And the effect was to give him far greater power than his muscles and bones already had: Even as Payne's fingernails bit into his forearm and she struggled in the manner of a death throe, nothing registered.

He wanted to kill. And he was going to—

"Wrath!"

As with Payne's defense, whoever was yelling his name didn't matter to him. He was locked on this path of murder, all sense of what was happening lost to the—

Someone else came and started yanking at him as that name-hollering thing got louder.

Beneath him, Payne was submitting, the fight slowly leaving her body, that eternal stillness exactly what the rage in him wanted. A little longer was all it would take. A little more pressure. A little—

A loud, repetitive noise sounded right in front of his face. Over and over and over again, like a bass drum, the beats perfectly spaced. The only thing that changed was the volume.

It increased.

Or maybe it was gradually cutting through his fury.

Wrath frowned as the racket continued. Lifting his head, he stopped squeezing so hard for a moment.

George.

His beloved, docile golden retriever was directly in his grille, barking loud as a shotgun, sure as if he were demanding that Wrath cease and desist right this moment.

All at once, the reality of what he was doing flooded into him.

What the fuck was wrong with him?

Wrath released his hold, but he didn't have a chance to jump free. Whoever was pulling at his shoulders took over, tearing his heavy weight off the female fighter.

As he landed on the mat on his back, the retching and heaving breaths of his opponent mixed with the curses of whoever else was with them—as well as a soft whimpering.

"What the *fuck* are you thinking!" Now someone else was in his face. "You nearly killed her!"

Putting his hands up to his head, a cold sweat bloomed over every square inch of him. "I didn't know . . ." he heard himself say. "I had no idea—"

"Did you think she could breathe like that!" It was Doc Jane. Of course—she was down in the clinic and must have heard the barking or . . .

And iAm was with them. He could sense the Shadow even though the guy was as usual not saying much.

"I'm sorry—Payne . . . I'm sorry."

Dear God, what had he done?

He abhorred violence against females. The problem was, when he was sparring with Payne, he didn't think of V's sister as one. She was an opponent, nothing more, nothing less—and he'd had the bruises and even a broken bone or two to show that when it came to her, no quarter was asked for nor given.

"Shit. Payne . . ." He reached out into the empty air, smelling the remnants of her fear as well as the scent that came with impending death. "Payne—"

"It's okay," the female said hoarsely. "Honest."

Doc Jane muttered a number of foul things.

"This is between me and him," Payne ordered her sister-in-law. "This is not your—"

As a round of coughing cut her off, Jane snapped, "When he nearly strangles you, it sure as hell is my problem!"

"He was going to let me go—"

"Is that why you were turning blue?"

"I was not—"

"His arm is bleeding onto the mat. You telling me your fingernails didn't do that?"

Payne caught her breath. "It's fighting, not Go Fish!"

Doc Jane lowered her voice. "Does your brother know exactly how far this is going?"

As Wrath added his own cursing to the fruit salad of F-words, Payne growled, "You are *not* to tell Vishous about this—"

"Give me a good goddamn reason why and maybe I'll consider it. Otherwise, no one tells me what I can and cannot say to my own goddamn husband. Not you, not him—"

Wrath was sure she was shooting a glare his way.

"—and certainly *never* concerning a fucking safety issue about a member of his family!"

The silence that followed was marked by rising aggression. And then Payne barked, "How many bones have you set on the King? How many stitches? Last week you thought I'd dislocated his shoulder—and

at no point did you feel the need to run to his *shellan* and report it. Did you. *Did you*?"

"This is different."

"Because I'm female? Excuse me—maybe you'd like to meet my eyes when you use that double standard, Doc?"

Christ, it was as if his mood had infected both of them. Then again, his actions had started all this. Fuck . . .

Rubbing his face, he listened to them go back and forth. "She's right."

That shut them both up.

"I wasn't going to stop." He got to his feet. "So I will tell V and we are never doing this again—"

"Don't you *dare*," the fighter spat before falling into another series of coughs. As soon as she recovered, she went back to being in his face. "Don't you fucking dare disrespect me—I come here to fight with you to keep my own skills up. If you took advantage of a weakness, that is *my* fault, not yours."

"So you think I was just being hard on you?" he asked grimly.

"Of course. And I hadn't tapped out yet—"

"Do you think for a second that would have gotten through to me."

A fissure of fear charged the molecules around the female.

"And that is why we will never do this again." He turned in the direction of Doc Jane. "But she's also right. This is not your business, so stay out of it."

"The hell I—"

"Not a request, Jane. An order. And I'll go see V as soon as I'm out of the shower."

"You can be a real prick, you know that, Your Highness."

"And a murderer. Don't forget that one."

He started off in the direction of the door, not bothering to take George's halter handle. When his trajectory got off, the dog course-corrected him by getting in the way and steering him to the proper exit.

"Locker room," he grunted when they entered the concrete corridor.

George, familiar with either the word or the postworkout ritual, helped him navigate down the hall, his paws clipping along across the bald floor.

Thank God the training center was a ghost town this time of day. The last thing he wanted was to run into anybody.

With the Brothers sleeping, the extensive underground complex was empty, from the gym and its equipment rooms, to the gun range and classrooms, to the Olympic-size swimming pool and the office that ran everything—as well as Doc Jane and Manny's operating rooms and recovery suites.

Although Payne had almost been a patient.

Shit.

Running his hand down the wall, he stopped when he got to an inset doorway. "You wanna wait here?" he asked George.

Going by the jangling of the collar and the bony *tha-bump*, the golden decided to sit out shower time which was fairly typical—not a big fan of hot and humid because of that long coat of his.

Pushing his way in, Wrath was able to orient well. Thanks to the closed-in acoustics and all the tile, things were easy to navigate by sound—and habit. Also, spaces that he'd spent a lot of time in back when he'd had some of his sight were so much easier to handle on his own.

Fuck. If that dog hadn't stopped him just now?

Wrath sagged back against the slick walls, letting his head hang loose. Jesus Christ.

Scrubbing his face, his brain played tricks on him, flashing images of what the aftermath would have been like.

The moan that rose up his throat sounded like a foghorn. His brother's sister. A fighter he respected. Ruined.

He owed that dog. As usual.

Stripping off his sweaty muscle shirt, he let it flop onto the floor as he shucked his nylon board shorts. Using his hand on the wall once again, he walked forward and knew when he got into the shower room because of the way the floor sloped. The faucet cranks were lined up on three sides and he zeroed in on them, feeling the slick circular drains under his bare feet.

Picking one at random, he turned on the water and braced himself against the cold rush that hit him square in the face.

God, that surge of anger. It was a familiar octane—but not anything he wanted back in his life again. That unholy burn had sustained him all those years between when his parents had been killed and when he'd met and mated Beth. He'd thought it was gone for good.

"Fuck," he bit out.

Closing his eyes, he braced his palms by the showerhead and

leaned into the heavy roping of his arms. His nasty mood made his head feel like it had a set of helicopter blades on it—and they were about two rotations short of separating his skull from the rest of his body.

God . . . damn.

He'd never thought about it before, but "insanity" was largely a hypothetical concept to the sane; a derogative slur to slam someone you didn't respect; a descriptor applied to inappropriate behavior.

Standing in the shower, he realized that true insanity had nothing to do with PMS or "hitting the wall" or going on a bender and trashing a hotel room before you passed out. It wasn't driving crazy or robbing a bank or temporarily taking your temper out on an inanimate object.

It was the removal of the world around you, a good-bye to sensation and awareness that was like a video camera manipulation—your internal shit got zoomed in and everything else, your mate, your job, your community, your health and well-being, went not just out of reach . . . but out of existence.

And the scariest part? This in-between when you had one foot in reality and the other in your own personal, living-breathing purgatory—and you could feel the former slip, slip, slippin' away—

From out of nowhere, Wrath's equilibrium went haywire, the whole world tilting on its axis to the point where he wasn't sure whether he'd fallen back or not.

But then he felt a sharp blade right under his chin, and realized that someone had grabbed hold of his hair.

"At this moment in time," came the hiss in his ear, "we know two things. But only one of them is a game changer."

NINE

This was a bad migraine.

As iAm cracked the door to his brother's room, the poor bastard's suffering stained the very air, making it hard to breathe—and even see properly.

Then again, everything was dark by design.

"Trez?"

The moaned answer was nothing good, a combination of wounded animal and sore throat from throwing up. iAm lifted his wrist into the light streaming in from behind and cursed at his Piaget. By this time, the SOB should have been solidly in recovery, his body digging itself out of the headache hole that had swallowed him.

Not the case.

"You want something for your stomach?"

Mumble, mumble, groan, mumble?

"Okay, I'm sure they've got some."

Mumble, moan, moan. Mutter, mutter.

"Yeah, that, too. You want some Milanos?"

Mmmmmmmmmoan.

"Roger that."

iAm shut the door and walked back to the stairs that took him down to the juncture between the hall of statues and the second-story foyer. Like the rest of the house, everything was silent as a tomb, but as he hit the grand staircase, his chef's nose picked up the subtle scents of First Meal being cooked in the kitchen wing.

The closer he got to the hub of *doggen*, the more his own stomach got to talking. Logical. After he'd finished making the Bolognese, he'd checked on his brother and then gone to the gym for hours.

Where he'd seen a hell of a lot more than just the inside of the weight room.

The last thing he'd bargained for was trying to pull the King off of that female fighter. He'd been coming to the end of his workout when he'd heard someone yelling and gone to check it out—whereupon he'd found, hello, the King pythoning that female.

Needless to say he had a newfound respect for that blind vampire. There were very few things iAm hadn't been able to move in his adult life. He'd changed a tire while acting as his own tire iron. Had been known to walk vats of sauce big as washing machines around a kitchen. Hell, he'd even actually relocated a washer and dryer without thinking much about it.

And then he'd had to lift that truck off his brother about two years ago.

Another example of Trez's love life getting out of control.

But down in the training center with Wrath? There'd been no budging that fucker. The King had been bulldog-locked on—and the expression on his face? No emotion, not even a grimace of effort. And that body—viciously strong.

iAm shook his head as he crossed that apple tree in full bloom.

Trying to budge Wrath had been like pulling on a boulder. Nothing moved; nothing gave.

That canine had gotten through, though. Thank God.

Now, ordinarily, iAm didn't like animals in the house—and he definitely wasn't a dog person. They were too big, too dependent, the shedding—too much. But he respected that golden whatever it was now—

Meeeeeeeeeeeerowwwwwwwwwwwwww.

"Fuck!"

Speak of the devil. As the queen's black cat wound its way around his feet, he was forced to Michael Jackson it over the damn thing so he didn't step on it.

"Damn it, cat!"

The feline followed him all the way into the kitchen, always with the in-and-out around the ankles—almost like it knew he'd been thinking benes about the dog and was establishing dominance.

Except cats couldn't read minds, of course.

He stopped and glared at the thing. "What the hell do you want."

Not really a question, as he didn't care to give the feline an opening.

One black paw lifted and then . . .

Next thing he knew, the goddamn cat was leaping into his arms, rolling over onto its back . . . and purring like a Ferrari.

"Are you fucking kidding me," he muttered. "I don't like you. Goddamn it."

"Master, what may I get for you?"

As Fritz, the ancient *doggen* butler, got up in his face big as a billboard, iAm took a moment to dial back to his happy place. Which, unfortunately, looked a lot like a *Saw* movie—the body parts of others all over everywhere.

But that was just a stress-induced fantasy. Like, he could remember once, a loooooong time ago, he hadn't been bitched about everything and everybody. Really. It was true.

Paw, paw, paw. On his shirt.

"Fucking hell." He gave in and rubbed that black belly. "And no, I don't need anything."

The purring got so loud, he had to lean in to the butler. "What did you say?"

"I'm happy to oblige whatever you require."

"Yeah. I know. But I'm going to take care of my brother. No one else. Are we clear."

The cat was now rubbing its head into his pec. Then stretching up into the itching.

Oh, God, this was awful—especially as the butler's already droopy face sagged down to what were no doubt knobby knees.

"Ah, shit, Fritz—"

"Is he ill?"

iAm closed his eyes briefly as the female voice registered. Fantastic. Another party heard from.

"He's fine," iAm said without looking at the Chosen Selena.

Leaving the kibitzers in the dust, he went into the pantry with the freeloading cat and . . .

Right. How was he going to get the load of post-migraine recovery rations down from the shelves with his arms full of—

What was its name?

Fine. It was Goddamn Cat, then.

Looking down into those wide, contented eyes, iAm thinned his lips as he rubbed under its chin. Behind an ear.

"Okay, enough with this." He played with one of the paws. "I gotta put you down now."

Assuming control, he took the cat out of its recline and went to put it down on the—

Somehow the thing managed to claw its way into the very fibers of his fleece and hang off the front of him like a tie.

"Are you kidding me."

More purring. A blink of those luminous eyes. An expression of self-possession that iAm took to mean this interaction was going to go the cat's way—and no one else's.

"Mayhap I shall help?" Selena asked softly.

iAm bit out a curse and glared at the cat. Then at the Chosen. But short of taking off his pullover? Goddamn Cat was sticking with him.

"I need some of those Milanos up there?" The Chosen reached up and took a bag from the Pepperidge Farm munchie department. "And he's going to need some of those tortilla chips."

"Plain or the lime flavor?"

"Plain." iAm gave up the ghost and resumed servicing Goddamn—and the cat immediately went into full La-Z-Boy again. "He's going to want one of the Entenmann's pound cakes. And we're going to bring him three ice-cold Cokes, two big Poland Springs, room temperature, and a partridge in a pear tree."

After one of his headaches, Trez wanted hydration, glucose, and caffeine. Made sense. Twelve hours of no food was bad news. And then there was the heaving he got to party down with.

Five minutes later, he and the Chosen and Goddamn Cat were heading for the third floor. And at least iAm managed to help with things by tucking the long water bottles under his pits. Fritz had also provided one of those handled Whole Foods bags for the rest of it.

Christ, he would have infinitely preferred to make this trip by himself.

"He likes you very much," the female commented as they ascended.

"He's my brother. He'd better."

"Oh, no—I meant the cat. Boo adores you."

"The feeling is *not* mutual."

iAm had every intention of hitting the female with an "I got this" when they finally showed up at the bedroom door—but Goddamn still wasn't going anywhere.

Which was how the Chosen Selena ended up in Trez's crib.

Exactly what the situation did not need.

Thank you, cat.

As the door was swung wide, light sliced in, and as luck would have it, the shit spotlit Trez as that big, ugly lug shot up.

Someone had caught the female's scent.

Oh, FFS.

And P.S., why couldn't the fucker look worse? His brother should be roadkill nasty after the way he'd spent the daylight hours.

"Where shall I set this?" the Chosen asked either or both of them.

"Over on the desk," iAm muttered. It was the farthest point away from the bed—

"Leave us," came a grunt from the patient.

Okay, thank God Trez was finally having a moment of clarity. The Chosen could keep going about her business, and he and his brother could try the whole come-to-Jesus thing again . . .

iAm became aware that no one was moving. Trez, however, was still upright and the Chosen was deer-in-headlights frozen. And they both were looking at him.

"What?" he said.

When light dawned on Marblehead, iAm narrowed his eyes at his brother. "Are you serious."

"Leave us," was all the bastard said again.

Goddamn Cat stopped purring in his arms, as if the animal knew that bad juju was flooding into the room.

But here was the thing: You couldn't deal with stupid—and iAm was just about ready to stop trying.

Turning to the Chosen, he said in a low voice, "Watch yourself."

On that note, he took Goddamn and his own sorry ass out of there.

No doubt for the best. He was feeling like going Wrath on his brother, and nothing good was going to come of that.

Striding to the stairs, he retraced his steps. Sometime along the

way, he got to tending to the animal in his arms again, fingertips finding that chin and settling into a tight circular stroke.

Back down in the kitchen, which was now full of staff on shift once again, it was time to part company with his shadow.

"Fritz."

The butler rushed over from the crudité arrangement he was working on. "Yes, master! I am eager to be of aid."

"Take this." iAm peeled the cat off himself, prying both of its front claws out of his fleece. "And do whatever it is you do with it."

As he turned away, he felt like glancing back and making sure Goddamn was okay. But why the fuck would he do that?

He had to get to Sal's and check on his staff. Usually he hit the restaurant in the early afternoon, but shit had not been "usual," what with that migraine: Every time his brother had one, they both got a headache. Now, though, with Trez rebounding and no doubt soon to be on the grind with that Chosen, it was time to get back on his own track.

If only to keep himself from going psychotic.

Jesus Christ, Trez was now going to fuck that female. And God only knew where that was going to land them all.

Just as he hit the exit, he called out over his shoulder, "Fritz."

Through the din of First Meal prep, the *doggen* answered back, "Yes, master?"

"I never find any seafood in this place. Why is that?"

"The King does not favor any manner of fin."

"Would he allow it in here?"

"Oh, yes, master. Just not upon his table, and certainly never upon his plate."

iAm stared at the panels of the door in front of him. "I want you to get some fresh salmon and poach it. Tonight."

"But of course. I will not have it ready afore First Meal for you—"

"Not for me. I hate fish. It's for Goddamn Cat. I want him served that regularly." He pushed the door open. "And get him some fresh veggies. What kind of cat food does he eat?"

"Only the best. Hill's Science Diet."

"Find out what is in his food—and then I want everything hand-prepared. Nothing out of the bag for him from now on."

Approval bloomed in the old *doggen*'s voice: "I'm sure Master Boo will appreciate your special interest."

"I'm not interested in that bag of fur."

Totally annoyed with himself and everybody else on the planet, he got the fuck not just out the kitchen, but out the entire mansion. Good timing. The sun had set and the light was draining from the sky.

He loved the night and took a moment to breathe in deep. The cold winter air made his sinuses sing.

If he had been his own male, free of the tether of his brother and the prison imposed upon Trez by their parents, he would have chosen such a different existence. He would be out west somewhere, living off the land and far from anyone else.

It wasn't just that he was a recluse by nature. He saw no value in what so many others did. In his mind, the world simply did not need another iPhone, or faster Internet service, or a twenty-seventh *Real Housewives* franchise. Hell, who the fuck cared if your neighbor had a bigger house/car/boat/trailer/mower. Why be bothered if somebody had a better watch/ring/phone/TV/lottery ticket. And don't get him started on sneakers. Fashion-forward anything. Makeup ads, movie-star drama, manic home-network shoppers and mindless human drones who actually believed what their preachers forced down their throats.

And no, it wasn't just humans who bought into all that shit.

Vampires were equally guilty—they just clothed their cow mentality in superiority over those rats without tails.

So many sublimating who they really were to the dictates of what they were told to want, need, seek, acquire.

Then again, he hadn't managed to break free of his brother's drama, so who was he—

As his phone went off in his fleece's pocket, he shoved a hand in and grabbed it. He knew who was calling him even before he looked at the screen, accepted the ring-a-ding-ding, and put the cell up to his ear.

What small part of him had flared to life died in the center of his chest once again.

"Your Excellency," he greeted the high priest. "To what do I owe this honor."

As Assail paced around his kitchen, he checked his watch. Turned in front of the sink. Strode back toward the bar. Checked his watch again.

Ehric had left about twenty-one—no, twenty-two minutes ago—

and the trip that he'd been sent on should have required twenty-five at the most.

Assail's heart pounded. He had a plan for the evening and this first piece was as critical as the conclusion.

He took out his cell phone and dialed—

The double beep that went off indicated that a vehicle was entering the garage.

Assail ran to the mudroom, threw open the reinforced door, and tried to see into the black-tinted windows of his bulletproof Range Rover. Had the cousins in fact secured . . .

Protocol was to wait for everything to be closed up again before exiting any vehicle, but impatience and that fear that was plaguing him threw the sensible rule right out the dormer: Striding fast over the bald concrete floor, he zeroed in on the SUV as Ehric cut the engine and got out along with his brother.

Before Assail could make an assessment of his cousins' faces, or start barking demands for explanation, the rear door opened slowly.

Ehric and his brother froze. Like they maybe hadn't had a lot of control over their cargo—and knew anything could happen next.

The older human female who emerged was five feet tall and stocky as a bureau. Her hair was thick and white and curled back from her lined face, and her dark eyes stared out bright and intelligent from a heavy overhang of lid. Beneath a shaggy black wool coat, her dress was a simple, bag-like blue flowered frock, but her short-heeled shoes and her matching bag were patent leather—as if she'd wanted to wear the best she had and that was all that was in her closet.

He bowed to her. "Madam, welcome."

Sola's grandmother held her little purse just under her bosom. "My things. I have them."

Her Portuguese accent was heavy, and he had to sift through the words to translate.

"Good." He nodded at the cousins and at the command, they went around to the back of the SUV and took out three modest mismatched suitcases. "Your room is ready."

She nodded curtly. "Proceed."

As Ehric came around with the luggage, he popped a brow and he was right to be shocked. Assail didn't take kindly to being ordered around.

Allowances would be made with her, however.

"But of course." Assail took a step back and bowed again, indicating the door that he'd stepped out of.

Regal as a queen, the little old lady clipped along across the floor toward the three shallow steps that led into the house.

Assail jumped ahead to open things up. "This is our utility room. Onward unto the kitchen."

He fell in behind her, swallowing his impatience. Yet there was no hurry. He had to make sure that the legitimate face of Benloise's empire was empty of its art dealers and office workers before he could go there. And that would be a good hour at least.

He continued on his tour. "Beyond, the eating alcove and the entertaining space." As he walked ahead into the tremendous open space that overlooked the Hudson, he regarded his sparse furnishings with a new eye. "Not that I care for entertaining."

There was nothing personal in the house. Just the "staging" that had been installed to sell the property, anonymous vases and rugs and set pieces of neutral sofas and love seats. The same was true with the bedrooms, of which there were four down below and one on the second floor.

"My office is over here—"

He stopped. Frowned. Looked about.

Had to backtrack to the kitchen in order to find the various parties.

Sola's grandmother had her head in the Sub-Zero refrigerator, rather as if she were a gnome looking for a cool place in the summer.

"Madam?" Assail inquired.

She shut the door and moved on to the floor-to-ceiling cabinets. "There is nothing here. Nothing. What do you eat?"

"Ah . . ." Assail found himself looking at the cousins for aid. "Usually we take our meals in town."

The scoffing sound certainly appeared like the old-lady equivalent of *Fuck that*. "I need the staples."

She pivoted on her little shiny shoes and put her hands on her hips. "Who is taking me to supermarket."

Not an inquiry.

And as she stared up at the three of them, it appeared as though Ehric and his violent killer of a twin were as nonplussed as Assail was.

The evening had been planned out to the minute—and a trip to the local Hannaford was not on the list.

"You two are too thin," she announced, flicking her hand in the direction of the twins. "You need to eat."

Assail cleared his throat. "Madam, you have been brought here for your safety." He was not going to permit Benloise to up the stakes—and so he'd had to lock down potential collateral damage. "Not to be a cook."

"You have already refused the money. I no stay here for free. I earn my keep. That is the way it will be."

Assail exhaled long and slow. Now he knew where Sola got her independent streak.

"Well?" she demanded. "I no drive. Who takes me."

"Madam, would you not prefer to rest—"

"Your body rest when dead. Who."

"We do have an hour," Ehric hedged.

As Assail glared at the other vampire, the little old lady hitched her purse up on her forearm and nodded. "So he will take me."

Assail met Sola's grandmother's gaze directly and dropped his tone a register just so that the line drawn would be respected. "I pay. Are we clear—you are not to spend a cent."

She opened her mouth as if to argue, but she was headstrong—not foolish. "Then I do the darning."

"Our clothes are in sufficient shape—"

Ehric cleared his throat. "Actually, I have a couple of loose buttons. And the Velcro strip on his flak jacket is—"

Assail looked over his shoulder and bared his fangs at the idiot—out of eyesight of Sola's grandmother, of course.

Remarshaling his expression, he turned back around and—

Knew he'd lost. The grandmother had one of those brows cocked, her dark eyes as steady as any foe's he'd ever faced.

Assail shook his head. "I cannot believe I'm negotiating with you."

"And you agree to terms."

"Madam—"

"Then it is settled."

Assail threw up his hands. "Fine. You have forty-five minutes. That is all."

"We be back in thirty."

At that, she turned and headed for the door. In her diminutive wake, the three vampires played ocular Ping-Pong.

"Go," Assail gritted out. "Both of you."

The cousins stalked for the garage door—but they didn't make it. Sola's grandmother wheeled around and put her hands on her hips.

"Where is your crucifix?"

Assail shook himself. "I beg your pardon?"

"Are you no Catholic?"

My dear sweet woman, we are not human, he thought.

"No, I fear not."

Laser-beam eyes locked on him. Ehric. Ehric's brother. "We change this. It is God's will."

And out she went, marching through the mudroom, ripping open the door, and disappearing into the garage.

As that heavy steel barrier closed automatically, all Assail could do was blink.

The other two were equally poleaxed. In their world, dominion was established through force and manipulation by individuals of the male persuasion. Position was earned or lost by contests of will that were often bloody and resulted in a body count.

When one came from that orientation, one most certainly did not expect to be castrated in one's own galley by a woman who didn't even have a knife. And would likely have to get up on a stepladder to remove said anatomy.

"Don't just stand there," he snapped. "She's liable to drive herself."

TEN

". . . only one of them is a game changer."

As the running shower continued on like nothing was doing, the pleasant sound of falling water reverberated through the locker room—and Wrath's head remained locked in its torqued-back position: With a dagger at his jugular, and a heavy hand on the braid that ran down his back, he was going nowhere.

Gritting his teeth, he didn't know whether to be impressed or to encourage that blade to head home.

But he was not suicidal. "What are they, Payne," he gritted out.

The female's voice was a low growl right in his ear. "We both know that you can get out of this if you choose to. In the blink of an eye, you can overpower me—you more than proved it back in the gym."

"And the second?"

"If I got to you once, I can do it again. And maybe next time I won't waste my breath trying to prove the fact that I'm your equal."

"I am the King, you realize."

"And I'm the daughter of a deity, motherfucker."

With that, she released him and stepped back.

Covering his genitals with his hands, he turned to face her. He'd never seen what Payne looked like, but he'd been told that she was built along the lines of her brother, tall and powerful. Apparently, she had the same jet-black hair and those pale, icy eyes, too—and the intelligence was something he could judge for himself.

She also, evidently, had the balls.

"I can kill you," she said, grimly. "Anytime I want. And I don't need a conventional weapon, either. You are stronger, yes—I give you that. But there are things I am capable of that you can't imagine."

"Then why didn't you use them."

"Because I don't want to put you in a grave. You are needed here. You are critical for the race."

Goddamn throne. "So what you're saying is that you would have let yourself die back in the gym?"

"You weren't going to murder me."

Oh, yes, I was, he thought with self-disgust. "Look, Payne, we can go around in circles about this for the next year and a half and it would get us nowhere. I'm not sparring with you again. Ever."

"You don't honestly expect me to accept an argument based on my sex."

"No, I expect you to respect my relationship with your brother."

"Don't pull that old-school BS with me. I am of maturity, and mated at that. I don't subscribe in any way to my brother having some kind of dominion over me—"

He jerked forward on his hips. "Fuck that. Vishous is my brother. Do you have any idea what it would do to him if I killed you?" He gestured with one hand to his head. "Can you get off your high horse for one second and consider that? Even if I didn't give a rat's ass about you, do you think I would do that to him?"

There was a pause, and he had the sense she was going to respond. But when nothing came back at him, he cursed.

"And yeah, you're right," he hedged. "You fight well enough to be a Brother—and I sparred with them for years, so I should know. I'm not stopping this because you're a frickin' girl. It's for the same reason Qhuinn and Blay can't go out into the field together, and why Xhex, if she ever decided to fight with us, wouldn't be allowed to be on the same squad as John. It's why Doc Jane wouldn't operate on your brother or you. Some things are just too close, feel me?"

Against that rushing backdrop of the running water, he heard her walk around, her bare feet nearly soundless on the tiles.

"If you were his brother instead of his sister," Wrath said, "it would be the same. The problem is me, not you—so do yourself a favor and get off this feminist pulpit you're on. It's boring me."

A little harsh, maybe. But he'd already proven that being civilized was outside his wheelhouse at the moment.

More silence. Until Wrath almost threw his hands up in frustration—but remembered his hey-nannies didn't need to be on parade. "Come on, Payne. I can totally appreciate your pride being injured. Except I want you living and breathing more than I care about your feelings getting hurt."

There was another long stretch of quiet. But she hadn't left—he could sense her presence almost as if he could see her: She was right across the tile from him, standing between him and the exit.

"You believe you would not have stopped," she said roughly.

"No." He closed his eyes, regret stinging his chest. "I know it. And like I said, that part has nothing to do with you. So please, for the love of God, drop this and let me finish my shower."

When there was no more conversation, Wrath felt his temper start to boil again. "What."

"Let me ask you something."

"Can't this wait until—"

"The Brothers spar together, correct."

"No. They're too busy taking off-duty knitting classes."

"So why don't they work out with you anymore?" Her voice got lower. "Why don't you keep sharp with them? Did it change after you took the throne?"

"After I went completely blind," he bit out. "It changed then. Do you want an exact date?"

"I wonder if I asked around whether people would agree with that."

"Are you suggesting I can actually see." He bared his fangs. "Seriously."

"No, I'm questioning whether your brothers would have gone to the mat with you once you properly assumed the crown upon your brow. I have a feeling that answer would be no."

"You want to explain why this is relevant," he cut in. "Because your other option is to watch me lose my shit again—and we both know how much fun that was the first time."

When she spoke next, her voice was farther away and he had the sense that she had gone over to the archway that led to where the lockers were.

"I think the only reason why we spar is because I'm female." As he opened his mouth, she talked over him. "And I think you would continue to fight with me if I were male. You can keep telling yourself it's about my brother, that's fine. But I believe you are more chauvinistic than you know."

"Fuck you, Payne. For real."

"I'm not going to argue with you. Why don't you ask your *shellan*, though."

"What."

"Ask her how she feels about dealing with you."

He jabbed at the air between them. "Get out. Before you give me a reason to put you in another fucking choke hold."

"Why doesn't she want you to know where she goes while you're working?"

"Excuse me?"

"Females don't keep secrets from mates who respect them. And that's as far as I'm going to take this. But blind or not, you need to get a clearer picture of yourself."

Wrath marched forward over the wet floor. "Payne. Payne! Come back here this fucking minute!"

He was arguing with himself, though.

The female had left him alone.

"Fuuuuuuuuuuuuuck!" he screamed at the top of his lungs.

Fuuuuuuuuuuuuuuck, Trez thought as he breathed in again.

Recovery from a migraine was all about a soft landing for your return to consciousness. Usually the prescription was food and actual rest—because shit knew that even though you were in a dark room with nothing but Howard 100 streaming through your iPhone, you weren't hanging proper with the sandman.

At the moment, however, he was seriously reconsidering years of get-back-to-normal trial and error: As the door shut behind his brother, and Trez was left alone with the Chosen Selena, every cell in his body went on full tingle.

Oh, man, he had to will on a lamp, even though it was a little early for his retinas to handle any real light—

Hello, goddess.

Selena was tall, and though she wore the traditional white robing of her station, it was clear she was built exactly like a female should be: Nothing was keeping down those curves of hers, not even all that draped fabric. And talk about your beautiful faces. She was all pink lips and pale blue eyes, her features perfectly symmetrical and engineered to catch a male's stare and hold it. Then there was the hair. Long, thick, and the color of midnight, she wore it in the style of the Chosen, all coiled on the crown of her head.

So that all you could think of was taking it down and running your fingers through it.

She was perfect in every way.

And would not give him the time of day.

Which made her appearance up here with his bag of shit all the more remarkable.

"You have been gravely ill," she said softly.

Trez's eyeballs rolled back in his head. That voice. Shit, that *voice.*

Wait, she wanted him to respond, didn't she. What had she—"Nah. I'm great. Just great."

And becoming hard as a rock, fuck him very much. God, he hoped she didn't catch the scent of his arousal.

"What may I do to help you?"

Umm . . . how 'bout drop the robe and hop up on this bed. After which you can ride me like a pony until I pass the hell out.

"Would you care for some of this food?"

"What food?" he mumbled.

"Your brother prepared for you that bag."

Had the bastard even been here? he wondered.

"You just asked him to leave?"

Guess so. "Oh, yeah. Right."

Trez eased back against the pillows and winced. As he went to rub his temples, he sensed her approaching the bed—and with a fast move, he yanked the heavy duvet higher on his belly.

Sometimes "naked" meant so much more than just "I don't have any clothes on."

Man, her expression was so worried. To the point where he had to force himself to remember she'd blown him off before. Which she really had.

Yup, as faulty as his short-term memory was—at least when it came to, like, his brother being in the room—he could recall exactly where he'd been when he'd seen this female last . . . as well as her less-than-enthused response to him.

He also remembered precisely how he came to know (of) her. He'd heard her name as soon as Phury had released the Chosen from the Scribe Virgin's Sanctuary and Selena, along with the others, had started living off and on at Rehvenge's Great Camp up in the Adirondacks. He'd even caught sight of her from time to time, but shit had been going down with Rehv and he'd been distracted.

That had passed, however. And he and iAm had gone up there at Rehv's request recently—which was when he'd met her properly, one-on-one.

Okay, iAm had been with him, but he'd likewise put the guy out of mind. Then again, the moment he'd seen that female he'd forgotten his own name, most of his English vocabulary, and seventy-five percent of his sense of balance.

Instant. Cosmic. Attraction.

At least, on his part.

She was less struck stupid, of course—although he'd had hopes. And stalker tendencies. For the past week, he'd hung around the mansion for however many nights in a row, hoping to see her in the midst of one of her visits to service the Brotherhood. Because, hey, nothing says, "I wanna date ya," like grounds for a restraining order.

Eventually, he'd won the lottery and managed to "run into her." Like the simp he was, he'd told her she was beautiful—and not in a pickup-line kind of way. He'd actually meant it. Unfortunately, and unlike the countless human women he macked on, she'd remained unimpressed.

So again, why the visit up here?

Not that that was a question he was going to look too closely at.

"What may I get you?" she said. And man, that earnest concern put him to shame.

"Ah . . . actually one of those Cokes, please?"

Oh, yeaaah, the way she moved as she went over to the bag she'd put down. So smooth and even, her hips shifting under that robe, her shoulders counterbalancing, her . . .

He averted his eyes from her posterior assets.

Although, *dayum.*

As she came over to the bed, he moved himself closer to the middle of the mattress, hoping she would sit down. She didn't. She bent at the waist and handed him the plastic bottle. Then she stepped back, keeping a respectful distance.

The soda let out a hiss as he unscrewed the cap.

"Please tell me what ails you."

Her hands twisted in front of her, wringing, wringing.

"Just a migraine." He took a long draft off the bottle. "Wow, that's good."

The view was better.

"What is it?"

"Coca-Cola." Trez paused before his second hit, realizing she wasn't asking about the Real Thing. "A migraine's a kind of headache. No big deal."

Well, except for the fact that his lasted up to twelve hours and made him feel like death.

Her beautiful eyes narrowed. "If it's not of concern, why was your brother so worried?"

"He's like that. A hysteric." Trez shut his lids and draaaaaaaaaaaaaank. And once more. "Nectar of the gods, for real."

"I've never thought of him in that manner. But of course, you know him better."

As she hovered, he wished she were half as interested in the fact that his chest was on full display: He wasn't arrogant, but usually the females looked at him and didn't look away.

"Don't worry, he'll be fine," he grumbled. "And so will I."

"But you've been up here all day—since you came home last night."

He was about to get truly annoyed with himself when he thought . . . wait a minute. "How'd you know that?"

The fact that she glanced away quickly made him sit up again.

"Your brother mentioned something about it downstairs."

Doubt that. iAm rarely talked to people unless he had to.

So she must have been looking for him. Right?

Trez let his lids lower. "Hey, do you mind sitting down here—I'm finding it hard to keep looking up at you."

Liar.

"Oh, but of course."

Niiiiiice.

As she eased herself onto the bed and arranged her robing, he knew he was milking it, but come on. He'd spent a considerable amount of time lying on the tile in front of the toilet merely hours ago.

"Are you sure you are not in need of a healer?" she asked, her eyes hypnotizing him to the point where he just watched her blink, those long lashes swooping up and down. "And be of truth this time."

Oh, he wanted to tell her one kind of truth, all right. But there was no reason to act a fool.

"It's just a headache that lasts awhile. Honest. And I've had them all my adult life—my brother doesn't get them, but I heard my father did. They're not a party, but nothing that'll hurt me."

"Has your father passed?"

Trez tightened his face to make sure he showed nothing. "He's still living and breathing. But he's dead to me."

"Whatever for?"

"Long story."

"And . . . ?"

"Nope. Too long, too complicated."

"Did you have other plans this evening then?" This was said with a quiet challenge.

"Are you offering to stay with me?"

She looked down at her hands. "This . . . long story of your parents. Is that why you have a last name?"

How did she know . . . ?

Trez started smiling, and it was a good thing she was ducking his eyes or she would have gotten a whole lot of his pearly whites.

Someone had indeed been checking up on him—and wasn't that interesting.

As for the last name? "That's just made up. I work in the human world and I needed a cover."

"What manner of work are you engaged in?"

Trez frowned, picturing the inside of his club—and then the inside of that bathroom he'd used as a fuck palace how many times?

"Nothing important."

"Then why do you do it?"

He took a final long draw on his Coke and stared into space. "Everyone's got to be somewhere."

God, he really didn't want to get into that part of his life—to the point where if she had to leave because the convo ran out of gas, fine:

In a flash, images of him having sex with that long succession of human women flashed in front of his eyes, taking Selena's place until he couldn't even smell her anymore.

To Shadows, the corporeal body was an extension of the soul—a reality that was perhaps self-obvious, but in fact, far more complicated in the way the s'Hisbe viewed it. Bottom line, what you did to your body, how you treated it and cared—or didn't care—for it, was directly transmuted to the very core of you. And as sex was by its very nature the single most sacred act of the physical form, it was never to be undertaken lightly, and certainly never, ever with dirty, nasty humans—particularly the pale-skinned ones.

To Shadows, pale skin equated to illness.

But the rules didn't stop at the doorstep of Homo sapiens. Making love was completely ritualized in the Territory. Sex was scheduled between couples, or halves, as they were known, formal scrolls being exchanged across marbled corridors, consent requested and given through a series of prescribed directives. And when all was agreed upon? The act was not completed during the daylight hours, and never, ever without a bathing ritual first. It was also announced to all and sundry, a special banner hung upon the chamber door, a genteel way of stating that unless the place was on fire or someone had an arterial bleed, there was to be no disturbance until one or both parties emerged at some future time.

The trade-off for all the barriers? When two halves hooked up, it could last for days.

Oh, P.S., no masturbation, either. It was considered a waste of communion.

So, yeah, his people wouldn't have just frowned on his sex life; they would have handled him only with barbecue tongs while wearing a Hazmat suit and a welding mask: He'd banged women at eleven a.m. and three in the afternoon and waaaay before dinner. He'd taken them in public places and under bridges, in clubs and restaurants, in bathrooms and seedy hotel rooms—and in his office. In only maybe half the cases had he known their names, and from that august group, he could recall maybe one out of ten.

And only because they'd been weird or had reminded him of something else.

As for the pale-skinned thing? He hadn't discriminated. He'd had all races of humans, some even at the same time. The only sector he hadn't fucked or been sucked off by had been males, but that was only because they didn't appeal to him in the slightest.

If they had, he'd have gone there.

He supposed all was not lost. Shadows did believe in remediation, and he'd heard of cleansing rituals—but there was only so much a guy could do to repair damage.

The irony, of course, was that he'd taken a sick pride in ruining himself to the extent he had. Juvenile, sure, but it had been like he was middle-fingering the tribe and all their ridiculous bullshit—especially the queen's daughter, who they all thought he should be in a big hurry to nail on a regular basis for the rest of his life.

Even though he'd never met her, wasn't interested in being a sex toy, and had no intention of volunteering to be locked in a gilded cage.

But it was funny. In spite of everything that he hated about the traditions he'd been born into, he found himself finally kinda seeing a point to them: Here he was, in his post-migraine float, within kissing distance of a female he was dying to worship with his body. And guess what. All that rebellion he'd enjoyed so much was making him feel filthy and totally unworthy.

Not that the actual act would ever occur with Selena—he was a slut, but he wasn't delusional.

Shit.

With a groan, he let himself fall back against the pillows again. In spite of the Coke and its one-two punch of sugar and caffeine, he was suddenly sucked-under-the-ocean exhausted.

"Forgive me," the Chosen murmured.

Don't say you're going to go, he thought. Even though I don't deserve you in any way, please don't leave me—

"Do you need to feed?" she asked in a rush.

Trez felt his jaw drop open. Of all the things he'd been prepared to hear . . . Not. Even. Close.

"Mayhap I'm being too forward," she said as she lowered her eyes. "It's just that you seem so very tired . . . and sometimes that is what helps most."

Holy . . . crap.

He couldn't tell whether he'd won the lottery . . . or been sentenced to death.

But as his cock twitched with demand, and his blood roared, the decent part of him that he had long buried spoke up in a quiet, persistent way.

No, it said. Not now, not ever.

The question was . . . who was going to win, the angel or the devil in him?

ELEVEN

Wrath hit the compound's underground tunnel at a hard pace, his shitkickers beating out a thunderous pounding that echoed all around until he was his own marching band. By his side, George was going at triple time, his collar jingling, his paws clipping over the concrete floor.

The trip from the training center to the mansion took two minutes at least, three to four if you were having a convo and strolling. Not this time: George halted him in front of the secured door a mere thirty seconds after they'd left the office through the back of the supply closet.

Mounting the shallow steps, Wrath felt around for the security pad and entered the code. With a *cha-chunk* like a bank vault unlatching, the lock disengaged and then they were proceeding through a passageway to the next lock point. Clearing that, they emerged into the cavernous foyer, and the first thing Wrath did was sniff the air.

Lamb, for First Meal. A fire in the library. Vishous smoking a hand-rolled in the billiards room.

Shit. He had to disclose to his brother what had happened with Payne in the gym. Hell, technically he owed the guy a *rythe*.

But all that could wait.

"Beth," he said to the dog. "Seek."

Both he and the animal tested and retested the air.

"Upstairs," he ordered, at the same time the dog started to walk forward.

As they got to the second-floor landing, her scent became stronger—which confirmed they were headed in the right direction. The bad news? It was coming from over on the left.

Wrath strode off down the hall of statues, going past John and Xhex's room, and Blay and Qhuinn's.

They stopped before they got to Zsadist and Bella's suite.

He didn't need his dog to tell him he'd reached their destination—and he knew exactly whose room they were in front of: Even out in the corridor, the pregnancy hormones thickened the air to such an extent, it was like hitting a velvet curtain.

Which was why his Beth was in there, wasn't it.

Females don't keep secrets from males who respect them.

Goddamn it. Do *not* tell him his mate wanted a kid and was doing something about it without even talking to him.

Gritting his teeth, he raised his knuckles to knock—but ended up pounding on that door. Once. Twice.

"Come in," the Chosen Layla said.

Wrath swung things wide and knew exactly when his *shellan* saw him: The smoky smell of guilt and deceit flowed across the room at him.

"We need to talk," he snapped. And then he nodded in what he hoped was Layla's direction. "Please excuse us, Chosen."

There was some conversating between the females, stilted on Beth's side, nervous on Layla's. And then his mate was off the bed and crossing over to him.

They didn't say a word to each other. Not when she closed the door behind them. Not as they walked back down the hall side by side. And when they got to the entrance of his office, he told George to stay outside before shutting the pair of them in together.

Even though he was intimately familiar with the arrangement of the pansy-ass French furniture, he put his hands out, touching the backs of the silk-covered chairs and a delicate sofa . . . and then the corner of his father's desk.

As he went around and sat upon his throne, he locked his hands on the great carved arms—and gripped them so hard the wood creaked in protest. "How long have you been sitting with her."

"With who."

"Don't play dumb. It doesn't suit you."

The air stirred in the room, and he heard her footfalls on the Aubusson carpet. As she paced, he could just picture her, her brows down hard, her mouth tight, her arms crossed over her chest.

The guilt was gone now. And in its wake, she was as pissed off as he was.

"Why the hell do you care," she muttered.

"It is my every right to know where you are."

"Excuse me?"

He jabbed a finger in her general direction. "She is pregnant."

"So I noticed."

His fist slammed down so hard the phone disconnected itself. "Do you want to go into your needing!"

"Yes!" she yelled back. "I do! Is that such a goddamn crime?"

Wrath exhaled, feeling like he'd just gotten hit by a car. Again.

Amazing how hearing his greatest fear spoken aloud was so devastating.

Taking a couple of deep breaths, he knew he had to choose his words carefully—in spite of the fact that his adrenal gland had opened up full-bore and was pumping enough OMG into his system that he was drowning in terror.

In the silence, the phone's dial tone and then *meep-meep-meep-*reconnect-me was loud as the curses running through both their heads.

With a shaking hand, he patted around until he found the receiver. Replacing it in the cradle took him a couple of tries, but he got there without smashing anything.

Dear God, it was quiet in the room. And for some reason, he became preternaturally aware of the chair he was sitting in, everything from its hard leather seat, to the carved symbols under his forearms, to the way his lower back was scratched by the relief that rose up behind him.

"I need you to hear this," he said in a dead voice, "and know that it's the God's honest. I will not service you in your needing. Ever."

Now it was her turn to breathe out like she'd been socked in the gut. "I can't . . . I can't believe you just said that."

"It is never, ever going to happen. I will *never* get you pregnant."

There were few things in life that he knew with greater certainty. The only other that came to mind was how much he loved her.

"Won't," she said roughly. "Or can't."

"Won't. As in, will not."

"Wrath, that's not fair. You can't just put that in stone like it's one of your proclamations."

"So I'm supposed to lie about how I feel?"

"No, but you can talk about it, for God's sake. We're partners and this affects us both."

"Discussion is not going to change where I'm at. If you want to keep wasting time with the Chosen, that's your decision. But if the gossip is true, and it does bring on your needing, know that you'll be drugged to get you through it. I'm *not* going to service you."

"Jesus . . . like I'm some kind of animal who needs to go to the vet?"

"You have no idea what those hormones are like."

"This. Coming from a male."

He shrugged. "It's a verifiable fact of biology. When Layla was in hers, we all felt it throughout the house—even a night and a half after she was over it. Marissa was drugged for years. It's what's done.' "

"Yeah, maybe when a female isn't married. But last time I checked, my name was in your back."

"Just because you're mated doesn't mean you have to have children."

She was silent for a time. "Does it not even occur to you for a second this might be important to me? And not as in, 'Oh, I need a new car,' or . . . 'I want to go back to school.' Or even, 'How about we have a fucking date once in a while in between you getting shot at and doing a job you hate.' Wrath, this is the foundation of life."

And the gateway to death—for her. So many females died on the birthing bed, and if he lost her—

Fuck. He couldn't even go there in the hypothetical. "I will not give you a young. I could doctor up the truth with a lot of meaningless bullshit and soothing words, but sooner or later, you are going to have to accept—"

"*Accept it?* Like I got sneezed on by someone with a cold and I just have to resign myself to coughing for a couple of days?" The astonishment in her voice rang out clear as that anger of hers. "Do you even *hear* yourself?"

"I'm really fucking aware of every word I choose. Trust me."

"Okay. Fine. Why don't we put the shoe on the other foot. How about I say . . . how about this—you're going to give me the child I want, and that's just something *you're* going to have to get used to. Period."

He shrugged again. "You can't force me to be with you."

As Beth gasped, he had some sense they'd entered a new dimension in their relationship—and not a good one. But there was no going back.

Cursing under his breath, he shook his head. "Do yourself a favor and stop sitting with that female for hours every night. If you're lucky, it hasn't worked and we can just forget about all this—"

"Forget about—wait. Are you—are you—have you lost your fucking mind?"

Shit. His *shellan* didn't stutter or stumble, and she rarely swore. What a trifecta.

But it didn't change anything. "When were you going to tell me?" he demanded.

"Tell you what? That you can be a real asshole? How about right now."

"No, that you were deliberately trying to start your needing. Talk about things that affect us both."

What would have happened if she'd suddenly gone into her time when they'd been alone together during the day? He might have given in and then . . .

Not good. Especially if he later found out she'd been marking time with the Chosen for specifically that purpose.

He glared at her. "Yeah, when exactly was that going to come up in conversation? It wasn't going to tonight, right? Were you saving it for tomorrow? No?" He leaned into his desk. "You knew I didn't want this. I *told* you so."

More pacing: He could hear her every footfall. It was a while before they stopped.

"You know what, I'm going to leave right now," she said, "and not just because I have to go out tonight. I need to not be around you for a while. And then, when I come back, we're going to talk this through—both sides of the issue—no!" she ordered as he went to open his mouth. "You don't say another goddamn word. If you do, I have a feeling I'll be packing my bags and taking off permanently."

"Where are you going?"

"Contrary to popular belief, you do not have a right to know where I am every second of the day and night. Especially after this diatribe."

Cursing again, he popped his wraparounds off and rubbed the bridge of his nose. "Beth, listen, I'm just—"

"Oh, I've listened to you quite enough for the time being. So do us both a favor and stay right where you are. At the rate you're going, that desk and that hard chair are all you're going to have, anyway. You might as well get used to them."

He closed his mouth. Listened to her walk off. Heard the doors slam shut in her wake.

He was about to jump up and go after her, but then he remembered Doc Jane saying something about John Matthew's MRI at that human hospital. Had to be where she was going—she'd said it was important for her to go with him.

Abruptly, he remembered the seizure, and what had gone down in the middle of it. He'd confronted Qhuinn afterward about what John had tried to communicate to Beth—if something was being said to his *shellan*, he was going to know the details, thank you very much.

I will keep you safe. I will take care of you.

Okay, file that under WTF. Normally, Wrath had no beef with John Matthew. In fact, he'd always liked the kid—to the point where it was kind of creepy how easily the mute fighter had entered all their lives—and stayed there.

Great solider. Good head on those shoulders. And the lack of a voice wasn't a problem except for with Wrath because obviously he couldn't see to read ASL.

Oh, and as for the blood test that said he was Darius's son? The more time you spent around the kid, the more obvious the connection was there.

But he drew the motherfucking line when any male tried to come between him and his mate, blooded brother or not. *He* was the one who was going to keep Beth safe and cared for. Nobody else. And he would have confronted John afterward . . . except the oddest thing was, the kid didn't seem to know what he'd said either: John wasn't well versed in the Old Language enough to hold a conversation in it, and yet Blay and Qhuinn had both confirmed that that was what he'd appeared to be mouthing.

But whatever. John was going for some treatment, and on the Beth front, he was ultimately not going to be a problem. This baby stuff, however . . .

It was a long while before Wrath peeled his clawed hands free of the throne's armrests, and as he fanned them out, the joints burned.

At the rate you're going, that desk and that hard chair are all you're going to have.

What a mess. But the bottom line, granite truth was . . . he just couldn't lose her in pregnancy. And as bad as it was to have this rift between them, at least they were both still on the planet and going to stay that way: There was no way in hell he was going to voluntarily risk her life just for some hypothetical son or daughter—who, by the way, assuming they survived into adulthood, was liable to suffer under this royal legacy as much as he did.

And that was the other big part for him. He wasn't in a hurry to condemn an innocent to all this King crap. It had ruined his life—and that was not an inheritance he wanted to share with someone he would undoubtedly love almost as much as his *shellan*—

Shifting in the throne, he looked down at himself—and frowned.

Even though he couldn't see anything, he realized . . . he had an erection. A throbbing, straining arousal was pushing against the fly of his leathers.

As if it had somewhere to go. Like, now.

Putting his head in his hand, he knew exactly what that meant.

"Oh . . . God . . . *no*."

"Would you like to feed?"

As the Chosen Selena waited for a response to her question, she did her best to ignore the fact that the incredible dark-skinned male in the bed before her was naked. He had to be. With the sheeting rolled down to his waist, his chest was bare, his chiseled pecs and his roped shoulders illuminated by the soft light in the corner.

It was difficult to imagine why he would bother with anything below the hips.

Dearest Virgin Scribe, what a sight to behold he was. And a revelation—although not because she was ignorant or naive. She might have been sequestered up in the Sanctuary since her birth a century ago, but as an *ehros*, she was familiar with the mechanics of sex.

Regardless of training, however, the act had not yet been her destiny. The previous Primale had been killed in the raids just after she had matured, and his replacement hadn't been named for decades and decades and decades. Then when Phury had assumed the mantle, he'd changed everything and freed them all whilst taking a *shellan* to whom he was monogamous.

She had always wondered what sex was like. And now, looking at Trez, she knew viscerally why females submitted themselves. Why her sisters had primped and prepared for their "duty." Why they had returned to the dormitory afterward with an incandescence to their skin, their hair, their smiles, their souls.

It was overwhelming to experience this firsthand—

Abruptly, she became aware that he had not answered her.

As he continued to just stare up at her, she wondered if she'd offended him. But how? It was her understanding that he was without a mate: He'd come into this house with his brother, not a *shellan*, and there was never a female up here in these quarters.

Not that she'd noticed his every move.

Just most of them.

As her cheeks flushed, she told herself that surely he must need a vein after all he had suffered? In fact, the toll of his illness showed in his face . . . his hard, beautiful face with its almond-shaped dark eyes and prominent, carved lips and high cheekbones and strong, heavy jaw. . . .

Selena lost her train of thought.

"You can't mean that," he said roughly.

His words were deeper than usual, and had the strangest effect on her. All at once, that blush on her face bloomed inside her entire body, warming her from the core out, loosening her in way that made her fear her future a little less.

"I do," she heard herself say.

And this would not be a duty. No, in this quiet, dim space between them, she wanted him—at her neck, not at her wrist—

Madness, an inner voice warned. That was not appropriate, and not just because it blurred the lines of the work she did here in this house.

Closing her eyes, she hated the fact that, by all that was reasonable, she *should* turn and walk out of the room right now. This male, this resplendent male who was capable of melting even her stiff limbs, was not her future. Not any more than the Primale was—or any male, for that matter.

Her future had been determined even before she had been swaddled in her first robing as a Chosen.

After a long moment, he shook his head. "No. But thank you."

The rejection made her nauseous. Mayhap he sensed the inappropriate desires on her part? And yet . . . she could have sworn he felt similarly. He had stopped her by the stairs that one time, and she had been so sure he had wanted . . .

Well, at least then she'd been in her right mind enough to try to warn him off.

After they'd parted awkwardly, however, the way he'd looked at her had lingered, and that was when she'd begun to watch him from the shadows.

He was not staring at her like that now, though.

And it had all changed for him with her offer. Why?

"You'd better go." He nodded to the door. "I just need to eat something and I'll be fine."

"Have I offended you?"

"Oh, God, no." He shut his eyes and shook his head. "I just don't want to . . ."

She couldn't catch the rest of whatever he said, because he rubbed his face and muffled the words.

Abruptly, Selena thought about the books she had read in the Sanctuary's sacred library. So many details of lives lived down here on Earth. So rich and surprising, the nights and days. So vivid the histories, until it had seemed as though she could reach out and touch this other plane of existence. She'd been hungry for this other side, developing an addiction to its stories in all their glory and their sadness: Unlike many of her sisters, who merely recorded what they were shown in the seeing bowls, she had been voracious in her free time, studying the modern world, the words used, the manner in which people conducted themselves.

She had always had the conception that that was as close as she would ever get to having freedom of choice and any kind of destiny.

And that was still true, even after Phury's liberation.

"Goddamn, female, don't look at me like that," Trez groaned.

"Like what?"

He seemed to roll his hips, and when he mumbled something she also couldn't catch, she breathed deep—and, dearest Virgin Scribe, the scent that was poured of him was nothing short of ambrosia in the nose.

"Selena, you gotta go, girl. Please."

He arched back into the pillows, his magnificent chest tightening, the veins in his neck standing out. "*Please.*"

Obviously he was in pain—and she was somehow the cause.

Selena fumbled with her robing to keep it in place as she got to her feet. With an awkward bow, she dropped her head. "But of course."

She didn't remember leaving the room or closing the door, but she must have: She ended up out in the hall, standing halfway between the locked vault that led into the First Family's private quarters and the stairwell that would take her back down to the second floor. . . .

Next thing she knew, she was up in the Sanctuary.

Bit of a surprise, actually. Usually, when she was done with any duty upon the Earth, she would wend her way north to Rehvenge's Great Camp. She enjoyed the library there—its fictions and biographies were just as gripping, and somehow less intrusive, than the volumes up above in the Sanctuary.

But something in her had taken her to her former home.

How different it was, she thought as she looked around. No longer a bastion of monochromatics—now only the buildings, constructed of pristine marble, were white. Everything else glowed with colors, from the emerald of the grass to the yellow and pink and purple of the tulips to the rushing pale blue of the baths. But the layout was the same. The Primale's private temple remained close to both the scribing cloisters and the enormous marble library as well as the locked entrance into the Scribe Virgin's private quarters. Off farther in the distance, the dormitories where the Chosen had had both their repose and their meals were adjacent to the baths and the reflecting pool. And then opposite all of that was the vast treasury with its objects, oddities, and bins of precious stones.

Oh, the irony, though. Now that there was color to please the eye? Everything was empty of life, the Chosen having flown the coop and spread their wings.

No one had any clue where the Scribe Virgin was—nobody dared ask, either.

The absence was strange and disconcerting. And yet welcomed as well.

As Selena's feet set to walking, it was clear that she had some sort of destination in mind, but she was unaware of it consciously. At least that was not unusual. She was always one to be in her head, usually because she was thinking about what she had watched in the seeing bowls or read in between the spines of those leather-bound volumes.

She was not considering the lives of others at the moment, however.

That dark-skinned male was . . . well, there didn't seem to be enough words to describe him in spite of her extensive vocabulary. And the recalled images from just now in his bedroom were like the newly arrived color up here—a revelation of beauty.

Locked in thoughts of him, she kept on strolling, proceeding past the scribing center, down the lawn to the dormitories, and then farther onward until she approached the forested boundary that, if entered, magically spit you out in exactly the same place you had walked into.

It wasn't until it was too late that she realized where her feet had taken her.

The hidden cemetery was bracketed on all sides by an arbor, the knoll purposely shut off from view by a netting of leaves that was verdant and thick as a vertical lawn. The entryway was likewise obstructed by an arch strung with vine roses and the pebbled path that snaked into the interior was barely wide enough for a single person.

Selena had no intention of going in—

Her feet broke that covenant of their own volition, moving forward as if the servants of some larger purpose.

Within the confines of the bracketing trees, the air was as temperate as ever, and yet a chill went through her.

Wrapping her arms around herself, she hated everything about the place—but mostly the stillness of the monuments: Set up upon white stone pediments, the female forms were in various poses, their graceful arms and legs angled this way and that about their naked bodies. The expressions on the statues were serene, their unblinking eyes gazing upon the afterlife in the Fade, their lips turned up in identical, wistful smiles.

She thought again of the male in that bed. So alive. So vital.

Why had she come here. Why, why, why . . . to the graveyard—

Her knees buckled at the same time tears broke free of her heart, her weeping taking her to the soft ground, the racking sobs making her throat hurt.

It was at the feet of her sisters that she felt the destiny of her early death freshly.

Over the course of her life, she had assumed all angles of her upcoming demise had been explored.

Being around Trez Latimer told her she was wrong about that.

TWELVE

The Benloise Art Gallery was located in downtown Caldwell, about ten blocks away from the skyscrapers and only two from the shores of the Hudson. The plain, unassuming building was three stories high, with a double-height gallery space on the first floor, staff offices in the back, and Benloise's bowling alley of an office just under its flat roof.

As Assail parked his Range Rover in its rear alley, he breathed in deeply. He hadn't done any coke before he'd left home because he wanted to keep sharp. Unfortunately, his body was twitchy from the lack of stimulation, and an addict-like preoccupation with what he hadn't done muddled his mind.

"You want us to come in with you?" Ehric demanded from the backseat.

"Only one."

Assail got out and waited for them to decide. Damn it, his hands were shaking, and in spite of yet another round of flurries falling from the sky, he was starting to sweat.

Should he just do the coke? He was close to nonfunctional like this.

Ehric joined him, coming around the back of the SUV. "What ails you?"

"Naught."

A lie on so many levels.

As they approached the back door, Assail gave up. Digging into the breast pocket of his Tom Ford coat, he pulled out his dark brown vial. Unscrewing the black lid, he filled the interior spoon with a serving of white powder.

Sniff.

He repeated on the other side, and then took a single, double-barreled huff that ensured everything got home.

The fact that he immediately downshifted into "normal" was another warning sign he chose to ignore. Calm and focused was *not* what he should be feeling after two hits—but he wasn't going to waste time on it. Some people had coffee. Others had a different coca product.

It was all about whatever got your move on.

As he came up to a heavy steel door—which was a security measure disguised as a commentary on the industrialism of the art market—there was no reason to ring any bell, and certainly not to knock. The three-inch-thick monster was hardly something to waste one's knuckles on.

And indeed, things were opened promptly.

"Assail? What you doing?" the Neanderthal on the other side demanded.

Such an inspiring command of English grammar. And the greeting also told him that Benloise and his men didn't know who had done the kills in West Point the night before—otherwise one could assume this titan of intelligence would not be so banal.

Those black masks they'd worn had been such handy equipment. And disabling those security cameras a critical tactic.

Assail smiled without flashing his fangs. "I have something to give your employer."

"He expecting you?"

"He is not, no."

"Okay. C'mon."

"This is my associate, by the way," Assail murmured as he stepped into the office area. "Ehric."

"Yeah. I figured. C'mon."

Striding through the high-ceilinged space, their footfalls on the concrete floor echoed up to the exposed ductwork and wiring above. Talk about organized chaos. A lineup of serviceable desks, stacks of filing cabinets, and random pieces of oversize "art" choked the huge space. No workers. No phones ringing. The legitimate face of Benloise's wholesale drug business was on after-dark shutdown.

As expected.

Out in the gallery space proper, he shot a quick look around as the guard who'd let them in disappeared through the hidden door to the second floor.

No one but a pair of guards standing watch by the way up to Benloise's office.

Assail regarded the men. Their stares were sharper than usual, their weight shifting incessantly, their hands moving around as if they felt the need to constantly reassure themselves they were armed.

"Lovely evening, is it not?" Assail commented as he nodded subtly at Ehric.

As the guards froze, his cousin took the cue to go on a wee walkabout, the vampire strolling around an exhibition of shredded newsprint molded into various phallic symbols.

"A little on the cold side, of course. But the flurries are rather picturesque." Assail smiled and took out a Cuban. "May I light up?"

The one on the right pointed to a laminated notice on the wall. "No smoking."

"Surely there can be an exception in my case?" He clipped the cigar's end and let the butt fall to the ground. "Yes?"

The guy's muddy brown eyes flicked down. Returned. "No smoking."

"Nobody here but us." He outed his lighter. Popped the top.

"You can't do nothing like that."

Mayhap Benloise specifically screened them for a lack of vocabulary? "In the stairwell, then?"

The genius glanced over at his partner. Then shrugged. "Guess it's okay."

Assail smiled again and flicked up a flame. "Let me in, then."

It all happened so quickly. The one who'd been doing the talking twisted his torso and popped the latch that sprang the door—as, at that moment, the other chose to take a stretch, curling his arms out from his body.

Ehric materialized directly before the back cracker, clapping his hands on either side of his astonished face and snapping that neck around. Not to be o'ershown, Assail stabbed forward with the knife he had surreptitiously taken out of its hip holster, catching the guard who'd been enforcing the rules directly in the gut. Next move was to disappear his lighter and clap his hand over the man's mouth—stifling the grunt that threatened to give them away.

To finish things up, he freed the blade with a jerk and moved upward.

The second stab went between two ribs directly into the heart.

The man dropped to the floor in a loose shamble.

"Tell your brother to ready the Rover," Assail whispered. "And drag this out of the way. He's going to take a minute or two to bleed out and that heavy breathing is audible."

Ehric went into cleanup mode, grabbing thick ankles and pulling the dying man behind one of the vertical displays.

Meanwhile, Assail slipped into the hidden stairwell and lit the cigar, puffing up clouds of smoke as he moved the broken-necked guard's hand in the way so the door stayed propped open. Ehric joined him a split second later, accepting his own Cuban and likewise lighting up as he let things shut behind them.

The linguist who'd gone to check with Benloise peered over the banister above. "What you doing?"

So that phrase was both a greeting and an inquiry. One shall make a note of that, Assail thought.

He blew out a blue stream and indicated the closed door panels. "They said we couldn't smoke out in the gallery."

"You can't smoke in here, either." The man glanced over his shoulder as if his name had been called. "Yeah, okay." He turned around again. "He said he'll be a minute."

"I believe we'll join you, then."

The bodyguard just wasn't on his A-game tonight, was he. Instead of controlling the situation, he simply shrugged and permitted his enemy to get closer to him, to his boss.

Such a gift.

Assail typically took his damned time, but not tonight. He and Ehric hoofed it up the metal flights at a good clip.

He was halfway to goal when he realized he'd made a mistake. Likely because of the coke: There were video cameras all over the facility's interior—and yet he had done nothing about them.

"Faster," he hissed under his breath to his cousin.

Reaching the top landing, Assail bowed to the guard. "Where would you like me to put this out?"

"I don't fucking know. He shoun't told you to light up."

"Oh, well, then."

Ehric, on cue, pulled another dematerialization, appearing behind the guard. With a slap, he covered that mouth, and yanked the guard back.

Presenting Assail the perfect captive target.

With a vicious move, he sliced his blade across that throat easy and quick as a cough. Then it was another case of drag-off once again.

Assail barged through the office door, pushing it wide. Across the vast space, Benloise sat alone behind his raised modernist desk, the glow of the lamp by his side pulling his features out of the darkness so that he rivaled some of Goya's best portraits.

". . . I'm coming up north right now—" Benloise stopped short, his visage becoming instantly impassive. "Permit me to call you back."

Caldwell's drug wholesaler hung the phone up so fast, the receiver banged into its cradle. "I believe I told you to wait, Assail."

"Indeed?" Assail looked over his shoulder. "Mayhap you should be clearer with your subordinates. Although, God knows, it is so hard to find good help, is it not."

The natty little man sat back in his throne-like chair, his expression unchanging. Tonight's bespoke suit was in a deep navy blue that emphasized his perma-tan and dark eyes, and as always, his thinning hair was slicked back from his forehead. One could smell his cologne from across the office.

"Excuse me for rushing you," the gentleman said in that educated, I'm-not-a-drug-dealer accent of his. "But I have another appointment."

"I would certainly hate to detain you."

"And your purpose is?"

Assail nodded once, and that was all it took. Ehric flashed behind that raised desk and locked on the wholesaler, dragging him out of his heavy chair by the head. A Taser later, and Benloise was a limp doll in that very nice-fitting navy blue suit.

As his cousin threw the man over his shoulder in a fireman's hold, no words were exchanged. No reason to—they had sketched this out beforehand: the infiltration, the securing, the removal.

Of course, it would have been so much more satisfying to stage a

Hollywood movie confrontation whereupon Assail answered the wholesaler's question as to purpose in violent detail. The real world of kidnapping and intimidation, however, did not afford such immediate gratification.

Not if you wanted to get your man and keep him.

With Ehric tight on his heels, Assail fell into a jog, crossing the office's glossy black floor and descending the stairs with alacrity. As they hit the gallery space, there was a moment of pause, a quick check for sounds of incoming confrontation.

None. Just the muffled pant of the stabbed guard's dying breath and the copper scent of blood from his gut wound.

Out through the staff-only door into the office space. Passing by those desks and the hanging mobile made of mangled car parts.

The Range Rover was parked so close to the rear exit, it was practically in the building, and with sure moves, Assail opened the backseat and Ehric threw Benloise in there like a duffel bag. Then it was a case of *slam, slam, screech*.

They were off and cruising at the speed limit between one heartbeat and the next, Assail in the front passenger seat, Ehric sitting behind him with their cargo.

Assail checked his watch. Total elapsed time was eleven minutes, thirty-two seconds, and they had a good number of hours before sunrise.

Ehric took out a set of handcuffs and clipped them to the "art dealer's" wrists. Then it was a case of slapping the motherfucker awake.

When Benloise's eyes opened, he recoiled like he was in a bad dream.

In grim tones, Assail finally answered the question that had been posed to him. "You have something that is mine. And you're going to return it to me before dawn—or I will make you wish you were never born."

A half an hour after the epic confrontation with her husband, Beth was in the back of the Brotherhood's Mercedes S600 with her half-brother beside her and Fritz behind the wheel. The sedan was brand-new, the wonderful smell of fresh leather and varnish like aromatherapy for rich people.

Too bad the sniffy-good wasn't doing a damn thing for her mood.

As she stared out the tinted window, the descent down the snowy mountain to the rural road at its base seemed to go in slow motion—although maybe that was because the sound track to the trip, which should have been Vivaldi or Mozart if you went by the ethos of car commercials, was the toxic tennis match of that happy little chat with Wrath.

Shit. Her *hellren* had always been autocratic—and again, that had nothing to do with his station in life: Screw the crown; it was his personality. And over the last couple of years, she'd watched him throw that attitude around in countless situations, whether it was with the Brothers, the *glymera*, the staff—hell, the TV remote. But with her, he'd always been . . . well, not subservient. Never that. She'd always had the sense, though, that he deferred to her. Whatever she wanted, when she wanted it—and God save the fool who got in his way.

So yes, she'd assumed the kid thing would be the same—that he'd cave, given how important having a baby was to her.

Instead? Total opposite—

A soft touch on her elbow reminded her of two things: One, she was not alone in the sedan's vast backseat. And two, she wasn't the only person who had problems.

"Sorry," she said as she dropped hands she wasn't aware of having brought up to her face. "I'm being rude, aren't I?"

Are you okay? John signed in the dim interior.

"Oh, yeah, absolutely." She patted his heavy shoulder, knowing this whole thing with the seizures had to be weighing on him: the trip into town, the MRI, the results that were going to follow. "More important, how are you?"

I guess Doc Jane made it to the medical center okay.

"Yup." Beth had to shake her head, her gratitude to Jane and her human partner, Manny Manello, choking her up. "Those two are amazing. Human health care is expensive and tough to navigate. How the two of them pulled this off, I have no idea."

Personally, I think it's a waste of time. He turned his head away. *I mean, come on. I've had the episodes for how long? Nothing's ever come of them.*

"It's safer to get everything checked out."

John's phone went off with a *bing!* and he tilted the screen so he could see it. *It's Xhex.*

"So she made it there okay, too?"

Yeah. He exhaled in a hard rush. *This whole being-driven-in thing is ridiculous. I could make the trip in a heartbeat.*

"Yeah, but if you're just a regular human, you'd come by car. Easier to keep the lie up, you know."

Even better, we could have scrapped this bullshit. He laughed a little. *I'll tell you, I'm sorry for whoever meets Xhex at the door. She was prepared to do a sweep of the entire hospital complex—and when she's like that? You don't want to tell her no.*

The respect shining in his eyes was a stinger. Considering the way Wrath had acted.

"Xhex is one lucky female," Beth said roughly.

It's the other way around. Trust me—why are you looking like that?

"Like what?"

He seemed to flush. *As if you're going to cry.*

She batted away the concern. "Allergies. I always get watery eyes this time of year. Maybe I'll pick up some Claritin while we're out tonight."

In December? Really?

As she became the one who was looking away, Fritz picked up speed along the rural straightaway. Slowed down coming into a curve. Reaccelerated when they were out the other side. The Mercedes handled everything with total ease, the ultra-padded seat absorbing the shifts of her body, a gentle warmth being pumped onto her feet.

They should have put the tagline "Ambien Edition" on the car.

Although again, any rock-a-bye-Benz-y effect was wasted on her.

She had a feeling there was going to be no sleep at all until she and Wrath worked things out—or . . .

Another tap on her arm. *You know, you can talk to me about anything.*

Beth swept her hair back . . . only to pull it forward over her shoulders again. Where the hell to go with that. There were so many choices—but John had enough on his plate already.

Beth. Seriously.

"How about we get through this with you and—"

It'll give me something else to think about, and I could use that right now. When she didn't respond, he signed, *Come on, please. I'm worried about you.*

"You are a total love, you know that?"

And you're not talking, are you.

She stayed quiet for a while. Up ahead, a sign for the Northway appeared, the "I-87" glowing in the headlights. If they got on and kept going, instead of taking the first of the downtown Caldwell exits, they could be in Manhattan in about an hour. Farther south than that would put them into Pennsylvania and then down to Maryland and . . .

"You ever wish you could just get away sometimes?" she heard herself ask.

Before Xhex came around? Sure. But now . . .

God, to think Wrath was the one she wanted to bolt from. Never saw that coming.

What's going on, Beth.

There was another long silence, during which she knew he was hoping she'd string some nouns and verbs together for his benefit.

"Oh, you know, just a marital moment."

He shook his head. *Been there, done that. It sucks.*

"Too right."

Finally, he signed, *You can use Darius's house, you know. If you need some space. You gave it to me, which was great—but I always think of it as half yours, too.*

She pictured the Federal-style mansion deep in human territory, and her chest burned. "Thanks, but I'll be okay."

And even if she wasn't, the last place she wanted to go was where she and Wrath had fallen in love.

Sometimes good memories were harder to bear than bad ones.

Can you at least give me a topic? My head is running in all kinds of directions.

It was going to take them another fifteen, twenty minutes to get to the St. Francis medical complex. Long time to sit in this awkward silence. And yet it seemed a violation of her and Wrath's privacy to talk about the baby thing . . . or maybe that was just an excuse to hide the fact that she didn't want to burst into tears.

"Do you remember anything about your seizures. I mean, like, when you're in them?"

I thought we were talking about you.

"We are." As he glanced over at her, she met his eyes. "You were telling me something. Halfway through, you looked up at me . . . and you were mouthing something. Can you remember what it was?"

He frowned as though he were running a check of his memory

banks, his gaze going unfocused. *I really can't . . . I just . . . I got up to the top of the stairs, looked into Wrath's study, saw you . . . and then it wasn't until Xhex took me down the hall to our room that my lights really came back on.*

"They say it was in the Old Language."

John shook his head. *Not possible. I mean, I can read it some and understand a little if someone talks to me. But I can't speak it.*

She inspected the ends of her hair, even though she knew there were no split ends; one of the *doggen* had trimmed it just last week.

"Well, is there something you want to tell me anyway?" She glanced over. "You can be honest with me about anything. Wrath has, like, a dozen Brothers. I only have you."

John frowned again. *No, I—*

A sudden trembling scrambled his hands, choking off whatever he was signing—and then he jerked back in the seat, his body going rigid.

"John!" Beth reached out to her brother. "John—oh, my God . . ."

As his eyes rolled back in his head, the whites flashed like he was dying. "John—come back . . . !"

Jerking forward, she knocked on the partition. "Fritz!"

As the butler dropped the smoky glass, she barked, "Hit it—he's having another seizure!"

Fritz's shocked eyes flipped up to the rearview. "Yes, madam. At once!"

The old butler stomped on the gas, and as the Mercedes torpedoed up the Northway's entrance ramp, she tried to help John. The seizure had taken him over, though, his back straight and unforgiving as a ramrod, his hands curled up to his chest and cranked into Dracula claws.

"John," she begged in a cracking voice. "Stay with me, John. . . ."

THIRTEEN

"Tell me he's coming around again."

As Assail spoke, he stared out the front windshield of the Rover, the hilt of a dagger locked in the grip of his right hand. They were deep into the woody fringes of Caldwell's zip code, no lights from dwellings twinkling through the tree line, no other vehicles coming or going along the icy, two-lane country road.

Benloise had roused briefly, only to "pass out" again. Which could well be a lie.

"Not yet," Ehric muttered. "But he's alive."

Not for long.

"And naked," the fighter tacked on.

Assail wrenched around just as his cousin collapsed his hunting knife. Naked, indeed. Benloise's bespoke suit had been beshredded, the fine navy fabric in tatters, the silk shirt underneath unfit even for a housecleaner's use. All jewelry had been removed as well, from the Chopard diamond watch to the gold signet ring, from the link bracelet to the cross on a thick gold chain.

The booty was bundled into a cup holder, along with a cell phone that had had its battery removed so that any GPS signal would be cut off. The clothing had been left wherever it lay.

Mayhap he was indeed unconscious. Difficult to imagine the man not struggling through that.

"How much farther?" Assail demanded.

"Right about here would be sufficient," Ehric said.

The male's brother hit the brakes, threw the gearshift in park, and killed the engine. Immediately, Assail got out, looked around and reconfirmed their isolation. No lights from any dwelling. No sound of any traffic. No one anywhere.

"Shut off the headlights."

With the flurries having abated and the moon making its appearance through spotty clouds, there was more than enough illumination coming through the pine trees.

Assail sheathed his dagger and then cracked his knuckles. "Get him up and out."

Ehric manhandled the deadweight with admirable aplomb, given that Benloise was unclothed and limp, a piece of luggage that had no handles, as it were.

The drug wholesaler returned to consciousness just as he was mounted against the icy cold contours of the Rover, and the jerk that announced his wake up was carried through to all his limbs, his arms and legs jangling like those of a puppet.

The cousins pinned the man against the SUV—and the great Ricardo Benloise no longer seemed powerful at all: He'd always looked commanding in his fancy suits, but without benefit of those carefully constructed jackets and slacks, he was just a compilation of shrunken hollows, his ribs standing out in sharp relief, his soft belly protruding over bony hips, his knees wider than his thighs and his calves.

"Let us not waste time," Assail said in a low tone. "Tell me where she is."

No response. Benloise's body might have been weak, but his mind, his eyes were sharp as ever: Though he was at a mortal disadvantage, his will was unbending.

That was not going to last.

Assail drew his arm across his own torso and cuffed the man with the back of his hand. "Where is she!"

Benloise's head ripped to the side as the slapping sound rang out, blood speckling Ehric's jacket.

"Where is she!" Assail hit the wholesaler again, his knuckles clapping hard enough to sting on the follow-through. "*Where is she*!"

The cousins hitched their prisoner up higher as he began to sag.

Assail snapped a hold onto the man's throat and helped in the effort until Benloise's feet dangled six inches off the snow. "I will kill you. Here and now. If you do not tell me where she is."

Benloise's eyes rolled around, but eventually met Assail's. And yet he said absolutely nothing.

Assail tightened his grip until the airway compressed. "*Marisol.* You tell me where you have taken her."

Benloise's mouth cranked open as he fought for oxygen, his thin arms pulling against what held them, his legs kicking so his heels pinged into the quarter panel.

"Marisol. Where is she."

Those eyes never left Assail's—to the point where, under different circumstances, one might have respected the man's obstinacy. Now it was a lightning rod for frustration.

"Where is she!"

With his free hand, Assail reached in between the man's legs and twisted the balls that had tucked in tight to the torso.

The scream that rose up was caught at the throat, Assail's hold silencing the sound. And he wanted to do so much more, but he couldn't kill the bastard. Not yet. Ordering his hand to release the airway, it was a moment before the digits obeyed.

Benloise coughed and gasped, blood from his split lip falling upon his naked chest.

"Where is she!"

Not one word came in manner of reply.

The bastard was not going to break. Not this way, at any rate—and as Assail's palm itched for his dagger, he didn't trust himself with that sharp blade.

Gutting the motherfucker was not what he ultimately wanted.

Assail moved in close. "I want you to pay careful attention now. Are you with me?"

Benloise's head lolled, but his eyes did stay open—so Assail went around to the back of the SUV. Popping the hatch, he lifted out the bound and gagged man they had kidnapped before going to the gallery.

Benloise's brother put up no fight at all. Then again, Ehric had snuck behind Eduardo in his home and punched a syringe full of heroin into a thick vein in his neck. The man was now also naked, and the far fitter condition of his body suggested that he was both younger and more vain—he had a spray tan over some measure of muscular development.

Assail threw him at Benloise's feet.

He didn't expect the surprise to sway things. But what was coming next would.

While the elder Benloise watched, Assail rolled the unconscious man onto his back, removed the gag, and took out a second syringe. In its fragile belly, Naloxone, the antidote used commonly in emergency rooms to combat opiate overdoses, was a clear liquid—and as he jabbed the needle into Eduardo's arm vein, it wasn't long before the pilot light came on again.

Eduardo woke up in a rush, torso jerking off the snow.

Assail took the man's jaw in a hard grip. Wrenching the head around, he growled, "Say hello to your brother—let us be polite."

Eyes popping wide, Eduardo immediately started speaking in Spanish, and Assail cured him of the impulse by taking out his dagger and pointing it in his face.

"Your brother has a place where he takes people to kill them. Where is it?"

"I do not know what you are—"

Assail straddled the man and grabbed the hair on the top of his head—as Eduardo used a great deal of product, it was a greasy mess, but he managed to get a passable hold. Putting the blade under the man's chin, he made sure to speak nice and slow.

"Where does he take people. I know there is a place, private and secure. Not at his house. Not downtown."

The elder Benloise brother finally spoke in a rush, the words to his brother guttural and punctuated with ragged breaths. In response, Eduardo's eyes became even larger, and one didn't need to know Spanish to catch the drift: You say anything and I will kill you myself.

Assail put his body between the two and got down eye-to-eye with Eduardo. "I'm going to hurt you now."

Pick a place, anyplace.

Assail decided to start with the shoulders. With a quick stab, he thrust the blade deep into the flesh below the collarbone—painful, but not fatal by a long stretch.

As his ears rang from the screaming, he kept the dagger in place. And his grip on the hilt.

"Where is it?" When he didn't get an immediate reply, he twisted the knife. "Where does he take them?"

More twisting. More screaming.

Which was when Ricardo spoke up again, his voice cutting through the drama to reinforce his message. Agony was going to win, however—Assail would make sure of that.

Backing off and giving dear boy Eddie a moment to rest and recover, he watched the hilt of the dagger move up and down in time to tortured respiration.

Oh, how the mighty had fallen. Eduardo was always the nattily dressed financial controller. But here he was, hair a mess, eyes bloodshot, snow smudged all over his naked skin.

Assail regarded him with all the compassion one would bring to still-thrashing roadkill. "Don't listen to him. If you do, I will kill you slowly. The only way to save yourself is to tell me what I need to know."

Ricardo barked something sharply.

"Do not listen to him." Assail kept his eyes locked with Eduardo's. "Talk to me. Save yourself."

Eduardo kept trying to see his brother, but Assail shifted positions with that panicked stare until Eduardo moaned, his eyes getting hidden amidst his crinkled face.

Assail gave him some more time, until patience was lost. Reaching out for the dagger, he announced, "I'm going to hurt you again—"

"It's north!" Eduardo yelled. "On the Northway! North! Southern side of Iroquois Mountain! Only road up to the property breaks off from the base! Go a half a mile and you'll see the drive!"

Up against the SUV, Ricardo exploded, fury evident in every syllable even if the sentence particulars were lost for lack of translation.

Assail breathed in deep through his nose. There was no scent of subterfuge coming from Eduardo. Fresh blood, of course, and the acrid sting of terror. Also, a rather touching shame that reminded Assail of root vegetables fresh out of a cellar.

The man had spoken the truth as he knew it.

"Put Ricardo back in the car," Assail said gruffly—

"Wait," he called out as the cousins complied. "Turn him back around."

Assail shifted so that he was behind Eduardo and propping the man's floppy torso up. Staring across the distance between Ricardo and himself, he said darkly, "You take from me, I take from you."

Jerking the dagger free of the shoulder meat, he streaked the blade directly across Eduardo's throat.

Ricardo tried to look away, his torso twisting between the cousins.

"This is only the beginning, Ricardo." Assail shoved the choking, bleeding man out of the way like the garbage he was. "We are just starting the now."

He closed in on Benloise. "I did, however, believe it was important for you to have one last memory of your brother's weakness. Just think, if he had been as strong as you, he could have died honorably. Alas, not his destiny."

Assail got into the passenger seat in the front. Retrieved his vial of coke.

As he snorted two spoonfuls into each nostril, the cousins put Ricardo into the rear compartment, and the squeal of duct tape being ripped free attested to how secure his relations were making things.

Reaching up and clicking on an overhead light, Assail unfolded a New York state map marked with three red As on it—and had no idea where to look.

Ehric got behind the wheel and put his iPhone in Assail's face. "It's a five-hour trip."

Assail's head started to buzz. Even with Benloise in their custody, he was terrified about what was being done to Marisol. Five hours was so long. Too fucking long in light of the previous twenty-four she'd already been gone.

Damn it, why did Benloise have to be so strategic.

"Then we must needs get driving," Assail gritted out.

FOURTEEN

The Commodore was arguably *the* place to live in downtown Caldwell. Rising up over twenty floors high, the condo building overlooked the Hudson River and was cut up into large block apartments that had plenty of square footage as well as state-of-the-art kitchens and bathrooms. Floor-to-ceiling glass windows meant the views in all four directions were as much a part of the decor as anything the owners put into the spaces, and there were rumors that celebrities, looking for a break from Manhattan, used them as drop pads.

Speaking of which, there was even a helicopter landing square on the top.

iAm got off at the eighteenth floor and hung a right. Down about a hundred feet, he stopped in front of a door marked 18A and popped the copper lock he and his brother had insisted on installing when they'd moved in five years ago.

Walking into the three-thousand-square-foot condo, his Merrells didn't make much noise even though the polished floor was bare of rugs and the modernist furniture was minimal not just in terms of style, but amount.

Damn . . . that view was still amazing. Especially like this, at night with no lights on inside: The city had its evening face on, everything sparkling, from the patchwork of lights left on in the skyscrapers to the double arches of the twin bridges to the stripes of red taillights and white headlights moving next to the shore down below.

So easy to forget that the heart of Caldie was a dirty place with as much poverty as wealth—if not more: Up here, insulated from reality, with the wailing sirens and stench of garbage so far removed, it was tempting to believe in the sanitized version of the 518.

But he was no fool.

Across the way, there were sliding glass doors that led out to the terrace, and after hitting the lights, he crossed over and opened one up, a cold gust rushing in and agitating the stuffy interior air. His visitor wasn't due for an hour yet, but he wanted to make sure the place looked lived-in. Doubling back to the open kitchen, he made some discreet clutter by popping a couple of already clean dishes into the rack by the sink and littering up the counter with . . . let's see . . . a spoon or two. A half-eaten bag of Cape Cod potato chips that were stale. An issue of *GQ* that he flipped through and left open to a page with a jacket Trez would like.

Then he got the coffee started.

He and his brother had no intention of ever coming back here, but he had to keep the place going because it was important that the s'Hisbe have no idea that they'd moved: A search party in Caldwell was not going to be a value add. Especially if it somehow culminated in a visit to the Brotherhood's mansion—

iAm pivoted to the glass door. Out on the terrace, a figure had materialized from the black night like a wraith, its robes thrashing in the stiff wind racing up the slick side of the building.

"Welcome," iAm called out to the high priest in a flat tone. "You're early."

Okay, which one of them had lost track of time?

The figure came to the doorway, walking in such a controlled, smooth manner you'd swear he was on a hover pad.

"Am I invited in?" came a dry voice.

iAm's heart skipped one single beat.

Fuck, that was *not* the high priest.

With those robes covering everything from head to foot, he'd assumed he knew who had come to him.

This was worse. So much worse.

The executioner's hood should have tipped him off.

"Well, am I, iAm." You could practically hear the nasty smile. "Such alliteration on that."

"Yeah, come in," iAm said, subtly tucking a hand under his jacket. With a flick, he released the holster's strap across the butt of his Glock. "Never expected you in my house."

"Interesting. I didn't think you were that naive." The male had to duck to make it inside. "And isn't this your brother's, too?"

Christ, all iAm could think of was the Grim Reaper.

Then again, s'Ex, as the Shadow queen's enforcer, had killed enough things to fill a graveyard or two. And he was built for bringing death. The male was seven feet tall and over three hundred pounds—easy. And that voice, coming from under the hooding? Pure evil.

"So I heard you never let AnsLai in," he said as he closed the slider. "I'm touched."

"Don't be. Actually, the high priest thought this place was too contaminated by our contact with humans. Coffee?"

"Like this is a date?" As opposed to the high priest, s'Ex didn't have any patience for the rules of court or the formality observed between members of the s'Hisbe. Then again, the supreme ruler didn't keep him by her side for his charm. "And yeah, why not. I like the idea of you waiting on me."

iAm ground his molars, but he wasn't going to get pissy. The s'Hisbe had raised the stakes about a thousand miles by sending this guy instead of the high priest, so things were already starting off on a bad foot.

Going around the granite counter, he took two mugs down from the glass-front cupboard and hoped the bastard didn't want milk in his. As he waited while the coffeemaker burbled and hissed to the end of its cycle, the last thing he expected was for s'Ex to come over and sit down on a stool—normally the enforcer would have cased the place.

Unfortunately, this probably meant he already had.

"So you and your brother been busy lately." s'Ex put his massive forearms on the counter and leaned into them. "Well, have you?"

"You mind taking that dress off." iAm stared right into the mesh that covered that face. "I want to see your eyes."

"How romantic."

"Not even close."

"You know, you haven't got a leg to stand on when it comes to demands."

"You hate wearing that goddamn hood. Don't front."

"Unlike some people, duty doesn't chafe my ass."

"Bullshit."

The short pause told him he'd gotten through on some level. But that didn't last. "Coffee's finished. Bring me mine, would you."

iAm turned away so that his tight jaw wasn't on display. "Sugar?"

"I'm sweet enough as it is."

Yeah. Right.

iAm brought over both mugs. "If you want a straw for this, you're SOL. Sorry."

s'Ex revealed himself with a quick, no-fuss jerk of the headdress—in spite of the fact that that thing must have weighed thirty pounds.

And yup, underneath was exactly what iAm remembered. Dark, dark skin. Cunning black eyes. Head with the ceremonial shaving patterns. White tattoos down the throat that continued around every square inch of his flesh.

And P.S., those tats were not made by ink. It was poison, injected into the skin in a pattern such that when the dermis died, it "discolored." Most males, to prove their masculinity, had a small one on their arm—and were sick for days. Nobody, but *nobody* had the likes of what s'Ex did.

The bastard was a monster. Especially as he smiled—for some reason, probably the testosterone overload, his fangs were always fully descended.

"Happy now?" he drawled.

"Not the word I would use." iAm took a draw off the rim of his mug. "So to what do I owe this honor."

Or kick in the nuts, as was the case.

s'Ex smiled a little—which was worse than his full-on grin. "So you and your brother have been busy."

"You already said that."

"I've paid you a couple of visits here. Nothing special—just a flyby or two. The pair of you haven't been hanging here lately. Busy with the females?"

"Working."

"Night and day, then. Wow . . . worried about money? Do you need a loan?"

"Not from you. I can't afford the vig."

"Too right." Black eyes narrowed on his own. "So where are you."

"Around. Here now, obviously."

"I don't think you live here anymore."

"Then why are you sitting on something I own."

"I'll bet if I go in your room, the closet's empty."

"And I assume breaking and entering is part of your 'flybys'—unless you've changed your style."

s'Ex eased back and crossed his arms under his robes. "Now how rude would I be if I did something like get in here and sniff around. It would be unthinkable."

"You're saying you haven't done that." iAm rolled his eyes. "Really."

"No. Or I could be lying. Kind of like you are about living here anymore."

"Maybe you've just come while we've been out."

"Okay, let's look at tonight. Why are you in your coat? Why are the spoons on the counter clean? Oh, and that magazine? Last month's. And yet it's been open like you've been 'reading' it." He even did the air quotes. "And one, already-opened bag of chips does not a full pantry make."

Goddamn it. "Isn't *GQ* contraband in the Territory?"

s'Ex smiled again. "Her Royal Highness likes to keep me happy. What can I say."

Either that or the queen herself was scared of the guy.

iAm lowered his lids to half-mast. "Talk to me."

"I thought I was. Or were we using sign language and I missed it?"

Except the enforcer got serious, frowning into his mug, going still.

And the longer the silence lasted, the stranger things got. s'Ex didn't waste time, and he had no patience—ordinarily, the fucker was as decisive as a chain saw.

iAm waited things out for two reasons: One, what other choice did he have. And two, he was used to that by now.

Thanks to Trez's shit, he'd had a master class in nothing-I-can-do.

s'Ex's eyes shifted back over. "The high priest is coming to tell you that Trez's time is up. The queen wants what she's been promised and the daughter is ready to receive him. Any delay from this point on is going to have measurable repercussions. So, no lie, if you've got any way of making your brother toe the line, do it. Now."

"She's going to get you to kill him, isn't she," iAm said grimly.

The enforcer shook his head. "Not yet. I'm going to start with your parents. Your mother first. Then your father. And it's not going to be pretty." The male's stare never wavered. "I've been ordered to tie her up and shave her head first—then rape her and cut her so she bleeds out slow. Your father is going to watch it all and then what I do to him will be worse. If you honor them in any way, talk to your brother. Get him to the Territory. Make him do the right thing. She's not going to stop until she gets him—and just so we're clear, I will not hesitate to do my job."

iAm braced his hands on the granite counter and leaned into his arms. The situation with their parents was . . . complicated, to use a Facebook term. But that didn't mean he wanted them dead and/or desecrated.

As s'Ex got to his feet and slung his executioner's hood over his shoulder, iAm heard himself say, "You didn't touch your coffee."

"You might have poisoned it." The enforcer shrugged. "I don't take chances with anybody—sorry."

"Smart." iAm measured the male. "But then, you're a real professional."

"And I have my reputation for a good reason, iAm."

"I know." He cursed under his breath. "I am well aware of your work."

"Don't pull my trigger. I didn't have parents, and wish I had. I'm not looking forward to this."

"Goddamn it, it's not up to me." iAm curled up two fists. "And I don't know if Trez is going to care, to be honest. He hates them."

s'Ex shook his head. "That's not good news. For any of you."

"Why the hell can't she just get someone else."

"Not a question I'd be asking if I were you." s'Ex looked around the apartment. "Nice place, by the way. Just my style—and I've been enjoying the view while I'm here."

iAm narrowed his eyes at the odd tone in that deep voice. Son of a bitch . . . "You get it, don't you."

"What? How someone would want out of the Territory. To be free to live their own life." Abruptly, s'Ex's face turned into a mask. "Don't know what you're talking about."

The enforcer turned away and stalked back to the slider. As he moved, his robes wafted behind him, his body shifting with the grace of a predator.

"s'Ex."

The male looked over his shoulder. "Yeah?"

iAm reached out and took the coffee he'd poured for his guest. Lifting it to his lips, he drank long and hard, finishing the shit on a oner even as it burned its way down to his gut.

As he put the empty mug back down, the enforcer bowed. "You have more honor than most, iAm. And that's why I came to you. I actually like you—not that that's going to help you much further than tonight."

"I appreciate it."

The enforcer looked around, as if he were storing the memories for later. "Back at the s'Hisbe, I'll do what I can to delay things, but this is on you. Your brother may be the one with his neck in a noose—but you're the guy who's going to have to get him where he needs to go."

"He's not clean, you realize."

"How so?"

"He's been fucking humans. A lot of them."

s'Ex threw his head back and laughed. "I should goddamn hope so. If I were on the outside, I would."

"Bet your queen won't feel like that."

"She's your ruler, too—and I wouldn't play that card if I were you." s'Ex pointed his forefinger across the distance. "She'll put him through a cleanse, and if he survives that—which is not a foregone conclusion—he'll never be the same. You need to shut your fucking mouth on his love life, trust me. Oh, and AnsLai doesn't know I've come. Let's keep this our little secret, shall we."

After the enforcer went out and disappeared into thin air, iAm strode over and closed the door. Then he proceeded directly to the bar at the far end of the open space and poured himself a bourbon.

Looked like Trez's get-out-of-jail-free card had a hole in it: His sex addiction was not going to be the turnoff they'd been hoping it would.

Great.

And if s'Ex hadn't shown up here and told him to keep all that fucking on the QT? God only knew what would have happened.

He hadn't even heard about cleansing, but he could guess.

One thing was sure: He never thought in a million years he'd ever owe that coldhearted executioner a solid. Then again, it looked like Trez wasn't the only one balking at the restrictions of the Territory.

The question was . . . now what. And he had about ten minutes to figure the shit out before the high priest got here.

FIFTEEN

"I never expected to see you again. They said you'd left town."

As St. Francis's Chief of Neurology leaned into the computer screen, the guy seemed to be talking to himself. And sure enough, as Manny Manello didn't answer him, he didn't seem to care.

Beth stepped in a little closer to take a look herself—although, come on, it wasn't as if the multiple views of her brother's brain up on that monitor meant anything to her. Hopefully, however, this guy in the white coat with the impressive credentials came at things from a different angle.

The dim anteroom they were all squeezed into was like something out of a *Star Trek* episode, high-tech equipment whirring and blinking, the massive MRI machine in the chamber beyond kept separate by a thick plate-glass window. And actually, the neurologist, sitting in front of that banked console, was kind of like Lieutenant Sulu as he faced off at the computer screens, the keyboards, a telephone or two, another laptop.

"How long did this most recent seizure last?" the neurologist asked absently.

"About fifteen minutes," Beth answered as John glanced over at her.

"Any numbness or tingling?"

When John shook his head, Beth said, "No. Nothing."

John had come out of the hollow doughnut about ten minutes ago and changed from his hospital johnny back into his relatively innocuous-looking jeans and Giants T-shirt. The IV that had pumped contrast into his body was out of his arm, a little white Band-Aid in the place of its needle, and his shitkickers were back on.

He'd left his weapons at home.

Xhex, however, was fully loaded as she stood next to him, a black Nike baseball cap pulled down low over her eyes. Payne was the other backup, the fighter dressed in black and wearing the same kind of loose coat John's wife was.

Beth did a retug of her own Bos Sox hat. It had been a while since anyone had seen her in the human world, and she didn't know anyone in particular at the hospital—but there was no reason to layer on more complication to this trip.

Oh, God, please let this be okay, she thought as that doctor scrolled through all the images again.

Right behind him, not that the man was aware of it, Doc Jane was also peering over his shoulder at the black-and-white pictures—in full ghost mode.

The more eyes, the better.

"What do you see?" Manny demanded.

To his credit, the neurologist didn't spin back around until he was good and ready—and he addressed John when he finally faced the crowd.

"There's nothing abnormal in there that I can see."

Cue the collective sigh of relief. And the first thing John did was grab Xhex's tight body and haul her in close, the world obviously disappearing for them both.

As Beth watched them, she knew she should be focused on the good news. Instead, all she could think of was how she was not only alone while she waited to hear whether her brother had some kind of embolism or tumor or heaven only knew what horror in his brain—but there was a big-ass metaphorical pink elephant between her and her husband that was not going to go away anytime soon.

Pink. As in baby-girl color.

Or maybe not. Maybe it was pale blue.

"All of the brain structure is normal. . . ."

The doctor launched into a whole lot of physician-speak that luckily meant something to Manny, given the nodding. But the lovebirds ignored all that, and their self-absorption was actually a beautiful thing to see.

At least until tears of relief mixed with tears of sadness, and everything went wavy for Beth.

Time to excuse herself.

Murmuring something about making a phone call, she ducked out into the hall. The imaging facility was isolated in the basement of one of the many St. Francis buildings, and outside of it, there was a whole lot of nothing going on: no patients in transport, no carts of supplies rolling by, no staff rushing around in soft-soled shoes.

Putting her head into her hands, she eased her butt against the wall and slid down to the floor. Thank God John seemed okay. So at least one part of her family was all right—

I need you to hear this and know that it's the God's honest. I will not service you in your needing. Ever . . .

Shit, she thought as she rubbed her eyes. Now she had to go back home and deal with all that.

A little while later, the group emerged from command central, and she shimmied to her feet, trying not to look anything other than relieved at John's scan.

The neurologist was staring at a check in his hands and shaking his head. "Jesus Christ, Manello. Did you win the lottery?"

Kinda. Thanks to Darius's investments, fifty grand to the neurology department as a donation was no BFD.

And to think, all the white coat had had to do was shove her brother into his pinging machine for about a half hour.

"I'm just grateful you got us in," Manello murmured.

The doctor turned to John as he folded the check and put it in his pocket. "So, yeah, I still recommend the anti-seizure meds, but if you're dead-set against them, the only thing I can tell you is, try to keep track of the whens and wheres. See if there's a pattern—maybe there is, maybe there isn't. And know that I'm here if you need me. Remember what I said, though—just because I can't see anything doesn't mean you're out of the woods. The episodes are happening because there's something wrong. Period."

"Thanks, man." Manello put out his hand. "You're the best."

The former colleagues clapped palms. "Anytime—and I mean

that. And . . . you know, if you ever want to come back, they'd take you in a heartbeat. You're missed here."

Manny's eyes shifted over to Payne, and the secret smile that hit his lips was another source of awwww.

"Nah. I've got it good now, but thanks."

Chatter. Chatter. Good ol' days. Bye. Thanks again.

And then the vampire contingency split off once again from the human one, Manny leading them out through a maze of bare tiled corridors that looked exactly the same—to the point where she began to become convinced they were lost. Wrong. Either their man in front had a compass implanted in *his* frontal lobe or he remembered well his decade working in the place—because eventually they hit ground level and went out the revolving doors they'd entered.

Fritz was waiting by the curb, that huge black-on-black Mercedes looking like it belonged to a diplomat. Which was another reason the car was so useful: People tended to err on the side of not screwing with it, like its inhabitants were really important or heavily armed. Fritz got more wave-throughs at stop signs and parking garages than she'd ever seen. Then again, he drove in the exact opposite way he moved.

The elderly butler didn't have a lead foot. The damn thing was made out of tungsten—

Let's go back now? John signed in front of her face—like maybe he'd been trying to get her attention.

"Wha—oh, sorry." She pushed her hair back. "Don't you want to go with Xhex?"

"I'm heading to the club," the female said. "With Trez out, I need to check the traps."

And that was a good, plausible excuse—except it was impossible to ignore the side glances being shared among the group.

"This isn't about me," she muttered.

Of course it isn't, John signed. *You're doing a favor coming back with me. You know, to keep me company.*

Fritz was only too happy to jump out and get her door for her, and as she ducked into the back of the sedan, she caught sight of Manny giving Payne a smooch, and John lip-locking with Xhex.

As a wave of dread came over her, she thought fondly of getting drunk as opposed to confronting her husband. The only problem was, that wasn't going to solve anything, and besides, she had always despised women who got lit. Nothing uglier or more pathetic.

John got in on the other side, and then the Mercedes floated off, following the lane out from under the porte cochere and into the roadway that went around the medical center. With signs like Emergency Room, Farnsworth Rehabilitation, and Yardley Spine Center, it was like a highway with exits to towns you really didn't want to visit.

Next to her, her brother kept looking over, like she was a stick of dynamite and he was measuring how much wick was left before shit went Technicolor boom.

"I'm fine."

Okay, I won't press. But here.

"Huh?" He answered her question by passing over a white handkerchief. "Why do I need—"

Fantastic. She'd started tearing up.

Really, truly fantastic.

As she blotted away tears she hadn't been aware of crying, she shook her head and let it all fly: "I want a baby."

Holy crap . . . that's awesome, her brother signed. *That's—*

"A nightmare, actually. Wrath's a no-go."

Oh, her brother mouthed.

"Yeah. Pretty much. And I found out right before we left."

My God, you shouldn't have come.

"I needed to get out of that house. And I wanted to help you."

Well . . . Wrath's probably just worried about you. It's a scary thing for females. At this, his face got tight. *I mean, Xhex isn't into kids, and I gotta tell you, I'm relieved.*

Twisting the cotton square in her hands, she let her head fall back against the rest. "But if I'm willing to assume the risks, I feel like he should go along with it. And by the way, it wasn't like he laid his argument out in terms of being worried for my health. It was just, 'I'm not servicing you.' Period."

John whistled under his breath.

"I know. Not our best moment." She glanced back over at her brother. "I envy you and Xhex so much. You guys are so in sync."

Ha! You should have seen us a year ago. John shrugged. *I didn't think we were going to make it.*

"Really?"

Shit, yeah. She wanted to go out to fight, and like, that was fine with me—until it really dawned on me that she could get hurt. He circled his hand next to his brain. *Fucked my head up bad. I mean, as a male, your woman is your thing in a way I don't think you females can appreciate. When it comes to Xhex, I am literally not in control of my emotions, my thoughts, my actions as they relate to her safety. It's a kind of psychosis.*

When she didn't respond, he touched her arm to make sure she was paying attention. *Sounds a lot like what you and Wrath are dealing with. Yeah, you can be all, 'It's about a kid,' but given the mortality rates for females? In his mind, it's probably about your survival—and he's picking that over any kind of son or daughter.*

God, maybe it made her a bitch, but . . . she really didn't want to see Wrath's side of things. Especially not spelled out so rationally—assuming that was, in fact, how her man felt.

She was still too hurt and angry.

"Okay, fine, maybe that's all true. But let me ask you a question—would you ever deny Xhex a child if she wanted one?" When he didn't answer, Beth said, "See? You wouldn't."

Technically, I didn't reply.

"It's in your face."

Yeah, but, it's easy for me to be all like, whatever—because she doesn't want one. Maybe I'd feel differently if she did. The risks are real, and there's only so much medical management can do.

"I still say it's my body, my decision."

But you're his primary concern. So he does get a vote.

"A vote's one thing. The royal veto's another." She shook her head again. "Besides, if you're able to articulate the position of a bonded male? So should he. He doesn't get a pass just because he's the King." As sound bites came back from the confrontation, she got nauseous. "His solution is to drug me. Like I'm some kind of animal. I just . . . I don't know if I can get over this."

Maybe you should take a break. Like . . . get away until you aren't so pissed off. Then come back and talk it out.

She put her hand on her stomach, and as she measured the fat padding that was now there, she felt so damned dumb for sitting on her ass eating ice cream with Layla. She wasn't any closer to her needing—whenever, if ever, that came, it was clearly going to be on its own schedule. All she'd done was make her pants tight and drive a wedge between herself and her husband.

In the words of Dr. Phil, How's that working for ya?

Great, Phil. Just awesome.

Hell, maybe she should watch OWN more often. Dr. Phil reruns were on for, like, five hours every morning, Monday through Friday. Surely he'd done a show on couples who disagreed over the baby thing.

Why don't you go stay at our father's house, John signed.

She thought of the mansion. "Yeah, no. I don't want to even think about that place."

As if on cue, images of her and Wrath from back in the beginning hit her hard—especially the memory of their first official date. God, things had been so perfect back then, the two of them falling in love so easily. Wrath had had her over to the house and dressed in a Brooks Brothers suit for the one and only time in their relationship. They'd sat at the dining room table and Fritz had waited on them.

That's when Wrath had told her she tasted like—

With a groan, she put her head in her hands and tried to breathe calmly. Didn't work. Her brain seemed to have the mental equivalent of an arrhythmia, thoughts and memories from the happy past and worries about the grim future mixing into a jumpy, jerky mess.

The only thing she was clear on?

John was right. She couldn't go back home yet: The instant she saw Wrath, she was going to light into him, and that was going to get them nowhere.

God knew they'd already had that conversation once. A repeat was just going to make things harder.

"Okay," she heard herself say. "All right. But I need something to eat first."

It's a deal, John signed.

SIXTEEN

As Wrath took form by the race's clinic, he sensed Vishous materializing beside him—and resented the fact that he was required to have a fucking babysitter. But at least V's medical knowledge was going to be a value add.

"Fifteen feet straight ahead," his brother announced. "Four feet of cleared pavement in front of you. Then it's snow-covered ground."

Wrath threw out one stride and hit hard asphalt. With his next step forward, the snow absorbed his shitkicker.

There was no bringing George to this. Blindness was not a virtue in times of peace for a ruler. During war? It was a critical weakness—and nothing said lights-out better than a Seeing Eye service dog.

Naturally, the retriever had been apoplectic at being left behind—but with Beth already pissed off at him, of course he'd had to alienate his damn dog. Next thing to work on? The Brotherhood. Although that set of hardheaded motherfuckers was too tenacious to be put off by anything less than an H-bomb.

"Stop," V said.

Wrath came to a halt even though he had to grit his molars. But it was better than walking into the side of the building.

There was a pause, during which V put in the code that changed every evening, and then they entered the shallow lobby, that trademark antiseptic hospital smell announcing that they were indeed in the right place.

And shit knew he felt sick: His chest was aching, his head was pounding, and his skin felt too small for his bones.

Clearly a case of asshole-itis.

And it was probably terminal.

"Greetings, my lords," came a tinny female voice—and even through the speaker, it was filled with awe. "We're sending the elevator for you at this moment."

"Thanks," V gritted.

Yeah, the brother hated Havers for a variety of reasons. Then again, so did Wrath.

Just think, when the good doctor had tried to kill him a couple of years ago, it had seemed like such a big deal. Now? Compared to the likes of Xcor and the Band of Bastards, one white coat with a bow tie and horn-rimmed glasses coming after him was a goddamn cakewalk.

Shit, he wished he could go back to his father's era, when people respected the throne.

There was the sound of an elevator opening and then V touched the back of Wrath's arm. Together, they entered the compartment, and after a *bing* and slide of the doors, a sinking feeling confirmed they were heading underground.

When the doors reopened, Vishous got careful with the leading: He closed in so he was shoulder-to-shoulder and stayed that way, no doubt looking to casual viewers as if he were just a bodyguard doing his duty to the King of the race.

Instead of functioning as a surrogate set of eyeballs.

A sudden murmuring in the waiting area was a sure sign they'd walked into a public place. And the reception at Reception was likewise electric.

"My lord," some female said, as a squeak broke out like a chair had been shoved back. "This way. Please."

Wrath turned his head to the voice and nodded. "Thanks for fitting us in."

"Of course, my lord. It is a rare honor to have your presence in our . . ."

Blah, blah, blah.

The good news was that he was fast-tracked to a private area with minimal interruption. And then it was a case of waiting. It wouldn't be for long, though. He was willing to bet Havers would put his running shoes on to get to wherever they were.

Not that that tight-ass pussy would know what Nikes were necessarily.

"Do, like, all hospitals have to have Monets in them?" Vishous groused.

"Guess the posters come cheap."

"This is an actual painting."

Oh. Yeah. Clearly, they were in a VIP suite. "Leave it to Havers—a cliché even while at Sotheby's."

"He probably brought it over from the Old Country. Tasteless fool. Once you've seen a fucking water lily, you've seen them all. And I hate pink. I really hate pink. Although lavender is worse."

As Wrath put his hands out to feel around, he thought of the Impressionist paintings he'd seen back when his eyesight had worked a little. Talk about blurred vision—nothing like a half-blind painter's smudgey art being viewed by a half-blind ass-hat.

Surrealists with their razor-sharp edges had been much better if he'd wanted to—

Wow. His brain really didn't want to think about why they were here.

"There's an examination table directly in front of you."

"I'm not getting examined," Wrath muttered.

"Fine, someone's grandmother's silk sofa is to your right."

As he rerouted and took the couch route, he thought of how much he loved having his own in-house docs. Too bad Doc Jane and Manny couldn't answer his questions in this case. And yeah, he supposed he could have gotten the information another way—like have Fritz come here and ask things. But sometimes firsthand was the only way to go: He wanted to catch the scent of the physician when the male spoke. It was the only way to be sure it was the truth.

"You going to tell me what this is about," V demanded.

A flicking sound was followed by a scratch, and a moment later, the scent of Turkish tobacco did away with most, if not all, of the bleachy ferment of oh, so many Lysol moppings.

When Wrath didn't say shit, V cursed. "You know, Jane can do this, whatever it is."

"She know about vampire needings? No? Didn't think so."

That shut the brother up for a minute.

In the silence, Wrath had an overwhelming need to pace—but that was a no-go, assuming he didn't want to run over all of Havers's fancy furniture.

"Talk to me."

Wrath shook his head. "Got nothing good to say."

"Like that's ever stopped you before, true?"

Fortunately, Havers picked that moment to come in—only to immediately stop short just inside the exam room.

"Forgive me . . ." he said to Vishous. "But there is no smoking here."

V's tone was bored. "Our species doesn't get cancer—or is that a newsflash to you."

"It's because of the oxygen tanks."

"Is there one in here?"

"Ah . . . no."

"Well, then I won't go looking for one."

Wrath cut off any further debate. "Will you shut the door." You fucking idiot. "I just have to ask you a couple of questions. And tell your nurse to leave, would you."

"Of . . . course."

Fear spiked the air as the nurse departed and the door was shut, and Wrath didn't blame the guy for being nervous.

"How may I be of service, my lord?"

Wrath pictured the male from memory, imaging that Havers still had those glasses on his Ivy League–looking face, and that white coat with his name stitched next to the lapel. As if there might be some confusion around his clinic as to who he was.

"I want to know what you can do to stop a female's needing."

Crickets. Whole lot of crickets.

Well, except for V muttering something that probably started with F and ended in U-C-K.

After a moment, there was a creak, as if the good doctor had sat down next to Wrath's sofa. "I, ah, I am unsure how to answer that, my lord."

"Give it a shot," Wrath said dryly. "And quick. I don't have all night."

Quiet sounds suggested the male was fiddling with things. A pen?

Maybe a stethoscope? "Has she . . . has the, ah, female . . . has it commenced?"

"No."

The silence that followed made him wish he hadn't come here. He wasn't walking out now, though, and not just because he'd lost track of where the door was already. "It's not my *shellan*, by the way. It's a friend of mine."

Jesus Christ, like he had an STD or some shit.

But at least that loosened up the doctor. Instantly, the male's vibe calmed and his mouth got to flapping. "I have no good answer for you, unfortunately. Thus far, I have found no way to halt the time's commencement. I have tried various drugs, even those available on the human market—the issue is that vampire females have an extra hormone that, when triggered, creates an overwhelming, system-wide response. As a result, human contraceptive pills or shots don't have any effect on our females."

Wrath shook his head. He should have known—nothing about the reproductive cycle of a female vampire was easy.

Dumb-ass Scribe Virgin. Oh, sure, go ahead and create a race of people—and while you're at it, why don't you saddle them with some really tough shit. Perfect.

Havers continued, his seat creaking again as if he were changing positions. "Easing the female during her suffering is the only method I've had success with. Would you require a kit for your associate, my lord?"

"Kit, as in . . ."

"For treatment of the needing."

He thought of Beth sitting in that room with Layla. God only knew how long that had been going on—but more to the point, he was afraid it had worked: He'd totally gotten sprung in his *shellan*'s presence. And yeah, that was not unusual, except for the fact that they'd been arguing and sex had been the last fucking thing on his mind.

Her hormones might well be in flux already.

Either that or he was paranoid.

Also a possibility.

"Yeah," he heard himself say. "I want one."

There was the sound of something being written down. "Now, I will need the male in charge of her to sign for this, either her *hellren*, her father, or the oldest male of her household. I don't feel comfortable sending these levels of narcotics out into the world unaccounted for—and of course, there will have to be someone there to administer them to her. Not only will she in all likelihood be compromised by the needing, but let us be honest. Females don't have the best heads for these things anyway."

For some reason, Wrath thought of Payne accusing him of being a misogynist.

At least Havers totally lapped him on that one—

Oh shit, how was he going to sign anything? Back home at his desk, Saxton always marked the signature line with a series of raised—

"I'll sign for it," V interjected sharply. "And my *shellan*, who's a doctor just like you, will take care of everything else."

"*You* are mated?" the physician sputtered. As if there were a greater chance of a meteor dropping on his clinic. "I mean—"

"Give me the paper," Vishous said. "And your pen."

Cue more scribbling in an even more awkward silence.

"What is her weight?" Havers asked, as there was a shuffling like he was putting something in a file.

"I don't know," Wrath said.

"Would you like me to see the female in question, my lord? She may come here at any time that is convenient, or I could provide a home visit—"

"One thirty-six," V said. "And enough with the conversation. Get us the drugs so we can get the hell out of here."

As Havers tripped over his own loafers to leave the room, Wrath leaned back until his head hit the plaster wall he'd been unaware of being behind him.

"You want to tell me what the fuck this is about now?" his brother bit out. "Because I'm jumping to a lot of conclusions at the moment, and neither one of us needs that—when you could just answer the cocksucking question."

"Beth has been hanging out with Layla."

"Because she wants . . ."

"A young."

A fresh influx of Turkish tobacco hit Wrath's nose, suggesting the brother had just taken a deep drag. "So you're serious about not wanting a kid?"

"Never. How's 'never' sound?"

"Amen to that." Abruptly, V's shitkickers made tracks around the room, and man, that pacing stuff was something to envy. "It's not that I don't respect Z and his little slice of nuclear. Thanks to those two females of his, he seems almost normal—which is a miracle in and of itself. So power to him, true? But that shit ain't for me. Thank God Jane feels the same."

"Yeah. Thank God."

"Beth's not on that train?"

"Nope. She's not even in that station, that town, or that part of whatever country your metaphor lives in."

Wrath rubbed his forehead. On the one hand, it was great to have someone agree with him about the no-young issue—it made him feel less like he was doing something wrong or being cruel to his Beth. On the other, that accord Vishous had with Jane? It wasn't that you wished the shit you were going through on your brother. Not at all. But damn, he could have walked a marathon in those comfortable shoes, thank you very much.

As his brother paced and smoked, and they both waited for Havers to return with the knockout drops . . . for some reason, he thought back to his parents.

The memories that he had of his mother and father were all about the Norman Rockwell—well, dub in the Old Country language and change the stage set to a medieval castle theme. But yeah, those two had had the perfect relationship. No arguments, no anger, just love.

Nothing had ever come between them. Not his father's job, not the court they lived in, not the citizenry they served.

Perfect harmony.

It was yet another standard set in the past that he was failing to live up to—

V let out a strange sound, part gasp, part curse.

"Swallow your smoke wrong?" Wrath said dryly.

Right next to him, the chair where Havers had been sitting didn't creak so much as curse—like V had thrown all of his weight into the thing.

"V?"

When the brother finally answered, his voice was low, too low. "I see you . . ."

"No, no, no." Wrath burst up. "I don't want know, V. If you're having one of your visions, do *not* tell me what it—"

". . . standing in a field of white. White, white is all around you . . ."

The Fade? Oh, fucking hell. "Vishous—"

". . . and you are talking to—"

"Hey! Asshole! I've told you all along, I don't want to know when I'm going to die. Do you hear me? I don't want to know."

"—the face in the heavens."

"Your mother?" Christ knew the Scribe Virgin had been MIA and then some lately. "Is it your mother?"

Shit, he didn't want to encourage this. "Listen, V, you gotta pull back. I can't handle it, man."

There was a low curse, as if the brother were collecting himself. "Sorry, when it hits in a rush like that, it's hard to stop."

"That's cool." Even though it wasn't. Not by a long shot.

Because the problem with Vishous's premonitions—aside from the fact that they were always about people dying? No timeline. That stuff could be about Wrath keeling over next week. Next year. Seven hundred centuries from now.

If Beth died . . . he wouldn't want to live—

"All I can say is"—V exhaled again—"I see that the future is in your hands."

Well, at least that was generic and obvious, like an astrology report in a magazine—the kind of thing anybody could read into and feel as though it applied to them.

"Do me a favor, V."

"What."

"Don't see anything else about me."

"Not up to me, true?"

Too right. Just like his own future.

But the good news was . . . he wasn't going to have to worry about Beth's needing. Thanks to this miserable little visit, he was going to be able to take care of her when it came.

Without running the risk of pregnancy.

SEVENTEEN

THE YEAR 1664

"Leelan?"

When there was no answer, Wrath, son of Wrath, knocked again upon his chamber door. "Leelan, *may I enter?"*

As King, he waited for no one, and there was not a body who permitted him to do aught.

Except for his precious mate.

And as with this eve, when there were festival gatherings, she desired to pretty herself in privacy, allowing him access only when she had prepared herself for his viewing and adoration. It was utterly charming—as was the manner in which their mated space was scented because of her oils and lotions. As was the way, even a year after their union, that she still ducked her eyes and smiled secretly when he wooed her. As was waking up every dusk with her against him and then fading off to rest at the dawn beside her warm, beautiful body.

But there was a different edge to it all now.

When was the waiting going to be over . . . and not about gaining entrance unto their room.

"Enter, my love," came through the stout oak panels.

Wrath's heart jumped. Turning the heavy latch, he shouldered the planks open . . . and there she was. His beloved.

Anha was across the room, by the hearth that was large enough for a grown male to stand in. Seated at her dressing table, which he'd had moved by the fire for to ensure warmth, her back was to him, her long black hair lying in thick coils down her shoulders to her waist.

Wrath breathed in deep, her scent more important than the oxygen that filled his lungs. "Oh, you look lovely."

"You have nae seen me properly—"

Wrath frowned at the tightness in her voice. "What ails you?"

His shellan *turned about to face him. "Naught. Why do you ask?"*

She was lying. Her smile was a faded version of its normal radiance, her skin too pale, her eyes dragging down at their corners.

As he strode across the fur rugs, fear gripped him. How many nights since her needing had come and gone? Fourteen? Twenty-one?

In spite of the risk to her, they truly prayed for a conception—and not simply for an heir, but as a son or daughter to love and nurture.

Wrath sank to his knees before his leelan, *and indeed he was reminded of the very first time he had done as such. He had been right to mate this female, and righter still to place his heart and soul within her gently cupped hands.*

She alone he could trust.

"Anha, be of truth to me." He reached up and touched her face—and immediately retracted his hand. "You are cold!"

"I am not." She batted him away, putting her brush down and getting to her feet. "I am dressed in this red velvet you prefer. How can I possibly be cold?"

For a moment, he nearly forgot his concerns. She was such a vision in the deep, rich color, the gold thread upon her bodice catching the firelight just as all her rubies did: Indeed, she was wearing the full set of jewelry tonight, the stones glinting at her ears, her neck, her wrists, her hands.

And yet, as resplendent as she was, something was not proper.

"Do rise, my hellren, *" she commanded. "And let us proceed down unto the festivities. All and sundry are awaiting you."*

"They may tarry longer." He had no intention of budging. "Anha, speak unto me. What is wrong?"

"You worry over much."

"Have you bled?" he asked tightly. Which would mean that a young was not within her.

She put a slender hand over her belly. "No. And I feel . . . perfectly well. Honestly."

Wrath narrowed his eyes. There was, of course, another issue that could be upon her heart. "Has anyone been cruel?"

"Never."

In that, she was lying for certain. "Anha, do you think there is aught that escapes my knowledge? I am well aware of what transpires about court."

"Do not concern yourself with those half-wits. I do not."

He loved her for her resilience. But her bravery was unnecessary—if only he could find out who was tormenting her, he would take care of it. "I believe I should readdress the gossips."

"You say nothing, my love. What's done is done—you cannot undo the presentation. Trying to silence any and all criticism or comment upon me would lead to an empty court."

It had all started that night when she had been brought to him. He had not followed proper protocol, and in spite of the fact that the King's wishes ruled o'er the land and all its vampires, there were those who disapproved of so much: That he had not undressed her. That he had given her the ruby suite of gems and the queen's ring—and then conducted the mating himself. That he had immediately moved her in here, to his private quarters.

His critics had not been appeased in the slightest when he had consented to a public ceremony. Nor had they, even a year later, warmed to his mate. They were never rude to her in his presence, of course—and Anha refused to say a word about what happened behind his back.

But the scent of her anxiety and depression were too well known to him.

In truth, the court's treatment of his beloved angered him to the point of violence—and created a rift between him and all who surrounded him. He felt as though he could trust no one. Even the Brotherhood, who were supposed to be his private guard and those whom he should have faith in above all others, even those males he was suspicious of.

Anha was all he had.

Leaning down to him, her hands cradled his face. "Wrath, my love." She pressed her lips to his. "Let us proceed unto the festival."

He gripped her forearms. Her eyes were pools to drown in, and the only terror he knew in this mortal coil was that someday they might not be there for him to stare into.

"Halt your thinking," his shellan *beseeched. "There is naught that will happen to me now or ever."*

Drawing her against him, he turned his head and laid it against her womb. As her hands threaded through his hair, he studied her table. Brushes, combs, squat bowls of chromatics for her lips and her eyes, a cup of tea beside its pot, a wedge of bread that had been nibbled upon.

Such prosaic things, but because she had gathered them, touched them, consumed them, they were elevated to the heights of value: She was the alchemy that turned it all, and him, to gold.

"Wrath, we must needs go."

"I do not wish to. This is where I wish to be."

"But your court awaits."

He said something vile that he hoped became caught in the folds of velvet. Given her soft laughter, he ventured it had not.

She was correct, however. There were many gathered for his attendance.

Damn them all.

Rising to his feet, he proffered his arm unto her, and as she looped hers through the crook of his elbow, he led them out of their chamber and past the palace guards who lined the hall. Some distance thereafter, they descended a curving stairwell, the sounds of the gathered aristocracy growing ever louder.

As they closed in upon the great hall, she leaned on him more, and he puffed out his chest, his body growing in stature as a result of her reliance upon him. Unlike so many courtesans, who were eager to be dependent, his Anha had always retained a certain prideful decorum within herself—so when, on occasion, she did require his strength in some way, it was a special gift to his most masculine side.

There was naught that made him feel his male sex more keenly.

As the cacophony became so loud it swallowed the sounds of their footsteps, he leaned unto her ear. "We shall bid them a hasty good evening."

"Wrath, you must avail yourself of—"

"You," he said as they approached the final corner. "That is of whom I must be availed."

When she blushed beautifully, he chuckled—and found himself in fervent anticipation of their forthcoming privacy.

Rounding the last turn, he and his shellan *came up to a set of double doors that were for their use only, and two Brothers stepped forward to greet them in the formal proper manner.*

Dearest Virgin Scribe in the Fade, he detested these gatherings of the aristocracy.

As trumpets announced their arrival, the portals were thrown wide and the hundreds assembled went silent, their colorful dress and sparkling jewels to rival the painted ceiling above their coiffed heads and the mosaic floor below their silk shoes.

At one point, when his father had still been alive, he could remember being quite awestruck by the great hall and the finery of the aristocracy. Now? Even though the facility's confines were as vast as a hunting field, and its dual hearths the size of civilian dwellings, he had no such illusions of grandeur and honor.

A third member of the Brotherhood spoke in a booming voice. "Their Royal Highnesses, Wrath, son of Wrath, ruler of all that is within and without the race's territories, and Queen Anha, beloved blooded daughter of Tristh, son of Tristh."

In a rush, the obligatory applause rose up and rebounded upon itself, each individual's clapping lost within the crowd's. And then it was time for a royal response. According to tradition, the King was never to lower his head to any living soul, so it was the queen's duty to thank the assembled with a curtsy.

His Anha performed such with unrivaled grace and aplomb.

Then it was the gathereds' turn to acknowledge their fealty with bows for the males and curtsies for the females.

And now, with the group formalities exchanged, he had to go over to the line of his courtiers and greet them one by one.

Striding forth, he could not recall what festival this was, what turn of the calendar's page or phase of the moon or change of season it marked. The glymera *could think of countless reasons to congregate, most of which seemed rather pointless, considering the same individuals showed up in the same venues.*

The clothes were e'er different, of course. And the jewels upon the females.

And meanwhile, whilst gourmet dinners were prepared and picked at, and slights and offenses were exchanged with every breath, there were issues of substance to be dealt with: suffering of the commoners because of the recent drought; encroachment on the part of humans; aggression from the Lessening Society. But the aristocracy worried not about such things—because in their view, those were problems largely confronted by the "nameless, faceless curs."

Contrary to the very basic laws of survival, the glymera *saw little value in the population that harvested the food they consumed and built the structures they lived in and stitched the clothing that covered their backs—*

"Come, my love," his Anha whispered. "Let us greet them."

Lo, it appeared he had halted without knowing.

Resuming his footfalls, his eyes focused upon Ench, who was as always at the front of the line of gray-robed males.

"Greetings, Your Highness," said the gentlemale—in a tone as if he alone were master of ceremonies. "And you, my queen."

"Enoch." Wrath looked down the courtiers. The twelve males were arranged by virtue of hierarchy, and as such, the last in line was barely out of his transition, from a family of great blood but lowly means. "How fare thee."

Not that he cared. He was far more interested in who amongst them had upset his beloved. Surely it must be one, if not all: She had no handmaidens, at her own request, so these were the only figures she had any contact with at court.

What had been said. Who had said it.

It was with no small amount of aggression that he proceeded down the line and greeted each one according to protocol. Indeed, this ancient sequence of private address in the midst of a public gathering was a way of acknowledging and reaffirming the advisers' position within the court, a declaration of their importance.

He could remember his father doing precisely thus. Except the male had seemed to actually value the relationships with his courtiers.

Especially on this night, the son was not where the father had been.

Who had—

At first he assumed his beloved had tripped and required more of his arm's strength. Alas, however, it was not her footing she lost. It was her balance. . . .

And all of it.

The dragging sensation on his forearm turned his head, and that was how he saw it happen, the vital form of his shellan *going loose and toppling downward.*

With a shout, he reached out to catch her, but he was not fast enough.

As the crowd gasped, Anha fell upon the floor, her sightless eyes staring up at him, but seeing nothing, her expression as blank as a mirror with no one before it, her skin even paler than it had been up in their chamber.

"Anha!" he screamed as he crumpled to the floor with her. "Anha . . . !"

EIGHTEEN

Sola woke up with a start, her face whipping off a cold, concrete floor, her body stretched out unnaturally. Flipping herself off her belly, her brain processed the status of her location in a split second: Cell with three solid walls and one with bars. No heat, no window, recessed light high above, stainless-steel toilet.

No cellmate, no warden that she could see.

Next check-in was her body: Her head had splitting pains at the nape and in the front, but that wasn't as bad as what was going on with her thigh. That bastard with the dark birthmark covering half his face had shot her about six inches above her knee—the fact that she could lift her calf off the floor suggested he hadn't gotten bone, but talk about a case of the ouches. The burning sensation coupled with the throbs was enough to make her nauseous.

Silence.

Across the basement, over on a wall, a pair of chains had been bolted into the concrete, and the wrist latches that hung off their ends were a promise of horror.

Well, that and the stains between and below the setup.

No security cameras that she could see. Then again, Benloise was cagey. Maybe he'd use a camera phone to replay his version of home movies?

With no idea how much time she had, she got to her feet—

"Fuck."

Putting weight on her right leg was like taking a hot poker and shoving it into her wound. Then pulling a Chubby Checker twist.

Let's try to avoid that, shall we.

As she eyed the toilet, which was a good five feet away, she cursed again. This leg of hers was going to be a major tactical disadvantage—because it was hard to walk without doing a zombie foot drag—which made noise as well as slowed her down.

Trying to whisper her way over, as opposed to creating a major audible disturbance, she used the loo but didn't flush. Then she backtracked to where she'd been. She didn't feel the need to test out the bars or see whether the door was locked.

Benloise wasn't into shoddy construction and wouldn't employ someone that stupid.

Her only shot was to try to overpower that guard with the gun, and how that was going to happen in her current condition, she hadn't a clue. Unless . . .

Resettling down on the ground, she sprawled herself out in exactly the same position she'd woken up in. Closing her eyes, she was momentarily distracted by the beat of her own heart.

Loud. Really damn loud.

Especially as she thought of her grandmother.

Oh, God, she couldn't end here. And not like this—this wasn't an illness or an accident on a highway. This was going to involve suffering deliberately inflicted, and afterward? Benloise was exactly the kind of sick fuck who'd send a piece of her back to be buried.

Even if the recipient was an innocent party to all this ugliness.

As she pictured her grandmother having only a hand or foot to place in a casket, she found her lips moving.

God, please let me get out of this alive. For vovó's sake. Just let me survive this, and I promise you I will get out of the life. I will take her and go somewhere safe, and I will never, ever do a wrongful thing again.

Distantly, she heard a clank like a door was being unlocked, and then muttering.

Forcing her breath to be even, she watched through the veil of her hair, listening to footsteps get closer.

The man who came down the staircase was the one with that huge birthmark on his face. Dressed in black combat pants and a muscle shirt, he was grim, hairy, and mad.

". . . goddamn idiot, dying on me. Least that shut him the fuck up—"

She closed her eyes . . . and there was another clank.

Abruptly, his voice was much closer. "Wake up, bitch."

Rough hands grabbed her arm and flopped her over onto her back, and it took all her self-control not to gasp in agony from her head and her leg. "Bitch! Wake up!"

He slapped her across the face, and as she tasted blood, she figured he'd split her lip—but whatever pain flared up was a drop in the bucket to that thigh of hers.

"Bitch!" Another slap, even harder. "Don't you fucking play with me!"

Her chest jerked up as he grabbed the front of her parka and ripped it open—and as her head scraped across the concrete, she couldn't keep in the groan.

"That's right—I'll wake you the fuck up." He yanked up her shirt, and there was a little pause. "Nice."

Her bra had a front fastener and he snapped that free, icy air hitting her skin.

"Oh . . . that's . . . yeah . . ."

She gritted her teeth as he felt her up, and had to force her limbs to stay limp as he went for the waistband of her pants. Just like with the flare she'd found in the trunk, she had one shot at this, and she needed him well and properly distracted.

Even though she felt like she was going to vomit again.

The guard stripped her jeans along with her panties off in a series of harsh tugs, her bare ass slapping against the cold, scratchy floor as he yanked and pulled.

"You owe me this, bitch—now I gotta tell him about that little shit you killed—what the fuck with your boots!"

He frantically pulled the laces free and yanked the things off, one after the other. And while he worked on her, there was the temptation to try to kick him in the face, but she wouldn't have enough power at this angle to really do damage—and if she fought back too soon and lost, he was no doubt going to chain her to that fucking wall.

As his hand went between her legs, she couldn't fight her body's panic at the invasion—no matter what her brain commanded, her thighs pressed shut around his wrist.

"You awake now?" he gritted. "You want this, don'tcha."

Relax, she told herself. You're waiting for one thing and one thing only.

His hand retreated. And then the sound of a zipper being yanked down gave her the extra incentive to let her legs fall open. She needed him to try to mount her.

And what do you know, he gave it a shot.

Shoving her thighs even wider apart, he got down on his hands and knees and began to crab-walk into position.

One shot. And she took it.

With a sudden burst of energy, she jacked up and nailed a grip on the motherfucker's nuts like she intended to castrate him. And gee whiz, that was exactly what was on her dance card.

Wrenching as hard as she could, she ignored the screams of pain in her thigh and her head and twisted with every ounce of strength she had. The guard let out a high-pitched holler, like a lapdog that had fallen into a deep fryer, and listed to the side.

That was all she needed. Throwing him off of her, she jumped to her feet as he cupped his cock and balls and curled into a ball.

Looking around quickly, she needed . . .

Limping across in her socks, she unlatched one of the chains that had been intended for her and dragged it back across the floor. Coiling it up around her fist, the heavy links formed a cage around her tight hand.

She went across and straddled the man's head and shoulders. "You want a good fucking, asshole? How 'bout this."

Lifting her arm high above her head, she brought the weight down with as much force as she could, striking at his cranium. The man immediately let out a roar and tried to cover himself up top, his arms forming a barrier around his skull.

Fine. Lobotomy later.

She went for below his ribs, for the soft field of flesh that protected his kidneys and his spleen. Over and over again, until he attempted a new defensive crouch. Back to the head—harder this time, until she broke a sweat even though she was mostly naked and the cellar's air temp had to be in the fifties.

Over.

And over.

Again.

Anywhere she could find a place of vulnerability.

And it was the strangest thing: She had all the strength in the world during the beating; it was as if she were possessed, her injuries fading into the background in deference to the superior need to ensure her own survival.

She had never killed anyone before. Stolen from people? Ever since she was eleven, sure. Lied when she had to? Yup. Broken into all kinds of places she hadn't been welcome in? Nailed it.

But death had always struck her as a level she didn't want to go to. Like heroin to a pot user, it was the granddaddy of them all—and once you'd crossed that line? Well, then you really were a criminal.

In spite of all that, however, some minutes or hours or days later . . . she stood over a bloodied mess of a body.

Sucking breath down into her lungs, she let her arm come to rest by her side. As her strength ebbed, her grip on the chain relented and the links uncoiled themselves from her fist, falling to the floor in a hiss.

"Move," she panted. "You have to move."

Jesus . . . when she had prayed for survival, she hadn't considered that God might give her the power to break one of his Ten Commandments.

"Move, Sola. You must *move*."

Dizzy, nauseous, with a headache that was so bad her vision fizzled in and out, she tried to think.

Boots. She was going to need boots—they were more critical than pants in the snow. Scrambling around, she picked up the first one she came to, only to have it slip right out of her hold.

Blood. There was blood all over her, her right hand especially.

Wiping her palms on her floppy parka, she went back to work. One boot. Then the other. Laces sloppy but double-knotted.

Back to her victim.

She paused for a beat to take in the mess.

Shit, she was going to be seeing this on the backs of her lids for a very, very long time.

Assuming she survived.

Making the sign of the cross over her chest, she got down next to the man and patted around. The gun she found was a godsend; so was the iPhone that was . . . shit, password protected. Plus it wasn't getting a signal, although maybe that would change when she was aboveground.

All she needed was the emergency call feature and then she could toss the thing.

As she leaped out of the cell, she slid the bars shut behind her. She was pretty sure that the bastard was dead, but horror movies and the entire Batman franchise suggested that belt-and-suspenders were a good call when it came to bad guys.

Quick survey. Two more cells just like the one she'd been in. Both empty. That was it.

Outside of the open area, there was a short hall and then that set of stairs, and it took her forever to get over there. Goddamn leg of hers. Pausing before she went up, she listened. No sounds of anyone moving upstairs, but there was a distinct smell of cooked hamburger.

Guess it was her kidnapper's last meal.

Sola stuck to the wall side of the steps, the gun out in front of her, the shuffling of her right boot kept to a minimum even though she had to stop and catch her breath twice.

The first floor had plenty of lights going on and not much else: There were a pair of cots in the corner, a galley kitchen with dirty dishes in its shallow sink—

There was somebody lying on a third cot by a bathroom.

Please let that be the other dead guy, she thought. . . . and shit, what kind of night was this that that was even on her radar?

The rhetorical was answered as she went in for a closer look.

"Oh—" Clamping a hand over her mouth, she turned away.

Had she done that with the flare? Jesus . . . and that smell hadn't been from somebody doing a DIY Big Mac. That was human flesh burned to a crisp.

Focus, she needed to focus.

The only windows in the place were the squat prop-open casement ones that you usually saw in basements and they were mounted high off the floor so there was no seeing out. And there were only three doors: the one she'd used to come up from the basement, the other that was open and flashing a toilet seat, and the last . . . which certainly looked reinforced.

It had a punch bar on the inside.

She didn't bother to look for any more weapons. The forty she had in her hand was sufficient, but she did go across to snag an extra clip from the kitchen counter—

Hello, Powerball winning ticket.

Car keys had been thrown casually with the clip, and if she hadn't been so afraid for her life, she would have taken a moment to cry like a little girl.

Yeah, sure, whatever car she'd been in probably had a GPS tracker like the phone.

But compared to the option of getting out of wherever she was on foot?

She'd take it in a heartbeat.

Limping to the door, with her vision going wonky on her, she hit the bar—

And smacked right into the steel panel.

Nothing budged.

Trying again and again, she found the door locked from the outside. Damn it! And as she checked out the car keys, there was nothing else on the ring. No—

Oh, right, she thought.

Mounted beside the door, there was a small square security sensor.

Of course you'd fingerprint it—on the outside *and* on the inside.

Glancing over her shoulder, she looked at the body across the way—specifically the hand that had flopped off the cot and was hanging halfway to the floor.

"Fuck me."

Going back to the dead guy, she knew dragging him over was not going to be a party. Especially with her leg. But what other choice did she have?

Glancing around, she—

Over in the corner, at a makeshift desk, there was a rolling chair, like you'd find in a proper office. It even had padded arms.

Better than yanking him across the floor, right?

Wrong. Stuffing flare-in-the-face guy into the thing was harder than she'd thought—and not because rigor mortis was an issue, as he'd apparently died not long after she'd melted his puss off. The problem was the chair—it kept slipping out of reach every time she got the deadweight—ha, ha—anywhere near the padded seat.

Not going to work. And P.S., the stench of that flesh was like a football coach urging her stomach to punt.

Breaking off with the corpse, who was now half off the cot, she scrambled for that bathroom, and the dry heaves were soooo helpful: First of all, there was nothing in there to toss, and second, if she'd thought her concussion was bad before?

Back at the dead guy's side, she went around to his shoulders, grabbed him at the armpits, and dug in with her good leg. His boots banged into the floor one by one as she got him completely off the makeshift bed, and those Timberland heels scraped their way over to the door. Fortunately, the guard had arms long enough to be a center for the Knicks, so she was able stop a good four feet away from her target.

His elbow even bent in the correct direction.

The thumb went right where she needed it, and the light at the base of the reader went from red to blinking orange.

The instant she got out of here, she was going to jump into that damn car and hit the gas—

Red.

The reader went back to red. So his print didn't work.

Dropping his hand, she sagged in her skin and hung her head. As a wave of pass-out threatened, she took some deep breaths.

The other guard was now locked in the cell all the way in the basement—and she'd barely been able to get this one across the damn floor. How the hell was she going to hump the man she'd killed up here?

Other man she'd killed, that was.

And shit . . . she'd locked him in downstairs. If that cell was print-locked, too? She was liable to starve to death first.

Unless Benloise got here soon.

Leaning up against the wall, and bracing her hands on her good knee, she tried to think, think, think. . . .

Looked like God had taken her prayers literally: She'd gotten out of the trunk after her first "Help me, Father." The second "Dear Lord, please let me get free" had only sprung her from the jail, but not the house.

As she offered up a third prayer, she got real specific.

Oh, Lord, I promise to get out of the life if you let me see my grandmother's face once again. Wait, wait, that could happen if she were on the verge of death and somehow vovó came here or to a hospital. *Dear God, if I can just look into her eyes and know that I am home safe with her . . . I swear I will take her somewhere far away and never again put myself in harm's way.*

"Amen," she said as she struggled to straighten.

Reaching deep, she found the strength to weave her way back to the stairwell and—

Sola stopped. Pivoted back to face the counter where she'd found the car keys and the clip. Locked eyes on a solution that was at once utterly repugnant, and evidence, arguably, that God was listening.

It appeared as if things were looking up.

In a sick way.

NINETEEN

"There it is," Assail said, pointing through the windshield. "The turnoff."

He had waited a lifetime for the nearly hidden, evergreen-choked lane that finally saw fit to make an appearance about fifty feet ahead.

As Ehric's phone had prescribed, they had followed the Northway all the way through the Adirondack Park, past a place called Lake Placid as well as some mountain that, considering what they had in the back, was rather fitting.

Gore Mountain.

And hadn't he seen something about a ski resort called Killington? His kind of recreation, indeed.

It had been such a long trip. Hours and hours, each mile under the tires of the Range Rover like an endless succession of hurdles to be surmounted.

"Thank fuck," Ehric muttered as he wrenched the wheel and they bumped onto a miserable stretch of earth.

The ascent that followed was best suited to goats, and fortunately the Rover's superior traction turned whatever version of Goodyear they were riding upon into quite passable hooves. It was, however, another endless delay, to the point where Assail became convinced that they had chosen the wrong way: although Benloise himself was with them, one wouldn't have put it past the man to have some sort of edict in place whereby if he didn't contact the captors within certain parameters, whoever was in custody would be eliminated.

Assail propped his elbow on the door and leaned his face into his open palm. The fact that his Marisol was a female made him ill. Males could be hard enough on members of their own sex—thinking about all the things that could be done to a woman was a nightmare he prayed had not been made manifest.

"Faster," he gritted.

"And run the risk of losing a shock absorber? We must needs get down off this pile of rock."

Just when Assail was ready to roar, the end of the trip presented itself abruptly and without fanfare: A single-story concrete structure with all the charm of a kennel came into view, and before they even closed in, he popped his latch and began to jump out—

At that very moment, the door to the place swung wide.

And for the rest of his life, he would never forget what came out of there.

Marisol was naked from the waist down, a parka that he recognized flagging wildly behind her as she lurched into the night. Spotlit and blinded by the headlights, she glowed red, blood streaking down her legs and up her ghostly torso, her face grim as death as she pointed a gun straight in front of her.

"Marisol!" he screamed. "Don't shoot! It is Assail!"

He put his hands up in the air, but it wasn't as though she could see him. "It is Assail!"

She stumbled to a stop, but like a good girl she kept that gun up as she blinked myopically. "Assail . . . ?"

Her voice cracked with a despair that changed him forever: As with the vision of her, he would hear that tone frame the two syllables of his name for years yet to come.

In his nightmares.

"Marisol, darling Marisol . . . I have come for you."

He wanted to tell Ehric to kill those lights, but he didn't know who else had been in there with her and whether anyone would be chasing after her.

"Marisol, come unto me."

The way her hand shook as she brought it to her head made him want to go to her. But she seemed unsure of what was reality and what might have been a phantom of her imagination. And with that gun, she was as dangerous as she was vulnerable.

"Marisol, I promised your grandmother that I would save you. Come unto me, darling one. Come unto my voice."

He held his arms out into the darkness.

"Assail . . ." As she took a step forward, he realized she was limping. Badly. But then, of course some of that blood had to be hers.

"She is going to need medical care," he said aloud. Damn it, how could he get her treated?

If she died on the way back . . .

How much of that blood was hers?

As she took another step and one more, and still nobody emerged in her wake, he had some hope that not all of what covered her was her own.

"Come unto me." As he heard his own voice break, he could feel Ehric shooting him a shocked look from the SUV. "My darling . . ."

Marisol moved that shaking hand over to shield her eyes, and for some reason, that brought the fact that she was naked into full focus.

His throat stung so badly he could not swallow.

Fuck this.

Assail shoved his gun into his belt and rushed forward to meet her more than halfway.

"Assail . . . is it really you?" she whispered as he came close.

"Yes. Please don't shoot—come unto me, darling one."

As she let out a sob, he grabbed her and hauled her up against his chest, the muzzle of that gun of hers going right into his sternum. If she pulled that trigger, she would kill him outright.

She did not.

With a sob, she gave herself over to his strength, and he held her up from the ground as she crumpled. She weighed nearly nothing against him, and for some reason, that terrified him even more.

Accordingly, he allowed only a moment of communion—and then he needed to get her safe.

Swinging her up into his arms, he turned and ran for the bulletproof Rover, ran into those headlights as if they were a heavenly safety zone.

Ehric and his brother anticipated what he wanted to perfection.

They jumped out of the Rover and left open the backseat doors—whilst they removed Benloise from the rear and kept that man away from sight.

Marisol did not need to know of his presence.

Placing his female in the back, Assail broke out the sleeping bag he had packed, along with the water and PowerBars he had brought for her. Covering her nakedness, he held on to her as she fell into a fit of trembling.

"Marisol," he said as he pulled back. "Eat. Drink. Ehric, my cousin, shall take you—"

Her nails bit into his forearm even through the heavy sweater he wore. "Don't leave me!"

He touched her beautiful face. "I must needs work herein for a moment. Things must be attended to. I shall meet you on the road." He wrenched around. "Ehric! Evale!"

The two males came over—and for a moment, he considered driving her away himself.

But no, vengeance needed to be served, and he was the one to balance the scales.

"My darling, look unto my relations." As he eased back so they could lean in and show their faces, he was thankful they had his exact coloring, and that their features were so like his own. Indeed, the three of them had been mistaken for brothers. "They shall carry you unto safety and put their lives before your own. I shall join up with you anon. I shall not be long, I swear to you."

Her frantic, harried eyes bounced back and forth as if she were trying desperately to hold herself together.

"Go," Assail hissed, glancing at the facility. "Go now!"

And yet he found it impossible to turn away from his Marisol. She had been abused and her state of undress suggested that—

Ehric gripped his upper arm. "Be of ease, my cousin. She shall be treated as our precious sister."

Even Evale spoke up for once. "She will be well in hand, cousin."

Assail had a moment of connection with the males, words of gratitude clogging his throat. In the end, all he could do was bow unto them.

Then he had to lean back into the SUV. "I shall not be long."

On an instinct, without being conscious of deciding to do so . . . he kissed Marisol on the mouth.

Mine, he thought.

Forcing himself to refocus, he grabbed his backpack, shut the SUV's door, and stepped away. Ehric, bless him, was careful to turn the vehicle around so that Benloise was not illuminated in the headlights—and then the Rover sped down the uneven path.

Oh, how he wished that lane had been paved. He wished it were a fucking highway with a seventy-mile-an-hour speed limit. Or better yet, that they had come via helicopter.

After the headlights had disappeared, he took out a headset and put it on, clicking on its miner's light. Then he went over to Benloise, grabbed him by the duct-tape straps about his ankles, and pulled him across the snowy ground to the open entry.

Dropping the legs, he palmed his gun and pointed it at the man.

"Just to make sure you stay put," Assail ground out.

Pop!

Benloise jerked in tighter, trying to protect his gut—too late. The bullet was already in there and leisurely doing its job: While painful and debilitating, intestinal wounds took their own sweet time accomplishing their goal.

Although Assail didn't plan on keeping the bastard waiting long for his death.

Striding into the dwelling, he kept his weapon up and his eyes sharp.

What he found inside gave him pause.

Directly by the open door, a severed human hand lay discarded, as if its purpose had been served and it was no longer of value. The body it had been attached to was right there as well—no, that corpse had two hands . . . although no face to speak of.

So there was at least one other dead inside.

His Marisol had clearly fought for her freedom like a banshee.

Walking around the open floor space, he saw nothing of value or interest—or anything that could detain an individual. But over in the far corner, there were a set of stairs descending to a lower level.

He double-checked on his captive. Benloise remained writhing in the snow just outside the main door, his dark eyes open and blinking unevenly, his upper lip peeled back, his porcelain caps glowing in the ambient light.

Best to take him with.

Assail went over and yanked the man up to his feet. When Benloise failed to stand on his own, it was the work of a moment to drag his hundred-and-forty-pound weight into the interior. Then together, they promenaded over to the staircase.

Down into the underground, Benloise's useless feet bouncing behind them like balls.

And there was the evil.

The lower floor was made up of a large open space with three cells and a wall of horror. One of the cells was not empty. There was a man with a brutalized face and neck lying on his back, staring at what you could only hope was Hell. His right arm had been pulled through the iron bars, and the bloody stump announced that his was the hand that had been taken.

For a moment, Assail felt his heart sting with desolate pride. Marisol had gotten herself out. No matter what they had done to her, or how few her resources had been, she had triumphed over her captors, bringing them not just to heel, but to their graves. . . .

It was at that moment that he knew he was lost to her.

He was in love with this woman—and indeed, it was sick to feel those depths in the midst of this carnage and violence, but the heart was where it was.

And as Assail pictured his Marisol chained to that stained stretch of concrete wall, he became rageful to the point of insanity, a stampede of bulls racing through his body, their thousand hooves driving him into madness.

Wheeling around on Benloise, he bared his fangs and hissed like the vampire he was—

In spite of being shot, the drug wholesaler recoiled. *"Madre de Dios!"*

Assail scrummed down, getting in the man's face. "That is right! I am nightmare come upon you!"

There was only one chain hanging from the wall. The other was coiled on the floor inside the locked cell, the blood that painted the links proving it had been the murder weapon Marisol had used.

It would be put into service yet again.

Assail dematerialized through the bars and picked up the sticky, copper-scented links.

Oh, Marisol, would that you had not had to be so brave.

As Assail dematerialized back out, Benloise was no longer the in-control businessman who was used to holding all the cards. Unlike the dead bodies and the blood or even the loss of his brother and the threat to his own life—all of which he had been able to mostly retain his composure around—learning Assail's true identity sent him over the edge.

Whimpering, crying, praying, the man lost control of his bladder, urine pooling out of his shrunken cock onto the concrete floor.

Assail stalked over to the wall and reattached the chain. Fortunately, there was nothing fresh upon the stained surface. There was going to be, however.

Manhandling Benloise's shrieking, flopping, pissed-on body off the floor, Assail bit through the duct tape tethers at the man's wrists, and cuffed him to the wall Christ-style by shortening the lengths until his hollow torso was pulled flat.

Assail shucked his backpack and unzipped it. As he looked at the amount of explosive he had brought with him, he knew it was more than enough to blow the facility sky-high. He glanced at Benloise. The man was crying all over himself, shaking his head as if he were hoping to wake up.

"Indeed, you are truly conscious," Assail gritted. "That shall not last, however."

Pivoting to face the cell, he pictured his Marisol in there, terrified . . . and worse.

His heart thumped in his chest. If he blew this place up . . . Benloise would be home free, dead and gone—mayhap to Hell, but as one could not be sure of the afterlife until one got there, it seemed far more prudent to err on the side of real-time suffering.

He had intended to kill the wholesaler first. Then set the explosives and detonate them from a distance.

But that was not as equitable as it should be. Marisol had suffered—

A growl vibrated up through his chest . . . as though his very body were protesting at the prospect of being cheated of the death.

"No," he told himself. "Better this way."

Too bad only part of him believed it.

Assail rezipped his backpack and strapped the thing on again. Going to first one and then the other of the chains, he inspected them for security. Indeed, they were well and truly placed. The same was true for the cuffs upon those wrists.

Snapping out a hold, he took Benloise's chin and forced the man's head back.

With another hiss, he bit into the flesh by the carotid, ripping a hunk out and spitting it onto the floor. The blood tasted good in his mouth and his canines tingled in anticipation of more. Except they would be denied.

The bite was but a symbol of what as a male he was driven by instinct and custom to do in the protection of his female. And he would have torn the neck fully open if Benloise himself had not been into torture.

As his prey spoke in a rush in that foreign tongue, Assail fought the battle to leave the man alive. Cruelty was going to require self-control in this circumstance—and ordinarily that was not a problem.

Nothing involving Marisol had been ordinary, however.

Assail slapped the man into silence. Jabbing his forefinger into that face, he growled, "She was not yours to take. Do you hear me? Not yours. *Mine*."

Before he lost his hold upon his temper, he stalked off to the stairs, leaving the lights on so that Benloise was fully aware of where he was: a prison of his own making with naught but the remains of one of his bodyguards to keep him company.

Mounting the steps two at a time, Assail knew there was a possibility someone could come and free the wholesaler, but it was remote. Benloise was notoriously secretive, and with Eduardo dead, the only people who would miss him were guards and staff—and given the cagey manner in which the man operated, there would be a lag before the troops marshaled up conversation and discovered that each individual was not so much out of the loop as that there had been no contact from their superior to anyone on the team.

After that? It was an open question whether any of them would actually look for their boss. People who operated in the underground world scattered when it came to complications like this—no one was going to risk getting killed or handcuffed by the human authorities just to save somebody else's skin.

Benloise was going to slowly die, alone.

And when someone found the bodies inside the facility? This year . . . next . . . a decade from now?

The cover Benloise had constructed was going to be blown.

Upstairs, Assail performed a sweep of the open room. He found two more phones, which he turned off, removed the batteries, and slipped into his pack. He left the guns and ammo, and was careful to shut the door and test that it self-locked.

It did.

Walking around the squat little building, he found a petroleum tank in the back. Locating the gauge, he noted that it was only a quarter full. Given how cold it was at this elevation, he guessed that the supply would run out within a day or two.

The bodies would be stored in a rather cool environment. Good to keep down the smell, not that there was going to be much of that getting out, given the small windows upstairs, all of which were closed.

He was about to take off when he noticed a car parked off to the side.

Heading over, he lifted its camouflage cover and tested one of the doors. Locked.

If he blew it up, the fireball would attract attention, and that was not desirable. He let the tarp fall back into place.

Closing his eyes in preparation to dematerialize, he saw his Marisol coming out of that door. And it was as he shuddered that he became one with the night air, casting his molecules to the south, to a rest area approximately twenty miles down the Northway.

Re-forming, he got out his cell and dialed Ehric.

One ring. Two. Three.

"She is just fine," his cousin said by way of greeting. "She has eaten and had some water. And she is anxious to see you."

Assail sagged in his own skin. "Well done. I am where we agreed."

"Did you accomplish all and sundry?"

"Indeed. Is there anyone upon you?"

"Neither in front nor behind, and we are but two miles from you."

"I shall wait here."

Hanging up, he stared at his cellular device. His first instinct was to get her to his home, but she was going to require medical attention—and she would want to be cleaned up and clothed before her grandmother saw her.

Assail's next call was to his own home, and when the heavily accented female voice answered, he found himself blinking away tears.

"Madam," he said roughly. "She—"

"Not dead," the old woman moaned. "*Meu Deus*, tell me she—"

"She is alive. I have her."

"What? You say again, please."

"Alive." Although he wasn't sure about any kind of "well" part. "She is alive and within my care."

Frantic speech now, in the mother tongue. And though Assail knew none of the words, the meaning was not only clear, but something he agreed with.

Thank you, Scribe Virgin, he thought, even though he was not religious.

"We are far from Caldwell," he told her. "We may not make it before dawn, in which case we shall be home after sunfall."

"Speak to her? May I?"

"Of course, madam." Up ahead, a pair of headlights mounted a rise on the highway and came down toward him, paring off on the exit ramp. "I need but a moment, and I shall put her on."

The Range Rover piloted directly over to him, taillights flaring as Ehric slowed.

"Here she is, madam," he said as he opened the rear door.

Marisol was wrapped in that sleeping bag, and her color was better—at least until she looked at him and what little blush she retained in her cheeks immediately disappeared.

As Assail felt confusion, Ehric twisted around, glanced at him—and recoiled. With a quick circle, he indicated his own face.

Oh, shit. Assail must have blood all over his mouth.

"Your grandmother," he blurted, shoving the phone at Marisol.

Sure enough, that did the trick to redirect his female's attention—and as she reached out like he was offering her a lifeline, he reshut the door.

Wheeling around, he headed to the public facility behind him at a dead run, located the men's room portion and entered the lineup of urinals and toilet stalls.

Over at one of the sinks, he looked into the flat panel of stainless steel that served as a mirror.

"Fuck."

Not what any female wanted to see, especially after she had been subjected to a capture: His face was indeed covered with blood, his jaw and lips marked with the stain—and his fangs . . . the tips of his fangs showed.

Hopefully the gore of his visage had been what she'd reacted to.

Bending down, he attempted to turn on the water and cup his hands, but the faucets were the kind one had to hold in place to make operational. The process took him too long, filling a single palm and bringing it to his face over and over again. And then there was nothing to dry himself off with.

Sloughing his hand down his features, he assessed his hair, which thanks to Paul Mitchell had retained some semblance of attractiveness—

Was he honestly trying to better his looks in this situation? How ridiculous.

As he strode back to the Range Rover, he knew he was going to have to make a third phone call when his Marisol was done with her grandmother: his female was going to need medical treatment.

Where to go, though? In the Old Country, there had been no physicians of the race available for him and his cousins. Fortunately, however, he and his relations had been able to rely on a human or two who would come after hours and ask no questions.

He did not have such arrangements in the New World.

Accordingly, there was only one person he could contact—and hopefully there would be a solution that was up to his standards.

Marisol deserved the best. And he would settle for nothing less.

TWENTY

Sitting in the back of the Mercedes, John Matthew watched through the windshield as his sister hesitated on the threshold of their father's house. The mansion's double-size door was wide-open, and he'd gone inside and turned on the front hall light for her.

Her silhouette cut through the glow that spilled out into the night, the black shape like a shadow thrown.

Jesus . . . if she had a child, it was going to be the future King or queen. And didn't that add another facet to the should-we-or-shouldn't-we stuff.

"May we depart, sire?" Fritz asked from the front.

John whistled an ascending note, then rubbed his face and eased back into the seat. He was fucking exhausted. The contrast they'd put into his arm had made him feel weird, and then there was the crackling anxiety he'd had inside the MRI while the machine had ping-ponged around him. Open MRI, his ass. Yeah, sure, it was better than being pumped into that jumbo tube and sealed in tight like he was toothpaste, but it was hardly an easy-breather situation.

Oh, plus, you had hanging over your head the happy ax of maybe you *hadda two-mah*. To quote Arnold.

At least he didn't have to worry about that, apparently. And screw the anti-seizure drugs. He was going to be fine. He was tight. Yup. Totally . . .

Shit. What if he had an episode while he was out fighting?

Whatever. He couldn't worry about that—

With a *bing!*, his phone announced a text had come through. Palming the thing, he frowned at what Tohr had sent out to everyone: *Xtra presence needed at clinic. ETA of visitors, 55 mins. Check in w status, STAT.*

John tapped out a quick reply: *On way back. Am avail . . .*

He wasn't sure how to finish things. As soon as they got home, he was going to ask Fritz to pack up the stuff Beth had asked for . . . and then find Wrath. Talk about your aw-shits. Telling the King that his mate wasn't coming home for the day was going to be about as much fun as one of his seizures, but someone had to let the guy in on her plans—and evidently it wasn't going to be Beth.

She'd told him flat out that she wasn't in a big hurry to talk to her husband.

Or be around him, evidently.

After leaving the medical center, she'd asked Fritz to drive them around for a while before she'd settled, at John's suggestion, on an all-night Chinese restaurant on Trade—that just happened to be, oh, hey, right down the street from the Iron Mask: It wasn't like John couldn't take care of his sister—but it was good to know there was plenty of backup available a little over a block away thanks to his mate and her twelve-ton bouncer squad.

While they'd eaten, Beth been mostly quiet, although she'd had a hearty enough appetite—she'd finished her beef with broccoli and then polished off his KPC along with a half dozen fortune cookies. When they were done, she hadn't wanted to get back in the car yet so they'd strolled up Trade Street for a while until there was no more time left.

Obviously, she'd been torn about staying in town or going back home.

Man, he felt for her. What a mess.

And it was funny, as much as he hated getting in the middle of things, there was nothing he wouldn't do for her. Nothing.

God, what had he been mouthing during that seizure . . . ?

About twenty minutes later, Fritz brought them safely to the Brotherhood's secret compound. Circling the fountain in the center of

the courtyard, he pulled into a space between Rhage's purple GTO and V's brand-new black-on-black R8.

The Brother still had the Escalade, of course. Just the newest version of it.

Getting out, John walked with the butler to the grand entrance. Unlike his father's other place in town, this mansion was more fortress than home, its great stone walls rising up from the earth, as indestructible as the mountain they were built on.

If the eastern seaboard was carpet bombed for some reason? This place, Twinkies, and cockroaches. That was all that was going to be left.

John tapped the butler on the arm just as Fritz reached for the massive door's bronze handle. *You'll get her things?*

"But of course." The *doggen* looked worried. "Just as she asked."

The implications of the queen crashing somewhere other than in her own bedroom with her mate had not been lost on Fritz—but he was far too discreet to ask questions or make a fuss. Instead, he just radiated anxiety—to the point where if you'd had marshmallows and a stick, you probably could have made s'mores from the *doggen's* aura.

Entering the vestibule, John put his face into the security camera and waited for a response. Ever since the First Family had moved in, there were no keys to the house, no way of gaining access unless you were let in by someone already in the interior.

And a moment later, the lock was sprung, and they were allowed to step through into the majestic front foyer. So much gold leaf, so many crystals, and those colored marble columns? It was a czar's palace relocated to the mountains outside of Caldwell.

How had his father pulled it off? John wondered. In, like, 1914?

No clue. And even more impressive? For nearly a century, Darius had somehow been able to keep humans from prying into the private property, the *lessers* locked out of it . . . and the *symphaths* clueless as to its coordinates: This location, and its underground training center, had not been compromised in all its history. Even during the raids.

Quite an accomplishment. Quite a legacy.

God, he wish he'd known his father. Wished the Brother was still around—because he could sure as hell have used some advice on how to tell Wrath what was going on.

Pausing in the middle of the depiction of an apple tree in full bloom, John let Fritz go right ahead, the butler mounting the Buckingham Palace–worthy staircase at a spry jog.

Wrath was undoubtedly upstairs in his study—but first, he needed to get a translator.

Fuck.

Who the hell could he ask to—

"Where is she?"

John closed his eyes at the demand . . . and it was a minute before he could turn to the billiards room: Sure enough, standing right under the arch, the King was dressed in black leather, his hands locked on his hips, his jaw jutting forward.

Even though he was blind, and his eyes were hidden behind those wraparounds, John felt like the male was staring right. Fucking. At. Him.

All at once, the ambient noise John had been unaware of hearing went dead quiet: The Brothers who were playing pool behind Wrath suspended all movement, all talk, until only tracks from Eminem's *The Marshall Mathers LP 2* were left thumping in the background.

"John. Where is my mate."

In the face of that glare, John walked forward. Yup, nearly all of the Brothers were in there with Wrath—no doubt they'd tweaked to his mood and had circled the wagons.

Sifting through the big bodies, he locked eyes with V and signed, *I need you.*

Vishous nodded and handed his cue off to Butch. Crushing his cigarette out in a crystal ashtray, he came over.

Wrath bared his fangs. "John, as God is my fucking witness, I will cut you if you don't—"

"Easy, there, big guy," V gritted out. "I'm going to translate. You want to hit the library where we can—"

"No, I want to fucking know where my *shellan* is!" Wrath boomed.

John started signing, and whereas most of the time people translated half sentences sequentially, V waited until he'd finished the whole report.

A couple of the Brothers muttered in the background as they shook their heads.

"In the library," V ordered the King in a way John never could have. "You're gonna wanna do this in the library."

Wrong thing to say.

Wrath wheeled on the Brother and went for him with such speed and accuracy no one was prepared: One minute V was standing next to the King; the next he was defending himself against an attack that was as unprovoked as it was . . . well, vicious.

And then things went shit-wild.

Like Wrath knew he was on the thin edge of a bad ledge, he broke off from V, and went total wrecking ball on the billiards room. The first thing he ran into was the pool table Butch was chilling next to—and there was barely any time for the cop to get that ashtray up off the side rails: Wrath grabbed the gunnels and flipped the thing like it was nothing but a card table, the mahogany and slate-topped behemoth flying up so high, it wiped out the hanging light fixture above, its weight so great it splintered the marble floor beneath on landing.

Without missing a breath, the King EF5'd into his next victim . . . the heavy leather sofa that Rhage had just leaped up off.

Talk about your couch-icopters.

The entire thing came at John at about five feet off the floor, the pair of ends trading places as it spun around and around, cushions flying in all directions. He didn't take it personally—especially as its mate do-si-doed with the bar, smashing the top-shelf bottles, liquor splashing all over the walls, the floor, the fire that was crackling in the hearth.

Wrath wasn't finished.

The King picked up a side table, hauled it overhead, and pitched it in the direction of the TV. It missed the plasma screen, but managed to shatter an old-fashioned mirror—although the Sony didn't last. The coffee table that had been in between the two sofas did that deed, killing the muted image of the two Boston guys and the old man from Southie with the baseball bat shilling for DirectTV.

The Brothers just let Wrath go. It wasn't that they were afraid of getting hurt. Hell, Rhage stepped in and caught the first couch before it tore a hunk off of the archway's molding. They just weren't stupid.

Wrath - Beth x Overnight = Psycho-hose Beast

Better to let him wear himself out trashing the place. But, man, it was painful to watch—

John jumped to the side as an entire keg came flying at his head. Fortunately, Vishous was able to grab it before the thing hit the mosaic floor out in the foyer—which would have been a bitch to fix.

"We gotta keep him contained," someone muttered.

"Amen," somebody else replied. "He gets free in the house, and it'll be shit even Fritz won't know how to clean up."

"I'll take care of it."

Everyone turned and stared at Lassiter. The fallen angel with the bad attitude and even worse taste in just about everything had appeared from out of nowhere—and was looking serious, for once.

"What the fuck is that?" V demanded as the angel put a thin gold pen up to his own mouth.

Turned out it wasn't a fancy Bic. With a quick puff, Lassiter discharged a tiny dart across the room—and when it hit Wrath in the shoulder, the impact was as if the King had been struck by a bullet in the chest.

He went down hard, his body stiffening and then falling like an oak.

"What the fuck did you do!" V pulled a Wrath and went for the angel. But Lassiter got right back in the Brother's face.

"He was going to hurt himself, the house, or one of you assholes! And don't get your fucking panties in a wad. He's just going to have a little nap—"

Wrath let out a soft snore.

Moving carefully, the Brotherhood closed in like they were checking out a grizzly and John went with them. As a circle formed around Sleeping Beauty, there was a lot of cursing under breaths.

"If you've killed him—"

Lassiter put his gold whacker away. "Does he look dead."

No, actually, the poor bastard looked like he was at peace with himself and the world, his coloring strong, his body so relaxed his shitkickers were lolling to the sides.

"Dearest . . . Virgin . . . Scribe . . ."

Everybody looked to the archway. Fritz was standing there with a Louis Vuitton duffel in one hand and the expression of someone witnessing a car accident on his face.

John closed his eyes.

He hoped like hell Beth had gone into that house, locked the door like she promised, and laid low during the daytime.

One of the pair of them was down hard. No one needed a second.

TWENTY-ONE

After Fritz and John left, Beth finally stepped into her father's house—and as she entered, time's relentless forward movement reversed itself. In the work of a moment, minutes, hours, days . . . then weeks and months . . . disappeared.

Abruptly, she was who she had been before meeting Wrath—a twenty-something human woman living with her cat in a cramped studio apartment, trying to make a go in the world with nothing and no one behind her. Sure, she had loved parts of her job, but her boss, Dick the Prick, had been a leering, misogynistic nightmare. And yeah, she'd been paid okay, except there hadn't been much left over after her rent—or chance of advancement at the *Caldwell Courier Journal*. Oh, and romance of any kind had been as fictional and far-off on the horizon as the Lone Ranger.

Not that she'd been interested in men, really. Or women, at all.

But then this one time, at band camp . . .

Shutting the door, she was careful to lock herself in. Fritz had a key, so whenever he arrived with her stuff he'd be able to get in—but no one else would.

As the silence in the house surrounded her, it felt like bars on a cage. How in the hell had she ended up here? Spending an entire day without Wrath? As early as the night before, at their place in NYC, a separation like this would have been unthinkable.

Walking into the parlor on the left, she wandered around, remembering how, when she'd initially come here, she'd been convinced Wrath was a drug dealer, a criminal, a killer. At least she'd been wrong about the first two—and he'd proved that last one by nearly murdering Butch O'Neal in front of her in an alley.

Following that little horror, they'd come here—where they'd found Rhage in the downstairs bath, stitching himself up. It was after that that Wrath had taken her though the painting, down the lantern-lit stairwell underground . . . and into a hidden lair.

Where he'd told her who she really was.

What she really was.

Talk about falling through your rabbit holes. Except it had made sense of so much that had confused her—the disconnect to the people around her, her sense that she didn't belong, her restlessness that had been ever-increasing as she approached her transition.

To think she'd assumed that all she needed was to get out of Caldwell.

Nope. Her change had been coming, and without Wrath, she would have died. No doubt.

He had saved her in so many ways. Loved her with his body and soul. Given her a future she hadn't even dreamed of.

Right now? All she wanted to do was go back to their beginning. Things had been so easy then. . . .

Going over to the floor-to-ceiling depiction of a French king, she hit the hidden switch that released the oil painting in its two-ton gold-leaf frame. As the thing swung open, she half expected the way down to be pitch-black—after all, no one had lived here for how long? But as with the way everything was still vacuumed and dusted and polished, the gas lanterns flickered in their wrought-iron cages, the rough stone steps and walls curving down into the cellar.

Jesus, it still smelled the same. A little musty and damp, but not dirty.

Trailing her hand over the uneven stone, she descended into the underground. The two bedroom suites at the bottom gave her a left and a right choice, and she picked the one on the left.

The one that had been her father's old hideaway from the sun.

The pictures of her were still where he had placed them, all kinds of photos in so many different frames covering the writing desk, the side tables by the bed, the mantel over the fireplace.

The particular image she was looking for was by the alarm clock.

It was the only one of her mother, and yup . . . just a quick glance at the woman and she was reminded of where she'd gotten her thick black hair and the shape of her face and the set of her shoulders.

Her *mother.*

What kind of life had the woman lived? How had Darius come to her? From what Wrath had said back in the beginning, the pair of them hadn't been together for very long before she'd found out what Darius really was—and bolted fast. It wasn't until she'd discovered she was pregnant that she'd gone back to see him, scared of what she was bringing into the world.

She had died in childbirth.

And Darius had stayed on the sidelines after that, hoping that their daughter wouldn't take after the vampire side of things.

Some half-breeds never went through the change. Some didn't survive the transition. And those who did make it through and came out the other side as vampires were subject to different, unpredictable biological rules. Beth, for example, could go out in the daylight as long as she wore sunscreen and sunglasses. Butch, on the other hand, couldn't dematerialize.

So God only knew about the pregnancy stuff. But if she was lucky, she would go into her needing and Wrath would somehow come around and she'd give birth to . . .

Well, then again, that was how her mother had died, wasn't it.

"Crap."

Sitting down on the mattress, she put her head in her hands. Maybe Wrath had a point. Maybe the whole conception thing really was too dangerous to mess around with. But that didn't excuse the way he'd treated her, and it didn't end the discussion.

Christ, as she sat down here, surrounded by pictures Darius had had taken of her, she was even more convinced she wanted a child.

Dropping her arms, she took out her BlackBerry, put her password in, and checked to see if any messages had come through that she hadn't heard. Nope. Turning the thing over and over in her hands, she idly wished it was an iPhone. V, however, was not just anti-Apple; he was convinced Steve Jobs's legacy was the root of all evil in the world. . . .

Sometimes couples did better over the phone.

And whereas Wrath hadn't played nice, that didn't mean she had to follow the example. If she intended to have some space for the next twelve hours or so, she really needed to pay him the courtesy of telling him herself—not use her brother as a messenger.

The trouble was Wrath didn't have a cell phone anymore. No need for one—when he'd officially taken over the King duties, he'd been "retired" from the Brotherhood by custom, law, and common f-in' sense. Not that it had kept him from getting shot.

There were plenty of phones at the mansion, however.

Six a.m. He was probably still working at his desk.

Dialing the digits, she listened to one ring. The next. A third.

There was no voice mail for Wrath anymore because the *glymera* had so totally abused the number they'd been given. Which was how he'd ended up with the e-mail account from hell.

The next number she tried was for the handset by their bed, the one that was so unpublished, she'd never actually heard it ring before. No answer.

She had several choices at this point. Training Center's clinic—in case he was injured. But how would that happen? He didn't leave the house anymore. Kitchen—except Last Meal was almost on the table and Wrath probably wasn't going to be in all that chaos without her: Even though he'd never said so, she had the feeling that crowded, noisy rooms made him uncomfortable because his senses of hearing and smell got overloaded, making it difficult for him to place people in space.

There was only one other number to try.

As she got the person out of her contacts, another slice of the past came back to her.

She pictured Tohr coming in through the sliding glass door of her old apartment, the Brother looming large as any nightmare should. But he had been, and always was, an ally. That night that they'd shared Sam Adams and oatmeal cookies and *Godzilla* had been the start of a true friendship.

He was in such a different place now. Losing Wellsie. Finding Autumn.

And Beth wasn't the same, either.

As the call went through, there was only one ring before things were answered: "Beth."

She frowned at the odd tone in Tohr's voice. "You okay?"

"Oh, yeah. Definitely. I'm glad you called."

"Ah . . . why?" Had Wrath told the Brotherhood she wasn't coming home? Probably not. "Never mind. I just . . . I'm looking for Wrath. Do you know where he is? I tried the study and our rooms and he didn't pick up."

"Oh, yeah. Definitely."

WTF? "Tohr. What's going on."

As true fear took root in the center of her chest, her mind got away from her. What if—

"Nothing. Honest—well, we've got an unexpected VIP coming into the clinic, so I'm scrambling to get coverage."

Ah, snap. She was being paranoid. Better than being right, though.

"As for Wrath, last I saw, he was . . ." There was a pause. Then a shuffle like the guy was switching the phone to his other ear. "He was taking a little breather."

"Breather as in?"

"He was asleep."

Beth felt her jaw hinge loosen. "Asleep?"

"Yeah. He was resting."

"Really."

Here she was, putting herself through the wringer, confused about what to think and feel, running their entire relationship backwards and forwards, planning conversations, tying herself in knots. Meanwhile, he was just, you know, pulling a siesta.

"Well, that's great," she heard herself say. "I'm really happy for him."

"Beth—"

"Look, I have to go." Yup, she was busy, busy, busy. "If he wakes up, tell him . . ."

No, not that she'd called. Men weren't the only ones allowed to keep their pride; women didn't have to be the "weaker sex."

"Actually, I'll tell him myself. I'll be at my dad's, cleaning things up today." Yeah, 'cuz the house was such a mess. "But I'll be back at nightfall."

The honest relief coming through the line was striking. "Oh, that's good news. I'm really glad."

"Okay, well . . ." Somehow she couldn't bring herself to hang up.

"Beth? You still there?"

"Yeah. I am." She found herself rubbing her thigh up and down. "Listen, can I ask you something?"

"Sure. Please."

After all, Wellsie and Tohr had had their arguments—some of which Beth had heard firsthand back before the beautiful redhead had been taken way too soon. Man, Wellsie had been unafraid to say exactly what she thought to anyone, including her *hellren*. She was never a hothead without a good reason, of course, but you hadn't necessarily wanted to cross her if you didn't have to.

People had respected her.

What did they think of me, Beth wondered.

"Beth?"

Certainly if there was anyone who could help her with Wrath, and keep it on the DL, it was Tohr. In fact, he was the one who usually got sent in when people needed help with their King.

"Beth, what's going on?"

Opening her mouth, she intended to vent, but there was one problem: The person she needed to talk to was Wrath. Anyone else was just filler.

"Do you still root for the monster?"

There was a pause. And then the Brother laughed in his trademark baritone. "Are you telling me there's another *Godzilla* marathon on?"

Beth was glad she was alone. Because she had a feeling the smile she was sporting was sadder than any tears.

She just wanted to go back to when things had been simpler. Easier. Closer.

"Just thinking about the good ol' days," she blurted.

Instantly, Tohr's tone tightened. "Yeah. They were . . . good."

Oh, shit. Even though he was in love with and mated to Autumn, it had to hurt to remember his first wife . . . and the baby she'd been carrying.

"I'm sorry, I—"

He recovered quicker than she did. "Don't feel bad at all. The past is what it is—good and bad, it's written and unchanging. And there's solace to be had in that."

Tears pricked her eyes. "What do you mean?"

There was a long pause. "The good parts are more luminous because you can trust them. And the bad parts can't get any more tragic for precisely the same reason. The past is safe because it is indelible."

Abruptly, she thought again of that first date she and Wrath had had upstairs. As much as hindsight painted it all with a rosy glow, that hadn't been exactly right, had it.

Come to think of it, he'd been angry when she'd first arrived that night. To the point where halfway through the four courses, she'd considered leaving.

Hardly the all-perfect that nostalgia repainted it as.

"You're right, Tohr."

"Yeah." He cleared his throat. "You know, it's not too late. You can still come back if you leave now."

"I don't have to worry about the sun, remember."

She could practically feel his shudder through her cell phone. "I got nothing to say to that. I really don't."

Taking pity on him, she changed the subject by promising to take care of herself and come home at nightfall.

After hanging up, she stretched out on her father's bed. Staring at the ceiling, she imagined Darius having done the same thing during the day—sometimes with Wrath right across the hall in the other chamber.

Wrath had been a real recluse before meeting her. He'd fought alone, slept alone, and most certainly had nothing to do with the whole throne thing: Until he'd mated her, he'd refused to rule.

She couldn't count the number of times people had thanked her for bringing him around—like her love was some magic potion that had turned a beast into . . . well, if not a completely civilized kind of guy, at least someone who was willing to live up to his responsibilities.

Had he really just gone for a snooze?

Then again, when was the last time he'd actually slept through the day? Not since before he'd been shot at.

Just before her eyes fluttered shut, she sat herself up and turned to the security alarm pad that was mounted by her head. Punching the proper code in, she armed things and then got horizontal again.

The eight-digit set of numbers? Her birth date, month, day, and year.

Another example of how, way before she had come into this vampire world, her father had been thinking of her: V might have been the one to install the state-of-the-art equipment and keep it all up-to-date, but Darius had chosen the code years ago.

Reaching over and clicking the light off, she resettled on top of the duvet.

Moments later, she was back at the lamp, turning it on again.

When you were without your husband, perfectly safe was relative.

TWENTY-TWO

Sola couldn't remember ever being so cold.

Wrapped up in a sleeping bag, with heating vents pile-driving BTUs into her face, she couldn't stop shivering in the back of the Range Rover.

Then again, there were a half dozen good reasons to be in shock, the kind that started with your head and put your body in a numb deep freeze.

Shifting her position, her thigh let out a scream—reminding her that there was also a physical imperative at work. How much blood had she lost?

"We are almost there."

Her head turned at the sound of that accented voice. Even though there was almost no light in the SUV, she could picture Assail's face as if it were spotlit: deeply set eyes the color of moonlight, slashing dark brows, full lips, hard jaw. The widow's peak and the jet-black hair.

Between one blink and the next, there was blood on the lower half of it . . . and very sharp teeth.

Or had that been a nightmare? She was having trouble figuring out what was reality.

She opened her mouth to speak. Nothing came out. "My head . . . not working right."

"It's all okay." As if on impulse, he reached out to her, but then dropped his hand like he didn't know what to do.

Sola struggled to swallow, her mouth dry. "More water? Please?"

He moved so fast, it was like he'd been waiting for a chance to do something. And as he cracked another Poland Spring bottle open, she went to push the sleeping bag away to free her hands—and got trapped. The nylon fabric seemed to weigh as much as a coating of asphalt.

"Be still," he said softly. "Let me serve you."

"My hands aren't working."

"I know." He brought the open neck to her mouth. "Drink."

Easier said than done. Her teeth started to chatter. "Sorry," she mumbled as water went everywhere.

"Ehric, how long," he snapped.

The Range Rover came to an abrupt stop. "I believe we're here—or somewhere."

Sola frowned as she looked over the shoulder of the driver in front of her. The rickety fence in the headlights was the kind of thing you'd see on a cattle farm—that had been deserted. Half of it was hanging at an angle, the old boards and rusted wire more tangle than organized form.

"Where are we going?" she asked hoarsely. "I thought . . . back home."

"We're getting you treated first." Assail repeated that thing where he reached out a hand and then put it back down before touching her. "You need . . . you're wounded and we can't let your grandmother see you like this."

"Oh. Right." Jesus, she'd forgotten she was half-naked, injured, and needed a good, long shower. "Thank you."

"Surely this cannot be it," the driver muttered.

Assail glanced out the windshield, and glared—as if things weren't what he expected, either. "Go up to that box."

As they approached what appeared to be a wooden birdhouse on a rickety stick, the driver put his window down—

A gruff, disembodied voice spoke out of the thing: "I gotchu. Go through the gates."

Like magic, the "distressed" gating system split right down the middle, moving apart smoothly and silently.

The road beyond was snow-packed but tended to. And some distance later they came to another barrier. This one was less flimsy, and taller, too, made of chain links that were rusty, and yet seemed solidly affixed to their posts. This time, they didn't have to stop—the fencing split before them, letting them pass through.

And so it went.

As they progressed, the gating systems became ever newer and more imposing until they came up to something that looked like it belonged in a government installation: Concrete pylons as big as the ones under Caldwell's bridges anchored a solid metal panel the size of a billboard. And stretching off in either direction? A twenty-foot-tall wall that had barbed wire up top and warnings to trespassers every ten feet.

Kinda Jurassic-parky, Sola thought.

"Impressive," the driver drawled.

As with the other entries, the way was opened before they could halt at the obvious check-in point, with its keypad, speaker, and monitoring equipment.

"Is this . . . an army base?" Sola mumbled.

Maybe Assail was an undercover cop—in which case . . . "Do I need a lawyer?" she demanded.

"For what?" Assail stayed focused on whatever was coming up, staring out the front windshield like he was driving the vehicle.

"Are you going to arrest me?"

His head whipped around, his brows down low. "Whatever are you talking about?"

Sola relaxed back into the seat. If he was lying, he deserved an Oscar. And if he wasn't—well, maybe this was God's way of answering her prayer: One sure solution for keeping her out of the life was to throw her into the court system.

The underground tunnel they entered was worthy of a Lincoln or a Holland with its fluorescent lighting and yellow line down the middle, and the descent tilted the Range Rover forward at an aggressive angle.

"Are we in Caldwell?" she asked.

"Yes."

Assail eased back, and in the now-abundant lighting, she saw him duck his right hand into his parka.

Sola frowned. "Are you . . . why are you palming a weapon?"

"I trust no one with you other than myself." He turned to her.

"And I made a promise to your grandmother. You shall be returned to her unharmed, and I am a male of my word. At least in this."

As she met his eyes, she had the oddest sensation settle into her chest. Part of it was fear, and that confused her. With the situation she'd been in, her savior had better be packing a forty and prepared to use it.

The other half of it was . . . not anything she wanted to look too closely at.

The tunnel terminated in a parking facility that reminded her of the one underneath the Caldwell Arena: shallow ceiling, plenty of spaces, the rising elevation that disappeared around a corner suggesting multiple floors.

"Where are we?" she asked as they pulled up to a closed door.

By way of an answer, the thing was thrown wide and a medical team came out, doctors, nurses, gurney and all.

"Thank the Virgin Scribe," Assail muttered.

Oh . . . shit. The white coats weren't alone—they were accompanied by three huge men: a blond with a face that belonged on the big screen, a military guy with a brush cut and an expression hard as a butcher's block, and then a truly terrifying backup who had a skull trim and a scar that ran across his cheek and curved into the side of his mouth.

No, this was not the U.S. government.

Not unless there was a covert hard-ass department.

Assail reached for the door. "Stay in the car."

"Don't go," Sola blurted.

He glanced back at her. "Be not afraid. They owe me this."

Her savior reached out again, and this time he didn't stop himself. He brushed her jaw so lightly that if she hadn't seen him do it, she wouldn't have noticed.

"Stay."

And then he was gone, the door shutting solidly. Through the tinted glass, she watched as a fourth man came out of the brightly lit hallway. Yeah, that was no accountant over there . . . With a floor-length fur duster and a cane, he was dressed like an old-school pimp, his cropped Mohawk and sardonic smile fitting the image perfectly.

The man and Assail offered each other their hands at exactly the same moment. And they stayed linked as they exchanged words—

Something was wrong. Assail started to frown; then looked downright pissed. But as the Mohawked man shrugged and seemed unmoved, Assail finally turned over his weapon and was patted down for his others. And only after his men got out and subjected themselves to the same treatment did the pimp nod at the team of doctors and nurses to go over to the vehicle.

As they reached out to open her door, a spike of fear had Sola pull the sleeping bag right to her chin—

The woman who stuck her head into the backseat was handsome, with short blond hair and dark green eyes. "Hi, I'm Doc Jane. I'd like to take a look at you, if you'll let me."

Her voice was level. Kind. Calm.

Yet Sola couldn't move or respond.

At least not until Assail appeared behind the doctor. "It's okay, Marisol. She's going to take care of you."

Sola found herself staring into his eyes for the longest moment. When she was satisfied with what she saw, she whispered, "Okay. Okay . . ."

And that was when her trembling finally stopped.

Assail was not happy about his empty holsters, but Rehv had made it clear: Either he and his cousins went in unarmed, or the human female was not going to be treated.

It was the only circumstance in which Assail would have consented to be vulnerable and he hated it. But needs must.

"And her name is Marisol," he heard himself say as the blond, female doctor began to speak in low tones. "Sola."

From over on the left, he could feel Rehv staring at him, and the Council's *leahdyre* wasn't the only one. The three Brothers on guard duty were too professional to show anything, but he could tell they were wondering why he'd turned up on their doorstep with a human woman. Who was injured. Whom he was willing to give his guns over for.

"No, you stay there, Marisol. We'll come around to the other side." The female doctor eased out and nodded to her team. "Vitals are low but stable. Gunshot wound to right thigh. Possible concussion. Shock's a concern. May have suffered other trauma she doesn't want to tell me about."

Assail felt the blood leave his head, but he didn't allow the inclination to pass out any further leeway—

"You," he called out sharply. "Stay back."

The male—or, God, was that actually a *human* man?—stopped short.

The main doctor, the female, spoke up. "This is my partner. Dr. Manello. He's—"

"Not to treat her." Assail bared his fangs. "She is unclothed from the waist down."

He was vaguely aware that everyone had frozen and looked his way. Was also aware of a scent that had suddenly entered the scene. He lingered on neither as he stared that man down, prepared to lunge at his throat if he continued around the back of the Rover.

The guy put his hands up as if he were faced with a gun. "Okay, okay. Let's relax. You want me out, I'm out."

Backing up, he stood with the Brothers, shaking his head, but saying nothing.

The female doctor put her hand on Assail's forearm. "We're just going to get her on the gurney. Why don't you come around with me. You can watch and stay close."

Assail eased off on his growl and cleared his throat. "I shall do that. Thank you."

Actually, he did more.

When the doctor opened Marisol's door, he hated the way his woman shrank back before she could catch herself. And then her eyes locked on his.

"Would you like me to help you out?" he asked roughly before any of the medical staff could move in.

"Yes. Please."

It felt so right to push everyone away and be the male who cared for her: Reaching into the SUV's interior, he scooped her into his arms, being careful to take the sleeping bag along with so that she was not exposed—

The hiss she tried to hold in made him nauseous, but he had to get her out—and once he straightened, she seemed to find an accommodation in his arms that didn't cause her too much discomfort.

Her head fell against his shoulder and stayed there.

"I shall carry her in," he informed the doctor.

"It's probably better to—ah, okay, all right." The blond healer put her hands up as his fangs flashed again. "That's fine. Just follow me."

The Brother Rhage was the first into the corridor, and the other two warriors hung back, bringing up the rear along with the cousins.

Assail walked as smoothly as he could, each stiffening of Marisol's limbs or sharp inhale communicating her pain directly into his own chest until it was his lungs burning, his breath catching, his leg that ached.

Going along, they passed by a seemingly endless number of rooms, some of which he looked into, most of which he didn't bother turning his head for. From what little he noticed, there were classrooms, an office that was empty . . . something that looked like an interrogation room. Just as he was becoming convinced they were heading for another zip code, the female doctor finally stopped and indicated the way into an examination room.

The gurney in the center was directly underneath a hanging set of lights, and as he went over and began to transfer Marisol onto the sheeted, padded surface, he was glad the healer didn't turn the chandelier on. It seemed far too bright already in the tiled room, the stainless-steel and glass cabinetry glinting at him, the rolling table with its instruments a threat even though those tools were supposed to help in the right hands.

Dearest Virgin in the Fade, Sola's face was gray from pain and exhaustion as she sat there, her knees up tight to her chest, that navy blue sleeping bag wrapped tight as a second skin around her.

"I'm going to ask all nonessentials to stay out in the hall," the doctor said, shooing the Brothers, the cousins, and that male healer out. "No, nope—we'll be fine. Right, bye-bye." Then in a lower tone, she hissed, "He's a bonded male. You want to deal with that if I have to do an internal exam on her?"

Bonded . . . male? Him?

As the Brothers began to argue with her, Assail nodded grimly at the warriors and Rehvenge. "There shall be no problems from me. You have my word."

Except then he wondered if Marisol's privacy didn't also deserve protecting from the likes of him.

"Marisol," he said softly. "Mayhap it would be best if I—"

"Stay."

He closed his eyes. "All right."

Going over to her head, he turned his back on her body so she could return eye contact with his face, but he could see nothing that would compromise her privacy.

The doctor stepped in close to her and spoke softly. Kindly. "If you could lie back, that would be great. If you don't feel safe, I understand, and I'll put the top of the bed up for you."

There was a long silence. "What was your name again?" Marisol asked roughly.

"Jane. I'm Jane. Behind me is my nurse, Ehlena. And nothing is going to happen here that you don't consent to, okay? You are in charge."

Indeed, he had a feeling he was going to like this physician.

"Okay. All right." Marisol grabbed his hand and eased back, grimacing until she was fully prone. "Okay."

He expected her to let go once she was settled. She did not—and her eyes didn't budge from his. Not as the healer unwrapped the sleeping bag and covered her with a blanket. Not as questions about a possible concussion were asked, and reflexes tested. Not as that thigh wound was poked and prodded at. Not even as a portable X-ray machine was brought over and a picture taken from several different angles.

"So I have all kinds of good news," the doctor said a little later as she approached with a laptop. On its monitor, there was the shadowy image of Marisol's thick, strong thighbone. "Not only is your concussion mild, the bullet passed cleanly through. There's no evidence that the bone is broken or chipped. So our main issue is the risk of infection. I'd like to clean things out thoroughly—and give you some antibiotics as well as some pain meds. Sound good?"

"I'm fine," Marisol cut in.

The doctor laughed as she put the laptop aside. "I swear you fit in here so well. That's what all my patients tell me. Still, I respect your intelligence—and I know that you're not going to want to put your health at risk. What I'm worried about is sepsis—you told me in the car that you were shot twenty-four hours ago. That's a long time for things to get cooking in there."

"Let us see this through, Marisol," Assail heard himself say. "Let us take the advice given."

Marisol closed her eyes. "Okay."

"Good, good." The doctor made some notes on the laptop. "There's just one other thing."

"What?" Assail asked, when there was a lengthy pause.

"Marisol, I need to know if there's anywhere else you might have been hurt."

"Anywhere . . . else?" came a mumbled response.

Assail could feel the doctor staring at him. "Would you mind excusing us for a minute?"

Before he could answer, Marisol squeezed his hand so hard, he winced. "No," she said stiffly. "Nowhere else."

The doctor cleared her throat. "You can tell me anything, you know. Anything that is pertinent to your treatment."

Abruptly, Marisol's body started trembling again—the way it had in the backseat of the Range Rover. In a rush, like she was ripping something off her skin, she said, "He tried to rape me. It didn't happen. I got him first—"

All at once, the sounds in the room receded. The idea—no, the reality—that someone had mistreated her, hurt her, scarred her precious body, tried to . . .

"Are you okay?" someone asked. The nurse. It must be the—

"He's going over!" the doctor barked.

Assail wondered about whom they were speaking . . . as he lost consciousness.

TWENTY-THREE

"Speak, healer," Wrath demanded as he stood over the motionless body of his shellan. *"Speak!"*

Dearest Virgin Scribe, she looked dead.

Indeed, immediately following his Anha's collapse, he had carried her back to their mated room, the Brothers going with him, the aristocrats and their worthless social gaming left behind. It was he who had laid his beloved out upon the bedding platform as the healer was summoned, and he who had been the one to loosen her bodice. The Brothers had departed as soon as the trusted physician arrived with the tools of his healing trade, and then it had been only the three of them, the crackling fire, and the scream that rebounded in his soul.

"Healer, what say thou?"

The male looked over his shoulder from his crouch beside Anha. With the black robes of his station flowing to the floor, he rather resembled a giant bird, imminently due to take flight.

"She is dangerously compromised, my lord." As Wrath recoiled, the healer rose. "I believe she is with young."

A cold draft hit him, rushing from his head to his feet, wiping out the feeling in his entire form. "She is . . ."

"With young. Aye. I could tell when I felt her belly. It is hard and distended, and you did say she recently was upon her needing."

"Yes," he whispered. "So this is caused by the—"

"'Tis not a symptom of early pregnancy as she is not bleeding. No, I do believe this malaise is accounted for by something different. Please, my lord, let us approach the fire to speak so as not to disturb her."

Wrath allowed himself to be drawn closer to the banked flames. "Is she ill then with fever?"

"My lord . . ." The healer cleared his throat, as if mayhap he was worried about a death that had naught to do with the queen. "Forgive me, my lord . . ."

"Tell me not that you have no explanation," Wrath hissed.

"Would you prefer I mislead you? Her heart is sluggish, her pallor is gray, her breathing is shallow and intermittent. There could be some internal difficulty that I cannae measure that she is succumbing to. I do not know."

Wrath shifted his eyes back to his mate. He had never been one to feel fear o'ermuch. Now terror slipped into his skin, possessing him as an evil spirit would, taking him o'er.

"My lord, I would tell you to feed her. Now and for as often as she may take the proceeds of your vein. Mayhap the charge of energy that comes with it with turn this about . . . certainly, if she has any hope, it is you. And if she rouses, I shall give her fresh water only, no ale. Nothing that will cause a further depression of her systems—"

"Get out."

"My lord, she is—"

"Leave us—now!"

Wrath was aware of the male stumbling to the door. And well the healer might—a murderous rage was risen in the chest of his King and liable to be directed upon any bodily form within reach.

As the door was shut once more, Wrath approached the bedding platform. "My love," he said desperately. "Anha, my love, rise unto my voice."

Back on his knees.

Wrath fell back upon his knees at the floor by her head. Stroking her hair upon her shoulder and down upon her arm, he was of care not to put any weight into his touch.

Measuring her breathing, he tried to will her into deeper breaths. He wanted to return to the night before, when they had awoken together and he had looked into her eyes and watched them sparkle with life. For truth, it twisted his mind to think he could remember with such specificity every-

thing about that moment, that hour, that night, the smells of the meal they ate, and the conversations they had about the future, and the audiences they went down to take in at court.

He felt as though the clarity of the remembrances should have been a door that he could go through and thereby take her hand, and smell her scent, and feel the lightness in the heart that came with health and well-being . . . and pull her back to the present in that state.

But that was only fantasy, of course.

Unsheathing his ceremonial dagger, he brought the flashing, polished blade up. When his heavy sleeve with its jewels and settings of precious gold got in the way, he tore his fine coat from his torso, pitching it behind him. As it landed with a scraping sound, all those meticulously affixed gems scratching at the hard oak, he slashed the knife edge across his wrist.

Lo, he wished it was his throat.

"Anha, verily, sit up for me. Lift your head, my love."

Propping her upon his free forearm, he brought the wellspring of his blood to her lips. "Anha, partake from me . . . partake for me. . . ."

Her lips fell open, but it was not her sweet acquiescence that rendered it such. Nay, it was only the angle of her head.

"Anha, drink . . . come back unto me."

As red drops fell into her mouth, he prayed that they somehow proceeded down the back of her throat, and thusly into her veins, reviving her by their purity.

This was not their destiny, he thought. They were to be together for centuries, not parted but a year after meeting. This was not . . . them.

"Drink, my love. . . ."

He kept his wrist in place until the blood threatened to pool out from her lips. "Anha?"

Dropping his head down onto the back of her cold hand, he prayed for a miracle. And the longer he stayed there, the more he joined her in a state that was but one heartbeat away from death.

If she passed, he was going to go with her. One way or the other . . .

Dearest Virgin Scribe, this was not them.

Wrath didn't wake up so much as surface from sleep like a buoy floating up from the depths to bounce on a choppy surface.

He was in the pitch dark of his blindness, naturally—and as always, he threw out his arm to the opposite side of the bed—

Crash!

Wrath lifted his head and frowned. Patting around with his hand, he encountered things that felt like books, a coaster, an ashtray.

Firewood burning.

He was not in his room. And Beth was not with him.

Flipping over, he jacked upright, heart skipping in his chest, the arrhythmia making him light-headed. "Beth?"

In the basement of his brain, he recognized that he was in the library downstairs in the Brotherhood mansion, but his thoughts were like worms in wet soil, twisting around incessantly, going nowhere.

"Beth . . . ?"

A distant whimper.

"George?"

Louder whimper.

Wrath rubbed his face. Wondered where his wraparounds were. Thought, yeah, he was on that couch in the library, the one in front of the fireplace.

"Oh . . . fuck me . . ." he groaned as he tried to get vertical.

Standing up was flat-out awesome. Head swimming, stomach clenched like a fist, he had to grip the arm of the couch or he was going to timber all over the place.

Lurching through dead space, he didn't make it to the doors so much as run into them, the hard panels punching back at his chest. Flubbering around for the handles, he popped the latches and—

George exploded into the room, the golden running around in circles, the sneezes suggesting he was smiling.

"Hey, hey . . ."

Wrath meant to make it back to the sofa, because he didn't want all the functional eyes in the house seeing him like this—but his body had different ideas. And as he went down on his ass, George took the opportunity to jump right in there, getting throw-blanket close.

"Hey, big guy, yup, we're both still here . . ." Stroking the retriever's broad chest, he buried his nose into that fur and let the scent of good, clean dog work some aromatherapy on him. "Where's Mom? Do you know where she is?"

Dumb fucking question. She was not here, and it was his own damn fault.

"Shit, George."

That big tail was banging against his ribs, and that muzzle was snuffling, and those ears were flapping around. And it was good, it was normal—but it didn't go nearly far enough.

"Wonder what time it is?"

Goddamn . . . he'd lost it at John and V but good, hadn't he. And that hadn't been the half of it. He had some vague memory of trashing the billiards room, flipping all kinds of shit, fighting with anyone who got too close—then it had been nap time. He was pretty sure someone had drugged him, and he couldn't say he blamed whoever had done it. Short of a tranq-induced lights-out, he didn't know when he would have stopped.

And he hadn't wanted to hurt any of his brothers or the staff. Or the house.

"Shit."

Seemed like that was the extent of his vocabulary.

Man, he should have let Vishous take him in here and tell him what was going on. But at least there were only two places his mate would go. One was Marissa's Safe Place, and the other was Darius's old house. And no doubt that was what John had been trying to tell him.

Fuck, he thought. This was not him and Beth. This was not where they were supposed to end up.

Matter of fact, things had always felt like fate with her; from the timing of when she'd come into his life to the completion that she brought to him, everything had always seemed like destiny. They'd had arguments, sure. He was a hotheaded asshole and she didn't take any of his shit. Duh.

But never this separation. Ever.

"Come on, bud. We need some privacy."

George hopped off and let Wrath push himself up from the floor. After reshutting the doors, he embarked on a game of find-the-phone. Talk about your emasculations. Hands thrust forward, torso bent, feet shuffling, he bumped into things and felt them up to figure out whether it was a love seat, an armchair, a side table. . . .

The desk seemed like the last fucking thing he ran into, and he discovered where the phone was when his man hand knocked the receiver off its cradle. Putting the thing up to his ear, he finger-tipped around until he located the buttons and then had to recock the dial tone before he could start dialing.

Picturing the ten digits with the pound sign and the star key at the base of the set-of-twelve arrangement, he punched in a seven-number sequence and waited.

"Safe Place, good afternoon."

He closed his eyes. He'd hoped it was closer to dark because then he could go looking for her. "Hey, is Beth there?"

"No, I'm sorry, she's not. May I take a message?" As he closed his eyes, the female said, "Hello? Is anybody there?"

"No message."

"May I tell her who's calling if she comes in later?"

He briefly wondered what the receptionist would do if he told her who it was. "I'll find her elsewhere. Thanks."

As he hung up, he felt George's big head nudge his thigh. So typical of the dog—wanting to help.

Wrath kept his finger on the toggle, pushing down. He didn't know if he was ready for another dial tone. If she didn't pick up at the next number? He was going to have no fucking clue where she was. And the idea that he might have to go to Vishous or John for that kind of information was too shameful to bear.

As he punched in a different sequence, he thought to himself . . .

I can't believe this is us. This just isn't . . . us.

TWENTY-FOUR

Turning her head on her pillow, Sola stared at the door of the hospital room she'd been given. She wasn't looking at it, though.

Instead, flashes of the abduction kept playing in front of her eyes, blocking everything out: Her arriving home and getting hit on the head. The car ride. The flare. The chase through the snow. Then the prison cell and that guard who'd come down to—

The knock made her jump. And it was funny; she knew who it was. "I'm glad you're back."

Assail eased the door open, and put only his head in, as if he were afraid of overwhelming her. "You wake."

She pulled the blankets up higher on her chest. "Never slept."

"No?" Pushing the door wider, he came in with a tray of food. "I had hoped . . . well, mayhap you would care for victuals?"

Sola tilted her head. "You have the most old-fashioned way of talking."

"English is not my first language." He put the tray down on a rolling table and brought it over. "It is not my second, either."

"Probably the reason I love to listen to you."

He froze as he heard her words—and yeah, maybe if she hadn't been hopped up on pain meds, she wouldn't have admitted such a thing. But what the hell.

Abruptly, he looked at her, an intense light in his eyes making them appear even more shimmery than usual. "I am glad my voice pleases you," he said roughly.

Sola focused on the food as she began to feel warm inside for the first time since . . . everything. "Thanks for making the effort, but I'm not hungry."

"You need food."

"The antibiotics are making me sick." She nodded at the IV bag hanging off the pole next to her bed. "Whatever's in there is just . . . awful."

"I will feed you."

"I . . ."

For some reason, she thought back to that night out in the snow, when he'd tracked her off his property and confronted her at her car. Talk about menacing in the dark—Jesus, he'd scared the shit out of her. But that wasn't all she'd felt.

Assail brought the one chair in the room over. Funny, it wasn't one of those rickety plastic jobbies that you normally found in clinics; it was like something out of Pottery Barn, padded, cozy, and with a nice pattern. As he sat down, he didn't fit in it, and not because he was overweight. He was too big, his powerful body dwarfing its arms and back, his clothes too black for the pale color—

There were bloodstains on his jacket, brown and dried. And on his shirt. His pants.

"Do not look upon that," he said softly. "Here. For you, I chose only the best."

Lifting up the cloche, he revealed . . .

"Where the hell am I?" she demanded as she leaned in and breathed deep. "Does, like, Jean-Georges have a medical division or something?"

"Who is this Jean-Georges?"

"Some fancy chef in New York City. I heard about him on Food Network." She sat up, wincing as her thigh let out a hey-girlie. "I don't even like roast beef—but that looks amazing."

"I thought the iron would be good for you."

The slab of beef was beautifully cooked, with a crust that cracked as he cut into it with—

"Are those sterling silver?" she wondered at the fork, the knife—the spoon that was still on a fancy folded napkin.

"Eat." He brought a precisely cut piece to her mouth. "Eat for me."

Without any prompting, her mouth opened on its own, like it was going to have none of the I-can-feed-myself delays.

Closing her eyes, she groaned. Yeah, she wasn't hungry. Not at all.

"This is the single best thing I have ever eaten."

The smile that lit his face made no sense. It was too bright to be just about her having some grub—and he must have known this, because he turned his head so she only saw a flash of the expression.

For the next fifteen, twenty minutes, the only sounds in the room, apart from the whistling heating vents, was that luxe silverware hitting a porcelain plate. And yup, in spite of her oh-no-I-couldn't-possiblies, she ate that huge slice of beef, and the scalloped potatoes, and the creamed spinach. As well as the dinner roll that surely was homemade. And the peach cobbler. And she even had some of the chilled bottled water and the coffee that came in a carafe.

She probably would have eaten the napkin, the tray, all that sterling and the rolling table if given the chance.

Collapsing back against the pillow, she put her hand over her belly. "I think I'm going to explode."

"I shall just put this out in the hall. Pardon me."

From her vantage point, she measured every move he made: the way he stood up, gripped the sides of the tray in long, elegant hands, turned away, walked smoothly.

Talk about your table manners. He'd handled the silver with a genteel flare, as if he used that kind of thing in his own home. And he hadn't spilled a drop as he'd poured her coffee. Or missed any food getting into her mouth.

A perfect gentleman.

Hard to reconcile it with what she'd seen as he'd handed her the cell phone to speak with her grandmother. Then, he'd been unhinged, with blood running down his chin as if he'd taken a hunk out of someone. His hands, too, had been red with blood . . .

Considering she'd killed everyone in that horrible place before she'd left? He'd obviously brought someone up with him.

Oh, God . . . she was a murderer.

Assail came back in and sat down, crossing his legs at the knee, not ankle to thigh as men usually did. Steepling his hands, he brought them to his mouth and stared at her.

"You killed him, didn't you," she said softly.

"Who."

"Benloise."

His magnetic gaze drifted elsewhere. "We shall not speak of it. Any of it."

Sola took elaborate care folding the top edge of the blanket down. "I can't . . . I can't pretend that last night didn't happen."

"You're going to have to."

"I killed two men." She flipped her eyes up to his and blinked fast. "I killed . . . two human beings. Oh, God . . ."

Covering her face, she tried to keep her head together.

"Marisol . . ." There was a squeak as if he'd moved that Pottery Barn chair even closer. "Darling, you must put it from your mind."

"Two men . . ."

"Animals," he said sharply. "They were animals who deserved worse. All of them."

Lowering her hands, she was not surprised that his expression was deadly, but she wasn't scared of him. She was, however, frightened of what she'd done.

"I can't get . . ." She gestured at the side of her head. "I can't get the pictures out of my—"

"Block them, darling. Just forget it ever happened."

"I can't. Ever. I should turn myself in to the police—"

"They were going to kill you. And do you think if they had they would have paid you any honor of conscience? I can assure you not."

"This was my fault." She closed her eyes. "I should have known Benloise would retaliate. I just didn't think it would be to this level."

"But, my darling, you're safe—"

"How many?"

"I beg your pardon?"

"How many . . . have you killed." She exhaled hard. "And please don't try to pretend you haven't. I saw your face, remember. Before you washed it off."

He looked away, and wiped his chin as if the blood were still on him. "Marisol. Put it away, somewhere deep—and leave it be."

"Is that how you handle it?"

Assail shook his head, his jaw clenching, his mouth thinning. "No. I remember my kills. Each and every one."

"So you hate what you had to do?"

His eyes stayed steady on hers. "No. I relish it."

Sola winced. Finding out he was a sociopathic murderer was really the cherry on top of the sundae, wasn't it.

He leaned in. "I've never killed without a reason, Marisol. I relish the deaths because they deserved what befell them."

"So you've protected others."

"No, I'm a businessman. Unless I am crossed, I am far more content to live and let live. However, I shall not be tread upon—nor shall I let those who are mine own be compromised."

She studied him for the longest time—and not once did he look away. "I think I believe you."

"You should."

"But it's still a sin." She thought of all those prayers she'd offered up and felt a guilt like she'd never known before. "I realize I've done criminal things in the past . . . but I never hurt anyone except financially. Which is bad enough, but at least I didn't burn their—"

He took her hand. "Marisol. Look at me."

It was a while before she could. "I don't know how to live with myself. I truly don't."

As Assail felt his heart pound in his chest, he realized he'd been wrong. He had assumed that getting his Marisol physically safe and taking care of Benloise would end this horrible chapter in her life:

Once she was within his own control, and he had ensured her return to her grandmother, then the slate would be clean.

Wrong. So damned wrong—and from her own emotional pain, he did not know how to rescue her.

"Marisol . . ." The tone in his voice was one that he had never heard before. Then again, begging was not his practice. "Marisol, please."

When her lids finally lifted, he found himself taking a deep breath. With them down, her stillness reminded him too much of the other outcome that could have been wrought.

What to say to her, though? "Verily, I can't pretend to understand this concept of sin that you uphold, but then your religion is different than mine—and I respect that." God, he hated that bruise on the side of her face for so many reasons. "But, Marisol, the actions you took were in the name of survival. Your survival. What you did back there is the reason you have breath within your lungs the now. Life is about doing what is necessary, and you did."

She turned away as if the pain was too great. And then she whispered, "I just wish I could have . . . hell, maybe you're right. I have to go back way too far with an eraser to get me out of where I was two nights ago. This whole thing is the culmination of so much."

"You know, if you so choose, you could change your course. You could stop having anything to do with the likes of Benloise."

A ghostly smile touched her lips as she stared at the door. "Yes. I agree."

He took another deep breath. "There is another way for you."

Even though she just nodded, he had the sense she had made peace with her retirement, as it were. And for some reason, that made him want to tear up—not that he would have admitted it to anybody, including her good self.

As she grew quiet, he stared at her, memorizing everything from her wavy, dark hair that had been thoroughly shampooed when she'd showered in her bathroom here, to her pale cheeks, to her perfectly formed lips.

Thinking of everything she had been through, he heard her say that she hadn't been raped—but only because she'd killed the bastard first.

The one in the cell, he thought. The one whose hand she'd used to get herself out of that facility.

His whole body ached for her, it truly did—

"I can feel you staring at me," she said softly.

Assail sat back and rubbed his thighs. "Forgive me." Glancing across the room, he hated the idea of using the door even though he probably should let her rest. "Are you in physical pain?"

Marisol turned her head back to him, her mahogany eyes searching his. "Where are we?"

"How about you answer my question first?"

"It's nothing I can't handle."

"Shall I get the nurse?"

He was in the process of rising to his feet when she put her hand out and stopped him. "No, please. I don't like the way that stuff makes me feel. Right now, I need to be one hundred percent connected to this reality. Otherwise, I think I'm back . . . there."

Assail eased down once more and really, truly wanted to go up north and kill Benloise outright. He quelled the impulse by reminding himself of the suffering the man was enjoying—assuming his heart was still beating.

"So where are we?"

How to answer that?

Well, as much as reality distortion was something she wished to avoid, it was *not* going to be with the fact that he was not human, but in fact, a member of a species she associated with Dracula. Thank you ever so much, Stoker.

"We are among friends." Mayhap that went a little far. But Rehv had provided what had been asked when it was needed—likely in response to the person Assail had "processed" if not directly on behalf of the King, then certainly and undeniably to his benefit.

"You've got some pretty fancy friends. Do you work for the government?"

He laughed. "Dear Lord, no."

"That's a relief. I was wondering if you were going to arrest me or try to get me to turn informant."

"I can assure you, the ins and outs of the human law system are of no concern to me whatsoever."

"Human . . . ?"

Cursing under his breath, he waved away the word. "You know what I mean."

As she smiled, her lids fluttered. "I'm sorry, I think I'm drifting off. All that food."

"Let yourself go. And know that when you wake, I shall take you home."

She jerked upright. "My grandmother is still in that house—"

"No, she is at my estate. I would never have left her where she was, exposed and vulnerable—"

Without any warning, Marisol put her arms around him, throwing them over his shoulders and holding on so hard, he felt every shudder of her body.

"Thank you," she choked out against his neck. "Without her, I have nothing."

Assail was so very careful as he returned the embrace, resting his hands lightly upon her back. Breathing in her scent, his heart ached anew that any male had touched her other than with reverence.

They stayed that way a long time. And when she finally eased back and looked up at him, he couldn't stop himself from brushing her face with his fingers.

"I am without words," he said in a cracked voice.

"About what?"

All he could do was shake his head and break the contact entirely by standing up. It was either that or he was going to get into that bed with her.

"Rest well," he said roughly. "At nightfall, I shall escort you safely unto your relation."

And then she and her grandmother could live with him. And that way he would know she would always be safe.

He would never worry over her again.

Assail hurried out before her eyes shut. He simply couldn't bear that image of her closed lids.

Stepping free of the room, he—

Stopped dead.

Across the corridor, his twin cousins were leaning against the wall, and they didn't have to look up or around at him. They were staring right into his eyes as he emerged—sure as if they had been waiting for him to come back out every second he'd been in there.

They didn't speak, but they didn't have to.

Assail rubbed his face. In what world did he think he could keep two human women in his house? And fuck forever—he wasn't going to be able to do that for a night. Because what would he say when it became apparent he couldn't go out during the day? Or have sunlight in his home? Or . . .

Overcome with emotion, he dug into the front pocket of his black slacks, took out his vial of coke and quickly dispensed of what was left.

Just so he could feel even slightly normal.

Then he picked the tray up off the floor. "Don't look at me like that," he muttered as he stalked away.

TWENTY-FIVE

"Wrath!"

As she called out her husband's name, Beth jerked upright off the pillows, and for a moment, she had no idea where she was. The stone walls and the rich velvet bedding were not—

Darius's house. The chamber that was not her father's, but the one Wrath had used when he'd needed someplace to crash. The one she'd moved over to when she couldn't sleep.

She must have finally passed out on top of the duvet—

Distantly, a phone started ringing.

Shoving her hair out of her face, she found a blanket over her legs that she didn't remember putting there . . . her suitcase just inside the door . . . and a silver tray set on the bedside table.

Fritz. The butler must have come sometime during the day.

Rubbing her sternum, she looked at the empty pillow next to her, the undisturbed sheets, the lack of Wrath—and felt worse than she had the night before.

To think she'd assumed they'd hit bottom. Or that space would help—

"Crap, Wrath?" she called out as she jumped off the bed.

Running to the door, she ripped it open, shot across the shallow hall, and careened into her father's chamber, diving for the phone on one of the side tables.

"Hello! Hello? Hello . . . ?"

"Hi."

At the sound of that deep voice, she collapsed on the bed, squeezing the phone in her fist, pushing it into her ear as if she could bring her man to her.

"Hi." Closing her eyes, she didn't bother fighting the tears. She let them fall. "Hi."

His voice was as rough as hers was. "Hi."

There was a long silence, and that was okay: Even though he was at home and she was here, it was as if they were holding each other.

"I'm sorry," he said. "I'm really sorry."

She let out a sob. "Thank you . . ."

"I'm sorry." He laughed a little. "I'm not real articulate, am I?"

"It's okay. I'm not feeling very with it, either. . . . I was just dreaming of you, I think."

"A nightmare?"

"No. Missing you."

"I don't deserve it. I was afraid to call your cell in case you didn't answer it. I thought maybe if someone was with you, they might pick up and . . . yeah, I'm sorry."

Beth exhaled and leaned back against the pillows. Crossing her legs at the ankles, she looked around at the pictures of her. "I'm in his bedroom."

"You are?"

"There isn't a phone in the one you used."

"God, it's been a long time since I've been to that house."

"I know, right? It brings up a lot."

"I'll bet."

"How's George?"

"Missing you." There was a muffled thump—the sound of him patting the dog's flank. "He's right here with me."

The good news was that the neutral subjects were the perfect way to dip their toes in the relating pool. But the larger discussion still loomed.

"So John's head's okay," she said, picking at the bottom of her

shirt. "But I guess you've already heard everything went all right at the medical center."

"Oh, yeah, no. Actually, I've been . . . kind of out of it."

"I called."

"You did?"

"Yeah. Tohr said you were sleeping. Did you finally get some rest?"

"Ah . . . yeah."

As he fell quiet, the second silence was the preparation kind, the countdown to the real stuff. And yet she wasn't sure how to bring it all up, what to say, how to—

"I don't know if I've ever told you much about my parents," Wrath said. "Other than how they were . . ."

Killed, she finished for him in her mind.

"They were a match made in heaven, to use a human term. I mean, even though I was young, I remember them together, and the truth is, I figured, when they died, that kind of thing was over with them. Like they were a once-in-a-millennium kind of love or something. But then I met you."

Beth's tears were hot as they continued to laze their way down her cheeks, some dropping off softly onto the pillow, others finding her ear. Reaching out, she snagged a Kleenex and mopped up without making a sound.

But he knew she was crying. He had to know.

Wrath's voice became thin, like he was having trouble keeping it together. "When I got shot that night a couple of months ago, and Tohr and I were hauling ass back from Assail's house, I wasn't afraid I was dying or anything. Sure, I knew the wound was bad, but I've been in a lot of bad shit before—and I was going to get through it . . . because no one and nothing was going to take me away from you."

Bracing the phone on her shoulder, she folded the wet tissue in precise little squares. "Oh, Wrath . . ."

"When it comes to you having a young . . ." His voice cracked. "I . . . I . . . I . . . oh for shit's sake, I keep trying to find the words, but I just don't have them, Beth. I simply don't. I know you want to try, I get that. But you haven't spent four hundred years seeing and hearing about how vampire females die on the birthing bed. I can't—like, I can't get that out of my head, you know? And the problem is, I'm a bonded male, so while I'd like to give you what you want? There's a side of me that isn't going to listen to reason. It just isn't—not when it comes to risking your life. I wish I were different because this is killing me, but I can't change where I'm at."

Leaning to the side, she pulled another tissue out of the box. "But there's modern medicine now. We have Doc Jane and—"

"Plus what if the kid's blind. What if they have my eyes?"

"I will love him or her no less, I can assure you of that."

"Ask yourself what we're exposing them to genetically, though. I manage to get along in life, sure. But if you think for an instant I don't miss my sight every day? I wake up next to the female I love and I can't see your eyes in the evening. I don't know what you look like when you dress up for me. I can't watch your body when I'm inside of you—"

"Wrath, you do so much—"

"And the worst of it? I can't protect you. I don't even leave the house—and that's as much about my fucking job as it is the blindness—oh, and don't kid yourself. Legally, if we have a male young, he's going to succeed me. He will not have a choice—just like I didn't and I hate where I'm at. I hate every night of my life—Jesus Christ, Beth, I hate getting out of bed, I hate that fucking desk, I hate the proclamations and the bullshit and being penned in the cocksucking house. *I hate it.*"

God, she'd known he wasn't happy, but she'd had no idea it went this deep.

Then again, when was the last time they'd actually talked like this? The nightly grind coupled with the stress of the Band of Bastards and their bullshit . . .

"I didn't know." She sighed. "I mean, I was aware that you were unhappy, but . . ."

"I don't like talking about it. I don't want you worrying about me."

"But I do anyway. I know you've been stressed—and I wish I could help in some way."

"That's my point. There's no help for it, Beth. There's nothing anyone can do—and even if I had perfect eyesight and the risks of pregnancy were no BFD? I still wouldn't want to dump this shit on the next generation. It's a cruelty I wouldn't do to someone I hate, much less my own fucking child." He laughed harshly. "Hell, I should let Xcor have the goddamn throne. Serve him right."

Beth shook her head. "All I want is for you to be happy." Actually, that wasn't true. "But I can't lie. I love you, and yet I still . . ."

Boy, did she get an idea of how he felt about the no-words thing.

He'd found a way to talk, though.

"I almost can't explain it." She curled a fist over her heart. "It's like this emptiness in the center of my chest. It has nothing to do with you or how I feel about you. It's inside of me—it's like a switch got flipped, you know? And I wish I could be more articulate than that, but it's hard to describe. I didn't even know what it was . . . until one of those nights, when Z took Bella down to our place in Manhattan and I babysat? I was hanging out in that suite of theirs, with Nalla asleep in my lap, and I just kept looking at all of the stuff they had in their room. The changing table, the mobiles, that crib . . . all the wipes and the bottles and the pacis. And I just thought . . . I want this. All of it. The Diaper Genie, and the rubber ducks, and the late days. The poop and the sweet bath-time smell, the crying and the cooing, the clichéd pink and the robin's-egg blue—whatever we get. And listen, I sat on it. I really did. It was such a shock that I thought—it's a mood, a phase, a rose-colored delusion I was going to snap out of."

"When did you . . ." He cleared his throat. "How long ago was this?"

"Over a year."

"Damn . . ."

"Like I said, I've felt like this for a while. And I thought you'd change your mind. I knew it wasn't a priority for you." She was trying to be diplomatic on that one. "I thought . . . well, now that I'm saying it, I realize I never did talk to you about where I was at. There just hasn't been time."

"I'm sorry. I know I already apologized, but . . . goddamn it."

"It's all right." She closed her eyes. "And I know where you're coming from. It's not like I haven't seen you every night looking like you wanted to be anywhere else but where you were."

There was another long silence.

"There's something else," he said after a while.

"What?"

"I think you're going into your needing. Soon."

Even as Beth's jaw dropped open, in the back of her mind, something kindled. "I . . . how do you know?"

The mood swings. The chocolate cravings. The weight gain . . .

"Shit," she said. "I, ah . . . oh, *shit*."

Annnnnnnnd that just about summed it up, Wrath thought as he eased back in the library's desk chair. At his feet, George was stretched out on the rug, that big, boxy head resting on one of Wrath's shitkickers as if offering support.

"I can't be sure." Wrath rubbed his aching temple. "But as your mate, I'm going to be affected as soon as your hormones start fluxing—my blood runs hotter, my emotions are stronger, my temper gets really touchy. Like, you're out of the house now, right? And I feel more myself than I have in about two weeks. But during that argument we had? I was kinda nuts."

"Two weeks . . . that's about the time I started checking in and then sitting with Layla. And yeah, you were really out there."

"Now"—he held up his forefinger to make the point even though she wasn't with him in person—"this is not to excuse the way I behaved. It's just context. I can talk to you over the phone like this and keep it together enough so I can explain myself. When you're with me? Again, not an excuse and not your fault, but I'm wondering if it didn't play a part in all of that."

As he leaned to the side and put his hand on his dog, George lifted his head, the golden seeking, sniffing, giving a little lick. Stroking the long waves that grew from that barrel chest, Wrath pulled them out and flattened them on George's forelegs.

"God, Wrath, when I didn't wake up with you just now . . ."

"Horrible. I know. It was the same for me—or maybe even worse. I wasn't sure whether I'd really fucked things up. Like, no-going-back-fucked-up."

"You haven't." There was a rustling, like she was shifting around on the bed. "And I guess I knew we've been kind of working in parallel for the last while. I just hadn't realized how much time we've lost—and other things. Going down to Manhattan, getting away together, really talking. It's been a while."

"Honestly, that's another reason I don't want a kid. I can barely keep connected with you at this point. I don't have anything to offer a young."

"That's not true. You'd make a wonderful father."

"In another universe, maybe."

"So what do we do?" she asked after a moment.

Wrath rubbed his eyes. Damn, he felt hungover as hell. "I don't know. I really don't."

They'd each said their piece in the way it should have been done in the first place. Reasonably. Calmly.

Actually, he'd been the problem on that one, not her.

"I'm so sorry," he said again. "It doesn't go far enough, on so many levels. But there's nothing else I can . . . man, I'm getting really fucking tired of feeling impotent."

"You are not impotent," she said dryly. "We've well established that."

All he could do was grunt in response. "When are you coming home?"

"Now. I'll drive in—I think there's an extra car here somewhere."

"Wait until after dark."

"Wrath, we've been through this before. I'm perfectly fine in the sunlight. Besides, it's nearly four-thirty. There's not much left."

As he pictured her out in the bright light of day, his stomach churned—and he thought of Payne calling him out on being a closet chauvinist. Compared to worrying about his *shellan*, it was so much easier to lay down an *I forbid*. The problem was what it did to Beth.

He really couldn't put her in a gilded cage just so he didn't have to freak out about her safety.

And maybe this pregnancy thing for him was just a deeper shade of that color of cowardice. . . .

"Okay," he heard himself say. "All right. I love you."

"I love you, too—Wrath, wait. Before you go."

"Yeah?" When there was only silence, he frowned. "Beth? What?"

"I want you to do something for me."

"Anything."

It was a while before she spoke. And when she was done, he closed his eyes and let his head fall back.

"Wrath? Did you hear what I said?"

Every word. Unfortunately.

And he was on the verge of throwing out a no-way, when he thought about what it was like waking up with her not beside him.

"Okay," he gritted out. "Yeah, sure. I'll do that."

TWENTY-SIX

As Saxton stared at himself in his dressing room's mirror, he pinched the butterfly ends of his bow tie and tugged the knot tighter. When he released the patterned silk, the thing kept its form and its symmetry like a pup well trained.

Stepping back, he smoothed his freshly shorn hair and pulled on his Marc Jacobs cashmere winter coat. He gave one sleeve then the other a tug; then he stretched out his arms so that the cuff links under his suit jacket showed.

They were not the ones with the family's crest on them.

He didn't wear those anymore.

No, these were VCA from the forties, sapphire and diamond, platinum setting.

"Did I do the cologne?" He looked at his Gucci and Prada and Chanel bottles, all of which were lined up on a mirrored tray with brass handles. "No comment from you all?"

A quick sniff of one wrist. Yes, that would be Égoïste, and it was fresh.

Turning away, he walked across the heavily veined cream marble floor and out into his white-on-white bedroom. Passing by the bed, he had an instinct to remake the whole thing, but that was nerves talking.

"I'll just double-check."

Plumping the pillows and rearranging the throw into the exact position it had been in when he'd gone in to dress, he glanced at the vintage Cartier clock on the bed stand.

There was no putting things off any longer.

And yet he looked around at the white chaise lounge and the white armchairs. Inspected the white mohair throw rugs. Walked over and made sure the Jackson Pollock over the fireplace was perfectly plumb.

This was not his old house, the Victorian that Blay had once spent a day in. This was his other place, a Frank Lloyd Wright single-story that he'd bought the second it had come on the market—because how could he not? There were so few of them left.

Of course, he'd had to do some clandestine remodeling and expansion of the basement, but vampires had long been working their way around humans and their pesky little building inspectors, et al.

Double-checking his Patek Philippe, he wondered why he was making this dreadful pilgrimage. Again.

It was like a horrible Groundhog Day thing. But at least it didn't happen with great regularity.

As he ascended the stairs, he was dimly aware of fiddling with his bow tie once more. Unlocking the door at the top, he emerged into a sleek forties kitchen with fully functional, modern repros of all those Hello, Lucy appliances.

Every time he walked through the house, with its Jetsons furniture, and complete and utter lack of frills, it felt like he was back in post-WWII America—and it calmed him. He liked the past. Liked the different footprints of the various eras. Enjoyed living in spaces that were as authentic as he could make them.

And it wasn't like he was going back to that Victorian anytime soon. Not after he and Blay had essentially started things there.

As he went out the front door, just the thought of that male made his chest tighten—and he paused, concentrating on the sensation, the memories that came with it, the change in his blood pressure and thought patterns.

After the two of them had broken up, which had been at his instigation, he'd done a lot of reading on grief. The stages. The process. And it had been funny . . . oddly enough, the best resource had been a little booklet he'd found on getting over the loss of a pet. It had questions that you were supposed to answer about what the dog had taught you or what you missed most about the cat or what your favorite moments with your cockatoo had been.

He wouldn't have admitted it to anybody, but he'd answered each one of them in his diary about Blay—and it had helped. Up to a point. He was still sleeping alone, and though he'd had sex, instead of wiping the slate clean, it had just made him ache even more.

But things were better than they had been. At least he had an operating principle that was halfway normal now: He'd been walking dead for the first couple of nights. Now, though, he had a scab over the wound and he was eating and sleeping. There were still triggers, though—like every time he had to see Blay or Qhuinn.

It was so hard to be happy for the one you loved . . . when he was with someone else.

Like all of life, however, there were things you could change and things you couldn't.

On that note . . .

Closing his eyes, he dematerialized and re-formed on a snow-covered lawn that was easily as big as a city park—and just as carefully maintained. Then again, his father hated anything out of order: plants, grass, *objets d'art*, furniture . . . sons. The grand manor house beyond was some fifteen thousand square feet in size, the different wings having been added over time by generations of humans. Staring up at it through the winter night, Saxton was reminded of exactly why his father had purchased the estate when some alumnus had left it to Union College—it was the Old Country in the New World, home away from the motherland.

A traditionalist, his father had relished the return to roots. Not that he'd ever truly left them.

Approaching the front entrance, the gas lanterns on either side of the mile-wide door flickered, casting ancient light on stone carvings that had actually been done in the nineteenth century as part of the Gothic Revival style. As he halted, he thought perhaps he would not ring the bell because the staff would be waiting for him.They, as with his father, were always in a hurry to get him in and out of the house—as if he were a document to be processed or a dinner to be served and cleaned up hastily.

No one opened the door preemptively, however.

Leaning in, he pulled on an iron chain with a velvet cover to generate the bell sound.

There was no answer.

Frowning, he stepped back and looked to the side, but that got him nowhere. There were too many manicured bushes to see into any of the diamond-paned, leaded-glass windows.

Being locked out of the house was such a testimony to their relationship, wasn't it: The male requests him to come on his birthday and then leaves him out in the cold at the front door.

Actually, Saxton had decided that his existence was now a fuck-you to his father. From what he understood, Tyhm had always wanted a young—a son, specifically. Had prayed to the Scribe Virgin for one. And then he'd been granted his wish.

Unfortunately, there had been a caveat that had turned out to be a deal breaker.

Just as he was debating whether to ring again, the door was opened by the butler. The *doggen*'s face was frozen as always, but the fact that he did not bow to the firstborn and only begotten son of his master was plenty of commentary on his opinion of who he was about to let in.

It hadn't always been like this in the household. But his mother had died, and then his little secret had come out so . . .

"Your father is currently engaged." That was it. No, May-I-take-your-coat?, How fare thee?, or even, Verily, how cold is this night?

Not even a conversation about the weather would be spared for him.

Which was fine. He had never cared for the guy, anyway.

When the butler stepped aside, and focused on the silk-covered wall opposite him, walking through that fixed gaze was like getting stung by an electric fence—although at least Saxton was used to it. And he knew where to go.

The lady's parlor was on the left, and as he entered the frilly room, he put his hands into the pockets of his coat. The lavender walls and lemon-yellow rug were bright and cheerful, and the truth was, even though putting him here was intended as an insult, he much preferred it to the wood-paneled gentlemale's equivalent across the foyer.

His mother had died about three years ago, but this was no shrine to the loss. In fact, he didn't have the sense that his father had missed the female.

Tyhm had always been most interested in the law—even over matters of the *glymera*—

Saxton stilled. Pivoted toward the rear of the room.

Distantly, voices mingled—and that was unusual. The house was typically silent as a library, the staff tiptoeing around, the *doggen* having developed a complex system of hand signals with which to communicate so they did not disturb their master.

Saxton approached a second set of doors. Unlike the ones leading out to the foyer, they were closed.

Cracking a panel, Saxton slipped through into the lofty, octagonal room where his father's leather-bound volumes of the Old Law were kept. The ceiling was some thirty feet high, the molding of all those shelves dark mahogany, the cornices over the doorways carved into proper Gothic relief—or at least a nineteenth-century reproduction of it.

In the center of the circular space, there was a tremendous round table, the marble top of which was . . . a bit of a shock.

It was covered with open volumes.

Glancing up at the shelves, he saw slots in the endless lineup of tomes. About twenty of them.

As a warning sounded at the base of his skull, he kept his hands in his pockets and leaned in, tracing the verbiage that was exposed. . . .

"Oh, Jesus . . ."

Succession.

His father was researching the laws of succession.

Saxton lifted his head toward the voices. They were louder now that he was in this room, although still muffled by another set of closed doors across the way.

Whatever meeting was taking place was in his father's private study.

Highly unusual. The male never let anyone in there—didn't even permit clients to come to the house.

This was serious—and Saxton wasn't stupid. There was a cabal against Wrath in the *glymera*, and obviously, his father was involved.

No reason for anyone to care about the next generation of King if they weren't trying to target the current one.

He walked around the table, locking eyes on each open page. The more he saw, the more concerned he became.

"Oh . . . shit," he muttered in a rare curse.

This was bad. Very bad—

The sound of a door opening in the study energized him. Jogging on the balls of his loafers, he scooted back into the ladies' parlor and reclosed the panels silently behind himself.

He was facing the John Singer Sargent over the fireplace when the butler called his name about two minutes later.

"He will see you now."

No reason to throw a thank-you out. He just followed in the wake of the *doggen*'s disapproval—and braced himself for more of the same from his father.

Usually, he hated coming here.

But not tonight. No, tonight, he had a far greater purpose than thwarting what was no doubt going to be yet another of his father's attempts to shame him into going straight.

Purrrrrrrrrrrrrrrrrrrrrrrrrrrrrrrrrrrr.

Trez frowned at the sound. Cracking one eye open, he found his brother standing over his bed, Boo the black cat in the male's arms, an expression of disapproval narrowing those icy eyes.

His brother's, not the cat's.

"Are you spending another night on your ass," iAm bit out.

Not a question, so why bother throwing out an answer.

Groaning as he sat up, Trez had to brace his arms to keep his torso vertical. Apparently, while he'd been out of it, the world had turned into a hula hoop and the planet was going around and around his neck.

Losing the fight, he flopped back down.

As his brother kept standing there, he knew that this was the siren call back to reality. And he wanted to answer it, he really did. His body, however, was out of gas.

"When was the last time you fed?" iAm demanded.

He shifted his eyes over and dodged the question. "Since when are you an animal lover?"

"I hate this goddamn cat."

"I can tell."

"Answer me."

The fact that he couldn't even think of when he'd . . . nope, total blank.

"I'll send someone," iAm muttered. "And then you and I are going to talk."

"Let's talk now."

"Why, so you can pretend you didn't hear it right later?"

Well, there was a thought. "No."

"They're going after our father and mother."

Trez sat up again, and this time he didn't need any extra help. Shit. He should have expected this from the s'Hisbe, but . . .

"How."

"How do you think?" His brother shifted his gentle scratching from the black cat's ears to under its chin. "They're going to start with her."

He rubbed his face. "Jesus Christ. I didn't expect the high priest would be so—"

"It wasn't him. Nah. He was the *second* person who came to see me last night."

"What time is it?" Although the fact that he could see out the windows into the night at least partially answered that one. "Why didn't you wake me up when you got home?"

"I tried. Three times. I was going to send for a crash cart if you didn't come around on this trip."

"So what did the high priest say?"

"s'Ex is the one we have to worry about."

Trez dropped his hands. Staring up at his brother, he knew he must have heard that wrong. "I'm sorry, who?"

"Not the kind of name I need to repeat, is it?"

"Oh, God." What the hell was the queen's enforcer doing paying a visit to his brother? Then again . . . "They're really upping the ante, aren't they."

iAm sat on the edge of the bed, his weight causing the mattress to shift. "We are at the impasse, Trez. No more pretending, no more persuasion. They've used the carrot; now they're going to use the stick."

As Trez thought of his parents, he could barely picture their faces. The last time he'd seen them had been . . . well, there was another thing he couldn't remember. What was crystal clear, though? The quarters they lived in. Marble everything. Gold fixtures. Silk rugs. Servants everywhere. Jewels hanging from lamps to create a sparkle effect.

They hadn't started out like that—and that was another thing he could picture: He'd been born in a modest two-bedroom flat in the far corner of court—nice enough by normal standards.

Nothing close to what they'd gotten when they'd sold his future.

And after that? While they'd upgraded to the best of the best? He'd been sent to be raised by the queen's staff, alone in a white room. It hadn't been until he'd refused to eat or drink for nights upon nights that iAm had been sent to him.

And that was how their dysfunction had started.

Ever since then? Somehow, iAm had become the one responsible for keeping him going.

"Do you remember when we saw them last?" he heard himself say.

"At that party. You know, for the queen."

"Oh . . . that's right." Their parents had been sitting with the queen's Primaries, as they were called. Front and center. Smiling.

They hadn't acknowledged him or iAm when they'd come in, but that was not unusual. Once sold, he had become the queen's. And once drafted into service to smooth things over, iAm was no longer theirs, either.

"They never looked back, did they," Trez murmured. "I'm just a commodity to them. And, man, they got a good price."

iAm stayed silent, as was his way. He just sat there, stroking that cat.

"How much time do I have?" Trez asked.

"You have to go tonight." Dark eyes shifted over. "Like now."

"And if I don't . . ." There was no reason to answer that, and iAm didn't bother: If he didn't get out of bed and turn himself in, his parents were going to be slaughtered. Or worse.

Probably much worse.

"They're such a part of the system," he said. "Those two really got what they wanted."

"So you're not going."

Once he set foot back within the Territory, he was never going to see the outside world again. The queen's guard was going to shut him in that maze of corridors, lock him up so that he was the male equivalent of a harem, separate him even from his brother.

And meanwhile, his parents would live on, uncaring.

"She looked at me," he muttered. "That night of the party. Her eyes went to mine—and she gave me this secret little smile of superiority. Like she'd made all the right moves, and the added benefit had been that she hadn't had to deal with me. What the fuck kind of mother does that?"

"So you're going to let them die."

"No."

"So you're going back."

"No."

iAm shook his head. "It's binary, Trez. I know you're pissed off at them, at the queen, at a hundred thousand things. But we've reached the crossroads, and there are only two options. You've really got to understand that—and I'll go back with you."

"No, you'll stay here." As his muddled head tried to wrap itself around the variables, his brain was all fizzle, no flash. "Besides, I'm not going."

Shit, he needed to feed before he tried to deal with this.

"Fuck, that human blood is for crap," he mumbled, rubbing his temples like maybe the friction could jump-start his IQ. "You know what? I really can't talk about this right now—and I'm not being an asshole. I literally can't think."

"I'll send someone." iAm got up and went to the door that separated their suites. "And then you need to make your mind up. You've got two hours."

"Will you hate me," he blurted.

"About them?"

"Yeah."

It was a long while before he got an answer. And the cat stopped purring, iAm's hand stilling at that throat.

"I don't know."

Trez nodded. "Fair enough."

The door was shut and his brother well on his way when Trez's brain coughed up a hey-wait.

"Not Selena," he called out. "iAm! Yo! Not Selena!"

He did not trust himself with her on a good night—the last thing he needed was to get close to her right now.

TWENTY-SEVEN

As Wrath knocked on the door in front of him, he didn't know what the fuck he was doing. Maybe he'd luck out and there'd be no answer.

He needed more time before doing something like this—

Denied. Things opened up and a deep voice said, "Hey. What's doing?"

As he tried to think of an answer to that, he closed his eyes behind his wraparounds. "Z. . . ."

"Yeah. Hey." The brother cleared his throat. Which really drove home the silence thing. "Yeah. So. What's up?"

Abruptly, like the universe was sending him a shot in the nuts, a young's cry rippled out. "Ah, listen, I was just getting her up. You mind?"

Wrath dragged a hand through his hair. "No, no, yeah, it's cool."

"You want me to come to your office afterward?"

He wondered what the room looked like, and painted the space according to what his Beth had said was in it. Cluttered, he thought. Homey. Cheerful.

Pink.

Nothing that Z would have been caught dead in before he'd met Bella.

"Wrath? What's going on here?"

"You mind if I come in?"

"Ah . . . sure. Yeah, I mean, Bella's working out so we've got some privacy. But you're going to want to—"

Chhheeeeeeeeeeeeeeeeeeep!

"—watch where you step."

Wrath lifted up his shitkicker and whatever toy he'd crushed reinflated with a wheeze. "Fuck, did I break it?"

"I think it's a dog toy, actually. Yeah, I'm pretty sure she picked it up from George downstairs. You want it back?"

"He's got plenty. She can have it."

As he shut the door, he was painfully aware that they were each talking about their young—only Wrath's had four paws and a tail.

Least he didn't have to worry about George succeeding him or being blind.

Z's voice came from deeper in the room. "You can sit on the foot of the bed if you go fifteen feet straight ahead of you."

"Thanks."

He didn't particularly want to park it, but if he stayed standing, he was going to want to pace and it wouldn't be long before he tripped over something that wasn't a toy.

Over in the corner, Z spoke softly to his daughter, the words rolling into some kind of rhythm like he was talking through a song. In reply, there were all kinds of cooing.

And then came something that sounded terrifyingly clear: "Dada."

Wrath winced behind his wraparounds, and figured he might as well get this over with. "Beth wants me to talk to you."

"About?"

As he imagined the Z he knew so well, he pictured the brother he'd been convinced was going to implode and take out half a dozen of them with him: skull trim, scarred face, eyes that had been black and opaque as a shark's until Bella had come. Then they had gone yellow—at least as long as he wasn't pissed off, and that didn't happen anymore unless he was out in the field.

Big turnaround.

"Are you holding her?" Wrath asked.

There was a pause. "As soon as I get this bow tied in the back—

hold on, girlie. Okay, up you go. She's in a pink dress that Cormia made her by hand. I hate pink. I like it on her, though—but keep that to yourself."

Wrath flexed his hands. "What's it like?"

"Not totally hating pink? Pretty fuck—ehrm, frickin' emasculating."

"Yeah."

"Do not tell me Lassiter's been metrosexualizing even you. I heard he talked Manello into going for a pedicure with him—but I'm praying that's just gossip."

It was hard to ignore how easily the brother was talking. Like normal, really. Then again, he had his family, his *shellan* was safe, and he'd been disappearing into the basement with Mary on a regular basis for how long now?

Nobody knew precisely what they talked about down there. But everyone could guess.

"Actually, I don't know why I'm here," Wrath said roughly.

Liar.

Footfalls came forward, and then there was a regular creaking, like the male had taken a seat in a rocking chair and was going back and forth. Apparently, Nalla liked whatever positioning had occurred, the young doing more of that cooing.

A soft squeaking suggested Z had picked up another toy and was keeping her occupied.

"This about Beth spending time with Layla?"

"Am I the only person who didn't know?"

"You don't leave your office much."

"One more reason not to want to have a kid."

"So it's true."

Wrath bowed his head and wished his vision was working so he could pretend to inspect something. The bedspread. His boots. A watch.

"Yeah, Beth wants one." He shook his head. "I mean, how did you do it? Getting Bella pregnant—you must have been terrified at the idea."

"There was no planning involved. She went into her needing, and when push came to shrug . . . I mean, I had the drugs. I begged her to let me take care of her that way. In the end, though, I did what a male does to see his female through it. The pregnancy was rough, but the birth scared me more than anything I've ever been through in my life."

And considering the guy had been a sex slave for how long? That was saying something.

"Afterward," Z said slowly, "I didn't sleep for a good forty-eight hours. It took that long for me to be convinced Bella wasn't going to bleed out and Nalla was alive and going to stay that way. Hell, maybe it was more like a week."

"Was it worth it?"

There was a long quiet, and Wrath was willing to bet his left nut the brother was staring at his daughter's face. "I can say yes because they both survived. If that hadn't been the case? My answer would be different—even as much as I love my daughter. Whatever, like all bonded males, Bella is the one I focus on before everything, even including my young."

Wrath popped the knuckles of one fist. Went to work on the other hand. "I think Beth was hoping you'd change my mind."

"I can't do that. No one can—it's the hard wiring of the bonded male. The one you really need to talk to is Tohr. I fell into this—and I am the luckiest bastard on the face of the planet that it happened to work. Tohr, on the other hand, he chose it. He somehow had the balls to roll the dice—even knowing the risks. And then his Wellsie died anyway."

Abruptly, Wrath remembered going down to the training center's office, looking for the fighter with all of the Brotherhood behind him. He had found Tohr sitting with John, a phone up to the brother's ear, an aura of desperation marking everything from his pale face to the grip he'd had on that receiver to the way his expression had frozen as he'd looked up to find them all there, in the doorway.

Jesus Christ, it was fresh as if it had happened yesterday. Even though in the intervening time, Tohr had mated Autumn and moved on, to the extent that any male would be able to.

Wrath shook his head. "I don't know if I can go there with the brother."

Cue another long stretch of quiet, as if maybe Z were thinking of that night, too. But then Zsadist said softly, "He's your brother. If he'd do it for anyone . . . it would be for you."

The minute Beth walked into the mansion's magnificent foyer, she stopped dead in her tracks.

At first, she couldn't put a name to the splintered pile of wood that was on its side under the billiard's room archway. But then the ragged green skin gave it away: It was the pool table. Looking like someone had had at it with a chain saw.

Going over, she peered in and felt her jaw unhinge.

Everything was trashed. From the sofas to the light fixtures, the TV to the bar.

"He's okay," a male voice said from behind her.

Wheeling around, she looked up into Z's yellow eyes. In the Brother's arms, Nalla was dressed in a darling pink dress with an empire waist and a flaring skirt she was going to grow into in a couple months. Talk about the cuteness. Little white Mary Janes flashed on her feet, and an off-center white bow tied back her multicolored curls.

Her eyes were yellow, just like her dad's, but her smile was all Bella, wide-open, trusting, and friendly.

God, it hurt to see them. Especially as she knew the cause of the destruction in that other room.

"He called me," she said.

"That why you came home?"

"I was going to anyway."

Z nodded. "Good. Last night was a thing."

"Clearly." She glanced over her shoulder. "How did he . . ."

"Stop? Lassiter darted him. He went down like a stone and had a good, long nap."

"That wasn't what I was going to ask, but . . . yeah." She rubbed her cold hands together. "Ah, do you know where he is?"

"He told me you asked him to talk to me."

As she stared across at Z, she thought of meeting him for the first time. God, he'd been terrifying—and not just because of the scar. He'd had a glacial glare back then, as well as the kind of deadly focus that had gone straight into the center of her chest.

Now? He was like a brother to her . . . except when it came to Wrath. Wrath would always come first for him.

It was true for all the Brothers. And considering what Wrath had done to the game room, that was not a bad thing.

"I thought maybe it would help." God, that seemed lame. "What I mean is—"

"He's gone to find Tohr."

Beth closed her eyes. After a moment, she said, "I don't want any of this, you know. Just so we're clear."

"I believe that. And I don't want this for the two of you, either."

"Maybe we'll figure it out." As she turned to the stairs, a wave of exhaustion hit her like a ton of bricks. "Listen, if you see him . . . tell him I've gone up to have a shower. It was a long day for me, too."

"You got it."

As she passed by the Brother, she was shocked when his hand landed on her shoulder and squeezed in support.

Good Lord, if you'd told her a couple of years ago that the fighter would be offering anyone anything other than a gun to the head? NFW. And the fact that he was currently holding a total Gerber baby in his heavily muscled arm, said daughter staring up at his scarred face with absolute and total adoration?

Pigs flying. Hell freezing over. Miley Cyrus keeping some clothes on.

"I'm sorry," she said hoarsely, knowing that the flip side to the Brotherhood's closeness was that they all truly worried about each other.

The problems of one were the problems of all.

"I'll let him know you're home safe," Z said. "Go have a rest. You look wiped."

She nodded and hit the stairs, dragging her tired body up one step at a time. As she came to the second floor, she stared through the open double doors into the study.

The throne and the huge desk it sat behind loomed like monsters, the old wood and ancient carvings a tangible representation of the lines of succession that had served the race for how long? She didn't know. She couldn't guess.

So many couples sacrificing their firstborn sons to a position that, from all she'd seen, was not just thankless, but downright dangerous.

Could she put her own flesh and blood there? she wondered. Could she sentence something she herself had had a hand in creating to where her husband sat and suffered?

Stepping over the threshold, she crossed the Aubusson rug and stood before just two of the symbols of the monarchy. She pictured Wrath there, with the paperwork and the grind, like a tiger trapped in a zoo, fed well, cared for relentlessly . . . nonetheless caged.

She thought back to working at the *Caldwell Courier Journal*, for Dick the Prick as a copyeditor for his boys' club while he tried to look down her shirt. She'd wanted to get out so badly, and her transition and meeting Wrath had been her saviors.

What was Wrath's?

How would he ever get out of this?

Short of abdicating, his only saving grace . . . was getting killed by Xcor and the Band of Bastards.

Wow. Great future there.

And her solution was to threaten her own life by trying to get pregnant. No wonder he'd lost his shit.

Running her fingertips across the complicated edging of the desk, she discovered that the curlicues actually formed a vine. And there were dates inscribed along the leaves. . . .

The Kings and the queens. Their children.

A long legacy of which Wrath was the current manifestation.

He wasn't going to give this up. No way. If he felt impotent now, walking away from the throne was going to send him right over the edge. He'd already lost his parents too soon—to release their legacy over to another? That would be a blow he'd never get past.

She still wanted to have a child.

But the longer she stood there, the more she wondered whether it was worth it if she had to sacrifice the man she loved. And that was going to be the result—plus, assuming she could get pregnant and deliver a healthy baby, if they had a son, he was going to end up here.

And if she had a daughter? Whoever she married was going to take over—and then her daughter would have the pleasure of watching her man go insane from the pressure.

Great inheritance either way.

"Damn it," she breathed.

She'd known Wrath was the King when she mated him—but for her, by then, it had already been too late. She'd been head over heels in love, and whether his job had been security guard or supreme head of state, she was getting hitched.

She hadn't thought of the future back then. Just being with him had been enough.

But come on, even if she had been aware of all the implications . . .

Nope. She still would have thrown on Wellsie's gorgeous red gown and marched down to have the crap scared out of her as Wrath had her name carved in his back.

Thick or thin. Richer or poorer, in human terms.

Child-filled . . . or childless.

When she finally turned away, she straightened her shoulders and walked out of the room with her head level. Her eyes were clear, her heart was calm, and her hands were steady.

Life was not an à la carte buffet where you got to fill your plate with whatever you wanted. You didn't get to choose your entrée and your sides and go back for more when maybe you had three bites of meat left and had run out of mashed potatoes. And hell, when she thought about it logically, getting True Love along with Happily Married and Hot Sex Life was already one hell of a trifecta.

There were good reasons for them not to have a child. And maybe it would change in the future; maybe Xcor and the Bastards would meet their graves, and the *glymera* would come around, and the Lessening Society would stop killing. . . .

Pigs flying.

Hell freezing over.

Miley planting her twerking ass in a chair and keeping it there as a public service.

As Beth headed for the private stairwell to the third floor, she wished she'd come to this conclusion before Wrath had gone to find Tohr, but that was yet another collision she had triggered that she couldn't undo.

She could stop this from going any further, though.

However much it hurt, she could choose another path and put them both out of their misery.

For God's sake, she wasn't the first woman on the planet who couldn't have children just because she wanted them. And she was not going to be the last. And all those females? They went on. They lived their lives and kept going—and they didn't have her Wrath. . . .

He was more than enough for her.

And anytime she thought he wasn't? She was going to go back and sit in front of that desk . . . and put herself deep in her *hellren*'s shitkickers for a mile or two.

She didn't want to let her father down and she hadn't even met him. For Wrath, being King was the only way to honor his—and not wanting to subject the next generation to the throne?

It was the only way to protect the children he would never have.

The Rolling Stones were right. Sometimes, you didn't get what you wanted. But if you had all you needed?

Life was good.

TWENTY-EIGHT

"Your cousin is getting mated."

As Saxton was led through the doors of his father's study, that was the greeting he received.

Here we go, he thought. And next time they talked, no doubt it was going to be about said cousin having a perfectly healthy baby boy who was going to grow up *normal.* Guess this was his birthday "gift"—a report on some relation living the right sort of life, with subtitles that he was a shame to the bloodline and a great waste of DNA for his father.

Actually, the happy little updates had started up soon after his father had learned that he was gay, and he remembered every single statement, arranging them like ugly figurines on the mantel of his mind. His absolute, bar-none favorite? The newsflash a couple of months ago about a gay male who had gone out with another gay male of the species, and ended up beaten in an alley by a group of humans.

His father had had no idea he was talking about his own son on that one.

The hate crime had been the capper on his first date with Blay, and he had nearly died from the injuries: There had been no going for medical help—Havers, the only physician in the race, was a devoted traditionalist, and was in the practice of turning away known homosexuals from treatment. And going to a human doctor had been a no-go. Yes, there were twenty-four-hour clinics open in the city, but it had taken all the energy he'd had left to drag himself home—and he'd been too ashamed to call anyone for help.

But Blay had shown up—and everything had changed for them.

For a while, at least.

"Did you hear what I said," his father demanded.

"How wonderful for him—which cousin is it?"

"Enoch's son. It was arranged. The families are going to have an eventing weekend to celebrate."

"At their estate here or in South Carolina?"

"Here. It is time for the race to reestablish proper traditions in Caldwell. Without tradition, we are nothing."

Read: You are worthless unless you get with the program.

Although naturally his father would couch the directive in much more scholarly terms.

Saxton frowned as he finally looked at the male. Sitting behind his desk, Tyhm had always been thin, an Ichabod Crane figure in suits that hung like funeral draping from his bony shoulders. Compared to their last visit, he appeared to have lost weight, his sharp features holding up his facial skin like supports under a pitched tent.

Saxton didn't look anything like his sire, that dark hair and those dark eyes, that pale skin and lanky body not what the genetic lottery had dealt him. Instead, his mother and he had been pea-and-pod in disposition and decoration, fair and gray eyed with a healthy glow to their skin.

His father had often remarked on how similar he was to his *mahmen*—and looking back on it, he wasn't sure that had been a compliment.

"So what are you doing for work," his father muttered as he drummed his fingers on the leather blotter.

Over the male's head, the portrait of his own father loomed with identical disapproval.

As Saxton was pegged with two sets of narrowed eyes, there was an almost irresistible urge to answer that question honestly: Saxton was, in fact, First Counsel to the King. And even in these times, when regard for the monarchy was at an all-time low, that was still impressive.

Especially to someone who revered the law like his father.

But no, Saxton thought. He was going to keep that to himself.

"I'm where I was," he murmured.

"Trusts and estates is rather a complicated field. I was surprised you chose it. Who are some of your more recent clients?"

"You know I can't divulge that information."

His father brushed that aside. "It would not be anyone I know, surely."

"No. Probably not." Saxton tried to smile a little. "And you?"

That demeanor changed instantly, the subtle distaste ebbing out and being replaced by a mask that had all the revelatory quality of a slab of slate. "There are always things to command my attention."

"Of course."

As both of them continued speaking in a volley, the conversation remained stilted and irrelevant, and Saxton passed the time by putting his hand in his pocket and fitting his iPhone to his palm. He had planned his departure, and wondered when he could take his cue.

And then it came.

The phone on the desk, the one that had been made to appear "old-fashioned," rang with an electronic bell that sounded as close to real as anything not actually brass could get.

"I'll leave you," Saxton said, taking a step back.

His father stared at the carefully hidden digital display . . . and appeared to forget how to answer the thing.

"Goodbye, F—" Saxton stopped himself. Ever since his orientation had been revealed, that was an f-word worse than *fuck*—at least when used by him.

As his father just waved him off, he had a passing relief. Usually, the worst part of any in-person visit was the departure: As he'd leave, and his father confronted yet another failed attempt to bring his son around, it was the walk of shame all over again.

Saxton hadn't come out to his family. He'd never intended his father to know.

But someone had blabbed and he was fairly sure he knew who.

So every time he left, he relived getting kicked out of this very house about a week after his mother had died: He'd been booted with his clothes on his back, no money, and nowhere to stay as dawn approached.

He'd learned later that all of his things had been ritually burned in the woods out behind the manor house.

One more handy use for all the acreage.

"Shut the door behind you," his father snapped.

He was more than happy to obey that one: Closing things silently, for once he didn't waste a moment on all the pain. Looking left and right, he listened.

Silence.

Moving quickly, he went back to the parlor and through into the library, pulling the doors shut behind him. Taking out his phone, he started snapping pictures, his heart beating as fast as he was tapping. He didn't bother to arrange angles or do anything sequentially—the only thing he cared about was that the focus and the lighting were good and that he didn't move—

The rumbling of doors opening directly behind him had him spinning around.

His father seemed confused as he stood in the doorway that led out of his study. "Whate'er are you doing?"

"Nothing. I was just looking at your volumes. They're quite impressive."

Tyhm glanced at the doors Saxton had shut behind himself—as if wondering why they were closed. "You should not have come in here."

"I'm sorry." Surreptitiously, he slipped the phone into his pocket, tilting his torso to the side as if to nod at the books. "It's just . . . I wanted to marvel over your collection. Mine are cloth covered."

"You have a set of the Old Laws?"

"I do. I bought them from an estate."

His father went forward and touched the pages of the closest volume open on the round table. The loving way with which he stroked those words, that paper, that inanimate object . . . suggested that maybe Saxton wasn't the biggest heartbreak in his life.

If the law let him down? That would break him.

"What is this all about?" Saxton said softly. "I heard the King was shot, and now . . . this is all about the succession."

When there was no reply, he began to think he needed to leave in a hurry: There was a high probability his father was in with the Band of Bastards, and it would be folly to think Tyhm would hesitate for even a second in turning his gay son over to the enemy.

Or in his father's case, the allies.

"Wrath is no King for the race." Tyhm shook his head. "Nothing good has come since his father was killed. Now, there was a ruler. I was young when I was at court, but I remember Wrath, and whereas the son cares not for the proper way . . . the sire was a stellar King, a wise male with patience and majesty. Such a failure of this generation."

Saxton looked at the floor. For some absurd reason, he noted that his own loafers were perfectly polished. All of his shoes were. Neat and tidy, arranged.

He found it difficult to breathe. "I thought the Brotherhood was . . . taking care of things rather well. After the raids, they have killed many slayers—"

"The fact that you use the word *after* to modify *raids* is all one needs to know. A shameful commentary—Wrath did not care to rule until he married that half-breed of his. Only then, when he sought to contaminate the throne with her bastard human genes, did he see fit to try to be King. His father would hate this—that human wearing the ring of his mother? It is a disgrace that cannot . . ." He had to clear his throat. "It simply cannot be supported."

As the implications dawned on Saxton, he could feel the blood drain out of his head. Oh, God . . . why hadn't they seen this coming?

Beth. They were going to take him down through her.

His father lifted his chin, his Adam's apple standing out like a fist in the front of his throat. "And one has to do something. One has to . . . do something when bad choices are made."

Like being gay, Saxton finished for the male. And then it dawned on him . . .

It was almost as if his father was joining the effort . . . only because he couldn't do anything about his own failure of a progeny.

"Wrath will be removed from the throne," Tyhm said with a resurgence of strength. "And another who has not strayed from the race's core values will be put in his place. It is the appropriate consequence for one who does not do things in the proper manner."

"I had heard . . ." Saxton paused. "I had heard that it was a love match. Between Wrath and his queen. That he fell in love with her when he helped with her transition."

"The deviant often couch their actions in the vocabulary of the righteous. It is a deliberate act to attempt to ingratiate themselves to us. That doesn't mean they have behaved well or that their poor choices should be supported by the masses. Quite the contrary—he has shamed the race, and deserves all that is coming to him."

"Do you hate me?" Saxton blurted.

His father's eyes lifted from the books that were going to be used to pave the way to the abdication. As their stares met across the blueprint for Wrath's destruction, Saxton was reduced to a child who simply wanted to be loved and valued by the only parent he had left.

"Yes," his father said. "I do."

Sola pulled the fresh jeans up to her knees and paused. Bracing herself, she eased the waistband over her thigh wound carefully.

"Not bad," she muttered as she continued to tug them all the way onto her ass, and then button and zip them.

Little loose, but when she put on the fresh white long-sleeved shirt and the cozy black sweater she'd also been given, you'd never know. Oh, and the Nikes were the perfect size—and she even liked the black-and-red color scheme.

Going into her hospital room's bath, she checked her hair in the mirror. Shiny and smooth, thanks to the blow-dry she'd given herself.

"You look . . ."

Wheeling around at the voice, she found Assail standing by the bed. His eyes burned across the distance between them, his body looming large.

"You startled me," she said.

"My apologies." He offered her a short bow. "I knocked several times, and when you didn't answer, I was concerned that you had fallen."

"That's really . . . ah, kind of you." Yeah, *sweet* couldn't be associated in any way with him.

"Are you ready to go home?"

She closed her eyes. She wanted to say yes—and of course, she needed to see her grandmother. But she was afraid to, as well.

"Can you . . . tell?" she asked.

Assail came over to her, walking slowly, as if he knew she was a hairbreadth away from spooking. Lifting his hands, he brushed her hair back over her shoulders. Then he touched the sides of her face.

"No. She will see none of it."

"Thank God." Sola exhaled. "She can't know. Do you understand?"

"Perfectly."

Turning to face the door out into the corridor, he offered her his elbow . . . as if he were escorting her to a party.

And Sola took it just because she wanted to feel him against her. Know his warmth. Be close to his size and strength.

It was a different kind of hell to be facing the prospect of meeting her grandmother's eyes.

"Do not think of it," he said as he led her down the long hall. "You must remember that. She will see it in your face if you do. None of it happened, Marisol. None of it."

Sola was dimly aware that the guards that had met them when they'd come to this place had slipped in behind them. But she had so many other things to worry about—and that bunch of men hadn't pulled any of those triggers as she'd come into the facility. Hard to imagine why they'd bother on the way out.

One of them jumped in front and opened the steel door for them, and the Range Rover was right where it had been parked. Next to it, Assail's two cousins were standing grimly—watched over by more of those incredibly dangerous-looking guys.

Assail opened the back car door for her and offered her his hand. She needed it. Humping herself up into the SUV caused her thigh to sting until her eyes watered. But as she was shut in, she managed to work the belt herself, pulling it out from her body and clipping it in place.

Sola frowned. Through the tinted glass, she watched as Assail went to each of the men, one after another, and offered them his hand. There were no words spoken, at least not that she saw, but there didn't need to be.

Grave stares met Assail's eyes and subtle nods were given with respect as if an accord had been reached among them all.

And then Assail's cousins hopped in the front, Assail got in the rear with her and they were off.

She had only a vague memory of all the gates and barricades they'd had to go through to get into the place—but she figured the way out would take forever.

At least she wanted it to. She had some hope that if enough time passed, she could convince her inner little girl that she hadn't broken the main Ten Commandment twice, nearly been raped, and had to deface a body to get herself out of hell.

Unfortunately, they were back on the Northway, heading south toward downtown Caldwell, a heartbeat and a half later. Or it certainly seemed like that.

As they zeroed in on the bridges that would take them over the river and through the woods, to Assail's fortress they went . . .

Great. Her brain was non-sequituring it up.

Rubbing her tired eyes, she had to pull things together.

It didn't happen.

"You know, you may have a point," she said quietly.

"About what," Assail asked from beside her.

"Maybe it was all just a dream. A bad, horrible dream . . ."

The Range Rover mounted the westbound bridge over the Hudson, and with traffic moving smoothly across the span, they were going to be at Assail's in only five or ten minutes.

Twisting around, she looked at the receding downtown, all those lights like stars having fallen to earth.

"I don't know if I can see her," she heard herself say.

"It didn't happen."

Watching that cityscape get smaller and smaller, she told her brain to do the same with all the sights and smells and sensations that were so close, too close: Time was a highway and her body and brain were traveling on it. So she needed to hit that fucking gas pedal and get the hell away from the last forty-eight hours.

Before she knew it, they were turning off onto the thin road that went down to the peninsula Assail owned. And then her stomach sank as that glass house came into view, its golden illumination pouring out onto the landscape as if the place were a pot of gold.

They went to the back, the headlights swinging around across the rear of the mansion. And there she was. In the window of the kitchen, head lifting to look out, hands reaching for a dish towel . . . Sola's grandmother was watching, waiting—now scrambling for the back door.

Abruptly, everything went out of Sola's mind as her hand fumbled for the latch.

Assail gripped her arm. "No. Not until we're in the garage."

Unlike the rest of the trip, getting undercover took forever, that reinforced door trundling down like it had all the time in the world.

The instant it thumped into place, Sola burst out of that SUV and ran for the door. It was locked, and in her jammed-up mind, the only thing that occurred to her was to grip the handle harder and yank and pull—

Someone unlocked it remotely, because there was a *clunk!* and then suddenly things sprang open.

Her grandmother was on the far side of a squat anteroom, standing in the center of the kitchen, that white dish towel wadded up to her face, the scents of home cooking like love in the air.

Sola ran forward as her grandmother opened the only arms that had ever been there to hold her.

She had no clear knowledge of what was said in Portuguese, but on both sides, words flowed fast. Until her grandmother pushed her back and captured her face in those weathered hands.

"Why for you this sorry?" the woman demanded, brushing tears away with her thumbs. "No sorry for you. Never."

Sola got pulled back in hard and held against that generous bosom. Closing her eyes, she sagged and let her brain shut down.

This was all that mattered. They were together. They were safe.

"Thank you, God," she whispered. "Thank you, dear Lord."

TWENTY-NINE

Of course it was Selena.

As soon as Trez heard the knock across his bedroom, he took a deep breath . . . and yup, her scent preceded her, drifting in under the door.

His body hardened instantly, his cock extending up his lower belly, pushing against the weight of the duvet.

Send her away, a part of him said. If you have any decency left in you—send her away. . . .

Not exactly the best argument: He was, after all, contemplating putting his parents in a grave—so how much Boy Scout could he possibly have in him—

He stopped that mental wheelspin in its tracks. At this point, he was so blood starved, he wasn't going to make any sense. Feed first. Then . . . think.

Right. Back to the Please, God, not Selena.

The problem was . . . who else was coming here to service him? He hadn't seen any Chosen in this household except for her and Layla, who was now out of commission. And if he didn't take the vein about to be offered, his only other option was to head out to the club and work his way through a half dozen human women—which was about as appetizing a prospect as drinking engine sludge.

There was also the issue that he was so far down into an energy wormhole that he wasn't sure whether even that would be enough. Another fun fact? He didn't think he could stand up to pull a pair of jeans on. So how in the hell was he going to go to the Iron Mask and—

The soft knock was repeated.

Pushing his hand under the covers, he shoved his erection around so that it would lie as flat as possible—and the contact made him grit his teeth.

You've got to do this with her, he told himself. Once and never again.

"Selena . . ." Shit, the sound of her name leaving his lips made him feel like his hand was back on his cock.

Oh, wait, he hadn't taken the damn thing off.

As she opened the door, he whipped his arm out from under—and glared at it to stay put.

Sweet Mary, Mother of God . . . to quote that Boston cop.

She looked as beautiful as always in that white robing with her hair up, but his starvation turned her into a transcendental vision—that went right to his hips. His pelvis immediately started curling, his cock begging for something, anything from her.

This was a bad idea, he thought.

And sure enough, Selena hesitated in the doorway, glancing around as if she recognized the charge in the air.

It was his last chance to send her away.

He didn't take it.

"Close the door," he said in a voice so deep it warped.

"You suffer."

"Close it."

Click.

There was only a single lamp on, that one by the chaise longue, and the butter-yellow light seemed to act as a sound buffer, everything inside the room amplified, everything outside silenced.

Then again, maybe it was the color of her eyes doing that.

As she approached, she pulled up her sleeve, exposing her pale wrist. And in response, his fangs didn't descend so much as punch out from his upper jaw—and shit, he didn't want what she was going to offer. He wanted at her throat . . . he wanted her naked and underneath his body, his canines in her neck as his cock—

Moaning, he kicked his head back and gripped the duvet in his fists.

"Worry not," she said in a rush. "Here, take of me."

In spite of all the air in the room, his lungs began to starve for oxygen, shallow breaths pumping in and out of his open mouth.

And then her hand brushed his arm, and he moaned again, trying to twist away. Gritting his teeth, he knew this was a *very* bad thing.

"Selena, I can't. . . . I can't do this. . . ."

"I don't understand."

"You should leave. . . ." Fuck, he could barely get the words out. "Leave or I'm going to . . ."

"Feed," she cut in sharply. "You need to feed—"

"Selena . . ."

"You must take my vein—"

"—you'd better go . . ."

They were talking over each other, getting nowhere, when she took charge of the situation. At first, he thought his brain was playing tricks on him—but no, that was the scent of fresh blood in the room. Hers.

She'd scored her wrist.

Big mistake.

With a roar, he went for her—and not her wrist. His hands unlatched from the wadded sheeting and he grabbed her, taking her by the shoulders and flipping her across his lap to lay her out flat on the mattress.

He mounted her a split second later, the duvet folding up between them, his hands pinning her wrists up on the pillows by her head.

One look in her shocked eyes stopped him dead. And yet he couldn't get off her.

Screw panting; he was breathing like a freight train, his body hard all over, his muscles twitching. "Shit . . ." he moaned as he dropped his head.

Get off of her, he ordered his body. Get the fuck off of—

The undulation beneath him took a moment to register. And then he realized it was her. She was . . . moving against him, and not as in she wanted to get free. Her eyes, once alarmed, were now glazing over, her lips parting as she arched into him.

She wanted him. Fucking hell, her scent was flaring into his nose, her blood running fast and hot as his own.

"Selena," he groaned. "I'm sorry. . . ."

"For what," she said roughly.

"This."

He struck her throat, fangs sinking deep, blood rushing onto his tongue, down his throat. And as he nursed at her, his body pumped against the wadded duvet, desperately trying to find her core through the layers of sheeting, his cock throbbing, the friction making everything worse.

As he drank hard, a growl reverberated out of his chest, filling the air with the sound of a male animal getting what he needed—or at least, part of what he needed. And in a way, maybe it was good that he was so blood starved. Otherwise, the sexual urge would have taken precedence.

As long as all he did was feed? They could come back from that.

Anything further, and they were—

Mine, a voice deep inside of him announced.

Mine.

Selena had thought she was prepared for this. She'd thought she was ready to come up here to this room, to find Trez in this bed, to have him at her wrist. She'd assumed she was ready to do her duty and keep the secret of wanting him to herself.

Instead, she was blown away. By the power of him unleashed, by the strike at her neck . . . by the sexual desperation with which she needed him. And there was more. Crushed under his great weight, feeling his hips surge and retreat on top of her, knowing that he was drinking of her vein, she was at least momentarily unafraid of the statues in the cemetery up above. How could she fear them now? Not with her body like this, with her arms and legs, her very sex, loose and hot and desperate to receive him.

Opening her eyes, she looked up at the ceiling beyond his dark shoulders. "Take me," she breathed into his growl. "Take me. . . ."

In response, his fingers slid up to her palms and steepled in between, holding instead of trapping as he nuzzled at her vein, his cheek stubbly against her skin. She had an instinct to part her legs, and as soon as she did, the pressure of his pumping torso zeroed in on that aching heart of her, pushing, rubbing—but it was too indistinct. She wanted it focused.

She wanted them both naked as he did that.

There was no moving, however. Trez had her pinned and the frustration she felt amplified the hunger that had taken root, the denial of what she wanted ratcheting up the need. Pushing against his palms, she got nowhere, her strength nothing compared to his.

"More," she moaned as she curled her spine upward, her breasts tightening painfully, her heart thumping under her ribs.

Each pull against her throat, every draw on her vein, all the suction he brought upon her, took her closer to some kind of precipice—and she'd never wanted to fall so badly before. Even though she didn't know where the landing would take her, she couldn't imagine that she could rise any higher without splintering apart.

She was wrong.

Except then he stopped.

With a curse, he seemed to have to force himself to retract—and even then, he didn't go far from her neck. With his fangs out of her skin, his head hung there for the longest time. Until he started licking at the puncture wounds to close them.

This can't be over, she thought frantically. This can't be—

"I'm sorry," he said in a guttural voice.

"Please . . . please," she said hoarsely. "Don't stop. . . ."

This brought his head up and around. And, dearest Virgin Scribe, he was magnificent. Thick lips parted, black eyes glossy, a high blush upon his cheeks, he was both satiated and hungry still, the male animal only partially fed.

And she was well aware what part of his meal was missing.

Yet when she tried to reach for him, her hands pushed against an iron hold.

"Take me," she begged. "Down below . . . I need you there—"

"Jesus *Christ*," he spat as he leaped off her, all but throwing himself from the bed.

Up on his feet, he seemed to lose coordination, but then he stalked off to the bathroom and slammed the door shut.

Cold rushed in all over her. And not just because his body no longer blanketed her own. It was shame. Embarrassment.

But how could she have gotten that wrong?

Sitting up required a couple of tries. And when she was finally off the pillows, she pushed at the mess of her hair and tugged the lapels of her robing back into place. Twisting around, she looked at where she had lain. Her blood was a bright red stain on the white sheets.

Her wrist was still bleeding from where she had scored it.

Taking care of that with her own tongue, she shifted her legs off the bed. They felt too weak to hold her weight, but she had no choice, save to call them into service.

Going over to the closed bathroom door, she placed her hand upon the panels. On the far side, she could hear him breathing hard.

As she opened her mouth, intending to apologize for her temerity and then take her leave—she took a deep inhale—

The scent of his sexual arousal was strong as ever, and she frowned. He wanted her, still. So why had he. . . .

At least her mortification could ease a little. "Trez?"

"I'm sorry."

Testing the knob, she found things unlocked—but as she began to open the door, he barked, "No! Don't—"

As the scent of that arousal grew even stronger in her nose, she peered inside. He was across the way, braced against the sinks, his head hanging low. And whatever torment he was going through, his body was clear with where it stood.

His erection was . . . just as incredible as the rest of him.

"Shut the goddamn door!" he hollered.

Except she wasn't going to listen to that. Not after her visit to the cemetery up above. Not after having been reminded as recently as this morning exactly what was waiting for her: Her body was just beginning its death process, but she knew well enough that once the joints began to grind, time was of the essence.

This could be her one and only opportunity to be with a male—and she wanted this. In fact, she would have wanted him even if her future weren't as yet breathing down her neck.

And his body desired hers. Clearly.

For all those reasons, she pushed the door completely open.

"Fucking hell," he muttered. Then more loudly, "Selena, *please*."

"I want . . . this."

His head shook. "You don't."

"I want . . . you."

"You can't—for God's sake, Selena, I hurt you."

"You did not."

He looked over the carved muscles of his upper arm. His eyes were glowing green. "Don't push me right now. You're not going to like what happens."

"Are you going to make me beg?"

His huge body swayed, as if she'd sucked his strength instead of given him more. "Don't do this to either of us, Selena. Not tonight."

She frowned. "Tonight?"

He grabbed for a towel and wrapped it around his hips. "Just go. I'm so . . . grateful you gave me what I need. But I can't do this right now."

Giving her his back, he stood there, staring at a blank wall.

Selena pulled her lapels closer. "What ails—"

"For the love of fucking God, I'm already fucking my parents over, okay? I do not want to add you to the list."

"Whatever do you speak of?"

When he didn't reply, she went over to him, her cloth-soled shoes making no sound. When she touched his shoulder, he jumped.

"Trez—"

He wheeled around and backed up at the same time, slamming into the wall. "Please—"

"Speak unto me."

His frantic eyes bounced around her face, her shoulders, her body. "I don't want to talk right now. I want . . ."

"What?" she whispered.

"You know what . . . goddamn me to hell . . . I want you. So you really fucking have to leave."

They stared at each other for the longest time. And then she decided to take control.

Reaching for the tie at her waist, Selena's hands shook as she pulled apart the bow and let the strip fall to the floor. Uncurling, the robing split asunder, exposing the center of her body, her aching breasts catching the two halves and holding them.

But her sex was on display. And his eyes went down . . . and stayed there.

Trez's lips parted, his fangs descending anew; and now she was the one weaving on her feet as her core responded even further, blooming between her legs, sending out a call.

Which he answered by falling to his knees.

She wasn't sure what she expected, but it wasn't what he did next.

Reaching up, he slipped his hands under the robe's halves and onto her waist. Warmth was her first impression—and that was followed by an immediate electric sensation, a sizzle that was transmitted from him to her through his broad palms.

He was so tall that his head came up to just below her breasts, and all she could think of doing was running her hands over his soft, tightly curled hair—

She lost that initiative as his mouth brushed against her sternum. And then her upper belly. And then her navel.

He was curling himself backward onto his heels as he went down, and she . . . was he going to—

Selena moaned and nearly fell over as he brushed the top of her bare sex with his lips; His grip on her waist was the only thing that kept her upright.

The nuzzling was soft and gentle, his face and nose rubbing on her pelvis, his lips kissing the outside of her cleft.

And she wanted more.

Just as she was trying to form words, his tongue extended in for a probing lick, the invasion so languorous, she wasn't spooked at how foreign it was. And then it came back, reentering, taking another taste of her.

He was purring now.

Falling forward, she put her hands on his shoulders and widened her stance—even as she became impatient with the effort it took to stay standing: She wanted all her concentration to be on him and what he was doing to her. Worrying about balance and coordination—

He solved that problem by lifting her off her feet and laying her down on the fur rug in front of the claw-foot tub.

Giving herself up to wherever this would go, she reached her arms over her head and arched her back, her breasts peaking and casting aside the robe halves, her body revealed to him.

"Fucking hell," he gritted as his eyes traveled from the crown of her head to her tight nipples . . . past the flat plane of her belly, to her sex and her legs.

His dark hand was a contrast to the paleness of her skin as he drew a lazy stroke from her collarbone to one of her breasts. Capturing the weight in his palm, she groaned and undulated, her knees bending up . . . and falling open.

His towel dropped away from his body, exposing his hairless beauty and his formidable sex.

"Take me," she ordered him. "Teach me."

THIRTY

His brother's tears had smelled like summer rain on still-warm asphalt.

As Wrath stalked his way back from the training center, every word that he and Tohr had shared, each syllable, and all the silences in between resonated like aches after a fight: Down to his bones, down to his marrow, he felt the remnants of the conversation they'd had by the pool.

One comment kept coming back to him.

They are as empty without a young as we are empty without them.

It was probably the only thing that really punched past all the fear: For him, waking up without Beth had been the worst kind of revelation—and if that was the way she felt without a baby, then it was going to be a cold-bed overtime for the both of them.

Look at him. He was in a life he hated, and he was one hallucination short of psychotic. He didn't want that for her—and he knew all too well how being with the one you loved wasn't enough if you were honestly, fundamentally unhappy.

The problem? The fact that he saw the light about where she was

coming from didn't change all the shit he was worried about. It just made him feel their incompatibility all the more viscerally.

George sneezed.

Wrath switched hands on the halter, leaned down, and patted the dog's flank. "This tunnel always gets to your nose."

God, what the fuck was he going to do? Assuming she was going into her needing that was . . . but maybe he was wrong and that would save them. Although that was for how long? Sooner or later she was going to become fertile.

When George signaled it was time to stop and go up the shallow stairs, Wrath punched in the code, opened the way, and a moment later, they were in the foyer and rounding the base of the grand staircase. First Meal had already been served, the Brotherhood in there talking, the voices deep and loud. Pausing, he listened to the group and thought of that night Beth had transitioned. She'd come up from the basement at Darius's, and he'd blown his brothers' minds by taking her into his arms in front of them.

Made sense. Back then, they'd never seen him like that around a female.

And when he'd returned from the kitchen with the bacon and chocolate she'd needed to satisfy her post-transition cravings, the Brotherhood had been down on one knee around her, their heads bowed, their daggers nailed into the hardwood floor.

They had been acknowledging her as their future queen. Even if she hadn't known it at the time.

"My lord?"

Wrath looked over his shoulder with a frown. "Hey, what's doing there, counselor."

As Saxton walked over, his scent was all about the not-good. "I must speak with you."

Behind his wraparounds, Wrath closed his eyes. "I'm sure you do," he muttered. "But I have to go to my Beth."

"It's urgent. I've just come from—"

"Look, no offense, but I've backseated my *shellan* for the last . . . shit, I don't know how long. Tonight, she's coming first. When I'm done, if there's time, I'll hitch up." He angled his head downward. "George. Take me to Beth."

"My lord—"

"As soon as I can, my man. But not a second sooner."

With quick efficiency, he and his dog jogged up the grand staircase and headed for the door that led up to the third floor—

From out of nowhere, a lurching sensation made him stumble on his feet until he had to throw a hand out and catch the wall.

The weirdness passed as soon as it hit him, though, his balance righting itself, his shitkickers once again solidly on the floor.

He turned his head left and right, like he had when he'd still had some vision to go by. There was nothing coming at him, however. No one pushing him from behind. No mad gusts of wind blowing in from the sitting room at the other end of the hall. No toys to trip over on the floor.

Weird.

And whatever. He just wanted to get to his Beth—and he sensed that she was upstairs, in their private quarters.

Waiting for him.

As he started up the final staircase, he thought of his parents. From everything he had been told, they had wanted him badly. No discord on that issue. He had been prayed for and worked for and given over to them by fate, or destiny, or luck.

He wished he and his Beth were on the same page like that. He truly did.

As Anha heard her name from a great distance, she felt as though she were drowning.

Sucked down deep into unconsciousness, she knew herself to be summoned, and she wanted to respond to the call. It was her mate, her beloved, her hellren *who was speaking unto her. And yet she could not reach him, her will tethered by some great weight that refused to let her go free.*

No, not a weight. Nay, it was something introduced unto her body, something foreign to her nature.

Mayhap the young, she wondered with horror.

But 'twas not supposed to be as such. The bairn she had conceived within her womb was supposed to be a blessing. A stroke of luck, a gift from the Scribe Virgin to ensure the next King.

And yet it had been after her needing that she had taken to feeling the illness. She had hidden the symptoms and the worry as well as she could, shielding her beloved from the concern that had bloomed within her. She had lost that fight, however, had fallen to the floor at his side at the festival. . . .

The last thing she had heard clearly was him calling her name.

Swallowing, she tasted the familiar thick wine of his blood, but the rushing power that came with imbibing from his vein did not follow.

The sickness was claiming her, piece by piece, robbing her of faculty and function alike.

She was going to die from whate'er this was.

Good-bye—she wanted to say good-bye to Wrath. If she could not reverse this, at least she could bid him sweet love as she went unto the Fade.

Summoning the dredges of her life force, she pulled against the rope that locked her unto her passing, yanking with desperation, praying for the strength she needed to see him one last time.

In response, her eyelids lifted slowly and only partway, but yes, she saw her beloved, his head bowed, his body collapsed beside their bedding platform.

He was weeping openly.

Her mind commanded her hand to reach out, her mouth to open and speak, her head to turn unto him.

Nothing moved; nothing was uttered.

The only thing that came of it was a single tear that gathered itself at the corner of her eye, plumping up until it lost hold of her lash and slipped down her cold cheek.

And then it was done, her lids re-closing, her good-bye given, her strength done for.

At once, a white fog boiled up from the corners of the black field of her vision, the wafting rolls of it replacing the blindness that was wrought upon her. And from out of its curls and strange illumination, a door arrived to her, coming forward as if birthed from the cloud.

She knew without being told that if she opened it, if she reached out for the golden knob and opened the portal, she would be welcomed unto the Fade—and there would be no going back. She was also aware of a conviction that if she did not act within a prescribed time, she would lose her chance and become lost in the In Between.

Anha did not want to go.

She feared for Wrath without her. There were so few to be trusted at court—so many to be feared.

The legacy left by his father had been a rotten one. It had just not been evident at the start.

"Wrath . . ." she said unto the fog. "Oh, Wrath . . ."

The yearning tone in her voice echoed around, rebounding in her own ears as well as the white-on-white landscape.

Looking upward, she had some hope that the Scribe Virgin would appear in robed splendor and take pity on her.

"Wrath . . ."

How could she depart the Earth when so much of her would be left behind—

Anha frowned. The door before her seemed to have moved back. Unless she had imagined it?

No, it was retreating. Slowly, inexorably.

"Wrath!" she shouted. "Wrath, I don't want to leave! Wraaaaaaaaaath—"

"Yes?"

Anha screamed as she wheeled around. At first, she had no idea what was confronting her: It was a little boy of mayhap seven or eight, black of hair, pale of eye, his body so painfully scrawny, her immediate thought was that she must feed him.

"Who ever are you?" she croaked. And yet she knew. She knew.

"You called me."

She put her hand upon her lower belly. "Wrath . . . ?"

"Yes, mahmen.*" The young focused on the door with eyes that seemed ancient. "Are you going to cross unto the Fade?"*

"I have no choice."

"Untrue."

"I am dying."

"You do not have to."

"I am losing the fight."

"Drink. Drink of what is in your mouth."

"I cannot. I cannot swallow."

The cadence of their words was increasing, faster and faster, as if he knew she was running out of time . . . and by extension, he was, too.

Those eyes of his, such a pale green . . . and there was something strange about them. The pupils were too small.

"I cannot drink," she repeated. Dearest Virgin Scribe, her mind was muddled beyond measure.

"Follow me and you will be able to."

"How?"

He held out his hand to her. "Come with me. I shall take you back home, and then you will drink."

She looked to the door. There was a pull to it, a draw that made her want to reach out and complete the cycle that had started as soon as she had fainted unto the floor.

But what she felt toward her son was stronger.

Turning away, she gave the portal her back. "Return me to your father?"

"Yes. Back to him and to me."

Walking forward, she clasped the warm palm of her son instead of the knob of the door, and lead her on he did, escorting her out of the white fog, away from the death that had come for her, toward . . .

"Wrath?" she whispered into the darkness that claimed them both.

"Yes?"

"Thank you. I did not want to go."

"I know, mahmen. *And someday, you will repay me thus."*

"I will?"

"Yes. And all shall be well—"

She didn't hear the rest of what he said: Just as a suction had pulled her under, a sudden explosion propelled her outward, the push hitting every part of her at the same moment. And then a great wind hit her in the face, stripping her hair back, rendering her breathless.

Anha knew not where she would end.

All she could do was pray that what had come to her was in fact her progeny . . . and not some demon to mislead her. The only thing worse than not going back would be to be cheated of an eternity with those whom she loved. . . .

"Wrath!" she screamed into the maelstrom. "Wraaaaaaaaaath . . . !"

THIRTY-ONE

Trez knew that none of this should be happening.

Not the way he'd taken Selena's throat instead of her wrist. Not that crazy-ass shit on the bed. And really, totally not the fact that she was laid out on the fur rug, her breasts bare to his eyes, her sex ready for the taking, her scent all about the aroused.

"Take me," she said in the sexiest voice he had ever heard. "Teach me. . . ."

Her stare was dead to marks on his, and on some level, he didn't understand. She'd turned him down before, and then . . . now she wanted him?

Who cares. His erection throbbed. *Who cares! Take her! She wants us!*

Us. Like there were two parts of him. And actually, that wasn't as moronic as it sounded. His cock was, in fact, talking on its own at this point.

"Selena," he groaned. "Are you sure? I get any more of you, anywhere . . . and I'm not going to be able to stop."

Hell, he was barely holding on to this pause.

She reached her hand out and ran it up his forearm, stroking him. "Yes."

"I shouldn't be doing this," he heard himself say.

Shut up! Sit down!

Great, now he was channeling Howard Stern's father.

"Selena, I'm not . . . worthy of this."

"I want you. And that makes you worthy."

I told you not to be stupid, you moron.

Yup, that was defo Ben Stern.

Trez closed his lids and swayed, thinking it seemed a goddamn cruel twist of fate to be offered this tonight.

"Please," she said.

Aw, fuck. Like he was going to say no to her?

When he opened his eyes again, he didn't know how he was going to get them both through the sex in one piece. It was the worst possible moment to open this can of worms, but he wasn't going to turn away from her: He was raw in places he didn't like to acknowledge even to himself, and this was going to be a Band-Aid, something that was going to help him.

Even though only temporarily.

And at least he could do his damnedest to make it good for her.

Moving up on Selena, he braced his arms on either side of her undulating body and slowly, inexorably brought his mouth down until it was barely a millimeter above hers.

"No going back," he growled.

She linked her arms behind his neck. "No regrets."

Fair enough.

To seal the deal, he kissed her, brushing his mouth against hers, plying at her until she opened herself on her own. His tongue had already penetrated into her sex—but only by a degree. Hell, he'd shocked himself with that licking. Now? There was no holding back. He extended himself into her fully, fusing his mouth to hers, tilting his head to the side as he drew against her lips.

It was the strangest dichotomy. He was so ready to take her, prepared to split her legs wide and drive into that hot, wet place between her thighs—and yeah, he wanted to mark her internally with his come, leave his scent all over her inside and out, make it so no male dared to touch her, look at her.

Yet he had all the time in the world for this kissing.

Then again, she was sweet as ice wine, smooth as double-batch bourbon, heady as port. And he was drunk before he even lifted his head for a breath.

But he wasn't going to stay forever. There was another place he wanted to get back to.

As he kissed his way down to her neck, he regretted the raw marks he'd left at her vein, and brushed them with his lips, once, twice.

"I'm sorry," he said, roughly.

"Whatever for?"

He had to reclose his eyes as that husky voice of hers penetrated his haze—and promptly sexed him up even more. What had she asked . . . oh, yeah.

"I shouldn't have been so rough."

"Well, I didn't mind being held down. At all."

Annnnnnnnnd didn't that get him seeing double.

"Are you going to return to where you were?" she asked.

Fuck yeah. "Yes . . . right now. If you want—"

The undulation of her body and that moan was the best "I do" he'd ever heard.

Trying to keep a lid on his inner beast, he kissed his way over to her collarbone and then had to pull back and just look at her. Her breasts were the most beautiful thing he'd ever seen: She was perfectly built, her nipples tight on top of the pale swells, her skin smooth, her breathing a taunt to his self-control.

He was as careful as he had been with her mouth.

Extending his tongue, he licked a circle around her nipple—and going by the way her hands speared into his hair, she approved.

"Oh . . ." she groaned.

He smiled before he sucked her in. Nursing at her, he eased onto his side and swept a hand down to her waist, her hip, her thigh . . . her inner thigh.

She gave way for him like water, her body loose and trusting as he suckled and inched his touch higher, and higher. He was almost at her core, and planning exactly where to stroke her when—

An image of a human invaded the space between his ears.

At first, he couldn't figure out what the fuck his brain had coughed up . . . but then he recognized the random woman as one he'd nailed in the back of a car over a year ago. And the clarity was a killer. He saw everything in HD, the lipstick smeared on her front teeth, the mascara smudges under her eyes, her botched boob job where one of her nipples was wall-eyed.

But none of that was the worst part.

No, the worst was the way her head moved up and back, up and back—because he was inside of her. His cock was in her sex, going in and out, the rhythm growing faster so that he could come and be done with the session.

His erection, the one that he was getting ready to slip into Selena, had been in a cesspool. Had been in . . . hundreds of dirty human women who hadn't brought up safe sex or STD tests or whether or not they'd already contracted AIDS from letting sluts like him into their panties.

The fact that he couldn't contract their diseases did not matter in the slightest.

Filthy was filthy.

Jerking back, he hissed and closed his eyes, trying to order an evac for all of that shit.

"Trez?"

"Sorry, I . . ." Shaking his head, he refocused on her breasts—and felt nauseous from self-hatred. "I'm just—"

Another human woman tackled his brain, this one that real estate agent he'd done at the warehouse he'd just bought: He pictured her hands spread against the wall as he fucked her from behind, her wedding ring flashing.

"I'm sorry," he grunted. And then it was more with the head shaking—like the memories were objects he could knock off his table of consciousness. "I'm . . ."

In rapid succession, he saw the brunette he'd let suck him off in his office. The redhead he'd done with that blond in the club bathroom. The threesome with those college girls, the Goth at the cemetery, the waitress at Sal's, the pharmacist when he'd gone to get Motrin one afternoon, the bartender at that place, the woman he'd seen at the car dealership . . .

Faster and faster, until the images were like bullets one after another after another, firing into his brain.

As he peeled off of Selena, it seemed both bizarre and totally appropriate that the only thing he could think of was that the Shadows were right.

Sex with humans had contaminated him.

And he was paying the price for the poison, right here and now.

Sitting at the kitchen table, Assail could only stare at his cousins. The pair of contract killers, drug dealers, and enforcers had not only washed up before the meal, they were now easing back in their seats and looking like they wanted to loosen their pants.

As Marisol's grandmother got to her feet again, Assail shook his head. "Madam, you must enjoy this food on which you worked so diligently."

"I am enjoying." She headed back for the counter and cut more bread. "These boys, they need to eat more. Too thin, too thin."

At this rate, she was going to turn his backups into—what was the expression, sofa potatoes?

And what do you know, even though those two males were stuffed, they took another slice of her homemade bread, and dutifully layered on the sweet butter.

Unbelievable.

Assail shifted his eyes over to Marisol. Her head was down, her fork testing the mettle of the food. She hadn't eaten much, but she had opened the copper-colored pill bottle Doc Jane had given her and taken one of the gray-and-orange capsules inside.

He wasn't the only one watching her. The eagle eyes of her grandmother were monitoring everything: Every move of that fork, each sip from her glass of water, all the non-eating that was going on.

Marisol, on the other hand, was watching no one. After the emotional reunion with her bloodline, she had closed up, her stare staying on the meal, her voice limited to yeses and nos about condiments and seasonings.

She had retreated to a place he didn't want her to dwell in.

"Marisol," he said.

Her head came up. "Yes?"

"Would you like me to show you to your room?" The instant that came out of his mouth, he glanced at the grandmother. "If you will permit me, of course."

According to the old ways, the senior female would have been Marisol's *ghardian*, and though he rarely showed respect to humans, it felt appropriate to pay mindfulness to the woman.

Marisol's grandmother nodded. "Yes. I have things for her. There."

Sure enough, there was a rolling suitcase parked by the archway into the great room.

As the grandmother went back to her own food, he could have sworn there was a slight smile on her mouth.

"I am just exhausted." Marisol got to her feet and picked up her plate. "I feel like I could sleep forever."

Let us not talk of such, he thought as he, too, stood.

After she kissed her grandmother's cheek and spoke in her mother tongue, he followed her, putting his dishes in the sink, and then going over to the suitcase. He wanted to put an arm around her. He did not. He did, however, pick up the luggage when she went for it.

"Allow me," he said.

The ease with which she gave in told him that she was as yet in pain. And assuming the lead, he took her out to the stairs. There were two sets: one that went up to his chamber, another that proceeded down into the basement, where there were five bedrooms.

The grandmother and the cousins were on the lower level.

Glancing over his shoulder, she was silent and grave behind him, her eyes drooping, her shoulders slumped from fatigue that was more than just physical.

"I shall give you my room," he told her. "In privacy."

It would not do for him to stay with her. Not with her grandmother in the house.

Even though that was where he wanted to be.

"Thank you," she murmured.

Before he knew what he was doing, he willed the reinforced pocket door out of the way, exposing the highly polished black-and-white marble stairs.

Oh . . . shit, he thought.

"Motion detectors, huh," she said, without missing a beat.

"Indeed."

As she mounted the steps, Assail tried not to notice her body's movements. It seemed the height of disrespect—especially as she was limping.

But dearest Virgin Scribe, he wanted her like nothing and no one else.

His quarters took up the entire top floor, the octagonal space providing three-hundred-sixty-degree views of the river, the distant urban core of Caldwell, the forested flats to the west. The bed was a circular one with a curving headboard, its platform set directly in the center of the room beneath a mirror ceiling. The "furniture" was all built-in: burled walnut cabinetry served as side tables, bureaus, and the desk area, absolutely none of it getting in the way of the glass walls.

Hitting a switch by the door, he triggered the drapes, which swept forth from their hidden compartments, their flowing lengths billowing as they locked into place.

"For your modesty," he said. "The bath is through here."

He reached around a doorjamb and flipped another switch. The color scheme of the bedroom was almond and cream, and it was repeated in the marble floors and walls and counters of the loo. Funny, he had never thought one way or the other about the decor, but now he was glad for the calming tones. Marisol deserved the peace she had earned in her hard-won battles.

As she walked about the bathroom, her fingers drifted over the veins in the marble as if she were trying to ground herself.

Pivoting around, she faced him. "Where are you sleeping?"

Never one to hesitate in stating his position, he nonetheless cleared his throat. "Downstairs. In a guest room."

She crossed her arms over her chest. "Isn't there another bed up here?"

He felt his brows lift. "There is a pullout cot."

"Can you stay? Please."

Assail found himself clearing his throat again. "Are you sure that's proper with your grandmother here?"

"I've got the heebs so badly, if I'm alone, I'll never be able to sleep."

"Then I shall be pleased to accommodate the request."

He just had to make sure that was all he did. . . .

"Good. Thank you." She eyed the Jacuzzi tub beneath its windowsill. "That looks amazing."

"Allow me to fill it for you." He went forth and cranked the brass handles, the rushing water crystal clear and soon-to-be hot. "It is very deep."

Not that he'd tried it out himself.

"There is also a *petite cuisine* here." He popped open a hidden door, revealing a squat refrigerator, pint-size microwave, and coffeepot. "And there are victuals in the cupboard above if you get hungry."

Indeed, he was a master of the obvious, was he not.

Awkward silence.

He shut the little cabinet. "I shall wait downstairs whilst you attend to your—"

Marisol's breakdown arrived without preamble, the sobs racking her shoulders as she put her head in her hands and tried to hold the noise in.

Assail had no experience comforting females, but he went to her without missing a beat. "Dearest one," he murmured, as he pulled her against his chest.

"I can't do this. It's not working—I can't—"

"Cannot what? Speak unto me."

Muffled into his shirt, her reply was clear enough. "I can't pretend it didn't happen." She lifted her head, her eyes luminous from the tears. "It's what I see every time I blink."

"Shh . . ." He tucked a strand of hair behind her ear. "It's all right."

"It's not. . . ."

Cupping her face in his hands, he felt both rage and helplessness. "Marisol . . ."

In lieu of a response, she grasped his wrists, squeezing—and in the tight quiet that followed, he had the sense she was asking something of him.

Dear God, she wanted something from him.

It was in the stillness of her body, the wildness of her stare, that grip upon him.

Assail closed his eyes briefly. Mayhap he was misreading this, but he didn't think so—although in any event, she could hardly be credited with sound thinking, given all she had been through.

He stepped back. "The tub is almost full," he said roughly. "I shall go confirm the accommodations of your grandmother, yes? Call upon me if you need aught before I return."

Indicating the in-house intercom, he hastily made his exit, closing the door behind him. Falling back against it, he wanted to bang his head a number of times, but did not want to alert her to his conflict.

Passing a hand down the front of his slacks, he intended to rearrange his erection into a socially acceptable position—but the instant contact was made, he groaned and knew he needed to take care of things.

He barely made it down into the bathroom off the first floor office. Locking himself in, he braced his hands on the marble of the sink and hung his head.

He lasted three rapid heartbeats.

The belt came undone with the alacrity of fabric falling apart, and the fasteners of his slacks were just as accommodating—and then his cock, his rock-hard, throbbing cock exploded out from his hips.

Biting his lower lip, he palmed himself and started stroking, his full weight leaning on that arm he had thrown out, the pleasure intense to the point of pain.

The moan he let out threatened to carry, but there was nothing to be done about that. He was too far down the rabbit hole to stop or even alter the course or his response.

Faster, up and back—until biting his lip wasn't enough: He had to turn his head into his arm and bite his biceps, his fangs sinking deep into the muscle through his sweater, through his shirt.

The orgasm hit him hard, the peaks sharp as knives going into him, the ejaculations caught in his free palm as he covered himself.

Even at the height of release, he honored his Marisol: He deliberately kept all images from his mind, determined to make this solely a physical act.

When it was done, he was not relieved in the slightest.

And he felt dirty even after he cleaned himself.

THIRTY-TWO

Beth found the medication kit on the sink in the bathroom. After freaking out about the condition of the pool table and everything else, she'd gone upstairs and immediately headed across the bedroom to take a shower—whereupon she'd discovered the black leather clutch on the counter between her sink and Wrath's.

At first, she thought it was a glasses case for one of Wrath's pairs of wraparounds, except it was soft, not hard.

And it was as she reached out to pick the thing up that the first wave hit her.

Hot, moist air bloomed all over her body, from the back of her neck to the lengths of her legs, from her face and throat to her belly and down to her feet.

As if she'd already turned on the shower.

Throwing off the sensation, she unzipped the two halves and opened the kit. Not sunglasses, no. Instead, there was a glass vial with a clear liquid in it, and three syringes, all strapped in like they were going for a car ride and wanted to follow the seat-belt laws. The label on the little bottle was facing in, and she twisted things in place to see what it said.

Morphine.

She'd never seen anything like this in any of Wrath's things. And it wasn't hard to extrapolate that he might have gone to Doc Jane—or hell, even Havers—to get prepared in the event she went into her—

Another blast of heat came over her, and she frowned up at the vent above her head. Maybe Fritz needed to have the HVAC systems looked at—

As her knees gave out without any warning, she barely had time to catch herself on the counter, the kit scattering into Wrath's sink, her two Chanel perfume bottles knocking over. With the groan of a wounded animal, she tried to haul herself up, but her body didn't listen to the signals.

It was on its own path.

A tremendous, volcanic power exploded out of her, robbing her of the strength to keep herself off the floor. Slumping down, she curled herself around her core, holding her lower belly, jacking her knees to her chest. The cool marble barely registered as the forest fire under her skin shifted into a driving urge, an overwhelming sexual need that required one and only one thing.

Her mate.

Flipping herself onto her back, she rolled over to her other side, and then onto her belly. Clawing at the slick floor, she rubbed her thighs together, trying to find some relief, some respite from the ache that was taking over everything.

How many hours? She tried to think—how many hours had Layla said this lasted?

Twenty-four? No, longer—

Beth cried out as another blast tore through her body, sweat bursting from her pores, fangs descending into her mouth.

And this was only the beginning, a distant part of her acknowledged. Just the first salvo—it was going to get worse: As time wore on, the hormones were going to render her incapable of anything but respiration.

To think she had volunteered for this?

Madness.

The needing was like a pair of fists torquing her body to the point where she knew she must have broken bones. No, no, this was going to kill her—how could it not? And the need for sex? It wasn't even about having a child. It was about survival—

Wrath.

Oh, God, he was going to come up here. Whenever he was done talking to Tohr. And he was going to find her on the floor—and then what?

Even through the maelstrom of hormones, she was able to think that through to its conclusion—he was going to be in a horrible position: either service her and live with consequences he hated, or watch her suffer.

Which he would never do.

Her palms squeaked against the slick floor as she pushed her thousand-pound torso up. Climbing the drawer pulls like they were a ladder, she had to take a break at the counter level, her vision swimming, her eyes struggling to focus as her body begged for sex it simply couldn't have.

Before she succumbed to this entirely, she was going to take care of things on her own.

Her hands were shaking so badly, it took her several tries to capture the kit, but eventually, she got the thing and brought it down to the floor. Time for another breather on the cool marble. But not too long a delay. The waves were coming harder and faster each time.

Fumbling fingers, the glass vial bouncing out of its tether, skittering away.

She was crying as she dragged her body after it, arm out, hand pawing—

"Beth," a voice said. "Oh, God . . . *Beth*."

A masculine palm came down from out of the sky, reaching for her, searching through thin air for her—and through the morass, she struggled to process the hows and whys—except then her body made the connection for her.

Wrath.

As his shitkickers came into her vision, her hormones blew up, responding to his presence by ratcheting up to a level that was Hell not just on Earth, but under her skin, boiling her blood, making her sex scream for what only he could give her.

But that could never be.

"Go . . ." she cried out in a cracked voice. "Drug me . . . or give me the—"

Wrath knelt down with her. "Beth—"

"Give me the drugs! I'll do it—"

"I can't let you—"

Pegging him with a hard stare, she didn't have any energy to fight with him. "Give me the fucking drugs!"

Wrath's body had begun to respond as he took the stairs up to their quarters—and by the time he made it into the bathroom, he knew exactly what was doing. As well as what the solution was: Every instinct in him was roaring to service his female, to ease her suffering in the only way that mattered.

Shaking himself, he dropped to his knees, patting around for her, following the sounds of her voice and the jerking movements of her body against the marble floor. She was incoherent, writhing in pain, lost to the throes of the needing.

"Give me the fucking drugs!"

It took a moment for her demand to sink in, and then he realized that this was a moment in life when the path that was presented had only two forks—and in his mind, neither was a good one.

"Wrath . . ." she groaned. "Wrath . . . just drug me."

He thought of the kit he'd left on the counter. All he had to do was open it, fill a syringe and inject the morphine into her. And then her suffering would be eased—

Only partially, a part of him pointed out—

A fresh onslaught of need crushed Beth's body, her gasp rising to the volume of another scream, her limbs knocking into him as she spasmed.

He wasn't sure exactly when his mind made itself up. But suddenly, his hands were at the button fly of his leathers, the medication forgotten, the direction chosen.

"Hold on, *leelan*," he grunted as he released his erection. "Hold on, I'm coming. . . ."

Too fucking right.

Except as he felt around for her legs and went to take her jeans off, it took him for goddamn ever: Her body fought with him, thighs scissoring as she twisted and turned on the floor—but when he finally got the fuckers off her legs, he didn't waste time. He forced her to be still, digging his hands into her hips, and then he—

Beth yelled out his name as he entered her, her nails tearing into his shoulders, her breasts shoving up against his chest. He came immediately, his balls tightening up and then releasing—and he wasn't prepared for the response from her. As she orgasmed along with him, her sex milked him, pulling at his length, all but yanking at him—

He came again. So violently, he bit into his own tongue.

Pumping against her, pumping into her, he went hard and wild—until his body took a short pause to recover. And that was when he felt the difference he'd made in her: She, too, was at a brief rest, the tension in her body uncoiling as if her very molecules were taking a deep breath.

But before he could congratulate himself, he sensed something else. Sorrow permeated the air, the sad spice of it stopping him and tilting his head down as if he could look her in the eyes.

"Don't cry," he said roughly. "*Leelan*, don't—"

"Why are you doing this?" she moaned. "Why . . . ?"

There was only one answer. For tonight. . . . and evermore: "Because I love you more than anything else."

More than himself. More than any future young.

Her trembling hand brushed his face. "Are you sure?"

He replied by beginning to move deep inside of her again, the rolling penetrations sliding him in and out of her slick sex. And her response? The sound she let out was part purr, part groan, her hormones cranking up again.

For some reason, he thought about Vishous's vision.

I see you standing in a field of white. White, white is all around you and you are talking to the face in the heavens.

Your future is in your hands.

Jesus Christ, he felt like the Fade was breathing down his neck, stalking him—and even though that was true of every living thing, he felt targeted, like his expiration date was around the next corner.

It didn't mean that Beth was going to survive him. Quite the contrary. The most likely cause of his own demise . . . was going to be hers.

Dropping his head into her neck, he jacked his arms under her body and got serious about the fucking. Giving in, giving up, going with it was just like jumping off a cliff—the leap was the easy part because the free-falling didn't cost you shit.

It was the landing that was a killer.

THIRTY-THREE

Sola closed her eyes as she urged her body deeper into the belly of the tub. As the water level rose up to cover everything but her neck and head, its warmth made her realize how cold she had been, not on the surface of her skin, but down in her marrow.

Staring at her body in the dim light, she felt divorced from it, and she wasn't an idiot. Letting some thug grope her so that she could survive the night had created the separation—the thing now was . . . how to get a connection back?

She knew one sure solution.

But he had left her up here alone.

Man, she was having a hard time taking Assail's very sound advice. Pretending those hours, that fear, the horror hadn't existed seemed just as challenging as getting through the experience itself. But what was her other option? She couldn't breathe the same air as her grandmother, with everything she had done and seen right in the forefront of her brain.

Looking down at herself again, she moved her legs. Through the undulating waves, the bandage on her thigh distorted and re-formed, distorted and re-formed. Reaching through the water, she pulled the thing off, the adhesive coming free easily. She knew she wasn't supposed to get the wound with its stitches wet—oops.

Where the hell had Assail taken her to be treated? That place had been big money, from that gating system to the medical facility to all those people. Her brain had been trying to make sense of it, and the only conclusion she still kept coming to was *government.*

Even though he'd laughed that off, she couldn't think of any other explanation.

But he hadn't arrested her.

Closing her eyes, she wondered how he'd known how to find her. And what exactly he'd done to Benloise. Shit, that image of blood on Assail's face, around his mouth . . .

Who was going to be in charge of Caldwell now?

Duh.

Lifting a hand out of the water, she pushed her hair back. The wetness was wicking up the length of it, warming the base of her neck, making her perspire.

God, it was so quiet here.

She had lived in that house with her grandmother for almost a decade and she was used to the chatter of a neighborhood: cars driving by, dogs barking distantly, children yelping and yelling as they dribbled basketballs in driveways. Here? Only the water moving against the tub as she shifted her legs around—and she knew the silence wasn't just because there were no other houses immediately around them. This place had been built like a fortress, and it had tricks. High-level tricks.

She thought back to that night she had first come here at Benloise's request. Her mission had been to spy on Assail and his castle—and what she'd discovered had confounded her: Those strange holographic curtains. The security cameras. And the man himself.

Maybe she was over-thinking things. Maybe Assail and his buddies were just hard-core doomsday preppers. . . .

Closing her eyes, she gave up on everything and just floated in the water. She could have hit the jets, but her body had been through enough agitation, thank you very much—

Abruptly, emotions bubbled up, too many to hold.

Jerking upright, water splashed out and hit the floor. "Damn it."

How long was it going to take before she felt normal? How many nights of the jitters, and distractions at meals, and hidden crying jags was it going to take?

Getting out, she snagged a fluffy white towel off the counter and winced as it came in contact with her skin. It was like her nerves were on high alert, weather vanes catching each pull of the terry cloth, every blow from the vents above, all the shivers of water evaporating—

"You are beautiful."

Her wet heel squeaked as she wrenched around to the doorway. Assail was standing in the shadows, a dark, looming presence that made her feel more than just naked.

There was an electric moment as their eyes met.

And then she dropped her towel. "I need you."

The sound of him exhaling was all about a kind of defeat, but she didn't care. She could feel the sizzle in the air between them, and knew it was not one-sided.

"Now," she demanded.

"How can I say no," he whispered in that accented voice of his.

He came to her and took her face in his broad, warm hands—and it was such a relief to have him bend down and brush his lips against hers, plying her mouth, soothing her while sexing her up. And then she was off the floor and in his arms, being carried into the bedroom.

With incredible gentleness, he laid her out on the fur duvet as if she were in danger of shattering—which was too right. Even as her body responded to him by loosening up and going liquid, she was on the knife edge of breaking apart.

But this was going to help.

She pulled his shoulders down to her as he settled beside her on the bed—like he was worried that trapping her in any way might panic her. Except she wanted his weight to tether her; she wanted the feel of him pressing her down into the mattress, replacing memory with reality, shifting her consciousness through contact.

Sola pulled him onto her. Splitting her legs to make room, the erection behind his fly went right to her core, the pleated wool pants he had on scratching against her sensitive skin, making her moan—in a good way.

More with the kissing, his tongue slipping into her mouth, his palms going to her breasts. He was better than the water in the tub for her aches and pains, especially as he rolled his hips against her, stroking her sex with the promise of his own, bringing her along nice and easy. And as her nipples tightened to the point of pain, he seemed to know what she needed next, breaking the seal on her mouth and kissing his way down to them.

His tongue was lazy as he licked around one and then the other—before sucking in a tip and pulling at it.

Arching into the pleasure, she stroked his hair back, the thick waves giving her more than enough to hold on to . . . as she looked into the mirror above the bed.

And watched him make love to her.

"Oh, Marisol . . . a feast for the eyes . . ." His lids were low as he lifted his head and looked down her body. "You are a male's dream."

Hardly. She was lean as a boy, with no hips to speak of and breasts that were barely big enough to need a bra—and yet like this, in this dim light, on this circular bed, under his straining watch, she was as voluptuous as any woman on the planet, fully sexualized and ready to be pleased by her man.

Even though he wasn't really hers.

Dropping his head back down, he attended to her breasts some more as his fingers drifted over to her hip and onto her outer thigh. Up and down he petted her leg, as he suckled and ground carefully against her—

And then his hand slipped between them, replacing his clothed erection, passing over her wet sex once, twice . . . and then rubbing.

He recaptured her mouth as his fingers delved in.

For a split second, she winced and stiffened, her body remembering the last time that had happened.

Assail immediately stopped everything. Staring down at her, his expression darkened to the point of violence. "How badly were you hurt."

Sola just shook her head. She didn't want to go there, not when relief was so close she could touch it.

"Marisol. How bad."

"I thought you said I'm supposed to forget it happened."

His eyes closed as if he were in pain. "I don't want you hurt—ever. But especially not like that."

God, he was beautiful, those handsome features of his pulled into agony on her behalf.

She reached out and smoothed his brow, erasing the lines that had been created. "Just be with me. Make it all about you and not . . . anybody or anything else. That is what I need right now."

* * *

Every time Assail thought his female was done surprising him, Marisol took him to another, deeper level. In this case, the idea that some man had brutalized her sacred body . . . Virgin Scribe in the Fade, his brain literally shut down from a traffic jam of aggression and agony.

And yet just her touch was enough to redirect him from the violence.

"Don't stop," she breathed as she nuzzled his throat—

Her innocent action triggered an immediate feeding response in him, his fangs dropping into his mouth, his urge to mark her by taking her vein almost as strong as his abiding resolve to never let her learn what he really was.

She had been traumatized enough—

Her hands went to his shirt and she tugged the thing free of his slacks. And then she went to work on his belt.

Except he couldn't be distracted. Not until he knew . . .

"What did he do to you?" he demanded.

As Marisol went still, a part of him wondered why he was pushing her, especially given the advice he'd insisted on imparting.

"I did what I had to, to distract him," she said tightly. "And then I went for his balls."

Assail exhaled. "I should have been the one to kill him."

"To defend my honor?"

He was dead serious as he looked at her. "Absolutely."

Her eyes seemed to cling to his. "You really are a gentleman under all of it, aren't you."

"I killed Benloise," he heard himself say. "In a way that made him suffer."

Her lids closed briefly. "How did you know he was the one who took me?"

"I followed you the night you broke into his house."

"So it was you." She shook her head. "I could have sworn someone was with me. But I wasn't sure. Jesus, you put me to shame when it comes to tracking somebody."

"Why did you go there? I have wondered."

The smile she gave him was full of irony. "Because he called me off of your trail—and refused to pay me the full amount I was owed. I mean, I was prepared to keep my end of the bargain, but something spooked him. You?"

He nodded once and took her mouth again, drinking in the feel of her, the taste. "No more of that for you."

"Of what?"

"That kind of work."

Her stillness returned, but only for a moment. "I agree."

God, that was what he needed to hear and hadn't known it: The idea of her staying safe gave him a rush so great he had to blink his way through it.

And as soon as it passed, Assail shed his clothes quickly, the fine fabrics floating off the edge of the bed onto the floor. Then he was skin on skin with her, poised above her parted thighs, his rock-hard cock nonetheless content to wait.

When he finally positioned his head at the entrance of her sex, he knew he was going to be lost forever if he completed the act. Or maybe that was a lie. Maybe . . . he had been lost since that first night he'd met up with her out in the snow.

Pushing inside slowly, feeling her arch up against his chest, watching her eyes roll back, he wished they had never met. As good as this was, he didn't need a weakness like her anywhere near his life. But like a wound filled with salt, she was permanently in his skin.

At least she was going to stay here with him and be safe.

That was his one solace.

Moving slowly, carefully, he eased himself in and out of her slick hold, his cock getting stroked on all sides. He had to grit his teeth and lock his lower back to keep up the steady, even pace—he wanted to go faster and faster, but that was not an option.

And yes, he knew exactly what she was after: She was using him as an eraser, and he was more than willing to fit the bill.

Anything for her—

Marisol repositioned her herself, wrapping her legs around him, angling herself so that he went even deeper. One stroke later and she was holding on hard to his shoulders. It was getting close for her, so close.

"I have you," he said into her hair. "Let yourself go and I shall catch you."

Her head threw back and her nails dug in and her body tightened, and he froze, feeling the tugs on his arousal, the subtle pulls that cranked him up.

Turning his head into her neck, he meant only to get closer, feel more of her, be further responsive to her needs.

But she moved unexpectedly, arching her body, shifting her position—and her neck pushed into his mouth . . . his fangs.

The scratch was minor. His taste of her was anything but.

Before he could stop himself, he scored her more deeply.

His Marisol moaned and swept her hands down to his hips, pulling at him as if she wanted him to start moving again.

"I'm on the pill," she said from a vast, vast distance.

His clogged mind didn't know what that meant, but the sound of her voice was enough to snap him back to reality. Lapping at the wound he'd made, he both closed it and took more of her blood into him—although it was such a small amount compared to what he wanted.

"Keep going," she said. "Please . . . don't stop—"

Assail was tempted to take that the wrong way and bite her properly, take from her completely. But he would not do that without her permission. Rape could happen in many different ways—and a violation was a violation, especially when only one side got pleasure from it.

He would, however, finish the sex.

Hitching a more complete hold on her, he drove in and relented, drove in and relented, swinging his hips.

At the last moment, he pulled out and came all over her lower belly, the jerking spasms kicking out his scent on her skin.

As much as he wanted more of this—and he intended to have her again, right now—he would not complete the act within her until she knew the full truth about him. Only then would she be able to honestly decide whether or not she wanted him as a lover.

With his lips at her ear, he said, "More, yes . . ."

The rippling moan she let out was the perfect reply. And before it had even faded, before her nails once again sank into his flanks and her legs squeezed his lower body closer to her, he began to move again, the sex tempered by his respect for her, and yet all the more vivid for the restraint.

He had never been with a woman or a female like this before.

After years of having had sex, he felt as though he was finally with someone for the first time.

THIRTY-FOUR

Kneeling before the bedding platform, Wrath kept time between his beloved's breaths, measuring her inhalations as they pushed weakly against the arm he had stretched over her waist. Longer and longer between the draws, slower and slower the exhales.

And meanwhile his own heart continued to beat, and his own lungs did their duty, and his body kept on.

It seemed so cruel—and he would have traded her his health in a moment. He would have given her anything of his just to keep her with him—and as that was not possible, he put his palm on the hilt of his jeweled dagger and brought it between them.

Focusing on her parted lips, he angled the blade so that it was pointed at the center of his chest. The supports of the platform were constructed out of stout oak panels, and they happened to be at just the right height for what he required: Bracing the base of the weapon's handle on the edge of the wood, he kept the dagger upright in his grip and leaned in, measuring the distance he had to close.

Putting his sternum to the tip of the blade, he pushed in enough to feel the pinch.

Satisfied with the angle, he turned the knife around and took the point to the wood itself, digging a circle out of the fibers, creating a lock for the base. As he chipped away, it seemed disrespectful to waste the last of his Anha's breaths on such efforts—he should be paying mind unto her, and her alone.

But preparations needed to be made.

If he lost her before he took care of this, he was liable to make a sloppy attempt, and he needed to make sure that there was no chance of survival—

"What . . . do you do?"

Wrath's head jerked up. And at first he could not comprehend the sight a'fore him.

His Anha had turned her pale face to him and was staring out from under heavy lids.

The dagger point slipped from the perch he was creating, sinking into the wrist of the hand he'd braced. The slice didn't register.

"Anha . . . ?"

Her tongue licked at the blood on her lips. "Our son . . ."

Verily, he did not hear whate'er it was she said. Tears came to his eyes and his heart pounded, and he wondered first if this was not a dream . . . a function of his having followed through with his own death, stabbing himself in the very place he felt the love for her most keenly.

Except no—she was reaching out to his face. Touching him with wonder—as if she too could not comprehend a return to consciousness.

"Anha!" He pressed his lips to hers and then brushed his own tears from her cold cheeks.

Abruptly, the healer's advice came to him and he rushed to put his wrist over her mouth. "Drink, my love—do not speak unto me yet. Drink. *First and foremost, you must* drink!*"*

His Anha struggled for only a moment before she swallowed properly once. And again. And a third time.

As she moaned and closed her eyes, it was not from discomfort or fear. No, it was from a vital easing, as if she were feeding a hunger that had pained her and the agony was relenting.

"Drink . . ." he said as everything went even blurrier. "My love . . . partake of me and come back. . . ."

Stroking her hair back, he eyed his dagger. And prayed that this miracle stayed with them both. That she remained revived and soon recovered—

"My lord?"

At the sound of a deep voice, Wrath snapped his head around without moving his vein from her lips. The Black Dagger Brother Tohrture was standing just inside the closed chamber door, having entered silently.

"She is roused," Wrath said hoarsely. "Praise unto the Scribe Virgin . . . she is roused."

"Yes," the Brother said. "And I must needs speak with you."

"Can it not wait." He refocused on his beloved. "Leave us—"

The Brother stalked over, and put his lips close to Wrath's ear, such that not a word traveled: "She looks as your father did."

Wrath blinked. Looked up. "Pardon?"

The Brother had the most incredible blue eyes, the color something that rivaled the pale aqua gems that had been specially purchased for Anha's spring gown.

Leaning back down, the words were whispered once more. "Your father presented thus the evening he died."

As the Brother straightened, those eyes of his never faltered. Neither did his expression. His very body.

A flash of anger had Wrath curling up a fist. The last thing he wanted intruding into this sacred space of hope was any memory of that other night of loss . . . when he had rushed for the castle upon a black steed, careening through the forests, risking his own life to return in time.

Indeed, much as he wished the chapters of that story to stay free of his mind, they came back to him with clarity: He had suffered an injury during the daylight hours, a slip and fall in his chamber that had rendered him upon a metal spike. The wound had made it impossible for him to dematerialize, but he had been well enough to proceed from the castle when he'd been called out unto one of the Founding Families.

When he had departed at the fall of night, he had not intended to return until the morrow.

The Brotherhood had come for him an hour later.

By the time he had gotten back to the castle, it was too late. His father was gone.

And as for appearances, some dead showed their provenance, it was true: the murdered, the maimed, the aged—in the case of his father, however, the King had just looked asleep, his body cleansed and dressed in ceremonial robes, his hair tended to, his gloves and shoes on as if he intended to walk unto his grave.

"What do you say?" Wrath shook his head. "I cannot . . ."

Another whisper in his ear: "Look unto her fingernails."

As Anha's eyes opened and widened at the sight of the Brother, Wrath leaned in and kissed her forehead. "Worry not, my love."

Instantly, she calmed under his touch and his voice, continuing to feed as her eyes reshut.

"That is right," he murmured. "Take what I provide."

When he was sure she had settled once more, he glanced down at her hands and frowned. Her nails were . . . blue.

His father's hands had been gloved.

"Come back," he said to the Brother roughly. "I shall call for you."

Tohrture nodded and walked to the door. Before he left, he said clearly, "Do not allow her to imbibe aught that has not been tasted."

Poison? Had it been . . . poison?

As their chamber was shut and relocked, Wrath felt a strange calm come unto him: Strength and purpose returned to him as Anha continued to pull against his vein, the sips turning into proper draws. And the more she took from him, the more that death color faded from her fingers.

After his father's death, he had been weightless in the world—until she had been brought to him and become his tether not just to the breaths in his chest and the beats of his heart, but his reign as King.

To think that his father might have been taken from him? And then his beloved female?

As he thought of Tohrture's expression . . . he knew that there were enemies in his court. Enemies capable of murder.

Anger boiled beneath his surface, changing him in the inside . . . in the way steel and iron were forged.

"Worry not, my love," he said, clasping her hand in his. "I shall take care of everything."

And blood will run like the tears you shed in your pain.

He was King, yes. But first and foremost, he was the hellren *of this magnificent female—and* ahvenge *her he would.*

THIRTY-FIVE

"Of all the things they had to be right about . . ."

As Trez lay flat on the slick floor of his bathroom, he put his forearm over his eyes. He was acutely aware that his cock was deflating, all that meaningless sex he'd had taking the wind out of his sails and then some.

But he was even more clear on who was next to him, naked on the fur rug.

Shit, he had to get that towel back on his hips and—

"Who is 'they'?"

Grabbing for the terry cloth, he couldn't even look at Selena. "My people."

"What are they right about?"

"Why are you still here?"

When he realized what that sounded like, he sat up—and caught her recoil. "Sorry—I just mean, how are you putting up with my crap."

Goddamn, she was utterly edible sitting there, that robe covering nothing but her shoulders, her breasts still peaked, her legs arranged so that if he moved just a little, he could see her . . .

Selena pulled the draping across herself—and as much as it pained him, it was the right thing on so many levels. He had ruined what had been happening between them.

But for the right reasons.

"I'm sorry," he said, thinking that he should have that tattooed on his forehead so he saw it in the mirror every morning, every night.

He should never have taken things as far as they'd gone. Ever.

"For stopping?"

"No, I'm not sorry about that." As she winced, he wanted to kick himself in the balls. "What I mean is . . . fuck. I don't know. I don't know anything right now."

There was a long silence. And then she said calmly. "You need to know that there is nothing you can't tell me."

"Be careful with that—Pandora's box is hard to close."

"Nothing." Her eyes were totally clear as she stared over at him. "I have nothing to fear—from you or by you. I do think you owe me an explanation, however. Assuming that you have no intention of continuing—and if only so that I do not blame myself for this."

Wow, okay. If he'd thought she was hot before? Now, she was in goddess territory: Physical beauty was one thing; having a spine was even more attractive.

And she had a point.

"All right," he said, feeling like a total reject. But she did have a right to know. "I've fucked a lot of human females in the last ten years—and none of that mattered to me until tonight with you. And I think I'm about to condemn my parents to a torturous death. Other than that, I'm fine."

Her brows rose. But she didn't recoil; she didn't run. There were a number of deep breaths, however. "Maybe we'll just take the second half of that first. What on the Scribe Virgin's Earth are you talking about?"

"It's a fucking mess—I'm a mess."

She waited, clearly expecting him to continue. "And you have told me nothing."

Staring into her eyes, he felt such respect for her. "God . . . how is it possible that you exist?"

"Still not telling me a thing." She smiled slowly. "Although I like the way you're looking at me."

Trez shook his head, knowing she deserved so much better than he could ever offer her. "You shouldn't. You really shouldn't."

"That's for me to decide. Now speak—if you're so determined to put me off of you, then use your words to persuade me of your ugliness."

"The sex life didn't do it already?"

"I am trained as an *ehros*. It is my expectation that males have carried their seed far and wide."

He narrowed his eyes: Her face had suddenly become impassive, and that was a serious-ass tell. "There's one other thing."

"Which is."

"I'm promised to someone."

She almost hid her wince. Almost. "Indeed."

"Yeah. Indeed. And if I don't show, my parents are going to get slaughtered."

"So you are not in love?"

"I haven't met her. And I don't want to."

Some of the tension left the Chosen. "You have no knowledge of her at all?"

"None. Except that she's the queen's daughter."

Those incredible eyes got wider. "You are to be royalty, then."

He thought of how much fun Wrath was having on his throne, and all the kicks and giggles Rehv was rocking as imperial head of the *symphaths*—and at least they were allowed out into the night. Well, kinda, in Wrath's case.

His future was going to be all about the gilded cage.

"My parents sold me when I was very young," he heard himself say. "I was never given a choice—and now? Unless I go back to the Territory, the pair of them aren't going to live long."

Selena's head eased to the side, her mind clearly working. "There is no chance for negotiating?"

"None."

"Can your parents not give the price paid back?"

He thought of his mother's cynical smile that night he'd last seen her. "Even if they could, I don't think they would."

Her brows rose again. "Are you certain?"

"It would be consistent with them."

"Have you not asked?"

"No, I haven't. But it would involve going back to the s'Hisbe, and that's not possible."

"Is there not someone you could send on your behalf?"

He pictured iAm going into the Territory. The contract was specifically for Trez, so it wasn't as if the high priest, or even s'Ex, could do a bait and switch. They could, however, take his brother hostage. Or worse.

And that would get Trez back.

"I don't think so. My brother's the only one, and I can't risk that. I won't risk him."

"And you think your parents will be . . ."

"No, I know they'll kill them." He massaged the nape of his neck. "You know, so much of this is sad—but I think the worst of it is the fact that I can't even pretend to be emotional about those two. It's, like . . . they made a deal with the devil. If something bad happens, they're just getting what's coming to them."

Unfortunately, however, regardless of what happened to his mother and father . . . the debt would still be owed.

Even if s'Ex carved them up into little bitty pieces, Trez would remain on the line for what they had contracted for.

What had been set in motion . . . could not be undone. And as he kept looking at Selena, he mourned that truth now more than ever.

Selena's hands were shaking. Had been ever since Trez had said that he'd been with . . . exactly how many human women? she wondered.

Dearest Virgin Scribe, she didn't even want to think about that.

She could, however, at least try to get her hands to stop trembling. As Trez fell silent, she splayed her fingers wide and flexed them, hoping that it would stop things before he saw through her calm facade: She had the very clear sense that if he became aware he'd upset her, he would never say another word . . . and this intimate space that had unexpectedly opened up between them was even more sacred than the sexual experience had promised to be.

"I did not have parents as such," she said quietly. "But I cannot imagine having a young and . . . selling them."

Trez nodded, his arm cocked high so that he could continue to rub the base of his neck. "I know, right? I mean, my parents did value me. The problem is, I was a commodity to them, something to be bartered. You expect that from car dealers and rug merchants and people who run supermarkets and malls. And listen, I wish I was one of those well-adjusted motherfuckers so I could be all like, 'They didn't want me, but I'm still of value, blah, blah, blah'—things haven't worked out like that for me, though. In my head . . ." He made a circle at his temple. "I'm not anything. I'm not . . . anything."

Suddenly, Selena wanted to weep. To stare across at this absolutely magnificent male . . . and know that in his heart, he saw nothing of what he was? It was a crime—a crime caused by the very people who should have cared most about him.

"Is that why you were with the humans?" she heard herself ask.

In the silence that followed, it was difficult to draw an even breath: She was frightened of his answer. For a whole lot of reasons.

"Yeah." He cursed under his breath. "Like, you know, I was with this woman—right before I got the migraine."

That was just the other night, she thought, wanting to cringe—

"And she was as empty as I was feeling. Just two hollow bodies clapping together. It didn't mean anything, and that's what I've been doing all these years. Physical exercise and that was it."

Selena struggled for the right thing to say, something that was even-keeled and signaled that she was comfortable with what he was telling her . . . when in reality it was ripping her heart out. Even though it shouldn't have.

She'd spent how much time with him? An hour? Two at the very most?

Impending death was making her reckless—

"I could save them," he said, almost to himself. "If I sacrifice myself, I can save my mother and father."

He shifted his head to the side sharply and a crack sounded out.

"Here," she murmured, moving behind him. "Allow me."

Pushing his hand out of the way, she gripped his iron-hard shoulders and squeezed as he had done, trying to work some ease into the muscle fibers. As she worked at him, his smooth skin slid over ropes of tension, but that was the only thing that seemed to be accomplished.

He groaned. "That feels amazing."

"I don't think I'm doing anything."

His hands briefly covered her own. "You are. More than you know."

Selena continued the massage and thought of her own past. "As I said, I didn't have a proper mother and father. I was raised with and by my sisters. I was needed to further the traditions, but I cannot say I was ever wanted by anyone. Claimed, as it were. So, in a way, I can imagine how you feel—bred but not born, as it were, because *born* implies you were hoped for, prayed for."

He leaned his head back and stared up at her. "Yeah. That's exactly it."

She smiled at him and pushed him back into position.

"If my parents are killed, I feel like I'm going to go to hell," he muttered.

"But you can't be culpable in this, because you never consented."

"I'm sorry?"

"You were promised when you were incapable of giving consent—indeed, it sounds as though they never even asked you. Therefore, your failure to perform, and any consequences thereto? They are your parents' to claim, not yours. This is about you and yet has nothing to do *with* you."

"God . . ."

When he didn't finish, she frowned. "I'm sorry. I don't mean to be presumptuous."

"You're not. You're . . . perfect."

"Hardly."

"I want to do something for you."

She stilled. "What?"

Because she had some ideas.

"Something worthwhile."

She eyed the fur rug she had been stretched out on. Oh, it would be worthwhile. . . .

"But I keep coming up with nothing."

Selena sighed. "Your presence is plenty."

Trez put his hands over hers again and pulled her forward so that she was draped over his back. Holding her there, he put his head against her own.

As he breathed in, his great torso expanding, she was lifted from the floor and brought back down. "Thank you," he said in a voice that cracked.

"I have done nothing."

"You've made me feel like I'm not evil. And tonight, that's everything."

"Oh, you are never that," she whispered as she pressed a kiss to his cheek. "Not you, not ever."

Closing her eyes, she held on to him, and found herself becoming connected with him at the soul level. To the point where she didn't know how to leave him. Not just tonight, but . . . whenever her destiny finally claimed her.

"Have you eaten?" he asked after a while.

"Actually . . . no." Her stomach rumbled. "And I am hungry."

"Let's go downstairs. My brother was making some of his sauce—or at least, I assume so. He does that every time I have a headache."

Selena relinquished her hold and went to ease back—

Without warning, her spine rebelled, the vertebrae locking into their position. Trez, on the other hand, got up easily enough—and as he extended his palm to help her up, she could only stare at it.

As confusion played over his handsome features, she figured she might as well accept the help. At this point, she was incapable of lifting herself off the floor.

"Slowly," she said gruffly. "Please?"

Trez frowned, but was gentle as he lifted her to her feet. "Are you all right?"

She bought herself some time by making a production of tying her robe together. Meanwhile, her joints were screaming, particularly her hips and back.

Forcing a smile onto her face, she tried not to get spooked. But this was how it had started for her sisters. Each one of them.

"Shall we?" she said with determination.

Trez's almond-shaped eyes narrowed even further. But then he shrugged. "Yeah, sure. I'll just pull on some clothes."

"I'll wait in the hall."

Through will alone, she made it across the bedroom and out into the corridor. By the time she closed the door behind her, she was choked of breath—

Instantly, her body experienced an internal shift of incredible power. In a way that meant only one thing: Someone was in her needing.

The queen? she thought with astonishment as she looked to the vaulted entrance of the First Family's private quarters.

Now that would be momentous.

Easing back against the wall, she thought of massaging Trez's shoulders and wished there was an equivalent for her own body. There was none. No cure, no slowing the disease.

No telling how long she had left.

THIRTY-SIX

Beth had no choice but to give herself up to her body's roaring demands. And the only respite she got? Every time Wrath released into her, there was a brief reprieve—before the grinding need started its ascent once again.

"Take my vein," Wrath said roughly. "Take it. . . ."

She didn't even know whether she was on her back or her belly, what room she was in, what time it was. But the instant his throat came up to her mouth, she was crystal clear on the bite: Her fangs punched out and she used them hard, cranking down on Wrath's flesh, breaking the surface and going deep, freeing up the other thing she needed from him.

Oh, the power of him. As her mouth was filled, she was struck once again by the incredible impact his blood had on her. With her strength flagging even as the needing raged on, and her body aching everywhere as if she'd been through a baler, she was nonetheless fortified from the very first draw, better able to continue—even though it wasn't like she had a choice.

As she had to release his vein to suck some air in, she couldn't believe she had volunteered for this. She must have been crazy, some stupid-ass romantic vision of having a baaaaaaaby getting in the way of twelve kinds of reality.

Relocking on Wrath's throat, he somehow managed to keep pumping even as she stayed on his vein, his erection going in and out, the deep digs and sharp removals resonating throughout her torso, her head rocking up and down, her hips absorbing his weight. Slick with sweat, their bodies moved together with such seamless communion, she didn't know where hers left off and his began.

A sudden change in tempo told her he was gearing up for another orgasm, and she needed it from—

Wrath reared his head back, and her fangs ripped his neck, but he didn't seem to care.

Didn't seem to even notice.

Jesus, he was magnificent: Through the haze of the sex, she watched him strain, his lips curling back, his own fangs getting exposed, his hair flowing away from its widow's peak as his sightless, pale green eyes flared wide and then squeezed shut.

And then it was her turn, her core grabbing at his arousal, greedy for what he ejaculated into her, the pleasure so acute that it was a kind of agony.

Just as the contractions were beginning to slow, she braced herself for the next wave, preparing for yet another next round of the bone-crushing urge to take over. . . .

When it didn't immediately come, she looked around, as if the needing were a third party that just might have left the—

Oh, wow. They were still in the bathroom. On the floor.

Wrath collapsed against her, his head falling so far, so hard that she heard his forehead knock against the marble.

As the respite grew longer, she probably should have started to go cold, but the inferno in her body kept both of them plenty warm—

A whirring sound from over the tub brought her head around. The shutters were going down for the day, the panels locking into place at the sills.

So this had been going on for . . . eight hours? Nine?

There were no sounds from downstairs, but then the Brothers had probably all been affected by her hormones. The females as well.

Wrath lifted himself up, his muscles straining, his arms trembling. "How are you?"

Beth opened her mouth to answer, but only a croak came out.

"You're going to want my vein still," he said, brushing a strand of hair back from her face. "You need it."

"What about—" As her voice cracked, she cleared her throat. "What about you?"

He looked gaunt, his cheeks hollowed out as if he'd lost twenty-five pounds—but he shook his head. "My only concern is you."

The image of him grew wavy as tears speared.

"I'm sorry," she mumbled. "Oh, God . . . I'm so sorry."

"About what?"

"This . . . whole thing."

He shook his head. "This would have happened sooner or later."

"But I—"

Wrath dropped his mouth to hers and kissed her softly. "No more of that. We go forward from tonight. Whatever happens . . . we fucking deal, okay?"

There was no time for her to reply. Abruptly, the needing geared up once again, that tide rising, the heat uncoiling in her sex and driving right into her heart.

"Oh, God," she moaned, "I thought it was over."

"Not yet." He didn't seem surprised at all. "We're not finished. . . ."

iAm was standing over the stove down in the kitchen when he sensed his brother's appearance. He didn't even need to turn around from the pot of stew he'd thrown together: the air in the room changed—and not in a good way.

Trez was also not alone. And he knew that not because he caught Selena's scent . . . but because he caught his brother's.

iAm cursed under his breath as he stirred. The motherfucker had bonded.

Fantastic.

Hell, iAm had had some hope that, with all the hormones flooding the household, whatever sex those two had gotten down with had been the result of someone else's needing.

Great theory. Except Shadows were immune to that kind of shit.

"You weren't supposed to be the one who serviced him," iAm muttered as he put more sea salt into the mix.

"Watch your tone."

iAm pivoted around and glared at the dumb-ass. "I have an idea.

How about you—for once—make a good decision about a female. Then I won't have to get pissy."

The Chosen standing beside Trez kicked her chin up. "If you want to blame someone, do not address him. I chose to go unto him even though you asked for another."

iAm turned back to his pot. "Great. Congratulations and welcome to the family."

His brother materialized over to him, spun him around and grabbed him by the throat. "Apologize to her—"

iAm leaned into the iron grip, baring his fangs. "Fuck you, Trez."

"You want a piece?" his brother growled. "You want a fucking—"

"Do it. I fucking dare you—"

"Don't push me—"

"I'm trying to save your ass! You fucking—"

As the pair of them escalated toward an implosion to rival Wrath's from the night before, the Chosen walked over and spoke evenly.

"He told me," she cut in. "Everything. And it strikes me that the two of you are alone in this situation. So mayhap Last Meal instead of fisticuffs, shall we."

iAm turned his head at the same time Trez did.

As the pair of them faced off at the totally calm and controlled Chosen, Trez did the unheard-of—and dropped his hand. Stepped off. Crossed his arms over his chest.

He was still furious to the core, but the call to heel was obeyed with such ease, you had to wonder if maybe the bonding bullshit might not be useful—to a point.

iAm glared at his brother. "I don't know what to say to you."

"Selena, will you give us a sec?"

The Chosen nodded. "Mayhap I'll just return up north. And give you two plenty of space."

Trez frowned. "You don't have to go."

Selena's eyes went back and forth. "Actually, I think I do. You know where I'll be—and please. Do not tear each other asunder. It will only make all of this worse."

iAm braced himself for a gag-worthy display of good-byeing, but the female further impressed him by bowing slightly and taking off. No muss, no fuss.

Shit, he could almost like her. If he weren't so angry at his idiot brother—

"I want to meet with s'Ex. Today."

iAm crossed his own arms and leaned back against the stove. "Because you think you're going to talk sense into him? I already got real with the bastard—and he's more than ready to do his job."

"Can you reach him?"

"Yeah."

"Tell him to meet me at noon at our apartment."

"That's the deadline for you to show at the s'Hisbe." When his brother didn't reply, iAm lifted his brows. "You aren't turning yourself in, are you?"

"Set up the meeting."

iAm cursed long and low. Yeah, he wanted to kick his brother's ass—but absolutely, positively didn't want anyone else to. "Trez."

"Do it."

"Not unless you tell me where you're at."

"I thought you wanted me to go back."

"So that's what you're doing? Tell me something, you planning on bringing your Chosen with you—make a happy little family or some shit?"

"She's not mine."

"Have you told your hormones that?"

Trez slashed his hand through the air. "I don't know what you're talking about—"

"And that's your fucking problem."

"Just call the executioner. That's all I've got to say."

As Trez turned on his heel, iAm spoke sharply. "I can't let you go back there."

Trez stopped. Looked over his shoulder.

"What," iAm groused.

"I just . . . I don't know. I guess I didn't expect that."

Time to go back to the sauce. Stew. What the fuck was he making again?

Popping the lid off, he remanned his spoon and stirred slowly. He'd handmade everything from the chicken stock to the spice satchels that were floating on the surface of the fragrant mélange.

"iAm?"

"I don't care if they die." He watched slices of carrots and squares of onions surface in the thick base. "I know I'm supposed to, because they're my parents, but I've thought about it and I'm sorry—if they can be selfish, so can I. My family is you and me, and I will choose us over anyone."

"God . . . I think I needed you to say that."

He shot another glare over. "You doubted it? Like, ever?"

Trez went across and parked it on one of the stools at the counter. "There are limits."

iAm had to laugh. "You don't say."

Going to the cabinets on the left, he took out two deep-bellied bowls, then sprang one of the drawers and got some soup spoons. Ladling the stew in, he served his brother first.

Trez tried some and moaned. "This is amazing."

When iAm gave the shit a taste, he had to agree, but he kept that to himself. Pride was an unattractive trait, even if it was well-placed.

"What are you going to do about the Chosen?" iAm asked.

Trez's shrug was just a liiiiiittle too nonchalant. "Nothing."

"Not sure it's going to work out like that for you."

Trez stared into the stew. "She's just one more reason to stay on the outside. Not that I needed it."

"She says you told her everything. That right?"

It was a long while before Trez nodded slowly. "Yeah. Pretty much."

"What exactly did you keep to yourself."

Those black eyes lifted after a while. "Seconds?"

iAm snagged the now-empty bowl and brought it over for a redo.

"I didn't tell her how bad it's going to get," Trez said softly as more stew was delivered.

"So you lied."

There was another long silence. "Yeah. I did."

Because after the queen was done eliminating their parents? The tribe was going to come after iAm. He was the next rung on the ladder of coercion because they couldn't touch Trez, after all. He had to be in one piece.

iAm found himself nodding. "Probably a good move."

THIRTY-SEVEN

It was easy to think of God while watching the sun rise over the Hudson River.

As Sola sat on the empty terrace of Assail's glass house, she stared across the cold, sluggish water. Little flashes of peach and yellow skimmed over the icy expanse as, across the way, that great orange orb crested over the skyscrapers of downtown.

She had made it out of that prison, she thought for the hundredth time. And whatever scars might have formed on the inside of her, her body was intact, her mind functional, and her safety, at least in the short term, assured.

Thinking back to all those prayers, she couldn't believe they'd been granted. Desperation had made her utter the words, but she hadn't really expected anyone to be listening.

The question now was . . . did she keep her side of the bargain?

Man, it would have been so much easier if an angel with wings had come down and freed her, magically depositing her here. Instead, she'd done the dirty work herself, Assail had been on cleanup, and one of those fierce cousins of his had been a chauffeur for the five-hour trip back to sanity. Oh, and then there had been all those people in that facility.

Mere mortals touched by the hand of God? Or a series of random events that just happened to roll out as they did? Was the fact that her life had been saved a case of divine intervention . . . or of no more significance than one bingo ball getting picked over another?

A shallow fishing boat puttered into view, its sole passenger steering the outboard motor from the back, controlling speed and direction.

Pulling the heavy duvet even closer around her body, she thought about all the things she'd done, starting when she was just nine or ten. She'd begun picking pockets, trained by her father, and moved up to more complex theft with his help. Then, after he'd gone to prison and she and her grandmother had moved here to the States, she'd gotten a cashier's job at a restaurant and tried to support them both. When that had proved too difficult, she'd put her experience to good use and survived.

Her grandmother had never asked any questions, but that had always been the way—her mother had been the same, except when it came to Sola's involvement in the life. Unfortunately, the woman hadn't lived long enough to make much of an impact, and after she was gone, the husband and daughter she had left behind had become thick as thieves.

Natch.

Sooner or later, she'd been bound to get caught. Hell, her father had been even better at it than she was, and he'd died in prison.

Picturing him the last time she'd seen him, she remembered him at his trial, dressed in prison garb, handcuffed. He had barely looked at her, and not because he was ashamed or worried about getting emotional.

She'd been no longer useful to him at that point.

Rubbing her eyes, she thought it was asinine to still be hurt by that. But after spending all her time trying to make him proud, get some approval, find any kind of connection, she had realized that to him, she was just another tool in his black-market workplace.

She had left the courtroom before knowing whether he was found guilty or not—and she had gone directly to his apartment. Breaking in, she'd found the stash of cash he kept in a crawl space cut into the wall behind the shower in the bathroom—and used that shit to get her and her grandmother free of his legacy.

The papers to enter into the U.S. had been falsified. The news they'd received about three weeks later from relations had been real: Her father had gotten life.

And then he'd been murdered behind bars.

With her grandmother not just a widower, but childless, Sola had stepped into the role of provider the only way she knew how, the only way that worked.

And now she was here, sitting on the deck of a drug lord's house, faced with the kind of moral dilemma she had never expected to come up against. . . .

Watching some random fisherman cut his engine and throw a line in.

Even though the guy had turned off the motor, he wasn't still. The river's current carried him along, his boat drifting across the view, a humble craft dwarfed by the distant buildings.

"You want the breakfast?"

Sola twisted around. "Good morning."

Her grandmother had her hair done in tight curls around her face, her apron tied on her waist, and a flash of lipstick on her mouth. Her simple cotton dress had been handmade—by her, of course—and her sturdy brown shoes were somehow fitting.

"Yes, please."

When she went to get up, her grandmother motioned downward with both gnarled hands. "Sit in the sun. You need the sun, too pale you are. You living like a vampire."

Ordinarily, she would have pushed back a little, but not this morning. She was too grateful to be alive to do anything other than comply.

Returning to the view, she found that the fisherman was disappearing on the right, going out of sight.

If she hadn't prayed, she would have gotten out of that place anyway. She was a survivor, always had been—and she had done what she had on a strange kind of autopilot, sucking in her emotions and physical sensations and doing what was necessary.

So if she looked at her future, at the currents in her life that were going to carry her out of view, so to speak . . . going legit was the smartest thing to do.

Regardless of any "agreement" she'd had with God.

She was going to end up in jail or dead—and she'd just dipped her foot in the icy cold of the dead scenario. Not where she wanted to end up.

Blinking in the gathering light, she gave up on the vision thing and closed her eyes, letting her head fall back. The warmth on her face made her think of Assail.

Being with him had been like touching the sun and not getting incinerated. And her body wanted more—hell, just the passing thought of him was enough to take her back to those moments in that bed, the night so quiet, the gasps so loud.

As her breasts tightened, she felt a welling between her thighs—

"Sola, you are ready," her grandmother said from behind her.

Getting to her feet, she leaned out over the glass balcony, trying to find her fisherman. She couldn't. He was gone.

Brr, it was cold out here—

"Sola?" came a gentle prodding.

Strange. Ordinarily, her grandmother's voice was like the woman's hands—never soft. In fact, she spoke like she cooked: out front, forthright, no holds barred.

But now the tone was as close to gentle as Sola had ever heard it.

"Sola, you come eat now."

Sola took one last stab at seeing her fisherman. Then she turned around and faced her grandmother.

"I love you, vovó."

Her grandmother could only nod as those ancient eyes of hers steamed up. "Come, you'll catch the dead of a cold."

"The sun is warm."

"Not warm enough." Her grandmother stepped back and motioned. "You must eat."

As Sola entered the house, she froze.

Without looking, she knew that Assail had come down the stairs and was staring at her.

Shit, she wasn't sure she could leave him behind.

After having been sequestered in his room for the last couple days, Trez found the world to be a stretch for the senses, like having a strobe light in his face and a pair of speakers up to each ear: Getting onto the Northway to head into downtown Caldwell, he found himself putting his sunglasses on and turning off the radio—

From out of nowhere, some dumb shit did a two-lane sweep and cut him the hell off.

"Watch where you're going!" he shouted into the windshield, pounding on his horn.

For a split second, he hoped the guy behind the wheel of the Dodge Charger decided to go road rage back at him. He wanted to hit something. Shit, it would probably be good practice for his meeting with s'Ex. Mr. Charger, however, just took his overload of testosterone and his pencil-size dick off at the next exit, jogging in front of a minivan and a pickup truck in the process.

"Asshole."

With any luck, the bastard would drive off into a ditch with no seat belt on.

About ten minutes later, Trez peeled off from the sixty-mile-an-hour-ers and entered a maze of one-ways. Confronted by all the traffic lights and the stop signs, his brain cramped up and he forgot the way to the condo—

When a horn sounded behind him, he locked his molars and hit the gas. In the end, he was forced to pilot around by tracking the Commodore's twenty-story-plus height, gradually zeroing in on the high rise and finding the ramp that led down into the parking garage. As he descended, he got his pass out from the visor, swiped it through the reader, and proceeded to one of their two reserved spots.

The elevator ride up took fifty years and then he was stepping off onto the carpet runner. Their condo was down a little and he used its main door, not the service one, letting himself in with his copper key.

As he came into the kitchen, he saw two mugs on the counter, an already open bag of Cape Cod potato chips, and the coffeepot half-full.

He paused over an open *GQ*. He'd already gone through it. "Nice jacket," he murmured as he shut the mag.

No reason to will on any lamps. The day was bright and sunny and all the glass let in plenty of light—

The towering black shape that arrived on the terrace was a harbinger of doom if he'd ever seen one.

Striding over, Trez opened the door by hand and stepped outside, closing things up behind him.

s'Ex's voice from under the executioner's hood was mildly amused. "Your brother invited me in."

"I'm not my brother."

"Yes. We've noticed." As the queen's hatchet man crossed his arms over his chest, his massive forearms bunched up even under the folds of fabric. "To what do you owe the honor of my presence?"

The fact that it was freezing cold out seemed appropriate. "I don't want you to fuck with my parents."

"Then you need to come back. That's it." The executioner leaned in. "Don't tell me you called me all this way in hopes of negotiating. Did you. Surely you are not that stupid."

Trez bared his fangs, but then dialed shit back. "There's something you want. Everyone has a price."

The executioner reached up and slowly took off that hood. The face behind the folds of black cloth was handsome as sin . . . and had eyes with all the warmth of winter granite.

"Why would I risk my own life for your parents? If I disobey an order, there are consequences—and none of you are worth them."

"You can talk to the queen. She listens to you."

"Assuming that is true, and I'm not saying it is, why would I do that for you?"

"Because there's something you want."

"Since you seem to know everything, what exactly do you think that is," the executioner said in a bored tone.

"You're stuck there as much as any of them are. I remember what that's like—and I can assure you, life on this side of those walls is so much better."

"Which is why you look like shit, then?"

"Think about it. I can get you anything on the outside. *Anything.*"

The executioner's eyes narrowed. "Sparing them is not going to save you."

"Killing them isn't going to bring me back. And that's why you'd do it, right? So go to the queen, tell her you've spoken to me directly—and I don't care whether you kill them. Then suggest that she strip them of everything they've been given—the quarters they live in, the clothes and jewels they've bought with the bounty they received, the food in their cupboards. Everything. That will make the queen whole again. She'll have lost nothing, be out nothing—"

"Bullshit. She doesn't have a half for her daughter. All that 'restitution' doesn't solve the fact that the princess has no mate."

"It's not going to be me. I'm telling you right now. You guys can fuck my father and mother up, you can threaten me with bodily harm, you can trash my house—"

"What if I just take you now?"

Trez outed the gun he'd shoved in his waistband at the small of his back. He didn't point it at s'Ex. He put it right under his own chin.

"If you try to, I'll pull this trigger. Then you have a dead body, and unless that daughter of hers is a sick bitch, she ain't gonna want me then."

s'Ex went inanimately still. "You're out of your fucking mind."

"Anything you want on the outside, s'Ex. You take care of this for me, and I'll take care of you."

As the queen's executioner considered the deal, Trez breathed smoothly, and thought of the only two people who really mattered. Selena . . . Jesus Christ, he wanted her, but he was no good for the likes of that Chosen. Hell, even if this flier of a negotiation worked, he was still going to be a pimp, and there was no changing his past.

And then there was iAm.

The idea of losing his brother was . . . he couldn't even put it into thought. But the male was going to be better off without him if he couldn't fix this problem.

"I'm surprised that you want to save your parents this badly," s'Ex said offhandedly.

"Are you kidding me? If they lose their station, it's worse than death for them. What they did to me has ruined my life and my brother's. That shit's my revenge. Besides, like I said, no matter what you do with them, I'm not going back there."

The executioner broke off and strolled the length of the terrace, his robing swirling around him like the promise of violence, the puffs of his breath like a dragon breathing fire.

After a long moment, he clasped his hands behind his back, and returned.

It was a while before he finally spoke, and when he did, he wasn't looking at Trez. He was staring at the glass of the apartment.

"I like this place."

Trez kept the gun to his chin, but felt a stab of . . . hope? Well, not that cheery an emotion, certainly. But maybe there was a solution after all.

s'Ex lifted a brow. "Three bedrooms, two and a half baths, nice kitchen. Plenty of light. But the beds are the best—big beds in there."

"You want this, it's yours."

As s'Ex's eyes slid back to him, Trez heard the phrase *deal with the devil* over and over in his head.

"It's missing something."

"What."

"Women. I want women brought to me here. I'll tell you when. And I want three or four at a time."

"You got it. Name the number and the hour and I'll bring them to you."

"So sure of yourself."

"What the fuck do you think I do for a living."

s'Ex's eyes flared. "I thought you were a club owner."

"I don't just sell booze," he muttered.

"Hmm, what a job." The executioner frowned. "Just so we're clear, she may order me to go after your brother."

"Then I'm going to have to kill you."

s'Ex threw his head back and laughed. "Very cocky."

"Let me make myself perfectly clear. You touch iAm and I will find you. Your last breath will be mine and your heart will still be warm when I take it out of your chest and eat it raw."

"You know, it's a wonder we don't get along better."

Trez put out his free hand. "Have we come to terms?"

"There is the queen to consider. I may not be able to sway her. And just so you're aware, if she doesn't go for it, your deadline will have passed."

"So kill them." He held s'Ex's black stare without wavering. "I mean it."

The executioner tilted his head, as if considering all angles. "Yes, evidently you do. Meet me here at noon tomorrow with a sample—and I'll see what I can do in the Territory."

Before s'Ex disappeared, the male clasped the palm that was offered briefly. And then he was gone, like a nightmare banished upon waking.

Unfortunately . . . Trez knew the male would be back.

The question was, with what kind of news. And what kind of appetite.

THIRTY-EIGHT

It was an hour past sundown when Abalone left his home, dematerializing off his side lawn. The night was bitterly cold, and as he re-formed on the estate of one of the *glymera*'s wealthiest families, he took a moment to breathe until his sinuses went numb.

Others were gathering, the males and females appearing out of the darkness, straightening their furs and fine clothes and jewels before striding toward the light.

With a heavy heart, he followed.

The grand carved doors of the mansion were held open by *doggen*, the staff unmoving in their livery, naught but blinking stops.

The lady of the house, such that she was, was standing under a chandelier in the foyer, her dress a bright red couture number that fell to the ground in drapes of silk. Her jewels were rubies, the flashes at her throat and her ears and her wrists an ostentatious display.

For no particular reason, he thought that the true queen of the race's red gems were much better, bigger, clearer. He had seen an oil painting of the majestic female back in the Old Country, and even distilled through paint and age, the Saturnine Ruby and its counterparts had had a resplendence that would destroy the pretense before him.

The hostess's mate was nowhere to be seen. But then again, that male had difficulty standing for long periods of time.

Not long for the world, he was.

The receiving line that had formed proceeded apace, and soon enough Abalone was kissing the powdered cheek of the female.

"So glad you could come," she said grandly, flicking a hand in the direction behind her. "The dining room, if you will."

As her rubies flashed, he pictured his daughter as such, a grand lady in a grand house with glassy eyes.

Mayhap the punishment for not going along with this affront to the throne was worth it. He had found love with his *shellan* for the years she had been on the Earth, but that had been luck, he'd come to realize. Most of his contemporaries, now slaughtered in the raids, had been in loveless, sexless relationships that had revolved around the party circuit instead of the familial dinner table.

He did not want that for his daughter.

Yet, if love had happened for him, surely there was a chance for her even in the *glymera*?

Right?

Walking into the dining room, he found that it was just as it had been when the King had addressed them all so recently: the long thin table was moved out and the twenty or so chairs were set up in rows. This time, however, the survivors of the aristocracy were settling in along with their mates.

Usually *shellans* were not included in Council meetings, but there was nothing usual about this gathering. Or the last.

And indeed, the gathered should have been more somber, he thought as he picked a silk-covered seat in the back: As opposed to showing any respect for the historical significance, the danger, the unprecedented nature of all this, they were chatting among themselves, the gentlemales blustering, the ladies casting their hands this way and that so that their jewels flashed.

Indeed, Abalone was alone in the back row, and instead of greeting those whom he knew, he freed the button on his suit jacket and crossed his leg at the knee. When somebody lit up a cigar, he took a cheroot out and did the same, just to give himself something to do. And as a *doggen* immediately showed up at his elbow with an ashtray on a brass stand, he nodded thanks and focused on tapping the ash.

He was small potatoes to all of them, because he had long ago decided that under the radar was best. His blood had seen firsthand the cruelties of court and society, and he had learned that lesson through reading the diaries that had been passed down to him. The truth was, he had financial resources that all of them in this room collectively could barely meet.

Thank you, Apple computer.

Best investment anyone in the eighties could have made. And then there had been big pharma in the nineties. And before that? The steel corporations and railroad companies around the turn of the century.

He'd always had a knack for where humans were going to want to go with both their enthusiasms and their necessities.

If the *glymera* knew this, his daughter would be a commodity of great value.

Which was another reason he didn't talk about his net worth.

Incredible how far his bloodline had come over the centuries. And to think they owed it all to this King's father.

Ten minutes later, the room was full—and that, more than the party-party affect, was the sign that the *glymera* had at least some appreciation of the magnitude of what they were doing. Fashionably late did not apply this evening; the doors were going to be locked right about . . .

He checked his watch.

. . . now.

Sure enough, there was a reverberation of sound as heavy wood slid home.

All and sundry sat and went silent, and that was when he was able to count the heads and find out who was missing. Rehvenge, the *leahdyre*, of course—he had allied himself with Wrath and no one was going to shake that tie. Marissa was also missing, although her brother, Havers, was here—but then she was mated to that Brother no one really knew who was supposedly from Wrath's line.

Naturally, she would be absent as well—

The paneled doors on the right side of the fireplace opened and six males walked in. Instantly, the assembled straightened in their seats. He recognized two of them immediately—the aristocratic-looking one in the front . . . and the ugly harelipped one in the back who had come to visit him with Ichan and Tyhm. The four in between were shades of the same dark hue: big-bodied, sharp-eyed fighters, who were alert but not twitchy, ready but not jumping the gun.

Their control was the scariest thing about them.

Only the unafraid could be that relaxed in this situation—

The lady of the house led her *hellren* in, the male bent like the head of the cane he used with his free hand, his hair white, his face lined like pleated drapes.

She sat him down as if he were a child, arranging his suit coat, smoothing his bright red tie.

Then she addressed the assembled, hands clasped like a soprano about to belt out an aria to a packed house. Her glow at the attention turned upon her was wholly inappropriate, in Abalone's mind.

In fact, this whole thing was a nightmare, he thought as he tapped his ashes again.

As her mouth got to working, spewing out thank-yous and acknowledgments, he wondered how things were going to fare for her after her "beloved" went unto the Fade. Undoubtedly, that depended upon the will and whether this was a second mating and if there were young of the blooded line preceding her in the race to the assets.

Ichan was the next to take the stage. ". . . crossroads . . . necessary action . . . work of Tyhm to expose the weakness set before the race . . . half-breed mate . . . quarter-bred heir . . ."

It was the rhetoric that had been spelled out to him, the recap simply posturing to pretend that this was the first anyone had heard of it. But all had been prepped, the expectations laid out beforehand, the repercussions avowed as necessary.

Abalone glanced over to the far corner of the room. Tyhm, the solicitor, was standing with all the prepossession of a coatrack, his long, thin body held tightly upon its vertical. He was nervous, his eyes both rapt and blinking over much.

". . . vote of no confidence must be unanimous for this super-majority of the Council. Further, your signatures will be affixed with seals upon this document prepared by Tyhm." Ichan held up a parchment with its Old Language symbols drawn with care in blue ink—and then motioned to a lineup of multicolored ribbons, a sterling-silver bowl of red candles, and a stack of white linen napkins. "All of your colors are present here."

Abalone glanced down at the massive gold signet ring that sat heavily on his hand. It was the one his father had worn, the crest carved so deeply in the metal that even after the passage of centuries, the outline, the swirls, the icons were obvious.

Verily, the ring's gold had no doubt been shiny back when it had been cast, but now it was matte from a patina of wear and tear well-earned by the males of his family. Honorably earned.

This was wrong, he thought once again. This entire construct against Wrath was false, drummed up only to serve the ambitions of aristocrats who were not worthy of the throne: They did not care about the purity of the heir's blood. It was just the vocabulary assigned to justify their goal.

"May we have a vote?" Ichan looked out over the crowd. "Now."

This was *wrong.*

Abalone's hand began to shake such that he dropped the cheroot on the floor—and he could not move to pick it up.

Say no to this, he told himself. Stand up for what is—

"All in favor, say, 'Aye.' "

He did not speak. Although not because he had the courage to be the sole "nay" when dissent was requested.

He did not open his mouth then, either.

Abalone hung his head as the gavel hit wood.

"The motion is carried. The vote of no confidence passed. Let us all now join as one to send this message of change out unto our race."

Abalone bent down and retrieved his cheroot. The fact that it had burned a small hole in the varnished floor seemed apt.

He was leaving a smudge on the legacy of his ancestors this night.

Instead of going forward to the parchment, he stayed where he was as each family representative and all the females went up and postured at Ichan, playing their part as seals and ribbons were affixed. It was like watching actors on a stage, each of them enjoying their moment in the light, the focus on them.

Did they know what they were doing? he thought. Turning over the reins to whom—Ichan? As a front for those fighters? This was disastrous—

"Abalone?"

Shaking himself at the sound of his name, he looked up. The entire room was staring at him.

Ichan smiled from up front. "You are the last, Abalone."

Now was the opportunity to live up to the name of his grandfather. Now was his moment to voice his opinion that this was a crime, this was—

"Abalone." Ichan was still smiling, but there was stark demand in his tone. "Your turn. For your blood."

As he put the cheroot down in the ashtray, his hand was shaking anew, his palm sweaty. Clearing his throat, he got to his feet, thinking of the bravery of his bloodline, the way his ancestor had done what was right in spite of the risk.

The image of his daughter cut through his wellspring of emotion.

And he felt the eyes of the others like a thousand laser sights trained on him.

With intent to kill.

As Wrath heard a knocking upon the vaulted door of his mated chamber, he cursed under his breath and ignored it.

"Wrath, you must receive whoe'er it is."

He took another spoonful of the rich soup that had been prepared before him from vegetables he had gone out and dug from the earth himself. The taste was subtle, the broth fragrant, the pieces of meat from a freshly dispatched cow hand-raised in his stables.

That he himself had killed.

The knocking came again.

"Wrath," Anha chided as she pushed herself up higher upon her pillows. "You are needed by others."

He had no sense of the time, whether it was light or dark, how many hours or nights had passed since she had come back to him. And he did not care. Just as he cared naught for the vagaries of court or the concerns of the courtiers—

More knocking.

"Wrath, give me the spoon and you answer that door," his female commanded.

Oh, that made him smile. She was truly returned.

"Your wish is my command," he said, placing the broad bowl in her lap and giving her the utensil he had used.

He would have so much preferred to continue to feed her himself. But to see her able to manage the effort without spilling and effect the process of getting further nourishment into her belly? It eased him in ways internal.

And yet sadly, a pall still hung over them both: Neither he nor she had spoken about the young—about whether or not what had befallen Anha had robbed them of their dearest wish.

It was too painful to speak of—especially in light of the revelation made by Tohrture—

"Wrath. The door."

"Yes, my love."

Stalking across the throw rugs, he was ready to behead whoever dared to intrude on the healing.

Except as he opened the heavy panels, he froze.

Outside in the corridor, the Black Dagger Brotherhood had amassed, their fighter bodies choking what was otherwise more than ample space.

Instinct to protect his shellan *made him wish for a dagger in his hand as he stepped out and closed the door behind him.*

Indeed, that urge to defend his turf had him curling his fists up even though he had never been trained to fight. But he would die to save her—

Without a word, their black blades came out, the torchlight catching and flashing across those killing surfaces.

Heart pounding, he prepared for an attack.

Except it was not: As one, they went down upon bended knee, bowed their heads, and struck at the ground, their daggers chipping up flakes from the stone floor.

Tohrture lifted those incredible blue eyes first. "We pledge ourselves unto you and only you."

And then they all looked up at him, their respect plain on their faces, those incredible bodies prepared to be called into service for him, by him—and only in that fashion.

Wrath put his hand over his heart and could not speak. He had not realized until this moment how alone he had been, just his shellan *and him against the world—which had felt like enough. Until now.*

And this was such the opposite of the glymera*. The courtiers' gestures were always done in public, and had no more depth than any performance—once executed, it was past.*

But these males . . .

By tradition and custom, the King bowed to no one.

And yet he bowed the now. Deeply and reverently.

Remembering words he'd heard his father speak, he pronounced, "Your vow is accepted with gratitude by your King."

Then he tacked on something that was all his own: "And it is returned. I pledge unto you, each and every, that I shall provide to you the very fealty that you have offered and I have accepted."

He met each of the Brothers in the eye.

His father had used these specially bred males for their brawn, but his alliance had been with the glymera *primarily.*

Instinct told the son the future was safer if the opposite was true: With these males behind him, he and his beloved and any young they might have would have the better chance of survival.

"There is someone who desires to meet with you," Tohrture said from his position on the floor. "We would be honored to stand guard here at your door whilst you attend to this necessary in your receiving chamber."

"I shall not leave Anha."

"If you will, my lord, please proceed unto your other chamber. This is one with whom you need to speak."

Wrath narrowed his stare. The Brother was unwavering. All of them were unwavering.

"Two of you come with me," he heard himself say. "The rest remain here to stand guard o'er her."

With a chuffing war cry, the Brotherhood rose en masse, their hard, frozen faces the very worst commentary on the state of things. But as they arranged themselves before his mated door, Wrath knew in his heart that they would lay down their lives for him or for his shellan.

Yes, he thought. His private guard.

As he departed, Tohrture fell in front of him, and Ahgony came in behind, and whilst the three of them proceeded forth, Wrath felt the protection cloak him to the point of chain mail.

"Who is awaiting us," Wrath said softly.

"We snuck him in," came the quiet reply. "None can know his identity or he will not last the fortnight."

Tohrture was the one who opened the door, and on account of his heft, there was no seeing who was—

In the far corner, a cloaked and hooded figure stood, but was not still: whoe'er it was, was shivering, the draping fabric about them animated by the fear they contained within their body.

The door was shut by Ahgony, and the Brothers did not leave his side.

Breathing in, Wrath recognized the scent. "Abalone?"

Ghost-pale hands trembled their way up to the hood and removed it.

The young male's eyes were wide, his face devoid of color. "My lord," he said, dropping to the floor, bowing his head.

It was the young, family-less courtier, the end of the lineup of dandies, the one who was there by the grace of the blood in his veins and nothing else.

"What say you?" Wrath asked, inhaling through his nose.

He caught the scent of fear, yes—but there was something more. And when he defined it for himself, he was . . . impressed.

Nobility was not ordinarily an emotion to be scented. That was more the purview of fear, sadness, joy, arousal . . . but this sapling of a male, barely a year out of a transition that had done little to increase his body weight or his height, had a purpose beneath his fear, a driving motivation that could only be . . . noble.

"My lord," he choked out, "forgive me my cowardice."

"In regard to what?"

"I knew . . . I knew what they would do and I did not . . ." A sob escaped. "Forgive me, my lord. . . ."

As the male broke down, there were two approaches. One aggressive. The other conciliatory.

He knew he would get farther with the latter.

Walking over to the male, he extended his palm. "Rise."

Abalone seemed confused at the command. But then he accepted the hand up and the direction that took him over to one of the carved oak chairs by the fireplace.

"Mead?" Wrath asked.

"N-n-n-no thank you."

Wrath sat opposite the male, his chair groaning under the weight in a way Abalone's had not. "Imbibe a deep breath."

When the command was obeyed, Wrath leaned in. "Speak unto me the truth and I shall spare you whate'er you fear. None can touch you—as long as you bear no falsity."

The male put his face in his hands. Then he breathed in deep again. "I lost my father before my transition. My mother, too, died on the birthing bed. In these departures, I am as you are."

"It is terrible for one to be left without parents."

Abalone dropped his hands, revealing eyes that were steady. "I was not supposed to discover what I found. But three dawns ago, I was down in the cellars of the castle. I could not sleep, and my melancholy caused me to walk in the underground. I was without a candle, and my feet were held within soft leather shoes—therefore, when I heard voices, they knew not of my approach."

"What did you see," Wrath asked gently.

"There is a hidden room. Beneath the kitchens. I had never seen it before, because its door has a facade to match the walls down below—and I would not have noticed it . . . except the false panel had failed to close properly. Caught upon a stone, there had been a crack through which mine eyes could focus. Inside, there were three figures, and they were circled about

a cauldron o'er a flame. Their voices were hushed as one of them added greens of some kind into whate'er they were warming. The stench was horrible—and I was about to turn around and proceed about my concerns . . . when I heard your name."

Abalone's eyes fixed on a middle distance, as if he were seeing and hearing anew that which he was recounting. "Except it wasn't you. It was your father. They were discussing how he had sickened and died—and attempting to determine the proper amount for someone of smaller stature." The male shook his head. "I recoiled. Then hurried off. My mind was twisted by what I had witnessed, and I convinced myself . . . I must have imagined thus. Surely they could not have been talking about your father, your mate. It was just—they had pledged their troth unto you and your blood. So how could they have such things pass from their lips unto the ears of others?" Clear, guileless eyes met Wrath's. "How could they do such?"

Tempering an inner fury, Wrath reached out and placed his hand upon the youth's shoulder. Even though their ages were not that far apart, he felt as though he were speaking unto one of a vastly different generation than his own.

"Worry not of their motivation, son. The impure are confounding to the righteous."

Abalone's eyes appeared to well. "I convinced myself that I had been mistaken. Until the queen . . ." He put his face back into his palms. ". . . Dearest Virgin Scribe in the Fade, when the queen went down unto the floor, I knew I had failed you. I knew I was no different from them who had caused harm, because I did not stop that which I should have known—"

To prevent a complete unraveling, Wrath squeezed that spare shoulder. "Abalone . . . Abalone, arrest yourself."

When there was a modicum of composure returned, Wrath kept his voice level, even though in his interior, he was seething. "You are not responsible for the actions of the nefarious."

"I should have come to you—they killed the queen."

"My mate is alive and well." No reason to dwell on the near loss. "I assure you, she is very well indeed."

Abalone sagged. "Thank the blessed Virgin Scribe."

"And you are forgiven by me and mine. Do you understand? I forgive you."

"My lord," the male said, dropping anew to the floor and putting his forehead to the black diamond ring Wrath wore. "I do not deserve this."

"You do. Because you came unto me, you can make the amends you seek. Can you take one of the Brothers down unto this hidden place?"

"Yes," the male said without hesitation. Springing to his feet, he put up his hood. "Now I shall show them."

Wrath nodded to Ahgony. "Go with him?"

"My lord," the Brother said, accepting the command.

"There is just one thing before you go," Wrath said on a growl. "Can you tell me who they were."

Abalone's eyes locked on his own. "Yes. Each of the three."

Wrath felt his lips lift in a smile even though he knew no joy or happiness in his heart. "Good. That's very good, son."

THIRTY-NINE

There was an advantage to living alone and being disowned by your remaining parent: When you didn't come home for an entire day, no one was gnashing their teeth over your possible demise.

Certainly cut down on the phone calls, Saxton thought as he sat across from the double doors of Wrath's study.

Rearranging himself on the ornate bench, he looked over the gold-leaf banister. Silence. Not even *doggen* cleaning. Then again, something was up in the house, something big—he could feel it in the air, and although he didn't have a lot of experience with females, he knew what it was.

Somebody was in their needing.

It wasn't the Chosen Layla again, of course. But he had heard that one female going into her time could spur others along, and clearly that had happened.

God, he hoped it wasn't Beth, he thought as he rubbed his tired eyes.

Things needed to be sorted before she—

"Do you know where he is?"

Saxton looked over the banister again. Rehvenge, the *leahdyre* of the Council, had managed to get halfway up the grand staircase without his presence even registering.

And apparently, something else was definitely up: As always, the male cut an imposing figure with his mink coat and his red cane, but his nasty expression put him into downright deadly territory.

Saxton lifted a shoulder to shrug. "I'm waiting for him myself."

Rehv stomped onto the second story and paced over to the study's doorway as if to see for himself that no one was in there. Then he frowned, pivoted on the heel of his LV loafer, and looked up at the ceiling—while discreetly rearranging himself in his pants.

At which point, he blanched. "Is it Beth?"

No reason to define what the "it" was. "I think so."

"Oh, for fuck's sake." The *leahdyre* sat down on the opposite bench and it was then that Saxton noticed the long, thin cardboard tube he was carrying. "This just keeps getting worse."

"They did it," Saxton whispered. "Didn't they."

Rehv's head whipped around and amethyst eyes narrowed. "How do you know?"

Do you hate me?

Yes, I do.

Saxton looked away. "I tried to warn the King. But . . . he was going to take care of his *shellan*."

"You didn't answer the question."

"I went to my father's house for a command performance. And when I was there, I figured out the whole thing." He grabbed his phone and scrolled through his photos, showing them to Rehv. "I snuck these. They're books of the Old Laws, all open to references of heirs and blood. Like I said, I'd hoped to get to him last night."

"It wouldn't have mattered." Rehv swept his hand over his cropped Mohawk. "They had all the wheels in motion already—"

Across the way, by the head of the hall of statues, the door leading up to the top floor opened. What emerged was . . .

"Holy shit." Rehv shook his head and muttered, "Now we know what the zombie apocalypse looks like."

The lurching, heavy-lidded, floppy-limbed nightmare bore only a passing resemblance to the King—the long hair, damp from a shower, still fell from that famous widow's peak, and the wraparounds were right, and yes, the black muscle shirt and leathers were his uniform.

But everything else was all wrong. He had lost so much weight, his pants were hanging loose as flags around his legs, the waistband sitting at his thighs, even the supposedly skintight shirt billowing off his chest. And his face was just as bad. The skin had shrink-wrapped around his high cheekbones and heavy jaw—and his throat . . . dearest Virgin Scribe, his throat.

His veins on both sides had been taken so often and with such force, he looked like an extra in *The Texas Chain Saw Massacre*.

And yet the male was floating on a cloud. The air that preceded him was soft as a summer breeze, his sense of satisfaction and happiness a bubble that surrounded him.

Such a shame to ruin it.

Wrath recognized the pair of them immediately, and as he halted, his head turned from side to side as if he were measuring their faces. Instead, Saxton was sure it was their auras.

"What."

God, that voice was hoarse, barely a whisper. There was strength behind it, though.

"We gotta talk." Rehv smacked the tube into his palm like it was a baseball bat. "Now."

Wrath responded with a vile string of curses. And then gritted out, "Fuck me, can you give me one hour to feed my fucking *shellan* after her needing?"

"No. We can't. And we need the Brothers. All of them." Rehv got to his feet with the help of his cane. "The *glymera* voted you out, my friend. And we need to drum up a response."

Wrath didn't move for the longest time. "On what grounds?"

"Your queen."

That already pale face turned positively ashen.

"Fritz!" the King bellowed at the top of his lungs.

The butler materialized from the second-floor sitting room, as if he had been waiting to be summoned for hours.

"Yes, sire?"

It was with utter exhaustion that the King muttered, "Beth needs food. Bring her everything she could want. I put her in the bath—you'd better check on her now. She was weak and I don't want her passing out and drowning."

Fritz bowed so low, it was a wonder his baggy face didn't brush the carpet. "Right away. At once."

As the *doggen* hurried off, Wrath called after him, "And will you take my dog out? And then bring him into my office."

"Of course, sire. My pleasure."

Wrath turned and faced the open doors of his study like he was going to the gallows. "Rehv, call the Brotherhood."

"Roger that. And Saxton needs to be in on the meeting. Someone's got to render an opinion on the legalities of all this."

Wrath didn't respond. He just went into the pale blue room, a living shadow in the center of all the fussy French furniture.

In that moment, Saxton could see the weight bearing down on the male, feel the heat of the fire that burned at those feet, sense the lose-lose that had presented itself in this bend in the road. Wrath was the bow of the race's ship, and as such . . . he was going to hit the glaciers first.

It was so thankless, all of it. The hours that male had spent chained to his father's desk, the paperwork passing in front of him, a blur of pages that had been prepared by others, presented by Saxton, ruled upon by Wrath, and sent back out into the world.

An endless stream of sucking need.

Getting to his feet, Saxton straightened the clothes he'd been wearing since he'd gone to his father's house and discovered the truth when it was too late.

Whatever was coming next? He was in Wrath's corner—and not just because his father and he were estranged.

He knew all too well what it was like to be forced into a mold you didn't fit—and then demonized for failing convention.

He and Wrath were kindred spirits.

Tragically.

In silence and with a heavy heart, Sola walked through the house she had shared with her grandmother, going from room to room, seeing everything and yet nothing.

"I can hire someone to do this," Assail said quietly.

Stopping in the kitchen, she stood over the little round table and looked out the window. Even though there were no external lights on, she pictured the back porch, seeing it covered with snow. Seeing him standing there in the cold.

Little frustrating. She had come here with collapsed U-Haul boxes to pack up personal stuff—not reminisce about this man. But as she opened cupboards and made estimates about how much wadded newspaper she was going to need, he was all that was really on her mind: Not the house she was leaving, not the things she was going to have to let go of, not the years that had passed since the autumn day she and her grandmother had come here and decided that yes, this house would do for the two of them.

Lot of time had passed.

And yet the only thing on her mind was the man standing behind her.

"Marisol?"

She looked over her shoulder. "I'm sorry?"

"I asked where you would like to start?"

"Ah . . . upstairs, I think."

Heading out into the living room, she picked up some of the unformed boxes, slipped some rolls of tape on her wrist, and took the stairs up. At the landing, she decided . . . her room.

It was the work of a moment to set up one of the medium-size boxes, the tape ripping out with a noise like fabric tearing, her teeth helping her scissor strips off, the four sides becoming solid and capable of holding things.

Her grandmother had been doing Sola's laundry long enough that the woman had known what clothes were favorites and had already brought them over to Assail's. What was left in the bureau were the second stringers, and she tossed them over without sweating any folding business: yoga pants that had been washed so many times they were dark gray, not black; turtlenecks that had lost their elastic around the throat but were still functional in a pinch; bras that were a little frayed at the cups; fleeces that had pilled up; jeans from high school that she used as a scale to judge her weight.

"Here," Assail said gently.

"What . . ." As she looked at his handkerchief, she realized she was crying. "Sorry."

Before she knew it, she'd sat down on her twin bed. And after blotting at her eyes, she stared at the handkerchief, running the fine fabric back and forth under her fingertips.

"What ails you?" he asked, his knees cracking as he knelt beside her.

Looking over, she studied his face. God, she couldn't believe she'd ever thought it was harsh. It was . . . beautiful.

And his extraordinary moonlight-colored eyes were pools of compassion.

But she had a feeling that was going to change.

"I have to leave," she said roughly.

"This house? Yes, of course. And we shall put it on the market, and you—"

"Caldwell."

The stillness that came over him was as pronounced as a burst of activity—everything changed, even as he remained in the same position.

"Why."

She took a deep breath. "I can't . . . I can't just stay with you forever."

"Of course you can."

"No, I can't." She refocused on his handkerchief. "I'm leaving in the morning and taking my grandmother with me."

Assail burst up and paced around the cramped room. "But you are safe with me."

"I can't be a part of the life you're living. I just . . . can't."

"My life? What life."

"I know what's coming next. With Benloise gone, you're going to need to get your product somewhere—and you're going to solve that problem in a way that puts you in charge of not just supplying Caldwell's many retail customers, but wholesaling the eastern seaboard."

"You know not what my plans are."

"I know you, though. Dominance is what you do—and that's not a bad thing. Unless you're someone trying to get away from all"—she motioned her hand back and forth—"this."

"You don't need to be a part of my work."

"Not the way it goes and you know it." She glanced up at him. "Might be true if you're a lawyer, but you're not."

"Yet you consider leaving me a better option?"

Funny, a part of her perked up that he was talking like they were a couple. But reality stomped that little wink of sunshine out. "You think you'll start another career?"

The silence that followed answered that one the way she thought it would.

His voice was annoyed. "I fail to understand the abrupt turnaround."

"I was kidnapped from my home, held against my will, and nearly raped." As he recoiled as if she'd slapped him, she cursed. "It's just . . . it's about time I go legit and stay that way. I have enough money so that I won't have to work right away, and I have another place."

"Where."

She ducked her eyes. "Not here."

"You're not even going to tell me where you're going."

"I think you'd come after me. And I'm too weak right now to say no."

A sudden scent spiked in the air and she looked around, thinking of those cologne inserts that came in magazines. But nothing had changed—it was just the two of them alone in the house, no Glade PlugIns in sight.

He came across the cheap carpet and loomed over her. "I do not wish you to go."

"Maybe it makes me demented, but I'm glad." She brought his handkerchief up to her mouth and rubbed it back and forth over her lips. "I don't want to be alone in feeling like this."

"I can keep you separate from the business. You won't have to know anything about the operations, distribution, cash positions."

"Except that for however long I'm your girlfriend, or whatever, I'm a target. And if my grandmother lives with you, too, she's a target. Benloise has family—not here in the States, but in South America. Sooner or later his body is going to show up, or his absence is going to be noted, and maybe they don't find you out. But maybe they do."

"Do you think I cannot protect you?" he demanded haughtily.

"I thought I could take care of myself. And that house of yours? I've checked it out, as you know, and it's a fortress, I'll give you that. But things happen. People get inside. People get . . . hurt."

"I do not want you to go."

She lifted her eyes back to his, and knew that she was never, ever going to forget the way he looked standing in the center of her little bedroom, hands on his hips, frown on his face, an air of confusion surrounding him.

As if he were so very used to getting his way in all aspects of life that he couldn't comprehend what was happening.

"I'm going to miss you," she said with a cracked voice. "Every day, every night."

But she needed to be smart. The attraction had been there from the very beginning—and him coming to save her had added another dimension to all that, an emotional connection forged in the kiln of her terror and pain. The problem? None of that was the basis for a solid relationship.

Hell, she'd met him while spying on him for a drug importer. He'd hunted her for trespassing. They'd both tracked the other through the night—until she'd watched him having sex with another woman for godsakes. Then came her near-tragedy and some mind-blowing sex that had been a double-edged sword in her recovery.

Sola cleared her throat. "I just need to get out. And as much as this hurts . . . that's what I'm going to do."

FORTY

Down here was better for the announcement, Wrath thought as he strode into the dining room with George at his side.

Taking his place at the head of the thirty-foot-long table, he waited for everyone to arrive. No way he was having this kind of a meeting while his ass was in his father's throne. Not going to happen. And there was no reason to exclude anyone in the household. This was going to affect everyone.

And no premeeting, also. He didn't need some private conclave with Rehv and Saxton where he learned the particulars and then had to sit around while they were regurgitated for everybody else. He didn't have a thing to hide in front of his family and nothing was going to make this any easier to hear.

Removing his wraparounds, he rubbed his eyes and thought of another reason he was glad he wasn't upstairs . . . too close to Beth. Fritz had assured him she was in bed and eating, but one thing he knew about his *shellan*? She was fully capable, even after the rigors of her needing, of heading down to see him and reconnect with the outside world.

If this was about her? She didn't need to hear it right now. Shit knew there was going to be plenty of time to tell her—

"Have a seat," Wrath muttered as he put his sunglasses back on. "You, too, Z."

He could sense Phury hesitating on the threshold of the room with his twin, and in the awkward beat that followed, Wrath shook his head. "No kissing the ring, okay? Just give me some space."

"Fair enough," Phury murmured. "Whatever you need."

So they'd been tipped off. Either that or Wrath looked as bad as he felt.

As the others arrived one by one or in small groups, he could tell by the scents who entered and in what order. Nobody said anything, and he imagined that Phury was giving hand signals to people, telling them to shut the fuck up and stay the hell back.

"I'm on your right," Rehv announced. "Saxton is next to me."

Wrath nodded in their general direction.

Sometime later, Tohr said, "We're all here now."

Wrath drummed his fingers on the table, his brain overwhelmed by the sad, anxious scents in his nose—as well as the silence. "Talk to us, Rehv," he demanded.

There was the soft sound of a chair getting pushed back on the rug, and then the *symphath* King and *leahdyre* of the *glymera*'s Council started wrestling with something. There was a pop . . . followed by an unsheathing rush.

Then parchment, a large piece . . . being unrolled. With a lot of something brushing the table.

The ribbons of the families, Wrath thought.

"I'm not going to read this shit," Rehv groused. "It's not worth my time. Upshot, they all put their seals on this. In their minds, Wrath is no longer the King."

A wellspring of anger jumped out of the throats of his household, many voices intermixing and lifting the roof, the sentiments all the same.

And actually, it was Butch's *shellan*, Marissa, who was hands down the most refined female in the house, who summed it up best:

"Those goddamn sons of bitches."

Wrath would have laughed under any other circumstances. Hell, he'd never heard her curse before. Didn't know she could pass that shit through her perfect lips.

"What are the grounds?" someone asked.

Wrath cut through the chatter with two words: "My mate."

Pin-drop silence ensued.

"The mating was entirely legal," Tohr pointed out.

"But she's not entirely vampire." Wrath rubbed his temples and thought of what he and Beth had done for the last eighteen hours. "And that means if we have young, neither are they."

Jesus Christ, this was a mess. A total fucking mess. He might have had a shot if he hadn't had any young—then the throne could have passed to his next closest relation. Butch, for example. Or any young that that brother and his mate would have.

Now, though . . . the stakes were different, weren't they.

"No one's a purebred—"

"—isn't the Middle Ages—"

"—we need to take them all out—"

"This is fucking ridiculous—"

"—why are they wasting time on—"

Wrath quieted the chaos by curling up a fist and slamming it down on the table. "What's done is done." God, this hurt. "The question is, what now. What is our response, and who the hell do they think is going to rule?"

Rehv spoke up. "I'll let Saxton tackle the legal aspects of the first part—but I can answer the second. It's a guy named Ichan, son of Enoch. It states in here"—rustling—"that he's a cousin of yours?"

"Who the fuck knows." Wrath shifted in his chair. "I've never met him. The question is, where are the Band of Bastards. They have to be involved in this."

"I don't know," Rehv said as he rerolled the proclamation. "Seems a little sophisticated for Xcor's tastes. Bullet to the brain is more his style."

"He's behind this." Wrath shook his head. "My guess is that he'll let the dust settle, kill this Ichan motherfucker, and get himself appointed."

Tohr spoke up. "Can't you just modify the Old Laws? As King, you can do anything you want, right?"

When Wrath nodded in Saxton's direction, the attorney stood up, his chair creaking quietly. "What the vote of no confidence does, from a legal point of view, is remove from the King all powers to command and rule. Any attempt now to change verbiage would be null and void. You are still King, in the sense that you have the throne and ring, but in practice, you have no power."

"So they can appoint someone else?" Wrath asked. "Just like that?"

"I'm afraid so. I found a hidden procedural note that in the absence of a King, the Council can appoint a ruler de facto with a supermajority, and that is what they have done. The passage was intended to be triggered in wartimes, in the event the entire First Family was wiped out along with any immediate heirs."

Been there, done that, Wrath thought.

Saxton continued. "They have triggered that provision, and unfortunately, from a legal standpoint, it is valid—even though it's being used in a way that was not contemplated by the original drafters of the laws."

"How did we not see this coming?" someone said.

"It is my fault," Saxton said roughly. "And accordingly, in front of you all, I tender my resignation and removal from the bar of solicitors. It is unforgivable that I missed this—"

"Fuck that," Wrath said with exhaustion. "I do not accept your—"

"My own father is the one who did this. Just as bad, I should have researched this. I should have—"

"Enough," Wrath snapped. "If you follow that argument, I should have known all along, because my sires are the ones who drafted that shit. Your resignation is not accepted, so shut the fuck up about all the quitting and sit the fuck down. I'm going to need you."

Man, he had such *great* interpersonal skills.

Wrath cursed some more, and then muttered, "So if I hear this right, there is nothing I can do."

"From a legal standpoint," Saxton hedged, "that would be correct."

In the long pause that followed, he surprised himself. After having been so miserable for not just the centuries before he'd decided to live up to his father's legacy, but the actual nights on the job, you'd think he'd be relieved. All that paperwork weighing him down, the demands from the aristocracy, the antiquated everything—oh, and then there was the stuck-in-the-house, only-sparring-with-Payne, dagger-hand atrophy that went along with everything.

To the point where he felt like a Hummel figurine.

So yeah, he should be pumped to be free of the bullshit.

Instead, he felt nothing but despair.

It was losing his parents all over again.

* * *

In the end, Wrath had to see the hidden chamber himself. Cloaking his form in a humble robe so that none would know it was he, he proceeded through the castle with Ahgony, Tohrture, and Abalone—who had resumed his disguise as well.

Moving quickly through the stone corridors, they passed members of the household, doggen, *courtiers, soldiers. Unburdened by all the bowing and the ritual greetings that would have been his due as King, they made excellent time, the finish of the castle growing coarser as they proceeded away from the court areas and down into the servants' purview.*

The smells were different, here. No fresh rushes and flowers, or hanging bundles of spices, or sweet-smelling females. In these extensive quarters, it was dark and dank, and the fires were not changed with rigid regularity, so there was a sooty undertone to every inhale. However, as they came upon the kitchen, the glorious perfume of roasting onions and baking bread elevated all that.

They did not enter the cooking arena properly. Instead, they took a narrow set of stone steps down farther into the underground. At the bottom, one of the Brothers took a lit torch from its perch and brought the flickering yellow illumination along.

Shadows followed them, scattering across the packed dirt floor like rats, tangling underfoot.

Wrath had never been down here. As the King, he was only ever in the prettified parts of the estate.

This was an appropriate place to do evil, he thought as Abalone came to a halt in front of a stretch of wall that appeared no different from any other.

"Here," the male whispered. "But I know not how they entered."

Ahgony and Tohrture began feeling around, utilizing the light to search.

"What of this?" Ahgony said. "There is a lip."

The "wall" was indeed a lie, a flimsy fabrication colored to appear as if it were part of the stone-and-mortar construction. And inside . . .

"No, my lord," Ahgony said before Wrath was even aware of stepping forward. "I shall go first."

With the torch held aloft, the Brother penetrated the darkness, the flames revealing what appeared to be a cramped workspace: Off to one side, there was a rough table on graceless legs, on which sat glass jars capped with heavy metal lids; a mortar and pestle; a chopping block; many knives. And in the center of the squat room, a cauldron sat o'er a fire pit.

Wrath strode over to its cast-iron belly. "Bring unto me the light."

Ahgony directed the illumination into the thing.

A vile stew, cold now, but clearly having been cooked, lay like the leftovers of a sewage flood.

Wrath dipped his finger in and brought up some of the brownish sludge. Sniffing it, he found that in spite of its consistency and the depth of its color, it had little fragrance.

"Do not taste, my lord," Tohrture cut in. "If you require that, allow me."

Wrath wiped his hand upon his cloak and went over to the glass jars. He recognized not the various twisted roots contained in the set, nor the flakes of leaves, nor the black powders. There was no recipe, either, no slip of parchment with notes for the preparer.

So they knew the ingredients by heart.

And they had used this space for some time, he thought, running his fingers over the pitted tabletop, and then going over to inspect the crude venting hole o'er the cauldron.

He turned to the assembled and addressed Abalone. "You have done honor to your bloodline. You have proven your worth this night. Go forth and know that what shall happen the now shall not fall upon you."

Abalone bent low. "My lord, again, I am not worthy."

"That is for me to decide and I have made my declaration. Now go. And be of silence of all this."

"You have my word. It is all I have to offer, and 'tis yours and no one else's."

Abalone reached for the black diamond and affixed a kiss upon the stone. Then he was gone, his shuffling footsteps retreating as he made his way back along the corridor.

Wrath waited until even his keen ears could hear nothing. Then in a hushed tone, he said, "I want that young male taken care of. Supply him from the treasury enough wealth to carry his generations forth."

"As you wish, my lord."

"Now, shut that door."

Soundless. Seamless. They were closed in with nary a squeak.

For the longest time, Wrath walked around the claustrophobic space, imagining the fire kindled and throwing off warmth as it broke down aspects of the plant material, the roots, the powders . . . turning nature's bounty into poison.

"Why her?" he asked. "If they killed my father and want the throne, why not me?"

Ahgony shook his head. "I have asked myself that. Mayhap they did not want an heir. Who succeeds you in your line? Who would be the next on the throne if you had no young?"

"There are cousins. Distant ones."

The royal families tended to have limited offspring. If the queen survived one birthing, they did not want to risk her unnecessarily, especially if the firstborn was male.

"Think, my lord," Ahgony prompted. "Who would be in line for the throne? Mayhap one who is soon to be born? They could be biding their time for a birth, after which they would target you."

Pulling up the sleeves of the cloak, Wrath looked down at his forearms. Following his transition, he had been inked with the family lines, and he traced what was permanently in his skin, tracking who was was living, who was dead, who had young, and who was pregnant—

He closed his eyes, the solution to the equation presenting itself. "Yes. Yes, indeed."

"My lord?"

Wrath let the cloak's sleeving fall back into place. "I know who they are thinking of. It is a cousin of mine and his mate is heavily with young the now. The other evening they were saying they prayed unto the Scribe Virgin for a son."

"About whom do you speak?"

"Enoch."

"Indeed," Tohrture said grimly. "I should have known."

Yes, Wrath thought. His chief adviser. Seeking the throne for a son who would carry the family fortunes into the future—whilst the male himself placed the crown upon his own head for centuries.

In the silence, he thought of his own receiving room, the desk with parchment covering every square foot of its surface, the quill pens and ink pots, the lists of issues for him to tend to. He loved all of that, the conversations, the judgments, the calming process of coming to a decision thoughtfully.

Then he saw his father's dead body with its gloved hands, and his shellan*'s blue fingernails.*

"This shall be handled," he declared.

Tohrture nodded. "The Brotherhood shall find and dispatch the—"

"No."

Both of the Brothers stared at him.

"They went after my blood. I shall shed theirs in response—personally."

The faces of the two trained and bred fighters became impassive—and he knew what they were thinking. But it mattered not. He owed vengeance unto his lineage and his beloved.

Across the way, there was a squat, coarse bench beneath the table and he pulled it out. Taking a seat, he nodded over at the cauldron.

"Ahgony, go forth and extol the life force of my mate. Make it known far and wide that she survived. Tohrture, stay herein with me, and await the return of the murderers. As soon as they hear the news, they shall come here again to make a second attempt—and I shall greet them."

"My lord, mayhap I could offer my service unto you in a different fashion." Ahgony looked at his Brother. "Let us escort you back to your mate, and allow us to engage whomever shall come here."

Wrath crossed his arms over his chest and leaned back against the wall. "Take the torch with you."

FORTY-ONE

Beth just had to go and look at herself in the mirror.

Even though she was in a whole new territory of exhaustion, she simply had to get out of bed, stiff-walk across the thick carpet, and zero in on the glowing light over the sinks in the bathroom. As she went along, her body was a contradiction of sore, tense muscles and liquefied, loosey-goosey innards—and her brain apparently had voted to go with the latter: She couldn't keep a thought in her head, fragments of the previous day and night burping to the forefront, but not having the traction to offer any concrete cognition.

Catching sight of her reflection, she was taken aback: It was as though she were looking at her own ghost—and not because she was pale. Actually, her skin was radiant and her eyes sparkling even though she was bone tired, like she'd gone to Sephora and had her makeup done professionally. Hell, even her hair belonged in a Pantene ad.

No, the specter part was all about the Lanz nightgown she'd put on: flannel, and big as a circus tent, the white-and-pale-blue pattern was like a cloud around her, billowing everywhere.

It made her think of *Beetlejuice*, the movie. Geena Davis and a lower-BMI, less angry Alec Baldwin stuck in the afterlife, prowling around their house in baggy sheets, about as scary as Casper.

Looking down, she bent over and picked up the drugging kit that had never been used. Rezipping it, she put it back where she'd found it, on the counter between their two sinks.

God, whether it was the aftermath or all the hormones still in her bloodstream, the whole experience was a dreamscape, as hazy a memory as it had been a wrenching, vivid experience.

But what had come before her needing was getting crystal clear. Like someone whose symptoms didn't tie together until they received a diagnosis, she thought back over the previous four months . . . and strung together the mood swings, the yearning for a child, the cravings, the weight gain.

PMS, vampire style.

This whole getting-fertile thing had been on its way for a while. She just hadn't strung together all the signs . . .

Refocusing on the mirror, she went in for a close-up. Nope, her features were all the same. She just felt as though they should be different.

Like with her transition.

Wrath had helped her through all that as well. And it was funny, as with the needing, she'd had vague weirdnesses for some time before her change had come, too: restlessness, appetite stuff, headaches in the sun.

She had to wonder if finding out she was pregnant was going to be as big as discovering she was a vampire.

Putting her hand on her lower belly, she thought . . . actually, it probably would be.

For some reason, she went back to waking up after her transition. First thing she'd done was go into the bathroom for the mirror. At least then she'd had fangs to show for all of it. Now, any changes that might be going on were on the inside.

At least her abdomen was still swollen. Although that was more likely just the weight she'd put on thanks to her Breyers diet.

Or she could be pregnant. Like, right now.

As she pictured the guy in the AT&T infinity x infinity commercial, she knew that even though Wrath had serviced her, she'd be crazy to think he'd magically turned a corner in the road and was suddenly going to be all happy-happy about starting a family.

Again, assuming she was pregnant.

Meeting the reflection of her own eyes, she wondered what the hell she'd put into motion. There were things in life you could undo.

This was not one of them—

Her stomach let out a noise like her heart was spelunking down to her butt. Glancing at the thing, she muttered, "Okay, people, let's all get along."

With her guts grinding on the food she'd thrown into them, she turned around and walked back for the bed.

Except that was not where she ended up.

Instead, she went into the closet, pulled on a blue bathrobe and shoved her socked feet into a pair of pink UGGs that Marissa had gotten all the females in the house as a joke.

The First Family's quarters were so sumptuous that Beth didn't spend a lot of time looking or thinking about the way they were turned out, and as usual, she was relieved as she left them. Yeah, sure, the place was lovely—if you were a sultan. For godsakes, it was like trying to sleep in Ali Baba's cave, jewels twinkling on the walls and the ceiling—and not fake ones, either.

And no, she'd never gotten used to the gold toilet.

The whole thing was absurd—

Holy crap, she thought as she locked the vault back up behind her. How did anyone raise a kid in that environment?

A kid that was halfway normal, that is.

Heading down the stairs to the second floor, she realized there was another aspect of the whole child thing she hadn't considered: She'd been so focused on getting one, she hadn't considered having one in this kind of life.

They'd be a prince or a princess. The former the heir to the throne.

Oh, and P.S., how do you tell a kid his or her father had been shot in the throat by someone who wanted the crown?

God, why hadn't she thought about any of this?

Which was Wrath's whole point, wasn't it.

Stepping out of the staircase, she went to Wrath's office, only distantly aware of conversation rising up from the foyer.

She was a little surprised that he wasn't behind the desk. She'd assumed when Fritz had brought up the food that her *hellren* had gotten sucked into work.

Stepping into the room, she stared at that huge wooden boat of a throne and then squinted, trying to imagine a son—or a daughter—

sitting behind it. Because screw the Old Laws: If they had a little girl, Beth herself was going to make sure her hubs changed the rules.

If the British monarchy could do it, so could the vampires.

God . . . was she really thinking like this?

Rubbing her temples, she recognized that all of this was the tip of the iceberg Wrath had been crashing into—and meanwhile, she'd been Fisher Pricing it in her head, enjoying an internal debate on cloth diapers versus Pampers, what kind of video monitor to buy, and whether or not she liked the new crib styles at Pottery Barn.

Infant and baby stuff. The kind of things she'd watched Bella and Z wrestle with, and purchase, and use.

None of what had been on her radar had been about raising children into adulthood. Which was what Wrath had been focused on.

Suddenly, the pressures inherent in that great carved chair had never seemed so real: Although she had witnessed them firsthand, the true burden of it all didn't really set in until this moment . . . as she pictured a child of hers sitting where her mate did every night.

She left the room fast.

There were two other places he would be—in the gym or maybe in the billiards room.

Oh, wait, no one was in there anymore.

At least until they got new furniture.

Man, what a mess this was.

Hiking up the nightgown and the robe, she hit the stairs at a trot—until the jiggling of her internal organs made her nauseous and she had to slow it down.

Crossing over the mosaic depiction of the apple tree, she figured she could ask whoever was in the dining room to—

The moment she came under the arches, she froze.

In spite of the fact that it was not mealtime, the entire household was at the table—and something awful had happened: Her family was like a collection of Madame Tussauds versions of themselves, the bunch of them arranged motionless in the chairs, with faces that had the right features, but expressions that read wrong.

And everyone's eyes were on her.

As Wrath's head lifted and angled her way, it was like her transition all over again, when she'd come out of her father's basement and walked in to find the Brothers at the table. The difference, of course, was that back then there had been surprise in the room.

Now, it was something altogether different.

"Who died," she demanded.

Back in the Old Country, Xcor and his Band of Bastards had stayed in a castle that appeared to have risen from the earth, as if the very stones of its construction had been rejected by the dirt, expelled like a tumor. Situated upon a scruffy, otherwise uninhabitable mount, the construction had glowered over the small hamlet of a medieval human town, the fortification not so much regal as resentful. And inside, it had been no less uningratiating: Ghosts of dead humans had wandered the many rooms and the great hall especially, knocking things off heavy tables, swinging cast-iron chandeliers, toppling stacks of burning logs from the fireplaces.

Indeed, they had fit in well there.

In the New World, however . . . they lived on a cul-de-sac, in a Colonial with a master suite the color of one's lower intestine.

"We did it! Verily, we have the throne!"

"We shall rule fore'ermore!"

"Huzzah!"

As his fighters congratulated each other and proceeded unto the alcohol, he sat upon the sofa in the living room and missed that castle's great hall. It seemed more fitting a space to play witness to the history they had set in motion and succeeded at.

Eight-foot ceilings and velour couches just did not make the grade for an event of this magnitude.

Besides, their castle . . . had formerly been the seat of the race's First Family. Wrath's dethronement announced at the very place he had been born and reared would have had such greater resonance.

Mayhap this weak, suburban locale was what was robbing him of the joy his fighters shared.

Except no, it was something else: This fight with Wrath was not over.

There was no way it ended here, like this. Too easy.

Reflecting upon his journey to this moment, Xcor could only shake his head. Before he had come unto the New World, flying across the ocean at night, things had seemed rather much in his control. Following the death of the Bloodletter, he had taken the reins of the soldiers and enjoyed centuries of conflict with the Lessening Society after the Brotherhood had come to Caldwell.

Eventually, however, after all their successes in the field, there had been no one save humans to chase after, and it was difficult to find much sport in those rats without tails.

He had wanted the throne as soon as he had landed because . . . it was there.

And perhaps he knew that unless he took the crown, he and the Band of Bastards would be hunted: Sooner or later, the Brotherhood would discover their presence and want to exert superiority over them.

Or eliminate them.

Through his efforts, though, those tables had been turned; he had gained power over them and their King. And that's what was so strange. The sense that he was in some way out of control now was illogical—

As Balthazar let out a whooping laugh and Zypher poured more gin—or was it vodka?—Xcor's temper lit.

"He has not responded yet," Xcor cut in.

The group of them turned upon him with frowns.

"Who has not?" Throe asked as he lowered his glass. The others had red plastic cups or were drinking from the bottle.

"Wrath."

Throe shook his head. "He cannae have one, as legally he is powerless. There is naught he can do."

"Do not be naive. There will be an answer to our cannon shot. This is not over the now."

He got to his feet, a restlessness drumming through his body, animating him with twitchy movements he struggled to keep within himself.

"With no disrespect intended," Throe hedged, "I fail to see what he can do."

Turning away from the joviality, Xcor said, "Mark my words, this is not over. The question is, on the basis of his reply, may we still sustain."

"Whither goest thou," Throe demanded.

"Out. And I shall not be followed, thank you."

"Thank you" was rather more like "fuck you," he thought as he dematerialized through the flimsy front door and reappeared upon the lawn.

There were no more houses in this part of the development, the only other structure a pump house for the municipal sewer system.

He tilted his head back and considered the sky. There was no light from the moon, a cloud cover that promised more snow blocking out the illumination.

Yes, in this moment of his triumph, he felt no great joy or sense of accomplishment. He had expected to be . . . well, *happy* would be one word for it, although that emotion was not in his lexicon. Instead, he was as empty as he had been when he'd arrived upon these shores and ill at ease to the point of anxiety—

Oh, fuck. He knew the cause of the worry.

It was his Chosen, of course.

Whilst his men enjoyed the illusion of victory, there was only one place he wanted to go—even though it would undoubtedly put his life at risk.

And go unto the north he did.

Traveling upon the frigid night air, his molecules scrambled in a wave to the foot of one of the mountains on the very farthest edge of Caldwell's territory.

Standing amongst the pines and oaks, his combat boots planted in the crusty snow, he looked up even though he could not see the apex of the mount.

He could not, in fact, see much more than that which was three feet afore him.

The great smudging of the landscape ahead of him was not based on the weather or the terrain. It was magic. Some kind of sleight of hand that he could not understand, but could not question the existence of.

He had followed his Chosen here.

Back when she had gone unto the clinic, and he had been terrified that the Brothers had hurt her in retaliation for feeding him, he had waited for her to emerge from treatment, and followed her here. Indeed, she had been manipulated into providing him with her vein. Had saved his life not through true choice, but a conceit created by Throe—and not for the first time did he regret sending that fighter unto the Brotherhood. If he hadn't sought to punish the male as such, neither one of them would have e'er met her.

And his *pyrocant* would have remained unknown to him.

For truth, lack of knowledge of that female's existence, of her scent and the taste of her blood, of those shattering, stolen moments in that car, would have been such a boon to him.

Instead, it was as if he had taken a saw to his own leg and cut it off.

He had unwittingly volunteered to cross her path.

Staring at the edge of the mist, he braced himself and crossed into the barrier. His skin registered an instant warning, his inner instincts activated by the force field, teased by a rootless feeling of terror. Proceeding forth, his boots crunched through the ground cover, only a slight rise informing him that he was, in fact, beginning the ascent up the mountain.

In this moment of triumph, the only place he wanted to be was with the female he could not have.

FORTY-TWO

Generally speaking, if your husband refused to say a word until the pair of you were behind closed doors and alone?

Shit was not going well.

As Beth heard the double doors of the study shut behind them, she went over to the banked fire and put her palms out to the heat. She was suddenly feeling very cold . . . especially as Wrath did not go behind the desk and sit down on his father's throne.

Her *hellren* settled into one of the two French-blue sofas, and the effeminate little thing let out a very unlady-like protest as his weight landed.

George settled at his master's feet, the dog staring up as if he, too, were waiting for the other shoe to drop.

Wrath just stared straight ahead even though he couldn't see a thing, his brow tight behind the bridge of his wraparounds, his aura black as his hair.

Turning, she backed her butt into the heat source and crossed her arms. "You're scaring me."

Silence.

"Why aren't you sitting behind the desk," she said roughly.

"It's not mine anymore."

Beth felt all the blood leave her head. "What are you . . . I'm sorry, what?"

Wrath took off his sunglasses and braced an elbow on his knee as he rubbed his eyes. "The Council has removed me."

"What the . . . fuck. How? What did they do?"

"It doesn't matter. But they got me." He laughed in a short burst. "Listen, at least now all that paperwork over there? Not my problem. They can govern themselves—have a ball infighting and arguing about stupid bullshit—"

"What were the grounds?"

"You know what's really fucked-up? I hated doing the job, and yet now that it's gone . . ." He rubbed his face again. "Anyway."

"I don't get it. You're the King by blood and the race is ruled by the monarchy. How did they do this?"

"It doesn't matter."

Beth narrowed her stare. "What are you not telling me?"

He burst up and walked around, having memorized the furniture layout long ago. "This'll give us more time together. Not a bad thing, especially if you're pregnant. And hell, if you have a young now, part of what I was all up in my head about is a non-issue—"

"I'm going to find out, you realize. If you don't tell me, I'll get someone who will."

Wrath went over to the desk and ran his hands down the carved edges. Then he fingered the top of the throne, caressing the ins and outs of the wood.

"Wrath. Talk. Now."

Even with her laying it down like that, it was a long while before he spoke. And when he finally did, his reply was nothing she expected . . . and as devastating as any piece of it all.

"They based it on . . . you."

Okay, time to have a little sit-down.

Going to the same sofa he'd sat in, she all but fell into the soft cushions. "Why? How? What did I do?"

God, the idea that she'd cost him the throne because of something she'd—

"It's not anything you've done. It's . . . who you are."

"That's ridiculous! They don't even know me."

"You're half-human."

Well, that shut her up.

Wrath came over and knelt down in front of her. Taking her hands, he held them in his so-much-larger palms. "Listen to me, and you have to be clear on this—I love you, all of you, each and every part of you. You are perfect in every way—"

"Except for the fact that my mother was human."

"That's their fucking problem," he snapped. "I don't give a fuck about their goddamn prejudice. It doesn't affect me at all—"

"Noooooot exactly true, is it. Because of me you're not sitting on that throne anymore, right?"

"You know what? The shit's not worth it to me. You're what's important. You're what matters. Everything else—every*one* else can fuck off."

She glanced over at the throne. "You mean to tell me you don't care that your father's seat is no longer your own?"

"I hated the job."

"That's not my point."

"The past is the past and my parents have been dead for centuries."

She shook her head. "Does that really matter, though. I know why you stuck with it all—it's for them. Don't lie to me—more important, don't lie to yourself."

He sat back sharply. "I'm not."

"Yeah, I think you are. I've watched you these past two years. I know what's motivated you—and it would be a mistake to think all that commitment up and disappears because some third party says you can't wear the crown anymore."

"Number one, it's not 'some third party.' It's the Council. Number two, it's a *fait accompli.* What's done is done."

"There must be something you can do. Some way around this—"

"Just drop it, Beth." He got to his feet, his head turning in the vague direction of the throne. "Let's move ahead—"

"We can't."

"Fuck that."

"It's one thing if you resigned, or abdicated or whatever the hell it's called. That's free choice. But you don't do well taking orders from other people." She tacked on dryly, "We've discussed this before."

"Beth, you gotta let this go—"

"Think about the future, a year from now, two years from now . . . do you mean to say you're not going to resent me for this?"

"Of course not! You can't change who you are. It's not your fault."

"You say that at this moment, and I believe you—but a decade from now, when you look your son or daughter in the face, you think you won't resent me a little for cheating them out of—"

"Getting shot at? Criticized by all comers? Placed on a pedestal you don't want to be on? Hell, no! All that shit is part of the reason I didn't want a goddamn kid!"

Beth shook her head again. "I'm not so sure about that."

"Jesus Christ," he muttered, locking his hands on his hips. "Do me a favor and don't make up my own fucking mind for me, okay."

"We can't ignore the possibility—"

"I'm sorry, did I miss something? Did some fortune-teller slip you a crystal ball or some shit? Because no offense, you can't look into the future any more than I can."

"Exactly."

Wrath threw up his hands and started in with the stomping. "You don't get it, you just don't fucking get it. This is done, it's zipped up. The vote of no confidence passed—I'm castrated as a ruler, I have no power or authority. So even if there was anything I could do from a legal standpoint? I'm not the person who can change things anymore."

"So who is?"

"A distant cousin of mine. Real peach of a guy."

Her *hellren's* tone suggested *peach of a guy* was a euphemism for *total fucking douche*.

Beth crossed her arms over her chest. "I want to see the proclamation or document—there had to be one, right? I don't think they'd just leave you a voice mail."

"Oh, my God, Beth, will you leave this alone—"

"Does Saxton have it? Or did they send it to Rehv—"

"Will you be fucking normal!" he hollered at her. "You just went through your needing! Most females are in bed for a week, why can't that be you? You want a young, go lie goddamn down—that's what you're supposed to do. I'm surprised with all that time you spent with goddamn Layla she didn't tell you . . ."

As he went on and on, she knew this was just steam being released through vocabulary. But they didn't have time for him to keep it up indefinitely.

Getting up from her seat, she walked over to him and—

Slap.

As Beth followed through with her palm, the sharp cracking sound faded in the room and her beloved mate shut up.

Staring at him calmly, she said, "And now that I have your attention and you're not ranting and raving like a lunatic, I'd appreciate your telling me where I can find whatever they sent us."

Wrath let his head fall back as if he were utterly exhausted. "Why are you doing this."

Abruptly, she thought of what he'd said to her when her needing had hit and he'd found her trying to get at the drugs.

In a voice that cracked, she replied, "Because I love you. And you either don't want to acknowledge it, or you can't see that far into the future, but this really, totally matters to you. I'm telling you, Wrath, this is the kind of stuff that people never get over. And like I said, you want to quit? Fine. That's your choice. But I'll be good and goddamned if I'm going to let someone take it away from you."

He brought his jaw back to level. "You don't get it, *leelan*. It's over."

"Not if I have anything to do with it."

There was a long moment . . . and then he reached out and crushed her to him, holding her so tightly she could feel her very bones bend.

"I'm not strong enough for this," he whispered in her ear—like he didn't want anyone to hear that coming out of his mouth. Ever.

Running her hands up his powerful back, she held him just as hard. "But I am."

It was forever.

Wrath waited in the hidden room that smelled like earth and spice for forever. In the blackness, his thoughts were loud as screams, vivid as lightning, indelible as an inscription in stone.

And just when he thought it would never happen, that he and his silent, stewing companion would be always in the dark, literally and figuratively, there was a rasping sound and the camouflaged panel began to slide back.

"No matter what occurs," he whispered to the Brother, "you are not to interfere. I hereby command you thus, and hear me well."

Tohrture's response was no louder than a breath: "As you wish."

The flickering light of a torch cast only shallow illumination, but it was more than enough for Wrath to identify the male: a cleric who was on the periphery of court . . . but whose father had been a healer for the race.

A keeper of herbs and potions.

The male was muttering under his breath. ". . . make more in a night's time. Cannae do that which is impossible . . ."

As the male went for the worktable, Wrath's body acted without benefit of his mind. Springing forth from the shadows in a sloppy fashion, he grabbed upon the thin upper arm, putting his strength into the effort without any finesse. In response, there was a high-pitched yelp of surprise, but then that torch swung about and Wrath nearly lost his hold as the open flames flashed close to his eyes.

"Shut the door!" Wrath called out as he attempted to catch the cleric around the waist.

Even though there was no comparison in their sizes, with Wrath twice as big, the cleric's robes were slippery to hold on to and the thrashing of his prey difficult to control. And that torch was a danger as both sought to control it: With shadows racing across the walls and the cauldron and the table, Wrath found his hands getting burned as he attempted to—

And then the cape he'd used to hide his identity was afire.

As a searing heat flashed up his side and headed for his hair, he jumped back and fumbled for his dagger for to cut the fabric free—except the blade was under his cloak. All he could do was feel the outline of the hilt in its holster.

Leaping back, he went to pull the voluminous wieght fabric o'er his head, but had to retract his hand with a shout of pain. In the next heartbeat, flames were all over him, and though he tried to bat them away, it was like fending off a cloud of wasps. Flailing, blinded by agony and heat, great woofs! *of sound bracketing his ears, he realized . . .*

He was not going to emerge alive from this.

Breath short, heart pounding, soul screaming from the unfairness of it all, he wished he was a different male, a male of the sword, not of the pen, one who could dominate another with alacrity and confidence—

The deluge came from above and it was foul-smelling, foul-tasting—and so viscous, it was more wet wool blanket than liquid. With a hiss and fizzle, and a stench that made his eyes water even more, the flames were gone, the fire out, the mad flailing over.

A great clatter ensued as Tohrture tossed the weighty cauldron aside. "Drink not, my lord! Spit it out if you have partaken!"

Wrath bent over and expelled what had been caught between his lips.

And when a rag was shoved into his hands, he was able to clear the dripping sting from his eyes.

Bracing his palms on his thighs, he breathed deeply in hopes that he would stop panting, his exertion making his head spin. Or mayhap that was the smoke. The pain. That mess that had been dumped upon him.

After a moment, he realized that the light had become steady and he glanced in the direction of the illumination. The Brother had captured control of the torch . . . as well as subdued the cleric, the male down and curled in on himself, his legs flopping about.

"How did you—" A round of coughing cut off Wrath's inquiry. "What did you wrought unto him."

"I cut the tendons behind his knees so that he cannot run."

Wrath recoiled at the thought. But the utility was well apparent.

"He is yours to do with what you will, my lord," Tohrture said, stepping back.

As Wrath looked over at the cleric, it was hard not to contrast the Brother's calm demeanor and successful effort with his own frazzled, frothing mess of a self: For Tohrture, the effect had been but the work of a moment to accomplish.

Shuffling over to the compromised male, he forced the cleric onto his back, and there was a slice of satisfaction as those eyes peeled wider when Wrath's identity became apparent.

"Whom do you serve," Wrath demanded.

The reply was a sputter that went nowhere, and before Wrath knew what he was doing, he gripped the cleric's dress and hauled him up off the packed dirt. Shaking him, that loose head flopping this way and that, Wrath was struck by a deep, abiding need to kill.

There was no time to examine the foreign emotion, however.

Dragging the male higher so they were nose-to-nose, Wrath growled, "If you tell me who else, I will spare your young shellan *and your son. If I find out there is even one that you leave out? Your family will be bound hand and foot, hung in my great hall by the ankles, and left to expire over time."*

Whilst Tohrture smiled a bloodthirsty grin, the cleric's face went e'er paler.

"My lord . . ." the male whispered. "Spare me as well—spare me and I will tell you all."

Wrath stared into those pleading eyes, watching tears well and fall . . . and thought about his shellan, *his father.*

"Please, my lord, show me mercy—I beg of you—show me mercy!"

After a long moment, Wrath inclined his head once. "Proceed."

In a shaky rush, names came forth, and Wrath recognized them all.

It was the entire composite of his advisers, starting with Ichan and ending before Abalone—who had already proved where his loyalties lay—

The inner vibration of violence began to ratchet up as soon as the final name was uttered and the cleric fell quiet—and the urge to kill would not be denied.

His hand was trembling as it fumbled for the hilt of his dagger, and he withdrew his weapon with herky-jerky motions, the angle wrong for removal, the blade getting caught in its sheath.

But he did manage to free it.

Letting the cleric fall back down to the earth, he clamped a hold on the male's throat and began to squeeze.

"My lord . . ." The cleric started to struggle, clawing at Wrath's wrist. "My lord, no! You vowed—"

Wrath lifted his arm high—

And realized he'd blocked a clear shot at the heart, the jugular, and the major organs with his hold.

"My looooooooooord—"

"This is for mine blood!"

He thrust all of his strength into the downward arc—and was meeting the horrified stare of the cleric as the razor point of the dagger pierced the male's right eye and proceeded apace into the brain behind it, stopping only when the entirety of the blade was embedded within that skull.

The body beneath his own went into immediate spasms, arms and legs thrashing, the remaining eye rolling back so that only the white showed.

And then all went still except for some minor twitching of the facial muscles and the hands.

Wrath slumped, falling off the now-dead body.

As he regarded the sight of that dagger protruding from a male's face, he was o'ercome with nausea and had to wrench around, brace his palms on the cool dirt, and vomit until his arms could no longer hold him up.

Rolling to the side, he laid his hot face on the inside of his muck-soaked arm.

He did not cry.

He wanted to.

As the realization that he had killed another being hit him, he desired to go back to the world he knew before this—where his father had died of natural causes, and his shellan *had simply had a dizzy spell because of a pregnancy—and the worst thing he had to worry about in court was that others gossiped over his choice of mate.*

This new version of reality was nothing he wanted to be a part of.

There was no light on this side. Just midnight black.

"I have never killed someone before," he said in a small voice.

For all his fierceness, Tohrture's tone was gentle. "I know, my lord. You did well."

"I did not."

"Is he not dead?"

Yes, indeed he was. "I meant what I said about his shellan *and son. They shall be spared."*

"Of course."

As the listing of names ran through his head, that urge to kill rekindled, even as his stomach was barely settling—and his efforts were a mockery compared to what the Brotherhood could do.

And indeed, he would not be alive the now if Tohrture had not stepped in.

Wrath pushed himself off the dirt, his head hanging low. How was he going to—

A large palm presented itself before him. "My lord, allow me to help you."

Wrath looked up into those bright, clear eyes—and thought that they were like the moon, shedding light upon the darkness, showing a path out of the wild.

"We shall train you," Tohrture said. "We shall teach you what you need to know such that you may ahvenge *your bloodline. I shall remove that body and stage it as if an accident befell him—that will give us the time we need. And from now on, food shall be prepared in your receiving quarters by our own personal* doggen, *not anyone affiliated with the court—and any and all victuals shall be brought in from the fields and sky by a Brother's own hands. We shall each eat and drink of it in your presence before you do, and sleep outside your rooms. This is our solemn vow."*

For a moment, all Wrath could do was stare at that palm, outstretched unto him like a benediction from the Scribe Virgin Herself.

He opened his mouth to offer thanks, but there was naught that came out.

By way of reply, he clasped that which was before him . . . and felt himself lifted up to stand squarely upon his own two feet.

FORTY-THREE

Fresh air was good for the mind and the soul.

As Layla strode out into the garden, she was careful across the ice-covered terrace, splaying her arms out, going slowly: She didn't want to run the risk of falling.

Funny how her assessment of everything from potentially slick surfaces to stairs to selecting food had intensified.

"Off into the night," she said to the young within her belly.

It was, of course, crazy to speak to that which had yet to be born. But she had some thought that if she could only keep the dialogue open, mayhap the young would continue to choose to stay around. If she could just eat the right things and not fall and get her rest . . . somehow, at the end of however many months, she could hold her son or daughter in her arms, and not just in her body.

Walking down onto the snow-covered lawn and away from the glow of the house, she found the boots she had snagged from the back hall to be warm, solid and comfy. The same was true of the parka and the gloves. She'd left the hats and scarves behind; she'd wanted the chill to clear her head.

Farther along the grounds, the swimming pool was sporting its winter cover, but she imagined it full of water lit from underneath, the azure waves inviting and soft upon the skin and joints. She was going to swim as soon as she could—and outdoors. Much as she appreciated the pool that was in the training center, the air there smelled of chlorine, and after having been used to the crystal clear, naturally fresh baths above in the Sanctuary, she didn't favor . . .

Abruptly, she stopped walking. Stopped with the distracted thinking. Stopped everything except the draw in her lungs and the beat of her heart.

Closing her eyes, she replayed what had happened in the dining room, seeing the anguish on Wrath's face as the announcement was made, hearing the indignation and aggression in the Brotherhood's voices, watching how Rehv kept staring at the King as if he were reading things she could not sense.

Xcor was behind it all.

He had to be. One did not go from orchestrating an assassination attempt to sitting back idly whilst the *glymera* gained procedurally what one wanted. No, he was lurking behind the scenes. Somewhere.

Stomach churning, she resumed her restless promenade, heading past the pool area and into the geometrically constructed formal gardens. And she kept going on their far side as well, linking up with the twenty-foot-tall retaining wall that ran all the way around the compound.

Continuing ever onward, her ears were numb. So was her nose. She didn't care.

Images of Beth appearing in the archway of the dining room and Wrath looking down the vast table at her warred with a far more traitorous and just as tragic montage of . . .

That which she refused to think of.

Or at least tried not to.

Had she really allowed Xcor into that car? Had he really sat next to her, unarmed, his menagerie of weapons left on the hood of the Mercedes . . . and talked to her? Held her hand?

"Stop it," she warned herself.

No good would e'er come of remembering that connection, that burning spark.

Layla slowed. Stopped. Recalled with great precision and no small amount of guilt the way Xcor had looked at her.

She knew so little about him—apart from his political aspirations, he was a total stranger, and a deadly one at that. And yet she had the sense, given his awkwardness with her, that he was not one who reveled in females very often.

With his facial disfigurement, it was obvious why.

But with her . . . he was different.

Aside from the pregnancy, which she had actively brought about, she had never affected much during the course of her life. But she could not stand idly by while there was mayhap even a little she could do to help Wrath in this horrible situation.

She had such guilt. Over so much.

She could, however, attempt to do something about it all.

Taking out her cellular phone, the one Qhuinn had insisted she take with her everywhere, she called up the dialing screen.

Xcor had told her how to call him, the digits engraved upon her mind the moment they had left his lips.

She had never imagined putting them into service.

With each finger tap of the screen, the phone let out a different tone, the sequence completed in seven contacts.

She hovered over the send button. And then she pressed it.

Her whole body was shaking as she put the thin, playing card–size device to her ear. An electronic ringing sounded once . . . twice. . . .

Layla wrenched around.

From over on the left, on the far side of the wall, she heard a distant sound, one so faint that if it hadn't mirrored exactly the rhythm of that which was in her own phone, she might have not paid it any mind.

The cellular device slipped from her grip and bounced upon the snow at her feet.

He had found them.

Standing in the shower at Assail's house, Sola didn't know how long she stayed under the hot spray, letting the water pound on her shoulders and fall down her back, closing her eyes and leaning into the wall.

For some reason, she was ice-cold—even though there was enough steam in the bathroom to qualify the loo as a sauna, and she was pretty sure she had increased her core temperature to a hundred and five.

Nothing was touching the deep freeze that had taken up res in the center of her chest.

She had told her grandmother they were leaving just before dawn for Miami.

In retrospect, investing in a safe place in the heart of Benloise's family business had been a dumb-ass thing to do. But with any luck, Eduardo, assuming he was still on the planet and the beneficiary of his brother's will, would be so busy enjoying the purchase of pale blue Bentleys and animal-print Versace sheets that he wouldn't come after the likes of her.

Assuming he even knew what his brother had done to her. Or planned for her.

Ricardo had kept so much to himself.

God . . . what had Assail done to that man?

A quick flash of that face of his, bloodied around the mouth and chin, increased her chill, and she turned around—

"Fuck!" she screamed as she looked out the foggy glass.

The male figure who had appeared in the doorway was still as a statue and powerful as a tiger. And he was watching her as a predator might.

Instantly, she was hot on the inside of her skin—because she knew why he had come, and she wanted it, too.

Assail strode to the glass door that separated them and tore it open. He was breathing hard, and in the inset light above her head, his eyes were bright as match strikes.

He stepped into the shower fully clothed, his Gucci loafers no doubt ruined, his dark brown suede jacket absorbing the falling water and turning the color of blood.

Without a word, he clamped his hands on her face and dragged her by the head to his mouth, his lips crushing hers as he backed her up against the marble with his entire body. Sola gave in with a moan, accepting his tongue as it penetrated her, gripping his shoulders through his fine clothes.

He was fully erect and he ground his hips against her, pushing his hard cock in and rubbing it against her belly, the gold H of his belt scratching at her. More kissing, the desperate, starved kind that you remembered even when you were eighty and far too old to think of such things. And then his hands were on her slippery breasts, his fingers pinching her nipples until the distinction between pain and pleasure disappeared and all she knew was that if she didn't orgasm in the next moment, she was going to expire—

As if sensing what she needed, Assail dropped to his knees, threw one of her legs over his shoulder, and went down on her, his lips eating at her sex in the same way he'd attacked her mouth.

This was sex as punishment, an indictment of her choice, a physical expression of his anger and his disapproval.

And maybe it made her a sick bitch, but she loved it.

She wanted him to come at her like this, pissed off and nothing but edge, pouring himself into her so she didn't have to feel as guilty . . . or as empty.

Gripping his soaked hair, she tilted her hips and forced him even harder into her, using her calf to his back so he found a rhythm that—

Sola bit down on her lip as she came wildly, her torso jerking against the marble with a high-pitched squeak.

Before she knew it, she was on the floor of the shower, stretched out in front of him as he peeled his soaked jacket and silk shirt from his carved chest. As he went for his belt buckle, she reached out for him, her hands impatient to get to that smooth skin and those hard contours of his.

He never said a word to her.

Not as he spread her legs wide and mounted her, not as his cock went in and he started pounding on her, not even as he braced himself above her and stared into her eyes as if he were daring her to leave everything he could give her.

Assail's broad back caught the spray, shielding her from it, keeping her vision clear—so she could see everything from his fierce expression to his bulging shoulder muscles to the shadows thrown by his pecs. His wet hair swung to the rhythm, drops of water leaving the tips of the waves like tears, and every once in a while his lip would curl back—

Dimly, something registered as not right, a red flag raised in the far recesses of her brain. But that was so easy to ignore as another surging release took over, shutting down thought so that sensation was all she knew . . . Assail was all she knew.

As her sex fisted his erection, he began to orgasm, too, his body rearing back—

No condom. Shit!

Just as the thought flashed through her mind, it was gone again, her release redoubling on itself so instead of pushing him back, she reached out and sank her nails into his hips.

It was right about when her own release was fading that things went . . . a little strange.

Her body stilled in recovery and she felt him kicking deep inside of her, finishing what he had started.

Except he wasn't done with her.

After he'd finished ejaculating, his pelvis locking against hers, he began to withdraw almost immediately. And she expected him to lie with her on the marble; maybe lift her up and carry her out to dry off and get in bed; maybe make a comment that, damn it, they hadn't been safe in the slightest.

Maybe tell her what he'd shown her: that he didn't want her to go.

Instead, he braced his upper weight on one hand and gripped his glistening cock with the other. Stroking himself, he groaned as if he were getting ready to come again.

The second orgasm shot out of him and he directed it all over her sex—and he didn't stop there. After he'd covered her core, he moved up, shifting himself so that he came on her stomach, her rib cage, her breasts, her neck, her face. He seemed to have an endless supply of releases, and as the hot jets hit her oversensitized skin, she found herself orgasming along with him, sweeping her hands up and down her body, feeling the hot mess he was coating her with, cupping her own breasts.

In that back room of her brain, she knew there was some other point to all this.

But as with the lack of a condom, she was too in the moment to care.

It was as if he were . . . marking her . . . in some way.

And that was okay with her.

FORTY-FOUR

Xcor was totally disoriented in the midst of the mist and knew that it was getting time to turn back. He'd been aimlessly tromping up the mountain for what felt like hours, and had still not reached any kind of summit or fortification. All he'd seen were evergreen trees. The occasional stream bed that was iced over. Deer prints in the snow—

His phone rang quietly in his pocket.

Even as he cursed the interruption, he recognized it was the proper cue to stop this madness, undoubtedly one of his Bastards checking in. Besides, assuming he discovered the Brotherhood's lair, what did he expect to do? Howl outside of the Chosen's window until she agreed to meet with him?

All that would do was get him surrounded by warriors—and although he'd heard that red was the color of love, bloodshed was no proper replacement for a rose.

Retrieving his cell, he answered it brusquely. "Yes?"

A sharp sound reverberated in his ear, shrill and loud enough that he pulled the thing away.

Returning it into range, he barked, "*What.*"

No reply.

"Damn it, Throe—"

All at once, every instinct he had or would ever possess started to scream—and not in warning as if he were about to be attacked.

Dropping his hand, he turned around slowly, afraid that it was some kind of internal misfire—

His breath left him on a long sigh as he beheld what had appeared afore him.

It was . . . her.

From out of the dense fog, his Chosen had materialized—and the impact of her presence leveled him even as he remained standing. Oh, lovely to behold, her gentle spirit making him feel the monster in him with great clarity.

"How are you here?" she asked in a trembling voice.

He looked around. "Where am I?"

"I—you mean you do not know?"

"The Brotherhood must not be far, but I can see or find naught in this godforsaken spell."

Wrapping her arms around herself, she seemed to be conflicted—but why wouldn't she be. He had to be close to where she stayed, although there was no judging whether that was in terms of meters or miles.

"How fare you?" he asked quietly. "I wish there was moonlight. I would seek to see you better."

But he could smell her—and that scent of hers. That *scent.*

"I called you," she whispered after a long moment.

He felt his brows lift. "That was you? Just the now?"

"Yes."

For a treacherous second, his heart beat faster than if he'd run up here to her. But then . . . "You heard."

"About what you did to Wrath."

"That was the Council's choice."

"Do not pretend with me."

He closed his eyes. Alas, he could not. "I told you the throne was to be mine."

"Where are your soldiers?"

"As if I have come this night to rout the Blind King out of his home?"

Her voice grew stronger. "You have taken what you want from him, and used his beloved to do it. Why bother with him now."

"He is not the one I came to see."

The Chosen's breath left her in a rush—even though the admission surely was not a surprise.

And God save him, Xcor took a step closer to her, even though by all that was right and proper, he should have run: She was more dangerous to him than any Brother, especially as the fine tremors that vibrated up through her slender body registered upon him.

He hardened fully. It was impossible not to respond.

"You know that, don't you," he said with a soft growl. "Were you calling me to see if you could sway mine actions? Go on, now. You can be honest—'tis just you and me out here. Alone."

She lifted her chin. "I shall never understand your hatred for that good male."

"Your King?" He laughed harshly. "A good male?"

"Yes," she countered with real heat. "He is an abidingly good soul who has a true love match with his mate—a male who pledges nightly to do his best for the race—"

"Truly? And how is he accomplishing that laudable goal? No one e'er sees him, you know. He ne'er goes out to mingle with the aristocrats or the commoners. He is a recluse who has failed to deliver in a time of war. If it were not me, 'twould be another—"

"It is wrong! What you did is wrong!"

He shook his head, at once admiring the principled naïveté and saddened that she was going to have to grapple with it. "'Tis the way of the world. Strength conquers weakness. It is as universal as gravity and sunset."

Even through her outerwear, he could tell that her breasts were pumping above her locked forearms, and his eyes dipped down before closing briefly. "I have ne'er cared for innocence," he muttered.

"Pardon the offense, then."

Lifting his lids, he said, "But I find that, as always when it comes to you, the revelations continue apace."

Her long hands reached out to him, pleading across the cold air. "Please. Just stop. I'll . . ."

When she could only swallow hard, he found himself going still. "You'll do what."

With jerky movements, she paced around before him. And as yet, he could not move a single muscle.

"What exactly," he asked deeply, "will you do?"

She stopped. Raised that lovely chin. Challenged him with her stare and her body, even though she was two hundred pounds lighter than he and utterly untrained.

"You may have me."

"Is it hot in here—or am I crazy?"

When no one answered her, Beth glanced across the study. Saxton, Rehv, and Wrath were all quiet as they took up space on the matched set of blue sofas. The first two were staring into the dwindling fire, and she didn't know where Wrath had directed his eyes.

Hell, even though he was in the same room with her, she didn't have a clue where he was.

Taking off her robe, she put it on the great carved desk and read the proclamation again. The chair she'd chosen was the one Rehv usually took, the soft-seated bergère, she thought he'd called it, off to the side of where Wrath's throne was.

She refused, in spite of what she held in her hands, to refer to the giant chair as anything but her mate's.

Looking back down at the parchment, she shook her head at all the symbols that had been so carefully inked. When it came to the Old Language, she was slow with the literacy thing, having to think of the definition of each character before she could string a sentence together. But what do you know—on the second trip through, everything was the same as the first.

Putting the stiff, heavy paper with all its colorful fringe back on the desk, she ran her fingers over the satin lengths that were secured by wax seals. The things were as narrow and smooth as the strips of ribbon used in the hair of little girls, perfect for tying onto a pigtail.

Not that she had baby on the brain or anything.

"So there's really nothing we can do about this?" she said after a while.

Man, she was hot. Flannel had not been a good choice—either that or it was stress.

Saxton cleared his throat when no one else volunteered to reply. "Procedurally, they have followed the rules. And from a legal perspective, their foundation is correct. Technically, as the Old Laws read now, any offspring of . . ." More throat clearing. And he glanced at Wrath as if to measure how volcanic things were going to get. ". . . the both of you would be bound for the throne, and there is a provision concerning the blood of our ruler."

Her hand went to her lower belly. The idea that a group of people would target her child, even though it was unborn and maybe not even in existence, was enough to make her want to go down to the practice range and squeeze off a couple of clips.

Back when she'd been in the human world, she'd been discriminated against as a woman from time to time, *cough*Dickthe-Prick*cough*. She'd had no experience with any racial stuff, however. As someone who had appeared Caucasian, even though, as it turned out, she was only half-white because she was only half-human, that whole side of things had never been an issue.

Man . . . to have an opinion about an individual based on characteristics attached to the sperm lottery was nuts. People couldn't help what sex they were coming out of the womb; nor could they change the composition of their parents.

"That *glymera*," she muttered. "What a bunch of assholes."

"I'm probably next by the way," Rehv said. "They know about my ties to you both."

She focused on the Mohawked male. "I'm so sorry."

"Don't be. I only stayed with the job to help you two and the Brotherhood." Then he tacked on dryly, "I got plenty on my hands up north to keep me busy."

That's right, she thought. It was so easy to forget that he was not only the *leahdyre* of the Council, but the king of the *symphaths*.

"And you can't throw them all out or something?" she asked the male. "I mean, as *leahdyre*, you can't—I don't know, get a new roster of people?"

"I'll let our good lawyer friend over here chime in if I get it wrong, but it's my understanding that membership on the Council is determined by family. So even if I did find grounds to boot the fuckers, they'd just be replaced by members of those bloodlines—who'd likely have the same opinion of things. But more to the point, what's done is done. Even if they were all turned over with new people? The action still stands."

"I just keep thinking there's something—"

"Can we stop this now," Wrath cut in. "I mean, can we just give this bullshit a rest? No offense, but the angles have been looked at, you've read the thing they sent over—what's done is done."

"I just can't believe it was so easy." She stared at the throne. "I mean, one piece of paper and it's over."

"I fear for the future," Saxton murmured. "That value system of theirs is not good for people like me. Or for females. We'd made such progress over the past two years—bringing the race out of the Stone Age. Now? That's going to be wiped clean—mark my words."

Wrath burst up. "Listen, I gotta go."

With long strides, he came over to her, one hand out into the thin air for her to grab onto and pilot him in the last couple of inches.

As she took his palm and pulled him down to her, she leaned her head to one side so he could kiss her jugular, leaned to the other so he could do the same on the left, and then put her lips in the way of his mouth so he could brush her there, too.

And then he and George left.

Watching him go, she hated how drawn he was, how weak, how wasted—although physically speaking that was more what she had done to him during the needing. Mentally and emotionally? Long line of people responsible for that.

Although she was one of those, too.

"There has to be a way," she said to no one in particular.

God, she prayed her *hellren* wasn't heading for the gym. The last thing he needed was more exercise—rest and food was what his body required right now.

But she knew that look on his face all too well.

FORTY-FIVE

Xcor had never been a male of letters. Not merely untutored in literature, he was, in fact, illiterate—and on a regular basis, Throe used words either in English or the mother tongue that he did not understand.

And yet one would suppose, even at his lowest level of ability, that the four one-syllable words just spoken to him—at least, if taken individually—offered no challenge to comprehension.

His brain, however, was refusing to process them.

"Whate'er did you speak?" he asked roughly.

As Layla repeated what she had uttered, her scent was infused with the sharp spice of fear: "You may have me."

Xcor closed his eyes and fisted his hands. His body had already translated her speech and answered of its own volition, his muscles twitching to get at her, take her down unto the cold ground, mount her to mark her as his.

"You know not what you say," he heard himself mutter.

"I do."

"You are with young."

"I . . ." Even with his lids down, he could picture her swallowing hard. "Does that mean you do not want me?"

He took a moment to breathe, his lungs burning. "No," he groaned. "It does not."

Indeed, as he imagined her with another, the lance of pain that went through his chest was sufficient to make him pale. And yet, in spite of the seed of another planted within her body, he would take her, have her, keep her. . . .

Except for one thing.

Opening his eyes, he reviewed all manner of detail about her, from her beautiful upswept hair to her fine, delicate features to that slender neck he wanted under his mouth. There was more to see, of course—but it was her face most of all that he needed foremost in his mind's eye.

It had been a kind of madness since the beginning with her—e'er since he had been brought to her under the maple in that meadow, e'er since he had been given her wrist and taken from her wellspring, he had been infected with an illness.

"Answer me one thing." His eyes continued to roam, measuring each nuance of her frightened, frozen expression.

"What?" she prompted when he did not immediately speak.

"But for the events that have transpired, would you have e'er offered yourself unto me?"

She dropped her stare. Tightened her arms about her heart. Hung her head.

"Answer me," he said gently. "Speak the truth so that we both may hear it aloud."

"But what is done is done, and—"

He reached out and tilted her chin back up with the softest of touches. "Say it. You must hear your own truth—and I promise you I have taken harder arrows than it."

Tears welled in her eyes, rendering them luminous, like moonlight upon the surface of a lake. "No. I would not."

He felt his body sway, surely as if it had been struck. But as promised, he stayed standing through the agony. "Then my answer to you is no. Even if there was a way to undo all this with your King—and there is not—I will never take you against your will."

"But I choose this. It is my choice."

Xcor shook his head. "Only through the prompting of something else."

He took a step back. "You should get back to . . ." He looked around at the mist, still totally lost. "Where'er 'tis you go."

"You want me." Now her voice was steady and sure. "I can sense it."

"Of course I do. But not as a sacrificial lamb to the slaughter. My fantasy . . . is not that."

"Does the reasoning matter?"

"Some gifts are more painful than insults." He went to turn away from her, and found himself immobile. "Especially when there is naught to be done about your Wrath. He has been replaced."

"If you removed one rightful King, you can remove another. You can put Wrath back."

"You give me too much credit."

"Please."

Her steadfastness angered him, even though it was a virtue, he supposed. "Why does it matter so much to you. Your life shall not change. You shall be safe here—or where'er. The Brotherhood is not dismantled—"

"They will come for you."

"Then we will kill them. I am hoping they shall see the benefits of bowing out gracefully."

Indeed, he couldn't believe he was saying that. But to not disturb her, he would let them and Wrath live—provided they did not get in his way.

Layla shook her head. "Their loyalty will not allow that." Her hands lifted to her cheeks and pressed in as if she were imagining the horror. "There will be war anew. Because of you."

"Then hate me. 'Twill be better for the both of us if you do."

She stared at him for the longest time. "I fear I cannot do that."

Xcor did his best to ignore the way his heart skipped. "I shall take my leave."

"How did you find this place?"

"I followed you home not long ago. You were in the car, returning from the clinic. I was worried over you."

"And why . . . did you come tonight?"

"I must go."

"Don't."

For a moment, he played out a dream whereby she said that and meant it for him personally. And not just in the hopes of persuading him over to her position.

That folly did not last. Especially as he pictured himself terrorizing that wounded human man in the deserted restaurant, for no other reason than that he could—and then remembered removing the spines of all those *lessers* and delivering them unto which member of the aristocracy? As if the recipient was even significant. After which he recalled decapitating slayers. Stabbing them in the gut. Breaking off their limbs . . .

There were so many acts of violence in his background.

As well as the depravity of what he'd been through in the Bloodletter's war camp.

On top of which was his face.

He meant to just start walking down the incline. Unlike her, he could not dematerialize—he had tried repeatedly to expedite the ascent thusly and failed in this fog.

Yes, he meant to leave her behind. For all the reasons he'd spelled out to her and also those he kept to himself.

Instead, he heard himself say, "Meet me under the maple tree. Midnight tomorrow."

"For what"—she pulled her parka closer as if she were to be eaten alive—"purpose?"

"Not what you are worried about."

Now he did pivot and start walking—until his thought processes cleared enough to stop him. Looking over his shoulder, he said, "Chosen. Do you know the way home?"

"Oh, yes . . . of course . . ." Except as she glanced around, she seemed to grow confused. "Yes, it's right over . . ."

She did not pause to hide her words. She honestly did not appear to know where she was.

Closing his eyes, he cursed. He should never have come herein—*ever.*

For what if he left her here alone, and she did not find shelter afore the sun rose? What if they were halfway to where she needed to be?

Putting his hands on his hips, he tilted his head back and searched the heavens, thinking maybe they could offer him some common sense—because he'd clearly lost his.

Of all the ways for me to die, he thought . . .

He'd never once considered it would be over a female.

* * *

As Trez surveyed the Goth crowd in the Iron Mask, he couldn't say he was thrilled to be back in the saddle again. His business had always been important to him—well, first it had been Rehv's gig; then when the Reverend had bowed out—or more like blown his way out—Trez had taken over the whole club enterprise. And yet, whether the place had been his or Rehv's, he'd loved running the operations, dealing with the people, planning for new sites, watching his money grow. Yeah, sure, the humans were a pain in the ass, but that was true whether you were driving in your car, shopping in a supermarket, or trying to make a living.

Granted, the drugs and drinking really didn't help that last one, but whatever . . .

Tonight, though, as he watched the dozen or so working girls make the rounds, sitting on laps, flirting, taking men by the hand and disappearing into the private bathrooms . . . he was sickened by it all.

Especially as he thought about what he'd agreed to do for s'Ex.

Man, it was so tempting to assume that he'd solved the problem . . . that keeping the executioner happy was going to make it all go away.

Wrong.

The thing was, he just kept thinking that if he only had more time, he'd find a way out.

"Any chance you're looking for me?"

The human female standing in front of him had long black hair—natch, so many of them did up in here—and a body that was curvy as a racetrack. Likely just as fast. And with skin artificially paled to the point of flour and lips painted the color of blood, she was a wannabe vampire in a world of posers, all juiced up on a persona likely birthed from a bipolar emotional landscape.

Not that he was generalizing or anything.

"No," he said. "I'm not looking for you."

"You sure?" She did a little turn in front of him, flashing her bubble ass. " 'Cause I'm worth the search."

In his mind's eye, all he could see was his Chosen, laid out before him, so beautiful and clean.

"Sorry," he muttered as he turned and walked away.

After Selena had left him and iAm in the kitchen together, she hadn't come back: When everyone had been called down to the dining room to hear the horrible news about the King, he'd expected to see her there. No-go.

And he wanted to head up to Rehv's great camp to see her. Things between them were too open-ended for his liking, but he had the sense that getting down to the nitty-gritty was going to make him feel worse.

Her as well.

He really just needed to let the whole sitch with her go—

From across the way, one of the professional whores, a brunette in skin-tight red leather, met his eye, and he did a quick head-to-toe on her.

Yeah, he thought. She'd do.

When he motioned for her to come over, she was more than happy to weed through the crowd and close the distance. "Hey, boss."

Shit, he really, totally hated doing this. "I got a private client I need some special services for. You interested?"

"Always." She glanced around. "Is he here tonight?"

"Remote location. Tomorrow at noon. I'm going to ask two others."

"Fun. Don't bother with Willow, though, okay? She's been a pain in the ass lately."

"Roger that."

"Thanks for thinking of me, boss." She smiled and gave him a hip check. "I'll be sure your buddy has a great time."

As she sauntered away, Trez thought about maybe, possibly . . . yeah, pretty much definitely . . . ralphing his dinner all over the polished black floor.

In search of fresh air, he made his way to the entrance, and fronted like he was merely checking in with Ivan and the new guy at the head of the wait line. And then he just started walking, hoofing it in no particular direction even though he didn't have a coat on and his Ferragamos were not good on the slick sidewalks.

In his solitude, he was far from alone: thoughts of Selena, his brother, his parents, crowded the space around him, making him consider seriously the merits of getting fucking plastered.

iAm had told him that the deal made with s'Ex was a dumb-ass fucking idea. And then promptly headed back for the kitchen to make cacciatore.

Still, all things considering, that convo had actually gone so much better than some of their others of late—

"You wanna buy some crack? H?"

Cocking an eyebrow, Trez glanced over at a white guy who was lounging up against the far side of a tattoo parlor. Classy.

Just as he opened his mouth to tell the guy fuck, no—the wind changed direction and he got hit in the face with a cream pie full of *lesser* scent.

It stopped him dead in his tracks.

"So what'll it be?" the slayer asked him.

Trez looked left and right for no particular reason—other than he was suddenly interested in buying something he was never going to use from an asshole who had no clue he was talking to the enemy.

Stepping into the darkness, Trez put his hand in the pocket of his slacks like he was going for his wallet. "How much?"

"For which one."

Trez kept up the ruse, glancing around like he was nervous. Up close, this was defo a *lesser*, the sweet stench so much worse than a seven-day-no-shower human working in a sweatshop—who just happened to be doused in baby powder.

And smuggling a dead raccoon under each armpit.

"Both. Hey, you mind if we step a little farther in?"

The slayer turned away and started quoting prices as he moved deeper into the shop's side alley. He did not make it to the cash-changing-hands part of the transaction.

Trez took control easily, coming at the bastard from behind, grabbing onto the head and snapping it around so that the only thing keeping it on the spine was the skin. Catching the deadweight by the torso, he pushed the slayer behind a stack of pallets and started going through pockets.

Ten baggies of powder. Twenty or so rocks—small scale. Seven hundred in cash, roughly.

Not major leagues. In fact, hardly remarkable for this part of town—except for the *lesser* part.

Shoving the still-moving corpse to the ground, he took out his phone and dialed up a number. It was answered on the third ring.

"Butch?" he said. "Hey, buddy—whatchup to? Uh-huh. Yeah. Right." He eyeballed the slayer and thought the sluggish machinations of the arms and legs were totally fly-on-a-windowsill. "Well, I got a friend I'd like you to meet. Nah, not the kind you'd want to bring home for dinner. Yeah, he's going nowhere. Take your time."

After he hung up, he looked at the packets in his palm. They were marked with the death symbol—in the Old Language.

Someone in the race was dealing, big-time. And they were working with the enemy to do it.

Next question? Who the fuck was it.

FORTY-SIX

It was getting close to dawn when Beth decided she just had to leave her and Wrath's set of rooms. He hadn't come back yet, and the prospect of spending another minute with the chaos in her mind was enough to make her want to take a bridge.

First stop? Layla's room, but the Chosen wasn't there. Probably a good thing as she supposed all she would have done was bug the poor female about early pregnancy symptoms—which was nuts on two accounts: One, if she had conceived, she was what, like twenty-four hours into it, tops? And two, Layla had had that horrible near-miscarriage.

Not exactly a good comp—if Beth didn't want to drive herself completely insane.

Walking back down the hall of statues, she figured . . . kitchen. Yeah, the kitchen was a good next stop—assuming she didn't want to bug Wrath down in the training center's weight room.

He clearly needed some space.

As she hit the grand staircase, she was finding it impossible not to parallel-process reality. The first layer was what was in front of her: Wrath and the dethroning, the sad quietness in the house, the stress over what the race's future held. The second level was wholly internal and completely physical: a twinge in her pelvis—was it implantation . . . or the coming of her period, which would mean no-go?; an ache in her breasts—symptom of conception . . . or the result of all that sex?; hot flashes—the residual of the hormonal imbalance . . . or flannel?

Only the severity of the situation they were in thanks to the Council's actions kept her from devolving completely into her body's minutiae. And meanwhile, in her heart of hearts, she didn't know whether she hoped she was pregnant . . . or hoped she wasn't.

Actually, that was a lie.

Putting her hand over her lower belly, she found herself praying that it hadn't worked. The only thing worse than Wrath losing the throne . . . was him finding out he was going to be a father right afterward.

If he was already feeling like he'd lost his parents' legacy, that was going to be like throwing him a boulder to catch while he was barely treading water: Undoubtedly, he was going to feel like he cheated his child, too.

Down at the foyer level, she crossed over into the dining room, and then pushed into the kitchen. God, the eerie emptiness—the galley was usually such an active place, even during the lulls between large household meals. To walk in as the shutters were coming down and have nothing on the stove, in the oven, or on the counters scared her.

Damn . . . what was going to happen now?

Was the Brotherhood going to split apart? Where would she and Wrath go? Technically, they shouldn't be staying in those overdone quarters on the third floor if they weren't the First Family anymore.

Actually . . . it would be a relief to get out of there.

Although the cause for the relo sucked.

Opening up the Sub-Zero, she saw . . . a whole lot of shit she didn't want to eat. But she should be hungry, shouldn't she? She'd only snacked on the stuff Fritz had brought her how many hours ago? And she certainly hadn't eaten anything during the needing.

She needed to pee.

Disappearing into the loo off the kitchen, she took care of business, washed her hands, and gave the refrigerator another try.

Someone had just put a big vat of something on the lower level. A quick peek under the lid and . . . cacciatore. Normally an entrée well worth tackling, especially because iAm must have been the one who made it. However, a quick whiff got her a big fat no-thanks from her stomach. Same thing when it came to the leftover ham. A plate's worth of Bolognese with linguini in a Tupperware container. Tomato soup . . .

Giving the freezer a try, she took out a box of plain Eggos . . . then put them back. "Meh."

Ice cream was a total no-go. Just the thought of that heavy-cream stuff made her want to throw up—

She hesitated as she looked down at herself. "Somebody in there?" she said to her pelvis.

Okay, it was official. She'd totally lost it.

After a trip through the pantry, which proved to be like trying to find something edible in the laundry room, for chrissakes, she doubled back to the fridge and made herself take out a Vlasic jar of butter chips.

"It's pickles, people," she muttered. "Pickles. Total cliché here."

Except when she twisted off the lid and looked at the slices dancing in their little pool of sweet brine, she grimaced and had to put them back.

As a last resort, she hit the vegetable drawer—

"*Yes*," she said in a rush as her hand snapped out for a grab. "Oh, yes yes yes . . ."

As she carried the bunch of organic carrots over to the knife drawer, she couldn't believe she was about to get it on with all that beta carotene.

She hated carrots. Okay, not completely—if they were in salads, it wasn't like she'd eat around them. But she had never in her life volunteered them out of the fridge.

Standing over the sink, she cut one free, got out a peeler, and made a neat little pile of bright orange strips in the stainless-steel belly. Quick rinse. Cut in the middle. Slice length-wise twice. And voilà, crudités.

Crunch. Munch. Swallow.

They were so fresh, they cracked every time she took a bite out of them, and the sweet, earthy taste was better than chocolate.

One more, she thought as she finished her last quarter. Except when she got to the end of number two, she thought . . . how about another.

As she worked her way through her third, she thought back to the Council's proclamation. Her motivation for trying to do something was such a no-brainer. Even though her mother's racial identity was not her fault, she still felt responsible for bringing the shit cart to Wrath's front door.

If she could only figure out a way around this . . .

On the Council's side, things were evidently moving ahead. An official swearing in of that Ichan guy had been scheduled—and Rehv had found out because, like an idiot, the Council's secretary had failed to take him off their blast e-mail list.

That was taking place at midnight.

She glanced over at the double ovens. The blue digital clock read four fifty-four. So they had nineteen hours.

What the hell could be done in nineteen hours?

Turning back to her stash, she—

The sound of the security system announcing the opening and closing of an exterior door was a surprise. Frowning, she went out by the pantry, pushed through one of the flap doors that the staff used . . .

Layla was coming out of the library, looking like she'd been in a car accident: Her hair was windblown, her face white as a sheet, her hands up to her cheeks.

"Layla," Beth called over. "Are you okay?"

The Chosen jumped so high she had to put both arms out to keep steady. "Oh! Oh—ah, yes. Yes, I am. I'm fine, just fine, yes. Thank you." The female abruptly frowned. "And yourself? Are you . . ."

So many ways to finish that for the female, given what was going on: Are you . . . suicidal? Are you . . . taking a break between wailing sessions? Are you . . . pregnant, too?

"Oh, yup, fine. Yeah, just fine. Yup."

Two could play at the deflection game.

"Well, I'm just heading upstairs. To go to bed. To have a shower, and go to bed." As Layla started taking off her parka, her smile was about as genuine as Courtney Stodden's. "I'll see you at . . . well, later. I'll see you later. Bye. Bye for now!"

The Chosen took to that stairwell like she was being chased, even though there was no one behind her.

As Beth returned to the kitchen, she felt bad that she didn't follow through on the female's obvious distress, but the sad truth was, she had so much on her plate . . . there wasn't room left for anyone else's drama-burger with a side of brain-fry.

Back at the sink, she peeled another carrot. Cut it in half and turned it around to—

The solution came to her with such clarity, she nearly sliced the pad of her finger off.

Putting down the knife, she picked up the two halves . . . and held them together, finding the puzzle fit that made them seem as if they were one.

Then she deliberately separated them. Reunited them. Separated them.

In both incarnations . . . the halves were still carrot.

Throwing the pieces on the counter, she took off at a dead run.

It was a fat round hedge that saved them both.

As Xcor materialized in the front yard of his suburban abode, he had to take a moment to collect himself—even though the sun was threatening in the east.

Talk about close calls . . . he'd barely gotten Layla back in time. And even the now, he was not sure he had succeeded.

But he had done his best.

Once it had become obvious that she suffered the same disorientation as he in the mist, he had taken her hand and started her up the hill. He did not ask her for confirmation that the Brotherhood's hidden compound was in fact at the top—for that information, he relied on the same principles that had constructed his far more appropriate lair back in the Old Country.

The higher the position, the more defensible it was.

Hustling her as fast as he could, he had ended up running them straight into a twenty-foot-tall stuccoed retaining wall—a very good sign that they were close to her homestead. The problem was, she'd been too turned about to dematerialize over the damn thing.

Confronted by the choice of right or left, he'd been well aware that upon his decision rested her safety.

On so many levels.

He'd been well aware that even if he could construct a suitable shelter for them, something capable of shielding them both from the sunlight all day long, her absence would be noted and questioned when she returned at the following sunset. How she would be able to present answers that would not complicate her life irreparably, he did not know.

He had picked to the right—on the theory that he wanted to do right by her, and therefore, that was the direction he would take.

When they'd found that well-trimmed, well-cared-for little

bush . . . and then a number of its identical siblings, it was clear they were on the trail of the main house. He did not take her all the way. He went far enough to find the first planting bed, and then had released her hand and hissed at her to go—go fast.

He, too, was out of time.

Xcor had watched her hustle forth for only a moment, and then she was lost into the mist, not even the sounds of her footfalls reaching his ears anymore.

It was as if she had disappeared forever.

And as much as a part of him had been tempted to sit and let the sun take him, he had forced himself away, triangling downward until he had tripped over, quite literally, a ploughed drive.

Although he'd only been able to see five feet afore him, the level surface provided him with an opportunity for alacrity unparalleled by the uneven ground. He had run flat-out, gravity in his favor, his only concern that someone would come barreling up the mountain and see him in their headlights.

That had not come to pass. He had made it to the leveling-off part and had eventually broken free of the misted, scrambled landscape.

The sense of dread he'd first experienced upon penetration stuck with him, however. What if Layla hadn't made it inside in time? What if someone had found her and questioned her? What if . . .

He had checked his phone to no avail and then been forced to close his eyes, concentrate, and pray that he had enough remaining strength and focus to ghost himself away.

The only thing that had made disappearing possible was that he couldn't die not knowing what had happened to her.

Taking out his phone once again, he had some errant hope that she had called and he hadn't heard the ring in his escape down the mountain. Alas . . . no.

Stalking to the colonial's front door, the faint glow in the sky made his skin prickle with warning and his eyes water—which ended as he burst into the house.

To a scene of abject debauchery.

The only thing that would have made it more complete would have been the presence of females. As it was, the air was spiced thick with rum and gin, crowded with hearty laughter, heavy with the kind of male aggression that surged after victory.

"You return!" Zypher called out. "He returns!"

The bellowing would have been loud enough to rouse the neighbors, if there had been any. As it was, it filled the house.

"And we have news," Throe said with satisfaction mildly tinted with drunkenness. "The induction ceremony is at midnight this coming eve. In Ichan's library hall. We have been invited, of course."

The temptation to tell them to go in his stead appealed. But he kept his voice quiet. With naught but a nod, he disappeared upstairs.

Fortunately, his soldiers were used to him retreating into his own counsel—and let him go.

As he shut the bedroom door, the noise below was dimmed, not extinguished; however, he was accustomed to tuning out that group of males.

Going over to the bed, which was a mess of sheets and tangled blankets, he sat down, disarmed, and took out his cell. Cradling it in his hands, he stared at the screen.

There was no way to dial her: Whatever phone she'd used had a scrambled account.

Lying back and looking up at the ceiling, he knew an emptiness that was a revelation.

The idea that she could be dead and he didn't know it hit him so deeply, he felt as if his personality had split in two.

Never to be united again.

FORTY-SEVEN

Where was he?

As Sola loitered in Assail's kitchen, fussing over the few things she'd repacked from upstairs, she kept looking over her shoulder, expecting to find him coming around the corner to try to persuade her to stay.

But he'd already done that, hadn't he.

In the shower.

Man, for once, memories of being with him didn't get her juiced. They made her want to cry.

"I no understand why we leave so early," her grandmother announced as she came up from the basement. "It is not even dawn."

Her grandmother was dressed in the yellow version of her house frock, but she was ready for the trip, her good shoes on, her matching handbag hanging off her wrist from its fake leather strap. Behind her, Assail's matched set of guards each had a suitcase—and they did not look happy. Although, come on, they hardly had faces built for the jollies.

"It's a twenty-three-hour drive, vovó. We need to get started."

"We are no stopping?"

"No." She couldn't take the risk with her grandmother in tow. "You can drive in the middle during the day. You love to drive."

Her grandmother let out a sound that for anybody else would have been an F-bomb. "We should stay here. Is nice here. I like the kitchen."

It was not the kitchen the woman was fond of. Hell, her grandmother could cook over a Coleman without blinking an eye—and had.

He's not Catholic, Sola wanted to say. He's actually an atheist drug dealer. Soon to be wholesaler—

What if she was pregnant? she wondered. Because she hadn't taken her pill for two days. Wouldn't that be . . .

Nucking futs, as they say.

Shaking herself out of la-la land, Sola zipped the rolling suitcase shut and just stood there.

"Well?" her grandmother taunted. "We go? Or no?"

As if she knew exactly what Sola was waiting for.

Or who, as the case was.

Sola didn't have enough pride left to try to be cool as she looked around again, searching the entry from the dining area, the archway that was used when you came from upstairs or the office, the shallow hall at the head of the basement steps. All empty. And there were no footsteps coming at a dead run, no thumping from overhead as somebody rushed to pull on a shirt and get to the lower level.

Shower time aside, how could he not see her off . . .

At that moment, her grandmother took a deep breath and the flat yellow gold cross she always wore around her neck caught the overhead light.

"We go," Sola heard herself say.

With that, she picked up her suitcase and headed for the back door. Outside, a totally lose-it-in-a-crowd Ford was parked close to the house, the rental agreement in the name of Sola's emergency identity.

The one nobody in Caldwell knew she had. And in the glove box, there was another set of documents and IDs for her grandmother.

Using the remote, she triggered the locks to disengage, and opened the trunk. Assail's men, meanwhile, were handling her grandmother with kid gloves, helping her down the stairs, carrying her luggage, and her coat, which she had obviously refused to put on in protest.

As they settled the woman into the passenger seat and her suitcase in the back, Sola searched the rear of the house. Just as before, she expected to see him, maybe running through the main room to get to her before she left. Maybe coming up from the basement and shooting through the mudroom to come out. Maybe skidding around the corner from having been upstairs . . .

At that moment, something strange happened. Every window in the house had a sudden shimmer to it, the glass panes between the sills and the flat plates of the sliding doors showing a subtle twinkle.

What the—

Shutters, she thought. There were shutters coming across the windows, the subtle movement the kind of thing you'd miss . . . unless you were looking in at the very second it happened. Afterward? It was as if nothing had changed. All the furniture was still visible, the lights on, normal, normal, normal.

Another of his security tricks, she thought.

Taking her time opening her door, she put one foot in and craned around. The two bodyguards had stood back and crossed their arms.

She wanted to tell them . . . but no, they didn't seem like they were interested in carrying a message back to Assail.

They looked downright pissed off now that they'd gotten her grandmother safely into the sedan.

Sola waited for a moment longer, eyes fixed on that open rear door. Through the jambs, she looked at the shoes and the coats in that back hall. So ordinary-looking—well, ordinary for a rich person. But the house wasn't Middle America anything, and not just because it was probably worth five million. Or ten.

Turning away, she slid behind the wheel, closed herself in, and got a good whiff of lemon air freshener. Under which was the faint stinky haze of cigarette smoke.

"I no know why we have to leave."

"I know, vovó. I know."

The tinny-sounding engine jumped to what little life it had and she put the car in reverse. K-turning, she gave that open door one last look.

And then there were no more excuses to linger.

Hitting the gas, she blinked hard as the headlights illuminated the driveway and then the one-lane road that would take them off the peninsula.

He was not going to come after her.

"You make a mistake," her grandmother said on a huff. "Big mistake."

But you don't know the whole story, Sola thought as she came up to a stop sign and hit her directional signal.

What Sola was unaware of, however . . . was that neither did she.

Assail watched the departure from the ring of trees behind the rear of his home.

Through the windows of the kitchen, he saw her standing by the table, rifling through a suitcase as if searching for something she was leaving behind.

Out here, my love, he thought. What you have lost is out here.

And then her grandmother made an appearance with the cousins, and it was clear that the female did not approve of the leaving.

Just one more thing to adore about her.

It was also obvious that the cousins were against this. Then again, they had never eaten so well, and they had respect for anyone who would stand up to them.

Not a problem with Marisol's *grandmahmen*.

As Assail played witness to his female searching about as if she were waiting for him to present himself, there was a small satisfaction in her sadness. But the overriding imperative was to convince his inner beast to let her choose the path she had.

He could not argue with the self-preservation—just as he could not vow to disengage from his business. He had worked too long and hard to fade into a lifestyle of sedentary nights . . . even if they were spent with her. Besides, he had the worry that things were not done with the Benloise family yet. Only time would tell if there was another brother out there, or mayhap some cousin with a greedy eye and a heart of vengeance for what had been served unto his blood.

She would be safer without him.

As Marisol put her luggage in the boot of the car, her grandmother was accommodated to the front of the vehicle. And there was another pause. Indeed, as she glanced around, he felt she must have seen him—but no. Her eyes passed o'er him in his shadowed hiding spot.

Into the car. Shutting the door. Starting the engine. Turning about.

Then all there was . . . were brake lights disappearing down his drive.

The cousins loitered only for a moment. Unlike his female, they knew exactly where he was, but they did not approach. They retreated into the house, leaving the door open for him to use when he could stand the rising sun no longer.

His heart was howling in his chest when he finally stepped free of where he had tucked himself.

Walking across the snow, his body was loose-jointed to the point where he wondered if he would collapse. And his head was spinning 'round and 'round—his intestines as well. The only thing that was solid were his male instincts, which were bloody incessant that he needed to go out to the road in front of her, brace himself before that cheap-ass car, and demand that she turn around and come back home.

Assail forced himself into his house instead.

In the kitchen, the cousins were helping themselves to leftovers specifically cooked for them and left in foil-wrapped servings in the freezer. Their affects were as if someone had died.

"Where are the cell phones?" Assail asked.

"In the office." Ehric frowned as he peeled a Post-it note off the package. "'Preheat to three seventy-five.'"

His brother went to the wall ovens and began pushing buttons. "Convection?"

"Doesn't say."

"Damn it."

Under any other circumstances, Assail would have found it impossible to believe that Evale was wasting his meager urge to speak on cooking. But Marisol and her grandmother had changed everything . . . for the short time they had been here.

Leaving his cousins be, he was not at all surprised they didn't offer to include him in the repast. After centuries of transient existence, he had a feeling they were going to become hoarders of those foodstuffs.

In the office, he sat behind the desk and regarded the two identical phones before him. Naturally, his brain went to how he'd procured them—and he saw Eduardo first upon the ground and then Ricardo strung up against that torture wall.

Ordering his hands to clasp them, he—

His arms refused to obey the command, and in fact, his body fell back into the chair. As he stared straight ahead at absolutely nothing, it was clear that his motivation had deserted him.

Opening the desk's center drawer, he took out one of his vials and fired up one nostril and then the other with cocaine.

The tingling rush at least got him sitting up, and a moment later, he did in fact take the phones . . . and hook them up to his computer.

His focus was artificial, the attention forced, but he knew he was going to have to get used to that.

His heart, black though it was, had left him.

And was on its way to Miami.

FORTY-EIGHT

It was in fact possible, if you ran long enough and hard enough, to make the body feel as if you had been in a fist fight.

As Wrath continued to pound his Nikes into the treadmill, he thought about his last sparring session with Payne.

He had lied to her. Back when he'd finally assumed the throne in a serious way, the brothers and Beth had confronted him with a set of "guidelines" intended to chill him out on the ol' physical-risk profile. Not exactly a happy convo, and he'd broken the rules at least once that everyone knew about, and a number of times that nobody had caught him at. And after he'd been discovered fighting downtown, he'd agreed anew to put up the daggers but for ceremonial work—and since then, the scent of his *shellan*'s disappointment had been enough to keep him in line.

Well, that and the fact that he'd lost his remaining eyesight entirely at about that time.

The bunch of them hadn't been wrong. The King needed to be breathing most of all; taking down slayers in the back of an alley in Caldwell could not be the primary directive anymore.

And no sparring with the brothers, either.

None of them wanted to roll the dice with possibly hurting him.

Except then Payne had presented herself, and though he'd first assumed she was a male, when her true identity had been discovered, he'd been given a pass . . . precisely because she was a female.

He thought of her sneaking into the males' locker room and putting that knife to his throat.

He supposed now . . . he could fight with anyone he liked. And that he owed her an apology.

Reaching down, he increased the treadmill's speed. This one machine had been retrofitted with hooks on the console and a padded belt that had been made for him. With bungee cords strung between the two, he could go hands off and still keep on the machine, the subtle pulls on his waist telling him where he was in relation to the running surface.

Handy on a night like tonight. Oh, wait . . . it was daytime, now.

Falling into a faster rhythm, he found that as always, his head had a way of floating above the exertion, as if with his body engaged and working, it was free to drift. Unfortunately, like a helicopter with faulty gauges, it kept ramming into rocky cliffs: his parents, his *shellan*, the possibility of a future young, all the empty years stretching out before him.

If he only had his eyesight. At least then he could credibly go out and engage with the enemy. But now he was trapped—by his blindness, by his Beth, by the chance that she was with young.

Of course, if she hadn't been in his life? He would have gone on a killing bender until he died honorably in the field. Although, hell, without her, he probably wouldn't have bothered doing anything about ascending in the first place.

He knew he should never have tried that fucking crown on his head.

After everything his father had done in such a tragically short time, he should have followed his first instincts and walked the fuck away. The race had been fine going rudderless for a couple of centuries; probably could have kept that shit up indefinitely.

He thought of Ichan. Maybe that SOB was going to discover that modern populations didn't need kings.

Or more to the point, maybe Xcor and the Bastards were going to learn that lesson.

Whatever.

Wrath went to increase the speed again—and found that he'd tapped the machine out on velocity. Cursing, he resettled into his already breakneck pace, and thought of his father, sitting behind the very desk that he himself could no longer see or use, parchment rolls and ink pots, quill pens and leather-bound volumes covering the carved surface.

He could just picture that male behind it all, sporting a half smile of contentment as he melted wax himself and pressed the royal crested ring into it—

"Wrath!"

"Wha—" Cue the squealing of rubber as he yanked out the safety key and jumped to the side rails. "Beth—?"

"Wrath, oh, my God—"

"Are you okay—"

"Wrath, I've got the solution—"

He could not fucking breathe. "About . . . what?"

"I know what we have to do!"

Wrath frowned as he panted and braced his hands on the rails in the event his jelly legs gave up the ghost and he torpedoed. And yet even through the hypoxia, his female's scent was strong with purpose and conviction, her natural undertones sharpened so they got through to him clearly.

Grabbing the towel he'd slung over the console, he mopped his face. "Beth, for the love of Christ. Will you please stop—"

"Divorce me."

In spite of all the exercise-induced suffocation, he stopped breathing. "I'm sorry," he said roughly. "But I did not hear that."

"Dissolve our mating. Effective yesterday—when for all intents and purposes you were still King."

Wrath started shaking his head, all kinds of thoughts jamming up his brain. "I'm not hearing you say that—"

"If you get rid of me, you get rid of the grounds they used. No grounds, no removal. You have the throne and—"

"Are you out of your fucking mind!" he bellowed. "What the *fuck* are you talking about!"

There was a slight pause. Like she was surprised he wasn't all into her bright idea.

"Wrath, seriously. This is the way to get the throne back."

As the bonded male in him started screaming at the top of its lungs, he was an inch from exploding—but he'd already trashed one whole room in the compound. And the brothers would kill him if he smashed up their weight room.

Attempting to keep his voice level, he failed miserably: "No *fucking* way!"

"It's just a piece of paper!" she hollered back. "What the hell does it matter?"

"You're my *shellan*!"

"It's all about carrots!"

Annnnnnnnnd that stopped him dead. Shaking his head to clear it some, he said, "I'm sorry—what?"

Little hard to transition from ending their relationship to root frickin' vegetables.

"Look, you and I are together because we love each other. A piece of paper one way or another is not going to change us—"

"No, absolutely not—I'm not going to give those assholes the satisfaction of fucking you over—"

"Listen to me." She grabbed onto his forearm and squeezed. "I want you to calm down and listen to me."

It was the weirdest thing. As wound up as he was, when she gave him a direct order like that? He followed like a foot soldier.

"Predate the dissolution of marriage—mating—whatever. Don't give them any rationale, you don't want to look like it's reactionary. Then decide whether or not you want to stay King. But that way? It's not my fault. Right now, like it or not, I'm the reason you're losing the throne, and I can't go through the rest of our lives feeling responsible for something like that. It'll kill me."

"Sacrificing you is not the way—"

"We're not sacrificing me in the slightest. I don't care about being queen. I care about being by your side—and no crown or edict or whatever is going to change that."

"You could be carrying our offspring right now. Are you saying you want to bring that young into the world a *bastard*?"

"They wouldn't be to me. They wouldn't be to you."

"But to others . . ."

"Like who? You telling me Vishous would think the kid's something less? Tohr? Rhage? Any of the Brothers—their *shellans*? What about Qhuinn and Blay—Qhuinn's not mated to Layla. Does that mean you'd look down on that child?"

"This household's not the 'others' I was talking about."

"So who is, precisely? We never see the *glymera*—thank God—and I don't believe I've ever met what you guys call a commoner. Well, except for Ehlena and Xhex, I guess. I mean, all these citizens of the race—they never come here, and is that going to change? I don't think so." She squeezed his arm again. "Besides, you were worried about putting our kid on the throne? This takes care of that problem, too."

Wrath broke off from her hold on him and wanted to pace—except he didn't know the weight room layout well enough not to land on his ass.

He settled for wiping his face again. "I don't want the throne enough to divorce you. I just don't. It's the principle, Beth."

"Well, if it makes you feel better, I'll divorce you."

He blinked behind his wraparounds. "Not going to happen. I'm sorry, but I will not do this."

His *leelan*'s voice cracked. "I can't spend the rest of my life thinking it's my fault. I just can't."

"But it isn't. It honestly isn't. Look, I just . . . I gotta let the past go, you know? I can't hold on to my parents this way. That shit isn't healthy." He let his head fall back. "Goddamn, I mean, you'd figure I'd be over it by now. Losing them, that is."

"I don't think people ever get past that kind of thing—especially the way it happened to you."

Flashes came back of his scrawny pretrans self locked in that crawl space, watching through a knothole in the wood as his parents were cut into pieces. It was always the same film reel, the same glints of sword blades and screams of pain and terror . . . and it always ended the same, with the two most important people in his life up to that point gone, gone, gone.

He wasn't going to lose Beth. Not even in a figurative way.

"No," he said with utter finality.

Reaching over, he put his hand on her womb. "I've lost my past and there's nothing I can do to change that. I will *not* lose my future—even for the throne."

FORTY-NINE

One of the problems with marriages, matings, whatever . . . was that when the person you loved laid down a veto? Not much you could do about it.

As Beth stepped out of the weight room with her *hellren*, she was popped-balloon deflated. Out of arguments, out of plans, she hated where they were, but all the avenues to a better place were obstructed by a "no" she couldn't get past.

Instead of following him into the showers, she went to the office and sat at the desk, staring at the laptop's screen saver of bubbles floating around the image of Outlook—

The hot flash came out of nowhere, blasting up through her pelvis and spreading like a brushfire to the tips of her fingers, the soles of her feet, the crown of her head.

"Christ," she muttered. "I could fry an egg on my chest over here."

Billowing the collar of the nightgown helped a little, but then the internal oven blast was over as quick as it came, nothing but the cooling sweat on her skin left behind.

Swiping the screen saver off, she watched as Outlook updated itself with a send/receive. The account that was configured on this computer was the general mailbox for the King, and she braced herself for a long lineup of unread e-mails to start appearing at the top of the list.

There was only one.

A tangible representation of the switch in power, she supposed . . .

Frowning, she sat forward. The subject line read: *Heavy Heart.* And it was from a male whose name she recognized only because it had been on the list of signatures on that fucking parchment.

Opening the thing, she read it once. Twice. And a third time.

To: Wrath, son of Wrath
From: Abalone, son of Abalone
Date: 04430 12:59:56
Subject: Heavy Heart

My lord, it is with a heavy heart that I greet the future. I was at the meeting of the Council and I executed the Vote of No Confidence, with its antiquated, prejudicial grounds. I am sick for myself and the race over the *glymera's* actions of late, but more so over my lack of courage.

A long, long while ago, my father Abalone served your father. Family lore has passed down the story, although its details are not widely known anymore: When a cabal went against your parents, my father took a stance with his King and queen and honored this bloodline of mine for e'ermore in doing so. In return, your father provided the generations of my family with financial freedom and social elevation.

I did not live up to that legacy this night. And I find that I cannot stomach my cowardice.

I do not agree with the actions taken against you—and I believe that others feel the same. I work with a group of commoners to help field their concerns and approach the *glymera* for appropriate redress. In my dealings with such citizens, it is clear that there are many at the root of the race who remember all the things your father did for them and their families. Although they have never met you, that goodwill extends to you and your family. I know they shall share my sadness—and my worry—as to where we are headed the now.

In recognition of my failure, I have resigned from the Council. I will continue working with the commoners, as they need a champion—and although I am sorely remiss in that role, I must try to do some good in this world or I shan't be able to e'er sleep again.

I wish I had done more for you. You and your *shellan* shall be in my thoughts and prayers.

This is all so wrong.

Sincerely, Abalone, son of Abalone

What a lovely guy, Beth thought as she got out of Outlook. And he probably needed to ditch the guilt. Given the aristocracy's steamroller approach to everything, he hadn't stood a damn chance.

The *glymera* had ways of ruining lives that had nothing to do with coffins.

Checking the clock on the wall, she figured Wrath would be along any minute. And then they would . . . well, she had no clue. Usually at this time, they were heading up to bed, but that didn't hold any appeal.

Maybe they could switch bedrooms today. She didn't think she could handle even seeing that bejeweled suite of rooms.

Idly heading over to Internet Explorer, she stared at the Google screen, shaking her head at the *I'm feeling lucky* line.

Yeah. Right.

God, if only V didn't hate everything about the Apple company, she could have had an iPhone in her hand and asked Siri what to do.

She so appreciated Wrath standing by their marriage, but jeez . . .

For absolutely no reason, that scene from *The Princess Bride* flashed through her mind—the one where they were getting married at the altar in front of that priest.

Meeeewidge, a dweam wifin a dweam—

Beth froze.

Then typed fast and hit that frickin' lucky button.

What came up was—

"Hey, you ready to head up?"

Beth slowly lifted her eyes to her husband. "I know what we have to do."

Wrath recoiled like someone had dropped a piano on his foot. And then promptly looked like his head was pounding. "Beth. For the love of fucking God—"

"Do you love me, all of me?"

He let his huge body fall back against the office's glass door as George curled in for a lie-down—like he expected this to be another long one. "Beth—"

"Well, do you?"

"Yes," her *hellren* groaned.

"All of me, human and vampire."

"Yes."

"And you don't discriminate one side versus the other, right?"

"No."

"So it's like Christmas. I mean, you don't celebrate the holiday, but because it's what Butch and I are used to, you, like, let us put up Christmas trees and decorations, and now everyone in the household does the present thing, right?"

"Right," he muttered.

"And when it comes to the winter solstice, I mean, if you were going to ever do one of those balls, you wouldn't think it was any more or less important or significant than Christmas, right."

"Right." This was spoken in a tone that suggested in his head, he was answering the question, *If I put the gun right here, and pulled the trigger, I could get myself out of this misery, right?*

"No difference. At all."

"None. Can we stop now?"

"My beliefs, my customs, just as important as yours, no difference, right?"

"Right."

"At all."

"Right."

She burst up from the computer. "Meet me in the front foyer in two hours. Wear something nice."

"What—what the fuck are you doing?"

"Something we'd talked about a while ago and never followed through on."

"Beth, what's going on?"

"Nothing." She ran for the closet so she could get into the tunnel ahead of him. "Everything."

"Why aren't you telling me?"

She hesitated before disappearing. "Because I'm afraid you'll argue with me. Two hours. The foyer."

As she bolted out the hidden panel, she heard her *hellren* cursing, but she didn't have any time to go into this with her man.

She had to find Lassiter. And John Matthew.

Now.

Selena experienced her first true lockup that morning.

Sitting at the kitchen table of Rehvenge's great camp, she was nursing a cup of coffee and a homemade scone when her mind began to agitate over the King's fate, Trez's kisses, iAm's hard stare, her own uncertain future. . . .

Most especially Trez's kisses.

She hadn't seen him in public or private since they'd left that bathroom and proceeded downstairs to find his brother in the kitchen.

She was kind of glad.

The unfinished business between them—the *sexual* unfinished business—was too intense for her right now. When she'd been in the moment, it had all seemed so natural, so predestined even—but with a clear head and wide-open eyes in the aftermath, she wondered what she had been thinking.

The future was coming, and it was going to be hard enough without the pressure of falling in love.

And that was where things were headed with him. . . .

As her brain twisted in her skull, she took a sip of coffee, burned her lip, and in her frustration, decided there simply wasn't enough sugar in with her caffeine. And she'd put too much of the grinds in the filter. And the water hadn't been cold enough, so there was a tinny aftertaste.

In reality, the mix was pretty perfect. It was her internal sense of self that she was struggling to get into balance.

But she could do something about the java, as the Brothers called it.

Reaching forward for the little sugar pot, she extended her arm from her shoulder, tilted her torso over her hips, and—

Her body didn't so much stiffen as freeze in that position—as if all the joints that were engaged had become solid at once.

Terror quadrupled her heart rate, sweat flushing across her face and her chest. And when she went to open her mouth to breathe more deeply, she found that even her jaw was stuck in place—although that may have been the fear.

Abruptly, the silence in the house pressed in on her.

There was nobody else in the cedar-shingled camp. The other Chosen had gone up to the Sanctuary to visit with Amalya, the directrix following Wrath's dethroning. Rehvenge was down in Caldwell. The *doggen* who now rotated between this location and the Brotherhood mansion had stayed in town in light of the sad news.

In a frantic calculation, she tried to remember how long it had taken her sisters to be permanently affected.

Not days. Maybe months in terms of Earth time?

Dearest Virgin Scribe . . . what if this was it?

Focusing all her energy, she tried to unhinge the locked doors of her joints, and got nowhere. Indeed, the only thing that moved were the tears that pooled in her eyes and slipped off her lashes. And it was so utterly bizarre: For all her immobility, she could feel everything. The hot paths down her cheeks. The warmth from overhead that drifted by her temples and the tips of her ears. The cool draft across her soft-soled shoes. The lingering burn on her tongue and the back of her throat.

She even felt the hunger she had been drawn to the kitchen to try to satisfy.

What was she going to do if she didn't—

The trembling began in her thighs, starting with a twitching and then emanating with greater bandwidth. Her arms were next. Then her shoulders.

As if her body were fighting to get out of its prison, shaking the metaphorical bars that had slammed shut around it.

"Hello?"

The male voice was distant, echoing forth from the lake side of the house, and she attempted to answer. What came out was a weak moan, nothing more—everything was vibrating: from her teeth to her toes, she was rattling to the point of violence—

Just as Trez entered, her body burst free of its invisible confines, her limbs exploding out, banging into things, flapping free. And then she collapsed, her head slamming down onto the lip of the coffee mug, the scone bouncing off its plate, the clattering of the sugar bowl and the thunderous impact of her chest on the table like a bomb going off.

"Selena!"

Trez caught her before she slid onto the floor, his great arms scooping her up and holding her tight as, inside of her body, everything that had been rigid became liquid: She didn't so much recline in his hold as melt into it. And not because she was aroused.

"What's going on?" he demanded as he carried her out of the kitchen and laid her on the daybed opposite the foyer fire.

Although she opened her mouth to speak, nothing came out. Instead, the details of the dark wood paneling and the river-stone hearth and the stuffed owl on the mantelpiece became hyper-clear, her eyes practically burning from the acuity of her vision.

Closing her lids, she moaned.

"Selena? *Selena*."

There was curious lethargy now, one so intense she could feel her energy being sucked down into a vortex she feared it would never be free of. Dimly, she was aware that she'd had the disease wrong. She'd always assumed it was in the joints, but in fact, it felt as though her muscles were the problem.

Out of superstition, none of her sisters had spoken of the particulars. All that she had ever been told of was the final stage.

Now she wished she had questioned those who had suffered. Es-

pecially when the slightest of stiffness had started up in her how long ago?

Quite a while.

She was definitely embarking on the final stage now—

Something brushed against her mouth. Something wet, warm . . . *blood.*

"Drink," Trez commanded. "Drink, goddamn it, *drink*. . . ."

Her tongue came out and tested the flavor, and the taste of him made her groan with thirst. She didn't think she could swallow, however—

Yes, yes, actually, she could.

Pursing her lips, she formed a seal around the cut he had made in his wrist, and oh, the glorious nourishment. With each draw, she felt a strength come to her, filling her up where the lethargy had left her hollow.

And the more she had, the more she wanted, greed growing instead of satiation.

But Trez didn't seem to mind. At all.

With gentle hands, he repositioned her so that she was lying in his lap, her legs stretched out, her arms over her head. And as she drank of him, he was all she saw, his beautiful almond-shaped eyes, his perfectly molded lips, his dark skin and cropped-tight hair.

Just as she had before in his presence, she could feel her priorities shifting back to that place of desperation, to the sexual drive that had wiped out her proper thinking to such a degree that it didn't exist at all.

Indeed, in the deep recesses of her consciousness, she knew that any action taken in this state of hers was more than likely to be regretted, but she didn't care. If anything, her first true episode of the sickness made her want to follow through with him more as opposed to less.

And maybe she could not fall in love.

Maybe . . . she could steel herself against that.

Rigidity, after all, was her future.

FIFTY

Standing in the doorway of his bedroom, John Matthew could feel a seizure threatening to break through.

As his sister continued to speak, and he felt his head nod, he retreated into that place where the epilepsy was birthed, some kind of tangle of electrical impulses threatening to take over everything—except he was done with that shit. Just as the hum started to rise, he cut it off by force of will.

Not. Gonna. Do. It—

Unbelievable to be channeling Dana Carvey from SNL. But there you go.

Plus it worked. Not right away, but gradually, that sizzle and burn started to fade, its lights-out crescendo receding.

"So . . . will you?" Beth asked, her eyes wide. "It's, like, in an hour. Lassiter needs that much time to get ready."

Refocusing, he strung together some semblance of what she'd been talking about, his brain linking the nouns and verbs until . . .

Oh, my God, he thought.

Man, for once, he was glad he was mute. Because if he'd had to speak, she'd know he was in some strange place emotionally. As it was, his hands were steadier than his voice would have been.

Something about her request was getting to him big-time.

It would be an honor, he signed.

Before he could drop his arms, his sister pitched herself at him, hugging him so tightly she nearly snapped his head off. And as he closed his eyes and held her in return, time stopped—

A vision struck from out of nowhere. One minute, he was standing outside his and Xhex's bedroom. The next?

All he could see was tears . . . except, no, it was rain. Rain on the windshield of a car—a car he'd loved. And then he was reaching forward for the ignition and—

Beth pulled back and he watched from a vast distance as her mouth moved and she told him more things. He nodded in the right places, but as soon as she left and he shut the door, all that part of it was gone.

Leaning his forehead on the panels, he had no idea why his eyes were watering up—or why his chest had swollen with such pride and happiness.

"You okay?" Xhex whispered from behind him.

Turning into the darkness, he nodded—and then realized she couldn't see him.

"Yeah, I know," she said. "But I have to ask out loud sometimes."

There was a click as she turned on the lamp by her side of the bed. Blinking in the illumination, he took a swipe of his face, making like he was just, you know, rubbing it or some shit. But she was a *symphath*—so where he was at was as clear to her as a billboard.

I don't get it, he signed. *Why am I so fucked in the head about her?*

His mate's gunmetal-gray eyes locked on him, and he did nothing to avoid that laser stare: If he wanted more information on all this, she was his best bet.

"Your grid has that shadow," she murmured, shaking her head. "I've never seen one like it. It's as if—I don't know, you're parallel-processing life? Or that . . ."

What, he demanded.

"There are two of you in there."

That's how it feels. He rubbed his already messy hair. *Especially around her.*

"She is your sister."

But there was more than that to it, he thought. Not romantically or anything. Still . . .

"Come on," Xhex said as she got out of bed. "We need to get ready. Goddamn brilliant idea of hers."

As his female walked up to him naked, her tight, muscular body had a way of clarifying things—suddenly he had sex on the brain and what a relief. At least that he could do something about.

"Let me help you in the shower," she said, reaching in between the folds of his robe and finding his hard cock. "You should be very, very clean for this."

John was more than happy to be led by the dumb handle into the bathroom, and when they emerged forty-five minutes later, he was more relaxed—and clean as a motherfucking whistle.

"Yes, the tux," his female said as he stood in front of their closet, staring at the stuff hanging from the rods. "No question."

Nodding, he went for the starched white shirt, popping it off its hanger and pulling it onto his shoulders. Xhex had to do up the buttons—for some reason his hands were jumping all around now like he was nervous. He got the slacks on just fine, though—not the suspenders, however. She had to take care of them. And forget about the cummerbund and the bow tie—he just stood there like a dairy cow as she made quick work of it all.

The nice thing was that he got to stare at her.

"Now the jacket." She held the thing out for him like she was the man, guiding the fine wool into place on his back, then turning him around and smoothing the lapels. "Damn . . ."

What? he signed.

Her stare was gleaming as she pulled a head-to-toe on him. "You make that look hot as hell."

John puffed his pecs, going all robin-breasted. Hard not to when your female was eating you up with her eyes like that.

And you're still naked. He smiled. *Your birthday suit is my favorite.*

Except she wasn't completely unadorned. Reaching out, he touched the necklace he'd given to her, the one with the big square-cut diamond in the center.

Xhex wasn't normally down for the sap, but she covered his hand with hers and brought his palm to her mouth. Kissing it, she murmured, "I know. I love you, too. Forever."

He leaned into her and brushed his lips against hers.

A couple minutes later they headed out, with her dressed in slacks and a black silk shirt. Which, next to the aforementioned birthday suit, was a pretty fine little outfit. Especially because for once, she'd put her feet into a spectacular pair of fuck-me pumps.

Something he planned to follow through on whenever they could catch a minute alone.

Other people were coming out of bedroom doors: Blay and Qhuinn, also in suits. Z and Bella, with little Nalla dressed in yet another pink confection of silk and tulle . . . which made her pretty much the most adorable thing he'd seen.

And he didn't even like kids.

As the group walked down the hall of statues and hit the stairs, there wasn't a lot of talking. Hadn't been since Rehv had put that proclamation on the dining room table. Wasn't going to be for a while.

This was going to help, however.

Down below in the foyer, still more from the household had gathered, but not Wrath or Beth yet, and John joined the crowd—which again was very quiet. Hell, even Rhage put the kibosh on his usual antics—although with that mouthy fallen angel yet to show—

"What the *fuck* is that?"

At the sound of V's voice, John turned with the rest of them . . . and when he saw what was up at the head of the grand staircase, he blinked once. Twice. Twelve times.

Lassiter was standing at the top of the carpeted steps, his blond-and-black hair styled in a pompadour, a heavy Bible under his armpit, piercings catching the light . . .

But none of that was the real shocker.

The fallen angel was dressed in a sparkling white Elvis costume. Complete with bell-bottoms, balloon sleeves, and lapels big enough to tent up the backyard. Oh, and rainbow wings that revealed themselves as he held his arms out, preacher style.

"Time to get the party started," he said as he jogged down, sequins winking and flashing. "And where the hell's my pulpit?"

V coughed out the smoke he'd just inhaled. "She's having you do the service?"

The angel popped his already mile-high collar. "She said she wanted the holiest thing in the house to do it."

"She got holey, all right," somebody muttered.

"Is that Butch's Bible?" V asked.

The angel flashed the goods. "Yup. And his BoC, he called it? I also got a sermon I did myself."

"Saints preserve us," came from the opposite side of the crowd.

"Wait, wait, wait." V waved his hand-rolled around. "I'm the son of a deity and she picked *you*?"

"You can call me Pastor—and before Mr. Sox Fan gets his panties in a wad, I want everyone to know I'm legit. I went online, took a minister's course in under an hour, and I'm ordained, baby."

Rhage raised his hand. "Pastor Ass-hat, I have a question."

"Yes, my son, you *are* going to hell." Lassiter made the sign of the cross and then looked around. "So where's our bride? The groom? I'm ready to marry somebody."

"I didn't bring enough tobacco for this," V bitched.

Rhage sighed. "There's Goose in the bar, my brother—oh, wait. We don't have a bar anymore."

"I think I'll just run an IV of morphine."

"Can I put it in?" Lassiter asked.

"That's what she said," somebody shot back—

"Oh . . . wow. That's, ah, quite a getup."

Everybody looked over their shoulders as Beth spoke up. She was coming in from the library, Saxton beside her, Rehv behind them. The latter had a parchment rolled up under his arm, and a bemused expression on his face.

"I know, right?" Lassiter said, pulling a pirouette, that cape thing splaying out.

Not that John Matthew paid any attention to the male. Or anybody else.

Without conscious thought, he walked forward toward his sister. She was wearing a simple white sheath dress, one that covered her shoulders and went below her knees. And as he came closer, he recognized it as something he'd seen the Chosen in the house wear when they wanted to be comfortable. Unlike them, however, her hair was loose and spilling down her back in black waves.

She looked innocent. And lovely. And perfect.

You are beautiful, he signed.

"Oh, thanks." She flounced the dress. "Layla lent this to me. So are you ready to walk me down the aisle?"

It was a long time before John could make his hands work right. And as he signed his reply, he thought that for all the bullshit the *gly-*

mera was throwing out, and the stress in the household, and the sadness over Wrath . . . this was something he felt as though he had waited a lifetime for. Something that he had crossed a vast distance to do. Some kind of goal that he'd wanted to meet while not being aware it was out there.

Yes, I am, he signed with pride.

Beth had never loved her brother more. As John Matthew stepped in beside her, she could sense his quiet strength resonating out to her—and she needed it.

Even though she had arranged everything, she had no idea how Wrath was going to react to this.

Glancing around her brother's big shoulders, she popped her brows again at Lassiter. At least her *hellren* would be spared the sight of the angel in that rig.

"You love it, right?" Lassiter asked, holding his Bible high. "I mean, you told me to go onto the Internet. I did. I even printed out my diploma or whatever the hell it's called."

Opening the cover of the King James version, he took out a piece of paper and wave it around. "See? Nice and legal-like."

Beth leaned in. "Wow."

"I know, right? Just like Harvard."

"Impressive."

"I'm totally framing that shit, wha-what." He put the thing away. "And after I was done, I researched human weddings. I knew I was going to need some ceremonial robes, and these were the ones I liked best. I found them at Gould's Costumes and More—boom! I'm nothing but a hound dog."

Beth rubbed her temples. Vishous. She should have asked Vishous to do this. "How'd you manage the hair?"

"Aqua Net. Hairpins. *Cosmo* December issue—for the holidays. Again, thank you, Internet."

Rhage shook his head. "Do you have balls? Or are angels born sac-less?"

Lassiter smiled slyly. "I do all right. Back in the Old Country, I used to chime noon and midnight."

Really, really, *really* should have asked Vishous. "Well, I appreciate everything you—"

As everyone went silent, she looked up to the head of the stairs. Wrath had appeared and was standing tall and proud, George by his side. Unlike John, he wasn't in a tux, but he had put on a certain suit she remembered.

It was the one he'd worn on their first official "date" at Darius'.

"What's the crowd for?" he said.

"Just come on down," she replied.

As he started his descent, her palms went sweaty—and then an instant later, the mother of all hot flashes hit, the heat searing through her.

Man, she couldn't wait until she was either pregnant or fully over the needing. Her inner microwave was driving her crazy.

As Wrath's only pair of non-shitkickers hit the mosaic floor, she thought that he couldn't have looked more magnificent. His hair was fanned all over his massive shoulders, the ends coming down to his hips, and with that tie at his neck . . . he looked like a powerful businessman. Who could kill if he were so inclined.

And didn't that get the hormones cranking.

"What are we doing here, Beth," he demanded.

"We're getting married."

As he recoiled, she rushed in before he could go on any kind of tirade. "You said my human customs matter—that they're equally important. So we're getting married. Right now. In my way."

He shook his head. "But we're already mated. Why—"

"So you can divorce me and keep the throne." As his jaw dropped, she cut him off. "In front of our family here. With a real live minister."

Lassiter raised his hand. "Happy to be of service. I also do christenings. Just sayin'."

Wrath shook his head again. "This is—"

"Are you saying my human side is of lesser value?"

"Well, no. But—"

"So then if we do the ceremony here and now, we haven't lost anything, have we. You can divorce me according to vampire law, we're still mated, *and* we've managed to keep the throne." She kicked up her chin even though he couldn't see her. "Pretty good math, don't you think?"

There was a beat of hushed silence. And then one of the Brothers said, "I fucking love this female. I really totally fucking *love* her."

FIFTY-ONE

As Wrath allowed himself to get maneuvered around the foyer, George, as always, went with him.

Frankly, even if he'd had his sight, he would have had to be led around.

He kept waiting for an inner NFW to sound out. But Beth had boxed him in, in the best possible way—she was right: If her cultural norms were as important to them as a couple? Well . . . if they were "married" in the human way, then they were mated. Period.

And yet, he wasn't sure how he felt. Then again, they'd done things according to his race's traditions originally—and although none of that had any resonance for her, she'd gone right along with it.

Seemed only fair that he do the same for her.

"You ready?" Lassiter asked him softly.

People were still shuffling about, moving around the great space of the foyer. "What are they doing?" Wrath whispered back.

"Forming two lines so there's an aisle that starts at the dining room and runs right to us. We're about five yards in front of the billiards room. She's disappeared—they've shut the doors so we can't see her."

Wrath thought back to when they'd been mated. The Scribe Virgin had been around then. Beth had worn Wellsie's red gown—and had nearly fainted as his brothers had carved her nine-letter name into his shoulders. John Matthew, Blay, and Qhuinn hadn't been in the picture then. Neither had Rehv and Xhex, Payne, Manny, the Shadow brothers, and others.

Or Xcor and the Bastards.

And since then, they'd lost Wellsie. No one else, however.

From out of nowhere, music flooded the foyer, a classical ditty he'd heard before, usually in chick flicks that involved . . . weddings, natch.

"Ready?" Lassiter asked.

"Yeah." Jesus, this was not what he'd expected to be doing.

"I just nodded to Fritz," the angel whispered. "And he's opening the doors."

Wrath cleared his throat and leaned in. "What . . . what is she wearing?"

"White. Calf-length. Loose. She's escorted by her brother and carrying a pink rose that Rhage took from a bouquet on the mantlepiece." There was a pause. "Her eyes are right on you, and that smile of hers? Million bucks, my friend. Million fucking bucks."

All at once, the shit about the throne and the other reasons they were doing this went away: As he caught the scent of his *leelan*, all he thought of was that she was everything to him—and not just because she might well be saving his throne, right here and now.

Oh, and holy shit, she might be pregnant, too.

"Dearly beloved," Lassiter began, "we are gathered here to witness the joining of Elizabeth, daughter of Darius, and Wrath, son of Wrath."

So they were leaving the formal vampire names out. Cool. Made it seem more human.

"Who gives this female—ah, woman's—hand in marriage?"

Wrath expected one of the brothers to translate John's response. Instead, the male communicated his reply loud and clear: He whistled an ascending note that declaratively announced he was the guy presenting his sister.

On instinct, and because he had no idea what the ceremony entailed, Wrath thrust out his palm. As it was clasped by John Matthew, the two of them squeezed hard, a vow given and acknowledged in the shake, an I'll-take-good-care-of-her exchanged with a You'd-better-fucking-do-that.

Cue the throat clearing. Like maybe a couple of the brothers were getting emotional.

Lassiter coughed a little and there was the sound of pages being flipped back and forth. "Ah . . . okay, look, I'm just going to wing it, all right? Is there any reason you two can't do this? No? Awesome."

Beth laughed. "I think you're supposed to wait for us to answer."

"All together then, shall we? And you guys in the peanut gallery, too—any reason this won't fly?"

The entire household as well as his *shellan* and himself shouted, "No!"

"Man, we're doing great." More flipping. "Yeah, they go on and on here. Wrath?"

For some insane reason, he started to smile. "Yeah?"

"Do you take this incredible woman who's just saved your ass as your wife? Will you love and comfort her, honor and keep her in sickness and health, and forsaking all others, be faithful to her as long as you both shall live— crap, I was supposed to do you before him, Beth. How about you answer?"

"No," Wrath cut in with a big grin. "I'll go first. Yeah, I do."

There was a sniffle from the crowd. At which point, Rhage's voice hissed, "What. This is beautiful, 'kay? Fuck all y'all."

"Now, Beth, do you take this hotheaded PITA as your husband? Will you love and comfort him, honor and keep him in sickness and health, and forsaking all others, be faithful to him as long as you both shall live?"

"I do," his Beth said. "Absolutely."

"Niiiice." Lassiter flipped some more pages. "Okay, rings? We got rings here, people?"

"Put my ring on her thumb," Wrath said, taking off the massive black diamond his father had worn. "Here."

"And he can use mine," Beth chimed in. "It's his mother's."

"Aww, that's some sweetness right here." Lassiter took Wrath's ring. "Okay, let's rock this out. I hereby bless these rings. Beth, take yours back and place it on any finger you can fit it on. Or, like, the upper knuckle—there ya go.

"Okay, repeat after me. Oh, shi—I mean, crap. I was supposed to do this with Wrath first, I guess."

"No," Beth said with another laugh. "Actually this is perfect."

"Perfect," Wrath agreed.

It was all just so . . . right. It was natural and real—and the lack of formality so worked, especially in light of the aristocracy's ridiculous value system.

Hell, Lassiter was a living, breathing antidote to all that.

"Okay, so, Beth, follow me. 'I, Beth, a totally awesome chick . . .' "

Beth barked out a giggle. "I, Beth . . ."

"Where's the 'awesome chick' part? What? Come on, I have a license from the Internet. I know what I'm doing."

Wrath nodded at his *leelan*. "He's right. You are, in fact, awesome. I think we need to hear it."

"Can I get an amen!" Lassiter shouted.

"Ammmmmmmmmen!" echoed throughout the mansion.

"Fine, fine, fine," she said. "I, Beth, a totally awesome chick . . ."

" '. . . take this meathead, Wrath . . .' "

". . . take this meathead, Wrath . . ."

" '. . . as my husband, to have and to hold from this day forward . . .' "

". . . as my husband, to have and to hold from this day forward . . ."

" '. . . for better, for worse; for richer, for poorer . . .' "

And suddenly it wasn't a joke. The further she went, the more serious Lassiter got, and the shakier Wrath's *shellan* became, as if the words she were speaking were ones of great value and meaning.

This was tradition for her, he realized.

She continued in a rough way, ". . . in sickness and in health . . ."

" '. . . to love and to cherish, until we are parted by death. This is my solemn vow.' "

". . . to love and to cherish, until we are parted by death. This is my solemn vow."

Lassiter turned another page. " 'I give you this ring as a symbol of my vow, and with all that I am, and all that I have, I honor you in the name of the Father, and the Son, and the Holy Spirit.' "

Suddenly, Wrath gritted his molars to keep his own emotions in check as she repeated the words, and slid the ruby on his pinkie.

"And now, my lord," Lassiter said smoothly. "Recite after me. . . ."

Beth had never been one of those girls who'd imagined her wedding. Acted it out with Barbies. Bought *Bride* magazine as soon as she hit her twenties.

She was pretty sure that if she had been, though, none of the hypotheticals would have resembled this in the slightest: surrounded by vampires, possibly pregnant, with a fallen angel in an Elvis costume mangling the ceremony from the Book of Common Prayer.

And yet as she stared up at her soon-to-be husband, she couldn't have pictured anything she would have liked more. Then again, when you were facing the right person? None of the things they talked about on television, no Vera Wang dress, no champagne waterfall, no DJ or place setting or party favor mattered.

" 'I, Wrath, take you, Beth,' " Lassiter started.

"I got this," her husband said in his booming voice. "I, Wrath, take you, Beth, as my beloved wife, to have and to hold from this day forward, for better, for worse; for richer, for poorer, in sickness and in health, to love and to cherish, till death do us part. This is my solemn vow."

Cue a serious case of the misties.

As Beth sniffled and smiled at the same time, Wrath placed the gigantic King's ring on the top of her thumb. With grave sincerity, he said, "I give you this ring as a symbol of my vow, and with all that I am, and all that I have, I honor you in the name of your Father, and your Son, and your Holy Spirit."

There was a round of applause, spontaneous and loud. And Lassiter had to shout to be heard over it, "By the power vested in me thanks to Google, I now pronounce you husband and wife! You may kiss the bride!"

The clapping got louder as Wrath put his arms around her and bent her backward so far, the only thing keeping her from the ground was his strength.

It was a move he did on a regular basis, an unconscious way of asserting and proving his physical ability to take care of her.

"Take my sunglasses off," he whispered as the curtain of his hair fell all around, giving them privacy. "I want you to see my eyes even if they can't see you."

Beth's hands were shaking as she reached up to his face. Sliding the wraparounds from his temples, his extraordinary stare was revealed, and she thought of the first time she had seen it: in the underground guest suite at her father's house.

They were exactly as they had been. Brilliant pale green, they glowed from within to the point where she had to blink, and not just from the tears in her vision.

"Beautiful," she breathed.

"Useless," he countered with a smile—as if he were remembering the same exchange.

"No, they show me all the love in your heart." She touched his face. "And that is *very* useful."

Wrath's mouth came down on hers, brushing once, twice. And then he kissed her deeply and slowly.

When he finally started to right her, she put his sunglasses back into place, and facing the household, she flushed as she looked at them all. So much love all around.

It made her feel invincible against whatever came at them.

Over the din, Lassiter shouted, "A-thank you, a-thank-you-vera-much."

Wrath bent to the side, flubbled George's ears and took hold of the dog's harness; then the three of them were walking down the aisle toward the dining room.

Somehow Fritz had managed to pull a banquet of food out of thin air, the table magically set during the ceremony with a simple but ample spread.

But first there was business.

As Rehv came in past the arches, he nodded to Beth and she leaned into her husband.

"It's time to sign," she said.

It was painful to watch her husband's unrestrained happiness tighten right up.

"Just the same, right?" she whispered. "We're married. We're covered."

"Yeah . . ." There was a long pause. "Yeah, I can do this."

Except he took his time going over to where Rehv was unrolling a parchment that had red and black ribbons streaming off its lower half.

"I have a blue pen for the signature line," Rehv said, taking the thing out of his mink coat. "This document has been prepared by Saxton, and it's been predated to three weeks ago. He's assured me that the wording is ironclad and nothing that they can dispute in any way."

"Ironclad," Wrath muttered.

Rehv put out the pen. "Sign it and I'll take care of the delivery—with pleasure."

Beth dropped his hand to give her man some space—but he didn't want that, clearly. Gathering her palm back, he stood over the parchment.

"What does it say?" he demanded roughly.

Beth looked over the symbols and saw nothing but patterns of blue ink.

"It says . . ." Rehv leaned in. "That the union is annulled."

"Like it never existed?" Wrath muttered.

Rehv tapped the parchment. "This is a political statement. A political function. This is not about the two of you."

"My signature's supposed to be on it. And her name's on there. So it *is* about us."

Rehv backed off, too. Then it was just Wrath and the writing he couldn't see.

All the Brothers and the members of the household hung in the periphery, everyone quiet.

He wasn't going to do it, she thought. He just wasn't going to be able to do it. . . .

FIFTY-TWO

Watching Selena take from his vein, Trez was totally content to blow off whatever was going on down in Caldwell for this.

He'd still been at the club, finishing up some accounting shit that should have been taken care of days before, when he'd gotten the group text about the gathering. And he'd immediately headed home—expecting to see Selena. When she didn't show, he'd told himself to chill, let her come when she did, blah, blah, blah.

He'd lasted about a minute and a half with that shit before ghosting out, leaving iAm looking grim in the foyer with Goddamn Cat, as he called the animal, back in his arms.

As soon as Trez had gotten up to the great camp, he'd sensed Selena's presence and become juiced—but that had all changed when he'd found her in the kitchen, in the middle of some kind of collapse. Come on, though—when was the last time she'd fed—

From out of nowhere, his cock and balls roared at the thought of her sharing this with anyone else, and to get himself back on the side of the angels, he focused on the pulls against his wrist, the sight of her lips against his skin, the reality that he was, in fact, the one taking care of her.

For how long, though, a part of him wondered.

"Shut up." As her eyes flipped to his, he shook his head. "Not you."

Tracing her hair with his fingertips, he marveled at the difference in them, how soft everything about her was, how she smelled like fresh spring air even though it was winter, how her lashes were long against her pale cheeks as she closed her lids.

He could have stayed like this forever.

But eventually she released him, retracting her fangs and her mouth. And then it was time for a little torture: Her pink tongue snuck out and licked at the puncture wounds, closing them up—cranking him up.

Reclining in his arms, her eyes were fuzzy under those heavy lashes, unfocused from satisfaction.

"I haven't stopped thinking about you," he said softly. "Not for a second."

"Yes?"

"Yeah." He nodded as he brushed her lower lip with his thumb. "And not just because we have . . . unfinished business."

Her smile would have knocked him on his ass if he hadn't already been sitting down. "That we do."

God, he loved the quiet here. No loud music, no humans cluttering the room, no pressures from the outside world—or the s'Hisbe. Not even the Brothers and their mates, as cool as they all were. Just the two of them.

As his erection thickened even further, he had to shift his hips under her head. And then he heard himself say, "I want to make love to you. Right now."

Shit, had he really put that out there? And yet, right now, all the reasons to keep tight in the head seemed so far away, nothing but distant thunder in a night sky that was for the moment clear and full of stars.

Except then a shadow crossed her face, the lazy satiation replaced by a doubt that made him want to kick himself in the zip code.

Instead of pulling away, though, her hand reached up and caressed his face. "I want that."

"You sure?" Fuck, he was hard. Too hard to do the right thing.

When she nodded . . . he knew they were both lost.

"Please," she whispered in a hoarse voice. "Put me out of this misery, take away the burn."

Her hand swept down her body, coming to rest on the juncture of her legs—and he almost orgasmed then and there, his balls tightening and his cock punching against his pants, until he had to grind his molars.

His first thought was to take her where they were. Not smart.

He wasn't going to stop, even if someone else came in.

With a surge of strength, Trez got to his feet with her in his arms, cradling her with care. "Where is your bedroom?"

"Upstairs. In the back."

Striding off, he carried her up the creaking stairs to the second floor, heading for a suite that was over the kitchen wing, kicking open the door. Inside, the Victorian furniture was all heavy mahogany with lots of curves, and the bed was a spectacular expanse of millwork, the perfect frame for her as he laid her on the velvet duvet.

Prowling up her body, he straddled her, being careful not to put any weight down. "I want to . . . see you."

Her hands went for the tie on her robe, but he stopped her. "No, I'd like to . . . do it."

The belt was as white and soft as the rest of what she wore, and as his dark hands loosened the bow, he licked his lips. Parting the two halves of all the draping, he took his time with the reveal.

"Oh, fuck . . ."

Yeah, her nipples tightened even more as the cool air hit them.

Unable to help himself, he leaned down and licked at one, sucking it into his mouth as he kept going with what she was wearing, sweeping the fabric off her. Then he took care of the other one as he stroked his way down to her thighs.

Her scent went right to his sex, his cock kicking again, trying to get out.

And shit, the sound of her moaning his name made him sag. But then he was back in action, touching her between her legs, finding the hot, wet core of her and rubbing the top. As her nails bit into his upper arms, he smiled against her breast.

"Come for me," he groaned as he suckled on her.

Right on cue, her body tightened, a cord yanking straight, her torso jacking against his chest as he switched to her mouth, thrusting his tongue into her as he helped her ride the orgasm out. When it was over, she collapsed, breathing hard.

"Please . . ." Her voice cracked. "I know there's more."

"Yeah, there is." He reared up and nearly ripped his shirt in half. "Fuck, yeah—shit, I mean . . . damn it."

He knew he needed to watch the language, and vowed to do better with the vocab.

His pants were treated no better than what had been on his pecs as he tossed them away, not even caring that they landed on one of the spires of the headboard.

"You are . . . magnificent."

As she spoke, Trez froze and met her eyes—except she was not looking at his face. Nope. Her stare was locked down below, and a quick peek of his own confirmed that his heavily aroused cock was straight and proud, ready to get the job done.

"May I touch you?" she said shyly. Except she was already reaching for him, her pale hand—

The growl he let out was loud enough to shake the mirror by the door, and he fell to the side. "Careful . . . oh, God . . ."

He was going to come, especially as she stroked—

"Oh, Jesus," he said on a hiss before he bit down on his lower lip.

Selena got on her knees, her heavy breasts swaying, her hair uncoiling from its chignon. Two-handing him, she found a steady motion, going up and down, up and down, popping over the top of his head and then finding his shaft again. And as she worked him, his hips countered her, the rhythm getting faster and faster.

With a sudden jerk, he pushed her onto her back and took her hands away from his body.

"But I want to—"

He cut her off with his mouth, licking his way past her lips. "I want to come inside of you."

Her smile was sexy as hell, her eyes sparkling. "And then I get to explore?"

"You are going to kill me, female."

As he mounted her, she parted her legs to make room. "You're the only one I'm thinking of," he heard himself say.

And what do you know, this time the past stayed away—probably because he'd spent the hours they'd been apart thinking of her on the floor of that bathroom, writhing under his mouth, wanting more. Yeah, the desperation to get into her, have her, orgasm in her, was stronger than all the things he hated about himself. Nothing was going to stop this now.

Especially as, during the time they'd been separated, he'd pointed one salient fact out to himself:

She had been with a lot of males, too.

That was part of her job—even though he hated to think of it. As a Chosen who served the blood needs of others, she had been trained sexually and been with the males she had served. It was the way things worked.

And as much as it depressed him, he supposed it put them on an equal footing—although the sex she'd been having had been part of a sacred role that saved lives. His had just been an addiction.

Past tense there, he thought. Nice.

Gripping himself, he angled his cock and closed the distance, pressing into her, finding the right spot. With a groan, he brought both arms up so that he cradled her head—and as their eyes met, he could tell she'd stopped breathing, as if bracing herself for his size.

"I'll go slow," he murmured, kissing her gently.

Her voice was a mere whisper: "Thank you."

As he inched into her, she was curiously still, her eyes closed, her fangs descending. And all he could do was stare at how beautiful she was against the bloodred velvet duvet, her black hair tangling on the pillow, her cheeks flushed.

"You're tight," he gritted out. "Dear God."

"Don't stop."

"I won't—"

"Do it, just do it."

Trez frowned, thinking that was an odd way—

It happened so fast that he didn't have a chance to stop it—Selena gripped his hips, locked him in place, and thrust herself forward, driving him past a barrier . . . that should not have been there.

As she let out a gasp of pain, nothing computed. "What the . . ."

He didn't finish the sentence. Couldn't finish the thought. The tight grip of her all around him was too much, and the orgasm that had been brewing kicked out of him, flowing into her body.

In response, Selena linked her legs around his ass, a sigh rippling out of her as he tried to keep any thrusting to a minimum. Virgin? Virgin . . .

And then he remembered, back in the bathroom . . . Take me, teach me.

Virgin.

Trez withdrew so fast, she winced—and he nearly ended up not just off the bed, but out of the room.

The blood on his deflating erection made his gut fist up. "Selena . . . Christ, why didn't you say something?"

Her eyes dropped from his as she pulled her robe together. She even redid the cloth belt before sitting up on the pillows. "I wanted you. I still do. It's as simple as that."

He reached up to loosen the necktie that was constricting his breathing—and remembered he was buck-ass naked.

"Not simple," he said hoarsely. "That is not simple."

The last thing he needed was another female he was obligated to wed: If Phury as Primale wanted him to follow through on this? What the hell was he going to do?

Especially because . . . he was falling in love with Selena.

As Trez stood naked on the far side of the room, Selena thought, Hmm, not what she'd been going for.

But she'd been right to keep quiet. At the last minute, she'd made a conscious decision not to tell him—for precisely this reason.

"How is— how— why . . ." The stuttering was not a good sign. "I thought you were an *ehros*."

"I am."

"So how are you a virgin?"

"I was not used in that manner."

He threw his hands up in frustration. "Why me?" Abruptly, he cursed. "I mean . . ."

"As I said, I wanted to be with you. I still do." After the strike of pain, she'd only gotten a hint of the pleasure—she wanted to know what else there was to making love.

Putting his head in his hands, he just stood there. "Christ."

"Just so that we understand each other," she said crisply, "I'm not expecting anything from you. If that's what you're worried about. There shall be no mating."

Not with her future. Although with the way Trez was looking, that wouldn't have been in the cards anyway—

"You sure your Primale will think like that?"

She kicked her chin up. "Who's going to tell him." When that seemed to stop him, she shrugged. "It shan't be me. And no one else is in this house with us. So if you do not, he will never know."

In truth, she wasn't sure what Phury would do if he found out—technically, now that she'd had sex with someone other than the Primale or a Brother, she was fallen. But it was hard to know in these new times how much of the old ways survived.

Not that it mattered. Her time was coming due.

Which was why, when Trez had paused after noting her sex was tight, she'd taken matters into her own hands. She'd been determined to not lose her chance, especially not after that episode downstairs at the kitchen table.

Abruptly, she thought of the one he was bound to—and felt a lance of pain through her chest.

"Worry not," she said with exhaustion. "There is nothing to be done."

"I do have honor, you know," he snapped.

"I mean no offense."

He closed his eyes and muttered, "You shouldn't be apologizing."

"I fail to see the problem. My body is mine to give and I chose you—and you wanted me."

At that, his lids rose. "I hurt you."

"What was painful was that you stopped."

Trez shook his head. "This is a mess."

"According to whom?"

"You don't know the half of it." But at least he came over and sat on the bed. Putting his head back into his hands, he exhaled hard. "I shouldn't have been the one, Selena. Anybody but me."

"Again, don't you think that's a judgment only I can make?"

"But you don't know me."

"I know enough." After all, he'd told her about the human women. His parents. His being tied to another. What else could there be?

"Nope. You don't—"

A sound cut through the room, and it took a moment for her to realize it was a portable phone ringing.

"Are you fucking me," he groused as he reached past her to the pillow. On it, a cellular device was sitting with its screen facing up, having clearly slid out of his pants pocket when they ended up on the headboard.

He checked the number—and then looked over to the clock. "What time is it—oh, shit."

"What's wrong?" she asked.

"I've got to take this." He glanced around as if looking for some privacy. "I'll be right back."

As she watched him go out into the hall, his naked body was resplendent—and just the sight of his backside was enough to get her assessing whether or not she'd ever get the chance to be with him again.

Closing her eyes, she stretched herself and found an ache in her pelvis that had never been there before.

Yes, it had hurt some. But not enough to make her regret anything—or not want to do it again.

Something told her it wasn't in her future, however.

She should have said something to him.

But there was no taking that decision back.

FIFTY-THREE

In the end, Wrath signed the goddamn dissolution proclamation.

His mother's ring on his pinkie finger was what made up his mind: That ruby was a symbol of Beth's solemn vow to him and it made him think about everything his female had done for him. In order to mate him, she'd put her faith, her heart, her future in him and his people, traditions, customs—turning away from her human side entirely, to the point where she had no contact with that race anymore, nothing outside him and his brothers, his job taking over both their lives.

She had gained much, sure. But she had lost everything she had ever known. And she'd done it for him, for them.

Right now, the most important thing was not the throne. No, it was living up to the standard she herself had set: He needed to put his signature where his mouth was. Even though he hated this whole fucking thing, from the aristocrats and the Band of Bastards to the sense of loss that came with this piece of cocksucking paper, he had to honor what he'd told his Beth.

Her traditions were just as weighty and important as his own.

If he didn't do this? He was treating her with the same disrespect the Council had.

And this *was* the most logical way to circumvent the *glymera*.

A nice little get-it-up-ya to their machinations.

"Where's the pen?" he growled.

When Rehv put the thing in his dagger hand, he squeezed Beth's palm. "Where do I do it?"

"Right here," she said roughly. "Here."

He let her lead the pen's nib to where there must have been a line, and then he scribbled his name.

"What happens now?" he demanded.

Rehv laughed with a nasty edge. "I roll this little missive up and shove it where the sun don't shine." There was the rustling of parchment. "They called for the 'crowning' to happen at midnight. Fucking shame I have to wait until then. Come on, Saxton, you need some food. You look like you're ready to collapse."

Wrath glanced over at the silent, unmoving crowd. "Well. Are you people eating or what."

As conversation jumped into the silence, like his brothers knew he needed the attention elsewhere, he took Beth's arm.

"Get us out of here," he said harshly.

"Roger that."

With quick efficiency, his *shellan* led him away from the noise and the food, and when he caught a whiff of burning wood, he guessed she'd taken him over toward the library.

"Lie down, George," she said as she pulled up short at what he guessed was the doorway. "I know, I know you don't want to sit out here, but we need a minute."

Good call, he thought as he dropped his hold and walked forward on his own, his dagger hand stretched out. When he felt the mantel, he wished he could see the banked fire. He wanted to poke something hot and make it sizzle.

A *click-click* told him she'd shut them in.

"Thank you," his Beth said.

He turned around. "Back at you."

"It's going to be all right."

"If you're talking about the Band of Bastards, I wouldn't be so sure. There'll be another angle. We've bought some time, but not solved the problem."

Man, the bitterness in his voice was so not him. But this situation had changed him.

Thank God his father was dead—and wasn't that something he'd never imagined thinking—

From behind him, Beth pressed herself against his body, her hands slipping up to his shoulders and rubbing the tight muscles. "It was a beautiful ceremony."

He had to laugh. "Elvis did do a great job."

"You know what's customary for humans to do after they make it official?"

"What?"

As her arms slipped around his waist, she came around, rose up on her tiptoes and kissed the side of his throat. And what do you know, his mood started to improve.

"Consummation," she murmured. "It's traditional for the man and wife to seal the deal, if you know what I mean."

Wrath started to smile, but then he remembered the last time they were together—and the circumstances. "Are you sure you're ready for that after . . . well, you know."

"Very sure."

To prove the point, she rubbed herself against him, and he had to curse. Instantly starved, he nonetheless reeled that wild side in as he dropped his head and took his wife's mouth.

"Pick me up," she said on a sigh.

As he complied, she pulled the dress she was wearing to her waist, her legs splitting to go around his hips.

"You're not wearing any panties," he groaned.

"I wanted to be prepared for this."

"Jesus, I'm glad I didn't know—I would have . . ."

He didn't bother finishing that one. Instead, as she tightened a hold around his neck, he reached in between them and unbuttoned his slacks. Instantly, his cock sprang free, throbbing and hot, and as he settled her a little lower, he found her core—

"Shit! What if you're pregnant?" he blurted, shoving her back. "Fuck—"

"Pregnant women have sex. Really. They do."

Stretching up, she sucked in his lower lip and then nipped it with her fangs. "Unless you're saying you don't want me?"

He weaved in his shitkickers. "*So* not the case."

He solved any confusion there by entering her slowly, pressing in, finding home in a gentle way. She didn't seem to hurt any, but he wasn't taking chances as his palms cupped her ass and he began to move her up and down on him.

"I love you," he said into her hair. "Forever."

As she murmured it back into his ear, a shaft of paranoia drained some of the heat out of his body.

Had his father said the same thing to his mother?

And he knew how that had ended.

From out of nowhere, V's warning came to him, about the field of white and the future in his hands. What did—

"Wrath," his wife whispered. "Come back to me. Focus on me here and now. . . ."

With a groan of submission, he let all the bullshit go, doing as she'd commanded, feeling and knowing only the sensation of him pumping in and out of her. The orgasm was a quiet one, a wave that approached and retreated with all the thunder of a summer breeze. But as he came inside his female and felt her contract around him, it seemed more powerful than all the ones that had rocked his balls.

He did not want to let her go.

Ever.

Outside of Selena's bedroom, Trez accepted the call—but didn't get a "hello" in.

"Where the *fuck* are you," the queen's executioner bit out. "And *where* is what you promised me."

Trez squeezed his eyes shut. "I'm on my way."

"Don't you fuck with me."

The connection was cut.

"Trez?" Selena asked from inside the room. "Is everything all right?"

Nope. Not in the slightest.

How was it noon already?

He pushed the door wide. "Yeah. But I gotta go."

Cursing under his breath, he went directly to his pants and yanked them on—and when his balls got caught in the zipper, he deliberately pulled up harder, the pain shooting through his pelvis and making him sick.

That little phone call from s'Ex was a reminder of all the reasons it had been a dumb-ass idea to come up here.

Virgin.

Fuck.

As he grabbed his shirt and stuffed an arm through a sleeve, he was acutely aware of Selena sitting silently on the bed.

Virgin.

Right on cue, all those women he'd fucked came back to him in a rush, once again crowding the space between them. And then he had a happy thought about the ones he was providing s'Ex today.

"That's not happening again," he said, motioning to the bed, to her.

Once was already too much.

In response, Selena's face gave nothing away, but her scent said it all: The sadness came out of her very pores.

And yet she met him in the eye. "As you wish. But I shall be here if you change your mind."

Man, she was nothing but self-possession as she stared him down, almost challenging him to stay away.

His self-control was not that good. But the situation he was in was that bad.

iAm was already at risk. If Selena were involved with him?

He didn't want her falling into his Hell.

Oh, and as for Phury? He felt like shit saying nothing to the Primale. Just another way he'd dishonored her—but nothing good could come of a reveal like that.

"I have to go," he muttered.

"As you wish."

He reaaaaallly wanted her to stop saying that.

Trez all but stumbled from the room, and he didn't remember anything of the trip down the stairs, through the dark house, and out into the bright, snowy side yard. Closing his eyes, it was a while before he could focus and concentrate enough to dematerialize . . .

. . . but he eventually made it to the Commodore, re-forming behind the rear service entrance's Dumpster. Stepping out from it, the deliverymen who were unloading commercial cleaning supplies into the holding area ignored him, and so did the bike messenger who was streaking down the back alley.

But there were plenty of people waiting for him up on the eighteenth floor.

As soon as he stepped out of the elevator, he cursed under his breath.

iAm was leaning up against the closed door, all casual except for the murder in his eyes. And with him? The whores Trez had arranged for s'Ex.

The queen's executioner was undoubtedly on the terrace outside. Or prowling around the inner rooms after having broken in, in a rage.

Trez shoved his hands in his pockets—no keys. Fuck.

Did he forget them? Or were they on the floor of Selena's bedroom?

Goddamn it.

"Missing something?" his brother drawled.

"Hey, boss," one of the prostitutes said.

"Boss—"

"What's up—"

The women spoke over themselves as they pumped their extensions and rearranged their bra cups. They were each wearing some version of keep-it-legal, but everything was short and tight and low-cut.

Not that they were going to stay clothed for long.

"Allow me," iAm muttered, taking out his copper key.

After doing the deed with the lock, he swung the door wide and nodded for the girls to go inside.

As they shimmied in, the male narrowed his eyes. "What the fuck are you doing?"

"Taking care of business," Trez hissed back. "The only way I know how."

Pushing past his brother, he strode into the living room. And just like the wraith he was, the executioner was waiting on the far side of the glass, his black robes wafting in the cold wind.

As the three prostitutes noticed him, they froze, either spellbound or scared shitless. Maybe both.

"Give me a minute, ladies," Trez said as he went to the sliding doors. "I'll send him down to you in the bedroom off that hall over there."

"Yeah, okay, boss," the one in the front answered.

He waited until they were out of the room before letting s'Ex in.

Good thing—the executioner was pissed off, all but tearing the hood from his head.

Jabbing a finger into Trez's face, he barked, "You be on time in the future. Or our agreement is null and void."

Just as Trez was about to get all up in the bastard's face, iAm stepped in. "We had a mandatory engagement for the King. Nothing we could get out of, and nothing that's going to happen again."

Black, glittering eyes swung in his brother's direction. "You make sure of that."

iAm nodded once, his face deceptively calm: His tell was the twitch in his left eyebrow—shit, Trez was going to hear allllll about this as soon as it was over.

Great. Something else to look forward to.

s'Ex reached up to the black brooch at his throat. Big as a fighter's fist, it was studded with black stones, the metal twisting in and around itself—and when he removed the thing, all those robes fell to the floor.

Exposing a pedestrian-looking wifebeater and a pair of black combat pants.

What was not pedestrian was the rest of him: Every inch of his skin was marked with that white ritual tattooing, his heavily muscled arms and shoulders patterned with the shit. And yet, he could still pass for human.

Good news for the prostitutes.

"In spite of the fact that you're late," s'Ex gritted out, "I did you all a favor."

"So our parents are alive?" Trez said.

"Oh, yeah, that, too. They are losing their quarters, however—at the queen's request. Last time I checked, your mother was having a nervous breakdown as her jewels were being repossessed." The executioner smiled slowly. "Her majesty is actually pleased with their suffering. If I didn't know better, I'd say you planned this all perfectly."

"What's the favor?"

"Her majesty is about to be occupied with things that don't involve you for a little while."

Trez narrowed his eyes. "How so?"

"About nine months."

"I'm sorry, what? I don't get what you're—"

"She's pregnant."

Trez stopped breathing. And then forced his lungs to get back with the program as he shot a glance over at his brother. "How the hell did that happen?"

"Of all people, I'd assume you don't need a diagram."

"But I thought her consort died ten years ago?"

"Yeah. Such a shame." s'Ex cracked his knuckles. "He had a bad fall."

"So whose is it."

s'Ex smiled with a sly edge. "It's a miracle."

Holy . . . shit.

s'Ex nodded. "The timing's good for you because she's going to have to wait to see if it's another daughter. At that point, the star charts will have to be read to figure out which will be the next queen. Obviously, if it's a son? You're screwed. If not, you might have a shot—after all, you were promised to that particular daughter. If another is to be queen? You're good."

iAm exhaled slowly. "This is . . . pretty fucking great news. Potentially."

"But you still owe me," s'Ex growled. "From now going forward? You take care of me . . . or I'll take care of you both."

"Don't worry about that." Trez jacked up his slacks, his mind reeling. "Whatever you need."

"That's more like it."

Jesus . . . this changed everything. Or at least, it could.

A far better outcome than he could have engineered.

As s'Ex's obsidian stare shifted to the hall the girls had gone down, Trez refocused. "A couple of rules."

The executioner glanced back. "I don't hear that."

Trez stepped in tight, meeting the huge male grille-to-grille. "The rules are this—you do not hurt them. Rough sex is okay if it's consensual, but no permanent scars or marks. And you may not eat them. Those are my only two constraints, and they are not negotiable."

With Shadows, you always had to set limits. Especially a Shadow like this one.

"Wait, are they yours?" the male asked.

"Yeah."

"Oh, shit, why didn't you just say?" s'Ex put out his palm. "My vow. Nothing permanent and no lunch."

What a relief, Trez thought as he clasped that hand and gave it a hard shake. "But I'm giving them to you for however long you want them. And the apartment, too, of course. When you want something fresh? You know where to find me."

As the executioner smiled and went to walk off, Trez snagged a hold on the male's arm. "One more thing—those are humans. As far as they know, vampires are fiction—and you need to keep it like that if you want this to continue."

s'Ex looked bored. "Fine. But it would have been more fun the other way."

As he stalked out of the room, his heavy footfalls echoed down the corridor, and then there were voices. Followed by a door shutting.

Trez went directly to the bar even though it was only just after noon, and picked up a bottle of Maker's Mark. He didn't bother with a glass; straight from the bottle was good enough for him.

As the liquor burned its way down to his gut, his only thought was that he should feel more relief than he did. Then again, he wasn't quite out of the woods yet.

And he'd taken the virtue of a good female about a half hour ago.

No get-out-of-jail-free card was going to change that.

"Nine lives," iAm said as he came over and put his hand out.

Trez passed the bourbon over. "Not yet—"

The moan that rippled distantly was female in origin. And so was the one that followed.

"He's going to do all three of them at once," iAm muttered.

A quick image of the executioner on his back with one female straddling his hips, another riding his face, all while he fingered a third made Trez take the bottle back and drink hard.

Goddamn, Trez thought, he hoped he could stay ahead of that appetite.

FIFTY-FOUR

Fresh snow began to fall at six, as if it had been waiting for the sun to drop below the horizon before it made its appearance—and by midnight, the storm wasn't showing any signs of lightening up.

As Xcor stared out his bedroom window, he tracked the thick flakes, thanks to the streetlights that marked the cul-de-sac's circle in front of the house.

"Are you coming?"

At the sound of Throe's voice, Xcor looked over his shoulder. His fighter was standing in the doorway, dressed in a proper suit.

His Chosen would be waiting for him, Xcor thought. In this bad weather.

Assuming she showed.

But he couldn't miss the crowning.

"Yes," he said gruffly, getting off the chair he'd pulled over to the window.

Gathering up his holsters, he strapped them on his shoulders and his waist and slid in various guns and blades. But as he went to pick up the scythe, Throe shook his head.

"I think you should leave that here, no?"

"She comes with me."

After Xcor put her on his back, he covered everything up with his leather duster. "Let us proceed."

As he walked by Throe, he refused to meet the male's eyes. He knew what he would find if he did and was uninterested in the scrutiny.

Joining the Bastards down below, he was silent as they filed out into the chilly evening and dematerialized from the backyard . . .

. . . to the formal grounds of Ichan, son of Enoch's modern house.

Through the swirling snow, he saw that others had already arrived, members of the Council in formal dress milling around the interior rooms, passing by the glowing windows.

The celebration was warranted, as this was, indeed, a triumph—or it should have been. But all he could think about was the female who was out in a meadow, hopefully bundled against the winter elements, waiting for him. Glancing up to the sky, snow fell into his eyes and he blinked.

How long would she stay there—

"This way," Throe said, indicating a front entrance that had all the subtlety of a billboard on the side of the highway. "As if one could miss it."

So many spotlights, all focusing on the colored glass around a red-painted door that had some kind of sun-like symbol in it.

"How garish," Throe muttered as they started across the snow. "Unfortunately, the inside is worse."

Xcor, on the contrary, didn't have an opinion about the decor. And he was unimpressed by all the uniformed staff who opened the way in and passed around little pieces of food on silver trays and took drink orders.

No, he was in a field far away, under a maple tree, waiting for a female to arrive so he could give her his coat against the flurries.

He was not here—

"May I take your coat?" a *doggen* asked at his elbow.

Shifting his eyes over, the butler stepped back. "No."

"As you wish, sire." The bow that he gave was so low, the *doggen* nearly touched the glossy floor. "But of course—"

At that moment, Ichan approached with all the flourish of a bandleader. Indeed, he was wearing a satin smoking jacket that was red as blood and a pair of loafer-shoes that bore his initials in gold thread. Quite a dandy, at least in his own mind.

"Welcome, welcome. Have a drink—Claus, serve them?"

Xcor let his Bastards answer for him, deciding to move off into another room.

And indeed, the aristocrats silenced as he passed them, their eyes widening from fear and respect—which was why he'd worn his weapons. He had wanted his personage to be a potent reminder of who was actually in charge.

As he proceeded around, he noted idly that Throe was correct about the furnishings. Modern "art" choked the spaces, filling up corners and walls, crowding chairs and tables and sofas that were so contorted, one had to wonder where a guest could actually sit down. And the color scheme was all over the place, the only commonality appearing to be that the bright, discordant hues affront the retina—

How long would she wait? Would she have worn a coat?

Of course she would have.

What if someone questioned why she was leaving? What if she was caught coming back into the house—?

"Xcor?" Throe said quietly.

"Yes."

"It's time." Throe nodded in the direction of a library that was nothing but shelving and books, the furniture having blessedly been emptied out.

Or at least, most of it. Centered in the middle of the space, there was a large, throne-like chair set up as well as a table with a big piece of parchment, wax for sealing, and many, many ribbons.

Ah, yes. The site of Ichan's precious little zenith.

Which was not going to last.

Xcor went over and stood at the room's entrance, meeting the eyes of each member of the *glymera* as they had to go by him. When there were none left to gather, he turned his attention to the assembled, his Bastards standing around him such that their bodies choked the way out of the library—

From behind, the main door opened one last time, a rush of cold, dry air barging in like an errant guest. Glancing over his shoulder, he frowned.

Errant guest, indeed: Rehvenge, the Council's titular *leahdyre*, strode in like he owned the place, his full-length mink coat sweeping after him, a red cane that was not an umbrella, helping him along.

He was smiling, purple eyes showing a calculation that was a warning.

"Am I late?" he shouted out. As he came up to Xcor, those eyes stared directly into his own. "I'd hate to miss this."

Who the hell had invited him, Xcor wondered. The male was solidly on the former King's side, a mole who was more like a jaguar in their midst.

From inside the library, Ichan turned in mid-gesture, a cigarette in an old-fashioned ebony holder waving about—only to freeze when he saw who had arrived.

Rehvenge lifted his cane in lieu of greeting. "Surprise," the male said as he barged into the crowd. "Oh, did you not expect me? I was on the list of invitees."

As Throe stepped forward, Xcor grabbed a hold of the male and dragged him back to heel. "No. He may not be alone."

At once, all of his soldiers' hands disappeared into their clothes. As did his.

And yet no Brothers showed up.

So this was a message, Xcor thought.

Ichan glanced across as if he expected Xcor to deal with the intrusion, but when nobody from the group of fighters budged, the aristocrat cleared his throat and approached Rehvenge.

"A word, if you will," Ichan said. "In private."

Rehvenge smiled as if he already had his fangs in the idiot's throat. "No, not private. Not for this."

"You are not welcome herein."

"You want to try to remove me?" Rehvenge shifted forward on his hips. "You want to try it and see how that goes? Or maybe ask those thugs over there to do it for you?"

Ichan gaped like a fish, his bravado gone.

"I didn't think so."

As Rehvenge reached into his coat, Ichan squeaked in alarm and the aristocrats in the room milled around like cattle about to be slaughtered.

Xcor just glanced over his shoulder again. The door had been left open, the staff having become too distracted to close it—or mayhap they had just up and disappeared.

Rehvenge had left the thing wide on purpose, hadn't he. The male was already planning his exit.

"I bring greetings from Wrath, son of Wrath," the male said, still with that shit-eating grin on his face. "And I have a document he'd like to share with you all."

As he took a cardboard tube out from under his arm and popped the lid free, the aristocrats gasped—like they expected a bomb to go off.

And mayhap there was a kind of one in there.

Rehvenge unfurled a parchment that had red and black ribbons hanging off its end. Instead of reading what had been inked upon it, he merely turned the thing around.

"I think you should do the honors," he said to Ichan.

"Whatever have you . . ." The words dried up as the male closed in on what was displayed before him. After a moment, he said,"Tyhm. *Tyhm!*"

"Yeah, I think you'll find that it's all nice and legal. Wrath isn't mated to her. He divorced her about three weeks ago—and I'm not a lawyer, but I'm pretty sure you can't base a vote of no confidence on an issue that doesn't exist."

The tall, thin solicitor stumbled over and tilted in, as if ocular proximity would increase his comprehension of whate'er was on there.

And indeed, the expression on his face was all the translation that the crowd required: Disbelief turned to a kind of horror, as if an explosive had in fact been detonated right in front of him.

"This is a forgery!" Ichan declared.

"It has proper witnesses—and I'm one of them. Maybe you'd like Wrath and the Brotherhood to come over here and testify to its validity? No? Oh, and don't worry. We're not expecting a response from you all. There is none."

"We leave now," Xcor whispered.

If he were Wrath, the next move would be to attack the house—and there was not enough cover inside here, that dreadful art and the large open spaces offering little for use as shields.

As the voices of the aristocrats mixed and grew louder, he and his soldiers dematerialized out onto the front lawn. Bracing for engagement, they outed their guns.

Except there was no one there.

No Brothers. No attack. No . . . anything.

The silence was deafening.

FIFTY-FIVE

As with all great shifts in life, the sun and the moon paid no attention to the drama on the planet, their schedules unaffected by the changing destinies down below.

It was well past midnight when Wrath woke up next to his *shellan* in their mated bed, his arm around her waist, his hand cupping her breast. And for a moment, he wondered whether any of it had happened—the needing, that shit from the Council, the response.

Maybe it had all just been a fucked-up nightmare.

Cozying in closer, he kept his arousal back. He was going to leave the sexual instigation to his *leelan*, at least until they knew whether she was pregnant. And if she was . . . well, then he wasn't sure what he was going to do—

Holy fuck, was he really thinking like this?

"You're awake," Beth said.

"How did you know?" he murmured into her hair.

She turned in his arms. "I just do."

They lay there for the longest time, and fucking hell, he wished he could see her properly. Instead, he settled for running his fingertips over her features.

"How do you feel?" he asked.

"Victorious." He could hear the smile on her face. "God, I love Rehvenge. He really took it to the Council."

When he didn't say anything, she sighed. "This is a good thing, Wrath. I promise you."

"Yeah, it is." He kissed her on the mouth, and then pulled away. "I'm starved. You want to eat?"

"Actually—no. I'm not hungry, but it's got to be time for First Meal. Unless we slept through it?"

"I think that time is past. And you guys call it breakfast, right?" He got out of bed and went over to let George in from the bathroom. "I doubt anyone else is up. That party went till five in the afternoon."

As he popped the door, the golden tackled him with the hellos, collar jangling, tail whapping into the doorjambs, Wrath's leg, the wall as he circled, circled, circled, and sneezed from smiling.

"Wrath?"

"Hey, my man," he said as he knelt down. "What's up, big man? Who's the big man—"

"Wrath."

"Yeah?"

"Let's go to work after you eat."

"You trying to get me back on the horse?" He stroked that smooth head as the dog sneezed again.

"Yes. I am."

He rubbed his own face. "Shower. Food. Then we'll talk."

"Work, you mean."

The good news, he supposed, was that no one was going to want anything from him in the loo. And as he stepped under the spray before it went warm, he didn't know why he was hurrying. That wife of his was going to snap his chain until he was back on the throne, pushing papers.

With that prospect hanging over his head? He should be handwashing himself in the sink and using a lady's fan to dry off—

At first he wasn't sure what he was hearing. But then, over the drone of the shower, he recognized it as retching.

He jumped out of the marble stall so fast, he nearly yard-saled on the slippery floor. "Beth! Beth—"

"I'm fine," she said from around the corner.

Rushing over to the toilet's separate little room, he threw out his palms and felt around, finding his mate on her knees in front of the bowl, one hand holding back her hair, the other braced on the seat.

"I'll get Doc Jane."

"No, you won't—"

She was cut off by a series of heaves, and as he stood over her, he wanted to be the one going through the gasping and the straining.

"Screw this," he muttered, stumbling forward as he went for the house phone—

Except it rang before he could pick the thing up to dial the clinic's extension. Shit, maybe V's wife was reading minds, too, now.

"Jane?"

"Ah, no, sire, 'tis Fritz."

"Oh, listen—could you get me—"

"Wrath, stop it. I'm fine," Beth said from directly behind him.

He wheeled around. His wife's scent certainly didn't suggest a health emergency—and that tone of hers was annoyed, not panicked. "Ah . . ."

"Whom may I bring for you?" the butler asked over the connection.

Beth cut in again: "Wrath, seriously. Don't bother the woman, okay? There's nothing going on."

"Then why were you throwing up?"

"I'm sorry?" Fritz said. "Sire?"

"Not you," Wrath muttered. "And either she comes here or—"

"Fine, fine, I'll go down to the clinic," Beth murmured. "Just let me get dressed."

"I'm coming with you."

"I had a feeling you were."

Exhaling a curse, he wondered how in the hell he was going to make it through this—either she was pregnant, in which case he was going to be scared shitless for how long? Eighteen months? Or she wasn't, in which case he was going to have to help her through her disappointment.

Or . . . shit, she could lose the young, too.

That was the third option—oh, God, now he felt like throwing up.

"Thanks, Fritz," he said, "I'll be down—"

"Sire, I just wanted you to know that there will be workmen in the house this evening."

"Workmen?"

"For the billiards room? The damage . . . was rather extensive. The floor needs to be entirely replaced, although the good news is that the original craftsmen are available. I hired them to come, and coordinated with Tohr. He was going to discuss this with you?"

"There's been a lot going on."

"But do not worry, sire. We have proper security measures in place. The workers have been background-checked by Vishous, and the Brothers will be on hand to supervise. I'm afraid there was no other option, assuming we wish to use the space again."

"That's cool. Don't worry about it."

"Thank you, my lord."

As Wrath hung up, he refocused on the issue of his female. Marching over to the closet, he yanked on his leathers and a muscle shirt.

"Let's go," he announced as he put George's halter on.

"Wrath, I'm going to be just fine . . ." There was a pause. "Oh, shit."

Her footfalls hurried by him, and headed back for the toilet.

Calmly, Wrath returned to the phone—and got the butler to connect him to Doc Jane.

It was a little difficult to argue with the hubs about a doctor's visit when Beth couldn't get her head out of the bowl. Every time she thought the nausea was over, she'd get to her feet, go back out into the bedroom—and two minutes later, she'd be on her knees again on the marble floor, heaving up absolutely nothing.

"I don't need to lie down," she groused as she stared at the ceiling over their bed.

When Wrath didn't reply, she turned her head on the pillow and shot a glare in his direction. He was sitting at the foot of the mattress, shoulders set, jaw locked, huge body still as stone.

"I'm fine," she tacked on.

"Uh-huh."

"This is going to be a really long couple of months if we worry about every little twinge."

"You just tried to throw up your liver."

"I did not."

"So you were working on your pancreas?"

She crossed her arms over her chest.

"I can feel you glaring at me," Wrath said.

"Well, I am. This is ridiculous."

The knock on the door was quiet. So was the "Hello?"

"Come in," Wrath said as he got up. Sticking his hand straight out, he waited for Doc Jane to come to him.

"Hey, you two," the female said as she entered . . . and slowed down to look around at the suite. "Dear God, check out this place."

"Over the top, right?" Beth said.

"Is it real?" Jane breathed as she shook Wrath's hand. "I mean, like . . . the rubies and the emeralds. On the walls?"

"Yeah, they're real." Wrath shrugged as if it were no big deal. "They were part of the treasury from back in the Old Country. Darius had them installed here."

"Pretty fancy wallpaper." Doc Jane focused on Beth and smiled as she came over, all business. "So I understand you've been sick."

"I'm fine."

"No, she isn't," Wrath cut in.

"Yes. I am."

Doc Jane put her old-fashioned bag down on the bedside table and cleared her throat. "Well, maybe we can just see how you're doing anyway. Can you tell me what happened?"

Beth shrugged. "I threw up—"

"Like two dozen times," Wrath interjected.

"It was not two dozen times!"

"Fine, three dozen—"

Doc Jane put up both of her palms and looked back and forth. "Um . . . you know what I'd like to do if it's okay with you, Wrath? How about I talk to your mate one-on-one—I'm not kicking you out. I just think maybe things will go a little better if she and I had a second alone?"

Wrath plugged his hands on his hips. "She threw up. At least a dozen times. If she wants to sugarcoat it, fine. But those are the facts."

"All right, thank you for that. I really appreciate it." The doctor smiled. "Hey, you know what would be helpful? If you went down and got her some ginger ale and saltines from the kitchen."

Wrath positively glowered. "You're giving me a job to get rid of me."

"As a bonded male, I know that you're going to want to take care of her. And I think, if she's nauseous, having those things in her belly might make her feel better."

"I can call Fritz, you realize."

"Yes, I know. Or you can do it yourself and provide for her."

Wrath stood there, frowning and gritting his teeth. "You know something, Jane, you're spending too much time with Rhage."

"Because I'm manipulating you?" The physician's smile got bigger. "Maybe. But if you leave right now, you can be back waaaaay before I'm finished."

Wrath was still muttering under his breath as he whistled for George and took the golden's halter. "I won't be long."

A warning, more than anything.

But he did leave.

Doc Jane waited for the door to close before shifting those level eyes back over. "So. Let me guess, you think you're pregnant."

Beth felt her mouth drop open. "Well, I . . ."

In a gentler tone, the doctor said, "You're not going to jinx it. Saying it out loud won't change anything, I promise you. I just want to know where your head's at."

Beth put her hands on her rounded stomach. "I don't know, I feel kind of silly. But this nausea is not like anything I've ever known. It's like—not really about my stomach? It's as if my whole body is queasy? And Layla threw up as soon as the miscarriage stopped."

Doc Jane nodded. "She did. But before we go too far comparing the pair of you, I want to remind you that every pregnancy is different. Even with the same woman. That being said, you have just gone through your needing, and maybe you are. It's probably too early to tell, though."

"That's what I was thinking. And yet . . . I don't know—I'm kind of taking this like maybe it's a sign. But, hell, maybe it means nothing at all."

"Well, I'll say this. The fact that you have some human in the mix? It adds on another layer of complication that is going to make diagnosis and treatment tricky. Which is why I wanted to have a candid conversation with you. I think it would be a good idea for you and me to have an idea of how and by whom you want to be treated if you are pregnant. I'd be more than happy to try to see you through things, but this is not my area of expertise. Now, Layla went to Havers—"

"I can't go there. Wrath will want to be with me during any appointments, and nobody's going to believe that we're not together if he shows up with me pregnant at that clinic. I mean, the last thing we need is for them to call us out on fraud grounds."

"I agree. So I have an idea."

"What?"

"There's a great ob-gyn in Caldwell—a woman. Everyone used to talk about her at the hospital. She's got a real feel for special cases and needs and I think we should have Manny reach out to her—see if she'll take you on as a private pay. Between me and Ehlena on the vampire side, and her on the human end? With the equipment? I'll feel more comfortable about all this."

Beth nodded. "Yeah, that's a good idea."

"Great. I'll get on it. In the meantime, I'll do an assessment on you here and give you something for the nausea—"

"Honestly, I'm okay right now. It only seems to happen when I stand up."

"All right, but let me do a blood pressure check on you, 'kay?"

"Help yourself."

As Beth put her arm out, she had a moment of total, stunned disbelief. Was it possible that all that sex had worked?

Like, for its true biological function?

Doc Jane slid the blood pressure cuff into place and the thing made little puffing noises as it was inflated, the squeeze on her biceps making her think about all the invasive stuff that was going to happen to her if she was, in fact, knocked up. Blood tests. Ultrasounds. Examinations. As someone who had been healthy all her life, she wasn't sure how she was going to handle it.

No going back now.

There was a long hiss as Doc Jane watched a little dial and listened through her stethoscope. "Perfect. Lemme get a pulse here." After a moment with her fingertips pressed into Beth's wrist, the doctor nodded. "Yup. Good."

The physician sat back and just stared at her.

"You're giving me a doctor look," Beth said, suddenly frightened.

"Sorry, it's a reflex." Doc Jane put her things back into her bag. "Here's the deal. I could get aggressive and climb all over you, but your pressure and pulse are great, your coloring's good, and you're not vomiting at the moment. I'd like to do a wait-and-see on this one—as long as you're not bleeding down below?"

"Nope. Not at all."

"Terrific. As long as you agree to holler if anything changes? I'll stay on the sidelines."

"Deal—"

Wrath burst through the door, with Fritz tight on his heels.

"Oh, my God," Beth said as she got a load of the . . . um, load . . . they were both carrying. "Is that a *case* of ginger ale?"

"Two," her husband announced. "And we left the backup one out in the hall."

Doc Jane laughed as she got to her feet. "Your wife's good to go right now. But she's promised me she'll call—and I have the feeling, if she doesn't, you will."

Wrath nodded. "You can bet your ass on that one."

Beth rolled her eyes, but inside, she didn't mind him being pushy at all. Her husband was going to take excellent care of her—whether or not she was carrying his child.

And that was love right there.

FIFTY-SIX

After Wrath showed Doc Jane out, he went right back to the bed. As he sat down, Beth took his hand and squeezed it.

"I'm going to be fine," she said.

God, he hoped so. "Are you yawning?"

"Yes. I'm suddenly exhausted."

"Let me get a ginger ale—"

"No. No, thank you . . . I just want to rest for a minute or two. Then I'll tackle the idea of putting something in there."

"Are you still sick?"

"No. I just don't want to be." Her thumb stroked back and forth over his palm. "We can do this, Wrath. All of it."

As he didn't want to let his paranoia out, he nodded. "Yeah. It's gonna be fine."

Except inside, he wasn't feeling that. At all.

"You should go downstairs and work," she mumbled, like she was already falling asleep. "Saxton stayed over. He could help you check e-mail and stuff."

As if the *glymera* were going to have anything to say to him tonight?

When he'd gone down to get the grub with Fritz, he'd run into Rehvenge, who was more than happy to report on Ichan's thwarted throning ceremony. Talk about your swagga—Rehv had been high as a kite with victory: The aristocrats had been shanked a good one, the leg they'd been standing on sliced off at the knee.

But there was no reason to be naive and assume they wouldn't get all up in his ass again.

They were just going to find another way to come at him.

Thanks to Xcor.

Man, if he could just get his hands on that son of a bitch . . .

"I can't sleep like this," Beth said. "With you hovering."

"I want to stay."

"There's nothing to be done here. We're in hurry-up-and-wait mode until we know one way or another."

"Who will feed you when you're ready?"

Her tone became gentle. "I did a pretty good job of that before you came around."

Well . . . crap.

In the end, he figured she needed the rest more than he needed to babysit a grown-ass female. After dropping a kiss or two on her mouth, he let George escort him out of the suite and down the stairs. Emerging on the second-floor landing, he stalled out. The last place he wanted to be was in that study—

The sound of hammering down below got his attention. What the . . . ?

"Stairs," he told his dog.

As George led him down to the first floor, the noises got louder, but they were still muffled—and his nose caught a whiff of concrete powder in the air. And something else . . .

"Hey," Rhage said. "What's doing?"

Wrath put out his hand and let his brother clap palms. "Nada. How's it going in there?"

"Taking up the floor. We've got some heavy-duty plastic sheeting in the doorway to keep the dust down—Fritz was hoping we'd leave it open so he could clean up every morning after they leave. We kiboshed that."

"Good call."

On the far side of that sheeting, male voices bantered back and forth against the din of hammers cracking into stone, the chatter casual and clearly born of great familiarity. "How many workmen?"

"Seven. We want 'em in and out as fast as possible 'cuz we're all a little twitchy—John's here with me."

"Hey, JM," Wrath said, nodding in the direction of the male's scent.

"He says hey—and wants to know how Beth is?"

"She's good. Real good—thanks for everything, son."

"He says, yeah, it was his pleasure."

Good kid. Turning into a great male, Wrath thought.

"So I want to go in and meet them," he blurted for no particular reason.

There was a long period of quiet—during which he was willing to bet Rhage and John were locking eyes and no-going each other.

"Good, glad you agree," Wrath muttered as he cued George.

The dog signaled that they'd come up to a barrier by halting, and Wrath reached out, his palm finding a sheet that was stiff and thick. Dropping his hold on the halter, he used two hands to pull it aside so he didn't tear it from its tethers above.

The voices stopped immediately.

Except for one that breathed, "Holy . . . *shit*."

All at once there was a clattering, as if tools were being dropped to the floor—and then a rustling.

Like seven males of some size had just gone down on their knees.

For a moment, Wrath's eyes teared up behind his wraparounds. "Evening," he said, trying to be all casual. "How's the work going?"

No answer. And he could smell the stunned disbelief—it was like sautéed onions, not entirely unpleasant.

"My lord," came a low greeting. "It is a great honor to be in your presence."

He opened his mouth to blow that off . . . except as he inhaled, he realized that was the truth. For each and every one of them. They were honestly in awe and overcome.

In a hoarse voice, he said, "Welcome to my home."

As John ducked under the sheet and stood behind Wrath, all he could think was, About fucking time.

The seven workmen were all kneeling on one knee, their heads bowed, their eyes flipping up and down as if Wrath were the sun and they couldn't stare at him for very long.

Then the King spoke, and the four simple words that came out of his mouth were transformative, the workmen looking up on a oner with . . . a kind of love.

Wrath made like he was glancing around. “So, how do you think this is going to go?”

The males glanced back and forth, and then the foreman, the guy who'd introduced the workers one by one while they were patted down, spoke.

“We're going to take up the floor. And put down a new one.”

More looking back and forth—while Wrath just continued to swing his wraparounds left and right as if he were taking in the view.

“Are you . . .” The foreman cleared his throat as if he were pained. “Would you prefer another team?”

“What?”

“Have we displeased our lord in some way to bring you herein?”

“God, no. I was just curious. That's all. I don't know anything about construction.”

The foreman glanced at each of his males. “Well, that's because it's beneath you, my lord.”

Wrath laughed in a harsh burst. “The hell it is. It's honest work. There's no shame in that. So what are your names?”

The foreman's eyes bugged like that was the last thing he'd expected. But then he rose from the floor and jacked up his tool belt. “I'm Elph. This is . . .” He whipped through the introductions quickly.

“You all have families?” Wrath asked.

“I got a daughter and a mate,” Elph said. “Although my first *shellan* died in childbirth.”

Wrath put his hand over his heart as if struck by something. “Oh, fuck. I'm so sorry.”

The foreman blinked at the King. “I . . . thank you, my lord.”

“How long ago was it that you lost her?”

“Twelve years.” The male cleared his throat. “Twelve years, three months, seventeen days.”

“How's your daughter?”

The foreman shrugged. Then shook his head. “She's okay—”

The one in the back, who'd said the *holy shit*, spoke up. “She's paralyzed. And she's an angel.”

The glare he got from his superior was immediate—like the guy didn't want Wrath bothered. “She's fine,” he cut in.

"Paralyzed?" Wrath seemed to pale. "From the birthing?"

"Ah . . . yeah. She was injured. She was delivered without assistance. Other than me who was of sorry aid."

"Where the fuck was Havers?"

"We couldn't get to the clinic."

Wrath's nose flared. "You're lying to me."

The foreman's brows lifted in shock. "It was no one's fault, my lord. Except for mine."

"I thought you were in construction. Or did you go to medical school?"

"I did not."

"So how was it your fault?" Wrath shook his head sadly. "I'm sorry. Look, I'm glad your daughter survived."

"It is my biggest blessing, my lord."

"No doubt. And I know you have to miss your mate like hell."

"Every night. All day. Although my second *shellan* keeps me going."

Wrath nodded like he knew exactly where the male was at. "I get that. I so totally get that. Something similiar happened to my brother, Tohr."

There was a long pause. Then the foreman said slowly, "I don't know what else to say, my lord. Other than you have honored us greatly with your presence."

"You don't have to say anything. And I should leave you guys alone. I'm taking up your time." Wrath lifted his dagger hand in a casual wave. "Later."

As the plastic sheeting fell back into place behind the King, the workmen were speechless.

"Is he always like that?" the foreman asked numbly.

Rhage nodded. "He truly is a male of worth."

"I didn't think he would be . . . like that."

"Like what?"

"So approachable."

"Based on what?"

"The rumors. They say he's aloof. Untouchable. Uninterested in people like us." The foreman shook himself like he couldn't believe he'd said that aloud. "What I mean is—"

"Nah, you're good. I can imagine where that comes from."

"He looks like his father," the older one in the back said. "Spitting image."

"You knew him? Wrath's dad, that is?" Rhage asked.

The older male nodded. "And I saw the two of them together once. Wrath the younger was five. He always stood beside his father when the King had audiences with the commoners. I had a property dispute with my landlord who was in the *glymera*. The King took care of me over that aristocrat, I tell you." An air of sadness overcame the male's entire aura. "I remember when the King and queen were killed. We were certain the heir had been slaughtered as well—by the time we learned otherwise . . . this Wrath was gone."

"I heard he was shot recently," the foreman said to Rhage. "Is that true?"

"We don't talk about it."

The foreman bowed. "Of course. I apologize."

"Like I said, you're good, don't worry. Come on, JM, let's leave these guys to work." As John nodded, Rhage tacked on, "Just let us know if you need anything."

John went to follow the Brother, but then paused in the split between the sheets. The workmen were still staring at where Wrath had stood and talked with them, as if they were replaying everything. As if they'd been witnesses to a historic event.

Stepping out, he wondered if Wrath was aware of the effect he'd had on them.

Probably not.

FIFTY-SEVEN

As Anha sat at her dressing table, she had naught but a lingering tiredness leftover from her episode: With every night that passed, she was feeling more herself, her body rebounding, her mind resharpening.

But everything had changed.

In the first, the Brotherhood had moved into the chamber next door. All twelve of them. And they rotated their service such that the door to her and Wrath's private space was never unguarded.

And then there was the food. Wrath refused to let her eat anything that he or the Brothers had not personally sampled first—following a wait period of quite some while.

And then there was the worry upon her hellren's *face, every time she caught him unawares.*

Speaking of worry, wherever was he?

"Your King shall return very soon."

She gasped and looked over her shoulder. Tohrture was sitting in the corner, "reading" from a book of sonnets. In truth, she did not think he traced the symbols a'tall. Instead, his eyes were on the blockaded windows, the door, her, the windows, the door, her. On occasion, he broke the rhythm by speaking with one of his Brothers or tasting food that was prepared at her hearth.

"Where has he gone?" she asked once again.

"He shall return soon." The smile was meant to be reassuring. The shadow in his stare was most certainly not.

Anha narrowed her eyes. "He has not explained any of this."

"All is well."

"I do not believe you."

The Brother just smiled at her in that way of his, giving her nothing to go on.

Anha put down her brush and turned fully about. "He thinks I was poisoned, then. Otherwise, why this protection. The cooking. The concern."

"All is well."

Just as she threw up her hands in frustration, the door opened—

She jumped to her feet so fast, her dressing table wobbled, bottles and pots falling over. "Dearest Virgin Scribe! Wrath!"

Jerking up her skirts, she ran barefoot across the oak floor to the horror before her: Suspended between the holds of two Brothers, her mate was bloodied everywhere, his simple shift stained down the front from his split lip and his contused face, his knuckles dripping onto the rug, his head hanging limp as though he could not lift it.

"What have you done to him!" she screamed as the chamber door was shut and locked.

Before she could stop herself, she flailed at the ones who held him, her fists making no impact as they maneuvered him over onto the bedding platform.

"Anha . . . Anha, arrest . . ." As they laid Wrath out, his left hand rose. "Anha . . . arrest.*"*

She wanted to clasp his palm and cling unto him, but he seemed hurt everywhere. "Who did this to you!"

"I asked them to."

"What."

"You heard me properly."

Sitting back, she found that now she felt like hitting him as well.

Wrath's voice was so weak, she wondered how he was still conscious. "There is a job that needs doing. By mine own hands." He flexed them and winced. "No others will suffice."

Anha glared at her mate—and then did the same to the assembled males, as well as the ones who were newly arriving, clearly coming in after they heard the shouting.

"You shall explain yourselves the now," she barked. "All of you. Or I shall take my leave of this room."

"Anha." Wrath's voice was garbled and he was having trouble drawing breath. "Be of reason."

She stood up and put her hands on her hips. "Am I packing my things or is one among you going to speak unto me."

"Anha—"

"Speak or I pack."

Wrath exhaled a ragged curse. "There is naught for you to be concerned with—"

"When you come upon our mated chamber looking as though you have been struck by a carriage, it is very much my concern! How dare you exclude me from this!"

Wrath lifted his hand as if to rub his face and then grimaced when the contact was made.

"I believe your nose is broken," she said flatly.

"Amongst other things."

"Indeed."

Wrath finally looked upon her. "I shall ahvenge *you. That is all."*

Anha heard herself gasp. And then her knees went weak and she lowered herself back down to the bedding platform. She was not naive, and yet hearing confirmation of that which she had suspected was a shock.

"So 'tis true. I was made to become ill."

"Aye."

Tracing the injuries upon her hellren *with fresh eyes, she shook her head. "No, I shall not allow it. If you must have revenge wrought, let one of these capable males do it."*

"No."

She glanced over at the heavy carved desk across the way, the one they'd recently moved in here, the one at which he sat so happily for hours upon hours, ruling, thinking, planning. Then she regarded his misshapen face.

"Wrath, you are not fit for the likes of a violent duty," she said hoarsely.

"I shall be."

"No. I forbid you."

Now he glared upon her. "No one commands the King."

"Except for me," she countered smoothly. "And we both know it."

At that there was a soft chuckle in the room—of respect.

"They did the same to my father," Wrath said in a dead voice. "Except they poisoned him to the point of his death."

Anha lifted a hand to her throat. "But no . . . he died of natural causes—"

"He did not. And as the son, I am obliged to right that wrong—as well as yours." Wrath wiped some of the blood off his mouth. "Listen to me now, my Anha, and hear this truth clearly. . . . I shall not be castrated in this by you or anyone. The soul of my father haunts me the now, walking the halls of my mind, talking unto me. And you shall do the same if they finally succeed in putting you in your grave. I have been fated to live with the former. Do not *expect me to do the same with the latter."*

She leaned in urgently. "But you have the Brotherhood. That is what they are for, how they serve. They are your private guard."

As she implored her mate, the sheer heft and number of the males pressed in upon her—in the very best sense.

"Command them," she begged. "Send them out unto the world to exact this due."

His bloodied hand reached out, and she thought it was to clasp her palm. Instead, it rested upon her gown, below the bodice . . . upon her womb.

"You are with young," he said roughly. "I can scent it."

She too had been thinking the same, although for different reasons.

Wrath's one working eye met hers. "So I cannot allow others to do what is my duty. Even if I could regard you knowing that I was so weak . . . I could never stare into the face of a son or a daughter with the awareness that I had lacked the courage to caretake for mine bloodline."

"Please, Wrath . . ."

"What kind of father would I be then?"

"One who is alive."

"For how long, though. If I do not protect what is mine, it shall be taken away from me. And I will not *lose my family."*

Overcome, Anha felt tears fall down her cheeks, the paths burning her face.

Dropping her forehead to the bloodied black diamond of the King's ring, she wept.

For in her heart, she knew he was right—and she hated the world that they lived in . . . and were, in time, going to bring forth a young into.

FIFTY-EIGHT

Downtown, in the urban heart of Caldwell, Xcor picked up a burst of speed in an alley, his combat boots crushing through the dirty, salted slush, frigid air rushing at his face, distant sirens and shouts offering a kind of narration to this battle.

Up ahead, the slayer he was going for was just as fast as he. The bastard was not as well armed, however—especially after he'd emptied his clip and then had, in the fit of a fifteen-year-old, thrown the autoloader at Xcor.

Great move. Right up there with crying for your mommy.

And then the chase had been on.

Xcor was content to allow the *lesser* to run his lack of a heart out. Provided that all the sprinting didn't lead to the kind of complication that had gotten in his way the other night.

He had no interest in fielding another human.

After another quarter mile or so, the slayer came to the titular end of the alley—whereupon he was forced to pull a music video, throwing his body at a twenty-foot-high chain-link fence and commencing to scale it with admirable aplomb.

Then again, the Omega had given him a kind of super-power following his induction.

Not that it was going to save him.

Xcor took three leaping steps and pitched his body into the air, his weight sailing upward and landing him upon the *lesser*'s back just before the slayer hit the apex of the fencing. Locking on and yanking hard, he peeled the undead free of the fencing, twisting in midair such that they landed with Xcor on top.

His scythe screamed to be let out to play. But instead of releasing her, he unclipped her little cousin from his hip.

The machete had a steel handle and a rubber grip, and it felt like an extension of his arm as he lifted it over his shoulder.

Now, he could end this quickly by aiming for the middle of the chest. But where was the fun in that? Slapping a hold on the face, he wrenched the head to the side and sheared off the ear—

The resulting scream was a kind of music, echoing in his ears.

"Other side," he grunted, forcing the head around. "One needs to match."

The machete's blade whistled through the air a second time, Xcor's accuracy such that nothing save the fleshy appendage was touched. And the pain was enough to incapacitate his prey—well, that and the fact that surely the slayer knew that what was to come was going to be so much worse.

Fear had a way of leading to paralysis.

And the undead was right to be terrified.

In a fast series of hacks, Xcor worked his way down the body, striking the blade deep into each shoulder to cut the tendons and incapacitate the torso—and then following through with the backs of the knees.

Sitting back, he watched the writhing and breathed in the stench—as well as the suffering: Being the cause of pain fed his inner beast, a meal consumed by the evil side of him—that just left him hungry for more.

Time to get a bit more invasive. And he decided to cut off the left foot—slowly. With half strength, he hacked once, twice . . . three times before the blade cut cleanly through. The right foot was just as leisurely a pursuit.

In the midst of his work, his mind retreated to thoughts that were sure to make him even more depraved.

He kept thinking about Wrath's end run. Tyhm, the lawyer, had made a subsequent assessment of the mating-dissolution document and deemed it legal—but Xcor knew the thing had been predated.

Do not tell him that the King hadn't signed on that line as soon as that no-confidence parchment had landed upon his desk.

Moving up to below the knee, he resettled into his work, and the rhythm of chops reminded him of the Old Country, when he'd cut wood to take the edge off his frustration.

The question he wanted answered was, how far did that piece of paper go? Had the King in truth turned aside his mate?

It is a love match.

As he heard his Chosen's voice in his head, a surge of power overtook him—and good timing as he confronted the *lesser's* thighs. No more holding back, now: He threw his muscles into his work, whacking through skin and bone, black blood hitting his face, his fangs bared.

The slayer was clawing through the snow to the pavement, fingernails ripping into the asphalt below as the screaming dried up in his throat, shock o'ertaking his breathing and heart rate, rendering him all but inanimate.

But he would not die like this.

Indeed, there was only one way to kill him.

Xcor reduced the *lesser* to pieces, leaving only the head attached to a block of the torso, pools of that black blood forming under the four compass points of where the limbs had been attached.

When there was nothing else to cut off, Xcor sat back on his haunches and took a breather. It was not so fun now that the slayer was compromised. The suffering was still there, but it was not so obvious.

Yet he didn't want this work of his to end. Like the addict holding on to a fix that was no longer sufficient for his needs, he nevertheless couldn't finish things.

As his phone went off, he was determined to ignore it. He didn't want to hear Ichan's bitching—that aristocrat had been leaving message after message trying to recoup his almost-there to the throne. And then there was Tyhm, also calling.

Their little cabal had failed, however—and Xcor's mind had yet to devise the next approach.

Lifting the machete high into the air, he then buried the honed steel blade right into the empty chest—and immediately had to rear back to shield his eyes and face from the brilliant flash of light and burst of heat.

As he was knocked over from the impact, his phone began to ring again.

"Goddamn it." Jabbing his hand into his duster's inner pocket, he took out the annoying device. *"What."*

There was a pause. And then the sweetest voice he'd e'er heard entered his ear.

"I'm waiting for you."

Xcor swayed even though he was all but prostrate upon the ground. Closing his eyes, he exhaled. "I am on my way."

"You did not come earlier when you had said."

Untrue. As soon as he could break off from the Bastards, he had spirited to the maple—and found his Layla's footprints in the snow. She must have returned to their meeting place the now, though.

"There were things I could not get out of." That fucking meeting. The unrest afterward. "But that is no longer true. Be assured."

He wanted to stay on the phone with her, except he terminated the connection. Jumping to his feet, he glanced down, and recognized that part of his anger had been from missing the chance to see her—

Abruptly, he cursed. The limbs he had cut into pieces had not been incinerated.

He was not going to clean up after himself tonight, however. Whatever humans found the remains could enjoy something to get worked up over.

Ghosting off to the north, he scattered himself upon the wind . . . and re-formed at the base of their meadow. Immediately he saw her, standing under that giant tree, her pale robing gleaming in the moonlight.

In a rush, he tried to dematerialize to her, too impatient to surmount the distance by foot. But his mind was too muddled for him to concentrate sufficiently.

Left to cross the distance physically, he began to walk, but soon he was jogging . . . and then flat-out running.

She was the only goal that mattered in that moment, and as he arrived before her, he was out of breath. Out of his mind.

In love.

* * *

Layla brought a hand up to her nose.

As Xcor arrived before her, the smell that swirled around him was vile, so sickly sweet that she choked. And he noted her reaction immediately, hiding his bloodied hands behind his back, stepping away so that she was not downwind of him.

"Forgive me," he said roughly. "I was in the field."

As there was nothing that carried the scent of the blood of their kind, she sighed in relief. "Our enemy?"

"Yes."

"Then that is right and proper."

As his eyes flared, she shook her head. "I have no issue with your defense of our race."

"That is refreshing."

She tried to imagine him fighting—and found it was not difficult in the slightest. With his thick neck and his gigantic shoulders, he was indeed bred for violence. And yet even with the stench of slayers upon his person, she had no fear.

"I waited in the snow for you," she whispered.

"I worried that you had."

"It is done then. The Council knows about Wrath, that is."

He narrowed his eyes. "So that is why you followed through to see me here? To gloat?"

"No, not at all. I'm simply hoping . . ."

When she didn't finish, he crossed his arms, his chest appearing larger than ever. "Put it into words."

"You know exactly that of which I speak."

"I desire to hear the words."

"Leave Wrath alone."

Xcor broke away from her, walking back and forth. "Answer me something."

"Anything."

"That is not a safe reply for you, Chosen." He glanced over, his eyes glittering in the darkness. "In fact, this meeting is not safe for you."

"You will not hurt me."

"Such faith you put in a monster."

"You're not a monster. If you were, you would have killed me that night in the car."

"My question is this," he evaded. "Did Wrath honestly forsake that

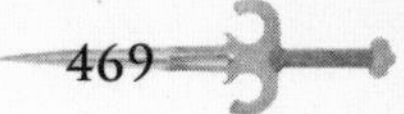

female of his? And you can attempt to lie to me, but I will know the truth."

Mayhap not, Layla thought. For she had practiced her response to just that inquiry. For hours.

Meeting his eyes steadily, she said without any change of affect: "Yes, he did. The proclamation was predated, but it is true. He has given up his only love to keep that which you endeavor to steal from him."

Hours in front of the mirror. She had sat in her bathroom, on the little padded bench, in the full glare of as many lights as she could turn on, repeating those words over and over again. Until they were rote—until their meaning was lost and they became only syllables. Until she could speak the lie with no hesitation or stumble.

And she knew that giving the partial truth provided her more credibility.

"Such a sacrifice," he murmured.

He, too, gave nothing away.

There was a long, long silence—filled by the pounding of her heart.

"Leave this unholy quest behind," she said. "Please."

"And what of your previous offer. Does that still stand."

She swallowed hard. On so many levels, she couldn't imagine having sex with him. He was an enemy sure as the Lessening Society was—and there was, in fact, a side to him that was monstrous. Moreover, she had never imagined bartering her body for something.

And she was not naive. Yes, she had felt an attraction to him when he had come to her and found her in that car. But this was a deal of business-like proportions.

Layla kicked her chin up. "Yes. It does."

"And if I agreed to your terms, would I have to wait for the birth of the young? Or could I take you immediately."

At that, the scenting upon the air changed, a dark spice flaring up and overtaking the stench that had made her ill.

Her hands went to her womb, a sudden terror seizing her. What if she endangered the young growing within her? Except the other Chosen had continued relations with the previous Primale, hadn't they. To no ill effect.

"You may have me whenever you wish," she said thinly.

"What if I wanted it here, and now. In the cold. Standing up, fully clothed."

Her heart thundered, her chest growing tight as she recognized his arousal—and feared it. Still, she held her ground, staying in touch with the fact that she had something he wanted, and with that reality, there was a chance Wrath and Beth and any young they might have could be safe.

"I would do as you asked," she heard herself say.

"All this for your King."

"Yes. For him."

Xcor smiled, but it was without warmth or humor. "I shall consider your terms. See me here on the morrow, midnight—and I shall give you mine answer."

"I thought that was why you called me here tonight?"

"I have changed my mind."

She expected him to dematerialize. Instead, he gave her his back and walked down the way he had come up, his heavy strides creating distance between them.

Closing her eyes, she—

"What did you say to him?" a male voice demanded from behind her.

FIFTY-NINE

Trez decided enough with the bullshit.

As he dematerialized back up to Rehv's great camp, he was ready to come clean, lay down the talk, set things straight with his Chosen. He and Selena had been circling each other for long enough, and now that he had some breathing room—for however long it lasted—he needed to make the situation with that female his priority.

Along with s'Ex's appetites, of course.

Fuck. Apparently that executioner had used the girls so hard that they'd been unable to work tonight. He'd gotten texts from all three of them—and the good news was at least they didn't seem to regret a damn thing: Each one of them asked if they could see the executioner again.

At this rate, they'd be paying him to see that son of a bitch.

Hell, they hadn't even brought up the money he'd agreed to pay them for their efforts.

Reassuming form in his usual spot on the side lawn, he was relieved to see a light on in that back bedroom of hers—and nowhere else. Thank God. Entering the house through the kitchen's rear entrance, he didn't call her name, didn't make a sound. Instead, he ghosted through the empty house, circling to the base of the stairs, ascending in a way that none of the steps creaked.

At the top landing, he went to the left, and when he got to the partially closed door, he could feel his chest grow tight.

"Selena . . . ?"

Her scent was in the air; he knew she was in there.

"Selena?" He pushed the door a little wider, and that was when he heard the sound of running water.

He had to duck his head under the low transom to enter, and as he went to the left again, he caught the humidity in the air, and the warmth—

Oh . . . man.

He found her in the tub. Head back on a towel, body stretched out in a deep pool of clear water, hands resting on the sides of the old-fashioned porcelain bath.

"I could have gotten up," she said without bothering to open her eyes. "But I wanted you to see me naked."

Trez cleared his throat with a cough—which was what you did when someone hit you in the solar plexus. "Ah . . . can we talk?"

"I think we have." Her lids lifted and she glanced over at him. "Or is there more?"

At that, she shifted her legs, the water undulating over that incredible body, her curves amplified as if she were moving . . . her nipples licked at and left wet to the air.

"There's more," he croaked as he ran his tongue over his lips.

"Then by all means, do draw up a chair. Unless you find that you'd like to join me."

Fucking *hell*. "Is there any way I can get you up and out of there. And dressed?"

"If you wish to do it yourself, by all means, oblige your impulse."

Yeah, because getting his hands on her naked was going to be suuuuch a big help.

Cursing under his breath, Trez went over and picked up a chair—because in the end, he was afraid that if he stayed standing he'd trip and fall into her. Literally.

As he sat down, he put his hands up to his face and scrubbed hard . . . and then all he could do was stay like that.

The water made a tinkling as if she were sitting up. "Trez? Are you all right?"

"No."

There had been so many times in his life when he'd fallen off cliffs, when things that he'd done or had done to him had come back to bite him in the ass. Never like this.

"Trez?" When he didn't answer her, she said, "You're scaring me."

"I'm . . ." Gee fucking whiz, where to start. "Selena, I'm really sorry."

"Why?" The tension was thick in her voice. "What are you apologizing for?"

Shame made his throat tighten up so badly, he could barely get breath into his lungs. "I need to be honest with you. Straight-up one hundred."

"I thought you had been."

All he could do was shake his head. "Look, you know that I have had . . . extensive dealings with humans."

"That wasn't exactly as you chose to phrase it previously," she remarked.

More with his head shaking. "My business is . . . it's a club. Do you know what that is?"

"Rugby? Or baseball?"

"A dance club. A place where people drink and . . . listen to music." Jesus Christ. "And do other things."

"Yes . . . ?"

He dropped his hands. She had sat up and her pink nipples were right on the edge of the water, the warm surface licking at them once again—not that she seemed to notice.

"Would you mind getting out and putting a robe on?" he asked.

"I have nothing to be ashamed of."

Fucking abso on that one. "I know. It's just hard to concentrate."

"Maybe I want you to struggle."

Okay, right, virgins were not supposed to be so tantalizing. Then again, she wasn't one anymore—he'd taken care of that.

Fuck. "Mission accomplished," he muttered.

"You were telling me about your work?"

He focused his eyes on the floor. It was simple white tile, old and well-scrubbed, the kind of thing that managed to look fresh even with its lateral cracks and occasional chips.

"Trez?" From the corner of his vision, he watched as she extended her foot and turned the hot water on for a refresh. "You were saying?"

Just do it.

Great, life had been reduced to a Nike ad.

"I traffic women. Do you understand what that means?"

She frowned. "You take them out into the street?"

"I sell them. Their bodies. To men, usually."

Cue the silence.

He met her in the eye. "I get paid for that. I sell them. Do you understand?"

After a moment, her beautiful hands receded from the sides of the tub and crossed over her breasts.

Exactly, he thought.

"And that's not the worst of it."

There was a very long pause. And then she said, "I do believe I should like to get dressed."

He got to his feet and headed for the door. "Yeah, I thought so."

Out in the snow-covered field, Layla wheeled around. She was about to scream when she recognized the male who had stepped out from behind the great tree. It was the soldier, the one who'd been injured and brought to the Brotherhood's training center. The one who had failed to correct her when she'd assumed he was affiliated with the Brothers.

The one who had brought her here to help Xcor that night so long ago.

"I'm sorry," he said, bowing low, his eyes still on her. "That is hardly a proper greeting."

She was about to curtsy when she recalled that he did not deserve the respect. He, like Xcor, was on the other side of things.

"You are looking exceptionally well this cold evening," he murmured.

His accent was not at all like Xcor's, each word pronounced perfectly, the voice well modulated instead of gruff. But she was not fooled. He'd used her as a tool once.

There was no doubt he would again.

"So what conversation were you having with him?" he asked, that stare narrowing.

Layla pulled her heavy robes more closely around her body. "I should think if you wish to know, you may inquire of him yourself. If you will excuse me, I shall take my leave of you—"

The hand that locked on her arm bit into her flesh, and his handsome face darkened to the point of menace. “No, I do not think so. I want you to tell me what you were discussing with him.”

Angling her chin up, she met the soldier in the eye. “He wanted to know if it was real.”

Those brows came down, his grip loosening some. “I beg your pardon?”

“The divorce proclamation. He wanted to know if Wrath has indeed given up his queen—and I assured him it was true.”

The soldier dropped his hold. “Assuming you can be trusted.”

“Whether I can or cannot be doesn’t change the truth. You’ll find out elsewhere, I’m sure.”

Probably not, actually, given the lack of contact the household had with the rest of the race. But mayhap this male would not know that.

“So it was an arranged mating the King cared naught for.”

“On the contrary, their love was obvious to all. He was well and truly bonded.” Layla forced her shoulders to shrug casually. “Again, you will hear this from others, I’m sure.”

Throe shook his head. “Then he could not have let her go.”

“Maybe you should consider this against any further ambitions you have for the throne.” She took a surreptitious step back. “A male who will set aside his bonded mate will do anything to keep that which others seek to take from him. The foe you are seeking out by your actions will not be beaten—and he will come for you all. Mark my word.”

“Fierce little thing, aren’t you.”

“Again, it is merely fact for you to discover at your leisure. Or not. Either way, it bothers me not.”

As he let her take another step away from him, she thought there was a good chance she was going to be able to depart.

“There was something else,” he said. “Wasn’t there.”

“No.”

“Then why didn’t he dematerialize?”

She frowned, having not considered that. “You’ll have to ask him.”

“Not his way.” The soldier’s eyes went down her body. “And I think I can guess. Be of care, Chosen. He is not who you think he is. He is capable of betrayals that a female like you couldn’t begin to contemplate.”

“If you will excuse me, I shall be taking my leave the now.” She curtsied and then struggled to focus, focus, focus. . . .

"Be of care."

Those words haunted her as she disappeared from the meadow . . . and found her way back to the mansion's front entrance.

As she contemplated the heavy door, a shudder went through her. That fighter struck her as more terrifying than Xcor himself: the latter would never hurt her. She didn't know how she was so sure of that, but it was like the beat of her heart—something she could feel in the center of her chest.

That other male? Not the case. At all.

Closing her eyes, she hated this in between with Xcor. How was she going to pass the hours before tomorrow at midnight? And why was he making her wait?

She already knew what his answer was going to be.

SIXTY

Selena put her full robing back on. Everything, undergarments and all. In spite of the fact that her hands were shaking so badly, she could barely marshal them.

When she finally walked out into the bedroom, she found Trez sitting on a straight-backed chair in front of the desk that she sometimes used to compose diary entries. And indeed, she was glad she had closed her leather-bound volume after she'd finished with last tonight's passage.

It was all about him, naturally.

And she had a feeling there was going to be an addendum.

He looked over at her, his dark eyes flashing for a moment. "You ready to do this now?"

Dearest Virgin Scribe, of all the things she thought he'd tell her . . . that was not it.

"How can you . . . sell them?" she said roughly.

He sighed. "They want the money. I make it happen. I make it safe."

"And they . . . you get paid for this as well."

"Yeah."

She had to sit down before she fell over—and went toward the bed before thinking, *No, not there*. Instead, she chose the loveseat that was in front of the fireplace. Settling in, she tucked her feet underneath her bottom and made sure the skirting covered all of her skin.

"How long?" she heard herself ask.

"Years. Decades. First I was a supervisor. Now I'm the boss."

"I can't imagine . . . that."

He rubbed his temples. "I know you can't."

Abruptly, Selena found herself struggling to stay still. Her internal compass was spinning around so fast, she could barely form a sentence. "You know what? Just tell me everything. At the moment, my head is making up all kinds of horrible things and I—"

"The worst part is that I've been with a couple thousand women. Easy."

At first, she thought, No, she couldn't have heard that right. But the wave of cold that went through her suggested that actually, she had gotten it correct.

"Thousand," she said weakly.

"That's a conservative estimate. Could be close to ten. Thousand, that is. Shit, maybe even more."

Selena blinked. Okay, when he'd maintained previously that it was "many" human women? She'd thought a couple dozen, tops. But the numbers he was talking about? Even by *ehros* standards, they were . . . unfathomable.

As she tried to imagine all the different scenarios he could have . . . "Were any of them women you . . ."

"Yeah. For a long time, I wouldn't sell a prostitute until I'd had her."

With a wave of nausea shooting through her gut, all Selena could do was stare at him.

"You are correct," she heard herself say. "I do not know you."

"God, Selena, I'm so fucking sorry—I should never have been with you. Not because I didn't want you, but because I . . . well, yeah, because I knew that this was the reaction I'd get if I told you the truth. And actually, last night, I came here to try to explain, but then I just . . ."

She put her face in her hands, images of him kissing her, caressing her, taking her, hitting her like blows. "I think I'm going to be sick."

"I don't blame you," he said bleakly.

And yet there was no reason to recast reality as a way to reclaim

virtue she had lost willingly. "I seduced you." She dropped her hands. "I asked for what I got."

"No, it is solidly on me—"

"Just stop."

"Okay. I'm sorry."

So was she. Because the sad truth was that she had enjoyed being with him. Indeed, while it was happening, it had been a kind of paradise. Unfortunately, that illusion was as transient as the act, and now that it was over? The pleasure was as if it had never been.

"Selena, whatever it is you're thinking, you can say it—"

"I wish I had been born into another life," she blurted. "I should have liked falling in love with a single male and finding a humble place in the world with him. I do not think I would have wanted for anything like that, no matter how little we had."

"That can still be for you." His voice became utterly flat. "That can happen—any male would want you."

Ah, yes, but there was only one person *she* wanted. And even if Trez had been a saint, which he clearly was not, she was still out of time.

"It's all right." She struggled to hold back tears—and was successful. After all, soon she would be alone. "It is what it is. I have learned long ago, there is no negotiating with destiny."

They fell silent for the longest time.

"I don't love her," he gritted out. "I don't know why I feel like I have to say that, but I do."

"The one you are mating? Yes, you said that before." Abruptly, she stared across the way at him, noting his lowered head, his aura of sorrow. "Ironic, but we are not so different, you and I."

As his eyes shifted to hers, she shrugged. "I have had no hand in my destiny, either. The tragedy is that some things follow us like shadows—they are with us wherever we go."

"Yeah. I just never cared about that. Until I met you."

She thought of the Sanctuary's cemetery, of her sisters who had been relegated to a shortened life span, and had had to wait to die in a prison of their own bodies. Then she remembered the feel of him moving inside of her, the liquid warmth flowing throughout her muscles and bones.

"Did you love them?" she asked.

"Who? Oh, the women . . . no. Never. At all. Hell, half the time I didn't really enjoy it." He cracked his neck like those shoulder muscles of his were stiffening up again. "I really don't know what the fuck I was thinking. I was out of control and just trying to get out of my own head. The problem is, all those women are inside of me now."

"Inside . . . ?"

"My people believe that you can poison yourself if you have . . . if you're with people the way I was. And I have—poisoned myself. It's eaten me up until there's nothing in here."

As he touched the center of his chest, she realized that he was, in fact, hollow, the light gone from his eyes, the animation lacking in his body, his aura dissipated as if it had never been.

Overcome with sadness, she shook her head. "You were wrong."

"About what."

So empty, he was . . . vacant down to his soul. "What I see now . . . is the worst part of it all."

As Assail stood on the shores of the Hudson, he was once again dressed in black with a black mask over his face. Behind him, Ehric was silent and at attention, wearing the same articles of clothing.

Both of them had guns in their hands.

"They're late," his cousin said.

"Yes." Assail listened hard. "We give them five minutes. Not one more."

Off to the left, about four meters into the tree line, his bulletproof Range Rover sat ass to the river, Evale in the driver's seat with the engine running.

Assail glanced up to the night sky. Following an earlier snowstorm, the moon now had some lazy clouds drifting over its face, and he hoped they took their own sweet time. More light they did not need—although the site was otherwise discreet enough: remote, in a bend on the shoreline, with forest that came nearly up to the river's frozen edge. Also, the way in had been a lumpy, bumpy barely-there lane, even the SUV struggling in its off-road mode—

"I am worried about you."

Assail glared over his shoulder. "I beg your pardon?"

"You do not sleep."

"I am not tired."

"You do too much of the coke."

Assail turned back around and prayed for the appearance they awaited for a fresh reason. "Worry not, cousin."

"Do you know if they made it to their destination."

It had been so long since Ehric had asked after anyone, that Assail had to pivot around once more. And indeed, his primary instinct was to shut the inquiry down quick, yet the true concern on that hard face stopped him.

He resumed watching the sluggish, icy water. "No, I do not."

"Will you call her?"

"No."

"Not even to make sure they are safe."

"She doesn't wish for that." And the whys of this waiting by the Hudson were proof of the soundness of her decision to leave him. "A clean break it is."

Even he heard the hollowness in his voice.

God, he wished to hell he had never met that woman—

The sound was at first indistinguishable from the ambient night noises, but the hum quickly became distinct: Coming from the left, it announced that perhaps their wait was over.

The fishing boat that puttered around the corner was as low to the river as a floating leaf and nearly as silent. As prescribed, there were three men in it, all of them clad in dark clothes, and each had a line in the depths, as if they were naught but plying what open water there was for a meal.

They pulled in bow-first.

"Catch anything?" Assail inquired as he'd been told to.

"Three trout."

"I had two last night."

"I want one more."

Assail nodded, putting his gun away and stepping forward. From that moment, everything went silently and with speed: a tarp was lifted and four duffel bags changed hands, moving from the boat to him and then to Ehric—who hung them off his shoulders. In return, Assail passed over a black metal briefcase.

The tallest of the men put in the code he had been given, popped the lid, inspected the layout of bundles of bills, and nodded.

There was a quick handshake . . . and then Assail and Ehric retreated into the trees. Duffels went in the rear, Ehric in the back, Assail in the passenger seat.

As they headed off, bumping back over the rutted lane, windows were cracked to catch any sounds or smells.

There was nothing.

As they came out to the road, they stopped and waited whilst still hidden in the trees. No cars coming or going. The coast, as the saying went, was clear.

On Assail's command, the gas was hit and off they went, into the night.

With five hundred thousand street dollars of cocaine and heroin.

So far, so good.

After extracting everything from both Benloises' phones, he'd combed through the numbers and the texts—particularly the international ones. He'd found two contacts in South America with whom there appeared to be a lot of communication, and when he'd called from Ricardo's phone, he'd been routed into a network of secured connections, a number of clicks occurring before a proper ringing started.

Needless to say, there had been a good deal of surprise after Assail had introduced himself and explained the purpose of his call. Benloise had, however, informed his compatriots of his new, biggest client—so it was not a complete shock to them that the one who had once been the wholesaler had become superfluous . . . and been eliminated.

Assail had offered them a deal to start the relationship off upon the right foot: One million in cash for half a million in product—as a gesture of good faith.

Partnerships had to be cultivated, after all.

And he had approved of the men sent to do the transaction. They were a clear step up from Benloise's street thugs, totally professional.

Now he and his cousins simply had to parcel the product for street sale, and connect with the *Forelesser* for distribution. And business could resume as if Benloise had never existed.

Perfectly engineered.

"This went well," Ehric said as they got onto the road that would take them out to Assail's glass house.

"Yes."

As they went along, he stared out the window, watching the trees pass by. A house. That hunting cabin.

He should have been more pleased. This was, after all, going to open up tremendous earning potential. And he loved money and all its power. Truly, he did.

Instead, the only thing on his mind was worry over where his female was whether she had in fact made it down to Miami in one piece with that grandmother of hers.

And there was nothing he could do about it.

She was gone.

Forever.

SIXTY-ONE

As Beth woke up, the first thing she did was a body scan for the urge to run for the bathroom. When that came back with a not-right-now, she pushed herself to a vertical and swung her feet to the floor. How long had she slept for? The shutters were still up so it wasn't yet daylight, but man, she felt like she'd been out for days.

Looking down at herself, she put her hands on her belly—

Holy crap, she didn't remember swallowing a basketball.

Under her palms, her stomach was swollen and hard, the protrusion such that she doubted she would be able to pull her pants on.

Her first instinct was to reach for the phone and call Doc Jane, but then she dialed back on the panic and got to her feet.

"Feeling okay," she murmured. "Feeling pretty good . . ."

As she went over to her closet, she felt like her body was a bomb about to go off—and, man, she hated it: She'd had no idea how much she took for granted in the health department until she'd deliberately tried to complicate herself—

For no apparent reason, the Saturnine Ruby slipped right off her finger.

Glancing down, she watched the ring bounce on the carpet—and frowned as she bent over and picked the thing up. She and Wrath had traded back for convenience because both had struggled with something that didn't fit—and the symbols of their marriage had meaning no matter whose hand they were on.

Or falling off of, as was the case—

"What the hell?" she breathed.

As she went to put the thing back on, she realized that her fingers were positively skeletal, the skin stretched over knobby knuckles and a sunken palm.

Heart starting to hammer, she rushed to the mirror in the bathroom, turning on the lights—

Beth gasped. The reflection staring back at her was all wrong—all totally frickin' wrong. Overnight, literally, her face had hollowed out, all the fat gone from her cheeks and her temples, her chin sharp as a knife, the tendons in her neck standing out in bald relief.

Stark fear speared into her chest. Especially as she lifted her arm and pulled at the skin on her triceps. Loose. Way loose.

It was as if she had lost twenty-five pounds within hours—except for her belly.

Trying not to completely freak out, she headed for the closet to find something she could wear. In the end, she pulled on a pair of drawstring sweatpants, and one of Wrath's few button-downs. The latter was like a cloud of fine white cotton around her—and that meant, as she had another hot flash, there was plenty of ventilation happening.

At least her slippers fit perfectly.

Heading down to the second-floor landing, she put her head into the study and didn't find Wrath at the desk. Maybe he was working out?

She was going down the grand staircase when she found him.

He and George were walking out of the dining room along with a string of *doggen*, the staff carrying all kinds of silver trays across the depiction of the apple tree in bloom.

The second he caught her scent, he stopped. "*Leelan!* Are you sure you should be up?"

Turned out the smell of the food was one hell of a distraction: the spike of hunger she got in response enough to halt her in her tracks.

"Ah . . . yeah, I feel okay. I'm hungry, actually."

As well as scared to death.

While the staff continued on into the billiards room, filing in past some sheets of heavy plastic, Wrath came over to the base of the stairs. "Let's get you into the kitchen."

Heading all the way down to join him, she let him take her arm, and leaned into his strength, taking a deep, easing breath. She'd probably just imagined everything up there. Really. Probably.

Crap. "You know, I slept well," she murmured as if to reassure herself. Which didn't work.

"Yeah?"

"Mm-hm."

Together, they walked past the long dining table, and went through the flap door in the far corner. On the other side, iAm was once again at the stove, stirring a great pot.

The Shadow turned—and immediately frowned as he looked at her.

"What?" She put her hands to her stomach. "What are you—"

"Nothing," he said, banging his wooden spoon on the steel vat. "You two like chicken soup?"

"Oh, yes, that sounds perfect." Beth hopped up onto a stool. "And some bread maybe—"

Fritz materialized at her elbow with a baguette and a plate with butter. "For you, madam."

She had to laugh. "How did you know?"

As Wrath sat on the stool next to her, George parked it between them. "I had him on standby."

A steaming bowl of soup was slid in front of her by the Shadow. "Enjoy."

"Him, too?" she asked of iAm.

"Yeah, the Shadow mighta been on it as well."

Picking up the spoon Fritz offered her, she dug in, aware the three males were staring at her—Wrath with such intensity, it was almost as if he'd gotten his sight back—

"Mmmmm," she said—and meant it. The soup was perfect, simple, not too heavy, and warm, warm, warm.

Maybe it was just that she'd been through the needing and not eaten for how long?

"So what's going on in the billiards room," she asked, to try to distract the males.

"They're cleaning up after me."

She winced. "Ah."

Wrath patted around for the baguette and broke off the hard end, putting it aside. The piece he then tore for her was soft in the middle, crunchy on the outside—and the butter he put on it was the unsalted, sweet kind.

The combo was great with the soup.

"Would you like something to drink?" Fritz asked.

"Wine?" iAm said—before catching himself. "No, not wine. Milk. You need the calcium."

"Good idea, Shadow," Wrath chimed in as he nodded at Fritz. "Make it whole—"

"No, no, that will make me gag." Annnnd didn't that stop all of them in their tracks. "Which was true before all the, well, you know. But the skim does sound good."

And so it went, the three of them waiting on her: More soup? iAm hit her bowl again right away. More bread with butter? Husband was on it. More milk? The butler raced for the fridge.

Being surrounded by all the normal really helped calm her down. But she felt the need to try to set the record straight before they fed her until she exploded.

"Boys. I really appreciate all this—but we don't know if I'm preg—"

She did not get to finish the thought, much less the sentence.

All at once, everything she'd eaten headed for the fire exit at the same time, her stomach contracting without warning.

She barely made it to the staff bathroom in time.

Yup, it all came up, from soup to bread, as it were. And then, even when she could have sworn not just her stomach, but her entire chest cavity was empty, the heaving kept her bent over the toilet until her eyes watered, her head pounded, and her throat was nothing but a raw, burning mess.

"Hey, how we doing?"

Of course, it was Doc Jane. "Hey, what's up—"

It was a long while before she could say anything else. And P.S., she really hated how the gagging sounds echoed in the bowl.

When there was a break in the action, so to speak, she rested her hot, sweaty forehead on her arm, reached up to flush again . . . and found that she didn't have the energy to pull the lever down.

"I think we need to get you to the doctor," Jane said.

"I thought you were one," Wrath bit out.

"Do we have to?" Beth countered—

The fact that she started throwing up again pretty much answered things, didn't it.

As Wrath stood just outside the staff bathroom by the kitchen, he was ready to scream at his lack of vision: There was nothing like having your mate in medical distress to get you good and pissed off that you were blind.

With his piece-of-shit pupils, he couldn't see her face to get a read on her coloring, her expression, her eyes. And his keen sense of smell? Out the window, too—the vomiting had clogged up his sinuses, making it impossible to tease out any emotional clues.

The one thing that was working? His ears—so that every new round of sickness went straight into his brain.

"Okay, let's go," Beth finally said hoarsely.

"Wait a fucking minute," he barked. "Go where?"

Jane's voice was level. "To the doctor—"

"You *are* a fucking doctor—"

V's mate put her hand on his forearm. "Wrath. She needs a specialist and we've found one."

WTF—? Wait a minute. "That does *not* sound like Havers," he gritted.

"It's not. She's a human—"

"Ohhh no, nope, not going to happen—"

Annnnnd cue another round of heaving.

Behind his wraparounds, he closed his eyes. "Fuck."

Against the horrible backdrop of his wife's suffering, Doc Jane started giving him all kinds of very rational reasons that his *shellan* had to be handled carefully. But, Christ, the idea she'd be going out in the human world, during the day—because hello, the cocksucking shutters just went down . . .

You know what? He really fucking wished life would take him off its shit list. He was getting pretty goddamn sick and tired of unwinnable situations.

". . . half-breed, unknown complications, incapable of making an assessment . . ."

He cut through Doc Jane's little speech. "No offense, but I'm not letting my wife go out there without serious-ass backup, and nobody can leave this house right now—"

"So I'll go with her."

Wrath glanced over his shoulder at the sound of iAm's voice. His first instinct was to go all bonded-male on the guy and tell the Shadow he had this, thanks. The problem was, he didn't have *shit*—and only an asshole stood in the way of his mate getting the medical treatment she required.

Wrath let his head fall back with a curse. "Are you sure she needs this?" he said, not really certain who exactly he was talking to.

"Yes," Doc Jane answered gravely. "I'm totally sure."

iAm spoke up again. "Nothing will happen to her on my watch. On my honor."

He had a feeling the Shadow was offering him his palm—and sure enough, as Wrath reached out blindly—natch—the other male caught hold of it.

"What can I do for you?" Wrath heard himself say as they shook.

"Nothing right now. Just let me take her."

"Okay. All right." Except as Wrath let go and stepped back, he was not at peace with any of this. What other choice did he have, though?

Shaking his head, he thought, see, this was precisely why he hadn't want a young. This pregnancy shit was *not* for him.

What the hell was he going to do if he lost her—

"Wrath," Beth said weakly. "Wrath, where'd you go?"

As if she knew he was two thoughts past sanity—heading into the weeds of wigging out.

"I'm right here."

"Will you take me upstairs? I think I should try and feed first, and I don't want to do it out in the open."

"Plus," Doc Jane murmured, "I need to call and see when she can fit us in."

"Wrath? Take me upstairs?"

Snapping into action, he went forward and gathered his beloved gently in his arms, lifting her from the floor.

And what do you know, instantly, he was grounded. Calmed. Prepared to hold his shit together if only to spare Beth the worry over him.

"Thank you . . ." she whispered as her head lolled into the crook of his arm.

"What for?"

She didn't answer him until George had guided them over to the base of the stairs and Wrath had begun their ascent.

Her reply was just one word: "Everything."

SIXTY-TWO

It was seven twenty-three in the morning when Sola stepped out on her terrace and saw the ocean properly.

"Almost worth the drive," she murmured to herself.

With the sun rising, the vast blue expanse of water melded with the color of the early sky, only the peach clouds of dawn marking the horizon in between the heavens and the earth.

Settling into a lawn chair, she groaned as every joint she had, and some she didn't know about, let out a holler. Man, she was stiff. Then again, a full twenty-four hours behind the wheel of a car would do that to a girl. And it wasn't just her bones that were aching. Her right calf was spasming, as if it were considering a full-on charley horse—in spite of the fact that she'd used cruise control a good eighty percent of the time.

Wow, the air was soft and nice down here, even in December.

And the humidity was awesome. Her skin was positively drinking up the moist air—her hair as well, her ponytail already corkscrewing at the end.

"I go sleep now," her grandmother announced.

Sola looked back through the screen door. "Me, too. I'll be in soon."

"No smoking," came the scold.

"I gave that up two years ago."

"And you're not doing it again."

On that note, her grandmother nodded and walked out of the shallow living area.

Sola refocused on the ocean. Her Miami place was on the fifth floor of an older building, the condo just an unassuming, fifteen-hundred-square-foot space that she'd bought a couple of years ago for all cash and then decorated out of Rooms To Go on the cheap. The complex had a pool and tennis courts, though—and it was mostly dead, what with the holidays approaching and the snowbirds yet to fly down for the rest of the winter.

Arching her back, she tried to give her spine a little relief. No such luck. She was probably going to need a chiropractor after that drive.

Good thing she was never going to have to worry about doing it again.

Shit, that was depressing.

Putting a hand into her back pocket, she took out her iPhone. No calls. No texts.

She hadn't thought leaving Assail would hurt this much. And yet, she couldn't say she regretted it.

What was he doing right now, she wondered. Probably settling in after a night of wheeling and dealing in the dark underbelly of the Caldwell economy.

Would he go back to that woman? The one she'd watched him fuck?

Closing her eyes, she breathed in deep a couple of times—and the fact that she could smell the brine in the air helped. She was not up there anymore, she reminded herself. She was not with him anymore—not that they'd really been together.

So what he did and who it was with? Not her issue.

Anymore.

This was going to be okay, she told herself as she put her phone back and stared at the ocean. She had done the right thing. . . .

And yet, even still, snapshots of Assail dogged her mind, barging in and taking over the beautiful view in front of her.

Bending down, she felt around her thigh and then pressed her fingers into the bandage. As pain shot up into her torso and raced her heart, she told herself to remember how she'd ended up here. Why she'd relocated.

Exactly how her prayers had been answered.

Yeah, the drive had given her something other than a sore body and a tired brain: all those highway miles had done wonders for her perspective on everything.

Up north, she'd told herself that her escape had been at her own direction.

But now, as that sun rose in front of her, the rays streaking out over the water, the dolphins frolicking in the morning waves . . . she realized, no. That had been a cop-out.

Because admitting to herself that she believed in God was too scary, too crazy.

Away from everything she had left behind up north, in a neutral territory where she was starting over, she was able to be honest with herself. That prayer she had offered up, that last one, had in fact been answered . . . and in coming down here, she was honoring her end of the bargain.

At great sacrifice, as it turned out . . . because she knew it was going to be a long, long time before she was able to stop checking her phone.

Getting up from the lawn chair, she went back inside, and as she paused to shut the door, she looked at the sliding glass . . . and remembered that first floor of Assail's house. And as she picked up the suitcase she'd left just inside the door . . . all she could think of was that she'd packed the clothes in it when she'd still been with him.

Same as when she brushed her teeth: The last time she'd used her toothbrush had been in his upstairs bathroom.

And as she got into the white sheets, she recalled lying next to him after he'd come to her in the shower and taken her with such incredible power.

Closing her eyes, she listened to the unfamiliar sounds around her—someone talking loudly in the parking lot out back, the person upstairs running their shower, a dog barking on the other side of the wall.

Assail's place had been so quiet.

"Shit," she said aloud.

How long was it going to take before she stopped measuring everything by what she had left behind?

It was just like it had been when her mother had died. For months afterward, the metronome of life had been driven by nuances of her mom: last movie seen together, the things they'd bought at the store just that afternoon, the final birthday present given and received, that Christmas—which, of course, no one had known would be the end of the tradition.

All of that relentless remembering had gone on for a good year, until each one of the anniversaries, internal and external, had been exhausted. Getting through them had been like punching through a wall each time, but she had done it, right? She had put one foot in front of the other until life had resumed a kind of normalcy—

Ah crap. She really shouldn't be comparing this walk away from a drug dealer to the mourning of the woman who'd given birth to her and raised her for how long before her grandmother had taken over?

But there you had it.

Before Sola finally fell asleep, she ended up reaching out to the bedside table, opening the drawer, and putting her father's Bible under her pillow.

It was important to keep a tie to something, anything.

Otherwise? She was terrified she was going to repack that goddamn Ford she'd rented and head right back. And that stupidity simply was not an option.

After everything that had gone down lately, she really didn't want to know what happened to people who broke an agreement with the big guy.

And no, she wasn't talking about Santa Claus.

SIXTY-THREE

Good thing Beth had never had a hypothetical fantasy about what it would be like to find out she was pregnant.

As she sat in a perfectly nice waiting room, surrounded by cushy, neutral-toned chairs, magazines about menopause and motherhood, and women who were either in their twenties or fifties, she was very clear that whatever came from this appointment, positive, negative or too-early-to-tell, she would never have cooked up this scenario:

Without her husband. Escorted by a Shadow with enough concealed weapons on him to blow up a tank—or maybe an aircraft carrier. Having taken a vein for *blood*, for chrissakes, some twenty minutes before leaving a house the size and make up of Versailles.

Yeah, not exactly shit that would get written up in, say . . . she picked up the nearest mag. *Modern Motherhood*, for example.

Flipping through the colorful pages, she saw all kinds of Happy, Satisfied Mothers holding their Heavenly Angels on Earth as they preached about the sanctity of breast-feeding, the importance of skin-to-skin contact, and making that critical, first postnatal doctor's appointment.

"I'm going to be sick," she muttered, tossing the propaganda aside.

"Shit," iAm said as he leaped up. "I'll find the loo—"

"No, no." She pulled him back down. "I meant, yeah, no, it was just a comment."

"You sure?"

"Absolutely. And next time I get annoyed, I promise to just say so. Not throw out a metaphor."

iAm had to squeeze back into his own stuffed chair: The Shadow was so big, he overflowed the armrests and the back cushion—and he attracted a lot of attention.

Although not because of his size, necessarily.

Every single woman who came in, walked by, or worked at reception looked at him—in a way that proved you weren't dead from the neck down even if you were pregnant or your ovaries were winding things up or you were frazzled from ringing phones, lots of patients and tons of paperwork.

"Have you ever been married?" she asked the guy.

Absently, he shook his head, those black eyes of his tracing around as if he were ready to defend her with his life.

Which was awfully sweet, really.

"Ever been in love?"

Another shake of the head.

"Do you want children?"

Looking over at her he laughed tightly. "Did I hear that you were once a reporter?"

"Is my who-what-where-why-when coming through again?"

"Yeah. But it's cool, I got nothing to hide." He crossed his legs ankle to knee. "You know, with everything going on with my brother all these years, I don't ever think like that, you feel me? I gotta get him sorted, and shit knows, that ain't been happenin'."

"I'm really sorry." She'd heard enough through the household gossip lines to get the gist of their situation. "To be honest, I keep expecting to come down one of these nights and find you both gone."

He nodded. "Might well happen—"

"Marklon, Beth?" a nurse called out from an open door across the way.

"That's me." Getting to her feet, she put her purse up on her shoulder and headed over. "Right here."

Jesus, talk about nausea: At the prospect of going in to actually meet the doctor, she thought, okay, now she really was going to throw up again—

The nurse smiled and stepped back, motioning to a little triage room behind her. "I'm just going to get your weight and blood pressure in here."

"Can you hold this?" she asked iAm, holding out her Coach bag.

"Yup."

As he took her purse, the nurse paused and pulled a head-to-toe on the Shadow. Then she flushed brilliant red, and had to clear her throat. "Welcome," she said to him.

iAm just nodded and kept scanning the back area. Like maybe a matched set of ninjas was going to jump out of an exam room or something.

Beth had to smile as the nurse refocused and got into the business of taking vitals.

After that was done, the woman escorted them down a hallway that had a dozen or so numbered rooms opening off of it. As they went along, the decor was the same brown and cream of the waiting room, with similar kinds of glass mounted, fake-textured "art" doing its best to give a noninstitutional feel to a place filled with medical equipment, and people in scrubs and white coats.

"In five, please," the nurse said, once again standing to the side.

As iAm passed by her, she took an extra step back, her eyes widening as if she liked the way he smelled.

The nurse shook herself and came in, closing the door. "If you could sit on the exam table, that would be great. And you can be anywhere you'd like, sir."

The Shadow chose the seat right across from the entry, staring at the door as if he were daring somebody, anybody to come through it.

With another smile, Beth had to wonder what the nurse would think if she knew he was prepared to jump anyone he didn't like the looks of. And kill them.

Maybe cut them up and put them into a stew.

God, she hoped it really had been chicken in that soup. . . .

"Ms. Marklon? Hello?"

She shook herself. "Oh, sorry, what?"

The history part of things went fast, because before her transition she'd been perfectly healthy, and it wasn't like she was going to tell them that a mere two years ago, she'd become a vampire.

Duh.

"And how far along do you think you are?" came the eventual question.

"I have no idea whether I'm even pregnant, to be honest. It's a possibility, though, and I am having a lot of nausea—I just want some reassurance everything's okay."

"Have you taken an over-the-counter test?"

"No. Should I have?"

The nurse shook her head. "We can do a blood test here if the doctor wants one. And as for the nausea, if you are pregnant, a lot of women get morning sickness that's more like all-day sickness in the first trimester—and yet it's all perfectly fine."

"Good Lord, I can't believe I'm talking like this."

The nurse just smiled and finished writing in the chart.

"Okay, now, if you'd like to change into this gown." A paper square was placed in her lap. "I'll send the doctor in."

"Thanks."

The door shut behind the nurse with a click.

"I can't leave you," iAm said as he got up, turned around and faced the wall—and put his head in his big hands. "But I would strongly suggest that you do not tell your husband you got naked with me in the room. I like my arms and legs just where they are, thank you very much."

"I agree."

As she made quick work of getting out of her clothes and into that flimsy gown, she really wanted Wrath with her. And actually, it was a good lesson for how much his presence calmed her out. They were so rarely apart, it was easy to forget what he meant to her, especially when things got stressful.

Annnnnd then it was a case of hurry up and wait.

"So if you were going to get married, what kind of woman do you want?"

iAm glanced over at her. "Can't we talk about baseball or something?"

Oh, crap. "Or guy, as the case might be. I'm sorry, I didn't mean to offend you."

He laughed again. "I'm not gay."

"So what would she be like?"

"Man, you don't quit, do you?"

Now it was her turn to laugh. "Listen, I'm sitting here, freezing cold in this paper doily, about to be told that I have the flu and shouldn't have bothered coming in. Do me a solid and get my mind off my reality, will you?"

iAm sat back in his chair. "Well, like I said, I haven't really given it a lot of thought."

"Can I set you up with someone—"

"No," he barked. "Nooooooooo. No, no, no, back right off the edge of that ledge, girlie."

She put out her hands. "Okay, okay. Just, I don't know, you seem like a good guy."

He didn't respond to that one.

And as he fell silent, she figured, damn it, she had made him feel awkward—

"Can I tell you something nobody knows?" he blurted.

Beth sat up straighter. "Yes, please."

The Shadow let out a long exhale. "The truth is . . ."

Oh, God, please don't let the doctor come in before he—

"I've never been with a female before."

As Beth's brows punched up to the center of her forehead, she gave them a strict lecture about resettling. She didn't want him to look up and see the shock on her face.

"Well, that's . . ."

"Lame. I know."

"No, no, not at all."

"Trez has been more than making up for it," he muttered. "If we averaged his sex life and mine, we'd still be on the Wilt Chamberlain curve."

"Oh, wow. I mean—"

"Before my brother bolted from the s'Hisbe, I was too goddamn shy. And then once the shit hit the fan with him? I've been trying to keep him from spiraling completely out of control. Plus, I don't know, I'm not into the sluts. Our tradition says you honor your body by sharing it only with someone you are halved with. Guess I can't get that bullshit out of my head."

After a moment, he glowered across at her. "What."

"I just . . . I've never heard you say that many words at once. It's nice to have you open up."

"Can we keep this between us?"

"Yes, absolutely."

She waited a couple of beats. "But if I meet someone, like, you know, who might make sense, can I introduce you two?"

He shook his head. " 'Preciate it. I'm not a good bet, though."

"So what are you going to do, live your whole life alone?"

"I have my brother," he said gruffly. "Trust me. That shit is more than enough to keep me busy."

"Yeah, I'm sure it is."

When he got quiet again, she assumed he was done talking. Instead, he spoke up one last time: "I only have one other secret."

"What's that?"

"Don't tell anyone . . . but I like that goddamn cat of yours."

Tilting her head to the side, Beth smiled at the Shadow. "I have a feeling . . . he's pretty fond of you, too."

It was a full hour before the door opened again.

And it was only another nurse. "Hi, I'm Julie. Dr. Sam's tied up in an emergency. She's really sorry. She's asked me to take a blood sample to speed things along?"

For a split second, Beth worried about that bright idea. There were anatomical differences in the two species. What if they found something—

"Ms. Marklon?"

iAm had said he was going to take care of any fallout, though, she reminded herself. And she could guess how he was going to do that.

"Yes, of course. Which arm do you want?"

"Let me take a look at your veins."

Five minutes, one alcohol pad, two sticks, and three filled vials later, she and iAm were alone again.

For a while.

"Does it always take this long?" he asked. "With humans?"

"I don't know. I was never sick, and I sure as hell never wondered if I was pregnant before."

The Shadow rearranged himself in his chair again. "You want to call Wrath?"

She took out her phone. "I'm not getting a signal. How 'bout you?"

He checked his. "Nope."

Made sense. They were in one of St. Francis Hospital's newer buildings, a twelve- or fifteen-story-high steel-and-glass number—and they were only on the second floor. In the middle.

Not a window in sight.

God, she wished Wrath were here—

The door swung open, and later . . . much later . . . she would recall the first thing that struck her:

I like this woman.

Dr. Sam was five feet tall, fifty years old . . . and all about her patient. "Hi. I'm Sam, and I'm sorry you've had to wait."

Shifting the folder she was carrying to her opposite arm, she put her hand out and smiled, flashing pretty white teeth and a face that had aged well naturally. Her short blond hair was a good dye job, and she had some nice gold bangles and a diamond ring on her left hand. "You must be Beth. Manny's an old friend of mine. I used to do ob-gyn consults for him in the ER from time to time."

For absolutely no good reason, Beth felt an absurd urge to cry—and tamped it right down. "I'm Beth. Marklon."

"And you are?" she said to iAm, also offering her hand.

"A friend."

"My husband can't be here," Beth said as those two shook.

"Oh, I'm sorry."

"He's . . . not going to be able to be at the appointments."

Dr. Sam propped a hip on the exam table. "Is he in the military?"

"Ah . . ." She glanced at iAm. "Actually, yes."

"Thank him for his service for me, will you?"

God, she hated lying. "I will."

"Okay, so let's get down to business." She opened the folder. "Have you been taking prenatal vitamins?"

"No."

"That's going to be first on our list." Dr. Sam glanced up. "I've got some good organic ones that won't make you sick—"

"Wait, so am I pregnant?"

The doctor frowned. "I—I'm sorry. I thought this was your ultrasound checkup?"

"No, I came in to find out whether I have a stomach flu or if I'm . . . you know."

The doctor pulled the chair the nurse had sat in up really close. Then she put her hand over Beth's. "You're very definitely pregnant.

And you have been for a while. That's why we need to get you on those prenatals right away—as well as try to put some weight on you."

Beth felt the blood drain out of her head. "I—that's not possible."

"Going by your HCG results, I'd say you're into your second trimester—although, of course, levels vary significantly. But right now you're over one hundred thousand. So as I said, I'm hoping you'll let me do an ultrasound so we can see what's going on."

"I . . . I . . . I . . . I . . ."

"Yeah, she'd like that," iAm said remotely. "Can you do it now?"

"I . . . I . . ."

"Yup, right now." Dr. Sam didn't move, though. "But let's make sure Beth's on board. Would you like some time with your friend?"

"I can't be four months. You don't understand . . . it's not possible."

Maybe this was a vampire thing, she thought. Like, the reading was wonky because she was a—

"Well, again, HCG levels are really only an indication in the very beginning—and solely in relation to how much they're increasing." The doctor stood up and opened a drawer, taking out a little boxy device that had a sensor attached to it by a thick wire. "May I check for a heartbeat?"

"It's not possible," Beth heard herself say. "It's just not."

"Will you let me see if there's a heartbeat?"

Beth collapsed back onto the table and felt the doctor put something the size of a thumbprint on her stomach—

A tiny little rhythm sounded out. "Yup, we have a heartbeat. Nice and strong. One forty is what we like to see, and you've got it down pat."

Beth could only blink at the ceiling tiles far above her. "Get the ultrasound machine," she said roughly. "Now."

SIXTY-FOUR

As John paced around the foyer's mosaic floor, he was acutely aware of two things: One, his sister had been gone for hours. And two, Wrath was at the end of his rope.

The King had taken up res on the final step of the grand staircase, his torso moving back and forth like the passing of seconds was being measured by his whole body.

For no good reason, John went over to the plastic draping over the archway into the billiards room. Work had progressed the night before—in spite of the size of the square footage, the floor was almost entirely up. Tonight, they were supposed to bring in a load of the new marble and start laying the stuff. Then they were going to have to work on the walls, which was going to probably take longer—

Wow. He was actually trying to distract himself.

Letting the sheeting fall back into place, he glanced over at Wrath. You'd think that at a time like this, John would be the worst person to sit with the guy, what with him being mute and the King being blind.

But Wrath didn't want to communicate, so, hey, it worked.

Everybody else had fled the scene after Beth had left with the Shadow—and John had meant to follow suit. Husband totally trumped

brother, especially when it came to shit like this. But once upstairs, even after he'd had a sesh with Xhex? His footfalls had taken him back down here.

And so he waited.

It was funny, he had the sense that if he'd been anyone else, Wrath would have thrown him out.

"Has your phone gone off?" Wrath demanded without looking up.

John blew a short, descending whistle, the closest he could come to a no. Then again, if he had gotten a call, they both would have heard the phone.

"Text?"

John shook his head, before remembering he had to whistle again—

Out of nowhere, the vestibule's bell went off, an image appearing on the discreetly mounted monitor by the grand entrance's acres of molding.

Beth. iAm. Outside on the front steps.

As Wrath jumped to his feet, John rushed for the access button before Fritz came, whistling in an urgent ascending call so that the husband knew the wife had returned.

The second he hit the unlock, the vestibule's inner door swung wide.

John would never forget what Beth looked like as she careened into the house: Her face was pale and drawn, her eyes too wide, her movements sloppy and disordered. She was carrying her coat instead of wearing it, and she let the thing, as well as her purse, fall unheeded to the floor.

Such pedestrian objects went scattering everywhere. A wallet. A hairbrush. A ChapStick.

Why was he noticing this—?

And then all he could see was his sister racing across the mosaic depiction of the apple tree in full bloom . . . as if she were being chased by a madman.

As she jumped at Wrath, it was not in joy.

She was terrified.

In response, Wrath held her effortlessly, lifting her off the floor, the strain gritting his jaw having nothing to do with how much she weighed.

"What is it, *leelan*?" he asked.

"I'm pregnant. I'm—"

"Oh, God—"

"—having a boy."

John threw a hand out to steady himself. He couldn't have heard that right. There was no way—

Wrath slowly let her back down to the floor. And then he took a little TO, falling onto that lowest step like his knees had given out of him.

And gee, what do you know, John did the same, a curious combination of despair and disbelieving joy taking the starch right out on him until he found himself sitting on the floor.

How was this possible . . . ?

In the silence that followed Beth's big announcement, Wrath couldn't get his brain to work. Or his arms or legs. As he fell down onto that step his ass had been warming, he felt like he was in some kind of nightmare.

"I don't . . . understand." A son? They were having a *son*? "Your needing was a night ago—two at the most."

"I know, I know," she choked out.

Instantly, he snapped into action. Fuck his own scrambled brain; his *shellan* needed him. Taking control of himself, he regathered her into his lap, aware that John and iAm were the only ones around—and he was glad of it.

"Tell me what the doctor said."

The scent of her tears killed him, but he kept tight as she cleared her throat a couple of times. "I was just going there to be told it was too early. I wasn't supposed to be four months along—"

"What?"

"That's what she said." Beth shook her head against his chest. "I mean, I know I've felt weird, but I thought it was just because the needing was coming? Instead, I was already—I mean, I guess I got pregnant before it even hit me."

Jesus . . . Christ.

She inched back. "Honestly, I noticed my clothes were getting tight about a month ago. Maybe a little longer? I thought it was stress eating, or because I wasn't making time for exercise? And then my moods starting getting wonky—and now that I look back on it . . . my breasts were sore, too. But I never got a period or anything. So I just don't know? Oh, God, what if I harmed the baby by being with Layla? What if—"

"Beth, shh—Beth, listen to me. What did the doctor say about the young?"

"She said . . ." His mate sniffled. "She said he was beautiful. He's perfect. He's got the heart of a lion—"

At this, Beth collapsed in a fit of sobs, the kind of thing that was a release of emotion more than anything else. And as he held her, he stared out over her head.

"A son?" he said roughly.

"The doctor says he's big and strong. And I saw him move," she said through tears. "I didn't know it was a baby, I thought it was indigestion—"

"So you were pregnant before the needing."

"That's the only explanation I have," she wailed.

Wrath held her even closer, right to his beating chest. ". . . a son?"

"Yes. A son."

All of a sudden, he felt the biggest, widest, happiest grin hit his face, the goddamn thing stretching his cheeks until they hurt, making his eyes water from the strain, pulling at his temples until they burned. And the joy wasn't just on his puss. A flush so great it burned him alive flooded through his body, cleansing him in places he didn't know were dirty, washing out cobwebs that had crept into his corners, making him feel alive in a way he hadn't been in a very, very long time.

Before he knew what he was doing, he burst to his feet with Beth in his arms, leaned back, and hollered at the top of his lungs, with more pride than his six-foot-nine frame could hold.

"A soooooooooooooooooooooooooooooooooooooon! I'm having a soooooooooooooooooooooooon!"

SIXTY-FIVE

Beth fell in love with her son at that moment.

As Wrath howled at the moon with fatherly pride, she smiled through her tears and worry. It had been so long since she'd seen him well and truly happy—and yet here he was, in the midst of news she'd expected him to freak out about, shining like the sun.

And their son was the cause of it.

"Where the hell is everybody," he bitched as he glared up the stairs.

"You just called them about two seconds ago—"

People came at a dead run, a traffic jam forming at the top of the stairs in spite of the fact that the thing was huge, the sound of big feet thundering down to the foyer as the Brothers came with their mates in tow.

"Here," she said, taking out a flimsy slip of paper. "Show them this—it's a picture from the ultrasound."

Wrath shifted her around so he was holding her with one arm—and he took that pic and thrust it out like it was billboard size and made of gold.

"Look!" he barked. "Look! My son! My son!"

Beth had to laugh even as her tears ran harder.

"Look!"

His Brothers formed a circle around what he was holding out, and she was astonished . . . every one of them had a sheen across their eyes, their manly, tight smiles proof they were holding their emotions in check.

And then she looked at Tohr. He was hanging back, with Autumn close to his side. As his mate glanced up in concern, he seemed to brace himself to come forward.

"I'm so happy for you," the Brother said roughly to both of them.

"Oh, Tohr," she blurted, reaching out her hands.

As the Brother clasped them, Wrath dropped his arm as if hiding the picture.

"No," Tohr cut in. "You keep that up, you feel that pride. I have a good feeling about this, and I'm rejoicing with you—all the way."

"Ah, fuck," Wrath said, yanking the Brother in for a hard embrace. "Thanks, my man."

There were so many voices, and people congratulating them, but there was one other face she wanted to see.

John was also staying on the periphery, but as he caught her eye, he started to smile—although it wasn't like Wrath's. He was worried.

I'm going to be fine, she mouthed.

Even though she wasn't sure she believed that. She blamed herself for not knowing she was pregnant, for trying to get that needing of hers started falsely—and especially for succeeding. What if that violent nausea had been a miscarriage in the making? What if—

Pulling herself back from the brink, she held on to two things—one, she'd heard that heartbeat, nice and strong; and two, the doctor had raved about the baby.

Abruptly, the sea of people parted . . . and then there they were.

Bella, with Nalla in her arms, Z standing beside his girls.

Beth broke down all over again as the female came forward. God, it was impossible not to remember how Nalla had started this, putting into motion the need that had become undeniable.

Bella was tearing up, too, as she stopped. "We just want to say yay!"

At that moment, Nalla reached out to Beth, a gummy smile on her face, pure joy radiating out.

No turning that down, nope, not at all.

Beth took the little girl out of her mother's arms and positioned her on her chest, capturing one of the pinwheeling hands and giving kisses, kisses, kisses.

"You ready to be a big . . ." Beth glanced at Z and then her husband. ". . . a big sister?"

Yes, Beth thought. Because that's what the Brotherhood and their families were. Close as siblings, tighter than blood because they were chosen.

"Yes, she is," Bella said as she wiped under her eyes and looked back at Z. "She is so ready."

"My brother." Z shoved out his palm, his scarred face in a half smile, his yellow eyes warm. "Congratulations."

Instead of shaking anything, Wrath shoved that ultrasound picture into his Brother's face. "Do you see him? See my son? He's big, right, Beth?"

She kissed Nalla's supersoft hair. "Yes."

"Big and healthy, right?"

Beth laughed some more. "Big and healthy. Absolutely perfect."

"Perfect!" Wrath bellowed. "And this is a doctor saying it—I mean, she went to medical school."

Even Z started laughing at that point.

Beth gave Nalla back to her parents. "And Dr. Sam told me she's delivered over fifteen thousand babies over the course of her career—"

"See!" Wrath yelled. "She knows these things. My son is perfect! Where's the champagne? Fritz! Get the fucking champagne!"

Shaking her head, Beth took a deep breath and decided to go with the moment. There was still a long haul in front of them, capped off with the delivery—which, Christ, was scaring the shit out of her already. With so many hurdles ahead, and so many unknowns, it was tempting to get lost in a tailspin.

But for the next hour, she just wanted to live with Wrath in all this high-octane joy—be a part of the celebration of this miracle.

So damn funny: All the while they had been fighting about children . . . they'd already had one cooking.

Life was really ironic sometimes.

Lounging back in her husband's arms, she just enjoyed watching him as he clapped his Brothers on the back, and even accepted a flute of Cristal from Fritz.

Her *hellren* was a tall guy. But right now? He put Mount Everest to shame.

"You can put me down," she said with a smile.

The frown that got shot her way was a brick wall if she'd ever seen one. "Absolutely not! You're my wife, and you're carrying my child. You'll be lucky if I let your feet touch the floor three years from now."

With that, he bent in and kissed her on the mouth.

Ah, hell, maybe she should have been all, "This baby is a *we* thing, not a *you* thing"—but that wasn't how she felt. She'd been so terrified he wouldn't accept and love a child, she was relieved and overjoyed that he was getting possessive already.

Falling in love, already.

Which was the best news for their unborn child: When Wrath, son of Wrath, decided someone was his? He would drag the moon down to Earth if they needed it.

The reaction was exactly what she had been too scared to wish for.

Wrath lifted his glass. "To my son," he shouted over the crowd. "And more importantly . . . to my wife."

As he turned his face to her, the love he felt made his eyes glow so fiercely, she could see the pale green light even through the wraparounds.

The household shouted in joy . . . and everyone drank.

Except her, of course.

Because she was pregnant, she thought with a bright smile to rival Wrath's.

Wrath rode the wave for as long as it took him. With his brothers surrounding him, and a new purpose jacking his shit up, he knew that this was one of the best nights of his life. Or . . . shit, it was still day, wasn't it.

Who the fuck cared, really.

It was difficult to explain, even to himself, what exactly had changed. But suddenly everything felt different, from the way he shook his brothers' hands to how he smiled at their mates to the hold he kept on Beth.

And she was the best part of everything.

With champagne flowing, and the laughter echoing around the foyer, he couldn't believe he had reached this moment in his life. Just a night before he had been throne-less and potentially mate-less. And here he was with the crown still on his head and his wife pregnant with his young.

Four months along.

He thought back, sifting through the weeks and then the months. There had been a night, about four months ago, when Beth had come to find him in the study during the day. They hadn't been together for a while at that point, what with everything going on—and he'd been shocked, in a good way, by how aggressively she'd gotten on him. Afterward . . . come to think of it, her scent had changed—deepening, although not in the way a vampire female's would with pregnancy.

All along, she had been with young.

Destiny had served them both up what she had wanted but feared would never have, and what he didn't know he'd needed.

As he heard his mate yawn, he went on instant alert. "Okay, time to go up."

The crowd calmed down immediately, and he could sense the focus on his Beth. She was going to get a lot of that from now on, not just from him but from his brothers. They were protective of her already. Pregnant? She was going to get that shit twenty-fold now.

"And I think I need to feed again," his Beth said as he started up the stairs, George leading him by subtle pressure on his leg.

"I gotchu." He frowned. "What did the doc say about the nausea?"

"She really does think I have the flu. But then, she doesn't know about the whole needing thing and maybe that's why?"

"I'll talk to Havers—you don't have to go see him."

"That would be great, actually. I'm really nervous."

"Don't you worry. I got this."

And he absolutely, positively did. He felt in control of the universe, an old, familiar part of him waking up once again.

George guided him to the door that opened up to the stairs to the third floor, and when they got to the top, Wrath went to the left.

As the vault was unlocked, he walked inside, taking her immediately to the bed. "You want me to run a bath? A shower? The sink?"

She laughed. "I just want to lie here. I feel like I've been on a roller-coaster ride that's been going too fast."

Sitting down beside her, he found her lower belly with his hand. "I love this."

"Love what?"

"This bump thing you got going on." He smiled. "That's our young."

"It sure is."

"I wish I could see it. That picture."

"Me, too."

"But this is good." He rubbed in circles, trying to imagine what his son would look like. "And he's strong."

"Yes. Just like his father."

"Here, take my vein." He extended his wrist to her mouth. "Please."

"Oh, thank you."

As her fangs sank into his skin, he wanted her at his throat but didn't trust himself. He was juiced up, and that kind of shit tended to like a particular outlet—and that was not happening while she was pregnant. Nope. Not with his son in there—

His wife's hand landed on his hard cock—and he nearly jumped out of his skin. "Fuck!"

She broke the seal on his vein. "We can have sex, you know."

"Ah, no. Nope."

"Wrath, I'm not sick—and it's not like we have to worry about whether or not I'm going to get pregnant." The smile on her face was all over her tone. "You got that job done just fine."

"I did, didn't I."

"I am so happy about this," she said, as he felt her touch his face. "About your response most of all."

Guess he'd surprised them both with his reaction.

Stroking her belly, he thought about what was growing inside of her. "You want to know what the best part of this is?"

"Tell me," she whispered.

"You have given me something . . . I didn't even know I needed. It's the greatest gift I will ever receive—it's, like, completing me already in places I wasn't aware were empty. And yet . . . in spite of all that? I don't love you one bit more. You are as important to me as you've always been." He curled down and pressed a kiss to the loose shirt she was wearing—it was one of his, actually, and wasn't that great. "I was wholly bonded to you before this, and will be after this—and forevermore."

"You're going to make me cry again."

"So cry. And let me take care of you. I got this."

"I love you so much."

He moved up to her mouth and kissed her once, twice, three times. "Right. Back. Atchu. Now finish feeding and rest—and I'll have food brought up."

"No food, please. Not right now. Your strength is all I need."

Amen to that, he thought.

Wrath stayed on the edge of that bed forever as she nursed against his wrist. Then he helped her to the shower, got her dried off, and put her between the sheets.

"I'm just going to rest a little," she said, already drifting off as the shutters started to rise for the night.

"However long you want."

A son. *A son.*

"I'm going to go hit the desk," he said—before stopping himself.

Funny, that was what he'd told her every night after First Meal, their joking way of acknowledging he was gonna go put his crown on and deal with shit.

"I'm so glad," she said in a sleepy voice.

Funny . . . right now? All that King stuff didn't seem like a burden anymore.

In fact, as he grabbed onto George's halter, it felt shockingly easy to go down the stairs and head for his study. And as he went into the room, he found the desk, walked around its carved corners . . . and paused before sitting in his father's chair.

It was with a sense of awe that he slowly lowered his weight. The throne creaked as it always did—and he wondered, as his father had sat in it, had it done the same? He didn't remember that detail from his youth and wished his memory was better.

Instead of calling for Saxton to come in, or checking email through his voice-activated computer, he frowned and tried to pull as many recollections out of the past as he could. They were hazy, the ones he did recall—because of his faulty eyes.

God, he'd never really thought of his wife's human side one way or the other—but he hoped like hell that the new DNA she was bringing to the table went to work on his defect. It would be so great if his son was born with good eyesight.

But if the young wasn't?

Then he himself had blazed the trail, and he would be there to support his son. Being blind wasn't great—but it didn't mean you had to miss out in life.

Shiiiiiiit, to think he'd been willing to sacrifice a child just because he was scared he or she might have a defect. Stupid. So stupid. And really fucking lame of him.

Thank Christ destiny had known better—

"My lord," Fritz said.

"Come on in!" Dayum, he was really cheerful—time to dial that down, if only so he didn't annoy himself.

"One of the workmen wishes for an audience."

Ah, yes. And for a moment, he reverted to his default to push things away, but then he got to his feet. "I'll come down—no."

With conscious thought, he sat back in the throne. "Send him up—escort him, though, will you? And get some brothers to help."

He wasn't ready to trust anyone but the people in his household.

"Right away," the butler said. "My pleasure!"

Looked like he wasn't the only one with his happy-happy-joy-joy on.

He glanced down to the floor. "I don't know what I'm doing here, George."

The supportive chuff he got in return was exactly the vote of confidence he needed. Fuck the *glymera*, for real.

A little later, Vishous's sharp voice cut into the room. "I got your visitor, true?"

"Send him in."

There was some shuffling and suddenly, the scents in the room changed—so overwhelmingly, Wrath recoiled.

He'd never known such . . . gratitude? Was that what it was? Reverence? It was a bouquet born of deep emotions, that was for sure.

"The foreman's bowing before your desk, my brother," V said. "His hat's off."

The fact that the foreman was crying was something Vishous judiciously left off the report.

Wrath got to his feet and went around. Before he could say anything, though, a stream of words fell from the humble male's mouth.

"I know it's you. I know it could only be you." The male's voice choked. "I cannot repay you—how did you know?"

Wrath shrugged. "I just figured your daughter probably needed a better wheelchair. And a couple of ramps."

"And the van. That van . . . how did you . . ."

"I'm guessing money's a little tight—although you take care of your family just fine. And as for the why, you're helping me here, I wanted to help you there."

"My second *shellan*, she cannot express her thanks enough. Nor can I. But we offer you this. As an unworthy tribute to Your Highness."

Wrath frowned, a sudden slice from the past coming back to him. And it made him blink hard.

He could remember people doing this with his father, offering the King tokens of thanks.

"I am honored," he said gruffly as he put his hands out.

What was laid across his palms was smooth, soft. "What is it?"

There was an awkward pause. As if the foreman didn't understand.

And that was the moment when Wrath knew he'd come to a crossroads. Oddly, he thought of his son.

Shifting the slight weight to one hand, he reached up . . .

. . . and removed his wraparounds.

"I'm blind," he told the commoner. "I cannot see. That's how I knew what would matter to you and your family. I've got some experience making accommodations in this world."

The gasp was loud.

Wrath smiled a little. "Yeah, that Blind King title isn't just gossip. It's the God's honest—and I am not ashamed of it."

Holy Shit . . . until he said the words, he hadn't realized how inferior he'd felt. How much he had kept hidden. How many apologies he had offered because of something that he had no control over. But that time was past.

Sighted or not, he had an example to set in this world—and he was goddamned if he wasn't going to live up to it.

"So please," he told the clearly astonished commoner. "Describe to me the gift that you pay me honor with."

There was a very long pause. And the foreman wasn't the only one who was surprised. V was emanating twelve kinds of OMG as he smoked like a frickin' chimney over in the corner.

The foreman cleared his throat. "It is—um, my mate, she weaves fabric in the traditional way from the Old Country. She sells it within the race for solace banners and clothing. This is . . . it is her finest weave, one that she did years ago and has not had the heart to sell. It took her a year to complete it—" The male's voice cracked. "She said she knows now why she could not let it go. She says to tell you she knows now, she was saving it in tribute for you."

Wrath put the wraparounds aside and ran his hands back and forth over the cloth. "I've never felt anything this fine—it's like satin. What color is it?"

"Red."

"My favorite color." Wrath paused. And then decided, Fuck it. "I'm having a son."

Cue the second gasp.

"Yeah, my love and I . . . we got lucky." Abruptly, the reality of his son not being the heir to the throne hit—and there was a sadness. There truly was—but also a kind of relief. "I will use this to receive him in. When he is born."

Annnnnnnnnnnnnd that would be a third gasp.

"No, he's not the heir to the throne," Wrath said. "My wife is part human. So he cannot sit where I do—and that's all right."

His son would make his own way. He was . . . free.

And as Wrath spoke his truth, without apology or explanation, as he cloaked himself in the vestments of honesty, as he said the words he had kept hidden without realizing he had done so . . .

He realized he, too, was finally free—and that his parents, if they had had a chance to look over his shoulder, would have approved of him.

Just the way he was.

SIXTY-SIX

The Caldwell Galleria Mall was open until ten o'clock at night.

As Xcor materialized in a hidden corner of its vast chain of parking lots, he then strode past the lines of parked cars, his long strides eating up the distance to an entrance that had some giant red sign over a multitude of doors.

He had no idea what he was doing here. About to walk around humans. With a purpose that, had one of his soldiers put such forth, he would never have let them get over it.

Pushing in through the glass portals, he frowned. Female clothes abounded on the left and the right, all manner of cheery colors—that made him think fondly of unleashing a flamethrower to put his retinas out of their misery.

Up ahead, there was section after section of glass cases with sparkling oddities in them, scarves hanging from racks, and mirrors—goddamn, there were mirrors everywhere.

Passing them by, he ducked his eyes. He didn't want the reminder of his ugliness. Especially not this night—

Did they even have what he was looking for in this place?

Prowling around the first floor, he could feel the eyes of the proper customers on him—and it was clear they were wondering if they were going to end up on the evening news in a bad way. He ignored them all and proceeded upward on a set of moving stairs.

It was on the second floor that he found the menswear department.

Yes, herein, all manner of masculine shirts and pants and sweaters and jackets were arranged on hangers and display tables. And just as with down below, music thumped in low tones overhead, whilst light streamed from the ceiling to set off the merchandise.

What the hell was he doing here—

"Hey, can I help you—whoa!"

As he wheeled around and settled into his attack stance, the black human salesperson jumped back and put his palms up.

"Forgive me," Xcor muttered. At least he hadn't outed one of his weapons.

"No problem." The handsome, well-dressed man smiled. "You looking for something specific?"

Xcor glanced around, and nearly walked back to that fancy stairwell. "I require a new shirt."

"Oh, cool, you got a hot date?"

"And pants. And socks." Come to think of it, he never wore underwear. "And undergarments. And a jacket."

The salesman smiled and raised a hand as if he were going to clap his customer on the shoulder—but then caught himself as he clearly rethought the contact.

"What kind of look are you going for?" he asked instead.

"Clothed."

The guy paused like he wasn't sure whether that was a joke. "Ah . . . okay, I can work with non-naked. Plus it's legal. Come on with me."

Xcor followed, because he didn't know what else to do—he'd gotten this ball rolling; there was no reason not to follow through.

The man stopped in front of a display of shirts. "So I'm going to go with the it's-a-date thing, unless you tell me otherwise. Casual? You didn't mention a suit."

"Casual. Yes. But I want to look. . . ." Well, not like himself, at any rate. "Presentable."

"Then I think what you're going to want is a button-down."

"A button-down."

The guy regarded him steadily. "You're not from here, are you."

"No, I'm not."

"I can tell by the accent." The salesman passed a hand over the dizzying array of folded-up squares with collars. "These are our traditional cuts. I can tell without measuring you that the European stuff isn't going to do you right—you're too muscled in the shoulders. Even if we could get the neck and arm size right, you'd bust out of them. Do you like any of these colors?"

"I don't know what to like."

"Here." The man picked up a blue one that reminded Xcor of the backdrop on his phone. "This is good with your eyes. Not that I go that way—but you gotta work with what you got. Do you have any idea of your size?"

"XXXL."

"We need to be a little more exact." The salesman got out a cloth tape measure. "Neck? Arms?"

As if to help the whole cognition thing, the man made a little circle in front of his own throat.

Xcor looked down at himself. He was wearing nothing but the cleanest muscle shirt he had, a pair of military combat pants, and his boots.

"I do not know."

The man reached out with the tape, but then hesitated. "Tell you what, how 'bout I give this to you—just wrap it around your neck and I'll read the number."

Xcor took the thing and did as asked.

"Okay, wow." The salesman crossed his arms over his chest. "Well, you won't be wearing a tie, right?"

"Tie?"

"I'll take that as a no. Will you let me measure your arm?"

Xcor extended his left one and the man moved fast. "That's almost normal in length at least. Width? You're talking the Rock territory, easy. But I have an idea."

A minute and a half of rifling later, Xcor had three different shirts to try on.

"What about slacks?" the salesman asked.

"I do not know my size or preference." Might as well be efficient. "The same is true about jackets."

"I had a feeling you were going to say that. Come with me."

Before he knew it, he was buck naked in a dressing room, jacking his body into the clothes, his weapons hidden under the pile of things he'd worn walking in.

"How is it?" his new best friend asked on the far side of the door.

Xcor glanced at himself in the mirror and felt his brows rise. He looked . . . not good, no. That would never be him. But he didn't appear as stupid as he felt—or as rough as he'd been in his own wardrobe.

Taking off the dark jacket that had been suggested to him, he strapped on his guns and knives and then put the thing back on. It was a little tight in the back, and he couldn't quite button it—but it was so much better than his bloodstained leather duster. And the pants stretched across his thighs only slightly.

Stepping out, he handed over the two other shirts. "I shall take all this."

The salesman clapped his hands. "Nice. Big improvement. You need shoes?"

"Mayhap later."

"We're having a sale at the end of the month. Come back then."

Xcor followed him over to the checkout, and took a pair of scissors out of a pen holder to cut the tags that were hanging off his wrist and his waist. "Do you have scent?"

"Oh, you mean cologne?"

"Aye."

"That's another department—across the way. I can show you where they are—actually, check this." He pulled open a drawer. "I have some samples here—yeah, old-school Drakkar. Égoïste—that's a good one. Polo—the original. Oh, try this."

Xcor accepted a small vial, popped the lid and breathed in. Fresh, clean . . . what handsome would smell like if it had a fragrance.

Basically everything he wasn't.

"I like this one."

"Calvin Klein Eternity. Very traditional—and the honeys like it."

Xcor nodded as if he knew what he was talking about. Such a lie.

The salesman rang up everything. "Okay, your total's five oh one ninety-two."

Xcor took out the bills he'd shoved in his back pocket. "I have this," he said, fanning the money out in his open palms.

The salesman's brows popped. "Yeah, it's not that much at all." There was a pause. "Do you . . . yeah, okay, I need five of those, four of these, and two of the little guys."

Xcor tried to facilitate the process of the man pulling specific denominations out that—apparently—meant something.

"And here's your change and receipt. You want a bag for your old stuff?"

"Yes, please. Thank you."

A big white bag with a red star was passed over the console. "Thanks for coming in—my name's Antoine, by the way. If you want to come back for shoes."

After shoving his former clothes inside, Xcor found himself bowing at the waist. "Your assistance has been much appreciated."

Antoine raised his palm like he was getting ready to do a clap on the shoulder again. But once more, he caught himself and smiled instead. "Knock her dead, my man."

"Oh, no." Xcor shook his head. "That shan't be necessary. This one I like."

Layla left the mansion at eleven forty-eight by sneaking out the library's French doors. No one seemed to notice; then again, Rhage and John Matthew were keeping an eye on the workmen in the billiards room, Wrath was up in his study with Saxton, Beth was at rest, the other Brothers were fighting, and Qhuinn and Blay were enjoying some quiet time on their night-off rotation.

Oh, and the staff were busying cleaning up after a celebratory First Meal.

Not that she was keeping track of everybody in the house.

Nah.

Dematerializing off the back terrace, she traveled to the meadow she was becoming so familiar with and re-formed at the base of the maple tree.

Dressed in her traditional robing, she had an overcoat on to keep warm, in the pocket of which she had put some Mace.

Qhuinn had insisted on teaching her self-defense as well as how to drive. So in case that other male showed up, she was prepared.

Slipping her hand into the coat pocket and palming the squat cylinder, she was careful to walk all the way around the tree. And note carefully the expanse of snow-covered meadow.

She was alone.

Dearest Virgin Scribe, was she really—

Down at the base of the rise, a figure presented itself out of thin air—and as the breeze shifted directions, she caught the scent.

It was him. And . . . something else? Some kind of fragrance that was at once masculine . . . and delicious.

Xcor took a long time to approach, his strides even and unhurried as he mounted the hill and came up to her, carrying something under his arm. Her body responded instantly to his presence, her heart racing, her palms sweating, her breath going short.

She told herself it was fear. And overwhelmingly, that was true. But there was something else. . . .

His clothes were different, she realized as he arrived before her. More refined. Attractive.

As if mayhap he had dressed for her?

Trying to relieve the burning in her lungs, she inhaled deeply and frowned. "You smell . . . different."

"Bad?"

She shook her head. "No. Not at all. And your clothes . . . you look very well."

He made no response and his face gave nothing away—so she could not draw any conclusion.

Silence stretched out. Until she couldn't stand it anymore. "Well . . . ?"

At least he didn't pretend to misread her prompting. "I have thought over everything that you have offered me."

And now her heart beat so loud, she could barely hear his deep voice.

"What say you?" she demanded in a hoarse voice.

"I agree to your terms."

It was what she had expected. And yet even still, she began to shake uncontrollably.

"In exchange for the use of you, I shall call off all of my efforts with regard to the throne."

At least there was solace to be had in that, except then she knew she had to live up to her end of the bargain.

"Worry not," he said gruffly. "It shall not be this eve."

Her relief came out in a very loud exhale—that made his face darken.

"Your reprieve is not indefinite." He took what he carried out from under his arm. "You will give me what I want sooner or later."

With a quick flap, he shook free what proved to be a blanket and laid it flat upon the ground.

Staring down at it, Layla didn't know what to do.

"Sit," he commanded. "And put this around you."

As she complied and was handed another wrap, she wondered what he was going to—

Xcor sat beside her and wrapped his arms around his knees. Staring ahead, his expression was inscrutable.

Taking his cue, she did the same. Even mirroring his pose.

At least she had saved Wrath. And provided her young was safe, she would continue to do whatever she had to for her King.

No matter what it cost.

SIXTY-SEVEN

The following evening, Beth lay back in her mated bed and held an extraordinary piece of cloth in her hands. "This was *made* by someone?"

"Yeah, the foreman's *shellan*."

Squinting, she tried to imagine how the incredibly fine and even weave could have been done by anything other than a machine. "It's totally amazing."

"I told them we'd use it for our son when he's born."

With a wince, she tried to ignore the spear of pure terror that shot through her. Wrath, who'd been panicked about the whole birthing thing before they'd conceived, seemed to be forgetting about that part for the moment. Her, on the other hand? More than making up the slack.

"Yes, of course," she murmured. "I love the color."

"I just had to do something for the two of them. He's a good guy. I didn't expect anything in return. . . ."

As Wrath walked out of the closet, he was dressed in his uniform, and she had to take a second to admire the view. His hair was swinging loose, almost to his tight ass. His magnificent arms were showing every muscle they had, thanks to the wifebeater. And those leather pants . . .

"So I guess she'd worked on that for a year—"

"Are you ever going to have sex with me again? Or do I have to wait five months?"

Stopped. Dead.

But at least she knew her husband was paying attention. "Come on, Wrath. Like I said yesterday, I'm pregnant, not broken."

"Ah . . ."

She stared at his hips, watching his arousal take shape, wanting that long, hard erection of his.

"Well, at least I know you want me," she murmured.

"Don't ever doubt that."

"So how 'bout now. Because you look . . . very fine." Her eyes did another up-and-down. "Did you get bigger all of a sudden? I mean, is that a baseball bat in your pocket or are you just glad to see me? Come over here and let me sample your goods, big guy."

He let his head fall back. "Beth . . ."

"Whaaaaaaat. What's the problem—look, we gotta talk about this. This abstinence thing is not good for you and me."

"My son's in there, okay? And it just—it doesn't seem . . . right."

Beth didn't mean to laugh, but she couldn't stop herself. "I'm sorry." She put her hands up as he frowned like he was pissed. "Honestly, I'm not making fun of you."

"Oh, really."

"Come here." She held her arms out. "And no, I'm not going to seduce you. Scout's honor."

He walked over in his bare feet, his black socks hanging from his deft hands. It seemed ludicrous to sit the King of the vampires down and give him a pep talk—especially when he was built the way he was. But she was going to go nuts if she couldn't have that sexual connection. And so was he.

"I'd like to be with you," she said, "but only if you're comfortable with it. It's not going to hurt the baby—you can call the doctor and ask her yourself. Or talk to Z—he and Bella were together while she was pregnant. She told me so. Talk to whoever you need to, but please rethink where you're at. Being with you has to have a place in all this."

As he cracked his knuckles like he was considering things, she stared at the tattoos that ran up his inner forearms.

She tried to imagine a son of hers with a set of those and reached out, turning one of his hands over so she could run her fingertips across the symbols.

"Will he get these, too?" So many names, she thought. "Or because I'm his mother, is he not allowed—"

"Fuck that shit. He can abso get them—and I'll have V do it. But only if he wants them."

"I'm surprised."

"About?"

"How much I want him to. I want him to be just like you."

There was a long pause and Wrath had to clear his throat. "That's just about the best compliment anyone's ever paid me."

"I don't know. . . . I just feel like you're the perfect man."

"Now you're making me blush."

She laughed in a rush. "It's true."

"I curse. Constantly. I have a short temper. I order people around—including you."

"You're also a great fighter. Great lover—although my son will never, ever have sex—nope, not going there, and if we have grandchildren, they will be immaculately conceived. Wait, where was I—oh, yeah, so you're also very loyal. You've never looked at another woman."

Wrath put his index finger up. "And that would be true even if I could see."

"And you're smart. Great-looking—"

He leaned in. "Are you trying to butter me up so I'll have sex with you?"

"Is it working?"

"Maybe." He kissed her lips softly. "Just give me a little time. Only yesterday you were rushed to the doc's because you were throwing up."

She ran her hand down his cheek and his hard jaw. "I'll wait for you. Always."

"I'm glad." He sat back. "So how's the stomach? You want food? The doctor said we need to put some weight on you, right?"

"Nothing appeals. But I will try some of those saltines and ginger ale in a bit. Layla swore by them."

"Good deal. When do you go back to the doc again?"

"Well, that was the other part of the appointment. iAm had to work a little magic on the poor woman—naturally, my bloodwork was nothing they'd ever seen before, although the pregnancy hormone numbers turned out to be right enough. She wanted me back in a month, unless anything changes. Doc Jane said she was going to try to get an ultrasound machine for the clinic—they have some portable equipment for ortho stuff, but there isn't one specifically for pregnancy that does three-D imaging. Unfortunately, that stuff's going to be hella expensive—"

"Whatever they need, they get."

Beth nodded and fell into silence.

After a moment, she picked up her husband's big hand and rubbed her thumb up and over that black diamond of his.

"What are you going to do tonight?" Even though she knew the answer.

"I'm going to hit my desk."

She smiled. "I love when you say that now."

"You know . . . me too." He shrugged. "It's funny, I felt really inadequate in that job. You know, when compared to my father, blah, blah, blah. But I was the one who didn't approve of me, not him. And I don't know, I've kinda let that bullshit go."

"I'm glad."

"Yeah, it's a good thing." He frowned. "I just wish there was some way to—I don't know, I liked helping that foreman. And there are more like him out there—there have to be. I don't know how to get to them, though. My father used to be all in with that shit, talking to people—real people, not that *glymera* bullshit—"

Beth sat up in a rush. "I have an idea. I know exactly what to do."

He glanced over at her—and the slow smile that hit his face was the sexiest thing about him. "You know what?" he said. "I love your mind. I totally do."

Wrath swung his leg out and around, bringing it in a full circle. And contact was made exactly where he wanted it—high up, and in the face.

Tohrture went with the impact, swinging in a circle, wielding his sword in concert so that the blade flashed right up close to Wrath's chest. Except it didn't quite make the distance. No blood was drawn, no clothing cut.

But Wrath knew better than to enjoy the small victory. Flipping backward off his feet, he somersaulted in midair and landed solidly, setting his fighting stance, raising both his daggers—

"Drop both blades," Ahgony barked.

Without missing a beat, he threw them away, confronting his opponent barehanded.

Tohrture came at him holding nothing back, neither speed nor strength, and Wrath became very still. At the last second, as the Brother's war cry was sounded out and echoed in the torchlit cave, Wrath flattened to the ground and caught the fighter at the ankles with an explosive lunge.

Tohrture fell forward—and as Wrath had learned, the last thing you wanted was a Brother with a sword in his hands on top of you. Scrambling himself out of the way, he jumped back to his feet. This was critical. Always back to your feet.

Tohrture was the same, upright a moment later, sword held high, eyes level. Both of them were breathing hard, and now, after how many fortnights into training, Wrath wasn't the only one with bruises.

The sword made a throaty whistle as Tohrture began to twirl it front to back on both sides of his massive upper body.

Wrath wasn't even aware of the assessments he was making—where the weight of his opponent was apportioned, where those eyes were looking, how the small muscle groups were contracting. But it was all part of his training, things that had once seemed foreign and were becoming second nature—

From out of nowhere, he was attacked from the back, an enormous weight taking him down to the floor. Before he could draw air, he was flipped over and held by the throat as a spiked glove made a fist.

Crack!

The impact stunned him senseless, his arms flopping to the packed-dirt floor.

"Call!" Ahgony yelled out.

Instantly, the weight was off him, Night jumping back out of the way, his face showing concern the now, not aggression.

Wrath forced himself to roll over and brace his upper body off the ground. Struggling to breathe through his bleeding mouth, he let the sanguinary rush clear out onto the dirt flooring with gravity's aid.

The pain had flared red-hot in his face, and as he waited for it to fade, he remembered back in the beginning of all this—how the sensation of injury had once flustered him, scared him, distracted him. No more of that. Now he knew the pattern of relief: how the numbness would inevitably come, how soon enough his mind would clear and he would be back on his feet.

Drop. Drop. Drop.

His blood was bright red as it formed a widening puddle under his face.

"That's enough for tonight," Ahgony announced. "Fine effort, sire."

Wrath pushed himself up upon his knees so his torso was upright. He knew better than to attempt to stand yet. His skull was too light for that. Wait . . . wait . . .

"Here, sire, allow me," Night said, offering his palm.

"Shall we call for the healer?" someone said.

Wrath closed his eyes and felt his body caving in. But then he pictured his beloved shellan, *lying on their bedding platform, her skin the color of clouds.*

Standing up on his own, he spit the remaining blood out of his mouth. "Again," he told the assembled. "We do it . . . again."

There was a beat of pause, the torchlight flickering over the other males in the secret training cave.

And then the Brothers bowed unto him in a way he had noticed they had recently started doing—not courtly, no, as it was not when greeting and leaving, as was aristocratic custom.

This was with respect.

"As you wish, my lord," Ahgony said. Before shouting once again, "Call!"

SIXTY-EIGHT

"Wither goest thou?"

Abalone paused in the process of pulling on his coat. Closing his eyes, he composed his expression before he turned around and faced his daughter.

"Nowhere, my darling." He smiled. "Are you proceeding about your lessons—"

"Why this letter?" She tapped the opened envelope in her palm. "Where are you going."

He thought of the proclamation that hung above the fireplace. The one that bore his father's name. And then worried over what she held in her delicate hand.

"I was summoned unto the King," he said tightly. "I must obey."

His daughter paled, crossing her arms around herself. "Are you coming back."

"I do not know." Walking over, he reached out and pulled her close. "That is up to his majesty . . ."

"Do not go!"

"You shall be provided for." Assuming the assets once given to his father by the current King's sire remained hers. But even then, he had hidden much in secret places. "Fedricah knows all and shall care for you." He stepped back. "I cannot shame our bloodline. Your future depends upon this."

If he did not make good on his cowardly action, he knew she could be next. And that he would not abide.

"Be well," he told her in a shaken voice.

"Father!" she screamed as he turned and headed to the door.

Nodding at the butler, he couldn't watch as the *doggen* stepped in and held his daughter back.

Outside, he could still hear his beloved young yelling his name and wailing. And it was a while before he was able to summon the concentration to dematerialize—although eventually, it happened.

Proceeding unto the address that had been given to him, he re-formed in front of . . .

Well, if this was where he was to be executed, it was an elegant enough place to lose one's life. The mansion was in the very best part of Caldwell, a Federal beauty with light glowing out of all of its windows and a cheerful lantern hanging in front of a beckoning entrance.

He could see figures moving inside. Large ones.

With fear tightening his throat and weakening his knees, he walked up to the front door. There was a button for chiming by the brass door handle, and as soon as he hit it, the broad portal was opened wide.

"Hi! You must be Abalone?"

All he could do was blink. The brunette in front of him was wearing loose clothes, her hair curling at the ends, her bright, blue eyes friendly and attentive.

"I'm Beth." She stuck her hand out. "I'm really happy you came."

He looked down at her hand and frowned. Was that . . . the Saturnine Ruby on her finger? Dearest Virgin Scribe, this was the—

Abalone fell to his knees before her, bowing his head nearly to the polished floor. "Your Highness, I am not worthy of—"

Two massive black boots came into his vision. "Hey, my man. Thanks for coming."

This had to be a dream.

Abalone lifted his eyes up, up, way up . . . the most tremendous male vampire he had e'er beheld. And indeed, with that long black hair and those wraparound sunglasses, he knew exactly who it was.

"Your Highness, I—"

"No offense, but could you get up? I'd like to shut this door. My wife is getting cold."

Scrambling off the floor, he realized he'd forgotten to remove his hat. With a jerky move, he ripped it from his head and put it in front of his body.

And then all he could do was look back and forth—and then behind, as two males so huge that they had to be Brothers, moved chairs across the foyer.

"Is this him?" the splendidly handsome one asked.

"Yup," the King replied, sweeping his arm to the right. "Let's go in here, Abe—"

"Are you going to kill me?" Abalone blurted without moving.

The queen's brows popped. "No. Good God, no—why would we do that?"

Wrath put a hand on Abalone's shoulder. "I need you alive, buddy. I need your help."

Convinced he was going to wake up at any moment, Abalone followed numbly into a lovely room that must have been for dining purposes, given its crystal chandelier and prominent fireplace. There was no long thin table, however, no row of chairs, no sideboard for serving. Instead, in front of the hearth, a pair of armchairs had been angled to face each other, and there were other comfortable sofas and seats set off to the side. A desk had been arranged in the near corner, at which there was a handsome blond male in a natty three-piece suit shuffling papers around.

"Have a seat, Abe," the King said as he himself took one of the armchairs.

Abalone obliged—'twas far better than a guillotine, after all.

The King smiled, his harsh, aristocratic face warming some. "I don't know how much you know about my father. But he used to do audiences with commoners. My wife read your e-mail the night of that Council meeting—and you mentioned you work with an organization of them?"

Abalone looked back and forth between the King and his mate, who had taken a seat on one of the other padded chairs—and was pouring herself a ginger ale.

The pair of them lied, he thought suddenly. They were very much together, their deference and devotion to one another obvious.

"Abe?"

"Ah . . ." Not at all what he had expected from this on any level—although he was o'erjoyed at the idea the *glymera* had been thwarted. "Yes, but it's . . . it's more of a loose affiliation, really. There are issues that need sorting, and—not that I was trying to step into your role—"

The King put up his hands. "Hey, I'm grateful. I just want to help."

Abalone swallowed past a dry throat.

"You want a soda?" someone asked.

It was a Brother with jet-black hair, a goatee, and icy silver eyes—as well as a set of tattoos on one of his temples.

"Please. Thank you," Abalone replied weakly.

Two seconds later, the fighter delivered a cold Coke in a glass. Which turned out to be the best thing Abalone had ever tasted.

Composing himself, he mumbled, "Forgive me. I feared that I had found your disfavor."

"Not at all." Wrath smiled again. "You're going to be very, very useful to me."

Abalone stared into the fizzing glass. "My father served yours."

"Yeah. Very well, I might add."

"Through your blood's generosity, mine has prospered." Abalone took another sip, his shaking hand making the ice tinkle. "May I say something about your father?"

The King seemed to stiffen. "Yeah."

Abalone looked up to the sunglasses. "The night he and your mother were killed, a part of my father died, too. He was never the same thereafter. I can remember our house being in mourning for a full seven years, the mirrors draped in black cloth, the incense burning, the threshold marked with a black jamb."

Wrath rubbed his face. "They were good people, my parents."

Abalone put the soda aside and shifted off the armchair, getting on his knees before his King. "I will serve you just as my father did, down to the bone and marrow."

Abalone was dimly aware that others had filed into the room and were looking at him. He cared naught. History had come full circle . . . and he was prepared to carry forward with pride.

Wrath nodded once. "I'm making you my chief cleric. Right here and now. Saxton," he barked out. "What do I need to do?"

A cultured voice answered smoothly, "You just did it all. I'll draw up the paperwork."

The King smiled and put out his palm. "You're the first member of my court. Boom!"

"I know where you went last night."

Xcor stopped in the middle of the alley—and did not turn around. "Do you."

Throe's voice was flat. "I followed you. I saw her."

Now he pivoted on his combat boot. Narrowing his eyes on his second in command, he said, "Be of care what you say next. And do not ever do that again."

Throe stomped his boot. "I talked to her. What the hell are you doing—"

Xcor moved so fast that it was less than a heartbeat later that the other male was up against a brick building, struggling to draw breath through the hold on his throat.

"That is not for you to question." Xcor made sure he did not take out a dagger—but it was tough. "What transpires within my private life is no concern of yours. And allow me to state this clearly—do not *ever* approach her again if you want to live to die of natural causes."

Throe's voice was strangled. "When we take the throne—"

"No. No more of that."

Throe's brows punched up into his forehead. "No?"

Xcor released the male and stalked around. "My ambitions have altered."

"Because of a *female*?"

Before he could stop himself, he palmed one of his guns and aimed it directly at Throe's head. "Watch your tone."

Throe slowly lifted his palms. "I only question the turnabout."

"It is not for her. It has nothing to do with her."

"What then?"

At least Xcor was able to speak the truth. "That male gave up a female he was bonded to in order to retain the throne. I have it on good authority of his actions. If he is willing to do that? He can have the fucking thing."

Throe exhaled slowly.

And didn't say anything more. The fighter just stared into Xcor's eyes.

"What," Xcor demanded.

"If you want me to say anything further, you're going to have to lower that weapon."

It was a while before his arm listened to the commands of his brain. "Speak."

"You are making a mistake. We were able to make great progress—and there will be another angle."

"Not from us there won't."

"Do not make this choice on an infatuation."

That was the problem, though. He feared he'd fallen far harder than that. "I am not."

Throe walked around, hands on hips, head shaking back and forth. "This is a mistake."

"Then form your own cabal and attempt to prevail. It won't work, but I will promise you a good burial if I'm still around to see to it."

"Your ambitions served mine own." Throe regarded him steadily. "I do not want to relinquish the future so blithely."

"I do not know this word 'blithely,' but I do not care of its definition. This is where we are. You may leave if you like—or you may remain and fight with us as we always have done."

"You are serious."

"The past does nae interest me as much as it used to. So go if you want. Take the others if you wish. But our life in the Old Country sufficed for many years, so I fail to see why the King's identity should be of such concern for you."

"That is because my blade had not been honed on the stone of the crown—"

"What shall you do the now? That 'tis all I care about."

"I fear I do not know you anymore."

"Once that would have been a blessing."

"No longer."

Xcor shrugged. " 'Tis on you."

Throe looked up as if searching for inspiration from the heavens. "Fine," he said tightly.

"Fine, what."

"Try as I might"—the male's face became grim—"my fealty is to you."

Xcor nodded once. "Your pledge is accepted."

But he wasn't fooling himself. Throe's ambition was between them now, and no exchange of words or even parchment was going to change that.

They were not done with this, not in the slightest. And mayhap it would take nights or weeks or years before the split came to the fore . . . but that which was due would follow them from this moment forward.

And he feared that the currency was female.

SIXTY-NINE

Sitting at his desk at the Iron Mask, Trez had had it with the whole club thing. The noise, the smell, the humans—hell, even the paperwork was getting to him.

Shoving away about a hundred and fifty receipts, he was ready to explode as he rubbed his eyes. And then, as he lowered his hands, his eyes readjusted to the fluorescent light, a pixilation fuzzing out his vision.

Another migraine?

He picked up a random piece of paper and checked to see if he could read the text.

No blind spot—yet.

Giving up on trying to get anything done, he sat back in his chair, crossed his arms over his chest, and glared across at the closed door. The distant thumping of the bass made him think he needed to get some earplugs.

What he really wanted to do was get the fuck out of here. And not just this club. Or the one that was going up in that warehouse across town. He wanted out of the whole cocksucking enterprise, from the booze sales to the prostitutes, from the money to the madness.

For shit's sake, every time he closed his eyes, he saw Selena's face. Heard her voice as she said she wanted to get dressed. Smelled the scent of her disappointment.

As he thought back over their "relationship," if you could call it that, he defined things in terms of pullouts. Failed conversations. Half-truths. Hidden secrets.

All his.

And it was weird. His brother had been yakking at him to clean up his act for how long? Telling him he had to get a grip and stop the sexing, warning him that time was getting tighter, hoping and praying that a turnaround would come—even when there had been no hope of that ever occurring. Meanwhile, he'd been balling whores in public places, getting migraines, and riding a huge wave of self-destruction—poppin' his collar and paying no attention.

In spite of all of iAm's best efforts, Selena had been the one to make him really see himself.

Seemed disrespectful to his brother to admit that, but there you go.

God . . . he prayed the queen had a daughter who was chosen. Maybe that way, at least part of this nightmare would be over—

The knock on his door was soft, and he caught a whiff of body spray even before the thing opened.

"Come in," he muttered.

The working girl who walked in was leggy enough to be a model, but her face wasn't quite there: nose a little too big, lips a little too small, eyes a little off center. And that was even after all the plastic surgery. Still, from a distance or in the dark, she was a goddamned knockout.

"I heard you want to see me?"

Her voice was up to phone-sex standards, deep and raspy, and her hair, as she pushed it over her shoulder, was naturally thick.

"Yeah." Good thing she didn't know him well enough to be aware he was half-dead. "I've got a special client who—"

"Is this the guy they've been talking about?" Her eyes widened in a rush. "Like, the sex god?"

"Yeah. I want to know if you can go to an apartment tomorrow and meet him." He and s'Ex had agreed to be on a once-a-week schedule, but when your blackmailer called you up and wanted a date? You went with it. "I'll introduce you and—"

"Oh, fuck, yeah. The other girls were talking about him—he's a stallion."

She started running her hands up and down her body, cupping her breasts and her sex.

"Tomorrow noon." He gave her his Commodore address. "I'll meet you there."

"Thanks, boss."

As her eyes narrowed, he had a feeling what was coming next. Sure enough, she said, "What can I do to show my gratitude?"

He shook his head. "Nada. Just come on time tomorrow."

"Are you sure?"

Staring across at her, part of him wanted to give in. It was so much easier that way—like falling backward into a swimming pool in July—splash, and you weren't hot anymore. The problem was, in that hypothetical, he didn't know how to swim. And every single time he let himself go just to get cooled down, he ended up underwater, unable to breathe.

The struggle to get to the surface simply wasn't worth the momentary relief.

"Thank you, baby girl. But I gotta pass."

The woman smiled. "You got a female there, boss?"

Trez opened his mouth to say no. "Yeah, I do."

Ha, he thought. Yeah, right.

After their happy little convo, Selena had not come down to the Brotherhood house again, and he sure as hell hadn't gone up to the great camp.

He could still remember exactly what she'd looked like as she'd stared at him. Eventually he'd gotten up and left her room—after the silence had stretched waaaaay out. Yeah, sure, he could have pressed her for some kind of closure or something. But the bottom line was, whether or not he had to go back to the s'Hisbe, he'd still contaminated himself.

What he had to offer her or anybody else wasn't worth the breath to apologize with.

"Ohhhh, that's big gossip," the whore said. "Can I tell the other girls."

"Yeah. Sure. Whatever."

She all but danced out of his office.

As the door reclosed, he went back to staring at it. On its flat plane, all he could see was Selena, sure as if she'd died and her ghost had come to haunt him.

For a moment, he was actually crazy enough to wish there was some unfinished business between them that he could use as an excuse to see her. Then again, the reality was, he could come at her in a thousand different ways . . . and all he had to offer was himself.

Not good enough yesterday. Today. Or tomorrow—

Deep inside of him, a shift began. At first he just recognized it as an errant thought. But then, as that thought resonated, he realized it went much, much further than that.

As he looked into the future, he saw nothing of substance in his life except his brother. iAm was it, the extent of any value he had in this world. And abruptly, the idea of turning himself over to the queen and her daughter, becoming a sexual slave imprisoned in the walls of the palace, used only for his cock and his ejaculate . . . didn't seem like anything very different from the way he had been living his life.

He'd been fucking things regularly and it hadn't mattered.

It wasn't like any of those women had meant a goddamn thing.

Why would the queen's daughter be any different?

Well, shit . . . the only thing that wouldn't be the same? His brother would be free to live his life.

Liberated.

And that would be the one truly honorable thing Trez could do.

Sitting back in his chair, he realized . . . not a bad way to end things.

Sola left her condo even though it was the middle of the night. She just couldn't stand the confines anymore, and the terrace wasn't doing it for her wanderlust.

Heading down the concrete steps, she went past the glowing pool to the pathway that cut through the bushes. On the far side, the beach stretched out a mile in both directions, the strong, warm wind hitting her in the face.

She picked right for no particular reason and put her hands in the pockets of her light jacket, feeling for her phone.

It had remained silent.

And as she looked out over the dark ocean and listened to the waves on the shore, she knew it wasn't going to ring.

Oh, sure, she'd get calls from her grandmother. Maybe the phone company. Maybe the repair shop for her new beater of a car.

But not from the 518 area code.

Stopping, she watched the moonlight that streamed from behind her touch the tops of the restless sea. Even though it made her queasy, she deliberately put herself back in the trunk of that car, feeling the cold and the vibration, the fear of knowing that whatever was coming next was going to hurt. A lot.

Holding all that tightly to her chest, she reminded herself yet again why the phone staying quiet was a good thing—

At first, she wasn't sure exactly what the tip-off was.

Not a smell, no; the wind was coming at her. And it wasn't the sight of anything—as she searched the landscape behind her, seeing scruffy bushes, another condo development, some kind of a lawn, a pool . . . there was nothing that moved. No sound, either.

"Assail?" she breathed into the wind.

She walked toward the bushes. Then jogged.

But when she got close to them? He wasn't there.

"Assail!" she called out. "I know you're here!"

Her voice didn't carry far because of the wind. Backtracking, she jogged closer to home. "Assail?"

Her heart was thumping in her chest, a treacherous hope vibrating through her until she felt like she was floating over the sand.

That optimism was like gasoline in a tank, however. The longer there was no reply, the lower the level got, until she slowed . . . stopped.

"Assail . . . ?"

She looked all around, praying to see him even though it was the last thing she needed.

But the black-haired man she was searching for did not answer her call . . . and eventually that sense that she was being watched went away.

As if the wind had taken it.

As if it had never existed.

On the way back to her place, she let the tears fall one by one without bothering to wipe them off. It was dark out. There was no one to see them.

And nothing to hide from.

She was . . . on her own.

SEVENTY

And so it went, the weeks and months passing, seasons changing from the bitter cold of winter to the wet, bracing winds of spring to the sweet-scented nights that promised an early summer.

By May, Wrath was used to measuring the time not by the calendar, or the up-and-down of the shutters of the mansion, or the meals at his own home.

It was by the nights that he spent hearing the stories of his people.

The real ones. The ones about life and death. And matings and divorces. And sicknesses and health. It was funny: As important as the vampire mating ceremony was to him, the human one he'd gone through with Beth got the metronome of existence better.

His audiences with the commoners were all set up thanks to quiet, steady Abe, a.k.a. Abalone, but Wrath's responses to things were his own. And there was so much to do, mediating disagreements in families, blessing the sons and daughters who were born, sharing grief with those who had suffered losses and joy with those who had had good fortune.

As always, Beth was by his side, sitting with Abe during the audiences, checking the paperwork with Saxton when it was required . . . growing bigger in the belly every moment.

"We are here, my lord," Fritz said from the front of the Mercedes. "At Master Darius's."

"Thanks, my man."

As he and George got out of the back, he paused and leaned in. "Hey, can you go and get more of those strawberries? She's got a craving for carrots again, too. And pickles. You better grab two of those jars with those tart motherfuckers."

"I shall be back right away, my lord! And I think I will get some of the frozen yogurt for her? She takes it with the chocolate chips?"

"Oh, shit. Yeah. And don't forget the beets. Or the beef."

"I shan't."

"Hurry, okay? iAm's bringing her in from Pottery Barn."

Wrath shut the door. "Let's do it," he said to George.

And the dog knew right where to go, leading him to the entrance—which Wrath opened with his mind. "Hi, honey, I'm home!" he hollered.

"Did you bring flowers?" Lassiter shouted back.

"Not for you."

"Damn it. Well, I'm on deck tonight with Tohr, so can we get moving? There's a full list of appointments, but I want to get back for *Hell's Kitchen*."

"Don't you DVR that shit?" Wrath groused as he and George went into the old dining room.

"Yeah, but I have poor impulse control. It was on at nine, okay? And I hate waiting. I put George's fresh water down by your chair, b.t.dub."

"At least you're a dog lover. That's the only thing that saves you."

"Ha! I have wings and a halo, you cranky son of a bitch. I'm already perma-saved."

"Just our luck."

"Hey, my brother," V said as he came through the archway and lit a hand-rolled. "Where's your girl?"

Lassiter cut in, "She's got to be coming back soon, right?"

Wrath had to smile as he took his seat. About the only time that annoying SOB got serious was when it came to Beth—and he had to admit, that was kinda endearing.

"She back yet?" Rhage asked as he walked into the room.

"How long can it take to order baby furniture?" Butch demanded while making his appearance.

"Weeks," Z answered. "You have no idea."

And so it went, everyone arriving with the same question, from Blay and Qhuinn to Phury and Rehvenge.

The only one who didn't ask it out loud was John—but he didn't have to. Beth's brother had been a quiet, worried presence since they'd made the announcement of the surprise pregnancy. And Wrath loved the guy for it. John never got in the way, but he was always there, listening to Beth, being supportive, talking with her, bringing her movies.

Funny, the gravity with which he treated the situation made Wrath think of Darius.

God, he wished the brother had survived to see what was coming in . . . was it only four weeks?

Jesus . . .

Every time Wrath thought about the impending *event*, he found he couldn't breathe. But he forced himself to remember all the checkups iAm had been taking his wife to. Beth was having a perfect pregnancy. She was healthy, happy, eating and drinking, and feeding well—not that Dr. Sam, the human physician she went to, knew about that. And the heart rate was great. And his son was great.

It was almost too easy.

Four weeks to go—

"*Leelan*," Wrath barked as he exploded up from his chair.

There were all kinds of deep-voiced greetings, but his brothers got out of the way so that she had a clear shot into his arms. And as he lifted her up, he was careful to put no pressure on her belly.

"How are you?" he whispered in her ear, knowing that one of these days, she was going to answer that she was having contractions.

"Fine and dandy. Oh, my God, I got the best stuff! I had to go blue—I mean, whatever, we're having a boy. The crib and dressing table are perfect—right, iAm?"

The Shadow answered, "Perfect."

No doubt the poor bastard had no interest in the shit at all, but that didn't matter. He was another one who had stuck by Beth and been her protector in the human world—and Wrath knew the why, of course. It was iAm's way of paying the household back for letting him and his it's-complicated brother stay at the mansion after their pad at the Commodore had been compromised. Plus, it was pretty obvi that he liked Beth in a nonromantic kind of way.

"Right? I know, right?" Beth hugged Wrath's neck so hard he couldn't swallow. "I'm so excited! I want to meet him now!"

"Is this nesting?" Wrath asked in the direction of where he'd heard Z's voice last.

"Yeah. And wait for it. You still have Diaper Genies and bottles to get through."

"We're going Born Free," Beth informed him, like he knew what that meant. "In case my milk doesn't come in."

Wrath just sat down in the chair and arranged her on his lap, content to ease back and let her enjoy making her report. And the brothers and the fighters? They rallied right around, asking questions like big brothers would.

Any one of them would have laid down his life for her or that young in her womb.

It was enough to make a male have to blink a little faster.

As Wrath held his female, he found his hand making a circle on her rock-hard belly and his brain reverted back to just before sunset. Once he'd gotten over his hang-up about sex, things had gone back to the way they'd been right after they'd met.

Hormonal surges being what they were and all.

This late in the game, they had to do it with her on top, and that was more than fine with him. He loved palming her now-heavy breasts with his hands and feeling her core take him in a new way because of the way her body had changed shape.

Matter of fact, maybe there was time for a quickie before—

"Hey, Abes."

"Yo, Ab."

"Whassup, Albacore?"

Naturally, Lassiter was the one who refused to get that name right.

As Abalone stuttered through his greetings, you had to smile. The guy still couldn't quite get used to the brothers, but they were used to him. And so was Wrath.

"My lord, my lady, good evening."

"Abalone, how's your daughter," Beth said.

"Yeah, Abe, how'd that date go last night?"

Pin-drop time. The Brotherhood had adopted the male and his only young, and woe was the young Turk who took the girl out and didn't treat her right.

"Well, I don't believe it was a love match. But she was returned a full thirty minutes before curfew."

"Good." Wrath nodded. "That means he can keep his legs. So what have we got on deck for us tonight?"

"It's a full roster," the aristocrat reported. "The first couple we'll see have just had a grandyoung, and they want to ask you if they may bring the mother in with the wee one. Their daughter is not married to the father, however, and they are concerned it will offend you."

"Absolutely not."

Abalone's tone remained calm. "But it's important to them that they ask permission and acknowledge this in person with you."

"Fine. Cool. When do I get to meet the kid?"

Abalone laughed. "Tomorrow evening?"

"I'll be here. And who's after that?"

"A cousin of mine, actually. He's seeking permission to . . ."

As the gentlemale went on and on, detailing the family interrelationships, Wrath was once again in awe. Abe was so low-key and respectful, never once stepping out of place, and yet every single fucking night he provided this wellspring of knowledge and compassion.

It was damn impressive.

And as Wrath sat back and listened to all the preamble, he was struck by how he could do this for fucking ever. He really could.

Especially with his *shellan* front and center, his dog next to him, and his brothers surrounding them all.

With a feeling of great dread, Anha put her hand upon her swelling belly, and watched her mate gird himself for the night ahead.

In the flickering light from the hearth and the candles, everything was different about him. She had noticed the change coming over the last number of months, but on this eve, all that had been subtle appeared to have coalesced at once, the culmination having arrived.

His body was different now, harder, more defined. Larger.

And his expression was not the same. At least, not when this new mood of his settled upon his shoulders.

As if sensing her regard, he looked over at her.

"How long will you be gone?" she asked. "And do not lie. I know for what purpose you are leaving."

He turned away from her, to the oak table on which clothing she had never seen before had materialized, brought in by the Brotherhood. Everything was black.

"I shall return at dawn."

His voice was lower than normal, colder than normal. And then she realized that he was putting on a leather strapping o'er his chest. Just as the Brothers wore.

"You are going to fight?" she whispered through a closed throat.

When he finally answered her, it was after he'd put two black daggers, handle down, over his heart. "I shall return at dawn."

"You're going to kill them, aren't you."

"Do you want me to answer that?"

"Yes."

Wrath, her mate, her love, the father of her nascent young, approached her where she sat afore her vanity mirror. When he got down upon his knees, it was a relief, because he was almost familiar that way. Especially as he looked into her eyes.

"I shall do what needs doing," he said.

She put her hands on his face, tracing the features, thinking back to all the dawns he'd come home bloodied and limping, swollen and stiff. But lately he had kept to his schedule with the males, and not returned injured.

So she should have known it was time.

"Be safe?" she implored. "We need you."

"I will come back unto you. Always."

At that, he kissed her hard, and then he left through the chamber door. Before it closed behind him, she saw that the Brothers had lined up on either side of the stone corridor, each with a torch.

They bowed to her hellren *as he walked out.*

Alone . . .

Dropping her head into her hands, she knew that all she could do . . . was pray.

SEVENTY-ONE

As Wrath saw the first of his appointments, Beth snuck out into the kitchen and snagged a bowl of fresh strawberries that Fritz had bought for her at the local Hannaford.

Man, after the past number of months, she had gotten used to the spoiling—a benefit Bella had told her to enjoy, but which had taken some time to become chill with: Everyone had been, and was being, so kind, the Brothers and their mates, the staff, John Matthew, the Shadows. It was incredible.

Just like the pregnancy.

By some miracle, she was trending exactly like a normal human pregnancy, well into her eighth month and feeling great. She had plenty of stamina, no swollen ankles, no stretch marks, and a baby that did laps under her rib cage every time she ate. Especially if there was sugar involved.

It was nothing that she had prepared herself for.

Disasters? Shit yeah, she'd been all about them. After that initial shock at the doctor's, she'd naturally gone right to the Internet and terrified herself stupid with all the different things that could go wrong. The one saving grace had been that, by that point, she'd already gotten herself out of that hairy first trimester when most miscarriages happened—although unfortunately, that needing that had kicked in was a wild card that she hadn't been able to fully relax about for another month.

But, yeah, the worry had mostly passed now that she was pulling into the final four-week lap. And sure, labor was going to be a bitch—but no, she wasn't going to try to white-knuckle it with a no-drug birth plan. And anytime she got a little rattly? She just reminded herself that millions upon millions of women and females had done this all before her.

What her birth plan *did* entail was iAm and Trez both being available at the drop of a hat for the next four weeks. Dr. Sam had promised to make herself free no matter the hour, day or night—a little commitment she suspected iAm had instilled with a mental sleight of hand.

He had worked a number of those, discreetly, of course.

And thus they'd been successful in keeping the race's identity on the DL.

She was hoping that, like a lot of women, she went into labor at night, so Wrath could be a part of at least some of it. But they'd both agreed—even though it was going to kill him, her safety and the safety of the baby came first.

And that meant she was going to have to go to Dr. Sam—

"Are the berries to your liking, madam?" Fritz asked.

Looking across her father's kitchen, she nodded. "They're perfect."

As the butler beamed like he'd won the lottery, she finished what was in the bowl and allowed him to take the thing from her.

Heading back out into the dining room, she was careful to make no noise as she went across to her padded seat.

Wrath was sitting in the armchair he favored, the one on the left, the one that Saxton's desk was behind. Across from him, in the matching chair, a male was sitting with his hands clasped hard on his knees, his shoulders hunched, his face gray. The clothes he was wearing were not fancy, just the kind of stuff you could get at Target, and his watch was nothing like a Rolex, just a matte black rubber–strapped one.

Wrath leaned forward and offered his palm. "What happened?"

The male rocked back and forth in the chair. "She . . ." All at once he looked at Beth, his face blanching even further.

As she stiffened, she put her hand over her belly.

Oh . . . hell.

"Talk to me," Wrath said in a low voice.

"She . . ." At this point, the male began to whisper so softly that nothing carried.

But it was clear Wrath understood every word. And as she watched her husband's hands clench, those forearms bunching up, she knew what it was about.

Deaths. From childbearing.

She had heard for so long about how the vampire race suffered on the birthing bed, as they called it, but she'd had no true appreciation for their losses before. Doing this with the commoners now? She was routinely horrified.

So many dead. Mothers and children.

Just as her own mom had died.

It was a tragedy that medical science couldn't seem to make much of a dent in. Say what you would about Havers: He had a clinic outfitted with all kinds of modern technology, and yet bad things happened. Seemingly all the time.

Wrath reached out his great arms and put his hands on the male's shoulders. He spoke softly as well, but whatever he was saying, the husband who had lost everything was nodding.

They stayed like that for a very long time.

When the meeting was finally over, the two of them stood up and embraced, the civilian so much smaller than her husband.

Before the male left, he kissed Wrath's ring.

Abalone escorted the commoner out, talking quietly with him, as Wrath slowly lowered himself back down. His brows were tight, his mouth a grim line.

As she stood up, she winced and had to stretch her back. Going over, she wanted to pull him tightly to her, but figured a reminder of the pregnancy was probably not what he needed at the moment.

"I can't help him," Wrath said in a voice that cracked. "I can't . . . help where he's at."

"Sometimes knowing you're not alone is enough."

"I'm not so sure about that."

But he took her hands and brought them to his lips, kissing her knuckles one by one. And as a sudden wave of exhaustion hit her, he seemed to recognize it.

"How about you head home?" he said.

"How did you know?"

"You just yawned."

"Did I?"

"Have Fritz take you."

As she arched her back, she wanted to stay, but had to be realistic. "Maybe walking around the mall for all that time was a little much."

"Go on, take a rest. I'll be home in a couple of hours and I'll put some shitty television on for us, 'kay?"

"That sounds like heaven."

"Good." He kissed her once. And then seemed to have to do it again. "I love you."

"I love you, too."

"Fritz!" her husband called out. "Car!"

She made sure to pet George a couple of times and tell him where she was going before she left. And then she was out into the night, getting into the rear of the Mercedes, heading for the mansion.

Letting her head fall back against the seat, she could feel herself already begin to doze off. "I'm afraid I'm not very good company," she said to Fritz.

"Just rest, madam."

"Good idea, Fritz."

As Beth departed, Wrath leaned back in the armchair, and was not at ease in the slightest.

. . . she died in front of me . . .

. . . held my lifeless son in my hands . . .

"My lord?"

"I'm sorry, what?" He shook himself. "What?"

Abalone cleared his throat. "Would you like a break, sire?"

"Yeah. Just gimme a minute." Taking George's halter, he said, "Kitchen."

Walking through the flap door with his dog, he was relieved that Fritz had already left and that the brothers stayed back.

Shit, the minute he'd smelled the pain and sorrow of that civilian, he knew that all had been lost for the male—and not in a material sense. People didn't get into that kind of agony over things. And as usual Abalone knew the full story, but Wrath preferred to let the people tell him the details in person; he wanted to hear things directly from them.

Childbirth had not actually claimed the female's life this time.

A car accident.

Wrath had expected it to be the former, but that was not the way destiny had played out. Nope, the female had lived through the birth and so had the child. They'd been killed by a drunk driver on the way home from Havers's clinic.

The casual cruelty of fate was sometimes a ballbuster on an epic scale.

Unbelievable.

Going over to the table, he pulled out a chair and sat down. He was pretty sure he was facing the windows—not that he could see out of them.

So many stories he'd heard, but this one . . . Jesus Christ, it got to him.

He didn't know how long he sat there, but eventually V put his head in. "You okay?"

"Nope."

"You want to reschedule, true?"

"Yeah."

"All right."

"V."

"Yeah?"

"Do you remember that vision you told me about. Where I was looking up at the face in the sky and the future was in my hands?"

"Yeah."

"What . . ."

Abruptly, he relived that civilian's anguish. "Nah, never mind. I don't want to know."

Sometimes, information wasn't a good thing. If that commoner could have seen the future, it wouldn't have changed the outcome. He would have just spent the remaining time with his female and his young terrified of what was coming.

"I'll clear the decks," the brother said after a moment.

The flap door closed with a *thump-bump*.

For no apparent reason, he thought of his father and his mother, and wondered what the night of his birth had been like. They'd never spoken of it, but he'd never asked, either. There had always been something else going on—plus, he'd been too young to care about that stuff.

As he tried to picture his own child's arrival, he couldn't imagine the stream of events. It was a hypothetical too emotionally charged to resonate.

But there was one thing that was abruptly crystal fucking clear.

He just wasn't sure how to get around it.

As he stewed on things, memories from the last couple of months filtered into him. Stories and problems, gifts given and received. After all the struggle he'd brought to doing the King's job before, it had been such a revelation to actually love what he was doing.

He hadn't even missed the fighting.

Hell, there had been too many other challenges to confront and overcome: Battles, after all, weren't always waged in the field, and sometimes enemies weren't armed with conventional weapons. Sometimes they were even ourselves.

Finally, he knew exactly why his father had gotten so much out of being on the throne. He totally fucking got it.

And it was funny: The one thing that so many of the people had in common was love for their family. Their mates, their parents, their children; all that seemed to come first.

Always.

Family first.

The next generation . . . first.

He thought back to the night his parents had been slaughtered. The one thing they had done before that door had been broken down? Hide him. Keep him safe. Preserve him—and it hadn't been about ensuring the future of the throne. That was not at all what they'd said as they'd locked him in that crawl space.

I love you.

That had been the only message that had mattered when their time had run out.

Not, *Be a good King*. Not, *Follow in my footsteps*. Not, *Make me proud or else. . . .*

I love you.

It was the tie that bound, even across the divides of death and time.

As he imagined his son coming into the world, he was pretty damn sure one of the first things he was going to say was, *I love you.*

"Wrath?"

He jumped and turned toward the sound of Saxton's voice. "Yeah? Sorry, just a little in my head."

"I'm finished with all my paperwork from last night and tonight."

Wrath turned back to the windows he could not see. "You worked fast."

"Actually, it's three in the morning. You've been sitting there for about five hours."

"Oh."

And yet he didn't move.

"Most of the Brothers left hours ago. Fritz is still here. He's upstairs cleaning."

"Oh."

"If you don't need anything—"

"There is something," he heard himself say.

"Of course. How can I help?"

"I need to do something for my son."

"A bequest?"

As Wrath started working the whole thing through in his head, he was a little freaked out. God, you'd think that great corners in life should come with a warning sign at the side of the proverbial road, a little yellow number that announced which direction you were going to go in, and maybe offered a "reduce speed" kind of advice.

Then again, he and his *shellan* had been pregnant months before her needing.

So life did its own thing, didn't it.

"Yeah. Kinda."

SEVENTY-TWO

It was as he had promised.

Wrath was good to the word he had given his shellan. *He was, in fact, back at dawn.*

As he rode toward home upon his horse, he was exhausted to the point of agony, unable to hold himself up for more than a walking gait. But then again, there was another reason for his slow progress.

Though he had gone out on his own, he did not return as such.

There were six dead bodies being dragged over the ground behind him and his steed, and two more to the rear of his saddle. The former he had tied with ropes at the ankles; the latter were secured to the horse with hooks and netting.

And the others he'd killed had not had enough left of their remains to take with him.

He could smell nothing but the blood he'd shed.

He heard nothing but the muffled rush of the bodies over the dirt of the road.

He knew nothing except that he had murdered each one of them by hand.

The wooded glen he proceeded through was the last distance to be crossed before the castle . . . and indeed, as he came out into a clearing, there it was, rising ugly out of the earth.

He did not relish what he had done. Unlike a barn cat who enjoyed his duty, the mice he had slain had not been a source of sly happiness for him.

But as he thought of his unborn young, he knew that he had made the world a safer place for his son or daughter. And as he considered his beloved mate, as well as the death of his own father, he was well aware that that which had been uncharacteristic to his nature had been very necessary indeed.

The drawbridge o'er the moat landed in a rush, providing him entrance as if he had been waited for.

And he had been.

Anha ran out onto the planks, the fading moonlight catching her dark hair and her red robes.

He had known her for so little time when judged by the passage of seasons. But through the course of events, he believed they had been together for lifetimes.

The Brotherhood was with her.

Pulling up on the reins, he knew she saw everything as her hands went to her mouth and Tohrture had to take her elbow to keep her upright.

He wished she had not come. But there was no going back now on any of it.

Dismounting, even though he was not even upon the bridge, he left his horse where it was and crossed onto the thick planks.

He thought perhaps she might run from him, but, no, it was the opposite.

"Are you well enough?" she said as she threw herself at him.

His arms were weak as they went around her. "Aye."

"You lie."

He dropped his head into her sweet-smelling hair. "Aye."

At least with her, he did not have to pretend. The truth was, he as yet feared for the future. He may have taken his revenge out on these traitors, but there would be more.

Kings were targets for the ambitions of others.

That was reality.

Closing his eyes, he wished there was a way out of the legacy—and he worried for his future son, if he had one. Daughters had a chance. Sons were cursed.

But he could not change who he was born to be. He just prayed for the courage that had served him this night to come again when it was needed most.

At least now he had proved to himself and his beloved that he was not just a leader in peacetime. In war, he could wield the sword if he had to.

"I love you," he said.

As his mate shuddered against him, he knew she was going to shudder again on the morrow evening—when she saw what he was going to do to the heads of those dead bodies.

Messages had to be sent in order to be received.

"Let us go unto our chamber," he said, tucking her into his chest.

As he nodded to the Brothers, he knew they would take care of his horse—and his prey. There would be time for the beheadings later. Now? He just wanted some sanity amid the madness.

Heading into their castle, she was, as always, his only tether.

"If we have a son," he murmured.

"Yes?" She looked up at him. "What for him?"

Wrath glanced down into the face that stared upon him, the beautiful face that defined his hours as well as his years. "I hope he finds someone like you."

"In truth?" she whispered.

"Yes. I pray for him to be half as lucky as I."

As Anha squeezed around his waist, her voice grew rough. "And for a daughter . . . a male half as good as her father."

Wrath kissed the top of her head and continued them onward, through the great hall and up to their chamber, the Brotherhood with them, but keeping a discreet distance.

Yes, he thought, to survive, one must not be alone.

And one must have a partner of worth.

Possess that? And you were richer than any King and queen who e'er roamed the earth.

SEVENTY-THREE

Wrath saw his mother for the first time in three hundred and thirty years that following day.

On some level, he knew it had to be a dream. He had been blind for too long to be seduced into thinking that reality had suddenly changed.

Plus, hello, she'd been dead for centuries.

And yet, as she came to him out of the darkness, she was as alive as he could have wished her to be, moving with ease, wearing a red velvet gown in the old style.

"*Mahmen?*" he said with wonder.

As he lifted his head, he realized with a shock that it was from his pillow. And shit, this was his room—he could tell by the subtle twinkling of the walls.

His first instinct was to flip over and find—

Beth was right beside him, lying safe and sound under the blankets, her face turned toward him, her dark hair all over the pillow that matched his own. And he could tell by the shape of her belly that yes, she was still pregnant—

Jesus Christ, he could *see* her.

"Beth," he said roughly, "Beth! I see you, *leelan*, wake upIseeyou-Iseeyou—"

"Wrath."

At the sound of his *mahmen*'s voice, he wrenched back around. She was right beside the bed now, her arms crossed, her hands tucked into the voluminous sleeves of that dress.

"Mahmen?"

"I do not know if you shall recall this, but you came to me once."

God, her voice was so gentle, just as he'd remembered—and he almost shut his eyes just so he could memorize the sound. Except no, he wasn't going to get cheated out of one nanosecond of sight.

Wait, what had she said? "I did?"

"I was dying. And you came to me from out of the mist of the Fade. And you told me to follow you home. You made me stop and return with you."

"I don't remember—"

"It is a debt I have owed you for a very long time." Her smile was peaceful as the Mona Lisa's. "And I shall repay it the now. Because I love you so very, very much—"

"Repay? What are you talking about?"

"Wake up, Wrath. Wake up right now." Abruptly, that voice changed, becoming urgent. "Call the healer—you must call the healer if you wish to save her life."

"Save her—Beth's life?"

"Wake up, Wrath. Right away, call the healer."

"What are you—"

"*Wrath, wake up*."

In a sudden rush, like he'd been catapulted out of REM sleep, Wrath shot upright. "Beth!" he screamed.

"What-what-what-what—"

As he twisted around to his wife, he cursed at the blackness all around him. Goddamn fucking dream, teasing him with what he didn't have.

"What?" Beth cried.

"Shit, sorry, I'm sorry." He reached out and soothed her, soothed himself. "Sorry, fucked-up dream."

"Oh, jeez, you scared me." She laughed and he heard her hit the pillow as if she'd let herself collapse. "Good thing we sleep with the bathroom light on."

Frowning, he turned to the side of the bed where his mother had stood and . . . "No, she wasn't really here."

"Who?"

"Sorry." Cracking his neck, he threw his leg over the side of the bed. "I'll be right back."

He gave things a good stretch, and as his spine let out a *snap, crackle, pop,* he thought fondly of the conversation he'd had with Payne as soon as he'd gotten home. They were going to start sparring again—and not because she was a female.

It was because she was a helluva good fighter and he wanted to get back in the game now.

In the bathroom, he petted George, who was curled up on the Orvis dog bed Butch had given him for Christmas—and then took a piss and had a face wash.

When he got back in bed, he intended to return to lights-out land. Except as he lay flat, he frowned. "Ah, listen . . . are you feeling okay?"

His Beth yawned. "Yeah, absolutely. But I'm glad I headed back here when I did—the sleep helped. And lying down feels better—I've got a stiff back from that mall crawl still."

Trying to sound causal, he asked, "When's your next appointment with the doctor?"

"Not till Friday. We're going weekly now. Why do you ask?"

"No reason."

As he fell silent, she curled in against him and let out a sigh like she was re-settling for the duration. He lasted about a minute and a half.

"What do you think about calling the doctor?"

"Calling as in—wait, you mean right now?"

"Well, yeah."

He could feel her recoil. "But why?"

Yeah, like he could tell her anything along the lines of, *My dead mom said so*. "I dunno. Just, maybe she could give you a checkup or something."

"Wrath, that's not appropriate. Especially considering there's nothing wrong." He felt her playing with his hair. "Is this about that civilian? Who lost his wife and baby?"

"It wasn't during childbirth."

"Oh. I thought that—"

"Maybe we could just call her."

"There's no reason to."

"What's her number?" He reached for his phone. "I'm calling her."

"Wrath, have you lost your mind?"

Fuck it, he'd just do 411.

Beth kept talking at him as he waited for the operator to come on. "Yeah, hi, in Caldwell, New York. The number of Dr. Sam—what's her last name?"

"You've lost your mind."

"I'm going to pay for the visit—no, not you, Operator." As the last name came back to him, he said it and spelled it twice. "Yeah, connect me to the office, thanks."

"Wrath, this is—"

Just as the call went through, Beth went quiet. "Beth?" he asked with a frown.

"Sorry," she said. "My back let out a twinge. You know what? I'm wearing running shoes next time I go walking like that. Now will you hang up and—"

"Yeah, hi, this is a medical emergency. I need Dr. Sam to come to our home, my wife's a patient of hers . . . thirty-six weeks . . . Symptoms? My wife's pregnant, how much time have you got?"

"Wrath?" Beth said in a small voice.

"What do you mean, you can't—"

"Wrath."

And that was when he shut up . . . and knew his mother had been right. Cranking his head toward his wife, he said with dread, "What?"

"I'm bleeding."

The definition of terror changed when things weren't just about you. And nothing was less about yourself than when you were thirty-six weeks pregnant, you felt a welling between your legs . . . and it was not your water breaking.

At first, Beth thought she'd lost control of her bladder, but as she moved the blankets aside and shifted positions, she saw something on the sheets.

She'd never seen blood so bright before.

And shit, her lower back was suddenly *killing* her.

"What's going on?" Wrath demanded.

"I'm bleeding," she repeated.

Things happened so fast at that point. It was almost like being in the back of a speeding car, everything whirring by too quick to catch: Wrath shouting into the phone, another call being made, Doc Jane and V arriving at a dead run. And then faster still, moving, moving, moving, everyone around her, while she felt curiously still and muffled.

When she was transferred onto the gurney, she looked over at where she'd been on the bed and shuddered at the neon stain. It was huge, like someone had poured out a gallon of paint underneath her.

"Is the baby going to be okay?" she mumbled, some kind of shock taking over everything. "Is he—is Wrath going to be all right?"

People offered her compassion, but no real answers.

But Wrath, the big one, was right by her side, holding her hand, orienting himself with the help of the side of the gurney.

John appeared as they hit the second-story landing. He was wearing only boxers, his hair all messed up, his eyes alert. He took her other palm.

She didn't remember much about the rush, rush, rush down into the tunnel—except for the fact that the pain was getting severe. Oh, and the ceiling lights were whipping by as she lay back, the rhythmic pulsing like she was in a *Star Wars* movie about to go into warp speed.

Why couldn't she hear anything?

As she looked at the people around her, their mouths were all going, their eyes meeting urgently over her.

"Is little Wrath going to be all right?" Even her own voice was on a fader, the volume turned way down. She tried to make it louder. "Is he going to be all right?"

And then they were dusting past the usual entrance into the training center, and going farther down—to an emergency door that had been created just for her, just for this situation.

Except this was not her birth plan. She was supposed to go into the human world, where there were people to take care of her and little Wrath, see to any problems he might have, be there for her and iAm if it was daylight, and big Wrath and John if it was night.

Little Wrath, she thought.

Guessed she'd just named their son.

As she arrived in the clinic, she just kept thinking she was not supposed to be here. Especially as she looked up at that massive operating chandelier in the main OR.

For some reason, she thought of all the times she had been down here, supporting a Brother injured in the field, or going to a checkup with Layla, or—

Doc Jane put her face in the way. Her lips moved slowly.

". . . eth? Can you hear me, Beth?"

Ah, good, someone had cranked up the volume on the world.

But her response didn't register. She couldn't hear her own voice.

"Okay, good." Doc Jane enunciated everything clearly. "I want to do an ultrasound to rule out placenta previa—which is a complication where the placenta ends up in the lower part of the uterus. But I'm worried you have an abruption."

"What . . . that?" Beth mumbled.

"Are you having pain?"

"Lower back."

Doc Jane nodded and put her hands on Beth's belly. "If I press—"

Beth moaned. "Just make sure Wrath is okay."

They wheeled the ultrasound machine over and her nightgown was cut away. As that gel was squirted onto her stomach and the lights dimmed, she didn't look at the monitor. She stared at her husband's face.

That wonderful, masculine face was utterly terrified.

He wasn't wearing his son glasses—sunglasses, rather. And his pale green, unfocused eyes were roaming around the room as if he were desperate to see something, anything.

"How did you know?" she whispered. "That I was in trouble . . ."

His eyes snapped in her direction. "My mother told me. In a dream."

For some reason, that made her cry, that image of her husband growing wavy as the out-of-control nature of life came home to roost in the worst possible way: She cared about nothing except the baby, but there was not a single thing she could do to affect any outcome. Her body and the young were rolling those dice.

Her mind, her will, her soul? All her dreams and desires, hopes and follies?

Not even at the table.

Doc Jane's face came back. ". . . eth? Beth? Are you with me?"

As she lifted her hand to get some hair out of her face, she realized they'd put a blood pressure cuff on her and run an IV. And that was not hair in the way; it was tears.

"Beth, the ultrasound is not showing me what I was hoping to see. The baby's heart rate is slowing and you're still bleeding heavily. We need to get him out, okay? I'm very sure you have an abruption and you're in danger as well as him. Okay?"

All she could do was look at Wrath. "What do we do?"

In a voice that was so cracked it was barely understandable, he said, "Let her operate with Manny, okay?"

"All right."

Doc Jane came back in view. "We're going to have to put you asleep—I don't want to do an epidural because we don't have the time."

"All right."

"I love you," she said to Wrath. "Oh, God . . . the baby . . ."

SEVENTY-FOUR

All Wrath had to go on was the smells in the room. Antiseptic in the air. Blood—that terrified him. Fear—from his Beth and the others all around him. Calm, cold reasoning on the parts of Doc Jane, Manny, and Ehlena.

Hopefully, that last one was going to be a lifesaver.

Abruptly, a new fragrance entered the mix. Astringent.

Then there was a squeak beside him, as if someone had pulled up a chair. After which a broad hand shoved him down so he was sitting, and took his own in a grip so hard the bones nearly crushed.

John Matthew.

"Hey, man," he said, aware that time had ground to a halt. "Hey . . . man."

In the end, all Wrath could do was squeeze her brother's palm back—and so the two of them stayed side by side together, frozen as medical terms were traded back and forth and there were metal clanging sounds and hisses and suction noises.

Doc Jane's voice was so even. Manny's replies were the same.

They were like the inverse of the situation: As things got scarier, they became more focused and in control.

"Okay, I've got him—"

"Wait, is it happening already?" Wrath demanded.

The ascending whistle next to him was the only reply he got.

And then . . . the sound of a young's first wail.

"Is he alive?" Wrath asked like a dumb-ass.

Another whistle.

And then he forgot about his son entirely. "Beth? What about Beth?"

No one answered.

"Beth?" he barked. "John, what the fuck is going on?"

The scent of blood was thick in the air. So thick. Too thick.

He couldn't breathe. He didn't think. He wasn't even alive.

"Beth . . ." he whispered into the darkness.

It was forever until Doc Jane came over to him. And by the closeness and direction of her voice, he knew she had knelt in front of him.

"Wrath, we've got a problem. The baby's fine, Ehlena's checking him out. But Beth is continuing to bleed even after I closed her uterus from the C-section. She's hemorrhaging very badly and there's no sign that she's clotting. The safest thing to do is a hysterectomy. Do you know what that is?"

She was talking to him like he was stupid—good thing, too.

"No." Even though he'd heard the word before. Hell, at this point, she would have had to define even the most common of terms.

"I need to take her uterus out. She's going to die, Wrath, if I don't. It means she won't be able to have any more children—"

"I don't give a fuck about anything but her. Whatever you need to do. Do it—*now*."

"Okay, let's move, Manny."

"Where's my son!" he called out abruptly. "Give me my son!"

Not even a moment later, a small bundle was placed into his arms. So light. Too light to be alive—and yet his son was warm and breathing. Vital.

He wanted to hold him because his *shellan* was in this child. In every molecule of his living body, she was with him—and that meant, as he kept the young up against his heart . . . he was holding his Beth.

"What's happening?" he whispered, not expecting a response.

He let the tears fall as they might. Probably on his son's face.

Who the fuck cared.

SEVENTY-FIVE

Beth came out of the fuzzy neverland like a cork surfacing on still water. Bobbing along, things came and went out of focus.

But the second her brain flipped back on, she yelled, "Wrath—!"

"Right here, we're right here."

Recoiling, she wrenched around in the hospital bed and felt an instant *oh, hell, no* from her belly.

And then nothing mattered. Sitting beside her bed, in a chair that wasn't big enough, her husband and her son were like two peas in a pod.

The weeping that came out of her was utterly uncontrollable, welling up so fast it all but exploded from her soul. And, man, her belly hurt like a bitch.

As she reached over the side of the bed, her IV pulled, but she didn't care. And her menfolk came to her, Wrath standing up with that newborn and easing down right beside her on the hospital bed.

"Oh, my God, that's my baby," she heard herself say.

Little Wrath—yup, she really had named him already—was the spitting image of his father. Even the dusting of hair formed a widow's peak in the center of his forehead. And like he recognized her somehow, he opened his eyes as his father let her take the precious bundle.

"Hey, there, big man."

Because even though he weighed how much? Seven pounds or something? The way that little one stared up at her, it was like he was already taller than his father.

"You are beautiful," she said to him.

And then she saw his eyes. The pupils were normal, the irises dark blue, not light green.

She looked over at her husband. "He's perfect."

"I know. They told me he looks like me."

"He does."

"Except for the eyes. But I would have loved him anyway."

"Me, too."

She cooed and fussed with the red fabric that the foreman's *shellan* had made by hand. Until she became aware that something wasn't right.

Her husband was way too reserved for this special moment. "Wrath? What aren't you telling me?"

When he rubbed his face, that terror she'd felt came back. "What. Is there anything wrong with him?"

"No."

"Where's the *but*?"

"They had to take your insides out. You were bleeding too heavily."

She frowned and shook her head. "I'm sorry?"

Wrath patted around until he found her arm. "Your insides are gone."

A cold rush hit her. "A hysterectomy?"

"Yeah. That's what they called it."

Beth exhaled. Another thing that hadn't been part of the plan. And it was a shock to realize that part of what defined her as a woman . . . as a female . . . was no longer with her.

But then she looked down at her perfectly formed, perfectly healthy little boy. The idea that she might not have had this moment? That she wouldn't be here with her husband and her son?

Screw the uterus.

"Okay," she said. "That's all right."

"I'm sorry—"

"No." She shook her head sharply. "No, we're not sorry. We have our family and we're very, very lucky. We are *not* sorry."

And that was when Wrath teared up, the crystal drops falling off his hard jaw onto the tattoos of his inner forearm.

As she stared at all the names, she smiled and pictured little Wrath, big and tall, strong as his father.

"We did it," she announced on a sudden rush of optimism. "We did it!"

Wrath started to smile, and then he found her mouth, kissing her. "Yeah. You did."

"It takes two." She stroked his face. "You and me. Together."

"I just got to do the fun part," he said with a grin.

A number of hours later, Beth got out of bed and had a sponge bath in the loo. Then she put on a Lanz nightgown and, with Wrath's help, walked out of the room with little Wrath in her arms—

To a standing ovation.

She'd intended to return to the mansion to find the household, but they had come to her. Nearly fifty of them, from the Brothers to the *doggen*, were crammed into the training center's concrete hallway, lining it all the way down and back.

Hard not to tear up.

But then, whatever. They were family.

"All hail the King!" came the chanting.

Cradling her son against her breast and covering L.W.'s ears, she started to laugh. And that was when she saw her brother. He was beaming, his smile so wide and proud, his hands locked in front of his heart like he was dying to hold the baby.

Limping over to him, she didn't say a word. She just passed L.W. over.

The joy she got in return as John awkwardly held the red bundle was pretty much the best thing in the world. Second only to Wrath's.

Abruptly, the crowd started chanting in the Old Language. *"All hail the King—"*

"Well, not really."

As Wrath said the three words, it was like he'd unplugged the sound to the whole world.

Frowning over her shoulder, she and everybody else just stared at the last purebred vampire on the planet.

Wrath cleared his throat and popped his wraparounds up to rub the bridge of his nose. "I abolished the monarchy last night."

Cue the crickets.

"What . . . ?" she said.

"You told me you didn't want to be the cause of my giving up the throne. You weren't. In the end, it was my choice. Sooner or later, someone else is going to make a run at me—and by extension you and him. And then if I die? My son's going to end up having to fight to keep something that shouldn't be decided by bloodline. It should be decided by merit."

Beth put her hands up to her face. "Oh, my God . . ."

"So we're a democracy now. Saxton helped make it legal. And elections are going to take place in a little while. I've talked to Abalone—he's going to coordinate it all. Hell, the guy already had a good slate of candidates. Oh, and the best thing? The *glymera*'s out of a job. I did away with the Council. See ya, motherfuckers."

"I'm *so* happy to be retired," Rehv cut in. "For real."

Wrath looked in Beth's direction. "It's the best thing for us. For L.W. And who knows—maybe he'll decide to run. But it will be his choice. Not a burden—and no one, from any segment of any society, will be able to tell him that the female he chooses isn't worthy. *Ever*."

At that, Wrath shoved his hand in the pocket of the black combat pants he was wearing . . . and took out a handful of . . . shavings?

No, they were fragments of parchment.

As he sprinkled them onto the floor, he said, "Oh, and I tore up that fake-ass divorce decree, too. Human ceremony's absolutely legal. But I figure our son has two kinds of blood in him, and I wanted both traditions to count."

Beth opened her mouth to say something. In the end, though, all she could do was step in against her husband's hard body and hold on.

Naturally, there wasn't a dry eye in the training center.

But that was what happened when an ordinary mortal . . . did something worthy of a superhero.

SEVENTY-SIX

It was a good month later when Wrath realized what V's vision had been all about. The face in the heavens, the future in his hands . . .

L.W. was already on a schedule, sleeping during the day, up all night—which was just perfect. Beth had bounced back from the C-section like a rocket, feeding well, eating well, and being the best damn mother on the planet.

Talk about your total natural. She was incredible . . . and so happy, so damned happy.

The reality of having a son was better even than the dream had been.

And oh, yeah, L.W. was taking to the on-the-planet stuff like a total trooper. Eating, pooping, sleeping, pooping, eating. He rarely fussed or cried, and had no problem being passed around at meals so each member of the household got a chance to hold him.

Even the dog and the cat liked him. The kid slept in a crib in the First Family suite, and apparently, George and Boo both thought of it as a guard station. When the retriever wasn't helping Wrath get around, he was right with the kid, lying in front of the damn thing, on guard twenty-four/seven. And when George was on duty with his other master? That feline was on shift as the baby slept.

So yup, it was on a blissfully normal night in June that Beth said she was going for a run after First Meal, and Wrath decided to take L.W. and his dog and the cat on a promenade around the first floor. The kid always seemed to like that, and as usual, the minute they started walking, his head began to crane around as if he were checking out the real estate.

They were in the library, going by the French doors, when L.W. let out a squawk and strained as if something had caught his eye.

"What is it, big man?"

Wrath repositioned his son—God, he loved that word, *son*—and then did the math.

"Is that the moon you're looking at? Must be—yeah, I think it is."

Unlatching the door, he opened the way out and took a deep breath. Summer was coming big time, the night warm as bathwater, and as L.W. stretched his arms up, Dads thought, yup. He was checking out the old man in the sky.

Or . . . the face.

With a feeling that reality was coalescing in some specific, magical way, Wrath turned his son upright and faced him outward.

Lifting him high.

Holding the future . . . in his hands.

As his son saw the moon for the very first time—with eyes that were as perfect as the rest of him.

"I'm going to give you everything I can," Wrath said gruffly, glad no one else was around. "Anything you need, I shall provide. And I'm going to love you until my last dying breath."

All at once, he realized he was not alone.

People were streaming out of the doors of the house. A great crowd.

Pivoting around, he held his son protectively, bracing himself for bad news. "What."

They came for Beth when she was on the treadmill. All of them. The whole membership of the Brotherhood.

But it wasn't Tohr who did the talking. It was Saxton.

And when he was finished, she went numb and nearly fell out of her Nikes.

Her trip back through the tunnel, heading for the house, had the same kind of dreamscape removal that she'd suffered from when she'd gotten into trouble giving birth. She didn't remember anything about the rush, not all the people with her, not anything that was said.

And when she came up to the foyer, and saw the others in the household gathered once again, every single one of them had the same expression she felt on her own face.

Destiny had taken the reins again.

And all they could do was go in the new direction.

She was leading the charge as they went around the first floor of the house, expecting at each turn to see Wrath and L.W.

The open door out onto the terrace provided the clue as to where they were.

As she stepped out into the night, she saw her husband holding her son up to the fullest moon of the season, the brilliant shining orb like the sun, the landscape bathed in white light.

It was as if he were making a sacred offering—

With a quick shift, Wrath turned on a dime, shielding their son with his massive arms. "What."

Even though Saxton had brought the information home, everyone looked at her.

Stepping forward, she wished she was in something other than workout gear. A ball gown, maybe.

"Beth, what the fuck is going on?"

She tried to get the words right, frantically stringing nouns and verbs together at random in her head. In the end, though, she kept it short and sweet.

Dropping down on one knee, she lowered her head. "Long live the King."

On a oner, the crowd behind her did the same, a chorus of those four words rising up into the night as their bodies lowered to the flagstone.

"I'm sorry." Wrath shook his head. "I'm not hearing that?"

She got up. But she was the only one.

"You were unanimously elected for life. King of the race. Abalone led the effort, and all those commoners you helped cast the votes. Every single one of them. You have been chosen by your people to lead. You are the King."

As the chanting started, Wrath seemed to have no idea how to respond. And it was such joyful chanting, female and male voices lifting up to the night sky, a celebration of the present and the future.

"And who knows," Beth said as she looked at their son. "Maybe if he grows up to be like his father, he'll be chosen, too. But it's up to the people—you put the right to vote in their hands, and they gave the throne to you."

Wrath cleared his throat. Again and again.

In the end, all he could do was whisper, "I wish my father and mother were alive to see this."

Beth wrapped her arms around her husband and son, holding them both. And as she looked over her man's shoulder and saw the face of the moon, she had a sudden sense that the realigning was over, the new era had finally arrived.

"I think they are," she said softly. "I think both of them are looking down right this moment . . . and they are very, very happy about it."

Parents, after all, were especially proud to see courage in their children rewarded by the world.

And to know that love abounded around them.

Everywhere.

Forevermore.